A FOOL'S ERRAND

IN ALL JEST
BOOK ONE

D.E. KING

To Gill, the best supporter anyone could have.

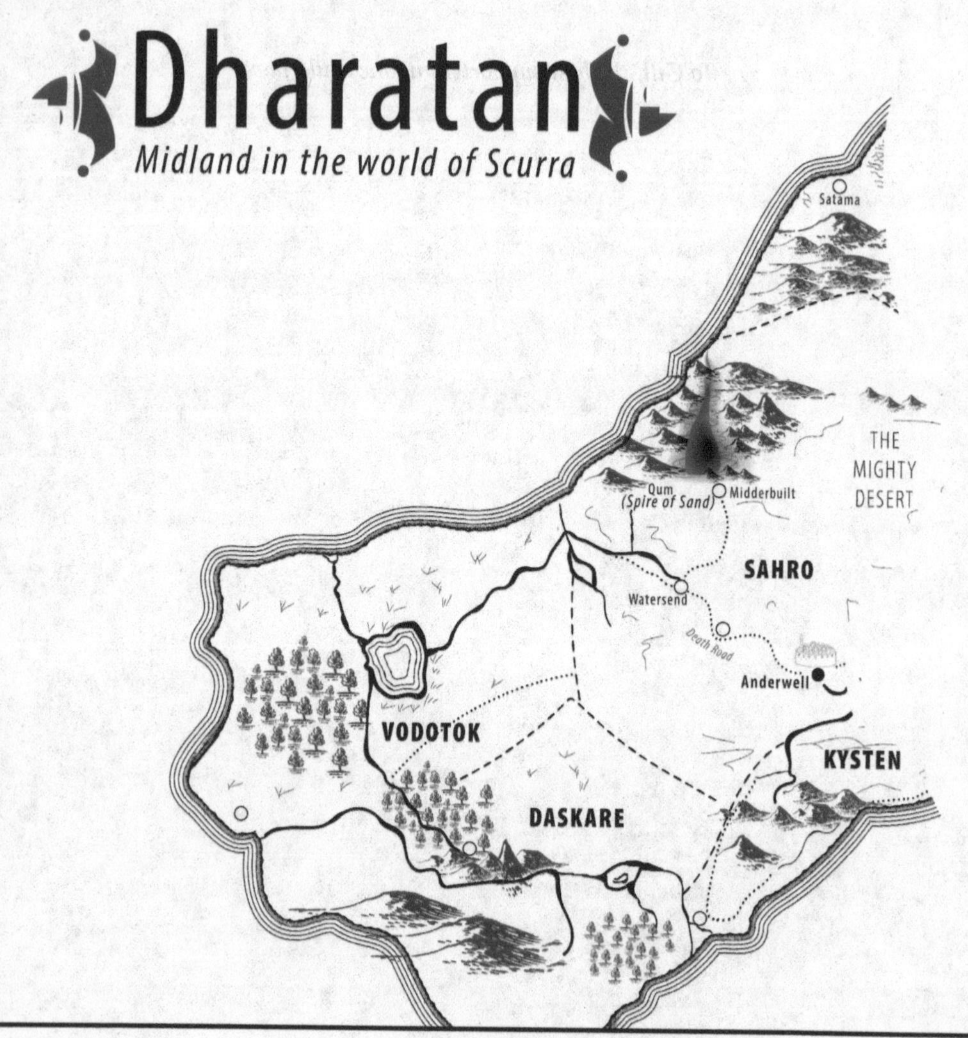

Dharatan
Midland in the world of Scurra
Satama
THE MIGHTY DESERT
Qum (Spire of Sand)
Midderbuilt
SAHRO
Watersend
Death Road
Anderwell
VODOTOK
KYSTEN
DASKARE

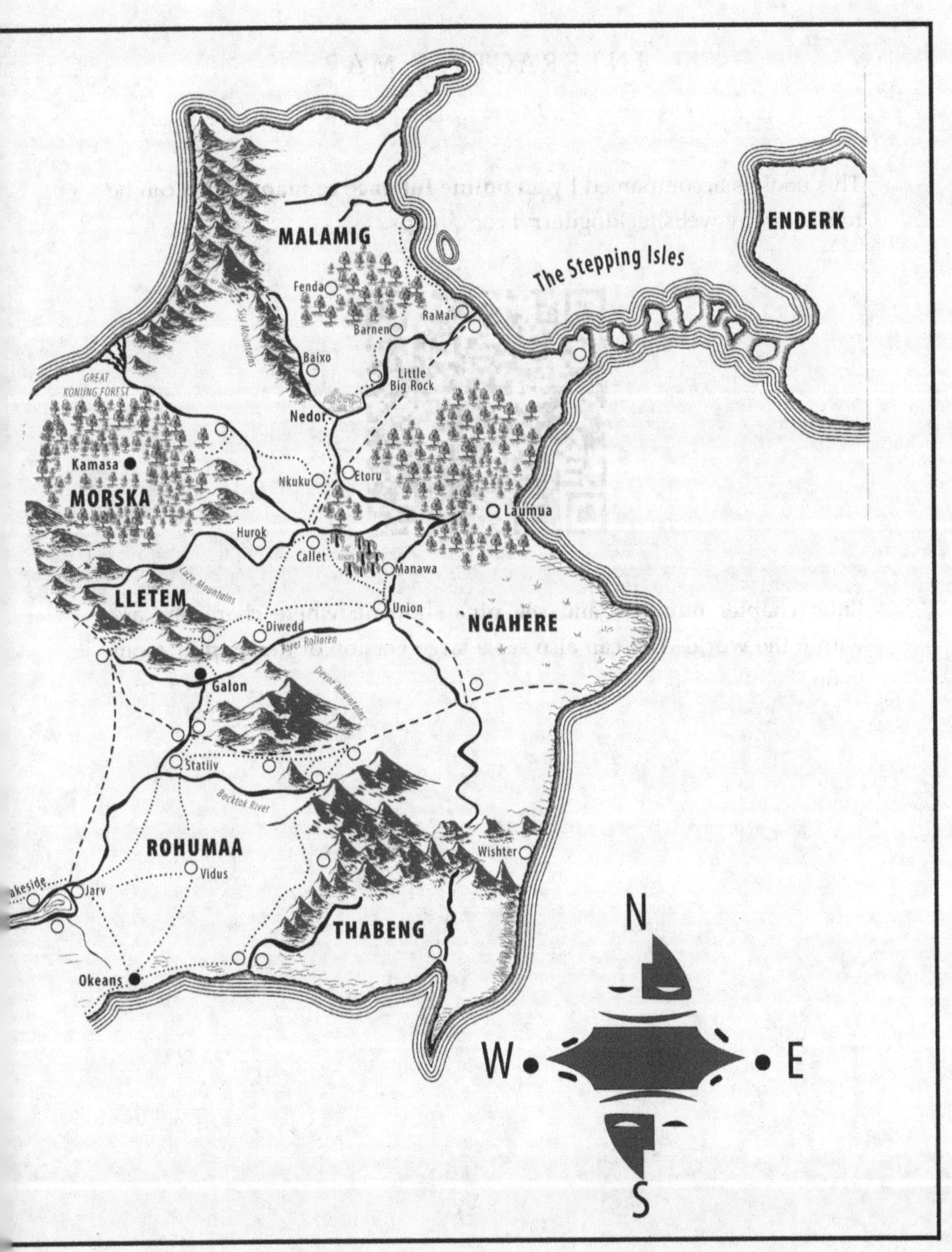

ENDERK
MALAMIG
The Stepping Isles
Fenda
Barnen
RaMar
Baixo
Little
Big Rock
Nedor
GREAT
KONING FOREST
Sisi Mountains
Kamasa
MORSKA
Nkuku
Etoru
Laumua
Hurok
Luze Mountains
Callet
THE IONEI
Manawa
LLETEM
Union
`NGAHERE
Diwedd
River Rolloren
Devor Mountains
Galon
Statiiv
Becktok River
ROHUMAA
Wishter
Vidus
akeside
Jarv
THABENG
Okeans
N
W
E
S

INTERACTIVE MAP

This book is accompanied by an **online interactive map**, which can be found on my website: kingdarryl.com/maps.

Enter chapter numbers and **see pins** showing where characters are within the world. You can also see a large version of the map to zoom in on.

1

LANI

The smell didn't bother her. In fact she couldn't smell it anymore, it was only because others always mentioned it that she was still aware of it.

It was the same with the little ones, they soon forgot the smell after days of carrying the pots. They were the ones who had to fetch the pots and carry them back here so Bragg Clothier could do his work. Lani's job was to work the vats.

She had been a carrier when she first came to Barnen, it was what all the lost kids did. In theory they were being cared for by Despring, the town's Thening priest, at his temple.

The priest pretended that they were all part of his flock and he cared for them as a parent would. Instead they were a workforce he gave out to his preferred merchants and craftsmen in the city in return for favors or coin.

Lani had been brought here when she was three or four. She couldn't really remember exactly when and it wasn't like anyone kept a record of that. If Despring knew any more he kept it to himself. She had tried to ask him once or twice in the early years but earned a whack across her legs or knuckles.

The cane he used seemed to be more for that purpose than helping him walk. Lani had noted he had no problem walking without it but often made himself out to be a little lame, particularly around the people he did business with. Little things she noticed.

She had lived in the old stable with all the other young ones up until recently. Now that she was older the priest's hospitality was gone. She had to earn what she got or Despring would put her out on the street, as he constantly reminded her.

As the boys got older they were apprenticed to local craftsmen, sent to work the Lord's lands or taken in by the guard. The girls had limited choices.

Lani had heard that in other places many of the young lived on the streets in a harsh life made up of scrounging and thieving. People didn't commonly steal here in Barnen. The work of the guards captain Kyro had seen to that.

Lani had seen the results of his tough stance on criminals. Maybe other captains didn't cut off people's hands or ears, or hang murderers above the market gate but it was how things were done around Barnen. She had heard some say that Barnen was the safest place in the realm.

Every year the city grew bigger, more people arriving from outside, and with them came those that thought they could outsmart Kyro. It meant the stockade regularly had someone on show, typically without a hand.

His eyes and ears throughout the city meant word traveled fast. Many feared him, although some of his men seemed to do as they please. Some things in Barnen happened out of sight.

Once Despring had cursed Kyro out loud for bringing her to the town, not realizing she could hear him. She tried to ask him what he meant and only wore another bruise for it.

She had a strange mix of feelings for Kyro de Guillan. There was some form of warm memory about him that she assumed originated from him being the one that had brought her to Barnen. She had learned that much about her past but no one would tell her any more. All she knew was that she had been alone and needed saving.

He had never spent any time with her since bringing her to Despring. She had often dreamed that if she went to him he would take her in and become her adopted father but the first time she had been caught for stealing some food he had broken that illusion.

She was only very young and didn't actually think he would cut off her hand but the way he had become so angry had frightened her. At times she felt she could still feel his grip on her arm even though it was more than five years later.

The last time had been the worst. One of his guards had found her inside a building she had no place being and dragged her to his office. While she had no stolen goods on her, there was a moment when she thought whatever it was that made him not punish her was gone. He had sat staring at her, saying nothing for minutes.

Lani had considered asking him about her history and why he had protected her from his own rules. Then he told her that he could do nothing more for her. He told her that the next time she broke any of the city's rules she would suffer the full weight of them, no matter what it was. He said that he had tried to give her every opportunity despite what had happened but she was an adult now and he could do no more. Before she could ask what he meant he had told his guard to get her out of his sight.

"You taking the piss, girl?" Bragg's voice brought her back from her daydream.

"That won't get any funnier, old man, no matter how many times you say it."

"You keep dozing off on your feet and one day we'll find you drowned in all that piss. I'll lose the whole batch of wool then. No one will want the dead girl's cloth."

"Fat chance of that, no one could fall asleep in all this."

Lani kept walking around in the vat; it was truly mindless but it paid her basic coin that allowed her meager survival.

Her feet were constantly wet, her skin puckered like the dried dates that she saw sometimes in the markets. The urine seemed to stop any diseases getting into her feet but it stung like hell if she had any cuts.

She was the only one tall enough to walk the vats apart from Bray Fuller, but his mind was going and he would be found standing still in a vat as often as not. The movement of pressing the fabric was as important as soaking, the wool needing the urine to clean out all the oils.

As jobs went it was probably the worst one in town but she'd been left with few choices. She'd tried to get a job as a server in an inn, but that didn't last long. A customer had grabbed a full hand of her butt and ended up with a broken nose for it. The landlord didn't take too kindly to that and wouldn't have a word of her explanation.

"What do you think you're there for, girl?" he had told her as he shoved her out the door.

She'd been lucky the patron hadn't come after her; she'd heard he was too drunk to remember her face, but had been some caravan guard who thankfully had left soon after.

The other girls she'd grown up with had mostly ended up in the whorehouses while a few of the meeker ones had become servants. Despring had tried getting her a servant role but she didn't know when to hold her tongue and didn't care for the haughty tones of the ladies and their friends.

She smirked as she remembered the last one who was complaining about the way she was brushing her hair. Lani had grabbed a full handful of it and ripped it out telling her she was lucky she didn't just cut it all off.

Despring had whipped her legs properly for that one. It didn't matter to Lani. She wasn't going to wipe the backsides of some proper ladies and be their slave. And she wasn't working a whorehouse either.

It left her standing in piss all day walking in circles wondering if this was as good as her life was going to get. The smell seemed to follow her around, others wrinkling their nose at her. Even her hair had a lingering smell.

It didn't really matter. She had no friends, and no boy in his right mind wanted to hang out with the girl who smelled like she'd peed her pants.

Spring was coming which she was thankful for, it meant the river would be warm enough for her to wash properly and remove the smell for a few months.

Her best bet was to learn off Bragg Clothier and find a way to become a Cloth Maker. She watched him every day she was here, seeing what he did, who he bought from, how the wool was prepared and treated.

Bragg had no children; his wife was barren or so he complained. Lani had never seen her in the yards. The business was Bragg's place alone and only traders, suppliers and the little ones came around here.

The Clothery was on the outside edge of the city close enough to the water that it needed to wash away all the run-off and dirt. Far enough away from the better folks' homes, that the smell of the vats and dyes didn't affect their posh lives.

"Enough then, girl. Let's get this fabric over to the washers before the light of the day is all gone."

Lani climbed out and she and Bragg drained the excess swill from the fabric, then moved it into a basket which they dragged over to one of the ladies that would rinse the urine and other ingredients out of the fabric.

She walked through the water trough to at least make a semblance of cleaning her legs. Weaving her way through the drying lines under the big outer roofline, she bade Bragg farewell.

He pulled a single coin out of his tunic pocket and handed it to her.

"Tomorrow then?"

Bragg shook his head. "Sorry, Lani, but there's not enough for tomorrow."

"I work hard, Bragg, you know it."

"You do good, girl, but I can't pay you for nothing. Sorry, but you know how it is. If I have extra I'll call for you."

"Okay." Lani knew she was being ungrateful but without the money she had little to get food with. "Don't forget me."

Bragg chuckled, "You know I don't. Now on your way, I've got things to do."

Lani turned and made her way back up Wool Street.

2

LANI

The winters in the northern half of Malamig were harsh, and this year had been a tough one. While Barnen wasn't as extreme as the very northern towns, it endured several cold months. The arrival of spring in Barnen was the time Lani enjoyed the most. The river was now ice free and it flowed stronger as the land began to thaw.

Soon enough would be the Day of Color celebration, the official beginning of spring. The week leading up to it was always a lot of fun, although the mess from the chalk march lasted for weeks after.

Barnen seemed to turn on a wheel from being a quiet cold city to a noisy festive place. Much like how she imagined Nedor was all the time. Not that she'd ever been there or was ever likely to go.

Hundreds of new people arrived in town full of life, new stories and energy. The inns and boarding houses were already filling up, and outside the old walls the temporary tent parks would burst into life.

Today the market square was alive with people and the noises of an eager audience, their attention captured by the three performers in the center of the square. With winter mostly past the troupes would start to travel, and the early ones always attracted the biggest attendance, people needing to see something fresh after being hemmed in the town for too long.

Lani leaned casually against the edge of a post set back from the main crowd, switching her attention between the act and the stallholders. Such a diversion was perfect for her, an opportunity to acquire fresher food without the normal risk it held.

Her life didn't offer much in the way of excitement – standing in vats all day and helping out the little ones was the sum total of it. Despite the threat of Kyro and his punishments Lani had found the rush of stealing occasionally gave her a thrill she couldn't resist. She was good at it and had only once been actually caught with anything in her hands.

Lani reached into her pocket and rolled the coin she'd earned with her thumb. If she spent this on something now there'd be nothing to feed the kin. As it was the single coin wouldn't get her much for them anyway.

As much as she wanted to just spend it all on herself, she knew if she didn't look out for them no one would.

She could hear the tone of Kyro's voice in her head when he had told her there would be no more chances. Did he really mean it?

Several town guards loitered about the edges of the crowd to make sure the enthusiastic small mob didn't get out of hand, but of course were as distracted as everyone else by the entertainers.

Sunlight reflected off the edge of a sword thrust high above the crowd, accompanied by the gasps from the crowd. As it reached its peak another followed it up. The main performer of the three stood underneath both blades juggling several brightly colored balls and almost absentmindedly caught and re-threw the swords as if they were just another ball.

The sound of a lute played by another of the group accompanied his act, the pace of the tune picking up to match the speed of the jongleur. The third of the team stood off to the side and occasionally lobbed an apple across the center of the square in time for one of the swords to slice it in half as it ascended, the two halves flying off into the crowd.

As the pace of the tune increased, Lani slowly moved across the back of the crowd and as she passed several stalls managed to slip some pastries and fruit into her shoulder bag without anyone the wiser. She continued her walk as if seeking a better position, acquiring a small pack of sweets wrapped in cloth from another stall, then stood at the rear of the crowd trying to peer over taller shoulders.

In feigned frustration she meandered her way away from the crowd and headed into West Road, sticking to the side under the shadows, taking a roundabout path to where she wanted to go.

No footsteps sounded behind her and no cry of alarm, so she relaxed a little, as much as she could, feeling pretty smug about her opportune timing. If she'd known of the entertainers in advance she still couldn't have planned it any better.

She began to imagine the taste of the pastries. It had been a long time since she had tasted something fresh from the baker. The days of porridge and stale bread were tedious and unchanging. It was hard to suppress the small grin on her face, and she decided to slip down Mill Lane and find a spot to taste one of them.

Crossing across the lane as she headed further towards the old mill, she was startled by a voice.

"Where you off to then, little Lani?"

The dread of hearing his voice made her heart start beating faster. She spun on her heel, using her right hand to block out the bright early sun rising over the market. One of Kyro's guards, Harsop, was heading down the road towards her. He was as recognizable by his bushy mustache as his bulging belly. On his tunic was their stitched badge showing the three triangles overlapping.

"What's it to you?" she threw back at him.

"If I'm not mistaken you've been helping yourself to things you're not been paying for, so what's in that bag of yours?"

"Just..." she stammered a little, "just my stuff. I've not taken nothing." Lani had been walking backwards away from him while she spoke; he was still a ways up the road, and the lane now felt confining with its close walls.

"Just stop right there! Don't make me chase you and we'll see exactly what you've got. I do like to catch myself a thief right before festival. Nothing Kyro likes more than a fresh hand to hang above the gates to remind everyone the price of stealing here. He'll be well pleased with me."

"You've got the wrong person, Harsop. You know I am no thief."

He feigned a laugh, forcing it out to mock her. "We all know your days of protection are over, don't we, Lani."

Lani's heel caught on a paver jutting up from the old lane and she stumbled backwards, ending up on her butt wedged against the lane wall and a barrel. As she climbed to her feet she scanned the lane quickly. He'd caught up to her now.

"Look at that, I didn't even have to break a sweat to catch you. You're making this too bloody easy, girl. Now, I want to see what's in your bag?" He reached out to grab the strap of her shoulder bag.

Lani turned her shoulder away from him, keeping the bag out of his reach.

"What do you think you're doing, girl. I've caught you and you're coming with me. So show me what's in the bag, unless you want to pay for your crimes in another way." His eyes ran down her body as he sneered at her. "I've been watching you, girl. You're that right age now. You shouldn't be hanging with the little kids when there's women's work you should be doing."

"I'm not one of your girls, Harsop. I've told you."

"Oh, look how sassy we are. You're in no position to be picking and choosing, are you?" He lifted her right arm in front of her face. "Will we take this hand, you think? It looks like a good one to lop off, thief."

Lani tried to free her arm but his grip was too strong.

"Stop your squirming."

With his right hand he reached out again, her body still turned against him so the bag was tucked behind her against the wall. He put his hand on her breast and squeezed, causing her to grimace.

"Looks like you're blooming nicely under here. Bit small for my liking, but girl, nonetheless."

Lani fought against his grip more, but he just gripped her even harder. Tears welled up in her eyes from the pain. As she tried to buck him she cracked her shin on the barrel, causing her to cry out.

"It ain't me that's hurting you, girl. It's your own fighting. Stay still and let me check you out," he chuckled. His slid his hand down her front and grabbed between her legs. "Now see how that's not so bad, girl. All you need do is let me take you down the back here and we can sort out this matter. No need for you to lose a hand, whatsoever."

"No," she cried.

Lani's vision was a little blurry from not being able to breathe, but she steadied herself as best she could. She tried to look back over his shoulder, looking for someone to help her but there was no one there. He'd been a lot smarter than she gave him credit for. The market was keeping everybody occupied. She knew what he was after and she wasn't going to let him take her down the alley.

"You'll do just fine. When I'm done with you, you can start earning your keep with my little crew."

He pulled her out from the wall and forced her to walk farther down the lane. Harsop let go of her right wrist to grab her arm from behind, just above her elbow so he could control her walk.

"Let go of me." It didn't matter what she said. He just laughed mockingly back at her.

He slowed as they approached a small cross lane, that ran parallel to West Road but down toward the river. It was unlikely anyone would be out down here, as much of this section of the town was storage or unused until harvesting started.

As they started to cross the lane his hand relaxed as he looked in both directions to check the way was clear. Lani took the opportunity the space provided.

"Wait," she said, turning slightly towards him.

"What do you want?"

"I'm coming with you, just stop hurting my arm. I know I've got no choice." She turned her eyes up to look at him, trying to put a smile on her face.

His eyes relaxed as she said it. It was enough of an unexpected interaction that he reacted without thinking. His grip eased enough that she could turn closer to him, bringing her body in towards his.

"Not here, girl, just a bit farther …"

He never finished the sentence. Her knee came up fast, as she drove it into his groin with all the force she could muster.

He let go of her and she kicked his shin as she jumped back. She saw him doubled over, his hands grabbing between his leg, catching his breath. As he lifted his head to her, she turned and ran.

"You'll pay for that, Lani! You can run all you want, I know where you live! You're mine now," he yelled behind her.

Rounding the end of the lane, she kept running down Mill Lane towards the river, out through the gate and across the rickety foot bridge.

She kept running, trying to not think about what had just happened but charging away from town. Just away from where he was.

Lani's lungs were burning from running. She finally fell to a stop, collapsing down behind a small thicket. It was enough cover to hide from a casual inspection but not enough to hide in for long. Her chest was heaving and her mouth dry. It took some time for the shaking to ease.

The other girls had warned her about what happened once you 'came of age', but she'd laughed them off and avoided everyone she could. She knew her safe place was the main reason he hadn't caught up with her before. Did he know about that now? Was that what he meant?

The thought made her shudder; that was her only safety, the only thing that was hers. Her stomach gave way and she vomited, tears streaming down her face as she emptied what little contents she had inside.

Her hands and body still shook but Lani stood up and hooked her little bag back over her shoulder. She wiped her face with her sleeve and looked around the thicket. There was no one following her from town. She kind of knew that Harsop wouldn't follow her, he'd just be waiting for her back in town.

Thunder cracked in the distance, pulling her out of her thoughts. Lani looked to the southern sky and saw storm clouds heading her way. Several large raindrops fell on her. A late afternoon storm wasn't what she needed right now. She knew she had to go back to town or find somewhere to rest out the night.

The thought of going back into Barnen frightened her more now than staying out here alone. She would have to get to her warren when she was calmer and check if it had been violated. The wind had whipped up now and the rain as falling heavier. The only safe way back there now would be through the drains but with storm rains about to fall she wouldn't get back in time to use them. No, there was no way she could go back to the city tonight.

Gathering her breath and looking out cautiously from behind the thicket, she couldn't see anyone else. Her choices were limited now, and the closest place was the woods west which the city used for logging. She would at least stay dry there. There was the woodsmen's cavern further north but she wasn't sure she had enough energy to walk that far.

3

LANI

The woods only provided some shelter from the rain and Lani was getting wetter. She was tired and her body felt like it was shutting down. Finally she slumped down against a tree and let the feeling of hopelessness wash over her.

She didn't care how wet she got anymore. She was cold already and that wouldn't change with more rain. Sitting there on the ground was enough. With her head buried in her knees she tried to fall asleep but it wouldn't come.

An image of the woodman's cave kept appearing in her mind. The vision of a dry warmer place to spend the night was appealing, except that she would have to move. Thunder cracked almost directly overhead from her and made her jump. The surprise broke the hold her thoughts had on her and she stood, unable to shake the feeling, to head to the cave. She pushed off from the tree that had been her shelter and trudged further into the woods.

Even with no one around she was startled every time her feet crunched through the undergrowth or a branch pulled against her arms. Her heart still pounded, her eyes naturally scanning every direction, all her senses on high alert. What light left with the cloud cover was almost gone as she broke free of the tree line into the small clearing in front of the cavern entrance.

Cautiously she crossed the open clearing towards the cave entrance, stopping on the well-worn road that ended in front of it. It was only twenty paces across – big enough to expose her, too big to easily escape.

Pausing to acquaint herself with her surroundings, she realized that something wasn't right and she wasn't alone. Even in the fading light she could tell the ground around the entrance was heavily disturbed, as if something had been dragged through it.

Lani stepped a little closer, the dry ground near the entrance drawing her towards it. As she got closer a familiar smell stopped her in her tracks. Despite the damp earthy aromas from the storm she knew this smell far too well.

That smell of rancid blood and dirty wounds had lived with her since she was small. When you lived on the street you often carried some type of wound that healed slowly or came across a body down some alley or lane.

There was no noise inside that she could hear. Without taking another step she reviewed her options quickly, her heart racing again. Was someone still in there? She listened, holding her breath, trying to detect if anyone was inside the cave.

She couldn't detect anything over the fall of the rain and wind in the woods. Despite those sounds there was unnerving stillness surrounding the area near the cave. She had few options now. She was exposed standing out in the open, and was drained. She hadn't eaten for two days and her mouth was dry and acidic from vomiting. Could this day get any worse?

Lani wanted to turn and run but she felt like she was being pulled towards the cave. Not physically, but it was as if her mind was being pulled there. She was just getting wetter standing in the rain. She either had to run or confront what or whoever was inside the cavern. She clenched her fists, scrunching her eyes as she cringed in on herself.

"Who's in the cavern?" she blurted out brashly, trying to mask her false bravado.

No response. More silence.

Despite a creeping sense of dread she tried to strengthen her tone. "I said, *who is in the cavern?*"

The cough sounded like an explosion out of the silence and was followed by a sickly gasp. "I can't move," the cracked voice gasped out of the dark cave.

A male voice. Another wet cough. Several gasps for air.

"I don't have much time left," was all he said. Nothing more.

There was a short scratching and a glow came out of the cave. A dull blue glow, enough to see within the cave but hardly enough to be noticed anywhere else. An unnatural glow that Lani couldn't recognize from anything she'd ever seen. *What makes a glow like that? Can I see him?*

"Are you alone?" she called out as she took several cautious steps closer to the cavern.

She could hear his wheezy half breaths, but no movement from within the cave as she waited for a reply.

"I am," seemed to scrape out of his throat with great effort.

Without other plausible options Lani cautiously crept closer. The trail leading up to her left away from the cave mouth, while steep and narrow around the rocks on the cavern roof, was clear and would be her best chance to escape if things turned bad. The glow weirdly didn't get any brighter the closer she got. It just had a hue that enabled her to see inside without giving off any bright light. She could see his body slumped against the wall barely inside the cave mouth. He wasn't going to be attacking her anytime soon.

Backing along the wall from the entrance, Lani got within five feet of the stranger. In front of him on the ground a small stone was giving off the blue glow. What light it projected added a ghostly hue to him, and he looked bad enough as it was.

On his lap sat an open journal and he had a quill in his hand as if he'd been writing in the dark. He put it down and barely lifted his head to look at her. "I won't hurt you, I can't move."

"What happened to you?" Lani was both concerned for him and wary.

"Bandits. Tried to take my satchel," he said, gasping for more air. "I got struck as I was finishing them off. A lucky strike."

"Lucky for who? You look like you're dying."

He closed his eyes. She could see the pain through his gritted teeth. His gaunt face was covered in grime and dried blood that he had likely wiped across his face. A straggly beard, dirty and dark, hung off him like it didn't belong.

"Can I help you?" It seemed pointless, Lani was no healer, but it didn't look like he was going to make it. There was no one around to help even if there was something to be done and she wasn't going back to the city tonight, no matter the reason.

It seemed like an age before he answered. "Nothing can be done."

Comfortable now that no one else was in the cave, Lani edged her way further in. His small sword lay near his limp left arm. He wasn't going to be using it on her anytime soon and she almost felt herself relax a little.

"Lani it's okay."

She froze dead. Her heart seemed to pause in her chest, and she couldn't seem to breathe as she struggled to stay upright, her legs ready to collapse under her.

"What did you call me?" How did he know her name? She had never seen him before, yet he knew her name. She had been starting to feel in control of the situation. Now she tried to gather herself together to dash out the cave entrance.

"I know things." It came out with a cough. Blood followed.

She knew she needn't be frightened of him physically, and yet she was more worried than at any time today. Her life in Barnen usually brought her few surprises, but here lay a dying man who crafted magic light and could read your mind.

"I know your name."

"How? I've never met you." The time it took between his replies was making everything worse, her impatience building with every pause he took.

"It's a bit like the blue light. I have some—" he paused "—skills. I could sense you out there in the woods."

Lani waited, he didn't seem finished.

"I helped you choose to come here."

"What do you mean?"

"I," he coughed, "spoke to your mind. Easiest way to explain it. Your mind let me know your name."

Lani shook from the wet and cold but also from what he was saying. "That sounds like magic, magic isn't real."

"It's real, Lani. You can see the light for yourself. How else would I know your name?"

She had no answer that would make any sense. Staring at the blue light, she realized there was something different about him.

"This hurts too much. I need to tell you something." He slumped in pain, windless. The wheezing for air increased, the wetness in the sound readily apparent. Every word came at a cost now.

"The bag..." More gasping. ".. Get it."

Past him on the far wall out of his reach lay a well-worn brown leather satchel, its strap coiled up underneath it.

"Who are you?" She knew he couldn't answer easily, but it was too much to take in. Why was he here and what bandits had he come across?

"The ... bag..." was all he could muster.

Lani cautiously stepped sideways around the bottom of his feet and across to the satchel, swooping it up with one hand, and backing back over to the wall.

As she opened the satchel she could have sworn she felt something move inside, but all she saw was something wrapped in a cloth pouch, a parchment folded sat on top and a small coin bag.

"In that pouch, there is an amulet, a dangerous amulet. I was taking it to a friend. They will know what to do with it. It must be delivered. Everything depends on it." The effort was drawing his last reserves. She watched him push himself back against the wall, grimacing in pain, to sit up a little more.

"It wasn't bandits exactly. Someone doesn't want that stone to make its way south. Someone knows I took it, they ..." He coughed, more blood coming out of his mouth. He seemed to be gritting through some pain. "... won't be happy about it. But..."

His eyes closed over a little. He waited and wheezed in some more air. Some more resolve. "It must be delivered. If it doesn't get there, no one will know what's coming."

"What is coming? Who did you take it from?" Lani rolled the clothed stone in her hand. She wondered what sort of amulet was worth dying for. Something very valuable, she imagined. If it was valuable she could trade it for money, get out of Barnen for good. She slipped it out of the cloth into her hand, her eyes captivated by its golden orange color, even in this poorly lit space.

"Oh, it's beautiful. Who did you steal it from?"

The silence in the cave seemed to hold for an age before he forced out a response. "It's worthless to anyone on this side of the Stepping Isles. It is no jewel… It's evil."

"Evil, you say? How can a stone be evil? I think you are lying to me to finish your deed. I think it's my amulet now and I'll decide what I do with it."

He gasped, horror written across his already deathly face. He dragged his right arm across his body and struggled with a pocket on the front of his gambeson. Without the use of his other arm he could hardly get his fingers inside. Bit by bit he reached in and pulled out something in his hand. He flicked it as far as he could toward Lani, as a small cloud of shiny dust flew in front of her, strange light bursting in tiny pixels from it and sharp crackling sounds.

Her concentration broke in fright at the strange cloud and noises. Looking down she felt the weight of the amulet unnaturally heavy in her hand, and without thought opened the pouch to it. The pouch seemed to draw it in like invisible tentacles, grasping it and dragging it in. As soon as it was all wrapped up, her head seemed to clear and the thoughts she had had seemed to slip away. It was as if she could see everything in a different light. She looked around but nothing had changed. The cave was still the same and the glow a deep blue that only just let off enough light.

"What did you do? What was that light? What is this amulet and pouch doing?" Lani dropped the pouch to the ground while fighting the part that had liked having it out.

"The pouch, it stops the evil creeping out … from that stone. It will try and protect you from it but only if you let it."

"I forgot to warn you about the pouch before you picked up the satchel. It was already working on you… the stone when you opened the pouch. Your greed was fueled by it. Without the pouch and the knowledge, you would just leave with it, and they will find you."

The effort was getting too much. He desperately tried to suck in bursts of air. His eyes stayed closed. He slumped and appeared almost asleep, or worse.

Lani moved closer, lifted a small water skin that sat beside him, and tipped some into his lips. He sucked it in as best he could.

"Who will find me?"

He grunted. She wasn't sure what to do. The fear had been replaced with concern. Concern for him, concern for herself. There was nothing she could really do for him now. The cut across his gut was too deep, and the amount of blood pooled in the dirt below him was too great. A small bunch of flies were already buzzing about and crawling on him. She made sure the stone was back in the satchel and snapped it closed.

Stepping around him, Lani gathered what he had dropped in the cave when he'd been dragging himself in. A coat, the sword and the satchel.

He lifted his head with a start. It caught Lani by surprise and she jumped back. He wheezed harder. His voice was almost gone.

"Let me finish my writing. Then I will tell you more."

Lani wrapped his coat around herself and watched him painfully writing words into the journal. She couldn't make out the ink from where she stood, not that it would matter as she couldn't read anyway. He struggled dipping into the small pot on the ground but eventually finished and closing the journal put his quill down.

"Listen now. You must… My name is Ashantha Pebruin. In this journal is all the knowledge my people will need to know—" he stalled, letting some blood run out his mouth "—about the amulet and what happened to me."

"What people?"

"I come from," he paused again, "a private group of people. They look after things without everyone knowing."

"What things?"

"Lani!" he barked at her. "I don't have long left, let me tell you."

She had to wait for him, the outburst causing him more pain. "Sorry."

"The amulet comes from Enderk. They want to do something bad with it. I made some notes." He wiggled the closed book on his lap. "There is something wrong with that stone, it tries to control your mind and make you do things. Don't let it out." He stopped, his head dropping to his left.

Lani tried more water but his mouth could hold nothing, he was slipping away. He grabbed hold of her wrist, surprising her. There was a strange strength in his grip belying the state of him. His dark brown eyes bored into hers. He said nothing to her but she felt sorry for him like she would do anything he asked, not that she could save him.

"A long way south. Callet…Go to Callet. Take the amulet and my journal.

"Lani. You must. Or all is lost. You must get to Bossu. He's safe. Trust only him with this. Bossu. Safe. He's the key. Only Bossu." His hand fell away as the last of his strength faded away.

"Where?"

"Callet… He's safe… Song…"

"Song? Do you mean strong?"

"Weaver… Song weaver."

"What was that?" Lani asked desperately, his words faint and empty as his breath died within him. "Don't die, tell me what you mean!"

His head dropped and his body slumped to his left onto the ground. A chill came across the cave and then passed, and a hollow whistle sound seemed to escape his mouth and blew from him out the entrance and off into the night. On his left hand a small ring went red momentarily and then returned to its silvery color.

All Lani could think was that this was a dream, it was too surreal to be true. She stared at his dead body, squatting beside him holding the water skin, the blue light was fading fast and the darkness was claiming back the cave.

Creeping to the back of the cave, stunned and silent she slid down the wall and sat in the farthest spot from the entrance. Her head ached.

Too much had happened today. The blue light finally went out, its very existence intrinsically linked to the dead man.

Too tired now to think or to move, Lani finally dozed off despite the dread and worry in her mind.

4

TILLANDRA

Tillandra rose from her bed, feeling older and colder this morning than she had for quite some time. What sleep she had managed had been fitful. That wasn't unusual, sleep wasn't something she got a lot of.

She was receiving a feeling she couldn't get a grasp on. Nothing she could put it down to but there was something wrong. Her senses knew it and she had lain awake much of the night trying to get a bearing on what it was.

Remembering that today was the council meeting for the Court, she sighed a little. The meetings were an effort at the best of times, but having a tired mind before it started was not going to help her. She grabbed a woolen poncho draped across her bed end and slipped it over her head, letting it wrap her in its warmth.

There was a knock at the door and Milfred let himself in, carrying her morning chai and some water.

"Hello, M-m-mother. I heard you were awake and thought you might care for this in here."

'Milfred, how on earth do you do that? I've been up not more than a few minutes and yet you have a hot drink ready for me."

"S'just my way, M-m-mother. You are up early today. A busy day ahead?" He had always refused to call her Tillandra to avoid his stutter.

"I can't say I slept that much at all last night," she replied. "Something seems to be on my mind, and I can't work it out."

Tillandra held the warm cup between her hands and blew across the mug before sipping lightly on the tea.

"I think I'll take breakfast in here this morning, I'd like some time to myself to clear my head."

Milfred nodded and headed out in his shuffling gait, shutting the door behind him.

I don't know how he does it, the little imp, Tillandra thought, laughing under her breath. Most people were 'little imps' to her. When you were over seven foot tall, the height could be a curse and blessing wrapped in one. She sipped some more of the chai, hoping it would warm out the cold feeling she had worn all night.

The chai was the greatest thing she had found in a very long time. It was a souvenir from Satama where she had found a unique tearoom in the back of an import/export shop. They sourced the tea from across the Western Sea. The brewers would reveal nothing more than that, and the unique combination of spice and tea was far superior to anything she could find elsewhere on Dharatan. She took another sip, letting the aromas creep up her nose and the liquid roll down her throat, warming as it went.

Sitting in her room Tillandra tried to work out what she was feeling. That was the problem with the visions she received, they came to her like puzzles. Often they came over many days in a series of impressions or images and she had to put them together to make sense of them.

This feeling was different. It felt sad and frightened more than anything else. She would have to wait until she received more before she understood it, she guessed. There wasn't anyone else in the college that had more experience with the premonitions that she could discuss hers with. And much of what she received had to be kept private. At times she wondered if she should journey to the Tellers. Could they teach her how to use her skill better?

The meeting today would start after the middle day meal and drag on late into the evening. They were the part she liked the least about her role. Having to make the final decisions didn't come easily to her. Most of the time she wasn't sure she was the right person to do that. Where she could, she let the vote unfold and avoided adding her own vote as the decision was already made.

She knew the Court was the only way they could manage what Anderwell had become. The Circuit was a thriving enterprise in its own right and there were too many parts for it to be managed by just one person. That didn't change the feeling of dread she got before each monthly meeting.

Once her chai and breakfast was finished she made her way to her office on the ground floor. Milfred had read her mind again and started the fire in there. Any chill the room would have had was mostly gone now.

Her desk was covered in papers, and several open books. The books readily drew Tillandra's attention. Research was her favourite thing. The larger of the two tomes was a book of crude maps. Map books had become a popular trend. A new group of cartographers were trying to out-chart each other. The competition didn't always make for better quality though.

Her experience on the Circuit told her how good the cartographer was, and this particular edition was one she liked for how close it was to her memories of the areas it covered. Reluctantly she closed it and its companion and moved them to a side table. The reports about the college, in front of her, had to be ready for the meeting, and poring over maps wouldn't help finish them.

A rap on her door grabbed her attention. "Come."

Milfred opened the door and stepped into the office. "Will you want to take lunch in here today?"

Tillandra pondered it for a moment, looking back at her desk. "Yes I think so, Milfred. I'm not ready for the meeting yet and I might have to work through and eat as I go."

He nodded, "Will you need anything else until then? I would like to start preparing things for the m-m-meeting."

"I'll be fine, Milfred. You have enough to do today and I won't be moving from here."

He left the room without another word and quietly closed the door behind him.

Tillandra looked back at the list of students she had been reviewing. The college still amazed her.

Some days she couldn't believe the world she now lived in and the good she knew they were doing. All of these students would have been lucky to survive on their own, cast out by their families or towns. Here in Anderwell they all had a place and for the special few amongst them maybe even more.

There was little to report on about them so she moved on to the issues she was facing with the growing numbers they were now trying to teach. They might have to change how things would work moving forward and that always stirred up the meetings.

5

TILLANDRA

*A*s Tillandra reached the bottom step she could hear raised voices coming from the entrance to the Map Room. She hurried along the corridor and as she turned the last corner could see Lionel and Beantic kneeling beside Milfred.

"What happened?" She struggled to control the tone of her voice.

Lionel stood up and turned to her. "He's okay now. He had a little incident with the door."

"What do you mean with the door?"

"I was finishing setting up, M-m-mother, and dropped one of the candles. As it rolled toward the door I reached out to stop it. I must have gotten too close." Milfred pushed himself up and slowly stood.

"You know the door is protected, Milfred."

"I know, M-m-mother. I didn't try to go in, I just reached out to stop the candle."

Tillandra could see the concern about what had happened on his face. She put her hand on his shoulder. "Do you feel okay?"

He nodded. "A little foolish but luckily I was just thrown backwards against the wall."

"Well that's a lesson I hope you won't need to learn again. No one without the ring can enter here. Hopefully you won't suffer too many bruises. We can finish off here, you go and rest your body."

"No, m-m-my job is to guard the stairs while you meet and fetch what you need. I can do that."

"You sure?"

"Yes. Please don't worry about me."

Tillandra patted him gently on the back and turned to the others. "Alright, let's get inside and set up, we have a lot to cover."

Lionel and Beantic gathered candles and cups from the table Milfred had set up outside the Map Room. Tillandra picked up her leather fold and grabbed one of the large water jugs. The room was dark and still. A faint glow came from the small blue lights in the center of the room.

Lionel began placing candles into the eight recesses around the large oval wooden table. He left the room and came back in with a lit taper, and set the candles alight.

Tillandra looked at the large table as it became visible. She always marveled at how the huge piece of wood had been placed here. It had clearly been cut from the base of a massive tree. It would have taken many people to move it and to smooth the surface.

As she placed her papers on it she ran her finger along the outline of the map carved into it. If any of the new breed of cartographers could see this map their minds would burst. She looked at the tip of Daskare, where she sat, and her eyes wandered up to the cluster of blue lights over Anderwell.

Not only was the map of Dharatan intricate and detailed, whatever magic directed their society showed the location of each of the ring wearers. The five of them who were based here in Anderwell were all clumped together on the map, making the light bigger and bolder.

She looked up as Toolet came into the room. "Good afternoon, colleagues."

Beantic hurried over and embraced her. "Hello, Toolet, I always miss seeing you when you're buried in your numbers."

"The lead up to these meetings is always a busy time, Beantic, the days just disappear."

"Can we finish bringing everything in while we wait for Junther?" Tillandra asked.

"It's all done, Mother, they can just settle in," Lionel answered for them.

Toolet unhooked herself from the bursting satchel over her shoulder. It took her several goes to hoist it up onto the table above her. Once she appeared satisfied it wasn't going to fall, she climbed up into her chair and shuffled the cushions there so she could easily reach the table.

Tillandra leaned back in her chair and let her eyes run over the line of masks on the far wall. There were lamps at either end and they cast a somber light over the exact likenesses of the members of their Court who were no longer with them.

She settled on the face of Ninarto, her mentor. Ninarto had been such a strong leader who everyone respected. Tillandra could only wish she had half of her talent. The disease that took her from them had been cruel. Over several years her body had slowly shut down on her until she was unable to breathe. They could never find a cause, or a cure.

I wish you were here to help me, Narty, there's so many things I don't understand.

The last of the group hurried into the room, a man of some age, his long silver hair parted exactly in the middle of his head with both sides flowing down to his waist.

"Am I the last?" he asked a little breathlessly.

"Yes, Junther," Lionel said.

"Sorry for that." Junther pushed the door closed with his only hand. While no one could physically get into the room, what was discussed was for no one else's ears either. The solid wooden door sealed tightly into its frame, blocking any sounds from leaving.

As Junther sat, Tillandra quickly looked about the group assembled, raised her bauble and tapped the table three times. The sound echoed around the hushed room. "Court is now in session."

"Hard to believe it's been another month already," chirped Lionel while tamping his pipe.

"It truly is, Lionel. It does feel that time is speeding up. As soon as I feel like I've finished my work from the last meeting I seem to be preparing for this one." Tillandra finished shuffling the papers in front of her.

"Junther, did you want to run through the notes from last time before we move on to the reports?"

He was sitting furthest away from her on her right and nodded as he lifted a sheet of paper. "There were only a couple of items that I haven't already heard back on. The first of those was to do with the missing funds from Vidus. Any word, Toolet or Lionel?"

"They showed up about a week after our last meeting, correct, Toolet?"

Toolet shuffled through her notes and nodded. "Yes, that's correct, I have them as received."

"What was the reason for the delay?" Tillandra queried Lionel.

"Nothing more than the weather from what I can tell. It's the first time that courier has been behind, so I don't have any other concerns, but I will be monitoring them over the coming runs. They are new to this area, so hopefully it is just about adjusting to the new routes."

Junther looked at Tillandra. "Settled then?"

Tillandra looked around the table. "Does everyone agree?" The others all nodded back at her.

"The last matter related to your questions about our security here in Anderwell, Mother. You raised questions about who was overseeing the guards and their training. Toolet, do you have an update on that?"

"I do. Did you want me to answer it now or as part of my report?"

"If you've got it covered in your report we might as well leave it in there then." Lionel put his paper down, lining up the sheets perfectly, tapping them multiple times to make sure they were all neat. He took his pipe out of his mouth and set to lighting it.

"I'll start like usual then." Tillandra looked down at her top sheet. "The College. We still only have the two Prospects. There doesn't seem to be much change there, but at the moment that shouldn't cause us any concern."

"Are they ever likely to be ready?" Beantic's head twitched as she spoke, her tic a constant whenever she spoke to others. "Are they real prospects or just the best hopes we think we have?"

"I'm not sure what you mean?" Tillandra felt a little annoyed by the question.

"Being the most recent person to take the Audition I feel like I have a good understanding of what it was like to be a Prospect. To me I knew I was ready. I knew I was the ONE." The last word was shouted, not by choice, but as a part of how her mind and body dealt with her condition. "Do either of the Prospects seem so confident?"

"Not all of them are as bold as you were, Beantic. And to be honest I don't know the answer. I'd be more concerned if we have to run an Audition, but as we don't, I feel like we don't need to worry too much about them at this point."

"My point is that we have to give up resources to train them. If they are unlikely to ever be right perhaps we should put them out to work and use the teachers more productively?" She placed her hands firmly down on the table in front of her as she finished, her head flick making the movement even more dramatic.

Tillandra always felt a little attacked by Beantic, but knew it was mostly because she came across as aggressive. She was working on practicing to not take it so personally and see through the manner of Beantic's delivery to the message underneath.

"Does anyone else feel the same way?"

The table was silent for a moment or two. Lionel exhaled a cloud of smoke and spoke up, "I understand Beantic's point, and to a degree share it, but for now I think we've other things to deal with. I don't feel we need to decide now."

No one else spoke up.

"Junther, record Beantic's concerns and I'll consider them prior to the next meeting." She took a deep breath. "Our Patroned are all fulfilling their roles. We have another season before I'd be considering looking for any changes amongst them. In the Gleemen we have a full class of those who have returned from the Circuit. Nothing much to report there. They are using their season off the road to refresh their routines."

Tillandra took a large sip from her cup, allowing anyone time to speak up if they had questions.

"Our Trainees are being sorted as usual, depending on what classes they show an affinity towards. I have a concern about a couple of the teachers we have. I feel like one or two of them are probably at the end of their time. I need to spend some time visiting their classes to settle on my decision. That means I will need your help, Lionel, to select their replacements from the current Circuit."

Lionel nodded but drew back in on his pipe and didn't reply.

"I am very excited about the Hospitality section. It's going a lot better than I expected at this stage, and it is going to open a number of new possibilities for us."

"Better food at our meetings?" Beantic laughed as she said it.

"Funny, Bea. The options for us to place people in kitchens, farms and the like is going to allow us much greater insight to what is happening. I am glad we did it. The numbers are small and it will decimate our numbers when we send the first batch out."

"There a Fool's Cart due soon, maybe that will provide some new likely candidates." Junther looked up from his note-taking.

"That's helpful. I think it is going to take some time to get the numbers to the level we need. Think about the scale if we were to just put one person in every major kitchen across Dharatan. It could take us years to get the right people."

No one else added a comment.

Tillandra continued, "I am starting to think about looking at our current crop of Trainees, and seek to move some of them. We've been so focused on our Gleemen, we're bursting at the seams throughout that part of the college. This brings me to the last matter, which is space. There's no capacity for us to fit in any more trainees within the Gleemen section of the college, and in fact the college as a whole is running out of room. Any ideas about how to handle this?"

"Do we need to keep taking on so many?" Toolet asked. "Everyone we train costs us double of someone who works around the city. We need more people working, not just at school."

"It makes sense to move people into Hospitality if that's short on numbers. I second what Toolet asks. Do we need to keep adding so many new trainees? From my perspective the Circuit is full and I can't see me fitting anyone new in for a year or more. So perhaps we need to start restricting them to only those who show some special talent?"

"If you look around the city you can see its suffering. Sorry, Toolet, but it is. Why not put more to work there? And what of our guards, weren't we going to bolster them?" Beantic shuffled around in her seat as she spoke.

"Okay, hold on, that's multiple things all at once. Can we stick to the topic?" Tillandra raised her voice a little.

"So what are you proposing then, Mother?" Junther quietly asked.

"That we move people out of the Trainees and into Hospitality, or if the need's there elsewhere as well."

Junther stretched out his neck and back and spoke a little louder, "All in favor then?"

Everyone at the table said, "Aye."

"Passed then."

"Good, I'll work out specifics then with you, Toolet, about what you need and I'll start bolstering the other group as well. I'll defer the discussion about the guards to her as well. That's all I've got for you all." Tillandra pushed her notes away and sat back in her chair.

6

TILLANDRA

*T*oolet stood up in her seat, something she always did when it was her turn to speak. It was either to make herself appear bigger or simply because standing on the floor wasn't practical around such a tall table. She cleared her throat and began.

"As my dear friend has so simply put it, the city is starting to look worse for wear. I've raised the matter before and there's not an easy solution except getting more hands to work on maintenance and cleaning. The cost of that becomes an issue as well. I'll get into the finances shortly but from the numbers I've calculated I can easily add another thirty or so people to the city crews for general work. That will free up some of my craftsmen to get started on the most important construction work."

"As for the city guard, we have an overall problem there."

"Which is?" Lionel asked.

"There's a particular set of needs for people to be guards and we can't grow the guards if we don't have the right type of people. I can't make a complete garrison with them all being less abled and we're not attracting in any new outsiders that might help me solve it."

"We don't have enough already?" Lionel spoke over the pipe still in his mouth.

"Not for a city this size. I'm also worried that as word about the size of the city spreads we're going to attract more of the less than ideal types. We simply don't have a force, we have a showing."

"Where would we get more of the 'right' types from then?" Junther asked.

"I don't have any idea. I need help."

"Sounds like I need to put word out on the Circuit for likely possibilities." Lionel put his pipe down on a plate and made a note on the top sheet of his papers.

"So who will train these new recruits if you do find them, Toolet? Without Ashantha to teach them how to fight, won't we just have a bunch of well-dressed outsiders?" Beantic's voice was raised more than usual.

"Easy, Bea. Captain Yelder is doing a fine job. He might not be as skilled as Ashantha, but then few are. And besides we can't sit on our hands while we wait for his return."

At the mention of their colleague's name Tillandra casually lifted her gaze up the table to the northern realms and towards The Stepping Isles leading to Enderk. As she did a gasp burst out of her mouth in surprise.

Everyone looked around at her.

"What is it, Tillandra?" Lionel asked.

She raised her hand and pointed to the table, "He must be back!"

They all looked to the end of the table near Beantic.

"It's been so long I didn't even pay attention to the lights. My goodness. And you haven't heard from him?" Beantic asked, looking back at Tillandra.

She shook her head. "Not a word. I wonder how long that's been there?"

The group rarely had reason to check on the locations of their small group, and the Court meetings were monthly.

"It's very strange he hasn't tried to contact me. I wonder what that means?"

The room sat silent for a few minutes while everyone considered the meaning of Ashantha's return.

"One can only hope this is good news. Having a light missing from the tables been quite disconcerting." Junther was always the most serious of them and Tillandra could see the concern on his face.

"It appears that's the same spot as when it was last visible on the map. Do you agree?" Beantic was staring at the light near her.

They all nodded in unison.

"Can you remind me why it was that the light disappeared, Tillandra?" she asked.

"He had a glove that blocked it. There was no way that he could wear the ring publicly in Enderk. His goal was to be captured as a slave and go unnoticed, apart from his obvious foreignness. If he was wearing such a ring he would have stood out. Not only that, if someone tried to remove it there would have been problems."

"Then we will have to wait until he sends word or contacts you, Mother?" Junther absentmindedly flicked his same ring with the thumb on his right hand.

"Yes, Junther." Tillandra stared along the large oval table to where Ashantha's light shone. Was she mistaken or did it look very weak? She shook her head. "Sorry, Toolet, why don't you continue, there's nothing we can do about Ash at this time."

"Thanks, Mother, and also you, Lionel. Before I go into the finances does anyone have anything they want to raise about the city?"

Tillandra leaned forward. "I am becoming worried about how much accommodation we have. When I am out, I get a sense that we're almost at capacity. Is that true?"

"It has been raised by our City Mayor. She's been concerned for a while now and wants an answer about when she can get more building underway in the western quadrant."

"What's the reasons against it?" Tillandra asked.

"Same as always. Money."

"Maybe you should go on to the finances then."

"Alright. As always the books of account are in my office if anyone wants to dig into the detail. I'm confident they are accurate according to the information I have received. The area that always worries me a little is the Safe Houses. I get reports about how much they hold, but no one ever audits them, so there's that possibility that they are incorrect."

"You think someone might be skimming them?" Lionel jumped in.

"I have no reason to believe that or the opposite. I'm just saying, again, that I don't actually know. At some point I think we need to audit them."

The room was silent while they considered it, before Tillandra spoke up. "Junther, please add a note that we need to consider auditing the Safes, and everyone give it consideration for the next meeting. Toolet, can you put forward the pros and cons of options on how and who might do that?"

"Yes, Mother. Overall we've grown our holdings which is unique in that it has happened over the winter in the north. Partly it's because Nedor has removed restrictions on traveling troupes, no thanks to Goran, and that has helped the flow of the Circuit to the north."

"But aren't they locked down up there through winter?" Lionel coughed slightly as he exhaled.

"These figures reflect what was taken prior to the slowing down. There's always a month or two delay in the numbers coming through, for obvious reasons."

"So how does that affect the city and our needs here?" he asked.

"You all know I prefer a conservative approach to our funds, particularly with the city growing but we're holding more than I think we need for the foreseeable future. I think it's time to release funds to start more construction here. Any objections?"

"How much construction?" Lionel seemed to be leading the questions about the matter.

"I think at least half of the remaining space we have there."

"That much?" asked Junther.

"Yes. We need to be catering for next year, not just now. I've looked at the calculations and because the north is about to open up I think we'll not touch our long term reserves at all. We can fund this from recent receipts and what I expect to come in."

No one else spoke up.

"We also need to take a good look at the guards' accommodation, I'm not sure we can grow them much further without more living quarters. I'll budget for that for our next meeting."

"Shall we take a vote then? All in favor of Toolet's request to commence construction?"

Everyone spoke their agreement and waited until Junther had finished writing it down.

"Anything else?"

"Not now, I need help from Lionel about finding possible recruits before I propose anything." Toolet sat down and appeared to relax a little.

"Lionel?" Tillandra turned to him.

"I think mine might be the quickest of all of you today. As Toolet just mentioned, the northern realms are heading into spring which means the Circuit will open up fully. There's a flurry of activity up that way but nothing out of the ordinary. The troupes and travelers all know their routes, and are well practiced at it."

He paused and took several sips from his cup. "I've placed several apprentices into some of the older troupes, all as helpers, but also I want to mix things up next year. We've had the same groups together for many years now, and I think it's a mistake. They can become comfortable with each other and they become too repetitive for the villages they visit."

"How did that go down?" Beantic asked.

"A few grumbles, but only because they have to look after someone new. I haven't made it public what my intention is for next year, so I'd appreciate it if that doesn't leave the room."

All the heads around the table nodded at his request.

"I haven't solved the problem of getting people based in Morska through the winter. We are allowed to travel through, but Kamasa is particularly difficult to get anywhere near. Things will slow down now through Kysten, Daskare and Vodotok due to autumn beginning down this way."

"What of the traveling fair idea in northern Kysten?" Tillandra asked.

"It wasn't ready for this year, Mother. There's a few things I still want to resolve about that, and I think I'll need to be there for the first time. It will be a certainty for next year."

"Anyone obvious you think might be the right candidates for teaching?" she asked again.

"There's a few that are getting long in the tooth. Several suffered longer winter illnesses this year by all accounts, so I'll draw up a short list. I think there's a couple of others that need to come in but who probably aren't suitable for teaching."

Tillandra moved forward in her chair and turned side on to the table, as she tried to stretch out her back and shoulders. It hit her like a blasting wind. What she knew as The Whistle came at her across the table, knocking her from her chair and onto the floor. She felt her head crack on the floor and just as the blackness fell over her she heard the name that always came with the whistle. Ashantha.

TILLANDRA

"Mother, can you hear me? Mother?"

Tillandra cautiously opened her eyes, and could see Beantic standing with Milfred beside her bed.

"Good, you're back with us. Dear Thenis, you gave us such a scare when you collapsed."

"I think I banged my head," she whispered, reaching up to the sore spot behind her right ear.

"When you fell off the chair you cracked your head heavily on the floor."

"Where are the others?"

"We suspended the meeting, we'll finish it off later. They're all downstairs waiting for you to wake up."

"How did I get…?"

"Lionel, Milfred and I carried you here. You've been out for quite some time. We were all becoming concerned."

"Can I get you a drink, M-mother?" Milfred asked.

She gently shook her head sideways. As she remembered hearing the name passing down the whistle, tears formed in her eyes and ran down her cheek.

"What is it, Tillandra?"

Closing her eyes, she gasped for breath, feeling the wrench of her heart, and dropped her head into her hands.

"Are you okay?" Beantic sounded concerned.

It took her a minute to compose herself enough to talk. "We lost Ashantha! He's gone."

The connection Mother Folly had with Ashantha was strong, after a lifetime working together. The magical connection she had to her Jesters was like an ethereal cord that snapped back at her when it was broken. It had only happened once before in her role leading their society, but each time it had hit her hard.

"But Ash, he wasn't sick? I thought he was gone away?" Milfred appeared perplexed by the news.

"We only just found him, Mother, I think you're confused." Beantic looked at her as if Tillandra was suffering from her head knock.

"The whistle, Bea, that's how I know. You heard it?"

"Yes."

"That happens when one of us passes and I hear their name on it. It is the most horrible way to find out."

"I will tell the others. They will want to know what happened."

"I don't know what happened. I'd say this is what's been behind my odd mood the last few days. He must have been very unwell, and I was feeling his life slipping away. If only I'd known."

She gazed across the room and out at the darkness of the early evening, her head still rattled by the effects of the connection breaking and banging it on the ground.

Tillandra nodded. "I must find out what happened. I need to follow his trail."

"Is that such a good idea after your head knock?" Beantic asked. "It's draining enough at the best of times."

"I need to do this, Bea. I will be fine."

Tillandra would need to compose herself to reach back out to his Majimag, the last trace of his spirit, and she needed to do it soon. There was always a trace that hung about for a brief period after a death. If she did it straight away she could connect to that and didn't need to use another life force. There were many things she could learn by touching his trace. She started to calm her breathing, and bring her mind fully back into the room, focusing on her present space.

Milfred trimmed the candles so that there was only a small amount of light in the room.

"I'll wait outside in case you need m-me." He and Beantic left the room.

Tillandra made herself comfortable and drew her focus to the center of her forehead. Within a minute she found herself in what they called the Void. She brought Ashantha's face to mind and began to seek out the trail.

The signal was weak and she was glad she hadn't left it any longer, as it would soon expire. He must have been very weak when he passed, she thought. It was very dark in the space where she found his body. It was barely visible to the naked eye but his form left other traces that Tillandra could see.

Her face tightened as she observed what she could. As her view improved she could see what looked to be a cave of some sort. Ashantha appeared to have taken several sword blows to his middle, and had died bleeding out. He was very thin, a shell of his former self. The toll of the mission had obviously been hard on him. Tillandra felt anguish from seeing how he had died and at losing such a good friend, coupled with guilt at having sent him to that fate.

The telltale lines were showing around his face. When one of their kind died the mask that they took on during the Audition peeled off and retained the look of its wearer. No one else knew of this, and even the students were not privy to the knowledge that they stored the old masks in the map room.

Her pain at seeing Ashantha's dead body had distracted her from her task. She scanned his surroundings looking for any other clues as to where he was. Lying beside him on the ground was what looked like his journal. A quill lay beside it, which she hoped meant he had been writing down what had happened to him in Enderk.

She became cautious when she sensed another person in the cave. She wasn't sure if others could sense her when she did this, nor what it might mean if they did. She drew in a few breaths and scanned the rest of the cave looking for the other presence.

At the back of the cavern she saw another body, slumped against the wall. There was little Tillandra could see of the person. They were huddled in on themselves as if sleeping. Carefully pulling back to not alert whoever was there, Tillandra retreated from the cave and brought her mind back to the void, and then into her room.

As she closed the connection she realized she had been holding her breath at the end, unsure of who the other person in the cave was.

The only other time she had done this before had been emotional but uneventful. She had observed a body and could confirm the passing, but this was different. Now she had more questions than answers.

She was most concerned about why he had not contacted her since his arrival back on Dharatan. That was most unlike him. What had happened on his mission over the water? His journal would be the only way they could find out now. Whoever the stranger was, they could not be left with his things. Those items needed to be retrieved and maybe whoever it was could provide important information about what had happened. Tillandra would like to speak to them very much!

"Oh, poor dear Ashantha!" she whimpered.

After a couple more breaths she rose, cautiously walked over and opened the door.

"Milfred, are the others still here?"

"Yes, M-mother."

"Help me downstairs please, we'll need to get back to the map room, there's much to discuss."

"Is that such a good idea? You look weary."

"I'm fine. It needs to happen, there's nothing that can be done about it. This changes everything. We'll need firewood for the map room as well, I think it's going to be a long night."

"I'll arrange it, M-mother."

He held her arm as they made their way down the stairs to the main room below, then he grabbed his coat as he swung the wooden door open and stepped out into the dark cool evening.

8

TILLANDRA

The room seemed darker despite the added firelight. Tillandra felt a chill that was deeper than the coolness of the room, and she knew it was the loss of Ashantha that lay deep in her heart.

Everyone was waiting on her. They had all expressed their concern about continuing so soon after what had happened, though she assured them she was fine. They still had much of their other business to cover but the death of one of their own raised new tasks that had to be handled quickly.

"So you are all aware that Ashantha has passed." Each of them nodded somberly. "There appear to be some unusual circumstances involved," she added.

Lionel looked about the table as he lit and puffed his pipe, "What do you know?" He directed the question to her.

"It happened while we were meeting, as you are aware. What you didn't know was that I had been sensing something out of sorts for the last few days, but had no inkling of what it was. I put it down to some type of mood. It caught me by surprise when the whistle arrived."

Tillandra felt giddy again; she braced her left arm on the table and breathed in and out a few times until it passed. No one at the table commented although she could see concern on several of their faces.

"We have the light to indicate roughly where he was. It seems he was in the middle of Malamig. He was in a cave, but I can only assume he had not been on the mainland long, as I've had no messages or word from him at all. That is what bothers me the most."

"Yes, yes," Beantic murmured back at her. "He was always one to talk a lot if he could. How odd." She was the youngest of the current court, her ascension into the Court having been only four years before.

"Was he ill?" Lionel queried, sitting back in his chair.

"I believe not. I was able to sense that he had been killed by the blade of a sword. There were several cuts to his midriff that looked fatal, and he appeared to have bled out in the cave where I located him."

The others all gasped out loud. It was the same thing that had shocked Tillandra, that one of their own had been violently killed. They were used to the occasional passing from within their family but normally it was age or illness, not violence.

"I can't be sure of the true cause, but it worries me, given his mission. There is more, though, and I am unsure what it means," Tillandra continued.

"There was another body in the cave where I found his trail. It appeared to be alive, but I couldn't latch on to it without giving myself away. From what I could tell, they may have been asleep or injured. There was an unusual presence surrounding this person, but I couldn't determine what it was. I know not whether they were the killer or whether they were a companion. I can't imagine he had that much that anyone would want to take from him. He looked very bedraggled."

The five members of the Court sat in silence. Tillandra rubbed at her temple, knowing it had been she who had sent him on his mission and in all probability brought about his death. The image of him lying gaunt and bedraggled in a remote cave, dying without reason or result, sat heavily on her heart.

Beantic broke the silence "Murdered? This is quite odd, especially for one as talented as Ash. There must be more to it. It seems so unlikely for him to be bested by just one individual."

"I know, I know, Beantic. That's my immediate thought as well. And the other body was not big. Scrying like this only shows a small part of what happened. I can only tell you what I could sense or see there. He is gone, though. There was no mistaking that."

Lionel inhaled deeply and coughed several times. "I am sorry as any for the loss of one of us, Mother. There is, however, the matter of his mission that lies unanswered now. I assume we all believe he made it to Enderk. With him passing without reporting in, it leaves us without any of the information we sought when you decided to send him there."

"*WE, Lionel*. It was all of us that decided," Mother replied forcefully.

"The council voted, Lionel, you're being petty if you blame it all on Mother," Junther crossly added.

"Perhaps, but you know I was not for it. Perhaps Toolet and I were correct after all." Lionel's eyes narrowed as he looked down his pipe.

Tillandra could feel anger welling up in her but she knew that was much because she partly agreed with him. "What point is there in us voting if we can't live by the decision? It was a majority decision. I do not feel good about what has happened, but perhaps, Lionel, you should consider the other side."

"Which is?"

"That what we sent him there to uncover was more valid than ever. If he was killed so soon after returning then it's highly possible that what he uncovered in Enderk was worth killing over. Have you considered that? And if that was the case, then his trip was even more important and timely than we'd considered when we sent him!"

The room had gone very quiet, Tillandra looked around at everyone; they seemed a little unsettled by her tone. It was rare she ever raised her voice to her colleagues. She was definitely feeling sensitive to what had just happened.

Lionel coughed again, his tone much gentler, "I had not considered that point of view."

"Can we look forward and not backwards? How do we find out what actually happened?" added Beantic, who had been quiet while they crossed words.

"There was one thing I saw that might offer us hope. He had his journal with him and it looked as though he may have been writing in it. A quill lay beside it."

"What of this other person? Were they a Derk?"

"That I couldn't tell, Toolet, sorry. I'd suggest they weren't, but I only got a fleeting look at them."

"That means we have an even bigger problem, Tillandra," Toolet continued.

"Such as?" Tillandra asked.

"Well, this person may well have knowledge that we need. Also they are about to learn what happens when one of us dies. The shedding of the mask."

Tillandra sat back in her chair; she hadn't realized how hunched over on the table she had become. She tilted her head to the left to stretch her neck before straightening it. "The worst part of it is that if they put on the mask it will wipe any knowledge they have that Ashantha might have shared."

"What do you mean?" Beantic asked.

"That's the curse of the mask, Bea. While you know what happens during the Audition, and the risk anyone takes when taking that test, where a trainee loses their mind if the Audition fails, a normal person untrained for such a test has their mind blanked if they happen to put on a mask."

"Oh my Thenis!" she exclaimed.

"Sorry, I forget there are some things you may still have not learned yet."

"We need to collect these things quickly then." Lionel sounded equally concerned. He turned to look at the part of the table map showing Malamig. "Who is that around Nedor?"

"That can only be Goran," Junther grumbled.

"Your favourite person," Lionel chuckled. "What is he doing near there? Surely Nordahl still has a bounty on his head?"

"That will last for as long as Nordahl lives. Goran's always been a risk taker, and if he's back in Nedor then he's playing with fire. Maybe he has a death wish."

"We all know your views on Goran, Junther. There's Clannack in

Ngahere, but the likelihood she could leave for an extended period is low. It would mean her giving up the position. We know how long it took to have someone in Vika's entourage. I'd not give that up easily."

"Hallendell?" Lionel asked.

"Last I checked she was on the road or in Kamasa. We would have a lot of difficulty getting her out. And it's a long distance north from there," Beantic answered.

"We have few realistic options. Even then it would take Goran the best part of a week or more to get there," Tillandra replied.

"I find it so frustrating that we can communicate between each other but have no way to easily communicate to the rest of our network. Surely we have a trustworthy Keeper up that way we could send out?"

"Yes, Toolet, I know. I've been trying to find ways to use the tokens but for now only those wearing a masks can speak to each other. Unfortunately as it's a mask we're wanting collected I'd be very reluctant to put anyone else at risk."

"This could get messy fast, Mother. If there's a mask out in the open and his journal, there's a lot of knowledge we don't want others to discover. We must act with haste!" Toolet's tone expressed her concern.

"Is Goran not a risk as well?" Junther spoke up again. "The reason he's acting as a Courier is because of the mess he made with Nordahl in Nedor. He set back our plans years, and I don't believe he has shown any remorse for it. Seeing him back near Nedor reinforces he's dangerous to us. How on earth did we ever let him sit the Audition?"

"Junther, he's one of us whether you like it or not. The mask accepted him and that can't be undone. You know that as well as I do." Tillandra's voice was again raised.

"You've always had a soft spot for him, Mother. It doesn't mean I have to agree. In my mind he should be back here where we can watch over him."

"Then what, Junther? We'd have one less of us on the Circuit. Or are you offering to take up a spot again to keep balance in our numbers?" Lionel stared across the table at his friend. "We all can't be based here in Anderwell, you know that as well as any of us."

Junther grunted back at him but said nothing else.

"Everyone, this isn't helping us. Can we debate Goran's future another time? Do you agree that he's probably our only choice at this time?" Tillandra asked.

Everyone nodded. Junther and Toolet a little reluctantly, Tillandra noticed, but at least they all agreed.

"Decided. I am unsure how he's going to locate her, I'll need to see what I can discover first. There might be a way I can help, but I will need to think on it. I will let him know what's at stake for him as well as all of us. Perhaps that might get him focused on what his role is. Much as my head hurts from all this arguing, and the bang to it, we need to press on with the rest of our business. Where did we get to before the whistle arrived?"

9

TILLANDRA

"*I* believe it's my turn to report," Beantic said as she stood. Her tick was active and she stood behind her chair grasping the back as if to hold it in.

"Are you alright?" Lionel asked.

"It's the stress that's activating it. I'll be fine."

"So, Bea, it seems there's about to be a lot of activity in your area. What else do you have to report on in the northern realms?" Tillandra asked.

"I've been trying to keep you up to date on the wheat shortage in the north. I received a worrying missive at the end of last week."

"What was that?"

"Mother, as I've reported before, the shortage came from ruined stores. This new report suggests that the stores were deliberately ruined."

Tillandra's eyebrows raised sharply. "How so?"

"It's widespread in almost every store in Malamig between RaMar and as far south as the northern outskirts of Nedor. It spans all the way to the Sisi Mountains and everywhere in between. While a weak crop could explain it, it is far too comprehensive in its extent for it to be just a bad season."

"How can your source be so sure?"

"They've been to over eighty percent of the store houses and looked at what happened. In every case, not just some, but every case, the attendants found dead rats that were unusual."

"Unusual?" Junther had stopped writing and was looking intently at her.

"Yes, they'd never seen this type of rat before. They were an unusual dark brown with a white tail, and they were all dead in the same buildings as where the wheat was stored."

"I've never heard of such a creature before." Junther started writing hurriedly on his papers.

"That's not the worst of it. It seems the seed crops were also affected. I have to say it is my conclusion that this was sabotage."

"Sabotage? That's a strong claim, Beantic," Lionel said.

"Yes, Lionel, it is. I have no other answer. Coupled with the reports of the Derks that have been spotted across the north, it has me deeply troubled."

No one spoke for a few minutes.

Tillandra broke the silence. "This is very serious. The reason we sent poor Ash away was mostly due to the increased presence of Derks spotted on Dharatan. Their numbers have increased in recent years as we all know but if they are behind this then it is a different matter altogether."

"Are we sure it's them? That seems like we're making connections without any proof." Junther raised his voice.

"Who else could it be, Junther?"

"Have we considered who profits from Malamig losing all its wheat?"

"That's a good question." Tillandra slowly looked around the table. "Bea, what about the other realms?"

"I've already been trying to work out if that's a likely scenario. Ngahere is set to profit initially from this and Nordahl has started purchasing from Vika. They don't have enough stored to truly profit from it though, so I don't see how they're likely to have set out to harm them this much."

"Morska already buys in more than it grows, Lletem is a delicate balance year on year, which leaves Thabeng or the southern realms. What of Daskare, Junther?"

"I've been trying to think through that while you were talking. My question was as much to me as anyone else. I can't see it, in truth. There's so much distance between them, wheat is the least likely trading commodity to ship so far from there. They'd lose a portion just in the travel and the amount needed would be too great."

"Has there been word of anyone opening up new farming zones, Bea?" Tillandra asked.

"Nothing in my reports for the last year that would suggest that. While we don't cover the whole countryside, I'd doubt someone could keep that amount of farming hidden for long."

Tillandra gently rubbed at the bruise on her head. "It was a worthy question, Junther, but I still feel that Enderk is involved in this. The question then would be why? Any thoughts?"

"It's the most important of all the food supplies. I could imagine it sowing unrest amongst the communities. Malamig doesn't trade wheat but they will have to buy it in, which will cost them, but I'd have to say the unrest is the only reason I can think of." Lionel was the quickest to respond.

"It would have had to have been a cleverly coordinated plan to get the infected animals over from Enderk and then transport them to the stores across Malamig. How did we miss something like this?" Tillandra looked at Beantic.

Beantic's head twitched repetitively, her mouth twisting a little each time it did. "Whether it was them or someone else, our network failed to notice whoever was at it. It would appear that we're only looking for information about what we know, in the safety of the cities and major towns."

"I agree, Bea, I'm not looking for anything from my zones that isn't part of the normal. Let's meet up later and work out what we need to get Lionel to spread for us."

"Thanks, Junther; if there are those at work around Dharatan with this level of sophistication, then I would suggest there's other things we're missing as well. I think the times are changing and we might not be adapting quickly enough."

"Anything else, Bea?" Tillandra asked.

"Nothing. I'm awaiting more information about the reported murders of the caravan, once again in Malamig. Until I have enough to inform you with, I don't want to jump to conclusions. I'm more worried about getting our hands on Ash's things than even the wheat."

"I'll worry about that, let's focus on improving what the Circuit is doing. My concerns haven't gone away over the last few years. There's something out there that's focused on our world, and we need to become more vigilant than ever. We should escalate the level of vigilance, Lionel. We've been at the basic level but that needs to change, you should send out the signal for a yellow alert."

"Noted, Mother."

"Junther, how about you?"

Junther put his quill down, and moved the papers with his hand before looking up. "Summer down south has been productive from an earnings perspective. Leolatod seems to be settling into his rule fairly nicely. Sadly that means he's cleaned house a fair bit, and change can be a little disruptive. I've had a snippet of a rumor they are constructing larger ships in Unkendt."

"For any purpose?"

"None that I know of. It seems to be experimental, I would imagine to be able to push further east and avoid the sea blockades along the coasts. It seems to be early stage at this point. There seems to have been some diplomatic arguments with King Anh. Daskare has been trying to get more gold, but Leolatod has upped the price to them. There was also a report of the Kysten border being fortified with more soldiers."

"That's not helpful," Tillandra replied.

"It's happened before as a way of sending a message. This time there appears to be an equally stern response from Anh. He has knights patrolling the border and everyone traveling across is stopped and interrogated, even simple traders. There's definitely no love lost there."

"Who do we have to give us more timely information?"

"The Keepers are our best eyes at the moment. I was going to petition that we consider getting Goran down there until today's news."

"Really?" Lionel sounded surprised.

"I don't like his methods, Lionel, but I am acutely aware of our lack of consistent information coming out of Daskare."

"So we need to consider moving someone then?"

Tillandra looked at Lionel and then to Junther. "I'm not sure we have anyone we can afford to move?"

"What about Gimbden?" Lionel asked.

Tillandra took a big drink from her cup, placing it down when she finished. "He's the most likely. It would make sense as we haven't been getting much of value out of Watersend. I have to make my annual trip to Midderbuilt soon, perhaps I need to move the timing of that forward?"

"Is it that time already Mother?"

"It is, Toolet. I have to swap out the Mother Stone, it's almost time. I would rather do it earlier than leave it late." Tillandra thought about the stones in the tower above them. Eleven perfectly carved clear stones circled around the larger Mother Stone. They were from the Citadel Stone that lived within Mount Qum. Each year the leader of their Court had to make the pilgrimage back to Midderbuilt to recharge the Mother Stone.

While it was gone the power of the stones in Anderwell was weakened, and Tillandra always felt the pressure of time when she made the trip.

"I have always worried about you making that trip alone, Mother." Junther's face was creased with concern.

"Are you suggesting I cannot take care of myself?" Tillandra raised her eyebrows at him.

Junther chuckled. "Of course not. Just that it's such an important item for us all, should anything happen to it..." He didn't need to finish the sentence.

"I would suggest that if we sent a whole party every year, it would attract a lot more attention. Besides the rule is only the mother can carry the Mother Stone, and must make the pilgrimage alone."

The table fell silent again.

"Well then, I should discuss this with Gimbden on my way there. He has been asking for a different placement, for some time now. Where would we place him? Kysten or Daskare?"

"I believe that Daskare would be the better place. I get a sense we're missing something down there," Junther answered.

"Bundok it is then," Tillandra stated. "Anything else?"

"Can we focus on expanding our reach down there overall, Lionel?" Junther queried.

Lionel nodded.

"And, Mother, perhaps the first of the Hospitality students to go out could go south as well?"

"Agreed." The room fell quiet again while Tillandra made a note on the page in front of her. "Oh, of course."

"What, Mother?" Lionel asked.

"With Ashantha passing I will have to go to Midderbuilt anyway. There will be a new ring."

"Where's the light?" Beantic asked.

Tillandra looked up from her paper. "What do you mean, Bea?"

Beantic pointed towards the location on the map where Midderbuilt was located. *"There's no purple light!"*

Tillandra nodded her head. "You're right." Concern crept across her face as she thought about it.

Lionel spoke up. "Maybe it takes time, Tillandra. We've never been in here when someone has passed before."

"True enough. Well, I will still need to collect a new ring from Tingfurlew."

"It seems you will need to decide on who will take the Audition as well."

Tillandra shook her head. "You're right. That adds all sorts of complications now, including heading south to the Carver. I will need to go to Midderbuilt soon if we're going to have an Audition in time."

Suddenly she could feel pressure building on all sides. Ashantha's loss was bad enough but now the need to replace him within two full moons added increased urgency. She had been sure that sending Ash was the correct thing to do, but now it felt like things were unravelling. Had she made a bad decision? Had she misread the vision she had?

Lionel's cough broke her out of her thoughts.

"If I am to get it all done in time I must leave within days. I will return here with the stone before I head south to the Carver. Junther, can you send a messenger there advising them of my plans?"

He nodded in confirmation to her. Tillandra picked up her bauble. "If there's nothing else?" She waited but no one else had anything to say, then she tapped the head of the bauble on the table three times. "Meeting closed. We've a lot to do, people, I think we may have to meet again before the next full session. Let me know if anything urgent comes up."

The room came alive with everyone getting to their feet. The door was opened and they carried their candles and drinks out to the table. Tillandra hurried off along the hall and told Milfred he was right to clean up as she got to the top of the stairs. Her heart was still heavy with the loss of Ashantha and she wanted some privacy to grieve.

10

LANI

*L*ani awoke, confused. A strange noise brought her back to consciousness. She couldn't see anything directly threatening and the realization of where she was quickly dawned on her. She wasn't sure if she was more surprised by the setting or the fact she'd slept until morning.

Sunlight was beaming into the cave entrance and she could see much more than last night. Her recollection of events came back to her clearly. She scanned the cave seeking out the source of the noise. There was only the dead man's body and no one else. He was exactly where he had been last night. The memory of him passing returned, and the whole encounter. She knew there was nothing she could have done to save him, but she felt bad nonetheless.

The rest of yesterday's memories returned as well, including the whole reason she had ended up out here. Harsop. Lani wrapped her arms around her legs again. Sleep hadn't taken away any of her concerns. While she felt refreshed a heavy sense of dread hung over her. She wasn't going to succumb to the black mood, not now. Sliding her back up the wall, she saw the satchel and picked it up as well.

Slinging the satchel over her shoulder, Lani squeezed it to check it still held the amulet. That was about as close as she wanted to come to the amulet after what had happened last night. She could still recall how it had taken hold of her thoughts, how she'd felt different but without any control over it. That was up until the man had thrown the shiny stuff at her. Well, she didn't need to look at it again, a lovely looking jewel like that would fetch her a good swag of money. Then it could take hold of someone else's thoughts for all she cared.

Calming herself, she knew that she couldn't stay here. The last thing she needed was to be caught beside a dead body with a bag full of things that didn't belong to her.

The people of Barnen and the guards would be bad enough but whoever the amulet belonged to worried her even more. The man had said they'd come for him because of it, then they killed him. Would they want to harm her as well? She didn't want to find out, not that she had any idea who 'they' were. She almost wanted to crawl up in a ball at the back of the cave and pretend none of this happened. Like her existence wasn't hard enough now that she had multiple people to worry about.

The noise was back, it came from the body. There were flies buzzing about the open wounds accompanied by several rats starting to poke at the body. She walked toward the body kicking dirt at them, and the rats scurried back under the wood stacks while the flies scattered up into the air.

While Lani hadn't seen many dead bodies, they weren't something that made her squeamish. She just accepted them for what they were, a body, and stepped over to it to see what else of value he might have. Something wasn't quite right about him, or his body, and it took her a moment to figure out what it was. His face was gone. She gagged a little bit and jumped back, turning away.

She took several breaths while looking out the cave entrance before turning back to him again. As horrific as it was, there was something about it which made her look nonetheless. She couldn't help herself. All that remained of his face was pink and fresh skin as if it was all new, but there was no blood. It was as if he'd shed his face like a snake does its skin. Lani stepped back from him, trying to work out how that had happened. She'd heard nothing while she slept and it wasn't as if an animal had attacked him.

The corpse didn't concern her but the sight of his missing face made her shiver. It was not normal, and she couldn't look as she tried to figure out what had happened. She caught sight of a dark object beside his head on the ground.

Stepping over his feet and around to where it lay, Lani picked it up. It felt like hard wood, smooth and polished like the fancy furniture some of the rich lords and ladies had. It was hollowed out and she turned it over, nearly dropping it when she saw what it was. The man's face stared back at her... or a replica of his face. The likeness was almost perfect except it was a healthier looking version of him, not the sick dying one she had seen last night. It was the most lifelike mask she had ever seen. The thought of wearing it caused her skin to crawl.

The wood-like material was almost weightless and was very shiny. It wasn't like any other type of wood she'd seen before.

Worse was the fact that it seemed to have fallen off his face. That made no sense to Lani; how did someone's face fall off? She recalled the strange blue light and the shiny flakes he had used last night, as well as the amulet. It was all some sort of magic.

She decided to keep the mask, it too probably had a value, and she stuffed it into the satchel before kneeling down to see what else he might have on him. Rifling through his pockets she found nothing at all except in the pocket where he'd dug out the sparkles. She managed to pull out a small drawstring pouch that appeared to be almost empty. When she poked her finger in, it came out with shiny pieces of sparkly metal that stuck to her finger despite her trying to fling it away. She wiped it on the wall and some of it came off but she quickly gave up worrying about it and put the pouch into the satchel as well.

The satchel had enough space in it so she grabbed his journal and put it in there as well. With a great effort she was able to twist the silver ring off his left hand; the surface of it had a pressed image of face on it, the same image that had glowed as he passed away last night. The ring felt strangely warm to her hands, which Lani knew was odd. The dead man was cold as the morning air. She rolled the ring around in her hand and it stayed warm. She looked at the image pressed on the surface, a hat with two points on it, above half of a face mask.

The mask on it struck Lani as significant, given what she'd just discovered. Without a stone in it the ring probably had little value. It was just a silver ring and the face on it was a little creepy too. She decided to try it on despite it being too big for her small fingers.

It slid easily onto her finger, much too big, then it shrank without warning. Lani pulled at it, but the ring was now nicely molded to the size of her finger and wouldn't budge. She stepped back and shook her hand frantically, but the ring wouldn't move. She tried twisting it and pulling but it refused to budge. It took her a while to calm herself back down and she stopped worrying about a ring on her hand and gave the body one last check.

The last thing she took from his body was a small knife tucked into his boot. Not that it had helped him, she thought. She tucked it into her boot anyway and made her way to the cave opening. Lani paused by the cave entrance listening to see if anyone else was out there, but all she could hear were some birds and a light wind licking its way through the woods around the cave.

The clearing was empty, as was the road that disappeared out through the cleared trees back toward Barnen. The path on her right that led up over the cave and the Fenda road was heavily disturbed. That had to be the way he'd gotten to the cave, she thought. As she thought about how much effort that would have taken, she remembered his name; Ashantha.

Much as she wanted to be safely away from the cave she also wanted to know more about what had happened. He had said he killed the others, which meant there were likely bodies. More bodies meant more loot. Maybe they had more of the amulets, she thought. It didn't matter that part of her was warning her to just get away and hide. She knew she had to go and look now.

Cautiously she crept up the path, stooped over trying to keep herself low. The path ran along the top edge of the cave, rocks on the lower side and the edge of the trees to her left. It was wide enough for a person to walk or even to lead a horse down, although quite steep. As it reached the top, she paused and stepped into the trees rather than continuing on the open path towards the roadway.

She stood still looking west along the Fenda road. Roads through these woods had been cleared a fair way to each side to help keep travelers safe. Off to the side of the road a short distance to the west, two clutches of birds were feasting. Lani knew that would be the bodies Ashantha had talked of, and she slowly move through the tree line towards the birds.

Aware she was now exposed to anyone coming along the road, she hurried herself. As she neared the bodies, she bent and picked up some stones. Hurling several of them at the gathering did little to interrupt the birds from what they were pecking at. She grabbed some slightly larger stones, and this time they connected with one of the vultures.

The bird screeched at her and launched into the air, the other birds following suit. She walked closer, shouting at them to help keep them away, when she noticed a sword on the ground. Lani picked it up, waving it in front of her helping to clear them all away. The unhappy birds had flown to the nearest trees and were seemingly fighting amongst themselves. They'd be back soon enough, she knew, this was too good a feast for them to leave for long.

Lani counted a total of seven bodies, strewn over a small distance, which the birds had begun on. Three of them looked noticeably different to the others. All three were dressed in the same dark black clothing – close fitting silky tunics and tights, a black belt at their waists, and hoods that extended from their tunics. There was something odd about the clothing. When she looked directly at it, the light seemed to react in a way that made the clothing seem almost fuzzy. It hurt her eyes to stare directly at it.

They all looked fit and like they knew how to fight. She knew that if Ashantha had been alone it would have been unlikely he would have survived as long as he had. Shaking herself to get moving, she inspected the bodies. She tried to ignore the skin where the birds had been pecking and the missing eye on one of them. The tunics held double fold pockets in the lower back that took some handling to get into. Each man had a small coin pouch but nothing else. She took them all.

As she gathered the pouch from the third man, Lani saw a ring on his right hand – an orange stone set in a muted silver. The ring was difficult to look at, her mind repelled by it. Dislike it or not, she knew it was worth something so she cut off some of the black tunic and used it to remove the ring from his hand. As she turned his arm and pulled it off, she saw a strange tattooed mark on the underside of his wrist. She held it in front of her for a moment. It was as if she should recognize it but couldn't think where from. Checking the other two she found they also had the same ring and the same tattoo.

The rings would all be sellable somewhere and she wasn't leaving behind anything she could make some coin from, no matter how horrible they made her feel.

When she checked the other four bodies she saw familiar faces from the city. Only one of them did she know much about, but they were all from Barnen. Lani looked at the man she had only known as Mister Rellings and felt sad, although she didn't know why. He had never done anything for her.

It felt different to go through these men's belongings but she did it nonetheless. They had nothing of value on them. If Lani had to guess they were most likely out hunting when they came across the men in black. Things hadn't worked out well for any of them. A distant neigh caught her attention and she looked up with a start, expecting to see someone riding towards her. Further along the road several horses were eating at the grass up near the tree line. They would look after themselves, she knew, either making their way back to town or someone would come across them.

Thankful that no one had shown up while she looted these bodies, Lani dropped the sword and headed to the tree line to the south. As she slipped further into the woods she allowed herself a small smile. If nothing else she had found herself a healthy small collection of coins and some jewels she could sell. As bad as yesterday had been there was a silver lining to it after all.

All she'd have to figure out now was how to handle Harsop and where she could offload these things without anyone pointing the finger at her.

11

LANI

The sound of hooves was unmistakable. They were coming fast from the east along the only road into the woodcutters' clearing. Lani had stopped in the woods back near the cave entrance, having discovered she still had some of the pastries from the market squashed in her pocket. The food was welcome, but the delay meant she now was stuck here unable to get away.

With it being so quiet in the surrounding area, she would have to wait out whoever it was before she looked to get away from the area. She was well hidden for now in a dense part of the wood slightly away from the trail above the wood storage cave.

As they came into the clearing the riders slowed their horses and moved through it more cautiously. Lani could recognize Kyro – everyone in Barnen knew the guards' captain – but she didn't recognize the other blonde man, and they led a riderless horse behind them.

Captain Kyro halted and dismounted, handing the reins to his man.

"Let me look in the cave, I see nothing out here to concern us."

"Agreed, captain." Lani recognized the deep voice belonging to Markahm and now that they were closer she could make out his features.

She watched as Kyro walked to the cave entrance, his right hand on the hilt of his sword. There was nothing Lani could do but lie still in the bush and let the scene unfold in front of her. If she didn't move, there was no way they would know she was there.

"Markahm, come. There's a body and it's not Rellings," Kyro called as he entered the cave. He hadn't bothered to unsheathe his sword as there would have been enough light in the cave for him to have seen there was little to fear.

Markahm tied off the horses and followed Kyro into the cave.

Lani could only hear voices now and not words, the detail lost in the confines of the cave. It wasn't until they came back out for air that she caught up on their conversation.

"That's the most horrible thing I have ever seen." Markahm coughed and shook his head.

Kyro was quiet for a few moments. "I have never seen the like of it, Markahm. What does that? How could someone's face have been removed like that without cuts and a lot of blood?" He spoke to himself as much as to his companion.

Markahm didn't reply. Lani could see him looking around the clearing nervously. "He's probably been dead since yesterday, that would match when the horse showed up."

"If I'm not mistaken there was more than one person in that cave."

"I agree. You could see they'd been in the back of the cave, past where his body lies."

Kyro appeared to be considering this observation. He glanced around the opening and the small clearing. His focus narrowed to the trail leading up the cavern side, where Lani had been earlier.

"He looks like a rough traveler but there's no way to recognize who he was with his face gone. I doubt he was killed for any belongings, although it looked as if a ring has been removed from his hand. Whoever was in there with him must still be alive. This trail looks like it's had fresh feet on it and we'd have seen them if they had come down the town road."

Markahm nodded his agreement. "Not much we can do for him now. We need to move that body out of there though. "

Kyro was slow in his response, "Aye, but I think I'd like to see first if we can find who was here, who killed this man. We can come back and handle it when we are done. It won't be going anywhere. Let's leave the horses and check what's up here before we make any more choices."

Markahm took the lead, a little more cautious as they climbed the path.

Lani held her breath as they edged their way up the path in front of her, not more than twenty paces away. She was far enough to not be seen, but any untoward noise and she'd be discovered. She knew she had done nothing wrong but with the spoils in her possession and all the dead bodies, an outsider like her would be an easy scapegoat for the murder. She didn't fancy the gallows today or any time soon.

The town guardsmen moved further up the path, and she could just see them as they headed over the crest, hands on their sword hilts. They would see the birds soon enough and make their way to the other dead.

She could hear them talking again and their footsteps sped up. Lani knew it was time to move. She would be stuck hiding here another night, or worse, found by Kyro. While the food she had was good, it was gone now and she was thirsty from a day without anything to drink. She was frightened and exposed and wanted the safety of her warren.

Stealthily she worked her way out south through the wood, remaining hidden from all sides. She figured Kyro and Markahm would want to thoroughly investigate these new bodies. They'd bury those bodies too, which would give her enough time to get back to town.

As she reached the southern edge of the woods she passed through the thinner scrub on its edge towards the main road that curled back around the river bend. It was about a quarter mile from where the roadway cut through the wood to the cavern. There was no expectation Kyro would be coming back yet, but Lani checked each way for any travelers.

The sun was reaching mid-morning heights, and it was a clear view all the way south and around the river bend. Lani needed to be across the river up over the small hillocks on the other side and down into the scrub that lay beyond to be sure of getting out of view of anyone on this side.

It was going to be a solid walk back across the hills to the southern side of town where the vineyards lay. There she could move along the creek bed she often used to cover her coming and going into town.

Checking each way again, she took off in a run. The distance seemed to be miles; the whole time she listened for the sound of someone calling at her, but no one did. By the time she closed on the river she felt like she'd run all day, her heart pounding as she scurried over and down the bank. Pausing briefly, she waded into the river holding her satchel above the water as it crept up towards her chest. While there was no ice to be seen, the water was as cold as she could remember it. She shivered almost immediately as it sucked any heat she had from her body. There was little choice she had to be on the other side.

Slow moving as the river was it still dragged her southward, which was fortuitous in its own right. She climbed out right beside a small rocky outcrop, which she could lie behind and be hidden from the other side of the river. She shivered now with all her clothing drenched, and had to empty her boots. The sun was warm enough to help thaw her out a little.

She could hear the distant creaking and groaning of a cart coming from the south. If she wanted to leave the outcrop she'd be seen by them. Instead she decided to let the sun warm her some more and wait out the cart before she moved on.

12

KYRO

"It looks as if we're a bit late, Markahm," Kyro said flatly.

The birds clustered in the grass ahead told the story before they got to it. Markahm brandished his sword, started yelling and charged at them, frightening them away. He stopped a bit before the bodies.

"Alright then, let's check all around outside the body area first," Kyro said. Both men worked their way in opposite directions in a circular path looking at the scene before them. As they met on the other side Markahm scratched his beard. "Ain't nothing good here, Kyro."

"You're telling me!" He shook his head as he surveyed what was in front of them. He could see the body of Norwlen Rellings in the grass and walked over to him to check whether he was still alive.

"Rellings?" Markahm asked.

Kyro nodded, finding it difficult to talk. Norwlen was one of the few people outside of his guards that he spent any time with. Over recent years they had become close and Kyro felt a pain inside at seeing his friend lying there amongst the dead. He shook his head and turned back to Markahm. "Them three all look like Derks if I'm not mistaken."

"Shall I?" Markahm gestured at the bodies.

Kyro nodded. "You check over there, I'll start here."

They both begun to look over the bodies more carefully, turning them over and checking the ground closely around them for anything that might provide more information. After he had searched over Norwlen's body, Kyro moved to one of the Derks. He hadn't said anything to Markahm but the black clothing they wore had brought back an old memory.

He pulled at the dark fabric and turned the body over. As he did so the man's left arm flopped over and Kyro caught sight of the tattoo on the underside of his wrist, causing him to gasp out loud.

"What is it, boss?"

Kyro stood quickly and stepped back from the bodies, looking hurriedly up and down the length of the roadway. "Did you notice that mark on their wrists?"

"Aye, I wanted to ask you if you knew what that was."

"Nothing good, let me tell you."

Markahm had stood as well and looked back at Kyro, his face showing more concern than it had earlier.

"The clothing looked familiar to me but that tattoo confirms it."

"What?"

"These Derks aren't just ordinary travelers. I don't know what they're called but I've seen the like of these once before."

"You have?"

Kyro nodded and rubbed his chin. "I've not told the details before because they didn't matter. You remember the killings on the RaMar road ten years or so ago?"

"Aye. That was about the time you came here, wasn't it?"

"Yes. We found one of the killers back then clinging to life. He'd been left by his partners and was trying to find safety. He didn't make it." Kyro was silent for a little as he recalled the day long ago. "He was dressed like this and had the same tattoo."

Markahm looked around the scene slowly as he appeared to think more about what he had just heard. "What does it all mean then?"

"I'm not sure but I can't see it's anything good. I doubt our city folk here were involved in anything to have crossed the path of these

Derks. It's probably more likely they stumbled across each other, leading to this."

"Why do they all wear the same things?"

"I had only ever seen the one before. I didn't think too much about the clothing back then, we had so many dead bodies and we interrogated the Derk until he died. He told us nothing and seemed almost relieved to die. All three of them wearing the same thing makes me wonder who they are though."

"Is it just me or does it hurt your eyes if you try to look at it too long?"

"I thought it was just me," Kyro replied. "Let's finish checking them all over. We need to look more closely at everything here, I don't have a good feeling about this at all."

"What about them?" Markahm pointed to three horses that were grazing near where the road went back into the woods.

"They don't look like they're going anywhere. Something must have spooked the one that ran back to Barnen, those would be the remaining horses of our folk. We'll get them when we're done here."

The men quietly went about searching the bodies and all the area around where the fight had occurred. When they had finished they both stood back, taking it all in again before Markahm spoke.

"What are you thinking, boss?"

"There's a few things that bother me."

"Such as?"

"Those Derks, they are all missing rings off their hands. Same finger and all."

"Ah yeah. That. Did you notice the pocket turned out on your one?"

"No, what do you mean?"

Markahm signaled him over and knelt down next to the body closest to him. "See here, that's a pocket in the top and it looks like it's been folded out to me. Same as that one over there."

Kyro stood up and went back to the Derk he had inspected. "You're right, this one too. I shouldn't have missed that. If you hadn't pointed that out I would have missed it. The fabric seems to blend together, there's something very different about the way it plays on your eyes."

"So someone has been here then?" Markahm queried.

"I think so. The rings was one thing but if their pockets have been emptied then no one here did that. I can't tell if there's anything missing from our folks' bodies. Those rings must have been worn for a long time on those Derks, there's a serious indent there and the tan marks."

"Could it have been the one in the cave?"

"He had nothing on him that I could see. If there was someone else in there that might make more sense now."

"What's that?" Markahm asked.

Kyro held up the small cloth-wrapped package. "Something else that's odd is what it is. It's a pastry."

"Pastry?"

"Yes. Like you can buy in the market around the main square. These small cloths are what they wrap them in. The pastry inside has been squashed like someone stood on it, and it hasn't been eaten."

Markahm shook his head. "I'm not sure I understand."

"If I had to guess then we've definitely got ourselves a looter. They took the rings but left the weapons. Someone who wanted items easy to pass along, and someone from Barnen or who was in Barnen very recently at the market. I think they dropped this in their haste to take what they could from these bodies."

Kyro watched Markahm take a few steps out of the circle around the bodies, looked down the road in both directions and then walked in a bigger arc.

"There's footsteps over here, captain. I'd say them be fresh enough to be today, not before," he said as he inspected the grass to the wood side of the bodies.

Kyro walked over. He too looked at the tree line, his hand resting on the hilt of his sword. He looked at what Markahm was inspecting and nodded. "You're right there. Let's wander down here and take a look. I bet they are long gone, but we best be sure."

They both unsheathed their swords and spread a little ways apart as they walked either side of the light foot marks in the longer grass.

"I'd say it's a smaller person. This grass ain't been bent too far, not as much as we're making in our steps," Markahm added quietly as they closed in on the edge of the wood.

Kyro pushed in through the undergrowth following the footsteps, which became lost amongst the brush and rocks. He stood still and looked about, his eyes struggling to pierce the low light amongst all the trees and see anything of use.

He pushed back through and spoke deliberately loud to Markahm. "Never mind now. We'll catch up with them back in town. Thieves get punished the same no matter where we catch them."

Playing along, Markahm replied, "For sure, captain, we'll find our looters soon enough."

They made their way back towards the bodies before Kyro spoke again. "There's not much more we can do here. I'll go get those horses and start ferrying the bodies back to the cave. You should make haste back to town and bring back some help and a cart, we'll need something to haul them all back."

"Aagh, you mean to do more with these back in town? Why don't we just bury them here?"

"I am not done yet. I want to inspect them a little more, and no matter who they are we should put them in the right place. Besides, we have to take our folks back anyway. We need to have the priests send them to Thenis."

"Dirty outlanders be as good in a ditch as any respect from Thenis in my view."

Kyro ignored him, knowing his bigotry was typical for the locals in Malamig. They didn't take as well to the Derks, the few that came through. As often was the case, the little you knew the more suspicious you became. Kyro wasn't happy about what he'd discovered. He had to think this through.

"On your way then."

"Keep your ears and eyes open, captain, we still don't know who is or isn't about here."

"Will do, Markahm, make sure you get back as soon as you can, I'll keep my wits about me till then."

Kyro watched Markahm walk back towards the cavern as he looked over all the bodies again. He hoped there were no more of these

Derks nearby. He turned and headed off towards the horses at the end of the road.

He had little time to contemplate what this all meant, by the time he rounded up the horses and lifted the heavy bodies up onto them, before leading them back down to the clearing outside the woodcutters' cave.

He was returning with his last load when he heard horses coming along the road into the clearing. With some relief he saw it was Markahm and several of the other guardsmen.

"Ho, Markahm."

"Ho, Kyro. You've moved them all then?"

"As you can see. Yes, I have."

"Esun is driving a wagon here, he's a way back along the road."

Kyro turned to the other man. "Harsop, you can wait out here and help Esun load these when he arrives. Keep an eye on all these horses too. Markahm, I want to inspect our other body in here."

Markahm climbed down off his horse and tied it back up to the rail before following Kyro into the cave.

"Set me one of them lanterns, Markahm, will you. I'd like more light."

Once the lantern was alight he stood holding it over the body while Kyro inspected the body more.

"I've not seen anything like what's happened to this face before, it's like it's been peeled off him. It doesn't look like that was what killed him either. There's no blood except from his stab wounds."

Kyro stood over the body and reluctantly bent down to lift the arms as he turned the body over a little. He had tried to avoid looking at the man's head up close but as he turned the body over he couldn't avoid it. A shiver ran up his spine and it took all of his willpower to inspect the body and not just let go and jump back up.'

"There was definitely another person over here," said Markahm.

"These pockets are all empty, it seems too. Most likely then that other person was our looter, as you suspected."

He put the man back down as something shiny caught his attention in the dirt. He ran his finger through it. "There's some little different colored flakes of metal here in the dirt as well, it's sparkling in the light."

"Looks like there's more of it on the wall there as well." They both looked at the smear down the wall. "So, traveling companions, you think?"

"That's still strange not to come seeking help but leave your companion and just head off. Unless you were up to as little good as those outlanders looked to be." Kyro stood up and looked over where Markahm had pointed.

"Or if you take people's faces. That's not something you want to get caught doing."

"Let's move this body out now. I don't think I'll learn much more from here. We'll cover his face with his coat, the men don't need to be seeing this. I'd prefer word of it didn't get out."

Markahm shut the lantern off, hung it back on the wall by the entrance then came and helped Kyro carry the body. They loaded it into the wagon that had arrived while they were inside. The other two guardsmen had finished loading the three outlander bodies.

"Let's have these all taken to the back of the yard then, and one of you go tell Dressing that there's some bodies he'll need to take care of. This one's face is pretty messed up, leave this coat over it, I don't want anyone seeing it, is that clear?'

Esun spoke. "It'll be done. You coming back now?"

"Soon, I'd like to just skirt around the area and see if anything else shows up. Markahm, you stay with me, we'll see you others back in town."

Kyro started walking away but stopped abruptly and turned back to Esun and Harsop, pulling something out of his pocket. "Do either of you recognize who sells these pastries?"

"I think a few people sell them in the market, don't they?" Harsop answered. "Why's that?"

"We found it near the bodies up top. It didn't look like it belonged to the bodies. It was as if the looter we suspect was there dropped it."

"I can ask around if you want?"

"Do that, Harsop, see if you can find out at least who it belongs to."

Kyro walked over and handed him the small package before he headed back to his horse.

Esun hoisted himself up to the front of the wagon and set about heading off down the road.

"What about these horses then, captain?"

"Keep them at the barracks for now, Harsop. We'll return them to the families later."

Harsop tied the spare horses into a chain and once mounted on his horse headed off with them behind Esun.

"Let's scout around the outside of the woods then, Markahm, and do a full loop. Let's stay wary. Who knows if there's more of those Derks about. I'm not happy there's a group of them together and armed. So much for the rules about them only coming over here alone."

As they rode their horses out the road and swept around the southern edge of the trees, Kyro couldn't help but wonder about what was going on. The three Derks were more than just travelers, that he knew, and he knew their kind were trained to be lethal. If he had to guess he'd say they were after the faceless man, and the men from Barnen had stumbled into something they weren't ready for. That would have allowed the faceless man to survive enough to finish them off. Knowing they were trained killers, what did that make this other dead man then? And who had got away?

13

LANI

Scurrying across the far side of the hills wasn't as easy as Lani had hoped. After the wagon had turned the river road toward the city out of sight, she had left the cover and gotten to the far side of the nearest hill. Using the vines and small scrub for some cover, she kept her eye nervously on the river road.

A lone rider came from the wood trail and was pushing hard for town. With the sun behind her she was mostly invisible and the blonde rider, Markahm, wasn't looking her way but riding hard.

She wondered why he was alone. They would have found all the other bodies like she had and she didn't know why he had left Captain Kyro alone with them. Anxiously she wondered what that meant. Had she left any clues?

Lani racked her brain to think about what she could have left behind. There was nothing she could recall. The only giveaway would be the things she had taken from the man in the cave and the other bodies. If Markahm or Harsop caught her with them she was as good as dead.

First she needed to get to her warren and hide those things while she worked out what to do. Barnen was not a place you could fence items you didn't own. Especially someone like her or the kin. To sell

74

them she would have to head to Little Big Rock but that would have to wait.

Barnen had been quiet and peaceful for as long as she could remember with Kyro at the helm, he wouldn't like this change. There'd be a push to know what was going on.

She had been so busy worrying about what might happen she wasn't watching where she was going. Lani put her foot into a hole, her leg giving out under her, and fell. She threw her arm out instinctively, but it was too late. She smacked her ear onto a rock, temporarily stunning her.

"Shit," she cussed to no one in particular.

As she sat back up her ear rang, and her vision was flecked with tiny dark spots. She'd seen spots before after a couple of nasty beatings. They never were a good sign. It meant she'd get the headaches next. These headaches made her gut wrench and any light caused her pain. Staggering up to her feet, she knew she had only a couple of hours before they would start. Her chest tightened. She knew she had to hurry back or she'd be easy prey for Harsop or others.

She'd almost forgotten Harsop with what had happened in the last half day. He seemed a tiny issue now compared to what had happened in the cave. Keeping herself lower than the ridge line of the small hill, she wouldn't be seen from the main road. Grabbing some grapes off the vines, she nibbled at them as she made her way through the vineyard, with one eye out for the farm workers.

Lani made it to the creek bed that fed the vineyard. The water hadn't run yet this week, the manmade gates at its head were only opened once a week to feed enough water down it to feed the grapes but not enough to make a floodway.

It was an easier path to follow back toward the river and town. It split in multiple directions and part of it worked its way around toward the southern edge of the town. The town wall was high on this side beside the river where it was made of the back walls of buildings, the rest free standing.

The scrub and trees were thicker this close to the river and town, and the vines were only planted out in the full sun, away from the shade of the walls and the trees.

Taking a break and rubbing the side of her head, Lani checked for anyone else near here. Getting into the city was easy but she didn't want to be seen. If any of the other street kids saw the satchel over her shoulder they would know she had a find, and would want to take it from her.

A sharp pain hit her behind her right eye. She winced and closed her eyes, breathing deeply to ease it off. Her balance wobbled a little but it was just an early hit. She still had time. Enough time, she thought, to get to the warren.

She was originally going to wait until dark before heading to the town side of the river, but the pain in her head meant she needed to go now. The quickest way would be to use the footbridge the vineyard workers used, but then she'd be heading in the workers' gate and too many people would see her. She moved further along to the east and stood under a tree for a minute or two waiting to see if anyone was coming. Time pressure meant she couldn't wait much longer.

She should be able to get over without being swept too far along, she would have to swim as much as she could to get over fast. Her aim was to land as close to the storm drain as possible. The city wall had a series of storm drains and grates that let out any excess rain water from the big rains. Channels inside the walls fed them and during the big storms, like yesterday, the water ran fast and hard, carting anything in its path away. Over the years, several bodies had been found trapped on the inside of the grates, pinned by water until they drowned.

One such grate was an entrance Lani used to get into the drains. Her warren was a hidden space she'd discovered that she could access from many directions. That was where she'd hide out until the headache had passed.

Checking the river banks and her line of sight and seeing no one about, she dropped into the river, the satchel tied up high on her back, and pushed off from the bank, her weakening arms struggling to guide her across the current. Bit by bit she closed in on the bank over on the town side of the river.

It took Lani more effort than she had hoped. She was only a dozen feet or so away from the footbridge by the time she clambered over the rocks and up against the slimy wall. She was soaked to the skin again and her head was throbbing. Allowing her breath to settle, she needed to concentrate with all her remaining focus. No one knew her warren and this was not the day to lead anyone to it.

She thought about what Harsop had said. He had threatened that he knew where she lived. Surely he meant with the others, not her warren. She was sure no one knew about it, but she would need to check.

For more than ten minutes she waited, gaining control of her breath and silently observing every sound around. It was only when her head was racked with another burst of pain that she forced herself to move. Cautiously she stepped rock by rock, hard up against the wall, small waves of water lapping at her soles, trying to suck her back in.

She edged up towards the grate of the storm water drain. Again she paused and breathed in, looking east, west, and through the bushes and vineyard for anyone that might notice her dark shape against the shaded wall.

Convinced she was safe, she edged to the rock line and pushed out the rock panel that she had loosened many years before. Back then she was tiny and the space was like a doorway. These days it was only just enough for her to get through. Shuffling her way inside, she placed the rock panel back in place. The ledge on the outside held it from any water pressure and she was sure to not use it enough to make it noticeably different to the rest of the wall.

Checking that it was set back in place, she crept along the drain wall, bent over to keep moving freely, the smell foul but familiar. Moving north under the wall, she reached a junction where a smaller drain joined the main channel. It was always dry unless there had been big rains. She climbed up into it and crawled along just enough to be unseen from the main drain, not that it was light enough down here to see much without a light.

She knew the way blind. It was her home, her drains. She knew them better than anyone in town. They had always been her salvation. The darkness helped her head, so little light made its way down there it eased the pressure building behind her eyes.

The only sounds were noises from the town above echoing down through the drains. She knew the pattern, the sounds, where they came from and what was danger or just normal.

Feeling safer now she edged quietly along the drain until she reached another junction. Heading left she made her way up a short distance until she reached the spot. Pitch black and not anywhere someone even with a light would notice. There was a path up towards an overhead grate that had long since been covered over. As she climbed up the rock work she found her way to a hardly noticeable dark wooden panel.

Taking a steel wedge she had carefully made, which acted like a special key with several counter hooks on it, she worked it to the left-hand side of the panel, and after a special twisting movement pushed the bolt on the inside across. Gently pushing in the panel, she swung herself up and into her warren.

Closing the panel and putting the bolt back into place, she paused and caught her breath. She didn't know why but her eyes were always able to see in the darkest of places. It wasn't really seeing like with light but she was able to make out the outlines of things that she'd seen in the normal light. It was if the memories were laid out like lines in the dark.

She had to let her eyes adjust and then she could make her way around the familiar space. Lani quickly changed out of the soaking clothes and hung them over a line she had fixed in one corner. Putting on dry clothes and wrapping herself in the deer skin helped fight back the chills she had.

Her head was starting to really kick her now, the pain driving behind her eyes and pushing at her eyeballs. She crawled to her mattress in the corner, and buried herself under the rugs and skins, the dark absorbing her as she drifted into a pained oblivion.

14

TILLANDRA

Evening was well set across Anderwell, and the air was deep with smoke from many chimneys. Living in a desert climate meant cold nights despite the daytime heat. Tillandra closed the window to her sitting room, shivering a little, and moved her chair over to the small fireplace. Milfred had set the fire earlier, with enough wood to last the night. She gathered her shawl about her as she sat and contemplated what had happened.

The day's events had left her weary, but hesitant to close down for the night. As Mother Folly it was her job to govern their 'family' as they liked to call it, and when problems arose, ultimately it was her job to solve them. There had been few events in her time as Mother that were anything like this.

Several times today she'd felt a different type of chill, tingling on her spine that felt distinctly like a premonition of things to come. She had felt it when she saw the second person in the cave beside Ashantha's body.

Tillandra had chosen intuition as her skill when she had passed the Audition. It was this ability she wanted to be enhanced, although many times it seemed as though whatever was behind the magic of the masks was a trickster.

Often the premonitions were about as clear as an early morning fog. You could see it but not through it. By the time she could see the situation clearly, it was guiding her on, was right in front of her face leaving her no time to prepare.

As many times as not, while she might get help to solve a problem from them, she ended up with a new problem as well.

The enhancement from the mask wasn't a clear-cut thing, what you received had no instruction, and you had to learn how to work with it. Tillandra didn't want to admit to her colleagues she struggled to use her power, and there was no one else to ask.

The mission to Enderk was one of those feelings that she had trouble locking down. At the time, there had been many heated debates amongst the Court about it. It had been an unusual time for everyone. In all her time she had never seen such emotion and anger amongst their group. She had been unable to explain fully why she felt it was necessary to send someone, which irked the Court members. They had claimed she was holding information back on them. There was no way she could tell them it was because she didn't actually know.

She hadn't been deterred though. That was her right. The final vote always lay with her, and now Ashantha's death lay at her feet. That had been hinted at in today's session, but she had already felt it, without anyone reminding her. She would always carry that burden now, and wasn't about to risk more people hastily. Tillandra had some concerns of her own about Goran but didn't air them to the others. Now she was worried she might be sending him into danger as well, and they couldn't afford to lose another.

Much of the reason she couldn't explain it was because it was different to her normal premonitions. Some of her intuitions were simply a feeling or vision that appeared to her. At other times there was an unseen presence that seemed to be directing her hand. It had been pushing her to send people to Enderk, or the Outland as some folk called it. She had felt the same presence only ever twice before. One of those times was when she first met Ash. He had turned up at one of their traveling circuses, deep in Vodotok, wanting to join. The Presence, as she'd come to call it, let her know that he was one they should take in, and all these years later, she had to wonder whether this was all part of the original prompt.

That feeling, of the Presence, was making itself felt again today. She knew she had to dig deeper into Ash's death but she didn't really understand why. Until a Collector could retrieve his things, there was little else they could do. His trail had long since gone. He was untraceable. The feeling lingered though despite her rational explanations to herself that there was nothing else she could do.

Or was there? Her role to explore their magic had led to discovering a way to use the connection between the masks for more than just talking. When the society had been formed there had been no guidance to the magic they were bestowed. When Tillandra had been elevated to the Court she had been assigned the role of exploring the rules of their magic. The other members had all agreed they were running blind without understanding what it was they were using.

Tillandra enjoyed researching and experimenting, looking to better understand the magic bestowed on them. She also saw it as an opportunity to experiment and see if there was more to what they could do.

One of these new methods was when she had accidentally been able to see through another's eyes. The mask was how they were able to speak to each other, but both parties were aware of it happening. Over many months she'd been connecting in a different way where she was able to see through the mask, as if she was inside it with the wearer.

Initially it had been by accident. When one of them initiated a normal call, they had to sacrifice an animal by placing the ring on it to gain access to its life force. None of them enjoyed that process, and because of it they always minimized the number of connections they made. Tillandra almost always vomited afterwards.

As a rule they used rats, as they existed in plentitude and were dirty pests that no one liked. It had been agreed this was the best way to do it, and subsequently that's what they all did. The limitation was that a rat was small and had a proportionally small life force, meaning the connection between each other was short. You also couldn't connect to more than one other person.

There had never been any discussion to try a bigger animal, and

Tillandra didn't even want to think about the physical reaction you might get. Instead she had been experimenting with multiple rats, and in one of those experiments she didn't connect audibly but was able to see through the mask.

It took her a lot of concentration and was exhausting and also an invasion of that person's privacy. When she did it she never knew in advance what that person was doing, and what she would see when she looked out.

Could she still connect to Ash's mask now that he had passed? There was no way to know unless she tried.

She stood and went to the stairs. "Milfred, are you there?"

It took him a few moments to appear at the bottom of the stair. "Yes, what can I get you?"

"You won't like it, but it's urgent. I need some rats." She could see the look on his face.

"Is that such a good idea?"

"It is, and I need them now."

"How m-many?"

"Two. I'm sorry, I don't like it any more than you but it must be done."

He turned and headed away, and Tillandra heard the door open and close. She retreated to her bedroom and prepared for what she was about to do, untying her boots and removing them.

He returned with a sack tied at the top, the live rats obvious from their squirming inside.

"Thank you, Milfred."

He didn't answer and left, closing the door after himself.

Sitting on a cushion on the floor, Tillandra slowly brought her breathing under control, slowing it down until it was almost stopped. She had her ring hand firmly placed on the bodies of the rats, through the sack. She began focusing on the place in her forehead between her eyes, and an image of Ashantha's face.

When the symbol of his face appeared in the Void she turned it with her mind, which was the difference to how they normally connected to each other. As it turned her vision moved so that she was looking out through the mask.

Suddenly she was jerked into what appeared to be a small dark room. As she adjusted to it she could tell it was an underground space with no light. The change of location in her mind was always very harsh and it took all of her concentration to retain her focus.

The room was small without any form of external window. There was a sleeping mat in a corner, a cupboard at one end and a table and chair. The vision she was seeing allowed her to see in the dark, and she could see many cushions on the floor and the bedding, as well as a body that appeared to be sleeping.

Scanning the body initially she learned little, she had only seen the person near Ashantha briefly and the clothing had been nondescript. It was an unusual experience due to the fact the mask was not being worn. Pulling back a little she realized why. The mask was inside a satchel that lay on the floor and that was where the center of her view was coming from.

Within the satchel she could sense something else. It was a strange sensation, but extremely unpleasant. She moved her focus away from it as it was causing her discomfort.

Looking back at the body, she noticed it was a girl, or more likely a young woman. She looked as if she was living a harsh life. She was very lean and her clothing, while not dirty, was worn and of average quality. She was not particularly big and most unlikely to have been able to best Ash in a fight. Had she just stumbled onto him and taken his things?

It was then she noticed the woman was wearing a ring. Not just any ring but one of theirs. Horrified, she moved in closer to check. It was definitely one of their rings, fitting tightly on her finger. It could only have been Ash's.

That made no sense at all, the rings were made only for one. Each ring was custom-made to suit the new member of the society. If the wearer of the ring died then it would change into a coin that could easily pass from person to person until it worked its way back to the Ring Master. She had been instructed that it wasn't possible for them to be worn by anyone else. Once the ring was on your hand it was not removable until you died. Tillandra could feel herself shaking her head, it didn't make any sense at all.

Her connection was weakening, which meant she had used up both of the rats and had little time left. She had wanted to work out where this woman was but there was nothing about the room that could help her, and with no outside view she couldn't anchor onto anything to see where it might be. It had been too long now, and she couldn't risk it any further. Changing her focus she sought to separate her vision from the mask. The dark room started to fade from view, before the sharp jolt brought her back to her bed.

The familiarity of her bedroom helped her to regain her sense of location, but the revulsion at what she had just done filled her stomach with nausea. She grabbed the pail close by and retched into it several times, her brow dripping in a cold sweat.

It took several minutes before she felt more settled. Her heart was a little jumpy and her stomach was still upset

She stood and placed the sack outside her door, knowing Milfred would deal with it.

Tillandra walked over and lay down on her bed. "Well that was quite unexpected," she said to no one but herself. "I must get to the Ring Master now, only he will understand this."

With that final thought Mother Folly drifted into an exhausted sleep.

15

KYRO

Kyro braced himself before the door, taking a deep breath, and then applied two sharp knocks with his knuckles. No quick reply came, but then he knew he would be made to wait, it was always the way.

"Come," filtered through the wooden door.

Kyro opened the door and stepped through. He looked around the room, spotting Lord Barnen standing at the open doors to the gardens. He closed the door behind him. "Lord Barnen, I have some news."

"Ah, Kyro, more news. Let it be good news for a change. I'm tired of this winter and all it has brought us." He beckoned him over with the goblet he held. "A drink?"

"Not for now, my lord, I have some things to attend to."

"As you were then. What's the news, man, you're not wearing a smile, so let me have it."

"There's been some trouble, outside of town…"

"What kind of trouble?"

"… We've found some bodies." Kyro knew he'd be interrupted all the way through, which irked him, but he was his lord. He was here to serve.

"Dead?"

"Yes, dead."

"Well go on then. If there's more, don't make me drag it out of you."

Relaxing his jaw, Kyro continued, "A riderless horse turned up at the west gate. The guards there alerted me to it. They were certain it carried the mark of one of our merchants. So Markahm and I set out to find its rider. His body turned up on the Fenda road near the wood cavern."

"I thought you said bodies?" Lord Barnen clanked his goblet on the sideboard and gathered a jug to top it up.

"His was one of seven dead men we found there, and one more in the cavern."

"Eight dead bodies. In Thenis's name, who killed all these people and what are you doing about it?"

"I'm getting to it, if you'd let me get there." Kyro regretted his words immediately.

"I beg your pardon, captain!" snapped Lord Barnen. "Let's remember who we are."

"Sorry, my lord." Kyro took a breath. "As best Markahm and I can determine, the man in the cave was the last survivor from the fight. It appeared he dragged himself to the cave and died there."

"Was he another of our citizens?"

"I can't say for sure."

"What do you mean you can't say for sure?" Lord Barnen's face was a bright red.

Kyro looked around to see if any of the serving staff were nearby, and lowered his voice. "He had no face."

He thought Barnen's eyes would pop out of his head. "I'm sorry, what did you say?"

"He had no face."

"Explain yourself, man! What do you mean he had no face?"

"As I said, my lord. I've not seen the like of it before. There was nothing there, just a blob of flesh. No blood, no eyes or even eye holes. No mouth or nose, just a flat head of skin."

Lord Barnen said nothing to him for several minutes and emptied the goblet he was holding.

"Is this some kind of joke?"

"Not at all, my lord. I'm deadly serious. I didn't want anyone else to know so we've covered the face and had him put out of sight."

"You brought him back here?" Lord Barnen's agitation wasn't lessening.

"Yes all of them, including the three that were clearly not of our kind."

"What do you mean not our kind?"

"The three were Derks, my lord, and didn't look like the friendly type. They were armed and dressed in identical clothing, like a uniform."

"I'm not sure there's such a thing as a friendly Derk is there? No, don't answer that. It's rhetorical. Are you suggesting that bands of armed Derks are roaming around my lands and killing my citizens?"

"Only four of them were ours I think, my lord. I'd believe the faceless man was from somewhere else."

"So who was the master swordsman then?"

"That I don't know either, he'd been looted. Nothing was left to tell us anything about him."

"This season just keeps on giving doesn't it? More crap every other week."

Kyro had nothing to say to that. His job was to protect the city, not take on all the burdens of the lord running it.

"So then, my captain, what do you make of it all?"

"Right now, I'm not going to jump to any conclusions but there's several facts I don't like."

"Such as?"

"Three Derks together, armed and attacking people, worries me. I had believed that the rule was they can only travel alone or they can't cross the bridge into Ngahere. Ever since anyone's known that's been what we've been told to watch for. That's my first concern."

"And then?"

"I've no idea who the faceless man was. He looked in a bad way as it was. He looked thin like he rarely ate. He was clearly of interest to the Derks but why, I have no idea. The only way to find out who he was and why they wanted him is to find the looter. And that's my third problem. It means we have a thief in our midst, and I don't like thieves at the best of times."

"That's a thing you've managed to keep well and truly under control, Kyro." Barnen had turned fully to look at him. "Up until now that is."

Kyro took in his large girth, the buttoned half coat he wore riding up on his ample belly almost comical. The man was unable to exert himself physically, limited by his size. Kyro looked at the sweat on his brow and how he struggled to stand. He wanted to tell Barnen to put the wine down and go for a walk.

"Meaning, my lord?"

"Well, meaning that if someone looted so close to the city, then there's every chance it's someone who lives here. I don't pay you to let your standards slip."

"Nothing's slipped here, my lord. But that's the concern I have too. The whole thing reeks of a mischief that has no place in my city."

"Whose city?"

Kyro cursed his words. "Your city, my lord. I take my role here very seriously."

"Don't be so precious, Kyro. It was a joke. Laugh for once, man."

Kyro looked at him, waiting for the next jibe.

"What do you suggest then, captain?"

He'd been thinking over this the whole ride back. The city had been restless ever since the wheat stores had been found compromised. It had been a harsh, slow winter and he didn't want people thinking his grip had slipped. He needed to let everyone know he was onto it.

"I was considering holding an open meeting."

"For what purpose?"

"To threaten our thief into taking an action. Either someone will expose them, or they'll flee. If they flee, then they take their ways with them. If they go back into their shell, time will catch them out, but the threat will be real to them. Or I will know who it was by their absence."

Lord Barnen didn't respond immediately, which surprised Kyro. He waited while he thought over Kyro's words.

"I actually like it. There's probably a need to rein in the masses a bit. Things aren't going to get any easier around here for a while. I've had notice that the whole region has trouble with wheat supplies. It seems the infestations weren't just isolated to here. I've no idea when we'll be getting a load from Nedor."

"That bad, is it?"

"Worse, I'll be paying half as much again as I would if it was local, and no doubt half of it will be that rubbish they ship in from Lletem. Everyone's sending emissaries to Ngahere but they are rationing who they give it to."

"There'll be a lot more grumbling then coming up to the Spring Festival if there's no wheat."

"Precisely. A little distraction and some reminder of who's in charge might be just the tonic I need to stop the merchants and nobles pestering me. Turning the focus onto something else might be ideal."

"So we should proceed, then?"

"Indeed. And meanwhile, how about you catch me this looter so we can hang their bloody hands above the gate while I deal with all this other nonsense."

He waved his arms about as if to signify the magnitude of his work.

"I'll do my best, my lord."

"When will we have this meeting then?"

Kyro nodded. "Would tomorrow suit?"

"Tomorrow?" Lord Barnen sipped on the wine, brushing his lips with his sleeve. "Why not. Can you get word out in time?"

"Leave that to me. They'll all be curious enough for an open meeting once word spreads."

Lord Barnen turned back to the garden, "Enough then. That will be all."

Kyro glared at the turned back, but nodded and left the way he had come. Despite how Lord Barnen irritated him, that had gone better than he thought it might. Now to find the looter.

16

LANI

Her left eye felt like someone had pushed a blade into it. She couldn't even relax the eyelid without the pain shooting around the side of her head and up into the center of her skull.

The darkness of her warren was Lani's only saving grace. She had learned many times when hit by these headaches that any light amplified the pain and duration of the attack. Her tongue was stuck to the top of her mouth, her throat parched. She desperately wanted something to drink but was stuck between the pain of moving for the relief of a drink or staying still where she was and avoiding any bursts of pain.

Cradling herself for what seemed ages she eventually relented, rolling slowly to her other side and dragging herself across the floor towards a box on the other wall.

Her ability to see the map of dark spaces she had already seen in the light allowed her to function in her warren. The small space wasn't far to cover except when every movement sent bolts of fire through your face and head. Using her right arm she grabbed a small jug of wine – water turned quickly down here in the dark – and tried removing the cloth that stoppered it with one hand while not dropping it at the same time.

The sips she took soured in her mouth initially but after a couple more she was able to swallow without pain, and her mouth felt more normal.

She put the bottle down on the floor, resting her head back onto her forearms on the floor; the discomfort of the hard stone didn't bother her, she didn't even notice. Ever so slowly the pain reduced a little back to how it was before she had moved. She lay there rigid, her head stuck in the grip of the headache until she dozed off.

Several more times she woke, taking more sips of the wine before drifting off again.

Gradually each time she woke the pain decreased. The debilitating headache became a more normal dull ache in her head and not her eyes. She was able to sit up and function more normally. She was glad she'd been able to make it back here before it had kicked in properly. Being stuck out in the open would have left her very vulnerable. Even more so when she was carrying a bag with loot in it.

Standing slowly, she raised her hand and found the low stone ceiling above her. It was only several hands high above her and uneven. The last thing she needed was to bang her head again on one of the rough protrusions.

Using her hand to steady herself she shuffled over to the opposite corner where a wooden peg was wedged. It took her several goes to pull it out and she squinted as light burst in. The sharp contrast to the dark room caused her pain behind her eyes which she kept closed for a minute. Lani turned her head from the light hole before reopening them.

While her ability to see outlines in the dark helped her, it wasn't a practical way to live down here. The small hole was the only remnant of what used to be an access hole into a small open shed at the back of a merchant's warehouse. At the time she was very small and managed to get through into the space below.

She never told anyone about it and liked the idea of a place that was all hers. There was a small air hole into the drains below the town. Over time she made the hole to the drains bigger and learned how to use that stone to close up the top hole. She was growing too big for it anyway so she sealed it in while allowing for the light hole to function without letting in the weather.

The light was needed, as was the knowledge of whether it was day or night above. The air from up there was fresher than the drains, which she preferred as well.

Lani had worked over many months to create an even space that would hold a small wooden door. The entry she fashioned allowed her the ability to crawl into the warren from a ledge in the outside drain. When she exited she had to crawl backwards and let her feet reach the ledge below.

While the access door set up in the wall of the drain kept it hidden from an unknowing eye, it also made it difficult for anyone that might discover it to have it open. The lock she had built into it was strong enough to protect it for her. Not that anyone had ever found it, that she knew of.

Over time the drains had filled with more silt and she rarely ever saw traces of anyone else down in them. Lani loved that she had this safe space to retreat to. Especially now that men were trying to trap her since she had grown older.

The thought triggered her memory of Harsop and his attack. She hoped when he said 'I know where you live' that he hadn't found this place. There was no way out if someone knew where it was and trapped her. That was the only risk locking yourself in, if someone trapped you in here you'd die, with no way out.

Lani was pretty sure he meant the old warehouse that the kids of the street had made their home. That was where people thought she lived, so it made sense he meant there. They all had set up a home of sorts there despite it being run down. No one had ever tried to evict them from it. She guessed it was as good a place as any to have them off the streets.

She'd have to deal with him when she went back topside. Maybe he'd leave her alone for now. She'd need to not get caught alone with him again, he'd be much more cautious next time. He had no proof she had been stealing so it was just his word against hers. He would try and make her life uncomfortable, that would be for sure, but he couldn't have her punished for what he thought.

The satchel lying on the floor caught her attention. Now if he knew about that then it would be a whole different issue. She did have things that didn't belong to her. Even if Ashantha had told her to take them. And the pouch of money as well. She picked it up and went and sat on the mattress on the floor. It was the only place she could comfortably sit down here.

She opened it and pulled out the largest thing her hand grabbed hold of, the mask. As she looked at it she felt a chill run up her arms. Looking at Ashantha's face took her back to sitting beside him as he died. She could hear his voice in the cavern.

You must take it to Callet.

It seemed as if he was there with her, as if the sound came from within the room not inside her head. She dropped the mask on the floor and shook her hand as if to flick off something on it. Her imagination must be playing tricks on her.

Tipping the rest of the satchel out onto the floor she then sorted everything that she had found. The coin pouch from Ashantha and one of the outlanders caused her to smile. Money was always hard to make here in Barnen. Her job with Bragg had become less reliable and he paid her only a pittance. The pouch held enough for her to feed the kin for weeks if she managed it well.

It had been taken from dead men that weren't from Barnen. She told herself they weren't going to be using it, so it wasn't really stealing. Why should the guards or the fat lord get it? They already had enough. *Those bandits had no rights anyway, and I was there at Ashantha's end. He said to take his things, so I did.*

She picked up the small handful of the coins and rolled them through her fingers, letting them fall back out again. *We deserve this as much as anyone else,* she told herself. Also lying on her mattress was the felt pouch, the black cloth she had wrapped the outlander rings in and the book Ashantha had been writing in.

She picked it up and opened it. There were few things written in the book. Lani couldn't read but it surprised her that many of the pages looked worn but there were few words or symbols marked on them. That didn't make much sense to her.

The gray felt pouch that held the amulet kept drawing her attention. Lani stared at it, recalling the feeling she'd had when she was holding it. It had felt like something was wrapping itself around her arm and crawling up it. She had lost control of her thoughts back then.

She reached out to the pouch, part of her wanting to look at it again. Before she got to it she came to her senses, pulling her hand away. Why was she trying to touch it when she had hated how it felt? There was definitely something not right about it. She could agree with Ashantha about that. Maybe it was because she had the headache and her resolve was weakened. She rubbed at the crown of her head automatically, where the headache still remained. The skin on her scalp was tight and unyielding.

Again she was drawn to take it out of the pouch and found her hands moving towards it. She pulled her hands back and held them together. Looking back at the pouch she could see it wasn't completely tied closed. She quickly grabbed the cord on it and tightened it close, and the sensation she had felt dissipated.

The amulet she needed to get rid of, and also the rings that she'd placed in the pouch with it. Not here in Barnen, she never offloaded anything here. The merchants would hand you over to the guards at a moment's notice. They didn't want to handle anything illegitimate either. She'd need to head south to Little Big Rock and try fencing them there. There was at least one contact down there she could think of that would like what she had to offer.

If she could get a decent price for them and add it to the money in the pouch she would have plenty to help feed the kin over the coming months.

That would have to wait though, she needed to keep the money hidden and wait until any trouble from Kyro's men disappeared. She could get by easily for a few weeks before having to worry about it.

It might be a good idea to head south for a little while anyway and be out of Harsop's way. She would just have to figure out how to manage the kin and make sure they didn't starve. Last time she had been away for a week and they had gotten themselves into all sorts of trouble.

Lani gathered all the items except the money and put them back into the satchel. She noticed the small knife in her boot and took it out. She thought about storing it with the satchel but decided it was a handy weapon to carry and tucked it out of sight in her boot. She stuffed a couple of coins into a hidden pocket and put the rest into the satchel as well.

She pulled the makeshift mattress she slept on away from the wall, and reached down into a little cavity she had carved there. The small packet containing her small blue brooch was still there. It was the only valuable thing she had. Supposedly her mother had given it to her, or so she had been told by Captain Kyro. He had told her to keep it safe and not let others see it, so she kept it here. She forced the satchel in there as well, which filled the whole space, and moved the mattress back into place.

With everything hidden, she began to relax again. There was no way she was connected to the deaths. No one had seen her, and there was nothing for anyone to find on her that would give it away.

The headache was just a dull crushing on top of her head now. She felt remarkably happier than she had, and changed her top. Lani felt ready to face the city and show up where she'd be expected to be seen.

17

LANI

The drains were empty and dark just the way Lani liked them, allowing her to lock her den and leave without anyone the wiser. With no one else around she could make her way through the tunnels to the exit she wanted.

Once she was into the main drains there were a number of way out to the streets above, each with its own benefits or risks. She chose the exit behind The Rolling Barrel. She had to clamber up the wall using a number of nooks and hand holds that she had created over time. Raising her head out through the metal grate she checked to make sure no one was close by. Where she exited sat at a narrow junction of the town wall and the inn wall. It was an unlikely spot for anyone else to be and only someone her size or smaller could use it. Once out of the hole she had to shuffle sideways up the slippery moss-covered paving to get to the yard at the back of the inn.

Lani brushed off her top and slipped around the wall into the inn's yard. Judging by the noise coming from inside the inn she guessed it had to be around noontime.

She crossed the yard and out into the road and headed towards the town center. Winter wasn't done with Barnen just yet and without sun the day was gray and gloomy. Lani stiffened a little with the chill and thought she should have brought something warmer to wear.

As she turned onto the market road she saw some of her younger kin and walked across the road to them. As she approached, one of the youngest of them, Ilker, a pasty boy of no more than seven, squealed in delight.

"Lani, Lani, I was looking for you. Where you been?"

Swooping him into her arms, Lani hugged him tight. The younger ones like Ilker were the most vulnerable. At his age, chances of survival were heavily dependent on the kin being able to keep food and shelter available and to keep predators at bay. Lani had always tried to look out for the young ones as best she could.

"I am right here, Ilky boy," she said, poking her tongue out at him.

"You been gone days, Lani. I worried."

She felt the eyes of the others on her as he wriggled about in her arms. "I got busy, Ilky, that was all. It was only a day and some."

"We missed you," he said.

"You miss me when I leave the room, Ilker." She looked at the others who ranged all the way up to fourteen. "Did you all eat?"

Several of them gave small nods, no one really looking directly at her.

"Really? Who cooked then? What did you have?"

One of the girls, Fioressa, looked up at Lani. "We had some oats. That's all what there was."

"Well I'll have to sort that tonight. I will. I've got me a coin so I can get us some proper vegetables from the market. We'll eat something better tonight without having to wait for what gets left."

Their faces brightened a little and small smiles appeared. Despring was meant to be providing for them, but apart from bags and bags of oats, what he left never seemed to stretch far enough. If they were horses they'd have fared better. When the other surprises turned up it was a matter of who found them first. If the older lads got them then the young kin never saw any of it.

"What are you all doing down here near the market at this time anyway?" Lani asked one of the slightly older boys.

Dorted began to answer. His speaking was an awkward process.

He could only use half his mouth after receiving a nasty beating when he was smaller. It had healed as it was broken and he didn't have full use of his facial muscles.

"Did ye na hear, whih ye bin?" He always sounded like he was accusing you of something, but he had learned to cut off a lot of what he was saying so he could get his message out. "Kyro brot a heap bodies."

Lani just let him finish, though others often jumped in and missed all he was telling. She had learned to be patient.

When he breathed in through his mouth, it sounded like he was sucking on something. "Ded bandets, lots of them. He talkin soon. We goin listn."

"Oh yeah, the bandits, I heard about that. I didn't know he was holding a town meeting though." Lani bluffed through it.

"Kyro's men were about telling everyone to come," Ilker added. "Harsop, he asked for you, he did."

"Why's that, then?" Her whole body tensed.

"He didn't say. He just asked."

"I don't like that one. He's trouble. What did you tell him?"

He had recoiled against her as she snapped at him. "Nothing, Lani, promise. Just you weren't here, didn't know where you were."

"Good." She paused, looking at the fear on his face. "You did good, Ilky. Real good." She took a deep breath and ruffled his hair.

Lani would deal with Harsop when she needed to. There was nothing she could do about it right now, except to not get caught on her own.

"We better get going then. Let's find out what it's all about," she added, putting Ilker back down and taking his hand.

In the time they had been talking, the number of people on the road had grown, and now a steady stream headed towards the market square.

The group of youngsters stayed mostly to the side and kept out of the way of the adults moving along the middle of the road. They all knew it was best to be as unseen as possible.

Harmless as they were, many of the city's residents didn't care for them. It didn't take much for some of the adults to clip one of the kids over the head or shove them as they passed. A man pushed through several of them muttering under his breath, "Rejects, get out of my way, waste of space you are."

The kids had heard it all before and none took too much notice. If it was just words, they felt lucky.

While Lani wasn't from here and she wasn't one of the harmed ones, she was as much an outsider as anyone else. She wished she could fit in better, but with her mixed eye colors and being an orphan she'd been made to feel unwelcome anywhere but with them.

BARNEN WASN'T THE LIVELIEST OF CITIES. IN FACT, LITTLE OF NOTE happened at all. Outside the main festivals the highest points of life were when any traveling troupes or teams passed through and put on a show in the square.

With winter only just coming to an end, a town meeting would prove to be the center of conversation for weeks. Gossip and rumor would be flowing more freely than the river on a rainy day.

Why was Kyro calling a city meeting, Lani wondered? There were rarely any full meetings and they never were for a good reason. Usually it was Lord Barnen imposing some new rules or taxes that had everyone in uproar and grumpy for weeks.

The market square was packed with bodies, living ones, all gathered in front of the stage that was a permanent fixture in the northern side of the square.

Lani and the young kin made their way to the eastern side and found perches on some barrels and a small wall so they could see without being in anyone's way, and out of the reach of any of the guardsmen.

"Lani!" a familiar voice called out.

Lani looked to her left and saw Beltima hurrying over to them.

"Beltima!" Ilky called out and jumped into her arms.

"Ilky, sweets. Such lovely hugs. I need hugs today."

"What happened to your face, Beltima?" The young boy spoke the words Lani didn't have the heart to ask.

"Nothing, Ilky. Here, sit with the others."

Lani gently put her hands on Beltima's shoulders. "You okay?"

Beltima forced a pained smile at her, and tilted her head to the little ones.

Lani nodded. "Is this what it has come to for you? Just come back to us, there's enough room."

"He'll not have any of that, and you know it."

"Who? Harsop?"

Beltima shook her head at her and looked quickly at the younger kin and back again, before putting a finger to her mouth. "It is what it is, Lani. I'm making the best I can of it while I work something else out."

"Like what?"

"I'm not sure yet. Don't you worry about me, girl. You need to be worrying about yourself."

"What do you mean?"

"You know what I mean. You're the next eldest in the group and he's been mentioning you recently."

"I had a run in with him a few days ago."

"And you've angered him now. He won't let up until he finds something else to take his mind off you. So be careful, or you'll be looking as good as me." Lani ignored the fake smile and looked at the bruised eye and side of Beltima's face.

"Enough of this, let's find out what this meeting is all about."

As they settled down she could see Lord Barnen and Kyro come in from the northern road towards the stage. Following them, the entire squad of his guardsmen walked all in formation. They then fanned out and made their way deliberately around the crowd to take up positions around the square.

As an air of tension crept across the square, the townsfolk slowly quietened as they observed the guardsmen getting into position, the air crackling with concern.

18

KYRO

Kyro stood on the permanent stage in the square looking across the forming crowd. Behind him stood the large frame of Lord Barnen, whose family the original town was named after.

Barnen had grown to city size and was no longer a town. He often thought the lord had grown alongside it. He too was bursting around the edges.

Kyro had watched the town grow and was dealing with all the issues that brought. Many of the people of Barnen had lived here all their lives and they made it still feel like a town, their town. Many outsiders were frowned upon unless they were just passing, including himself. Despite his decade of service to the town there was still a feeling of not being accepted. Until there was a problem that threatened them of course, then they were all his best friends.

He was still surprised that Lord Barnen had approved his suggestion of a public meeting. Kyro didn't get too much interference in doing his job protecting the city and the safety of the lord and his family, but he had learned that outside of that he did best to keep his opinions to himself.

The lord was prickly on a good day, and today was not a particularly good day.

They rarely had open meetings in Barnen. Typically a meeting was used to inform the masses about a change. Outside of some tax changes there had been little to trouble the citizens with in recent times. Kyro took great pride in knowing he had created the safest city in Malamig, albeit being heavy-handed with punishments in the beginning to put the fear of their life into anyone outside the law.

He waited another ten minutes, watching the way the crowd formed up, his men all positioned evenly about the square just in case the person he was looking for gave themselves away. The many voices were chattering and gossiping with their own tale of what had happened or theories of why the meeting had been called.

Kyro raised his hand, waited for most of the babble to settle down, and then called out in a loud and commanding voice. "Yesterday we found eight dead bodies out by the Fenda Road wood cavern."

There were loud murmurings and gasps at his words.

"Three of the bodies were outlanders from Enderk. Four of them were men from here and the other had some liking to a Mal. Right now we aren't entirely sure of his origin."

A voice rose above the others. "Three outlanders together, I thought there was meant to be limits on how they came and traveled over here."

"You're right to ask that question. I have no answer right now, but you know I will get to the bottom of it. They had no papers or anything that I can use to determine their reason for being near here."

He paused, gathering his breath and letting the gravity of it all settle in with the townsfolk.

"It seems that the unknown man was fighting on the side of our men and while it appears he was able to slay the Derks he fell to a wound he suffered in the fight. He wasn't from here. That I know. But, if he was close by, maybe he's known to someone here. If you had a visitor recently who has disappeared, bring it to our attention.

"Our goodly priest will be laying the bodies to rest by week's end." He turned and looked towards the side of the stage where the Thening priest Despring nodded in acknowledgment, his face devoid of any emotion. "We need to be sure he isn't known before then. We would like his valuables to be returned to his family if we can find who they are."

Kyro could see the crowd was becoming more restless now they knew most of what had happened, but he knew he had more to inform them of. Raising his hand out in front to silence the growing noise, he shouted more loudly, "That is not all of it!"

"Lord Barnen has agreed that it's more important you know up front what is happening to stop any silly rumors or gossip getting out of hand."

Many people turned their eyes to the lord who was sweating in his long coat despite the cool weather, and simply nodded along with Kyro's words.

Kyro wouldn't tell them all he knew but there was more than enough to share that would keep everyone on their toes and they wouldn't like all of it.

"We know that someone was out looting the bodies. We found an item that makes it clear the looter is from here. That means someone here in Barnen knows more than we do about this event. And that will not do!" His emphasis on the last phrase was heavy before he paused.

The crowd fell into an unnatural quiet as he looked over them, sweeping his view from left to right, pausing and holding the gaze of people in the crowd, letting the threat of punishment sink in. Amongst a group of the younger urchins, his eyes settled on the girl Lani. Inside his stomach turned as he thought about the symbol he'd seen on the wrists of the dead outlanders and the memory of what had happened to her mother.

A cough from Lord Barnen snapped him from his thoughts; he had lingered too long looking in that direction. She and the kids shrank back amongst the crowd, frightened by his stare. They were usually the brunt of any blame in the town, so focusing on them might give the crowd the wrong idea. He continued his look across the crowd, deliberately pausing on numerous people.

"Whoever knows about the deaths of these men and has found themselves with some things that do not belong to them needs to visit with me today!"

This stirred the locals up further.

Kyro added, "If you are here, come forth and see me before day's end and there will be no more than the loss of a hand for thieving. I want to know what happened out there! I will not tolerate any of you here that want to hide murder and thieving from me. Come sun-up tomorrow anyone found to be part of this will hang!"

At that Kyro stood back and the Mayor moved forward, as the crowd again fell into quiet. Lord Barnen's large girth was spilling over his trousers, held in by the strength of the buttons, his coat open at the front but masking the wideness of his sides.

"You know why I put Kyro in charge years ago. I was tired of the criminal influence around these ways and we've lived better now for years. I intend for Barnen to remain the safest city in Malamig!"

Kyro watched as he sucked in several more large breaths.

"We want to know more on this matter. That clock runs out at midnight. After tomorrow anyone caught handling goods from these bodies will hang, whether being the culprit or trying to trade in them."

Lord Barnen eyed the crowd with dark eyes, letting his words sink in, and there was almost complete silence. Kyro knew that there'd only been a handful of hangings in Barnen, several within the first eight week of his job, as he set about laying down the new law. While word of what happened kept everyone in check, the main townsfolk had all witnessed it and knew that what Lord Barnen said would be true.

"If that doesn't alert you to how serious I am on this matter, the following should. As of now the gates of the town are closed to normal passing."

The silence was broken by a rowdy outburst, the crowd coming alive with calls and talk.

"Closed! What for?" a voice carried over the rabble.

"Only those authorized by myself or Captain Kyro will be allowed to pass through. To do so you will need to carry a signed pass by one of us. It's for all our safety. We do not want these Derks wandering freely about our town, nor do we want anyone in who would break our rules."

The talk about the square was now intense, "How will we go about our work?" Another voice rose above the others.

Lord Barnen waved Kyro back toward the front of the stage, and raised his hand again until most of the noise had settled.

"None of you can go about your work or lives when such heinous acts go unpunished. Help us solve this and life can return to normal. Everyone needs to be wary, and pay attention to who is moving around our town. All our guards will be on extra shifts and manning every gate as well as patrols until we are sure our safety is not at risk."

"How long will that take?"

Kyro was becoming impatient for this to be over now. "As long as it needs to! Help us find who the looter is or spot anyone that doesn't belong and we'll let you know when all is clear. Rest assured though. We will solve this!"

Lord Barnen held up his chubby hands, "You know enough now! Get back to your work and help us find those who would circumvent our rule of law." At that he turned and moved to the stairs where his valet waited to help guide him down.

Kyro stood grimly looking over the crowd, his hand absentmindedly settled on the hilt of his sword. No single person or any group had stood out any more than any other, but he hardly expected anyone to give themselves away. It never worked that easily.

He waited there looking across the square until much of the crowd had dispersed, sure there would be many heated debates around fires and over pots of ale tonight. He made his way over and down from the stage towards where his second-in-command stood.

"Let's go, Markahm. After all that I need an ale."

19

LANI

*L*ani had seen Kyro's stare and felt like he had seen right through her. She knew he had no knowledge of her being at the cave or she would already be in chains. What was the item they had found out there? It worried her that she might have left something behind that would identify her. She had brought the satchel and her own bag back to her warren. There was nothing that identified her. But his stare, it was different. He looked at her and there was a query in his eyes, like he was thinking more than he should about her or them.

His gaze had fallen on them longer than seemed right. She didn't want to bring any more attention on her kin, they struggled hard enough as it was. She was as afraid of Captain Kyro as the others were. That was the right thing to do if you wanted to stay out of the jail or worse.

Several times before when she had been younger and caught taking some fresh food, she had been put before Captain Kyro. While his rules were harsh he didn't extend them to the youngest children. He had given her warnings and told her that she needed to make sure the kin stopped breaking the rules. He had given her leeway up until recently.

Now that she was older he had told her that the law would apply to her as well as anyone else.

Why had he stared at them? She half checked herself to see if she wasn't wearing something that would give herself away, but she knew there was nothing that would highlight her. Acting guilty was a sure way to be noticed. She needed to try and be normal. She had hidden everything, so there was no way they would be able to trace the dead bodies to her.

The crowd around the square was breaking up slowly. Some of the people shocked by the news wanted to discuss it, while others wanted to hurry home and make sure their things were all safe. The less scrupulous merchants would want to move some goods out of town before the gate security became a problem.

Would others take to the drains now to help get in and out of town? That was something she wasn't sure of. Nothing like this had happened before, so she would have to be extra careful. She hadn't ever seen anyone else down there but that didn't mean others didn't know about it. The last thing she needed now was guards poking around down there, especially Harsop.

As she rubbed her hands together she felt it. Ashantha's ring was there on her hand and she had completely forgotten about it. She couldn't feel it on her finger, it was only rubbing against it that reminded her. She quickly stuffed her hand into a pocket.

"What's wrong, Lani?" Ilker tugged at her arm.

She blinked and gently shook her head. "Nothing, Ilky, nothing. I was just daydreaming."

"You looked frightened, like you been spooked."

Grabbing his hand, she talked to them all. "Dead bodies enough to spook anyone, boy. Well, we know what Captain Kyro wanted now, don't we? We all have to look out for ourselves now, right?"

They all nodded heads and closed in tighter around her, their faces showing signs of worry.

"We stick together right?" She struggled with the words. What if she had to leave? What then? "I said we would get something to eat, so I need to go to a stall and buy from them. Let's get going."

They had joined the tide of people moving out of the square, and she steered them towards some of the market stalls that huddled together on the southern side of the square.

There was a particular stall that Lani was going to. She had on occasion bought from the lady that ran it, an older lady that had always treated Lani just like any other customer. She felt as if the lady actually looked after her better than others but wasn't sure why – just that the amount of food she ended up with seemed worth more than what she paid.

Standing to the side of the stall as hidden as possible, she waited until two other ladies were served. One of them gave her a sideways look, which Lani just turned away from. When they had gone she stepped around the side of the stall so the older woman behind the stall could see her.

"Hello there, young lass. Fancy seeing you here today."

"Everyone came in to hear what was going on."

"Yes, and a strange thing to be told it was too. I can't recall how long it's been since we had trouble around here."

"Longer than I've been here, I know that."

"Maybe it might be," she smirked. "That just makes me feel older and all."

Lani had nothing to say to that. Although her hair was mostly silver, there were still the odd strands of her original dark brown. She seemed spritely enough, though age wasn't something Lani had thought much about.

"Did you need something then?" the older woman asked, the corner of her mouth smiling gently.

"Well if I can? I've got a coin and I wanted to get something extra for my kin, we don't have much but oats and bread these days."

"Well show me that coin and let me find us something you can cook for 'em."

Lani cautiously pushed her hand into the pocket of her tunic and slipped one of the two coins she had placed in there. She leaned closer and handed it to the woman.

"Oh my, that's a big coin you have, lass. We can find you a good bunch of things for this." She pocketed it and grabbed a sack she had under the counter. "You'd be wanting to cook them some soup or the like I'd say?"

Lani just nodded, staying to the side of the stall as she waited. The younger ones were waiting just down the road as the stream of people left the square.

The farm lady handed the sack to Lani, who was surprised at how full it looked. "There you go. That is about right for the coin, I'd say."

"This seems a lot for just one coin?"

"Oh no, it's just about right I think. Don't you argue. I know my goods, young lass. I keep my eye around, and I know what you've been doing for all them young ones. I don't know if you're always up to good – I doubt you can be trying to survive in a city like this, but I'll help where I can."

Lani had no idea people even really noticed her. She wasn't sure if she was happy or scared that this woman had taken an interest in her.

"Don't be getting worried about what I said. Being an older person in the market with little to do, I notice more than I should. Just you know, girl, that you've done all right, you have. They wouldn't have gotten along so good if you weren't here. Now off with you. Go and feed that lot."

"Thank you," was all Lani could muster, dipping her head as she smiled and left. She caught up to the others who hungrily eyed the sack.

"We need to keep this lot hidden and get it home before any of the big ones see it, so form up around me and let's head there quick as we can. Stay on the main paths, and all."

The group formed up around her, Dorted grabbing hold of one side of the sack to help share the weight. They made their way toward the road to their hideout.

'Hideout' was a funny word. The street kids all called it that, but everyone in town knew where it was.

It had been an old stable that had survived a nasty fire in this older part of what was still a town back then. Several original houses and buildings, or their shells, still stood here, most left as they were, being too close to the river's edge which flooded in high water.

Gossip was that the owners had set the fire off and then demanded new plots in better ground. Nothing could ever be proven and they were slowly rotting away, all except the hideout. While it was still in much disrepair, the kids did what they could to make it keep out the weather.

It sheltered the smaller and younger kids and they stayed out of the way of any of the older crew who hadn't been pressed into service. Mostly the older ones lived in an abandoned house further along the river and the littler kids were definitely not welcome there. The arrangement worked as well as it could.

Lani was anxious being back here, she just hoped Harsop was being kept too busy to be remembering his threat to her. She wanted to be back in her warren but it would be strange if she wasn't seen doing her normal things.

The kids needed feeding anyway and she would take care of that before anyone came looking to take their food. Since they'd arrived back at the old stable most were milling about the yard area or playing in the dirt.

"We'll be needing some water for the pot and wood for the fire if I'm going to be making soup," she called out to those closest to her.

"Soup?" one of them replied.

"Well only if you keep it to yourself and help me get started, that is." Her reply set them into action. She watched them all fall into their assigned roles.

Who would take care of this lot if she left town? The thought conflicted her. She'd been anxious with the threats from Kyro and the Mayor trying to think whether it would be safer to leave. As she looked around at the little ones organizing wood in their makeshift rock oven she remembered what it had been like when she first turned up.

No one organized anything, you scrounged and scavenged for food wherever you could find it. Lani had been lucky, initially she'd been taken in by the priest until she had become familiar with the town. That only lasted six months and then she was put with the kin.

Since then it had become a struggle to make sure there was enough to eat. While the priest would leave oats, he rarely gave them anything else. They were allowed to pick items from a leftovers cart at the market. It was always hit and miss if they could be there at the right time that a trader threw out any older fruit or vegetables on the turn.

They'd take what they could though and whoever was leaving it, Lani was thankful for them. Once she'd become the elder in the group she'd made sure they all worked together, looking out for each other and that everyone got fed.

With practiced chaos a small fire was started and as it started to grow firewood was added to it, while others dragged the big old pot across the bench top they'd crafted from several partly burnt doors. They had all made do with what the buildings around them offered up.

"I want you lot to watch what I do again, you need to be able to do this yourself. You can't not eat if I get busy again. Do you understand?" She spoke to those perched around watching the water begin to steam.

It was like they needed 'mother' to cook even though there was nothing much to it. She went over to a small store box and pulled out a pouch. In it were some herbs and peppercorns.

Putting a small selection in, she stirred up the water and started pulling out the vegetables and roots from the sack. Where she had to, she peeled off the skins with her new little blade, but mostly it all went in. Chopping the bigger vegetables with her blade took time but it would be worth it. She used half the sack of produce, making sure they hid the rest.

It would just take time now, there wasn't any meat to go in it but this and a handful of the oats in it to add some starch would be the best meal they'd had in weeks.

Catching up on the latest silly tales and stories while they waited for it to cook, half kept Lani's mind off what was in her head. The activity was a pleasant relief from what she had faced in the last couple of days. Several of the youngest leaned into her so she could wrap her arms around them. It was the only comfort they would get.

The soup simmered away for an hour or so, slowly thickening as it all broke down, several of the kin taking turns to stir it with a wooden stick.

"Dorted, why don't you go and see if there's any old bread outside the bakers. Bread will be good with the soup."

He nodded at her and headed off out onto the street, Ilker following along beside him.

When they returned Lani was scooping bowls of soup out for everyone and the group gathered around their makeshift tables and took their fill – several bowls each for the larger ones. Everyone ate enough to see them through another few days.

Setting them all tasks to go clean their bowls and the pot in the river kept them all active enough until the day started to wane.

The chill of the evening crept into the barn and they all began making their way up into the remaining loft section which had the most shelter. They had gathered straw and rags and made small mattresses around the loft protected by a low roof. That, the sides, and the thin blanket they each had kept most of the chill at bay.

Only the few older ones lingered downstairs with Lani as the night fully settled in. Their chatter dwindled until without a spoken decision they all moved to their beds. She raised the ladder once she was up, sitting in the corner watching over the little ones, one eye on the lower area and the other on the small bodies as they slept, feeling like what little she did for this kin of hers wasn't all wrong.

20

TILLANDRA

Tillandra had known she would have to make the trip to Midderbuilt sooner rather than later, but her vision overnight sealed it for her.

There were multiple reasons for her to make the trip; Gimbden, the Mother Stone and collecting the new ring. Gimbden would be happy that he was getting to change location at least, although he too would be saddened by the news of Ash. While he could be told by anyone, or by talking through the masks, it was simpler to tell him in person since she was heading that way.

Any new ring and the Mother Stone could only be carried by her. She always looked forward to seeing Tingfurlew, the Ring Master, but never the long trip across the desert.

Her life would have been easier if she could communicate with him like she could the others in the Court, but he was not one of them. His role was unique and whatever rules bound him to the Jesters were different, and with no mask she could not connect to him.

The revelation that the girl was wearing Ash's ring troubled her. She had tossed and turned all night, trying to understand what that meant but no obvious answer came to mind. She would need to let the Court know about it.

During one of the few times she had slept through the night, a dream had come to her. She had seen a camel running west along Death Road through the desert. It carried a bag of unseen valuables, and a sense of urgency surrounded the whole dream. Like all of her visions their meaning was rarely clear but this one seemed as obvious as it could be. She needed to go, and now.

Tillandra knew Goran needed to be notified, but she wasn't willing to try another connection straight away, and she still wasn't sure how anyone could locate the girl. Before sending Goran on a wild goose chase, she needed to think more about it. Perhaps a solution might come to her on her journey across the desert.

She had risen well before the dawn, and prepared a note for Milfred and another for Bea. He would inform the court and no doubt they'd be upset with her for slipping away without warning. She had retrieved her travel kit, climbed the tower and taken the Mother Stone before heading to the western gate, her long strides helping her move at a faster pace than others would be able to walk.

As she closed on the gate, the weary guardsmen, bristled to attention recognizing Tillandra approach.

"It's early to be out, Mother," he challenged.

"It is, good man. I need to be passing through the gates early. I have a journey to make that needs no attention from the day folk."

"As you wish, let me see to the gate door for you," the guard replied. He had been about long enough to know that Mother Folly needed no retinue, or protection. He unlatched the door inset in the bigger gates and open it for her.

Tillandra stepped through the door and away into the cool morning air, conveying her thanks to the guardsman. She could hear the door being barred again, closed to the outer world. The road meandered west and north cutting back and forth around the rocky rises and harsh dirt landscape.

Anderwell was left mostly to itself due to the fact it wasn't in the most hospitable of areas. Sahro as a whole had a harsh and unpleasant climate with limited arable land. Even from when the city had just been known as Follytown, the only people that came there were those that needed protection from the outside world.

As a Humaas, her long muscular legs gave Tillandra loping powerful strides allowing her to cover the distance of an un-laden horse. By the time dawn was upon the land Tillandra was well gone from her home, and making steady progress. If her body held up she would be on the road for a week before she reached Watersend.

Sahro was a desolate place, a massive kingdom of desert that isolated it from everyone else. Few ever tried to go deep into the desert. Those who did never returned, its heart a burning land without cover or water.

The road along which Tillandra traveled had taken many years of building and was an important highway for much of the southern part of the continent. Each town or oasis along the trail had been placed at a set distance so that people could travel along it and still survive.

She slowed her march and climbed to the top of a dune topped with a rock tower. She took out her water pouch and sipped from it, looking over the sandy horizon. In the distance she could make out another tower. They were built like hollow pyramids that let the winds and sands blow through but held their height.

The desert made building a permanent road impossible. As soon as a path had been made it would be covered over and lost. The towers had been made to guide travelers from being lost. All you had to do was move from tower to tower.

She set out towards the tower ahead, thinking of the teams of dusters that traveled the road each year. They cleared sand from the towers and repaired them where damage had formed. Occasionally they found bones in the open bases where some traveler without guides had met their demise.

This first part of the trip west was always easier as few winds made it this far with much strength. Today it was almost still, allowing her to push hard and get to the oasis before the sun began to set.

While she was used to this trip the first few days were always the hardest. Tillandra was glad to reach the first oasis without too many aches and pains.

"Greetings traveler," the sole steward of the oasis said as she walked into the main tent beside the small water hole.

"And to you. Am I your only guest?"

"For now. Who knows who or what will blow in later. Shall I assume you will be staying the night?"

"Yes. I will be up and gone early in the morning, but for now something to eat and a hammock will do me well."

"One copper will cover your stay."

Tillandra reached under her robe and awkwardly took out several coins before selecting the right one. She handed it to him and headed to a far corner of the tent where a table had several covered plates.

Only one other person arrived before dark. Tillandra kept to herself and retreated to a hammock to sleep soon after, the only light some torches spread around the oasis.

Replenishing her water from the water hole, she also refilled her food pouch with dates from the communal food and left before the first rays of sun climbed over the road from Anderwell. She hoped the winds would stay calm and the road was straight and that she could make Hesb within the day, but doubted it.

All morning she followed the endless trail through the sand. Her height made it a little easier to see the distant towers across the undulating dunes and paths. There were few living creatures around. Occasionally the call of a distant bird, usually vultures, would catch her ear and she would look up to watch them. Even the life of a vulture out here was harsh. They hunted long and hard to find anything worth feeding on.

Twice she passed a trade caravan going the way she had come. The men and horses looked exhausted from the journey. Carts and wagons couldn't last the trip over the desert road, so eager merchants, wanting to get their goods east without the long trip around the bottom of Dharatan, were forced to travel this way.

Tillandra could easily pick the armed guards, knowing full well they likely carried gems from Watersend as much as anything else. She was seen as little threat and they never stopped, only waving or nodding as their paths crossed.

Just before middle day she arrived at the last small oasis before Hesb. It was empty apart from its steward.

"You're an odd one to arrive at this time," the old man called out to her as she came in.

"What do you mean?" Tillandra replied.

"It's a full day the way you've come, and best part of one the way you're heading. I know few who will travel through the night."

Tillandra moved under the cover of the tarpaulin trunk between the clumps of palms on the bank of the water hole. She unwrapped her head scarf and shook out the sand from it.

"Oh, my eyes are not so good, I didn't see you were Humaas from over there." The man had hobbled over to her.

"No need for long eyes out here, steward."

"Truth in that, young lass. Nothing but sand to be seen. Still, even with your pace, you must have been pushing hard to have made it here today."

"I left before the sun was fully up. What news from Hesb?"

"Little today, I'm sorry. The last two groups through here kept mostly to themselves and their guards had nothing at all to say."

"I passed them on the trail. Gem traders, I assumed, they gave me the once-over before hurrying by."

"It's rare that you see anyone that could threaten them out here, no one can travel through without passing our stops, we would know if there was trouble before it happened."

Tillandra nodded and pulled out her water skin.

"Help yourself to what you need. There's a jug on the table to your right, leave some coin in it for what you take. I leave it up to your honesty, I've no need to be making my riches at my age."

"Thank you."

Tillandra sat and looked at the small water hole. She had little time to decide whether to push on for Hesb today or spend the night here. Her pace had been good and she was here early enough to make it, but she would still be traveling the last of it in the dark. That was if she could keep up the same pace for the rest of the day.

Parts of her body were already aching and sore. It had been months since she had been on the road but she was confident she could push on through. As long as she didn't come across any headwinds or lose her way then she would be fine.

The urgent need to get answers to Ashantha's ring drove her forward. If this woman had the ability to hold on to the ring and the

Balance was thrown out, then their whole society was at risk. The timer began running as soon as Ashantha died and this trip of hers was taking her away from choosing who would face the Audition, as well as collecting Ash's things.

She stood up, knowing she couldn't lose any days on this trip.

"Doesn't look like you're staying, woman?"

"I have places I need to be, steward."

He chuckled. "At my age there's no place so urgent I need to be. I'm flat out trying to avoid to get to places."

Tillandra smiled at him and put a bronze coin in the jug as she gathered her things. "Keep well, old man."

LANI

*L*ani woke at first light. The ladder had been let down and as she stood and stretched she could see a couple of the kin were milling about in the common area. She joined them down below and sent several of them off to fill a large pot with water. When they returned she set to soaking a large bunch of oats in the pot.

"Ye want wood?"

"Yes, Dorted, that would be good."

She watched him head out to the back of the barn where they kept what wood they had. It was hard to remember he was just as young as Ilky. Not only was he big for his age, he acted much older. She had often wondered if that was because of the way he had been had been mistreated. Hearing someone else climbing down from the upper floor, Lani turned. "Do we have any turned fruit for our breakfast, Ilky?"

"I can go look." He hurried out onto the main roadway outside the barn.

Scrounging leftovers was one of the ways to add variety to what they ate. There was a collection of bins by the market where traders would throw out their spoiled or turning goods. There were only so many ways you could use oats and bread.

Ilker returned with a couple of bruised and soft apples. "Good work, Ilky. There's enough here we can use."

She showed him how to cut out the better portions and they added them to the pot, which now sat over a lit flame. Lani stood beside it letting the heat warm her body.

Lani felt better knowing the kin would have a stomach full of food today. The work Despring rented them out to do was never easy. Doing it on an empty stomach was always harder. She should see if Bragg had work for her. Until she could fence the loot she needed to keep earning what she could. He'd be cross with her for not showing up the previous couple of days, if he had work, but no more cross than any other day.

Standing by the small fire stirring the food made it easy to forget most of what had happened the last few days. She easily settled back into her role with the kin, not that she had chosen the role. It had just become what it was.

As the smell of the cooking porridge filled their hideout, the last of the sleepers rose and came down to the main area. She waddled over to the table with the heavy, large pot, minding not to burn herself. She only noticed Harsop standing in the door when she passed the first bowl, almost dropping it in the process.

Her stomach churned, her hands shaking a little, but she pretended not to notice and kept serving.

"Breakfast for you lot. That's a bit rich, isn't it," he snarled as he walked over. As he approached Lani's end she moved away from him around the table, sticking close to the kids. He stuck two of his thick fingers into the pot, scooping out some porridge and shoving it into his mouth.

"Bit bloody hot, that is." His mustache had caught some of the porridge, flecks of sticky white oats stuck on the dark hair.

"What do you want, Mister Harsop?" Lani asked.

"Funny you should ask, Lani," he sneered at her, brushing his mouth with the back of his sleeve. "You know very well what I am here for, girl. I told you what would happen."

Lani could sense that the youngsters were frightened by his

manner. She could feel tears welling in her eyes. Staring at him only brought back her memory of the other day.

"You go, Harsop!" Dorted shouted as he stood up from his seat.

Harsop laughed as he looked at the young boy. "What you going to do, Busted? Eh? You going to beat up on me?" His mocking laughter at the boy echoing around the otherwise silent room.

Dorted grabbed his bowl and threw it at Harsop, who easily pushed it away but he then started after him. Dorted turned and rushed towards the door.

"Run, Dorted. Run!" Lani shouted after him.

Harsop chased him as far as the door, "You'll keep, lad. I'll deal with you later." He turned and headed back toward the table.

Lani had used the distraction to dig out her knife from her boot, and had it slid it up in her sleeve, not sure what she could do with it but she wasn't going to give up quietly.

Harsop headed directly towards her but she moved the opposite way around the table. Several of the youngest were sobbing, the others just sitting nervously waiting to see what would happen, their food long forgotten. As he went back around the end of the table he pulled the pot handle and flung it across the floor, some of the contents spilling out.

"You lot don't deserve food here. You're all just a bunch of dumbsters and rejects. Should have been put down at birth. That's the truth of it. Now Lani here isn't playing along so you all need to be punished. "

He stopped and grabbed a girl from the table. "Who are you then, little one? I don't know your name."

Shaking with fright from the way he had yanked her up from the table by her skinny wrist, she replied meekly, "Fioressa."

"Well, Fioressa, you can come with me then if Lani won't behave. Nice name like that, you'll do well."

She squirmed in his grip as he half lifted her off the ground, her toes hardly touching the ground. She let out a scream of pain.

"Leave her alone, Harsop!" Lani shouted.

"Don't you tell me what to do, Lani. If you won't play nicely then this one will be the price."

"You're just bad, you are. How did you ever get to be a guardsmen? Put her down or Kyro will find out all about what you are up to."

He let go of Fioressa's wrist and she fell at his feet. "What did you say? You think our mighty captain would have time to listen to a dirty little grub like you? You heard his warning about you, any more trouble and you'll be suffering his punishments."

"You think he'd be happy with what you're doing? Maybe it's time he found out."

Harsop started towards her, his eyes boring in on her. "And what about the pastry he found out by those dead bodies? I seem to remember me thinking you had been stealing some of them. Think he'll believe a thief over me?"

Lani pulled the knife out and held it in her hand pointed at him, "You stay away from her, Harsop, and from me, you hear me. I'll cut you if you come closer."

Gasps came from the kin table, as she stood apart from Harsop; he had stopped and was looking at the knife and her hand.

"You think your little knife is enough to stop me, Lani? You've gone too far, you have, I need to teach you a lesson."

"I'm telling you again, Harsop. Stay away or you'll be explaining why you have so many cuts to your captain and I'll happily tell him."

"What's going on in here?"

Markahm and another guard had come into the barn, hearing all the shouting. "Put that knife down, girl, before you get yourself hurt."

"Not while he's here," Lani replied, less sure of herself now.

"What have you been doing, Harsop? You're meant to be patrolling not picking fights with girls." Markahm smirked as he said it and the other guard laughed.

Harsop stood back and looked darkly back at Markahm. "We have ourselves a troublemaker. She just threatened a guard, you heard it."

"I'll tell you what we have here, is you wasting time and frightening some young 'uns. The only trouble I see is what will happen if Kyro finds us wasting time here and the looter isn't found."

"You're no better than the captain with her. He said she wasn't getting no more protection but here you are doing his work just the same."

Lani watched Markahm's face turn sour, and his eyes narrowed.

"Oh really? That's one line you've crossed too many, Harsop. Consider yourself on night duty for the next two weeks."

"You can't!"

"I just did, and you can start tonight. A double shift might get you focused on what you're meant to be doing. Now out of here, do as you're told and leave this lot alone."

Harsop turned his face slowly to Lani; her skin crawled when his eyes met hers, she knew this wasn't over, his anger was there in his eyes but it was as dark as she had ever seen it. She looked away, her skin crawling, and all she could do was to stop herself being sick.

Markahm walked slowly up to her and leaned in to her ear. "And you put that knife away before you cut yourself. I don't know what was going on in here, but you don't be threatening people with that or you'll need to deal with me. Got it?"

Lani nodded and watch him leave the barn, then she dropped to the ground shaking, tears rolling down her face.

The kids left the table and came over to her, forming a group hug. Dorted snuck back in through the back door; he didn't come over but went to the big pot on the ground and rescued what he could, lifting it back up onto the table.

Lani got herself up. "Thanks, Dorted," she nodded, "come on, let's eat what we can then. Don't you worry about all that."

2 2

LANI

$\mathcal{A}$ somber mood filled the barn. While they had salvaged enough food for all the kin to eat, Lani hadn't been able to stomach anything. She was in no mood to go stand in the vats today but couldn't lose what little work she had.

She was as frightened of herself as anyone else. She'd never threatened anyone before and she knew that she wouldn't have stood a chance if Harsop had come at her, but she wasn't going to allow him to just take the girl. Lani didn't even know where the bravado had come from.

She wasn't the mother of the litter, they weren't hers to defend at all costs. That wasn't true though. She might not be their mother but without her how would they survive? She didn't know why she had taken on the role, the other older kin didn't. Beltima had never done more than what Lani asked.

Feeding them and organizing their habits was just an extension of how she'd survived when she came here. No one had done that for her. Back then they didn't even have this stable.

Maybe she hadn't done them a favor at all? Making them reliant on her and not standing up for themselves. She had grouped them all together, making them easier targets.

She needed to leave Barnen for a little while to fence the things she had found but they hadn't even fed themselves properly these last few days. How on Dharatan would they survive properly for a week or more, especially if Harsop now had it in for them all?

She was about to head out when Ilky came up to her. He seemed unsure of himself. "It's Fio."

"Yes, Ilky, what about her?"

"Well I've been sitting with her." He paused as if waiting to be told off. "Her arm, it's not right."

"What do you mean not right?"

"I think it's broke, Lani. She can't use it right, too much pain, I'm not sure it looks right."

"Okay then, we better check it."

Lani made her way up the ladder into the loft level. Fioressa was still lying on her bedding but now facing them as they came up.

"Fioressa, Ilky tells me your arm is hurting. Is that correct?"

She directed a stare at Ilky before she nodded her head to Lani.

"I'll need to look at it. Do you think you can sit up for me?"

Fioressa awkwardly sat herself up by dragging her butt backwards and using her right arm to help push her up; the whole time she cradled her left arm across herself, scowling once in what looked like pain.

Lani moved in closer, and trying to be gentle with her left arm lightly touched her fingers down the arm from the elbow to her wrist. Fioressa almost leapt in pain as she pressed around the upper wrist area where the bruising from Harsop's grip was.

"Sorry, girl, that isn't looking so good. Why didn't you say something?"

Fioressa's face dropped and she shrugged her shoulders.

"Never mind. I should have checked after it happened. Ilker, you need to go find me some splints I can use. About this long." She showed him the size of part of Fioressa's arm.

"Will it hurt?" Fioressa limply asked.

Lani shook her head. "No, all I am going to do is brace it so it won't hurt to carry it anymore." She could see Fioressa's face lighten a little at her response.

Ilky returned with a small bundle of wood bits accompanied by Dorted.

Lani sorted through the sticks and picked out two that were similar in length. "I am going to need something to wrap these on with, is there any spare cloth about here?"

The young ones all shook their heads but Dorted went and dug around where his bedding was. "Ya can tis, ya want." He handed over a thin purple scarf.

"That'll do, Dorted, if you're sure?"

He nodded at her and she took it, the edges already a little ragged. There were several rips in the fabric which made it easier for her to tear strips from it.

"Now, Ilker, come around here. Once I place the wood on her arm, hold it in place and don't move her." He gently held the wood, allowing Lani to grab the strips she had made. "It will hurt just when we tighten it, Fio, but that will settle once I stop. Okay?"

Fioressa nodded, closing her eyes.

Lani strapped the upper part of her arm and worked her way down, wrapping the strips around and then tying them off, so they would hold but could also be undone. Fioressa squirmed a little initially before settling again.

"Well there you go, that's all done," Lani said. She had an extra strip which she stuffed in her pocket so she could use both hands to feel her way down the arm. "That's set as good as I know how, I've seen them do it with legs on dogs. Now you just have to keep that on there until there's no more pain from squeezing. Okay?"

Again Fioressa nodded but said nothing, as she ran her fingers down her arm then lifted it. "It doesn't hurt to lift." A small smile was on her face.

"It won't either if it stays tight, but if you knock it, it will still hurt. Now you make sure you wear a long top over it so no one notices, right?"

Another nod.

"You know if some see that you're sore, they'll be drawn to hurt you more and tease you. So let's keep it as hidden as you can."

They all made their way down below, to find the barn was empty except for them.

"I've got to go to Bragg's and see if there's work. You lot will be okay now, right?"

They nodded and Lani headed out on the street, already late for a full day's work but hopeful Bragg would have something for her.

As unhappy as he was she had been missing, Bragg put her to work, but punished her by only giving her a half day's pay. By the time she returned there was little light left in the day. When she arrived back at the barn what she saw made her angry.

"What, no one has lit any lamps? What are you lot doing?"

As if on command some of them got up and started to go about lighting a few lamps.

"What's for dinner, Lani?" Ilker asked, his small face peering up at her as they gathered in the main areas.

"Why you asking me, Ilker? I'm not your mam. You can't just be waiting on me to feed you. Last night, that was special because I had something to share, but if something happened to me you can't not feed yourselves.

"Some of you need to go sort something. See what's been left out."

"Wot them veg you got?"

"Dorted, you going to need to use them for more than one night, you can't use them all at once." His eyes saddened at the answer.

They both looked disappointed but she didn't want to be their sole provider, that was setting them up for disappointment. If she was going to have to go away for a while then they'd need to take care of themselves. She didn't want to be worrying so much about them or she couldn't do what she needed to do.

"Go on, you need to sort it out, I've got to go out but I'll wait and see what you can gather." She went back and sat on the back wall, putting a small distance between her and the kin.

Harsop had a lot to answer for, breaking Fio's arm without even realizing it. His threats and attack this morning had just brought back all the problems in her mind. He wasn't going to leave her alone; how long could she hide from him, when would he grab her again like the other day? At least he was on night duty. That would buy her some more days before she decided when to leave town, and she could avoid him during the day.

Her mind ended back in the cave where she'd gone to hide. Nowhere around here seemed safe to her anymore. Could she tell Kyro? After what he had said the last time and the look in his face, she just knew he would blame her for anything that was wrong.

Did Harsop really think she was the looter? If he had told anyone then they would have come for her already. What was he up to? If she forced his hand and he told Kyro he thought she was the looter, there wouldn't be any way to stay out of trouble then.

Lani tried to calm herself. There was no way they could connect the pastry to her. Was there? Harsop seemed to have thought it through easily enough.

She already knew she had to go to Little Big Rock to fence the loot but this made her mind up. She needed to get away while Harsop was on night duty and before he got angry enough to tell someone else or make another move on her.

The kin would need some of her money. That was the best way to keep them okay while she was away. She just wasn't sure who to give it to now, who might keep Fioressa away from Harsop if he came back.

Lani slipped out the back of the barn, too distracted to say she was leaving, and headed back towards one of the entrances to the drains.

LANI

*L*ani shrugged off a twinge of guilt about leaving the smaller kin to themselves again. It wasn't her problem, she'd already made herself a bigger target, and all she wanted was the safety of her warren. Right now the dark and solitude would be a pleasant relief.

She swung out onto the main road and crossed from side to side, using the middle as she came to side lanes or smaller roads, not wanting to get surprised by Harsop or any of his pals. A few days ago her life in Barnen had been simple, she stayed to herself apart from her work with Bragg and looking out for the young ones. Now she had to worry about multiple problems.

To get into the drains she was always mindful to use a variety of entrances on the off chance anyone had an eye on her, that way she wasn't going to lead someone to her sanctuary.

As it was, the main roads were quieter than usual. The curfews and shutdown were already having an effect, making it easier to see if she was being watched. Further along Market Road she could see a patrol was loitering near one of the crossroads, causing her to pause and see what they were up to. It didn't take long to make out the silhouette and voice of Harsop in the patrol. They weren't moving in any direction but they were blocking the way she had intended to go.

Lani ducked along a side road and down a lane that she followed alongside a set of taller buildings with few windows. Halfway down the lane she climbed up onto a small wall and walked along the top of it as it climbed upwards on an angle, her feet confidently one in front of the other on the narrow brickwork.

Where it ended against the back of the building there were enough hand and foot holds for her to scale up toward the roof. The last part was the trickiest as she wasn't quite tall enough to fully reach the roof edge, and had to jump off the ledge on the top of the window and grab the edge of the roof.

She looked around to make sure no one was watching her and braced herself for the jump. As she leapt up and reached for the roof edge, her fingers slipped and she fell back. Her left foot landed solidly on the wall but she had thrown her right leg outward and she teetered perilously. Waving her arms madly, Lani brought her balance back to the middle of the wall and placed her right foot firmly behind her left.

Her heart was beating fast and she took several minutes to calm herself down. Her brain tried to talk her out of making another attempt. While it would be easier to move around at street level and less risky than making the jump, the likelihood of being spotted was much higher. She focused on what she needed to do and told herself she could do it.

This time she wiped her hands carefully on her tunic to make sure they were dry. She closed her eyes briefly and then leapt again. This time her fingers held and she hauled herself up onto the roof, the shingle not moving under her feet as she moved across it. The pitch on this roof was very steep and Lani had previously only ever tried it in dry weather. Luckily she was able to cross over to other flatter roofs and follow her way east towards her target. She took a break to perch on a roof and take in the town at night.

She was behind the square opposite to where they had watched Kyro the day before and could see down the winding road that led to Lord Barnen's manor. It stood out with its protective walls and the expanse of the property around it. While most other houses in Barnen were within space of each other, the Lord's manor had land and gardens as well as close proximity to the guards' barracks and quarters.

The Church of Thenis was located on the edge of this wealthier part of town. Despring the priest lived in a small manse attached to the back of the church. The church itself was quite large in proportion to the size of the town, its spire dominating the area.

A small movement caught Lani's attention and she had to look again to be sure she wasn't imagining it. A figure dressed all in black was making its way along the narrower lane towards the church.

She had to concentrate very hard to see them and it was only when they were forced to cross an opening where the light changed that she could do so. An uneasy feeling crossed Lani's mind. She was unable to stare directly at it without her eyes hurting. When she looked at the clothing the dead outlanders had worn, they had behaved the same way.

She stayed frozen where she was, far above them, watching the figure's pathway. She could see nothing for what seemed like half an hour, and her knees were starting to ache from squatting. Just as she was considering that she'd lost sight of them, the figure crossed the lane moving swiftly and soundlessly, but she could see their silhouette clearly enough.

They were dressed entirely in black with a wide hood across their head. She lost them again in the shadows until the shape appeared at the building next door to the church. With little effort and no noise they had forced the door open and went in, closing it behind them.

Lani tried to remember what the building was but she couldn't, although she was almost certain it belonged to the church. Because the building wasn't connected directly to the church, she wasn't so sure.

Her brain was spinning and her heart rate was high. Seeing one of these bandits alive was the last thing she had expected inside the town walls. How did they get in? Everyone was on the lookout for anyone unusual. It was very brazen of them to be walking the streets.

The other outlanders had been in a group. Were there any others around here now? Lani studied everywhere she could, her eyes seeing nothing out of the ordinary.

The building next to the church appeared undisturbed, no light showing through any window, the door still closed. From her vantage point on the roof, she could hear no sounds coming from within.

She hesitated. She wanted to see what they were up to, but the memory of Ash's dead body held her back, afraid to be anywhere near them. Ultimately her desire to know more won out. She couldn't wait any longer, not when this might be the only person that could answer questions about what she had found. She was relieved she didn't have the amulet on her.

Her knees burned a little as she forced herself up from the crouched position she had been in, then she eased her way step by step along the roof. She wished now she had taken one of the tunics when she had the chance, they were hard to see in the dark.

At the end of the building a ladder ran down the entire height of the building and she swiftly descended, partly sliding. She cussed as her left hand caught a rough edge, the sharp sting catching her unawares. The pain caught her focus and she landed a little more heavily than she wanted. She could feel a trickle of blood on her hand now.

The lane was lit enough from the moonlight and she could see she had a cut in her palm. When she sank her hand into her tunic pocket, Lani found the leftover strip of cloth from the arm binding she had made for Fioressa, and quickly wrapped it around her hand.

She stood with her back to the ladder, catching her breath and looking left and right making sure her minor disturbance hadn't alerted anyone. When she was satisfied no one was watching, Lani crept up to the edge of the warehouse she had climbed down, ducked across the gap, and crept down the side of what she realized was the undertaker's building that the sneak was in.

Careful to tread quietly, she made her way down the side alley until she was in line with the side of a window. She stood against the wall listening, calming her breathing as best she could. Several small shuffles could be heard through the wall, close enough to where she was.

She turned and leaned in towards the edge of the window. The outline of the caskets lined up against the far corner was the first thing she saw. She moved over a little further so she could see more of the room. Despite the poor light she could make out the silhouette of the intruder with their back to her while they moved along one of the bodies laid out on benches.

There were four benches with as many bodies, each covered in a canvas. The outlander had lifted the canvas on the far body and appeared to be searching it, lifting up an arm and checking the fingers.

As the outlander appeared to finish on that body, replacing the canvas so that it matched the others, Lani readied herself to slide back across the window before they turned.

"Oi, what are you up to?" The shout from up the alley caught her by surprise.

Turning to look, she recognized Harsop heading down the alley. His hand on his sword hilt froze her in her spot.

"Well, well. If it isn't Miss Lani. Some days you can't count all the luck you have." His voice was loud and carefree with no one else around.

Lani had forgotten about the bandit, but catching movement turned to see the face of the man looking directly at her through the glass. She could see his pale face and a dark goatee beard under his hood despite the minimal light. His dark eyes stared at her and a shiver raced up her spine. Back to the moment, she didn't wait another beat, pushing off the building to propel herself down the alley as fast as she could.

"Stop where you are, Lani!" Harsop's voice came from behind her.

LANI

She slid the grate back over her head to block off the entrance to the drain. The steel scratched and scraped on the compact dirt as she pulled it. Lani held her breath, her legs splayed out sideways with her feet wedged into holes in the walls to hold her in position.

She listened, waiting to see if anyone had followed her to this point. Nothing. The night was eerily quiet. The sound of the grate sliding would have been heard by Harsop if he'd been close enough, which she doubted. Running was always the easiest escape with him, she was so much faster than him.

Five more minutes passed without any hint of pursuit. Her legs were aching now and the sides of her feet were crushed into the cutouts. There was no more time to wait. One foot at a time she worked her way down the wall, trying to share her weight through her arms.

Once her feet touched the slimy floor Lani paused, letting her eyes adjust to the lightless drains. Satisfied as she could be that she was alone, she made her way through these very familiar paths stopping and listening regularly. The map lines she could see in her mind made it much easier. Her breathing was still rapid and short, her body on high alert. She was lucky again to not get caught although worse was the look she had seen through the windows. The outlander's eyes had spooked her more than Harsop. They threatened without her even knowing why.

Finally she crept into her warren and locked the small door behind her, the darkness wrapping her in a strange comfort. In here she always felt safe. Even if it was an unusual place to live, it was hers.

With it being night outside she plugged up the light hole with its wooden peg and fumbled around until she found the small lantern, which was the only light she used down here, lighting it and shuttering it right down so only the smallest of lights was given off. She removed her boots, changed out of her clothing into a shift, and hung her tunic and hose on a makeshift hook on the wall nearest her bedding.

She gathered her small skin of wine and poured herself a cup of it, her mouth dry now that the chase was over. Her heart rate was finally settling.

Lani tried to understand what had happened in recent days. Her simple ordinary life around Barnen had flipped on its head and now she found danger in almost every corner of the city. It was bad enough that she was having to hide and escape from one of the very people meant to be protecting the town, but having come face to face with one of the Derks inside the walls was worse.

Did Kyro know that an outsider was in town? Harsop wouldn't have seen him, he was only intent on catching her. Would Kyro even believe her if she told him? Going to Kyro would expose her to Harsop. She would have to find a way to let Kyro know that she had seen one in the town. Everyone needed to know.

Lani finished her small cup of wine and went and lay on her bedding, her brain still spinning from the chase and what she had seen. Despite it being late, she didn't feel tired. The act of lying on her bed was more one of comfort than any hope of sleep.

When she propped herself on her side, the light reflected off the ring on her hand. She'd forgotten about it. The way it had molded to her finger made it totally unnoticeable.

It was a strange looking ring, and she tried again to twist it, to pull it off, but it didn't move. The image of the clown mask looked back at her. It was a raised surface off the body of the ring. The hat had two tips to it, like some entertainers wore in the circus.

Annoyed about everything, she twisted harder trying to move it. It wouldn't budge, the clown's face almost mocking her efforts.

She stood and began to pace the room, all the time twisting and pulling at this rigid jewelry on her finger, inadvertently bumping into the few pieces of furniture in her room and once her head on the roof of the warren.

Sore and sorry, she slumped back on her bed, tears running from her eyes, "What is going on?" she said to the empty room. "More foul magic."

Magic was something that was never spoken about, an evil thing best not discussed. If Ashantha had magic, had he lied about who he was? Had he told her the truth about these dark-clothed men being bad? Was he the bad guy? Not for the first time she thought maybe he was just a thief, and his story to deliver the amulet was just to get it to whoever he worked for.

She thought back on the face of Goatee, and knew that he wasn't a good guy. That face and look belonged to someone bad. Her thoughts kept jumping back and forth between what Ashantha had told her and what she had learned since.

Lani sat in the corner holding the ring away from her body, half expecting it to laugh at her. She stared at it, waiting for it to do something. Nothing happened. She wasn't sure how long she sat there fretting, but the lamp light began to wane. So too her resolve.

Out on the street she had to show confidence in everything she did, otherwise she would never have survived the taunting and loneliness. Down here it was different, and while she always felt safe from people and the outside world, it was inside her head that her biggest battles were fought. Now more than ever.

It always came when she felt out of control. Her self-pity dragged her down, and it closed around her like a blanket she didn't want but took comfort in anyway.

A tear rolled down her cheek, she drew in her knees to her chest and wedged herself as far into the corner as she could, hiding the ring on her finger.

Why me?

Times like this she wished her mother were alive. Not that she could remember her. All she knew was that she had been killed. When Lani tried to picture her mother all she got was blackness and then emptiness. She tried to put a face to her using those from folk she saw about Barnen, but they never stuck.

Like now all she got was a darkness and emptiness that left her feeling sad and alone. She couldn't remember even what a hug felt like. Maybe her mother had never hugged her, or was she too young to remember?

She hated being touched though, so maybe she didn't want to be hugged.

Why didn't I die too? What life is this? I don't want this blasted ring, or his stuff. I don't want Harsop or the stupid kin. Leave me alone! Why can't you just leave me alone?

Holding her hand up in front of her face again she could have sworn that the clown was smirking at her. Like it was mocking her, as if knowing she couldn't wear the ring in public.

Her type didn't have jewelry or wear it. If they were seen with anything that didn't belong to them it would be considered stolen. While she didn't want the ring, she also didn't want to lose her hand over it.

She shivered at the thought. Their lot in life was bad enough, living hand to mouth on the streets, but losing a hand and being marked as a thief would be worse.

The last of the light disappeared and her space was now completely dark. She lay down on her cot keeping her hand out away from her body, and let sleep take her. At least there she had peace.

LANI

Unsure of how long she had slept, Lani got up and pulled the peg out of the hole in the ceiling at the corner of the room. A small amount of light squeezed its way through the gap, confirming that it was at least daytime.

The light was just enough to make the room's contents visible. With that change, it was easier to stay in tune with the town above. Usually she tried to spend some nights with the kin, but that was going to have to change now. This was the only truly safe place she had.

Changing into her street clothes, Lani hoped that if Harsop was patrolling at night then if it was early enough she might be safe to be on the streets for a bit. Somehow she'd need to work out his schedule so she could try and be above ground while he was resting or otherwise busy.

As she checked her pockets to see what was in them, the ring on her finger caught on the edge of one. She looked at it.

Cursing it all over again, Lani tried to pry it off her finger. It still wouldn't budge. Her hand looked a right state. The cut from when she'd climbed off the roof had mostly sealed up, but there was plenty of dried blood all over her hand and her bedding. She looked for the cloth she had wrapped around it but couldn't see it in the dim light.

No matter, she thought, *it's dried now. It just needs to heal.*

Between that and the ring she was going to need to cover her hands or others would be asking questions. Not that she was intending to be topside much. She would need food and drink but couldn't be seen out every day. That would just make it easier for Harsop to find her. How would she be able to work at Bragg's if she couldn't go topside? It didn't seem fair, all she wanted to do was just go about her days and now Harsop had cost her what little freedom she had. Maybe she could get one of the young ones to do things for her. Or would that put them more at risk? Like what happened to Fio?

Yes, it was dangerous right now but she had to get food and drink to last out the next few days while she planned her next step. Lani dug out the hidden pouch and took several more coins.

She grabbed the only cape she had and put it on in a way to cover her head. It was well worn and marked and wouldn't stand up to a close inspection but she felt at least she would appear different from a distance.

Near to the central square and markets was an alley that separated the back of several houses from the city wall. In it were several drain holes that were poorly maintained. Lani was still able to fit through one of them, although it was awkward, difficult to climb out, and left her exposed for longer than she would usually like.

She had checked both directions before squeezing through and was happy that no one had seen her. It wasn't an option she chose to use regularly and it was not a fast escape route. The wealthier residents in this section weren't keen on her type being around, and once before when walking down the alley she had been given a hurry up by a man who didn't think she was up to any good.

She paused briefly at a half barrel beside a building. It had a puddle of murky water that served to wash the dried blood from her hand. Carefully wiping it on her pants so as not to open up the wound again, she made her way to the market square.

Lani stood behind the market stalls and watched to see who was around. Most especially the guards.

She went to a shop beside the square that sold clothing items and shuffled up to the counter, the lady inside sneering at her when she turned to see who was there.

"I think you are in the wrong place, girl."

Lani hated the way everyone always assumed they weren't worthy of things like the other townsfolk. "You don't even know what I am after."

"I can only assume you want charity by the look of you," she said, her haughty tone grating on Lani.

"Do you sell gloves or not?"

"Yes we do but I doubt you can afford what we offer."

"You jump to a lot of conclusions for someone who thinks they're smart," Lani snapped back at her. "I just want some simple woolens and I can pay."

The women hesitated for a moment, looking around the shop as if to check Lani hadn't snuck in someone else with her who was taking items while she distracted them. It was a ploy they used occasionally but not now. "Let me see this money then before I waste any of my time."

Lani glared at her, the dislike of how the woman stared at her making her want to steal something just to spite her. She knew she could grab something and be out of the shop before the woman could catch her, but she didn't need the attention.

She reached into her pant pocket and pulled out one of the coins. "I have this and it should be enough for what I need. I don't need anything fancy."

"Obviously," the woman said, rolling her eyes as she looked at the coin in Lani's hand. She looked her over for longer than Lani felt comfortable with. "That seems a lot of money for someone like you. What was it the captain was telling us to do? Look out for suspicious people. Yes, that was it. Well perhaps I should find a guard."

Lani's heart jumped at what the woman said. She nearly turned and ran but knew then that they definitely would be looked for her. "How dare you! I work hard to make my money. You and your precious clothes wouldn't exist if I didn't do what I do for Bragg Clothier. Maybe I should tell him that he shouldn't sell you his cloth."

Lani's bluff seemed to work. The shopkeeper seemed shocked to be spoken to like this by Lani. Her cheeks flushed a little and she scowled back at her.

"I'm not sure about you but yes, it is coin enough. Let's get you something and have you out of here before you scare off my customers." She picked up a basket from the table behind her and banged it down on the bench before shuffling through. She pulled out several pairs of woolen gloves.

"Do you have any without the fingertips?"

The woman sighed and reached in again, pulling out a gray pair that were missing the tips of the fingers. "These are the only ones."

"They'll do then." Lani put the coin down on the counter, keeping her hand turned over to not show the cut, and pushed it to the woman.

The lady picked it up and threw the gloves in front of Lani. "Right, then. Settled. Off you go."

Lani knew she was paying too much for the gloves and was about to say so when the shop door opened.

The woman looked up, then quickly back at her and back at the new person. "Hello there, Miss Clara. Nice to see you. This one is just leaving. Come around over the side there and I will see to you."

She leaned forward and hissed at Lani, "Off you go, then, and make sure you don't be back again."

Lani sneered back at her and grabbed the gloves. She lingered a moment, wanting to stay and make this snooty woman uncomfortable in front of her customer but thought better of it. As she headed out of the shop she caught a quick glance of the lady starting to take off her dark green cape and shawl. Without showing her own face she hurried out of the store pulling the left glove on so the ring was hidden. She pulled on the other one and headed back amongst the stalls.

The morning sun was still low enough in the east that Lani could see it trying to rise above the buildings on that side of town. There were few people in the markets today and the stallholders were chatting amongst themselves as much as to any customers.

Many gave her a long look as she made her way towards her destination, looking closely over their wares as she passed them by.

The side she was headed for was the temporary stalls, for those who came and went. This is where the traders from out of town or further away took up shop when they were in town.

She was happy to see the grocer lady was back today. She only ever came for about a quarter of each full moon, so Lani had always figured she must be from a fair distance away. Whoever she was, she had never looked down on Lani, and many a time threw her a free piece of fruit as she went by, without expecting any payment for it.

"You're back again already?"

"Those young ones, they eat a lot when they can," she lied.

"Did you want some more then?"

"I need something just for me to see me through a few days, is all. You don't have everything I need, but those others," she pointed at the other stallholders, "they aren't as friendly to me as you are."

The woman smiled and nodded as Lani spoke.

"Could you help me?"

"Of course I can. What are you after?"

"I just want a little bread and cheese, and the rest I'll get from you here."

"Have you got some coin for me then?"

Lani blushed, forgetting she hadn't given her any money, and reached into her pants and pulled out a silver coin.

"This should do the trick, you only want a small amount then?"

"Yes, it's just for me for a few days."

"You wait here and mind my things then." Surprised she trusted her at all, Lani stood guard at her stall, the irony of it not missed on her.

Out of the corner of her eye Lani saw another stallholder who was looking her way. He was a strange looking man with a multicolored beard and dark hair pulled back and tied behind his head. His beard was almost comical. She realized he was a chalker, that his stall was full of chalk mixes and sticks of many colors. As he fiddled with items on his stand one of his hands went up and stroked his beard, adding new layers of color. Lani recognized him from Bragg's place. She was sure he stopped in there to do business from time to time.

The grocer lady came back and held out several small loaves of bread and a good sized chunk of hard cheese. "Will these do the job for you then?"

"They are perfect, thank you. You saved me a lot of hassle."

"Those other stallholders are okay, they are just wary of you street lot. They know there are those who like to help themselves."

Lani looked at the ground and about the stall. She couldn't look at the woman, knowing she often had helped herself. "Why do you trust me then?"

She chuckled. "How much fruit and veg you likely to run off with, then? If you need a piece to eat you just ask. Haven't I always given you things if I see you?"

"You have, you're more kind than anyone. It made me suspicious at first, but now I don't know?"

"I can understand that I guess. Ain't nothing to it, except I've seen my fair share of mistreatment of those who had no choice to their lot. Everything I got here," she waved her hands to encompass the stall, "if I don't sell it turns to mold. Can't sell rot. One bit of fruit won't cause me to starve. I just wish I could help more, but being away from here..." She stopped what she was saying.

"Where you from then?"

"Aren't you the chatty one today! We farm our lot a ways down towards Little Big Rock but inland a fair sum. That's why I only make it here on the moon turn."

"I wish there were more like you around here."

"They are a closed lot, these ones here. I was just telling the chalker here," she turned sideways a little and flicked her thumb towards the man with the colored beard, "what they are like."

Raising her voice a bit she said, "Didn't I, Rainbow?"

The man looked up at the name and a smile opened from within the hair as if it ran from ear to ear. "What's that you say, woman?" He made his way towards them.

"I was saying to the lass here how closed off many of this lot are." She nodded her head towards the main market.

"You'd think they were still in a little town out on the wilders. Many still remember old Barnen, not the city it is now. Who are you then, girl?" He reached out a hand to greet her, every finger an array of different colors.

Lani shook his hand gingerly, the cut still tender beneath the glove. "Lani." She couldn't help but grin a little when she took her hand back, the gray glove now dusted with color, her fingertips each a different shade.

"Oops, don't mind me, darn stuff, I can't get it off me." His smile seemed to shine extra light around his eyes. He hefted his thumb back towards the market. "Them all call me Rainbow. That's been my name as good as it need be. You can call me that too."

"To think I never knew your name, Lani," the farm lady said. "You best know my name too then. It's Pinqueth."

Lani smiled, feeling a little uncomfortable at all this familiarity.

"What did you need from me here? I still have this change."

"I just wanted some fruit. Berries and apples?"

Pinqueth grabbed a cloth and placed the bread and cheese in it then busied about picking out some of the fruit from her stall. "There you go," she said as put an ample supply of fruit into the cloth. "Will that do?"

"Ahh, yes. Thanks." Lani couldn't believe the coin that was there would cover it all. She was about to get more out of her pants.

"We're all square then," she said opening up a pouch tied about her waist and putting the coins into it.

"Thank... thank you," Lani stumbled across her words. She didn't know why this woman was always so generous to her, but she wouldn't argue.

Rainbow was pulling at his tunic, trying to get inside one of his pockets. He finally pulled out a little pouch tightly closed at the top. "Here you go, Miss Lani, here's a little something from Rainbow."

"You don't need to give me anything."

"Oh, but I do. You look like there's missing color from your life, lass. This here, it's a little pouch of color. If you feel a little dark you just open this and pinch yourself out some color. It's like magic." He laughed as he said it, repeating and laughing as he said the word 'Magic' again.

"I don't know what to say?"

"Thank you will do, girl. Now no more of it."

Pinqueth put her hand on Lani's shoulder, "I'll be pulling out of here today so you sure you've got all you need?"

She nodded her head, about to reply, when Rainbow piped up again. "Myself included. I think I've sold enough of me chalks for this trip to make a right old mess come festival time. I need to be getting myself down to Big Rock before some other cheeky chalker takes all my business."

"I am all good, thanks. I'll see you on your next trip then."

"Not if I see you first," Rainbow threw in before Pinqueth could reply. He laughed again and made his way back over to his stall.

"On your way, girl, and look after yourself."

Lani gathered up the bundle and looked around the market to make sure she was safe to head on.

LANI

ani was starting to leave when she paused and turned back to Pinqueth. "Why's it so quiet today? There's hardly anyone in the markets at all."

A frown came across the woman's face. "That's the truth and all. You're my third customer all morning. I wouldn't normally be able to count how many."

"But the lockdown of the gates, that wouldn't stop everyone, would it?"

"Oh, you haven't heard. One of the guardsmen was killed last night down by the church. There's a lot of gossip floating around the town but many people are scared and staying inside."

Lani gulped as Pinqueth told her.

"Yes, girl, we're all a bit worried, I tell you. That's one of the reasons I won't be lingering here today. I'd prefer to be elsewhere until this all settles down."

Lani didn't have much else to say. That was where she had been last night and where she'd seen the outlander. She unconsciously pulled her cape further up over her head, and wrapped it around her and the bag of food.

"I think it's best for everyone to stay inside until the guards have sorted this out, I do. You need to keep yourself safe, you do."

Pinqueth stared at her as she said it, and Lani thought she had lingered on that last part. Deliberately a small smile curled at the older woman's mouth, her gray eyes drawing her in.

"I… I will. Thank you, again." She hurried off away from the stall using other stalls to shield her and making her way towards Westgate.

Every sound now had her on edge despite it being daylight. With so few people out on the streets, anyone was a threat. Lani didn't want to stay on the Westgate Road so moved down a side lane. She kept looking over her shoulder and pausing at any cross lanes before bursting through them, half expecting Harsop to be there. He would have more reason that ever to be hunting her now. The dark-eyed man had seen her last night as well, would he be looking for her too? She needed somewhere hidden to stop and think things through.

At the back of the Motley Fool Inn, the stables and courtyard were deserted. Lani slipped through the half-closed gate making her way into the very back of the stables. She felt like no one was following her, but now was no time to be complacent. She climbed up into the hay loft and sat there waiting to see if anyone else came into the yard. It was one of the many places Lani had discovered she could access over the years.

While she waited, she nibbled on some of the berries in her bag; they were soundless to eat and moist enough she didn't need to find a drink.

When she was sure that the way was clear she clambered out the hay loft window and climbed down using the footholds on the outside wall until she could drop into the alley. The alley was completely shaded and the path had a permanent feeling of dampness. Moss climbed the side walls and the paving under foot was always slippery.

She jumped over the half wall into the back of their barn and made her way into the hearth they had made. Dorted and Ilker were in there arguing about something and both froze when they saw her.

She was about to say something when Dorted rushed to her and put his hand over her mouth shaking his head. Lani almost fell backward by surprise but managed to stay on her feet. Dorted turned to

Ilker and shook his head at him holding a finger over his mouth, and he then looked at Lani and pointed out the back. He removed his hand from her mouth and pointed up to the roof before grabbing at his ears.

Lani thought she understood and carefully made her way back out the way she had come, climbing over the half wall and moving back up the alley away from their hideout.

A few minutes later the two boys came around and followed her, neither saying a word, but Dorted still pointing away from the barn. At an alcove several hundred yards away from their hideout, they all gathered out of sight.

"What did you do, Lani?" Ilker demanded.

"Nah, Ilk," Dorted growled. "I told ya not her."

"But… but they said."

"Who said?" Lani asked.

"Me say," Dorted said to Ilker. "Guards. They look fa you."

Lani had been worried she would be linked into this just from being there last night; how would she be able to explain herself when it was Harsop who would have seen her down there?

"Why me?" she asked him.

He lowered his eyes to the ground.

"It's okay, Dorted, why me?"

"They say you killed him."

"Killed who? Who have I killed?" She knew what he meant but she was happy to play dumb for now.

"Harsop."

There it was, this was how he would get at her. "Harsop? Who did Harsop say I killed?"

"Na, Lani." It was even harder for Dorted to speak quickly when he was agitated. "It Harsop that's been killed!"

"What?" She gasped at the news. Lani put her hand out on the wall to brace herself, feeling all giddy. Now it made more sense. She steadied herself and realized what must have occurred.

"You okay, Lani?"

She didn't immediately reply. Harsop had been killed, it had to be the outlander, she knew, but she couldn't tell anyone that. No one could know she was there.

"I'm okay. That's a shock is all. Why are they blaming me?"

"You didn't do it did you, Lani?" Ilker's small face pleaded at her.

"I didn't do nothing, Ilky, I promise you."

"But the other day you threatened him, they all saw it, you had your knife."

"That was just to protect Fio, you know that, right?"

"He got stab many times," Dorted said, looking straight her. "I told Ilk, not you, you not stab."

"You're right. It wasn't me. I have never stabbed anyone. What am I going to do?"

"They've got that cloth I gave you, that you used on Fio's arm. They showed it and we recognized it. It was there they say, bloody and by his body."

She shook her head and anxiously looked about the alley to make sure they were alone. "I must have lost it somewhere. It wasn't me. You two have to go back, and I will have to find somewhere to hide."

Ilker grabbed her hand, making her wince, "You got gloves, Lani, they're like new."

She shook his hand off and hid her hands in the cape.

"It okay. Teller solve it." Dorted said.

"What?"

"Teller. Guards say one come. Read our minds they will. Solve it."

Lani knew the young ones told stories about Tellers to each other. She didn't know where they got the ideas from. "Just get back there. And you haven't seen me, right? Anyone asks, you haven't seen me or spoken to me. I will lie low until we know better. Okay?"

She pushed the boys out of the alcove and back towards the barn, "Go on. It's not safe if they are looking for me. Can you have someone tell Bragg I'm sick so he doesn't come looking for me either?"

Dorted nodded at her.

"But where you going to go, Lani?" Ilker was too young to understand.

"I'll be okay. I'll see you soon. Now go!"

She watched them walk down the alley, looking back over their shoulders. She flicked her hand to shoo them along before turning and scurrying back up the alley. What she needed most now was to be hidden in her warren and out of reach of anyone, guardsmen or the outlanders. Anyone.

Going to the market earlier without knowing about Harsop and getting away with it was a lucky break. She would be too scared of being seen now. With several days' food in hand, she could at least lie low until she came up with a plan.

Pulling the cape tightly about her she made her way cautiously back to the barn she'd hidden in earlier. Lani climbed up the outside of the stables at the back and returned to her hiding spot. It seemed like the best place to be until darkness fell.

The back door of the inn banged against a wall, and she could hear voices as several people came into the outside yard.

"I told you there's no one out here."

"We've been told to look everywhere, and I am not cutting corners."

"Fair enough. This yard's empty. No one hiding out would be dumb enough to be caught by Turp. No one seems to ever cause trouble here cos of him."

"Well, I've looked now so I can say we checked. Let's go check out the alley behind and scout along that way for a bit."

"Let me get me a smoke started first, then we can. I still don't know what Markahm suspects this girl for, I can't see how our Harsop be getting bested by a young gal like that."

"You think? But we saw her with that knife and all. She was well mad with him. Maybe she jumped him from behind and stabbed him before he could defend himself. Anyway, I don't know. Markahm just said bring her in as well as anyone else that Harsop had been making trouble with."

A silence fell, then the scratch of a flint. "There we go. I don't buy it myself but who knows right now? Everything around here's gone crazy if you ask me. There's something strange about it all. First them bodies, now this. I don't understand any of it."

"Me either, I tell you. Did you hear the captain has sent for a Teller from RaMar?"

"Really? I had not heard that."

Lani could hear them start walking again, their voices slowly moving away.

"Said he wants to get a reading about all of this – what's going on and who is involved."

Their voices moved too far away for her to continue hearing what they were discussing. Her head was spinning with that last part. She'd heard about Tellers. They were a strange group of people that could see things without their eyes. She hadn't ever seen one but heard they had some special form of magic. If one came they'd find her for sure. They'd find out everything, including where her stash was.

She was too agitated now to lie still, and climbed back down into the alley going the opposite way to the guards. She needed to get out of sight now, and she didn't want to wait a moment longer. She weaved through several lanes until she found a way down; it was more exposed than she liked but speed was the important thing now. Once underground, she stood still waiting to hear if anyone was following.

KYRO

Markahm walked into Kyro's office and made his way to a stool beside the fireplace. There were still embers smoldering there and he leaned against the hearth.

"No progress then?"

Markahm shook his head and sat on the stool. "The urchins didn't say as much, but she's missing from the stables. Several of them squirmed when we showed them the cloth we found near Harsop's body."

"Doesn't mean much. How would a small lass like that have butchered him that way?"

"Doesn't feel right to me, but like I told you I caught her waving a blade at him just the other day. He'd been in there causing trouble with them. Maybe he went a turn too far?"

"What sort of trouble?"

"I'm not entirely sure."

Kyro noticed Markahm look away and shift uncomfortably on his stool. "*Markahm?*" he asked much more forcefully.

"There's been word he's been running girls in town. Or protecting them that do."

"And you haven't brought this to my attention before now because?"

"I thought you knew. I thought you were turning a blind eye to it."

"A blind eye? When have you ever known me to turn a blind eye to anything?"

"Well..."

"Well, what?"

"Well, Lani."

"What do you mean, Markahm? Just spit it out!"

Kyro watched Markahm swallow and take a deep breath. "You've been protecting her over the last few years, captain. I know we let the little ones get away with trivial things, but she's not little. You would have punished others for some of the things she's done."

The room fell silent. Kyro knew he was right. He wanted to yell back at Markahm that it was none of his business, but it was. Here he had been pretending to run a strict set of rules when in fact he'd undermined it by his own actions.

"You're right," he said quietly. "I feel responsible for her care, for reasons I can't explain to you. I've allowed her to get away with a lot more leniency, but you heard me just the other week when I warned her."

Markahm nodded.

"I meant it, Markahm."

"I believe you, captain. But do you?"

"So back to Harsop. Could it have been an angry customer or a rival?"

"I don't think there are any rivals. No one else would dare. And with it appearing that you let him do it, no one else would dream of crossing your rules to run a competitive enterprise."

"For goodness sake. I didn't approve of him. I didn't know about it."

Markahm held his hands up and shrugged his shoulders.

Kyro leaned back in his chair, running his hands over his hair. "You don't think he had put Lani to work do you?"

"I can't say. What I can tell you is she and one of the bigger urchins were definitely not happy with him."

"Which one?"

"The lad with the face that got bashed in years ago. Remember him?"

"I do. What's his name?"

"I'm not sure. He was one of the lads that were right uncomfortable when we asked about the purple cloth."

"Why did you ask them about the cloth?"

"When we looked around the old stable we noticed one of the little girls had what looked like the same cloth wrapped around her arm."

"Oh really?" Kyro raised his eyebrows.

"Turns out she had a broken arm, and Lani had fixed it up. They claim that's what they were so angry about with Harsop. If I could understand that boy correctly, Harsop twisted her arm so hard he broke it."

"In Thenis's name, what is happening around this town? It appears I'm missing a lot of information. Is there anything else you're not telling me?"

"No, captain."

"There better not be. From now on, assume I didn't approve of anything. If it's against the rules, it's against the rules. I want to know. Got it?"

"Yes, captain."

"So we have no idea where Lani is at?"

"No. Want me to keep looking for her?"

"Yes, Markahm, I do, and anyone else who might be involved. This is a murder and suddenly our peaceful city is becoming just like all the others. I'm not going to sit idly by and let criminals take hold after everything we've worked towards."

He stared at Markahm as he thought about the last few days.

"Something's very amiss with all of this. I don't like not knowing what is going on. That needs to change. Why are the Derks around Barnen, for starters? The dead ones we found aren't just any old Derks either."

"So you said before."

"There is something very wrong about what they are up to, and we are going to need to find out what that is. If there are more of them then maybe Harsop stumbled onto one inside the city."

Markahm looked at him with renewed concern.

"That might explain the injuries he suffered. If they got in then maybe one of our citizens helped them. Perhaps we have intruders inside the city right now. You need to start looking at everyone."

"That, I'll gladly do. One of us getting killed, even an arse like Harsop, is making all the men a might jumpy. It will do us all good to go on an extended hunt."

"Dig deep, start going through everyone's affairs, into their warehouses, offices and homes. See if you can't unsettle whoever is behind it. And let's not forget maybe there's Enderk influence here we don't see."

They both sat wordless for a few minutes.

"Just don't go running off blade first, if you suspect anything bring them in nicely just for a discussion, we can lock them up once they are here. Did you spread that story about me getting a Teller?"

Markahm stood. "I did and the guards have been spreading it around the city. Maybe it will shake something loose. Either way, digging into things will please the guards. It'll be good to be busy. I'll go round up the men and let them know our plans."

"Watch to see if any of them have unusual errands to run after you tell them as well. We'd do well to keep an eye on our own ranks as well. Promise of gold can do funny things to a man's loyalties."

Markahm raised his eyebrows at that but nodded back at him, before turning and leaving.

The door never closed. The large frame of Lord Barnen pushed through.

"There you are, Kyro. I need to talk to you."

This couldn't be a good thing, Kyro thought. The man never waddled over to the guards' barracks. Something must be truly amiss if he didn't send a servant to fetch him.

"I wasn't expecting you."

"I wasn't expecting my city to fall apart overnight either, but there you have it."

"We're not falling apart, my lord. We've got something very amiss happening, true, but we'll get to the bottom of it and whoever's behind it will be sorry."

"Someone will be sorry, that's for sure." Lord Barnen stood before the desk, his pudgy palms face down as he leant forward. The meaning of his words was not ambiguous. "It was your idea to lock the gates and every day they are closed I'm down on taxes. This will not be a long-term fix, Kyro!"

"We are about to start going street to street shaking all the trees we can. Something will fall out of it."

"Hopefully you won't lose another of your guards."

"That was very unexpected. I've put everyone in pairs now until we uncover the person behind it."

"I am already getting complaints from some of the leading houses about business being interrupted. From all accounts the markets are near empty as well."

"Fear will do that to you. A few days of everyone camped inside getting on each other's nerves might be the catalyst we need to out the culprits."

"That's all well and good for you. How can we all eat if the markets are closed and nothing can get in through the gates? And more importantly if these houses decide it's safer for them elsewhere, like Little Big Rock, for example, then the city income will drop. And I won't tolerate that." He stood up and wiped his brow with his right sleeve. "You know we need taxes to run this city, Kyro. Less trade and bad deals means less taxes coming in."

Kyro listened as he carried on bemoaning his lot, despite him being richer by multiples than anyone else for furlongs around. None of the noble families in Barnen and the surrounding countryside stood close in comparison to the Barnen fortune.

"If I can't guarantee the safety of my citizens, captain, then I will need to review how things operate here. Is my meaning clear?"

Kyro nodded.

"I want a daily update, don't leave me in the dark. I was planning to head south soon after spring broke but if things are this unsafe around here best I don't leave our good people until it's resolved."

Kyro knew it was more fear for his own skin than anything else; in all his time here, he'd never seen Lord Barnen do anything but for his own self-interest.

"As you wish, sir."

"Right then." He turned and slowly moved himself out the office entry and down the hall, not bothering to close the door behind him.

Kyro sighed and stood, closing it himself, before sitting back down in front of the pile of papers. The paperwork never seemed to end for him. That was the problem. He spent too much time in here looking at papers and not enough time out on the street, like he used to. Kyro decided that needed to change, he'd tell Markahm to roster him on with the other guards. He needed to get things back to how they were.

LANI

*S*itting in the small room that was her warren, Lani looked at what her life amounted to. A small shaft of light squeezing through the roof hole highlighted all that was hers. She rubbed at her eyes. They were gritty from the lack of sleep. All night her mind wouldn't stop churning over all the things going on around her.

Her only comfort was that she felt safe here. This was her safety, the only place that no one could find her. Well, no one normal, that is. Had she heard the guards properly? A Teller was coming to Barnen.

Lani had never seen a Teller but everyone knew what they could do. They were able to see the future and read your past. She had heard about Tellers from some of the older kin. Their stories made them out to use magic. It was one of the few stories where people spoke about magic. Lani wasn't sure if all the stories were true but no one disputed they could see things others could not.

How long until they arrived in Barnen? She had no idea. For sure if they could see through events and who was involved, then they would be able to point her out. What if all they got were impressions, not whole pictures? She was at every spot when something bad happened. She was the only one.

The warren wouldn't be safe either, they would be able to see her here. Or would they? She knew no one she could ask if it was true or not.

Maybe the Tellers could lead Kyro right to her. She was the one with the loot, and hadn't come forward like the Mayor had ordered. She had been at the death of Ash and hadn't reported it to them. She had threatened to knife Harsop, and now he was dead, stabbed like she had threatened him.

Nothing about it looked good for her.

"It's all buggered. I'm screwed."

Tears welled in her eyes. Barnen was her only home, the only place she had really known. She wasn't sure how old she was when she was brought here, it was a guess, because no one knew her.

All they told her was that her mother had died and left her alone. She had been found by Captain Kyro and brought to the city. She had been handed over to the priest Despring for her care. Not that he did much for them, and before long he moved her into the old stables with the other kin.

She had been told nothing else, she wasn't even sure that Lani was the name her mother gave her, but it was all she could say when she arrived and it felt right to her.

She had grown up here and until the last week nothing had ever made her think this wasn't going to be her home for longer. At times the desire to know what had really happened tugged at the back of her mind, but she had no idea where to start, or what she was looking for. It didn't seem to matter; if she had belonged to someone else, her father or aunties, surely they would have come looking for her. No one cared or there simply was no one else.

This warren was her home. She shared it with no one, she couldn't afford to trust anyone else, taking this away meant there was nothing at all for her. For all her time in Barnen there was no one she trusted enough here to share this secret with. Yet Kyro might be bringing someone to expose that and there was nothing she could do unless she handed herself in. She didn't want to die from something she didn't do. Surely they'd believe her, she didn't do it.

Would it matter if they found out she didn't do the killing? Kyro and Lord Barnen liked to hang people above the gates to warn others.

If she stayed put here would he protect her or use her to lay down the law? The only other choice was to leave. To run. What did she know about running? The furthest she had ever been was Little Big Rock. Would that be far enough away? Lani doubted it. She would have to go further than that if she was going to hide from Kyro and the guards. It wouldn't take them long to find her down there if they wanted to.

Lani pulled out the pouch of coins she had stashed. She did have money now, she could get a room and some fresh clothes. She could clean up and hide away from here, start over somewhere new. What about her kin though? This money was meant to be for them. If she left and took it, who would care for them?

The light was almost non-existent from the roof hole so she pegged it closed and fumbled about lighting the lantern.

Opening the satchel Lani rifled through what was in there; the pouch she pulled out with the amulet and dark rings in it, carefully placing it to the side, unwilling to touch it for long. When she pulled the mask out, her fingers tingled at the touch of it. She dropped it on the floor, unsettled by that. Looking at the dark shadowy face made her feel even more uncomfortable, so she tried to not look directly at it.

She turned the journal over several times, and opened it up. She still couldn't see many words written in it, not that she could read them even if there were.

Everything she owned was now lying in front of her – a few belongings that made up her room, clothing, candles and this collection of coins and odd items. The most valuable of them didn't even come from Barnen and didn't belong here.

Where was it he had told her to take the amulet? Callet. How far away was that? He had said a long way south. Surely it couldn't be that far, could it? She could get a ride in Little Big Rock with the coins she had. If she could get all the way to Nedor she would be able to learn where Callet was. Someone there would know.

Or could she pay someone to deliver it? Lani wasn't sure if there was a way to make that happen. She knew Bragg had people ship his cloth but that was different to this. How would she know if they delivered it? Ashantha had warned her it was very dangerous. Maybe it would be better if she passed that danger on.

The only way she would find out was to get to Little Big Rock and look for a way to get rid of it.

There wasn't really a choice, was there, she thought. *To stay might mean I die for something I didn't do, or I go and try and find how to get it to Callet.*

LANI

Lani had made up her mind. There was no way she could live down here full time in Barnen. She would need food and supplies and with the city on lockdown the likelihood that someone would turn her in was high.

Little Big Rock was as good as here, she told herself. All she would need would be a little luck and she would get herself a ride south. Once away from there no one would know her and she could start over.

The only reason she was here now was because she had few options. Since being brought here as a little 'un she'd had to make do. It was the only 'home' she knew, and she had no feelings for it either way. Barnen was just the place she'd been living.

Her choices were different now; if she stayed she was as good as dead. There'd be no trial for one like her, she'd be found guilty for killing Harsop. If they found the loot she'd be blamed for more as well and she'd not come forward when told to. Murderers were hung, there was no other punishment here. If she was found then she'd be hung and that would be that.

She collected anything that might be useful to her on the road, including changing her clothes. Everything she was taking with her was within Ash's satchel. *It's not his anymore, it's mine.* It was a perfect size bag for her needs. She grabbed her cloak as she looked around the small room for what might be the last time.

Bolting the door from outside with the makeshift key, she lowered herself to the drain floor. She wedged the key back into the hole she kept it in. It was pretty unlikely anyone else would find it, and if she ever had to come back through here then having somewhere to hide might be useful.

Once she was back in the main drain, she looked back at the smaller tunnel, one last look at her only home to date. She pulled her old cloak over her shoulders, covering the satchel and her back. She listened for any sounds that shouldn't be down there and then set off for the exit by the river.

Part of her wanted to run and be as far away as possible, but the smarter part of her took it more cautiously than normal. The last thing she needed now was to get caught when she was so close to escaping. She thought she heard movement echoing along the tunnels at one point and found a culvert to hide in.

For what seemed an hour Lani stood frozen in the dark waiting to hear footsteps sloshing through the water, or something else to confirm her fears. Nothing came, and she had to force herself out of her hiding spot and onward to the grate near the riverbank. Her fear of getting caught fought with the need to get away.

Outside the city walls she edged along until she reached the workers' bridge. She wasn't going to get wet tonight, and with an almost moonless sky she hurried across the footbridge. It was a solid stone structure about a barrow's width across that led to the vineyards over the river. The door to it was long since locked for the night and no calls came out of the dark.

Lani didn't realize she'd been holding her breath until she dropped out of sight behind a bank on the other side. Looking back at the town wall one last time, she shivered in the evening chill before fixing the cloak around her shoulders tighter and heading off into the vineyards. She walked through the night, tripping a few times over roots and stones. Despite her knees and palms stinging from the falls she kept walking, putting as much distance as possible between herself and Barnen.

As dawn started to poke across the horizon behind her she followed her shadow down a trail that zigged and zagged towards the same direction the river headed. The road to Little Big Rock was on the other side of the river, which suited her for now. She knew she would have to cross, but until she had no other choice, the isolation suited her.

She stopped on the crest of a small rise in the trail. As far as she could see ahead was rolling hills, covered with scrub, some clumps of trees and rock. The road was visible on the other side of the river but this early in the day she saw no one using it. That wouldn't last for long. Now that the day was awake, riders would come down it quicker than she had walked last night.

For now, Lani decided she was best to travel at night and rest out the day hours. She carried on and left the trail a short distance ahead. In a small gathering of trees and scrub she found a suitable hollow in the rocks of the hill they backed up to that hid her from all distant views and the sun.

Settling in, she ate a small meal from her meagre supplies and sipped some of the wine she had brought. When she'd finished the wine she'd be able to fill the skin with fresh water from the river. She struggled to get comfortable, eventually folding the cloak into a cushion of sorts and wedging it behind her. It didn't help much and she squirmed and shifted most of the day, dozing off several times.

At one point her calf cramped and she half leapt awake, grabbing at it, cursing and shuffling until she could stop it from squeezing. She finally gave up and stood, stretching her body out. She was sweating from being tucked into the same spot without a puff of any breeze. She couldn't see out of the hiding spot across the river, and paced back and forth for what seemed another hour before deciding she'd had enough.

The afternoon was quickly slipping away and she knew it would be dark before long. It was enough for her, she gathered her things and pushed out of the scrub, checking if anyone was around before rejoining the trail and heading south again.

It felt good to be moving again and before long the knot in her calf began to ease. It was hard to judge exactly where she was but she knew there was a bridge somewhere to the south. She found it in the early hours of the morning. It appeared to only be her and a plethora of animals about and she'd been skittish for hours at every strange sound she heard.

Once she could make out the bridge ahead, she slowed and sought out an observation point to watch it for a while. She spent half an hour or more just watching and listening to see if anyone was guarding or traveling through the night.

On the other side of the river she could make out a mound that appeared to be covered in cloth. It was an unusual shape, and in the darkness and across the distance she couldn't see any more detail. No one seemed to be around and she hurried towards the bridge, careful to avoid tripping again on the dark trail. She positioned her left hand on the knife in her waist band, looking left and right for any signs of trouble. If it was anywhere she'd strike an opportunist it was here, she was certain of that. She slowed as she started over the bridge, focusing on any sounds that would alert her to a surprise.

Apart from the gentle splashing of the river against the bridge and river bank there was nothing else to be heard. She was so busy looking ahead and occasionally looking back over her shoulder that Lani almost walked straight into it. Just past the halfway mark almost all of the wood was missing. There were only the beams on the outside edges but nothing in between.

If she hadn't turned back just at that moment she would have fallen straight through. She stopped on the edge and regained her balance. She took a step back and looked at the broken timbers. The low light made it difficult to see the state of the wood on the other side of the gap. There were three options that she could see. Take a running jump and leap across the breach, cross on one of the old beams, or go further downstream and cross the river by foot.

Lani didn't want to get wet if she didn't have to. She needed to get to Little Big Rock as soon as possible and she would have to dry out before getting in through the town gates. The option to jump seemed her best option. She walked back a little to see how far she would need to be to get the right run up. The gap was wider than she was comfortable with and as she turned to check around, she felt her calf twinge again. Would it hold up to the run and jump? She would have to remember to jump off the other leg or it might knot up again.

Her confidence dropped as she leant down and rubbed the back of her leg. She wasn't sure if it would be a problem or not. She moved forward instead and looked at both of the main beams on either side of the bridge. The one to her left was worn and uneven as far as she could see in the light. The one on her right seemed to be in better condition. Lani took a tentative step and put her weight forward onto it to test how it would respond.

The beam was no wider than her foot and in some places less. She placed her full weight on it and waited to see if she needed to jump backwards. It seemed stable enough to her but as she settled on it, it made a loud creaking noise. Lani froze. She hadn't seen anyone around but if there was they would have heard that. She looked forward and tried to make her mind up. This beam or the jump?

"Who goes there?" A voice broke the night back behind her.

Lani nearly overbalanced in surprise. She turned her head and could see a man climbing up from under the bridge.

"You have to pay to cross my bridge," he called out.

"Your bridge is broken," Lani replied.

"Because too many people haven't been paying for its upkeep. Get back from there."

He was still a good distance from her but she needed to make up her mind now what she was going to do. It was unlikely she could take the run and jump now, he would catch up to her. She turned and tried to block him out of her mind. She moved her other foot off the solid bridge and out on the beam, losing her balance as she did so. She put it on the beam and corrected her balance.

"What do you think you're doing, woman? You'll fall. All to avoid paying a small coin."

She didn't pay any attention to him, and moved her back foot forward. The beam felt narrower underneath this foot when she placed it, and it took all of her concentration to stay upright. With her arms out to either side she took another step. And another. Ahead of her she could see the boards of the opposite side. She wished she could run on this beam but it was too narrow.

"You'll fall, fool."

Lani stopped. His voice broke her focus and she wobbled a little before correcting. She took more steps and finally reached the other side. Cautiously she moved onto the bridge proper before looking back at the bridge keeper.

"As good as a thief you are, lady. You come back this way again and I'll remember you."

Lani bowed at him, and turned towards the road. She kept going until she met up with Old North Road, the final choice in her journey.

Here she could turn right and head back to Barnen, or left and whatever the south could bring. She felt there was little choice, she made the main choice when she left Barnen, nothing had changed since then. It seemed ludicrous to her that this had all happened within a few days and now she was off chasing some tale from a dead man she didn't know. Everything seemed worse than a bad story from a drunk bard in an inn. Except she was living it.

She turned left and set off down the road, still a long way from Little Big Rock but resolute in what she was doing. She had to make it work now, there was no other choice. Once again as early light broke the night, Lani left the road and found shelter. Set back a good distance from the road was a vast woodland, and inside the edge of that she found a suitable spot sheltered by tree trunks and fallen debris.

She could see horses and carts making their way along the road throughout the day, without being seen by anyone. She passed much of the day inventing stories about the people as they came from one side of her vision to the other. When that became tedious she napped and nibbled at a small amount of food.

All that mattered was getting safely to Little Big Rock. After that she'd work out a plan.

LANI

*L*ittle Big Rock wasn't the sort of town that inspired anyone to hang around. It was a waypoint like many other towns. A place to stop safely and top up your supplies. Another town that hugged the river, a stepping stone on the road from Nedor in the south through Barnen and the Tree Roads to Hagel on the far north coast.

The town got its name from a rock about the size of several buildings perched precariously on the town edge and river bank. If you loitered long enough in one of the inns on the water's edge, you'd hear tales of how it was carried there by a gigantic ice bear back eons ago, and laid down while it drank at the river. No one ever explained what an ice bear was doing this far south where the climate was too mild for them to survive.

As the tales go, a lone swordsman jumped down from the rock and killed the bear while it lay there drinking.

Not that you can find any bones buried to prove this, though many have dug there looking. The rock itself sits unblemished and as imposing as it has always been. Its surface is so hard that despite numerous attempts no tools to be found in Malamig or beyond have been able to dent, chip or damage any part of it.

The morning Lani wandered into town, following along behind some carts that had traveled down the north road, was a gray and cold day. It allowed her to be wrapped up in her cloak and as nondescript as she could be.

She'd waited until the town gates had been open for several hours and those coming and going were not attracting that much attention from the guards before entering. She noticed they did seem to be paying a little more attention to those entering than usual.

She only ever came to Little Big Rock when she needed to sell any items she had taken. When she did, she always tried to arrive first thing in the day, take in a little of the town before fencing the goods and leaving immediately.

While she mostly trusted the fence she used, it made no sense to stay in town with extra money. Either she would be tempted to spend it or someone would try to take it from her. This time she'd need to find somewhere safe to stay so she could sell the jewelry she had and buy herself a ride.

She approached the gate.

"Where you coming from?" the guard to her left asked.

"Barnen."

"You traveled alone? Don't you know there's trouble up your way?"

"I followed others down here. It doesn't feel safe up there," Lani answered. "I thought it would be safer here."

"There's nothing safe here if you're living on the street, girl. We don't need no more beggars."

"I'm not a beggar. I need somewhere to stay."

The guard looked her up and down, and turned to one of his colleagues, a smirk forming on his mouth. The other guard winked back at him. "You want to follow the river down to where the Meet Market is. Just past that there's some accommodation that would likely suit you."

Lani nodded and moved forward. Not far inside the gates a small group of beggars sat in a group, with little enthusiasm for their task of attracting alms from passers-by. Lani could see most were small children and as dirty as her kin were but looking a lot hungrier. She knew things were no easier here for homeless ones than back in Barnen.

She had heard of the labor market down by the big rock, where the workers went each day to seek work. She wondered if that was also where the caravans and other travelers gathered? It seemed as good a place to start as any.

Following the town roads that ran parallel to the river, it wasn't hard to find the rock the town was named after. An open cobbled area lay beside the large rock. In line with the rock and in the middle of the square was a statue of a swordsman that Lani assumed was the hero of the tales.

At the back of the square a row of stalls circled the area facing a raised platform. A sole man was packing up his books and sheets on the platform but few people were left in the square. A couple of lads were loitering off on the far side, as if they had missed out on getting any work. A few stragglers were quickly following after men leading back towards the gate or into the town itself.

With no one left the traders still remaining were packing down their stalls. One woman had a small collection of bread in loaves and small buns and some other baked items. She stacked them into one basket and was starting to untie a skin roof over the stall.

Lani felt for a coin in her pocket, her stomach growling after her trip, and walked over.

"Are those pastries still for buying?"

The woman looked over at her arms still raised and fingers working on the knot holding the twine in place.

"Yeah they are, if you can wait one small bit until I'm done here."

"No rush for me." She waited until the woman had undone that one side and came around the front to her.

"Is this where the Meet Market happens then?" she queried the woman.

"It is. You not from around here then?"

Lani shook her head. "I've just come in from up north."

"Right. Well it's always an early start here and lasts only as long as there's people want workers and workers want work. I'd be done already if not for all the farmers coming on the one day. First time in many a while that there weren't enough workers for them all."

"What about those lads over there?"

"Well they're broken, that lot. Them two fools just come here every day to have something to do. One time they got picked by a foreigner and all sorts of commotion happened when he tried to bundle them up and take them with him."

"Oh."

"They'll be gone when the next fool's cart rolls through town.

The woman continued rolling up the cover, but was eyeing Lani up as she did so.

"So what's a lass like you want at the Meet Market?" she asked.

"I've heard of it back where I came from. Some of the lads come down here and work through the summer. I wanted to see it. I was hoping that I might find a ride south from here," Lani replied.

The woman looked her over at that. Her eyes were carefully watching Lani but her smile seemed genuine. "It all happens at dawn anyway so you've missed finding anything today. Not that there's any rides to be found here. Here, help me with this frame while you be chewing my ear off."

The woman pointed at the wooden poles sticking up from her cart. Cross posts were tied together forming a frame that the cover had been thrown over.

"Climb up on that stool there, and untie the twine, would ya? Be easier for a young lass like you than me climbing up there," the woman jested.

Lani looked at her, and while she wanted to eat some of the bread the woman had, she got up anyway. She took her gloves off and tucked them into her satchel. It was an annoying knot that took a bit of pulling and working to get undone. When it was done she moved around and did the other three without being asked.

"You made easy work of that, girl. My gnarly old fingers don't be working knots like they once could. Many thanks. Now you wanted something to eat, did you?"

"Yeah. One of them rolls, maybe. I walked in this morning and haven't had time to get bed nor food yet." Lani felt the woman looking over her again as if trying to work her out.

"How about you help me pack the rest of this down? Winter's almost gone, but my joints ache like demons until the spring suns heat eases them. This morning they've been causing me no end of grief. You help me and you can have that roll for naught."

An easy deal for Lani, she helped drag the skin off the top and rolled it up, loading it and the rest of her things into the hand cart that sat beside the fixed stall.

"Here you go." Lani caught the bread roll the woman tossed to her as she placed the last basket on top of the load. "You earned that, you did." The woman came fully around the stall in front of Lani.

Lani bit into it, the dried fruit in it making it a sweeter bread. "Thank you," she said through her full mouth.

"So you're looking for accommodation and a ride south, are you?" Lani nodded.

"Well, you don't want to head down that way." The lady nodded to her right. "The only inns down there are for men that want to find themselves a working girl, if you gather my meaning."

Lani blushed a little as she realized what the woman was saying. "Oh. Where's the best place to get a room then?" She stuffed the rest of the roll into her mouth.

"Hungry, aren't we?" She smiled at Lani. "My name be Arbery, and if my eyes don't deceive me you look like you could do with more than just a roll to eat. When are you wanting to head off?"

"Yeah, I came here first once I arrived. I wanted to see if I could find anyone traveling south. I'd have taken that instead of staying if I could."

"Well, like I said, this isn't the right place to find a ride. There's only work to be found at the Meet Market."

"Here, walk with me back to the bakehouse and you can share some breakfast with me and Dedrick. He'll have made something fresh from the ovens while he was baking and we always have more than we need. We have a couple of little rooms for travelers, you can see if they suit you once you've eaten."

A little surprised by the offer and immediately suspicious of anyone offering her something, Lani hesitated.

"Ain't no harm in some free food, girl. Thenis knows you look like you need it. Scrawny girl like you, no boys going to fall for your charms without some curves on ya. You don't want to stay, that's up to you, but might as well help an old duck like me move her stuff. Like I said, stuff hurts more than not these days. Do you have a name or shall I just call you girl?"

She paused maybe a little too long, her suspicious nature unsure of whether this older woman could be trusted. "I go by the name Tiber," Lani lied. "I will walk a little way with you if that's okay, but I won't put you out. I was glad to help."

"Come, don't come. Suit yourself, but I need to be on my way now, Tiber." With that Arbery starting walking the hand cart off down a side street heading back toward the town center from the jetty market.

Lani watched her walking away, uncertain if she should follow. She wasn't used to anyone wanting to help her type, but needed more information. The lady seemed to know about the right place to find a ride.

The lady started to disappear as she followed a narrow road around some buildings. Lani took off after her hoping that the offer of a meal was for real.

LANI

rbery moved at a quick pace pushing the cart in front of her, never stopping, not for people walking across in front nor the odd horseman. Lani was hard pressed just to keep up with her. It didn't seem to her that the woman was as sore as she made out, nor that she needed Lani's help. She wondered what the woman was actually up to.

They moved along roads that meandered and twisted between buildings. To Lani it seemed the buildings had been built before a road had been made, and now everything had to fit in around them.

Within a short while the warehouses started giving way to general living quarters with a mix of house and shopfronts and a lot more activity.

Arbery had been quiet throughout the walk but piped up as she turned to push the cart into a narrow lane. "Here's the bakehouse, come help me unload this cart and we'll get that food I promised."

Lani followed her down the lane and into a small cluttered courtyard behind the bakehouse. The backdoor was open and the big oven in the back was visible, smoke pouring from a chimney. She could feel the heat where she stood.

With only some empty baskets and a few leftover breads to carry inside the unloading was not much of a chore. Again she could tell Arbery was making more of the need for help that there actually was.

Walking through the back into the shop front, Lani was caught unawares by the heat emanating from the oven. The air was thick and steamy as they walked through it although Arbery didn't even seem to notice.

A deep gruff voice called from a deep cupboard alongside the ovens. "You're back finally, woman! I wondered if I'd be cooking and serving on my own till dark fall."

"That would be a first, you cheeky hog," Arbery shot back without emotion of any kind.

"Well make yourself a use, and pour us out some ale. I have a warm loaf for us," he finished off.

As the broad bald man made his way out of the pantry holding the fresh bread loaf he saw Lani and chuckled to himself, "I see you found yourself another stray?"

Arbery called back to him from the front of the shop, "This lass be calling herself Tiber. I found her down at the square. She's an out-of-towner and she helped me pack down and bring it back."

"Right then, lass. Dedrick be my name." He waved the loaf at Lani. "Might as well be helping us with this loaf, it's more than we need." He laughed at himself again as he moved into the shop.

Lani wasn't accustomed to people this welcoming and had no idea how to respond; she gave an awkward smile then followed him.

Arbery was latching the door closed and went behind the counter to gather some plates and utensils. Dedrick began cutting slices off the loaf, small puffs of steam escaping from it as he did.

As Arbery pushed by in the small space, she elbowed Lani towards one of the chairs beside the small rough-cut table they were gathering at.

"Sit yaself down there, girl. Not enough room in here to be loitering."

"This is all a bit much, I really didn't do much to help," stumbled helplessly out of Lani's mouth.

"Shush to you, there's enough here for all, I know you're not from here, and if I be reading you rightly you don't look much like you've eaten in some days," Arbery said back at her.

"Yes… No.. Well I am not from here, I am from up north and am heading south trying to find my sick pa," Lani answered back.

"Enough for now, lass. Just sit there and we'll all have something to eat." Arbery ended the conversation and carried on grabbing some cups and filled a jug of ale from a small barrel behind the counter.

There wasn't much talking while the food was being consumed. The simple meal of big chunks of bread, butter that soaked into the warm bread and some chalky cheese was to Lani like a feast at a lord's manor. She had run out of food the day earlier and was very hungry.

The thin ale tasted bitterer than Lani had had before. She usually only got some cheap homemade fruit wines and the occasional better wines if they were able to steal some.

Bitter or not, it quenched her thirst better than the river water had, and with the hot ovens in the back room, she was feeling a warmth she hadn't had since the summer.

Dedrick let out a coarse and loud belch as he finished a mug of the ale, patted his ample stomach and leaned back on his stool.

Arbery rolled her eyes but said nothing before looking at Lani. "I bet that feels a lot better?"

Swallowing a chunk of bread and cheese she answered, "I am not sure the last time I ate me bread that fresh, Arbery. But, oh my, I feel warmed and full now. Many thanks."

"I not going to be asking your story, don't be any of my business, nor Dedrick's. But I knows when I see someone lost in a place and you don't need to be finding your way down the other main street at the market square, only taverns and wench houses down there."

Lani blushed a little, as if the topic embarrassed her. She knew full well what the taverns and wench houses were like, but appearing a little naive about it all might work in her favor.

Surviving on the streets was her craft, and it wasn't often in Barnen anyone would offer up a meal like Arbery and Dedrick had without expecting more from her.

"I feel like I owe you something for the food, and I am glad I came this way and not the other. I can pay for my food if you'll let me?"

"Shush to you, I said. You helped me enough already. He makes plenty of the bread every day. We feed enough of the rats out back, so feeding a wee lass like you is no burden."

"Where you traveling to?" Dedrick said as he reached over and grabbed the jug, pouring himself more of the ale. He set the jug back with a clunk on the table, his mitts and strong arms more used to slinging around sacks of flour and the baking peel.

Lani picked up her cup and sipped some ale while she thought about how to answer.

"It's not much to tell. I just got here today by way of Barnen."

Lani paused and sipped some more ale. "I need to find me a place to stay a day or two while I find me a caravan or ride heading south."

There seemed little point hiding the actual facts of her journey, as long as that was all they knew. Word didn't need to be getting back to Barnen about her until she was well gone.

"You heading somewhere specific then?"

"Yes. I have to head to Nedor and on past there. My pa is sick and I got a message to go help bring him back."

Dedrick nodded his head as he watched her, no more questions coming from him.

Arbery had gotten up from her chair and unlatched the shop door, and started to clear the table. She said nothing while she got about her work.

Lani pitched in, helping to take the used plates and leftovers behind the counter.

Wiping her hands on an old cloth hanging on a wooden hook buried in the wall Arbery spoke again. "Tiber, you said? That's an odd name in Malamig."

Lani instantly became more wary. They were asking her lots of questions and she wasn't sure how well her story would hold up. She stepped her way out from behind the counter, her mind racing through options about how to get out quickly if she needed.

As if sensing her discomfort Arbery quickly carried on, "Yes, an odd name, but I like it. Well, like I told you, we have a small room out back in the yard. You can stay a day or two if you want. We often have travelers stay there, and I'd be happier knowing you were safe than how you might be finding a room out there." She pointed with a head flick and roll of her eyes out the doorway to the street.

Dedrick put down his empty cup on the table and added, "Right, I best make sure one of them is clean then," as if it was already agreed.

Lani piped up, "That's very generous of you. You've already been very generous, and I appreciate it. But I have someone I need to see first and I'm not sure if they will be able to help with a room or not."

A moment's silence fell between them before Arbery spoke up. "Well that's perfectly fine, Tiber. You know it's here if you need it. Do you know where you're going?"

"Yes, thanks." Lani didn't want to mention where she was heading to.

"You take good care of yourself." Arbery came back around the counter and laid her hand on Lani's shoulder.

"Thank you, Arbery. You too, Dedrick."

"You're welcome, lass."

"Right, I will be on my way. You sure I can't pay you for the food?"

"Be gone now. We've already answered that." Arbery removed her hand and pretended to flick her away.

Lani turned and opened the shop door. She stepped out onto the road outside and closed it behind her. She looked left and right, trying to find her bearings. Recognizing the way they had come, she turned and headed back down the road.

LANI

Out on the street Lani felt more comfortable. She was grateful for the food and how friendly the bakers had been but she was uneasy with someone being so welcoming. It wasn't something she was used to.

Her goal was simple. Get enough money from fencing the jewels to help her get somewhere new. Little Big Rock was too close to Barnen for her to feel safe. If Captain Kyro hadn't already sent word here, he soon would. Once they started hunting her then she wouldn't be safe here either.

She hadn't been any further than Little Big Rock before, so she didn't know what the next best town or city would be. Nedor was a long way away, as far as she had heard, and she wasn't sure the capital city was somewhere she wanted to try and live either.

One of the reasons she had headed to the Meet Market was that she knew how to get from there to the place she was heading now. This part of town was an area that most people didn't frequent.

Lani walked past the numerous inns and other venues that Arbery had warned her about, ignoring the catcalls of the doormen. A few streets later she turned into a small road that contained a number of larger warehouses with the occasional shopfront squeezed between.

The buildings weren't well maintained, the roadway was littered with rubbish and it ended at the town wall. There was no one on the road, which made Lani feel safer. She had never had any problems when she had been here before, but she had never had this type of bounty before either. While there was a rule that the thieves didn't take from other thieves, she knew it was safer to trust no one.

About two-thirds of the way along the road Lani could see her destination. Yerat's shop, for lack of a better name, was where Lani was headed. Years back one of the older kin had brought her here and introduced her to Yerat.

Whenever she had something to sell she always came back here. She didn't know if he gave her a fair deal or not but she preferred to deal with someone she knew, and the amount he had paid her each time was enough for her.

The door into the shop stuck on the floor and she had to lean into it and push hard to force it open, adding more scratches on the floor to those already there. A musty smell mixed with pipe smoke greeted her as soon as she stepped in.

Yerat popped up from behind the counter on the far side of the room, his narrow eyes squinting as he looked her over. He reached a hand up and scratched at his long nose before rubbing his wispy gray beard. He always ran his beard through his hand as if he was trying to stretch it, making it neat and tidy. The rest of him didn't match, his tunic grubby and patched, and his hair looked like it had never been brushed his whole life.

"Well look what the wind blew in." He stood up fully and put his hands on the counter.

"Yerat, it has been a while."

"That it has, Miss Lani."

"Miss. You are funny." She chuckled and walked over to the counter.

"I can only assume that in that bag of yours you have something you'd like to share with Yerat, and that this isn't just a visit to check on my well-being." His brown eyes twinkled in the lantern light as a smile formed on his face.

"How clever of you."

"How have you been, Lani?"

"Oh living the life of a queen, like normal." This time it was she who smiled.

"So Barnen hasn't changed then?"

"Not like that."

"What do you mean?"

"There's been trouble up there. Some outlanders fighting with locals and things."

"Yes, rumor of something unusual had reached the taverns around here. In times of change there's always opportunities for those who have an eye for it. What lovelies have you brought for me today? Some watches or necklaces?"

Lani shook her head and took the satchel off her shoulder, placing it on the counter.

"How rude of me, did you want some wine?"

"I'm okay right now."

He turned and grabbed a goblet from a shelf behind him. "Don't mind if I do." He took a healthy sip and put the goblet down on the counter.

Lani opened the bag and reached in, wrapping her hand around the cloth that held the rings. She looked up at Yerat. "I have a couple of rings and another unusual item."

"Oh, unusual! I like unusual. Show us these rings then and let's keep the unusual as a surprise."

She pulled the cloth out and clumsily unwrapped it, one of the rings falling out onto the wooden counter. Yerat reached out and picked it up as she finished opening the cloth and showing him all of them.

He turned and walked closer to the nearest lantern on the wall, and twisted the ring in the light. "And this isn't the unusual piece? Now you really have me intrigued. This is amber, girl. Rare as rare is. And you've got three of them. I know I shouldn't ask."

"Then don't."

Yerat chuckled again, and came back to the counter. He looked at each of the rings. "Lani, Lani! What a lovely haul you have here. I've not seen rings the like of these, but I've heard of something similar."

"Really?"

"Yes. These come from over the sea, without question. You don't get amber like this unless it's from Enderk. Which raises the question..."

"We don't need to raise the wrong types of questions, do we? You're either interested or you aren't?"

He raised his eyebrows at her. "See, that's what I like. As you're growing up you're getting smarter and more streetwise. Not like the little girl that came here with a friend the first time. No we don't need to ask those questions. But can you blame Yerat for asking?"

She just stared back at him, waiting.

"Of course I'm interested. I am not sure I can take all three though. These are nice but I am not sure I can sell all three in Big Rock without them becoming noticed."

"Can't you move them elsewhere?"

"Well I don't think they'll be wanted up in Barnen, which means south. Riverbend maybe, but most likely these need to be sold near Nedor, or further afield. I think one is good for me."

"How much?"

"Hold on there. First, let's see what your other goody is."

"If you thought those rings were special then you'll definitely like this." Lani reached in and put her hand onto the felt pouch. She took it out.

"Go on, open it up then."

Lani wasn't sure why but she suddenly felt reluctant to show the amulet. In the back of her mind she could hear Ashantha or what sounded like him, warning her to keep the amulet from others.

"Come on, don't tease me."

Lani shut out the voice in her head and peeled the pouch off the amulet. The stone appeared to take in the lantern light and shine brightly. Yerat stepped back slightly at the brightness.

"Oh my." He stared at the shining jewel in Lani's hands. "Where in Thenis's name did you find such a lovely piece like that?"

"Where doesn't matter, Yerat."

"Oh, but it does. This item will be sorely missed by its owner. They won't let up the search to get this back."

"What do you mean?"

"Look at it! It's beautifully crafted. I've never seen anything quite like it, and so much amber in one piece. Have you been raiding over in Enderk, Lani?"

Lani pulled it back from him. She could feel the amulet this time, it had a presence that was in the room, probing. Luckily she had the pouch under it, on her hand, so it wasn't touching her skin, but she wanted to put it back inside soon.

"No matter. Oh my. Oh my. What is Yerat to do with this? Can I?" He reached out to take it.

Lani looked at it and at him. "Do you need to?"

He looked back at her quizzically, "If I can't inspect it, I can't buy it. Can I?"

"Take the pouch too." She carefully passed it to him.

Yerat shrugged and let her slide the pouch with the amulet on it onto his palm. Once again he took it closer to the light to inspect it. "This is the most amazing piece of jewelry, Lani. In all my years I don't think I have seen such a piece."

"You know what it is I want you to tell me?"

"Yes, yes. How much. It's always the same." He was still ogling it under the lantern. "I am not sure I can even afford it."

"What do you mean?"

"I guess you aren't hearing me. This is a very valuable piece. Very! I am not sure I have enough to pay you its worth."

"How much?"

"A hundred gold or more."

Lani gasped.

"Like I said, girl. A lot!"

"I had no idea."

"Yerat doesn't have that sort of money on hand. And I'm not sure it would be safe to take it either."

"What do you mean?"

"Whoever used to own this will be very upset. They will want to find who passed this along."

"Isn't that what you're for? To discreetly move these goods along?"

"Some goods come with their own challenges. It would make it less valuable to the person taking the risk."

Lani shook her head. "Oh, I see what's happening here. Well, that person would need to consider the extra money such a piece would get for the risk."

Yerat grinned. He turned back to the light. Lani saw him take the amulet off his palm with his right hand and hold it up to the lantern. She wasn't sure that was the best thing to do. She could still remember how it felt when she held it.

The thud caught her by surprise. He had fallen to the floor and was out of sight.

Lani rushed around the end of the counter and saw him collapsed on the floor. His eyes were open but rolled back in his head. She went over and bent down over him. Unsure what to do, she slapped his face and tried to shake him. When he didn't respond she leant down near his nose to see if she could hear or feel him breathing.

There was no response from him, and she realized his skin was cold to touch. *That's odd*, she thought. *It's warm in here.*

She had heard of people dying suddenly before but this was very strange. Yerat was quite old. To her, anyway, but he had seemed perfectly fine just a moment ago. He had been very excited at the amulet, had it caused him a shock?

She tried to revive him again but he wasn't responding. Lani could see he was dead, she just didn't understand why. The amulet was still wedged in his right hand. She had to pry it out of his stiff fingers to get it. It was then she remembered that it didn't have the pouch under it. As soon as she touched it she could feel it just like in the cave. It felt like it had tendrils seeping out of it and crawling up her arm.

Standing up, Lani looked for her bag. The pouch of the shiny metal that Ashantha had used on her to free her from it, in the cave, was in the bag. The feeling on her arm grew, now it felt like someone strong had gripped her forearm and she could feel them all the way up to her elbow. Then she felt a sharp pain and cried out. She looked at her arm but nothing was there even though it had felt like something had pierced her skin. The amulet appeared to be flashing.

Lani shook her head, and looked around the floor for the pouch.

She stepped over Yerat's body and picked it up from where it had fallen. As soon as she brought it close to the stone it wrapped around the amulet and the feelings stopped. She tied off the end of it and put it on the counter.

Turning her arm and hand over, she checked for any marks. There was nothing on it. Her head felt clearer again and she knew that she had been affected by the amulet again. Shivers ran up her spine. What had just happened?

Now that her mind was clear she looked about Yerat's shop. Here was another dead body. She couldn't stay here. Cursing her luck, she knew she hadn't even managed to sell one of the rings to him. She bent down over him and felt through his clothing for any money. There was nothing on him.

He had to have some money here, she knew it. Lani opened a few cupboards and drawers looking for anything that might hold money but couldn't see anything obvious. She knew that every minute she stayed in here increased her chance of being found. While there was a rule to not thieve off a thief, she wasn't sure people would be too happy that Yerat was dead. And she didn't want to have to explain how.

Lani gathered the pouch and wrapped the rings again, putting them all back in her bag. She shook her head as she looked at Yerat one last time, and left the shop. Closing the door, she tried her hardest not to run. She stayed to the side of the road and walked away as if she had just finished a good deal with him.

What next? She hadn't secured the money she needed to buy a ride south, and now she was connected to another death. She needed to get away from this part of town, staying down here would be too close to Yerat. She needed somewhere safe, and knew just the place.

TILLANDRA

For the rest of the day all she could do was push herself from tower to tower, her concentration on the next one while keeping her speed up. Before she knew it dusk had crept up behind her and raced ahead of her. Orange flecks of light brought the sand alive on all sides like the embers of a bonfire.

With the dusk only a small moon was showing. If she didn't get within sight of Hesb soon the ground all around her would be dark. The last thing she needed was to twist something or have a fall. Tillandra forced her weary legs into a final push and was rewarded as the first twinkles of the city lights reached her.

Hesb was protected by a triangular wall that had three distinct corners. Atop each corner were fire towers and she could see them ahead of her now.

With relief she arrived and entered through the open gates. Desert cities rarely closed their gates. There was little that worried those who inhabited these remote cities. Hesb wasn't a city compared to anywhere else but in the desert if you had stone walls no matter your size you qualified to be called a city.

Tillandra loped her way to the western side and found a travelers' camp near the gates there. The camp held more people than she had seen in days, and having purchased her space she grabbed a bowl of a vegetable stew and some bread and took a seat in the common area.

To her side a group of men were happily discussing their recent travel.

"It's the best time of year on this road, for sure."

"Why's that then?"

"Much less heat during the day," the loudest of the group continued. Tillandra could see from his weathered face that he spent a lot of time on the road. "You're only battling the trail and the wind, not like summer. Then it's only madmen or double coin that puts people on this trail." He laughed at his own words.

"Makes sense. I've been down here once before, but this is my first time leading my own."

"Follow the towers and don't listen to any other nonsense. The only dead men on Death Road are those that think they're smarter than the desert." Another from the first group spoke up.

"What he says," the first man agreed, nodding as he said it through a half-full mouth.

"We lost our tail then," the first man that had spoken talked to the whole group. "I didn't think he would put down with us in a camp, no doubt he will be in the inn."

That brought a small burst of laughter from the others.

"I don't know why a southern knight would be out on this road in all their kit but I can't imagine them lasting in a full day's heat."

Tillandra was intrigued by this development and called out across the space. "A knight on the trail, you say?"

"Hello there, stranger. Yes I did. All the way from Daskare."

"Daskare? What on earth is a knight from down there doing traveling Death Road?"

"No idea. They've taken up residence in Watersend the last few weeks, and several of them rode to Fort Layden the same day we did. This one came here on his own."

Tillandra pondered what he said. "You think he's following you?"

The man looked over at her and shook his head. "I don't think so. They appear to be looking for someone, the way they were loitering around the camps. I would be surprised if this one comes any further. He will either stay here or return to Layden."

"That's the strangest thing."

"Isn't it just," the man said. "You heading that way?"

Tillandra nodded.

"Well you'll likely come across them then, for some strange reason they seem to have set up in Fort Layden and are watching the gates there."

"That is most unusual."

"You're telling me. I don't know why the city mayor is standing for it, although I wouldn't argue with them either." He laughed at himself again.

"Thanks, friend, for the information. It's always good to know what's ahead of you."

"Welcome."

Tillandra went back to the last of her meal and the men took up their group conversation again. She thought through what the knights being present in Sahro might mean. Unlike other realms, Sahro ran like a series of independent but connected cities, each one self-managing under guidance of the 'council' in Anderwell, as it was known to the outside world. They kept themselves deliberately aloof from the other realms.

To the outside they were an eccentric group of people that had little economic sense. With their land being mostly unusable there was only one thing the other realms were interested in. The jewels that came out of Midderbuilt and Watersend. If someone was trying to start forcing their way into her towns and cities then this was of major interest to her.

Tillandra made a mental note to alert Toolet that they might need more than just an expansion of the city guard. The rest of the towns and cities across Sahro might need some fortification as well. She shook her head and let her mouth form into a small smirk. *There's never a time without something else to worry about*, she thought.

Generally it wasn't known that the role of Mother Folly led the Court and as such was the ultimate ruler of the realm. Tillandra liked to keep it that way. Within their network she was who she was but to the mayors and other leaders across the realm she was at best just one of the council. To the person on the street she was just another person.

Exhausted from the day's travel she collapsed into her open bunk. When she removed her boots she could see she had done more than just wear them out, there were blood stains on her stockings. She had felt at least one blister forming through the day and that meant by now the skin was broken and worn away. There was nothing for it, she had no time to wait here and let them heal. Tillandra just hoped they would harden over the coming days. She hung her boots off the end of the bunk and settled into the gentle throbbing as she drifted off to sleep.

Again she worried about reaching out to Goran, but she had an idea that she was unsure of. When she got to somewhere private, in Fort Layden, she hoped, she'd reach out to Beantic and check her theory.

She was less energetic the next morning. Her body was suffering from the toll of the hard day through to Hesb. She put her boots back on despite the protests of her swollen feet, before standing gently.

Tillandra sought out supplies for the next leg of her journey, knowing that she would settle into it over a few more days, as she always had before, despite the short-term pain she was going to suffer. A few men with horses looked to be preparing to load up and set out as well; the road would be a little less lonely today if many were on it.

The next week passed in a continual pattern of the previous days with Tillandra pushing herself hard each day to reach a resting stop, before rising early and pushing on again. Halfway through the week her feet stopped aching and her strong frame settled into the journey, her muscles remembering her previous trips and adjusting to them naturally.

At the gates to Fort Layden she stopped and rested her left hand against the wall, looking back at the path behind her. She could only just make out the tower in the distance.

"Who are you and what is your business here?" a stern voice queried her.

Tillandra turned to see who the rude person was and saw two armed men approaching her. Their look alone was enough for her to know who they were, but the ice bear insignia on their breastplates and what she'd heard from the travelers confirmed it.

"Who is asking?"

"Just answer the question, lady." The one on the left was doing all the talking. Streaks of gray hair were visible under the hedge of his helmet.

"I don't know who *YOU* think you are, but unless things have changed around here, the Knights of Daskare have no rule in Fort Layden nor anywhere else in Sahro. So I'd suggest you go bother someone else." Tillandra caught sight of the local guards almost hiding in their hut.

"I do not like your tone, woman. Simply answer our questions and you can be on your way."

"Guards!" Tillandra called out to the local guardsmen. "Come here and move these knights on, they are bothering a traveler entering your city." The two guards reluctantly started heading over towards the gates.

The younger of the two knights turned sideways, his hand on the hilt of his sword.

"What seems to be the matter?"

"You know full well the matter here. These foreigners are stopping me from entering Fort Layden and have no rights to do so. I'd suggest you either remove them or arrest them."

The eyes of the guardsmen almost popped out of their heads at her suggestion. She knew why, these local men were no match for the knights. Any fight would be over quickly.

"They don't scare us. We've our job to do and we intend to do it."

"Then I suggest we're all about to find out what rule stands for in Sahro. Guardsmen, go and get your Mayor and the rest of the guard, and tell him that these two insolent little knights have threatened Tillandra of the Council of Anderwell and are to be arrested immediately." She walked forward directly at the knights, who both reluctantly stepped apart a pace allowing her to push her way through.

She turned as she passed. "I'd suggest you find your horses and get out of this town immediately or you will be arrested."

One of the guardsmen had already set off running. When Tillandra reached the other she angrily spoke to him, "And you. Take me to the Mayor. Now!" He didn't reply and turned to follow alongside her.

When they arrived at the Mayor's office the first guard was still trying to explain to him what was happening.

"What on earth is going on around here, Ernest?"

"Till… Tillandra. Uh. I… I am only just hearing about an incident." He stumbled over his words, surprised at her arrival.

"So you weren't aware you had Daskarian Knights roaming your town and harassing people as if they were your own guards?"

"Well, I knew they were here…"

Tillandra interrupted, "So you just let them do it?"

"Tillandra, it's not quite like that."

"Then how is it?"

Ernest Ferthing turned to the two guards. "You can go back to your stations now." The two men nodded and left. "It's complicated."

"Is it?"

"My men wouldn't stand a chance against the knights. They are local guards, not soldiers."

"And by not even pretending to be the law here, you've clearly shown that to them as well. This is disastrous, Ernest."

"What do you want me to do?"

"Your job, *Mayor*." She said his title with extra emphasis and watched him drop his eyes. "It's okay, I've threatened them myself. It seems a single unarmed woman was able to point out they should leave town immediately and I'd hazard a guess they have already moved on. Imagine what the supposed Mayor and guardsmen could have achieved had they even tried."

"Are you staying long?"

"Don't change the topic, Ernest. I'm very annoyed. And no, I will be gone in the morning. Do you think you can protect your residents and our town without me?" Tillandra was still standing imposingly in front of his desk.

"Yes, councilor."

Tillandra noted the use of her public title. She hoped that meant the seriousness of her message had been received. "Good. Then let me get to my accommodation and some food before I pass out. There'll be more to discuss on this later, mark my words." She turned and stormed out of his office without closing the door.

As she hurried out of the city gates the following morning, Tillandra wondered what she had uncovered. She surprised herself that she was able to sleep throughout the night without the worry of this new situation keeping her awake. Her physical exhaustion allowed her at least that small break. It hadn't been enough to prevent her dreaming though. This time it wasn't a camel but a wall of Skarian knights in front of her. Armed and fierce, they blocked her way. Now as she pushed forward on her journey she mulled over what it might mean.

The knights of the Church of Maltzer were a concern. The church in Daskare controlled much of the military might but the knights were their elite forces. Typically they protected the royal family, which was large. What they were doing in Sahro was something she needed to know.

At one of the towers less than an hour west of Fort Layden she found evidence of an overnight camp. As best she could tell it looked as if the two knights had got that far before settling in for the night. If she maintained her usual pace they would not be far ahead of her, unless they pushed their horses hard. She wasn't sure she fancied coming across them alone out in the desert. While they might have backed down in Layden they were definitely not acting friendly at all.

For the rest of her trip she kept an eye out for evidence of them but never came across them again. They had clearly pushed hard to their destination. When she climbed one of the last towers before Watersend she looked across the land ahead but couldn't see them. She was thankful for that.

The sparkling off the walls of Watersend was a welcome sight. Inset into the walls of the octagonal city were thousands upon thousands of beautiful gems, all placed high enough to be out of reach of people on the ground and so they caught the sun. At the right time of the late afternoon they would shine like a million colored stars across the walls.

She took a deep breath and pushed off the rocks of the tower and headed towards the eastern gate.

34

TILLANDRA

Only a few people waited ahead of her as Tillandra lined up to pass through the gates at Watersend. The city was named for the way the River Tek ended just inside the western walls. It was still a mystery to everyone how the water flowed up to the rock face, and simply stopped.

"Lucky last," said the guard as she approached.

"I'm glad I made it on time."

"Our spotters up above let us know if there's any last stragglers heading our way. We prefer to not lock anyone out here overnight."

"I'm grateful for it."

"Where are you heading?"

"The Clown Prince, at the northern end."

"I'm aware of it. You'll welcome an ale there I would say. Good evening to you, ma'am."

"And to you."

While Tillandra could almost taste the ale in her mouth, she was most interested in a bath and a change of clothes. She wasn't keen to remove her boots though. They had felt swollen for days and she'd been unsure if she could get them back on again.

She turned onto Broadway, which would take her most of the way to her destination, when she heard the sound of horses approaching from behind. She moved to her left to let them pass but they stayed behind her. She stopped and looked behind. What she saw didn't please her at all.

"You never learn then?"

The two horsemen from Fort Layden said nothing, but were clearly blocking her way. The sound of horses from the other direction as well caused her added concern. She turned to see four more horsemen, another two Skarian knights and two city guards. The city guards wore the sash of the Mayor's personal guard, and one of them rode forward while the others stopped.

"Why am I finding myself surrounded by armed men, captain?"

"Sorry, councilor. It's not meant to alarm you."

"What alarms me, captain, is that you're accompanied by men from outside Sahro, who appear fully armed. Two of these men I have already run into on my trip."

"Perhaps you could accompany me to meet with Mayor Pravat."

"Captain, as you can tell, I am dirty from my trip. I am well past tired and am very hungry. Tell the Mayor he'll have to wait."

"I don't think that will be possible."

"Excuse me?" Tillandra was becoming very angry.

"My instructions were to ensure you came this very night."

"That may well be your instructions, captain. Unless I am mistaken through I do not report to either you or the Mayor."

"I did not wish to imply you do, my lady. I was implored that it was very important that you came to the Mayor this evening, as soon as you arrived."

Tillandra took a moment to compose herself. She knew losing control of her emotions wouldn't serve her well here. As she reflected on what was happening, it appeared that she wasn't the only one here being directed. The four Skarian knights seemed to be the ones actually controlling the behavior of the captain and his guardsman.

The behavior of the two knights in Fort Layden coupled with their behavior now was very worrying to her. It occurred to her that she might actually need to meet the Mayor to learn what on Dharatan was happening in Watersend.

"Well?" the captain asked.

Tillandra looked again at the number of knights surrounding them. She didn't think she would physically come to harm, but she had no desire to be waylaid here in Watersend. Something was amiss, and she was now part of it. She thought about the object buried in the bottom of her bag which she needed to keep out of other people's hands.

"It seems we are at somewhat of an impasse. I really wish to be off to my accommodation but I also should heed the request of the Mayor. I will come, but under one condition."

"Which is?"

She beckoned the captain closer, and leaned in to whisper into his ear, "Can your guardsman be trusted?"

"Yes," he whispered back.

Tillandra stood back, and spoke so all could hear. "Have your guardsman," she pointed to the other guard, "take my things to The Clown Prince, and tell the innkeep there that I have arrived in Watersend, and will be needing a bed this evening."

The Captain considered what she was saying and nodded his head. He turned and waved the guard forward. Tillandra handed over her pack and quietly said to the guard, "Tell Wessen where I am going and that I will be there this evening without fail."

The man nodded, and turned around and rode off, the knights reluctantly letting him pass.

"Shall we then?" she asked the captain.

"Are you alright to walk?"

"I've walked this far, a few more steps won't kill me."

The group set off with the captain riding alongside her. Tillandra did not like the way the knights appeared to be in charge of this situation.

They arrived at the council buildings in the center of Watersend and the captain led her through to the main chambers. When they arrived she could see there were several other people in the room, including Gimbden, who stood behind the Mayor.

Nion Pravat got up from his seat and walked around the table to greet Tillandra. "Councilor."

"Mayor. I am told you'll be able to explain to me the unusual request placed on me."

The Mayor drew in a deep breath and gave a slight flick of his eyes to her left. "I do apologize for the inconvenience, but I felt it best once I knew you had arrived."

Tillandra let it pass without comment.

"I'd like to introduce you to our esteemed guest, Envoy Reyes. The Envoy has been visiting recently from Bundok, and I thought that what he has been discussing was worthy of your counsel."

"Is that so." Tillandra looked to where Pravat was pointing. The man was still sitting in his seat handling his food. He looked her way.

She said nothing else nor moved towards him.

"Sorry, Mayor Pravat, I didn't catch this person's name?"

Pravat's face flushed red. "Envoy, this is Lady Tillandra, Councilor of the Court of Sahro. I would suggest you treat her with the respect accorded to one of her position."

The Envoy raised his eyebrows, and slowly put the food down, wiping his hands on a napkin. He stood unhurriedly and stepped away from the table, before making a half-hearted bow to her. "My apologies, Lady Tillandra. Forgive me, you do appear a little well-traveled. I did not recognize your position."

"Envoy Reyes. Apology accepted. I do not believe I've made your acquaintance before."

"No we have never met, councilor. I believe the only councilor I have personally met was a gentleman by the name of Junther. Is that correct?"

"Yes one of us is named that."

Mayor Pravat interrupted. "Come and have a seat, councilor. I am sure you are thirsty and hungry after your travels."

"Thank you."

Once she had relieved her thirst Tillandra looked back at the foreigner. "What brings you to Watersend that's of such import, Envoy Reyes?"

Gimbden, who had been silent to this point, interjected, "Self-interest and bad manners, my lady."

The Envoy turned to look at him, his dark eyes firmly fixed on the fool. Gimbden was dressed entirely in black, a tight hood covering all but his face. He wore white gloves as if to highlight them as he moved them about.

"Oh nothing to trouble you, councilor. Just some matters of trade between Efitra and Watersend."

"Pfffft." Gimbden mimicked spitting out a drink as he said it.

Pravat turned to him. "Do you mind?"

"No, not at all. Do you?"

Pravat rolled his eyes.

"Do we have to put up with this buffoon?" The Envoy clearly was not impressed with Gimbden's presence.

"You can leave at any time. I can show you the way if you'd like?" Gimbden waved his hands as if indicating moving away into the distance.

"Please." Tillandra spoke up. "If it's just a matter of trade why do you come with a force of knights, Envoy?"

"It is my master's wish that all delegations from Daskare are well protected. I am but a humble servant."

Out of the corner of her eye Tillandra could see Gimbden's face ready to burst into laughter. She forced herself to focus back on the conversation. "I wasn't aware that there was any trouble around here that should cause you any concern?"

"One can never be too careful."

"So careful, that you would send them out on the road to other towns harassing people without any rights to do so?"

"I have no idea what you mean, councilor. Has something happened I should be aware of?"

Tillandra could see through his fake look of innocence. "You're denying you had men on the road to Fort Layden?"

"No, not at all. I simply stated that there was no incident I was aware of." He took a sip from his goblet. "I felt it would be worthwhile for some of my men to get a lie of the land."

"And why would that be?"

"Like I said, just some matters of trade."

"I'm all ears, Envoy." Tillandra was slowly forcing him to a point where he would have little choice but to explain himself. She wanted to get it out in the open so she could pause whatever was happening here.

"I can tell, my lady. It's most intriguing." Gimden stepped forward, unfolding his hands in front of himself as he approached.

Tillandra turned to look at Mayor Pravat.

He smiled at her. "It seems, councilor, that Daskare is very keen to make a more permanent road from Efitra to Watersend."

"Is that so?" She turned back to the Envoy. "I would think that would matter a lot to the council, Envoy."

"I don't think there's anything to be worried about. King Ahn wishes to shorten the distance our traders have to travel to Watersend. It's a very important city for us. The route through Vodotok adds unnecessary burdens on our traders, and we are unable to protect them."

"Currently a direct route would be through very empty land, it would not be an easy route for your traders."

"That is what I have been discussing with the Mayor."

Gimbden, who had appeared to be bursting at the seams since being cut off, sung out, "He has a plan. He has a plan!" He finished off his little song with a twirl, and promptly fell over flat on his back. "Oh dear."

Pravat shook his head. "There's a lot to consider." He turned to Tillandra, a pleading look on his face.

"How long are you here, Mister Reyes?" she asked.

"I must leave tomorrow. It is why I have been pressing for an answer from the Mayor. I felt we were at the point of agreement before your arrival." The last part was said with a snide tone.

"Such decisions should never be rushed, Envoy. I do believe I will need to think more on this and discuss it further with the Mayor. Perhaps we can send word to the King, when we have made our decisions."

The room fell silent, broken after a short while by a quiet snigger coming from the floor behind the Mayor.

"Ah... perhaps it would be best if I stay on a few days. It was impressed on me that I should return with an answer."

"Oh. But I can't say when we might have such an answer. It could be quite some time, I may even need to discuss with the rest of the council. Depending on this plan you've discussed I may well not have the authority to make a final decision."

The Envoy rolled his eyes. He wiped his hands on the napkin and dropped it ungracefully on top of his dirty plate as he stood. "I think it best I retire for the night." He turned to the Mayor. "Perhaps we might meet tomorrow to hear when you might be able to answer."

Tillandra stood also. Being nearly double the Envoy's height she deliberately wanted to impress on him who would be making the decision. "Good evening, Envoy. The Mayor will be able to advise you when the council has a decision. As previously mentioned, you would be wise to prepare for a lengthy stay if you wish to wait for it."

He bowed to her. "Councilor." He turned and repeated the motion to Pravat. "Mayor." He turned and headed across the room towards the double doors at the far end.

Just before he reached the doors, Tillandra called out. "Oh, Envoy Reyes."

He stopped abruptly and turned, "Yes, councilor?"

"I would recommend that, if you intend to stay in Watersend, you keep your soldiers very close. Should I feel they were a threat here or anywhere else in Sahro, I would be forced to ask for our mayors to take affirmative action. Understood?"

"Clearly. Is that all?"

"Good evening, Envoy."

He turned and left the room, the doors banging behind him.

Tillandra turned and looked down on Mayor Pravat. "As for you, I have no words. Whatever has been happening here I will deal with later. I am tired and now very grumpy. I will be going to my inn, and should anyone get in my way there will be trouble."

"Yes, councilor."

She turned and moved quickly across the room and out the doors.

"Wasn't that a whole lot of fun. I haven't had such fun in ages," Gimbden laughed, as he jumped up off the floor.

"Oh you can shut up too. Fool!"

35

TILLANDRA

Arriving at The Clown Prince she unwrapped her face and head. Standing just outside the entrance way, she shook off what was left of the sand that she had collected on the journey.

"Mind where you dump all your dirt there, traveler, we aren't your cleaners," a brusque voice called out through the open door of the inn. A middle-aged man, quite tall himself but with spindly legs that struggled to keep up his barrel-like stomach, stood at the door.

Tillandra turned to look at him and his face flamed red, "Oh. I am sorry, Mother. They warned me you were coming, but not that you were in such a state."

She laughed, "Now there, Wessen, I doubt you'd care so much really. You always were the least hospitable innkeep I've had the pleasure to know."

"I'll take that as compliment," he mockingly scowled. "You look like a woman who has taken a hard road to be here if I may compliment you in turn."

Clasping his shoulder with her hand and smiling back, she said, "That would be understating it, Wessen. I've been on the road nine days nonstop, straight from Anderwell, and then this nonsense with the Mayor."

"Nine days! Don't take it the wrong way, Mother, but that's a crazy schedule even for one as adept as you."

"My journey is most urgent and I can't afford the luxury of easy travel, but I can't go on another day until I rest some here. I fear my feet are all but broken."

"Well, get yourself inside and we can feed and water you for a start. You won't be resting much down in the main room, we've a full house. I am going to have to move some people about, there's not an empty bed to be had."

"I can perch anywhere, Wessen. At this point I could probably sleep standing."

"You'll have quarters. I was already arranging it. I'll have water drawn up for you. You're not putting your mess into my bed no matter who you are. Go in the main room and get some food before the blasted troup eat the lot."

"Did my pack get delivered?"

"It did. I have it safely out the back. I'll put it in your room for you."

She made her way to the main room filled with noisy cheer and a rich aroma of cooked meats. In many cities around Dharatan the court had set up friendly inns that discreetly catered for those of the circuit. It took a skilled innkeep to balance the privacy their members needed while appearing to be a normal inn, for anyone to frequent.

The Clown Prince was full of bodies, singing, laughter and the smells of many people drinking and smoking. Tillandra hobbled her way between the gathered groups until she found a free table.

She dropped heavily into the seat, glad to be off her feet. Wessen had organized food for her and within a few minutes she had a steaming bowl of stew and a mug of ale. She let the energy of the room relax her and used the chunks of bread to dip in the stew. She knew she was tired but the noise and laughter was a break from her own company.

She was finishing her meal when a slender man appeared at the chair opposite her, dressed in black.

"No pretty white gloves, Gimbden?"

He sat down across from her, "See, see... what blows with winds of sands, indeed. Who might guess today our very own Mother would pay a royal visit?" His voice was a lullaby of rolling tones and gentle edges that was like a song spoken.

"Gimbden, who else could make the very normal seem like their very own ballad. I nearly didn't recognize you before, talking so normally."

He chuckled. They reached out a hand to each other in what appeared an awkward clasping of their hands. The rings they each wore touched and a tingle of recognition ran through their fingers and hands.

"In All Jest."

"In All Jest," Tillandra replied.

"What brings you so far without message, may ask I?" he queried.

Tillandra picked up her mug to take a sip. After a small pause, she looked casually around the room, and replied, "Many strange things, Gimbden, but it needs to be told out of the earshot of others. Even then, there is some I cannot tell you. I had no choice but to hurry here. My needs are very urgent."

"On you, the journey's tale is worn like heavy cloaks."

The strange way that Dotokiens like him spoke usually slowed the pace of conversations, others having to understand what it was they said. Gimbden made up for it with his unique troubadour's voice.

She nodded her head, feeling weary despite the food and drink. Hopefully Wessen would be able to get her somewhere to sleep away from everyone else. Her feet were throbbing in her boots and her eyes strained in the dim light, her head crying out for rest.

"I certainly do not feel my best. We need to talk more about what just happened. Do you think you could use your working voice for me, I'm finding it hard to concentrate."

"Of course, Mother. I'm sorry. I realize that the method of you being brought to Pravat was unusual but I had to act swiftly or that fink Reyes would have had his way." He looked at those around them and leaned in close. "He was convincing Pravat Daskare would pay for the oasis, and way stations, along this new road."

Tillandra sat back, alarmed. "Really? And Pravat was going along with it?"

"You know what I've told you in my reports?"

"He's distracted by young women?"

"Distracted is one way to put it. Essentially it's about the only thing he thinks on. The Envoy brought a lot of bait from Daskare with him. The Mayor has had many young ladies to keep him company for this last week."

"I didn't think it was getting this out of hand. I just heard the most recent reports, Beantic didn't mention this."

"That's because she doesn't know. He's been bad but it hasn't affected anything major up until now. When I heard one of his knights telling him that you'd avoided them in Layden, I knew you were on your way here. I convinced Pravat he had to hold off until you arrived."

"Thank Thenis you did."

"The Envoy has been holding back the girls since it happened, I was concerned tonight they would seal a deal just so Pravat could get back to what he is interested in."

"This is too much for me to solve right now. Can you visit with me tomorrow?"

"I won't want to leave him alone too long, but I will find time. In the morning?"

"Make it after lunch, I think I will need a chance to think on everything that's come up on this trip first."

He stood and placed his hand on top of hers. "Get some rest, Mother. I'll see you tomorrow."

"Until then."

Tillandra finished her ale and tried several times to attract one of the serving girls. She went to get up to go get some more from the bar, but as she placed her right foot to stand a jolt of pain hit her from the outside of the heel. She almost lurched and fell over, but the grasp of Wessen righted her before that happened.

"I leave you for just a short while and you have too much ale already?"

Tillandra's face was twisted in a grimace "I only wish, Wessen. My right foot gave way on me. I really need to get out of these boots and soak for a while and see what damage I've done down there."

"Indeed. You won't be going anywhere soon if you can't even put weight on that foot."

"Time is of the essence, Wessen. As long as this nonsense with the Mayor doesn't interfere, I'll be needing to be out of here within another day."

"Not on these feet, I doubt."

"I'd hoped there'd be a team to hitch a ride with."

"There's none in the city, at all, right now. Only two have been operating over the last of the winter, and they both have been out of the city for half a week at least."

Tillandra shook her head in frustration. "I have no time for loitering. What about that bath?"

"Let's get you to the washroom and at least get these feet tended to."

Much as Tillandra was a private person, the pain in her foot overrode the thought of turning away his help, and with his support she made her way across the room and up the back stairs.

The sight that greeted her once she was able to wash and freshen up were two feet in a very poor state. Her right foot was swollen, and where a blister would have been many days before was a raw wound that had been bleeding into her stockings. It might have started small but now ran down the side of the back half of her foot and around the heel. She doubted she would be able to get either of her feet back into boots at the moment. One of the nails on her left foot had come away, and half that foot was black with bruise. Under her right foot the band from heel to toe was tight and inflamed and ached all the way up under her foot into the ball.

The lady that had helped her bathe had finished by rubbing in some salves but had left the wound open; she'd promised to cover it in the morning and bandage it. Tillandra cursed to herself, looking at the state they were in. She couldn't afford any delays getting to Midderbuilt, but unless she had a miracle she was stuck here in Watersend for several more days than planned.

She answered a knock at the door. "Come in."

Wessen came in and as he made his way over to her he shook his head. "Those feet aren't looking good at all, Mother."

"What can I say."

"I've made you up a room of your own down the hall here. Can you walk?"

"Yes, yes. I hope I didn't cause too much problem?"

"Not for me," he chuckled. "Never mind with that. Let's get you to resting."

"I wish it was that simple. I need you to do something for me straight away."

"Oh? What is that? "

"I need a rat, Wessen."

"Ugh. I'll see to it."

Tillandra could see on his face he didn't relish the task, but he turned and left. Once he arrived with the animal, she quickly contacted Bea about what she had wondered regarding Ash's ring. She waited for Bea to go and check and then connect back to her, confirming that the ring was still showing on the map and was moving. She now had her plan on how Goran could find her, but she couldn't do another connection now, she was exhausted and she'd already used the one rat she had.

She dropped the sack out the window and turned to the bed Wessen had prepared for her. Tillandra was out before her head hit the pillow.

36

TILLANDRA

Tillandra had woken with the early morning light and sounds of a waking city. The bed she had slept on wasn't particularly comfortable, but her exhaustion from pushing herself hard on the road would have made the floor seem soft.

She sat on the side of the bed and rested her wounded feet gently on the floor. It took some time for her to awkwardly walk to the table, drag a chair over beside the window, and seat herself.

She opened the window and sat looking out onto the road below. Her mind had been filled with memories of Ashantha, thoughts she had avoided during the arduous toil on Death Road. The relentless heat and constant pace she had kept up allowed her to avoid the inevitable blame she assigned to herself for sending him away.

A rap on her door snapped her from her dark thoughts.

"Yes?" she called out.

"Can I come in?"

"Wessen, is that you? Of course."

She turned away from the window as he came in. He carried a large mug in his hands.

"I brought this hot mead with me, in case you were awake."

"Very thoughtful of you, Wessen. I am very thirsty and hungry. I would have come down, but…" She looked down at her feet.

"Oh, dear. They haven't improved overnight. They look like they hurt."

"They don't just look it." She smiled at him. "It can't be helped. The swelling seems to have reduced overnight, which is a good thing. I can wrap them to protect them, but if I can't get them in my boots then that's another problem."

"I think we'd have trouble finding some readymade new boots for you." Wessen grinned at her.

"Indeed."

"Don't worry about moving, I can get food brought up here for you. I assume you will need to be resting here until they heal up a little?"

"That's not ideal, Wessen. The trip I am making is time sensitive. If I don't get to Midderbuilt and back in two moons, things will go very wrong."

"There's still plenty of time, Mother. Can't you just rest it out?"

"I don't want to leave it to chance. Any more word on the horse teams?"

"I'm waiting for a response, but I don't think the answer will change. There were no teams in town, and no idea when they will show back up. Teams need to rest as well. I don't think you'll be getting an answer you'd like anytime soon."

"A single day's delay I can stomach, any more than that is going to be a problem." She paused for a moment. "What can you tell me about the Skarian knights here in town?"

"That's only been a recent development." He rubbed his chin as he thought. "It hasn't been long, at best about a week. Gimbden would be better informed on the specifics."

"He'll be here around middle day."

"They haven't come to this part of town, but the troups have mentioned them. They seem to have been imposing themselves in the town, and there's nothing pleasant about their manner, apparently."

"I've had the misfortune of crossing them twice on my trip, so far. You'll need to be paying more attention to what they are up to. They are going to be around for a few weeks more. I might have forced the man they are here with to stay longer."

"The envoy from Daskare?"

"Yes. Good to see you're keeping yourself well informed."

"It's my job, Mother."

"I think you are going to want to speed up communication back to Anderwell. We should have known about this."

"Gimbden didn't pass it along?"

"He was focused on keeping Pravat from making a foolish mistake. He might not be in Watersend much longer either."

"Oh, really?"

"I was planning to move him. It's one of the reasons I am here."

"Was?"

"I need to find out more about this Envoy and what they are up to. The Church of Maltzer, or King Anh, is trying to have more influence here than they should. That worries me. I might have to hold off on that change until this is cleared up."

"And the rest of your trip is to Midderbuilt?"

His question prompted Tillandra's memory. "Yes. *Where's my pack?*"

Wessen got up and fetched it from behind the end of the bed. "Here you go."

Tillandra checked it over. It didn't look like anyone had opened it.

"No one has touched it, Mother."

"It wasn't your people I was worried about, Wessen. I didn't want to hand it to that guard yesterday, but I needed it away from the knights and had no idea what I was walking into when I met with Pravat and the Envoy last night. I can't believe I didn't think of it until now."

"You've pushed yourself hard. It's understandable."

"Not to me." She forced her hand into the open pack, moving things around until she could feel the pouch near the bottom. Her fingers worked the pouch open and she recognized the touch of the Mother Stone inside. She relaxed a little.

"Everything's alright?"

"Yes." Tillandra put the pack back on the floor. "I have to be in Midderbuilt soon, Wessen. See what you can do."

"I will. I'll leave you alone for now, but will get you some food brought up."

"Thank you." She watched him leave and turned back to watch the city outside her window.

The morning passed slowly for Tillandra as she thought over the events of the last few weeks. She had not long finished her midday meal when there was a knock at the door.

"Who is it?"

"Mother, it be I, and I it be," the lyrical voice answered.

"Come in, Gimbden."

The door swung open and he entered, closing it behind him. He was dressed in a simple tunic and tights.

"I've been waiting for you."

"I'm not late, am I? We agreed, we did, that now be the best time for me?"

Tillandra nodded. "We have much to discuss, Gimbden, best you grab a seat. There's wine there on the table."

He sat and poured himself a drink.

She turned away from the street, and stood slowly before dragging the seat back to the table.

"They look sore?"

"They are, but that's the cost of walking Death Road."

He dropped his Dotokien speech. "It's why I prefer a horse." A small smile formed on his face.

"Well, you might need one soon enough."

"Oh?"

"I have several things I need to do on this trip and one of them was giving you new orders."

Gimbden's eyes lit up. "Finally. Pravat is such a tiresome bore, I felt like I was being punished being left here so long."

"Not at all. As you know, placing someone takes time, we have to consider it carefully. If we put you somewhere then we can't easily pull you out again quickly. We've been trying to determine the best place for the move."

"And you have now?"

"Yes. You're to head to Bundok."

"Bundok? That's interesting given what's happening here."

"We didn't know about this latest event when we made our mind up."

"When do I leave?"

"Well, given what I've just learned, that might need to be delayed a little."

Gimbden's face dropped.

"Not for long. Would you not agree that this Envoy and the knights is concerning?"

"It is, Mother."

"Why did you not let Beantic know?"

"Like I said last night, it's only just happened. The Envoy turned up one day and by the next he was laying it on heavy with Pravat."

"He is definitely very forceful."

"Who will watch over Pravat if I am moved on?"

"We will have a new member within a month."

Gimbden's eyes opened wide with surprise. "Oh no."

Tillandra reached across the table and placed her hand on top of his. "It's Ashantha, Gimbden. He left us."

Gimbden closed his eyes and shook his head. He removed his hand from hers and covered his eyes. "What happened?"

Tillandra sat back and took a big gulp of wine. "He was killed. Somewhere towards the north of Malamig."

"Killed? Who would murder Ashantha?"

"We aren't entirely sure yet. You knew he had been away?"

"Yes. Beantic had told me that he was going to Enderk. Wasn't that over a year ago?"

"It was, and yes that's where he went. We needed to know what was happening over there."

"What did he tell you?"

"That's the thing, he didn't reach out to us." She could see the concern on Gimbden's face. "Now we don't know what he learned and who harmed him."

"Why are you here then, and not going to Malamig to find out?"

"There's a lot of things you've still to learn about our group. When one of us dies, we have to replace them."

"I'm aware."

"It has to happen within two moons. If not the Balance is broken and the consequences are bad. I'm the only member that can fetch the new ring for the Audition."

"Oh." His face showed recognition of something. "What of Ash's mask and ring?"

"Yes, well." She took another sip of her drink. "There's complications there as well."

"Such as?"

"We've sent Goran to collect his things. It appears someone might have been able to put on his ring."

"What? Isn't that impossible?"

"That's what we all understood. Which is another reason why I am on my way to Midderbuilt. The only person I think can answer that question would be the Ring Master."

Gimbden shook his head and stood up to pace around the room.

She continued. "That's why I tried to get the Envoy to leave. I can't spend days here in Watersend trying to negotiate with him, I need to get to Midderbuilt and back within time. If there's a new ring then we need to run the Audition."

"I see."

"I hoped that the pressure for him to get back to Daskare might mean he would leave without me having to deal with it. With him choosing to stay I need to deal with it before Pravat does something stupid."

"When doesn't he do something stupid?"

"Let's discuss what we know?"

"Okay. As I told you last night the Envoy wishes to setup this new road directly here?"

"Do you know why now?"

"There's hints of a disagreement between Vodotok and Daskare that's been a year in the making. I've heard of Vodotok imposing some large taxes on Skarians crossing their borders. They do it at every border crossing, so that's four times a trader can be hit with charges."

"That seems deliberate?"

"And it's only for Skarians, which I am not sure is widely known."

"That is news I wasn't aware of."

"I've told Beantic of it before, but given there's not been any major issues about it, maybe she was just watching to see what happened?"

"Perhaps. So this new road would bypass all of that."

"Yes. Efitra to Watersend would only cross Sahro, which removes all of those border crossings. And it would be quicker by at least a month."

Tillandra considered what he was saying. "It makes sense from a purely economic sense. What worried me most was him offering to pay for the costs."

Gimbden nodded. "He was offering to not only pay for the building of them, but the upkeep and security of them."

"That's what I thought you meant. Given what we've just seen with these knights, that would be a very unusual intrusion into Sahro by a foreign ruler." She looked around the room before talking further. "That will not happen. We have to cut this one off before it gets out of hand. I don't think I need to ask the rest of the Council's views on this, we would all agree that no other power can have their people stationed within these borders."

Gimbden nodded as she continued.

"Once this is resolved, it would actually be best that you do make your way to Bundok promptly."

"Why's that?"

"I would imagine King Ahn, or whoever is behind this attempt at claiming new land, will be frustrated. They will want to find new ways to get control. Having access to someone that was privy to the decisions in Watersend would be very appealing to them."

"Very clever, Mother. I see what you mean."

"Would they be watching the Mayor?" she asked.

"Who? The Envoy and his soldiers?"

"Yes."

"I imagine they have someone keeping watch. But, I don't know for sure."

"I want to instruct Pravat, but I don't want to bring their eyes down here." She pointed at her feet. "And I could do without having to boot these up today."

"I think I can handle that."

"I need more than just that."

"Name it."

"Wessen said there are no teams to take me to Midderbuilt, I need to find a way. I can't go by foot."

"There is a way, Mother, but it's a little unusual compared to the normal teams."

Her eyebrows peaked as she replied, "I'm listening."

"There's a camel team that mainly run fast messages and small deliveries. They are a rugged little team and they don't carry comforts with them."

"I am not so precious, Gimden."

"No, but right now you can't even stand."

"If I have to, I can travel. Don't mistake what you see."

He nodded. "Let me find if they'll do it. You're a Councilor, Mother, which may not suit their kind."

"I have no interest in what they otherwise do, if they can get me to Midderbuilt and back then I will pay them well and ask no questions. I'd want to slip out of here quietly. If we're going to lead the Envoy on a bit, then I'd like him to think I am still in town. I'm unsure that his visit is all about just this new road."

"Why's that?"

"I am not sure, it's just a hunch. Having you in Bundok would confirm or debunk that feeling, hopefully. If they have more of an interest in how things work here in Sahro I'd prefer to do what I am about to do without finding more knights on my tail."

"Then I best be gone and find what I can."

"Bring Pravat back as quick as you can, Gimbden. I want to stop this today."

"Understood, Mother." He stood, bowing slightly to her, and made his way from the room, closing the door behind him.

Tillandra sat back deep in the chair, gently moving her painful foot with a small grimace. *Of course I can travel if I want, it's just a little sore.*

LANI

*L*ani ran hard to get back to the main streets of Little Big Rock. As she approached the bakery she stopped and let her breathing calm down to normal. Just as she approached the door it opened, and a woman carrying a basket laden with cooked items exited. Lani waited for her then stepped in and closed the door behind her.

"You're back, girl." Arbery was behind the counter.

"Ah…yes I couldn't find who I was looking for, and you did offer a room. I was wondering…"

"Say nothing more, Tiber. We don't take back our offer."

"You're so kind. I don't know what I've done to deserve it."

Arbery laughed. "I don't know what it's like in Barnen, girl, but being friendly is normal for us. You don't have to do anything to be welcomed. Come on now, let me show you what we have. It's only simple but I think you'll find it good enough."

Lani followed Arbery out the back towards the courtyard they had come through earlier today. The building tucked away in the back of their yard had two doors. Arbery opened the one on the right, holding it for Lani to enter. The room was basic but clean, with a bed off the floor, a table and two chairs and a small window.

"Like I said, Tiber. It's simple but it will do, right?"

"It's perfect, Arbery. I plan to be moving on quickly anyway but a bed and shelter is all I need. How much will it cost?"

"We'll work that out later, if that's okay? I need to get back to the shop." She looked down at Lani's hand again, like she had done earlier, then quickly looked away and hurried back across the yard.

Lani wasn't sure why she was looking at the ring, but sought out her gloves from her satchel. She put them on and closed the door, settling in at the table to work out what had just happened.

Poor Yerat. He wasn't young, Lani knew that. But him just dropping dead in front of her was frightening. One minute he was praising the quality of the amulet and the next he was down on the floor. Lani didn't really know why people died when they got older, they just did. She wasn't pleased he had done it while she was there but she would just have to put it behind her.

It certainly complicated things for her. He was the only fence she knew here in Little Big Rock. She knew there would be others, but Yerat was one she trusted. As much as anyone trusted a fence. Her goal had been to get some money from him quickly and then get out of town using that money, and hide out further south.

It would look bad for her if she had been seen at Yerat's when word from Barnen about her reached the guards here. Lani closed her eyes. Her ability to replay everything in her mind had always helped her stay out of trouble before. As much as she could see, no one had seen her. There was no one visible on the street when she had gone down to his shop, but she couldn't tell if someone was looking from somewhere she couldn't see.

What she couldn't do was sit around and hope everything was going to work out. She needed to sell these jewels to fund herself while she worked out what she was going to do long term. At least Yerat had confirmed what she thought. The rings and amulet were definitely valuable, she would just need to find the right place to get rid of them.

Thinking about the amulet reminded her about the strange sensation she had felt in Yerat's shop. Lani pulled the sleeve of her tunic up and looked at her arm. There were still no marks on her skin. Could she have imagined it? *No,* she shook her head. The amulet had flashed and she could definitely recall the pressure on her arm. The amulet was not something she could take lightly, that was the second time now she had felt it reaching out. It needed to be kept in that pouch and off her skin. The sooner she could sell it the better.

The day passed slowly for Lani, as she hid out in the room. Later as the day began to wane the room became a lot cooler. Lani stood and wrapped herself in one of the blankets as she made her way to the small window that faced the bakehouse. Dedrick walked out of a small storage room, a sack of flour across his right shoulder, closing the door and latching it with his left.

His voiced carried across the yard. "I've been telling you it was this bad, Arbery, you just haven't been listening."

"You always exaggerate a thing, Dedrick, if I ran after everything that you warned of I'd be exhausted."

"Well there's little of it left and I can't afford to waste any of it. We'll soon enough be having to get emmer or we'll be the bakers without bread."

"Not that. I can't sell emmer bread, not when others have flour still. What's Jommy got to offer?"

"I told you he's got naught himself. While I know he will have enough to make sure the lord's bakers get their fill, even then I think he's likely to be running short before long. You have to plead our case to the Mayor."

"The Mayor isn't taking any more petitions about it. He's made it clear it's out of his hands, he's sent requests to the King to request support getting more flour north but he isn't getting any sort of response."

Dedrick carried the sack with him back into the rear of the bakehouse; Arbery followed him but their words were lost to her.

Lani wanted to warm up but wasn't sure she wanted to go inside. She walked over to the back of the bakery and immediately felt the warmth from the ovens. Arbery stopped at the back door with a tray of items in her arms.

"We been disturbing you with all our carry on?"

Lani smiled back at her.

"Well get yourself in here where it's warmer. There'll be a meal soon enough, get a drink and a seat and we'll be with you just now."

Arbery walked off into the baking area and Lani went inside. In the front room she ladled herself a mug of the thin ale they stored behind the counter and sat at the lone table. Arbery returned and quickly set about making a platter for their meal.

"I heard you before, Arbery, I can pay for my food please, I don't want to be causing you problems."

"It's not you that's causing any problems. The wheat shortage is what's causing our pain."

"I didn't know it was everywhere. I'd heard about it up in Barnen."

"Word is that it's a problem over most of Malamig."

"That's a problem for you then?"

"Yeah, that's where all the flour comes from. We don't use emmer or any other of the rough flours here, only wheat and some rye. That's why Dedrick's bread is so popular. For the common folk it's like king's bread."

Arbery walked over and put a plate of bread on the table and went back for the jug of ale she'd poured.

"The winter stores got spoiled, strange as it was. There's been plenty of rumor about it but whether someone got to it or it was just Thenis's plan, who'd know. Facts is facts though and there's not enough flour to go around. We've all but run out now. A couple more weeks' worth and that's all we have left."

"What happens then? How will you make bread?"

"That's what you would have heard us arguing about. I've been trying to buy some but the whole town is low. Our options are about run out now. Little Big Rock will be without proper bread before we know it."

Dedrick walked into the room carrying a steaming pot. "Don't you be worrying the lass about it, we've still got bread to eat for now. Something will come, it always does."

"We ain't had this little supply in as long as I've known you, Dedrick Baker, and you know it. Let's eat what we have and be grateful for that then. Thenis has always provided for us and I believe he will again."

While they ate Lani mostly looked down at her plate. The room felt very small and uncomfortable to her.

Dedrick belched after a large drink. "So what's your plans then, young Tiber?"

Lani had hoped she wouldn't have to deal with any more questions about her plans. "Tomorrow I'll be wanting to find myself a ride south."

He laughed at her.

"What's so funny?" She blushed at his response.

"Sorry, lass. There won't be any rides tomorrow, it's the Mayor's birthday festival. Everyone in Little Big Rock takes the day off."

"Oh, really?"

Arbery answered. "Mostly that's true. I doubt you'll get a ride out until the day after. Anyone that's come here will want to enjoy the festival. It's when the Mayor opens the first of the wines for the year, there's a bit of custom to it. You'll find that everyone gets through their business in the first part of the morning before shutting down for the day. You might get to ask at the agents if any are open."

Lani felt frustrated. She had hoped to catch an early ride out of Little Big Rock and put it all behind her. "Where would I find them?"

"You'd want to be looking round the stabled inns down toward Blanchard's Gate on the southern wall. That's where most of the agents are and where most of the outers stay over." Dedrick pointed through the wall behind her as he said it.

"Thank you. I will head down there early and see what I can find out. Where does the festival happen?"

"Down in the market square there'll be musicians and actors and all them arty types. They seem to travel in for it, now it's not too cold for their precious selves." He emptied the last of his ale and put his mug down on the table.

"Is that the market square where I met you yesterday, Arbery?"

"No lass, that's the Meet Market where we were. That's a tiny square. The main square is right near the middle of the town, it's twice the size or more. You'll know when you see it."

"Will I see you down there?"

"Once we're finished the morning bake, we will be meeting up with friends. Keep an eye out for us."

"I will. Can I help you clean up these?"

Arbery stood. "Just put your plate in the tub by the back door."

"Thank you again. I might turn in for the night, so I can be up early."

"You do that then. Let us know if there's anything you need."

Lani took her plate and placed it in the tub of other dishes on her way out to her room. She locked the door once inside and cursed her luck about the festival. With little else to do she crawled into her bed and drifted off to sleep.

ARBERY

$\mathcal{N}$ ormally, Dedrick would have headed off down to an ale house to meet up with several other shopkeepers in their street, but she had held him back.

"It's one of their rings, Ded."

"You sure of it? I didn't see it myself."

"I double-checked it the second time. I'm as sure as I can be without forcing her to show me."

"I don't understand why she didn't know about us then?"

"Me either, Dedrick. I thought that's the point of us having those rooms."

Arbery had met Goran, one of a group he had called the Travelers, about two years before. On a supply trip to Riverbend, she had met him in the inn she stayed over at. After they had got to know each other, he had asked if she knew of a safe and quiet place for him and some occasional friends to stay in Little Big Rock.

She had mentioned they had two small rooms behind their bakery that they kept for anyone who was on hard times. He had asked if he could check them out the next time he visited that way. Arbery was always looking for ways to top up what they earned from the bakery, so the idea of the occasional guest was something she was happy to entertain.

He had turned up a few weeks later and was very happy with the rooms. He stayed several nights with them, and explained that there was a group of people like him that had previously used a boutique inn, on the southern side of Little Big Rock, but it had burned down in a fire and they needed a new place.

After a few more visits, which he paid a healthy amount for, he revealed more to them. He showed them his ring, and a copy of a stone token. His explanation was that the rings were very rare, and they would be unlikely to see more than one or two people in a year wearing one. The stone token they would see more regularly. The token bearers were message couriers for his friends and they would pass through every month or so.

The man, Goran, had said that anyone that brandished the ring or token would not need to pay them directly. They should just keep a tally of nights they stayed and he would make sure they were paid twice a year for the stays, if that was acceptable to them. Both Arbery and Dedrick were excited to be involved with them. The extra money had been more than welcome.

On his last visit he had suggested that his colleagues were considering finding bigger premises. He had said there were more people they needed to house, and in many cities and some larger towns they had an inn, managed by local keepers, that catered to all their needs. Arbery had pitched to him that they would be interested in running such a place, if they were suitable for such a role. He indicated that could be mutually beneficial and would discuss it more with his colleagues at their next meeting.

She had been eagerly hoping to see him again, as the idea of running an inn appealed to her.

"If it hadn't been for her needing to take her gloves off this morning I would never have known. I saw it again when she came back. I tried not to be too obvious, but she seemed to notice me and seemed uncomfortable about it."

"Goran told us that they all were told who we were and how to find us. You sure it's not a copy?"

"How would I know, man? He said that only their small group wore a ring, and anyone else carried the token. He would have told us if there were fakes. Something doesn't feel right to me."

"She doesn't look threatening to me."

"I can't tell you why, but there's something not right about it, we've never had any problems before. They all announce themselves when they come, never been any secrecy about it."

Dedrick nodded as she spoke.

"When was the last courier through here?" she asked him.

"Only a week ago, I'd say."

"That means it will be a month or more before we see anyone heading south."

"Why, what are you thinking?"

"We need to get a message to them. I think it would look good for us if we were this observant and let them know of it. Don't you think?"

He chuckled. "You've got your heart set on being an innkeep, dear. Haven't you?"

"It's not just that. We do well from what they pay us. If they get an inn, that will all go away. And what if we run out of wheat? What do we do for money then?"

"I think we'll be alright. We always are, but I hear what you're saying. You're smarter about things like that, so if you think we should get a message to them, then we should."

"Well, it will be too late by the time the next courier comes through."

"So, what then?"

"I'm just thinking out loud, but maybe I should try going to River-bend for some wheat? I could try and get a message to them from there, if I can. That place where I first met Goran down there, they stay there. It's one of their inns. I'd bet I can get word to him from there."

As they sat there thinking through the conversation they could hear the sound of hooves clopping on the road below.

After a few moments Dedrick added, "How about you make a trip for the wheat and be offering this lass a ride? Then you gets to keep an eye on her a bit more and maybe figure this out."

Arbery looked through the dim light at him, a soft smile on her lips.

"That is an excellent idea, my dear. A very excellent idea. We'd need to be subtle about how we set that up with her. She's already a bit suspicious, if my gut is correct."

Dedrick nodded. "Let's see what happens tomorrow. If she finds a ride we'll reconsider what needs to happen. Something might come up without us having to plan too much."

"Okay, that seems good enough for now. I feel better about all of this now. I know she's not done us any wrong but I'd feel better knowing we told them anyway."

LANI

Little Big Rock was different to Barnen in so many ways. It was smaller and had grown organically without planning or restriction. Roads were haphazard and Lani struggled to find the logic in them.

She had never paid attention to how Barnen had grown when she was small but this is probably how it looked to others back then.

Mapping things in her mind was easy enough for her to do, storing images of what she saw was automatic, but making sense of them took more effort. She walked around another curving road noticing how even the buildings were not quite straight either. They curved a little as if to match the road.

While the whole day was a holiday, Arbery had told her that most of the townsfolk would be bustling about this morning taking care of normal things before they lunched and began festivities.

True enough there was a fervor amongst those who were out, rushing in different directions to complete what tasks they had to. The road she was following headed towards the center of town, further from the river.

Taking on board Dedrick's advice, she took a left turn at a major intersection, in a more southward direction. The street she was on was wide and busy with carts and people. The sides were a mix of stores, all of which were closed except a small tea house she walked by. A sweet aroma of incense drifted out as she passed by, the room inside quite dark. She could see nothing through the window.

In the distance, behind the buildings, she could make out the wall of the town. It wasn't as tall as every building but she could distinguish its shape behind many of them. There were fewer shops now, and large warehouses or stores accompanying large fenced yards became the norm. It was clear she was in the right part of town to find the shipping agents and booking desks, but like the rest of the town everything was closed up.

She took a break at the gates to one yard, watching a boy grooming some horses. He'd be no more than seven, Lani guessed, looking at him, but his lot in life seemed better than her kin back in Barnen. Despite the fact he was working on the holiday, he seemed well fed and his clothing was all in good order and clean.

Lani wondered how Ilker and the others were doing. At this time of the day they were likely all out collecting pots and working for Bragg. Hopefully one of them had cooked food for the others.

There was little she could do here. She checked all the nearby streets, noting each of the agents she'd want to be coming back to in the morning. She made her way back the way she had come towards the center of town.

Once she was back at the intersection she had veered off from earlier, she changed direction towards the town center. Lani could see where it led, widening even further as she neared the big market square.

This was more like the market she was used to in Barnen, a wide-open area with stalls and carts spread in an orderly fashion. Despite the holiday, it seemed business was business and the traders were taking advantage of all the extra people in town.

To the far left of the square a large stage had been assembled which she assumed was for the festivities later in the day. Cloths of many colors had been tied together to form long ropes and they hung forming multiple catenaries. They connected to building corners and tall poles to create a complete loop of the entire square.

Lani wondered why Arbery and Dedrick didn't have a stall in this market. It was clear there were many more people here than the Meet Market would offer and today of all days she guessed the food would sell out quickly.

Her nose was twitching at the array of aromas coming her way. A light breeze carried pinches of spices, warm meats and wisps of citrus fruits. Her mouth watered even though she wasn't hungry, thankful for the free breakfast she had been given.

As she passed between rows of stalls, the logic of the way they were set made some sense to her. All the food stalls were in one set of rows, around the northern edge of the square. There was then a gap to the area she assumed would be most popular, temporary inns and vendors of ales and wines. Several guards were already positioned behind them, no doubt set for a long day of keeping the peace.

The stage formed the next part of the outer edge of the square. She stood in the open area, rough cobbles underfoot, dark with years of trampled dirt and goods, but coarse enough that they weren't slippery. Lani looked around slowly taking it all in; so much of it was familiar, the nature of the buildings, the clothes of the people but yet it was fresh, something new. She stopped admiring the square and moved out of the open area, her natural suspicion of everyone reminding her to not linger too long where anyone could see her.

She made her way across to the other traders on the southern sides. One was already surrounded by a small throng of people and as she got closer she could see why. She recognized the chalker from Barnen immediately.

As she tried to recall his name, she heard his voice talking to the people gathered around.

"You'll be wanting the best chalks that you can get. You all know that the colors run dry early in the season so don't be hesitant. Rainbow's chalks they the first each year and always the best. These colors been brewing all winter long, they're deeper and richer than you'll have come Thenis month."

Hearing his name brought a smile to her face; there was something warming about him, like the touch of sunshine on a cold day. He had said he was moving on from Barnen, he might have even passed her on the road.

It crossed Lani's mind that he might well be heading south after here and maybe he would be someone to talk to in case there was ride in it for her. More and more people surrounded his stall seeking his chalks, so it wasn't easy to get close to see him.

His voice lifted to match the crowd and Lani enjoyed hearing the tone of it as he told stories about the chalk and made it sound as if his was the only one they should have in the whole of Malamig.

Person after person pushed out of the crowd, a grin covering their face, several pouches in their hands, speckles of colored chalk on their fingertips.

She eventually worked her way through the crowd up to the stall and watched in awe as Rainbow coaxed the throng in front of the stall. As his chalk was selling, the pouch around his waist was filling with coins. It bulged with all the money he was collecting.

He noticed her there at one point, giving her a wink before turning back to encourage the next group which colors they should purchase.

The novelty wore off on Lani after a short while and she made her way back into the square. The sound of lutes and singing now starting to fill the square, the different sounds competing with each other from different corners and the raised voices from vendors rounding out the cacophony of noises.

Lani had always liked markets, the vibrancy of them had everyone in good spirits, but it also made it much easier for a thief to do their work. She had already talked herself out of stealing anything here. She wanted no additional attention but still her eyes scoped out the crowd, taking in all the potential marks. And noticing those who were taking advantage of it.

She'd found a perch up against a building sitting on top of some crates. Her perch was near the road she'd come along to get to the square. Lani figured it was as good a spot as any to watch for Arbery and Dedrick if they were coming down to the square.

After a while watching with no result, she decided to head back towards Rainbow's stall. If there was a chance of getting a ride with him, she might even not have to spend any money. He seemed to be genuinely friendly and he certainly was making more than enough selling his chalk.

When she got there his stall was empty. She managed to catch the eye of a person working in the stall next to his.

"The chalker's gone then?" she asked.

"Yes, about an hour ago," the woman answered.

"Don't know if he's coming back?"

"No idea, girl. He sold out of everything he had. I don't think anyone would bother trying to restock through this crowd." The woman waved her hands at the crowd in the square.

"You're right. Thanks." Lani was disappointed she had missed that opportunity. Perhaps she could find where he was staying and get to him before he left.

She started pushing her way through the crowd. As she made her way closer to the section of the square where the temporary bars were located, she almost walked right into him.

"If it isn't the young lass from Barnen!" His voice carried so much warmth in it she couldn't help but smile.

"Rainbow! I just went back to your stall, but you were all packed up."

"Yes, Lani, it was the easiest day I've had so far. I think I could have said nothing and they would have still bought everything."

She couldn't believe he remembered her name. "How did you remember my name?"

"I don't forget names, that's something old Rainbow has learned over the years. You never know when they will come in handy." He laughed as he said it and clapped his hands, creating a small cloud of colored chalk. "I can never git rid of the stuff."

Lani wasn't sure what to say to him. She wasn't certain she wanted to come right out and ask for a ride.

"So what brings you down here, Lani?"

"Oh... I ... am traveling south, to see someone."

"Are you now," he smiled at her. "Anyone I know?"

Her face went red.

"I'm just joking, my dear. Of course I wouldn't know them."

Lani needed to change the subject. "Are you staying around here?"

"Oh no, I always try to only sell my things once each season in any one place. If I stay around then the mystery goes away."

It seemed to Lani that his smile never left his face. "Where are you going next?" she asked.

"I tend to zigzag my way down to Nedor. My next trip will be west to Rochos."

"Oh."

"What's up?"

"When I saw you I thought you might be heading in the same direction I am. I thought..."

"Sorry, my dear. If I was you'd be welcome to travel along, but I have to be over that way and I think you need to be heading south quickly, correct?"

Lani was taken aback by that last part.

"Don't worry, Lani. I can read people's eyes. You'll be just fine. Trust yourself and you'll be safe."

"Where's our beers, Rainbow?" Two men had crept up behind him and one of them clapped him on the shoulder.

He turned to them. "I was just talking to this young lady."

Before he was able to turn back around to her, Lani quickly moved back out through the crowd and away from him. She wasn't sure what he meant but the way he said things felt like he could understand what she was thinking. She was thankful for the crowd and merged into it with ease, flowing with the tide of people away from where they had been speaking.

Several minutes later a hand grabbed her shoulder and she spun in fear, one hand clamping on her satchel and the other the wrist of her assailant.

"Lo, Tiber, easy there, girl. I didn't mean to frighten you."

She looked into the familiar face of Dedrick Baker and with relief released her grip on his arm.

"Oh it's you."

"Sorry for startling you there." His deep warm voice helped to calm her. "Come on with us, we're just here in that circle." He placed his hand behind her arm and guided her with him, his solid frame clearing a path much easier than she had been able to.

"Look who I found. Poor lass, I near frightened her out of her skin."

Lani saw Arbery turn and smile as she approached.

"I wondered where you might be, Tiber, glad we could find you, this crowd can get a bit manic as the day wears on. Best a girl like you have some company, if you get my drift."

"I was beginning to feel a bit out of my depth, to be honest. That's why Dedrick startled me so much. Is it always this busy?"

Arbery smiled, "You ain't seen the half of it. We'll stay until the night fun begins but later on when everyone is well full of drink and song, it gets too much for us."

Arbery turned to the group. "This here's a traveler staying at ours. Her name's Tiber."

Those in the circle that could hear nodded or raised a mug of cup to her.

"Here, let me get something in that cup for you. I'd name them all but you'll not remember them." Arbery poured ale into her cup and went back to talking to the woman beside her.

Lani enjoyed the barrier the group gave her from the outside jostling and even a little from the noise.

As the sky turned dark, fires were lit around the square and also torches on the building walls. As the ale and wine took its grip her group soon started to talk of the shortage of wheat. It appeared the group was made up of several other cooks and bakers like her hosts.

"There's nothing to be done for it, Dedrick," a wiry man almost directly opposite Lani spoke up. His bushy black mustache was untrimmed over his lips and, damp with ale, wiggled as he spoke.

"You're calmer about it than me, Chiver." Dedrick's mood had darkened.

"What's to be done about it otherwise? My da always told me to only worry about them things you could control. I'm no farmer, nor merchant. So there's nothing I can do to control when we're going to get more flour. I choose to accept it."

"I'm not willing to admit defeat. I was an apprentice the last time I made emmer bread and while it will do to eat I can't believe the prissy nobles and mayor don't still have flour. They be hoarding their own supplies, in my view."

"So you're going to steal from them, are you? Word I heard is they are as bothered as the rest of us. The bailiff's been about and he knows the town is angry about it. We're all going to suffer this summer, that's no doubt."

One of the women in the group near Arbery cut in. "Worse news, or gossip maybe, but I heard the seed stock was damaged as well. There's some saying the planting of this year's crop wasn't as good as it could be and much of it hasn't taken."

Chiver turned to her. "Where did you hear that, Scyllia?"

"One of my contacts who maids in the Mayor's hall. She said they are all in a fuss about it. She only catches parts of it but they've been talking about how to feed the town if there's no wheat at all."

The group went silent for a bit, everyone topping up their drinks. It was Arbery that spoke next.

"It's like I told you, Dedrick, word is there's ample supply with our man in Riverbend. If you won't accept emmer then there's no choice but to go and buy it from there."

Dedrick said nothing; his face had a dark look about it and he focused on his ale.

"If you were going to do a trip we'd throw in for stock as well," Chiver added. The lady beside him nodded along.

"Us as well," another of the group said, two down from Dedrick.

"That's all well and good, Jessup Chiver, but I can't leave the bakehouse."

"Who says you've got to go, oaf," Arbery laughed. "I've been there on my own before and I can do it again. They load it all up. All I've got to do is drive the nags there and back."

"What about the market stall then? You want me to do that too?"

"We'll get by without it. You'll save more flour not having to bake for it, and can just look after the shop while I'm gone. It's not that big a trip and I'll not be hanging around down there."

"I don't feel so good about you on your own," Dedrick repeated.

"What's our option, Dedrick? You going to go and leave me to bake the bread?"

He spurted his drink he'd just put to his lips. "Not while I still breathe."

The group broke into good-hearted laughter and smiles, the tension broken for the moment by the jest. No one said anything while Dedrick looked at Arbery and the others, wiping the ale off his lip.

"She won't be on her own. I can go with her," Lani spoke up. "I'm going south so I'll keep her company as far as this place you mentioned."

Dedrick looked at her, and she could see him thinking it over. "Riverbend, that's the place. But you won't be coming back with her."

"I'll be able to couple up with other traders or a caravan when I have the load. There's always others on the road, you know that," Arbery answered.

Everyone went silent again. Lani watched Dedrick. It took him a good few minutes to think it over before he nodded at Arbery.

"Decided then. I'll go. You all need to sort me out coin for your needs, but the bulk of the wagon will be for ours. I'll bring you back what I can fit." Arbery looked around the group. "Best no one else knows my plans either."

Lani took another sip of the ale in her cup.

Arbery leaned in to her. "Now he's made his mind up we'll be off as quick as possible. But I'm guessing that won't bother you none?"

"No, Arbery. That suits me just fine. I hope that was okay me throwing my answer in?"

"It was perfect, girl. I didn't want to force you. It's not my role to make people do something they might not want, but it did cross my mind how lucky it was you showed up when you did."

Lani laughed.

"What's so funny?"

"Well I was just thinking how lucky it was I bumped into you in the market. You've housed and fed me and now you're taking me south like I wanted. You have to let me pay for it."

"You being daft again, girl, I'm having to go anyway. It's going to be safer with the two of us. You'll be doing me a favor."

"I can't keep taking your charity, Arbery. It's not right."

"We'll sort something on the road. There'll be rooms and food to pay for. You can help me with that. Okay?"

Lani nodded, a smile forming on her face.

40

LANI

What had seemed like a good idea in the middle of the festivities had become a rush to be ready. On their way back from the town center the previous night, Dedrick had gone and gathered the horse and cart that would be their carriage south. They had all retired early, the plan being that Arbery and Lani would set off as early as possible.

It was still dark and no sign of sun-up but Lani had been woken by the sounds of Dedrick getting things ready for their trip.

She had given up on getting back to sleep after he woke her. The trip was playing on her mind now and she rolled over trying to find a comfortable spot. It had sounded like Riverbend was a full day's ride away in the cart. It would be slow going compared to riding a horse, but her choice was already made.

Speed didn't really matter as long as she was further away from Barnen. It had been a stroke of luck to find a ride so quickly and more luck that it was someone friendly. This was all new for her. She had never been further than Little Big Rock before. Lani checked the satchel and made sure she still had everything, mostly checking her coins.

The money she had wouldn't last forever once she had to start paying her way. She knew she would need to be cautious. She would try again to sell the rings. There were always people keen to buy jewelry and once she was way from here, she didn't have to always look for fences.

Lani had no idea what the cost of the trip would be to reach Nedor. She hoped selling the rings would cover it. Not that she cared about sleeping rough if she had to along the way.

As the first light of the morning rose across Little Big Rock they were loaded and ready to leave. Arbery and Dedrick had hugged several times before he finally let them go.

"We'll be fine, man. All up it's a day there, then a day to supply and a day back. You'll forget I was even gone."

"I'd be happier knowing I was there too."

"You've got this lot to tend to and you know it."

"Well that doesn't make me care any less. Your staff is right there behind your seat. I hope you don't need it."

Arbery pushed away from him and climbed up into the cart. "Right then, Tiber. We're off now." She turned and waved back at him as they started down the lane. Lani waved as well looking back at the large man.

Once outside the town walls the road opened before them and Arbery was able to get the horse trotting at a steady pace.

The sky was a rich blue, with only occasional wispy cloud trails in small pockets breaking up the clearness of the day. The sun sat high in the sky and before them the bare roadway passed through fields of long grasses. Nothing was farmed close to the town gate; it was open land that left an open view for the town's defenders.

"I guess you've not been this way then before, Tiber?"

Lani glanced at Arbery. "No, I have not been this way while I be old enough to remember. My pa would know when, I'll be able to ask him when I get to his side."

"Well there isn't much to make of it, this road seems to never move at least until we hit the first river bend and there the farmlands start again."

"Why is there no farms on this side of the town, would this be not good land to use so close to the gates?" Lani queried.

"The story be that back in the time of the Seven Lords' War the farms that were here turned against the town, or the marauders used them to surprise the town. So little of the tale is truly known but they say once the town was regained and the last of the battles over, the Mayor of the time made it law that this side would forever be an open plain. That way no one could ever sneak up again," Arbery told her as she stared at the road ahead.

"Truly? I've not heard anything much about that before."

"Many people don't know. Strangely it's as if it wasn't important."

"How do you mean?"

"There is much lore we hear from the bards and minstrels that is kept alive by their tales. Have you heard any?"

"I haven't seen many bards, mostly they seem to tell tales of what I thought was just story."

Arbery chuckled. "I forget you are younger. Did your parents not also tell you stories about things?"

Lani looked away, taking time to compose an answer, "I haven't spent too much time around them. My father is mostly on the road and my mother died when I was younger."

"Oh, I am sorry."

There was a silence for a while, neither breaching the awkwardness that had formed.

Lani looked at the surrounding countryside on both sides, long grasses bent in the gentle breezes rolling up from the south east, the road to the south weaving its way in line with the river they followed. Far off to the right the mountains ran in parallel to the line they traveled, the view occasionally broken by clumps of trees. There was steady traffic heading south until closer to middle day when they started passing riders heading north.

Arbery broke the silence first. "Where did you live without any parents?"

Lani had come up with a story that was kind of true, to tell anyone that asked. "I was taken in by the priest and looked after there for many years. He took in many of us and the only stories we got were the teachings of Thenis."

"Ah yes, they tend to stick to their script, the religious ones. Well, you should learn to listen to the tales of others a little more now that you're grown. There is always much truth in the stories. The tellers embellish them to make them more interesting to hear, and shorten then to the most important parts. It's usually how we keep the history alive."

Lani looked at her with raised eyebrows. "Usually?"

"I am a bit older than you and I've heard many of the stories and songs over and over, but they all mostly end before they talk about the Seven Lords' War. There is no one telling anything before then."

"Is that when our history began then?"

Arbery shook her head, "Nah, dear, think about that. If there was a war with Seven Lords then they had to have armies and history. The beginning must have been long before that."

"Oh." Lani blushed, feeling a little daft for the silly question.

She shifted on the bench trying to find a spot on her butt that didn't already ache to little avail, as the wooden plank they sat on was unyielding. There was more traffic in both directions now, the faster messengers or hard-ridden horses caught and passed them from behind, and some coming from the other way. Most paid no attention to them, though very occasionally one would nod at them, or call out a greeting as they passed.

They ate while moving. Arbery had explained to Lani that River-bend was a hard ride in this cart and she wanted to get there before dark. The food she had packed was mostly bread and cheese with some nuts and fruits, all of which was finger food and easily eaten while bouncing around.

The road worked slowly further away from the river, following the easier flatter land. On their left the ground had become rockier and more undulating, not ideal to carve out a road from.

Lani reopened the conversation with Arbery. "Why do you think there's no history about the war then?"

Arbery looked at her and took a short while to answer. "See, you've got the bug to think too." She chuckled. "I'm not smart enough myself to know." She paused as she steered the horse around a twisted stretch of the road that led down over a bridge across a stream. The bridge was only wide enough for one carriage or cart.

"I have heard a couple of stories but they were told by a strange old man who you could mistake for being one of the loons."

"The loons?" Lani asked; she hadn't ever heard that name before.

"Yeah, the loons. That's the term given to those whose mind cracks, when they don't make much sense anymore."

"Oh, the crazy ones?"

"Yes I guess that's the other way of describing them. When their minds have gone off on them they tend to speak nonsense most of the time. This old fellow seemed to be like that but Dedrick and I got to thinking after, how he actually seemed to be acting it. There was something not right in his manner."

"Why would he be acting that?"

"Well the story wasn't one many had heard and it stretches belief a little, so I think he found it easier to be a loon and people took it only for the humor and strangeness without questioning him."

"What did he say?"

"A lot of talk of war and the seven realms, before what he called the Splitting. He talked that much was lost and all the lords have been taken away. Then he kept saying about the future they watch for, when the splitting ends and the orange wave will come again."

"Orange wave? What on Thenis is that?"

"No one knows. No one really took much notice of what he said. It did make me wonder about the war and why no one talks about before it."

"Well I'll be sure to listen harder now, that's for sure," Lani replied.

"Good luck finding another loon like him though."

"Why's that?"

"These days the loons all get taken away whenever a fools' cart hits town."

"Where do they take them?"

"I've never heard. To be honest I don't think anyone knows."

They lapsed into another silence as the afternoon progressed, the noise of the wheels and the horse's feet their only constant. The sun had dropped to the tips of the Sisi mountains off to their right and the cart crested the hill they had been climbing slowly for much of the last hour. The land ahead changed dramatically, farms sprawling off to the eastern side of the road which was tracking closely to the river.

Past the farms Lani could see the walls of the city and the small procession of people on the road making their way back there as the daylight was beginning to end.

Arbery piped up, "That's our destination, Tiber, the city of Riverbend."

"I think my butt will be glad of that."

Arbery chuckled, "It's not the most comfortable of ways to travel, that's for sure, but I need this cart if I'm to bring back a load of flour. And it's only a day each way, I've enough padding for a day's ride."

The farms were filled with crops of low vegetables on this side of the city. There were plenty of locals moving along the road to keep the rest of the ride more interesting, the new distractions helping her not think about the aches she had acquired over the day.

41

LANI

*E*ntering the city meant getting in line at the gates and being checked over by the guards. Everyone around them seemed frustrated by the inspections, their impatience to get inside and on their way obvious.

"Ain't nobody seen any of these so called bandits, them guards on about. All it done is slow the average person down," said a man in the line ahead talking to his neighbour.

"You're right about that. Three days of it and all it has meant is I end up late home. They'll lose interest in it like everything else they come up with," the man alongside replied.

"Makes you wonder where these smart leaders of ours get their brains from."

Arbery leaned in to Lani. "Sounds like there's something changed here. I've not had to be inspected like this when I've been down to Riverbend before."

The line to the gate was moving at a glacial pace and what had started as a somewhat patient group turned sour the longer they waited.

As their turn approached Lani could see, from the scowl on his face, that the guardsman wasn't enjoying this any more than those waiting.

"Keep it down back there. We've been told to check for strangers following on from what's been happening in some other towns. We know as little as you do, but if you don't like it, take it up with the Mayor."

"How come he got straight through?" the man in front of their wagon asked.

"Because he's my neighbour and I've known him since we were both lads. Now who are you and what's your business?"

"Do I look like a bandit? Chaelbn is my name, and I stay in the back quarter where I've lived all my live."

"Show me your forearms."

Chaelbn pulled his sleeves up and showed his arms to the guard.

"In you go then." The guard stepped aside, leaving a small gap between the gate and the other guards lined up watching everyone moving towards the city.

Arbery nudged the horse forward slowly so it was alongside the guard. "We're been on the road down from Little Big Rock, what's happening here in Riverbend that has the city shut down?"

"Trouble, that's what. I've no time for gossiping about events. My job's just to check all that try to come in. What's your business here in Riverbend?"

"We're here for supplies to take back home. We need to find an inn for the night."

"Can you show me your forearms?"

They both leaned towards the guard and held out their arms.

"Alright, you can move your wagon in through the main gate over there." He pointed to the side where several of the other guards were moving a barrier open for them.

Lani watched Arbery pull hard on the reins to turn the horse. The nag wasn't having much of it and tried to pull back against the reins. The mini battle persisted for a minute or so. Behind them several frustrated people started calling out to move it along. The guardsman used his staff to prod the shoulder of the horse, making it buck sideways and pull off in a hurry. The wagon lurched a little as it pulled sharply off its line.

It began to move with the horse, despite it pulling sideways against them, to a small cheer of delight from those behind them. Everything moved in slow motion, the horse pulling hard to its right, the wheels moving forward and the wagon trying to spin sideways on the packed roadway.

Just as the wagon straightened up in the direction of the wider entrance, a loud cracking of wood could be heard. Lani watched in despair as the back right wheel spun away on its own. It made it a few feet before falling on its side, and the wagon dipped badly to that side. While the back of the empty wagon didn't fall all the way to the ground, the lurching was enough to throw Lani out. She fell sideways, landing solidly on her right shoulder.

"Hold up, HOLD UP!" Arbery yelled at the horse, finally pulling it to a stop as it bumped into the other guards clearing a way for it.

"Watch what you're doing driving that wagon, woman," one of the guards barked at her.

"Frying toads!" Arbery cussed looking back at the lurching wagon. "You alright, girl?" she called to Lani.

Dusting herself off and wincing a little at the stinger on her shoulder, Lani stood up. "Nothing bust here, Arbery, except that wheel."

Lani watched Arbery come around the back of the wagon, pointing at the guards on that side. "Well, don't just be yelling at me, come on, we need a hand unless you want this blocking up the gate all rest of the day."

Several of the guards walked towards Lani, one of them leering at her as he went by, making her skin crawl.

"You want to learn to drive this thing properly before you go getting your tunic in a twist, woman," the older of the two barked at her. They made their way to the wheel and rolled it back to the side of the wagon. "We'll lift the wagon bed, you need to push that on."

"I know what to do," Arbery snapped.

Several of the men in the line alongside joined in, and the wheel was pushed back on without much effort. Lani didn't know much about wagons but she could see where the end of the axle was split.

"The pin's sheered out of the wood. I'll have to get to a wainwright and fix this up. Curses! We've little time for loitering about."

The older of the guards that had helped spoke to Arbery. "You'll have to walk the horse now. One of you will need to make sure that wheel stays on. Come on, let's get you through here before any more delays happen."

"Can you walk alongside that wheel and keep it on, Tiber?"

"I'll do my best, Arbery." Lani moved alongside, not sure what she could do if it was to slide off again.

Arbery started walking the horse gently forward and the guards let them into the city, more than likely glad to see the back of them, Lani thought. They made slow progress, with Arbery calling back to her whenever she was about to change direction. So far the wheel had stayed more or less in place. If it looked like it was slipping she found she could lean against it with her shoulder and push it back up the axle.

Riverbend was a flat city, sided against the river much like Little Big Rock was. The roads were busier than Lani had seen further north, which only allowed them to move very slowly. Their ability to maneuver was nonexistent, and the further they crawled away from the gates the further they moved from any help.

While it was painstakingly slow Lani was able to take in much of the roads they were moving along. She spotted several strips of shops likely to house jewelers or traders that might be interested in buying one of her rings. She felt safe enough from Barnen now that no one would be any the wiser about where they had come from.

The journey ended when they managed to get the wagon partly into the yard of an inn.

"Alright, Tiber, let's get ourselves a room then I'll set out to find us someone to fix that wretched wagon."

Lani gladly left the side of the wagon and, wiping her brow, followed Arbery inside the inn. The building was split by the entrance. A main room and bar were to the right and what seemed to be the accommodation to the left and upstairs.

As soon as they had settled into the room Arbery turned to her.

"Let's not labor about here, Tiber. The day's ending soon enough and the keeper gave me someone to seek out to fix that wheel."

"You want me to come with you?"

"I thought you might want to."

Lani wanted the opportunity to head back to the shops she had seen. She was thinking of an excuse when Arbery spoke again.

"It's okay if you don't. I can't spend important time debating it with you. I need to be gone."

"I'll stay, sorry."

Arbery turned and left the room. Lani thought she seemed a little annoyed but didn't care particularly much, she had her own task to complete.

After waiting a few minutes Lani dug into her bag. She pulled out one of the amber rings. She held it up to look at it and was happy enough to just try her luck selling the one. She didn't even know if she could find anyone this late in the day. Tucking it into her pocket, she slung her satchel over her shoulder. If by any chance someone was interested then maybe they'd want all three.

Locking the door on her way out, she hurried down the stairs and out onto the street.

42

LANI

There were more than enough people moving about Riverbend that Lani could blend in and go unnoticed. Time wasn't on her side, she imagined most traders would be closed by nightfall.

Running off from the northern side of the road were numerous small lanes. They were full of small stores and workshops crammed together. The lanes were narrow and didn't allow for wagons or horses to move through. The canopies of the stores on each side almost touched in the middle.

She ignored the first couple then wound her away up the next, quickly passing the clothes and leather stores. Smaller connecting lanes allowed her to cross eastward midway along until she found one that seemed to be more suited to her needs. It was mainly jewelers and metal workers with some other services mixed amongst them.

Lani walked back and forth along the lane several times. Closest to the main road were the craftsmen's stores. They were well kept shops and one of them appeared to have a private guard inside. That one she gave a wide berth.

In Little Big Rock she had never had to work out who to go to, she only could use a fence, and she'd been introduced to Yerat. She felt uncertain about what type of vendor would be right for what she was trying to sell. Several of the shops were run down and appeared to have more trinkets than jewelry.

Furthest from the main road a man had come out onto the doorstep of his shop and waited for her to walk that way. He was dressed in a plain tunic and tights, with a wide dark green belt around his waist set with a large brooch in its middle.

"What's a shabby looking young woman doing wandering up and down this lane?"

"I'm from out of town and I'm just trying to see which store best suits what I'm after."

"You've got money to spend then, lass? Well come into Lerkein's shop, there's plenty of great looking pieces in here for you to consider." He went back inside.

Lani made her way through the open door into a small shop with a cluttered array of display boxes and tables. Lani took in as much of the store as she could; it definitely was a trader shop and not a jewelers.

"What is it you're looking to buy, if I might ask?"

Lani stopped and looked him over. He looked nothing different to the storekeepers she played against in Barnen, except he knew nothing of her.

"Well in fact, Lerkein, much as some days I'd like to buy something, I'm more in the selling business."

He shifted on his feet and stood up from leaning against the counter. "Oh you are, are you?" A smirk came across his face, "What makes you think I'd be needing to buy anything else." Sweeping his hand around the room, he said, "I've got me plenty here already. What I need is some buyers."

Lani kept her eyes on his, knowing a sale was always hardest when you weren't known or when you were known too well. When she had walked in it had appeared to her that little in the shop had been moved in a very long time. Most of the trinkets and bric-a-brac seemed covered in a lot of dust. There was no way he made a living from selling it. Unless she was mistaken, he made his money trading things not on display.

A fence was a fence no matter what town you were in and Lerkein's shop smelled strongly of one. It was the type of place she needed but her job was to make him think she could wait.

"Well if you aren't in the buying business then I guess I walked into the wrong store."

"Perhaps. Perhaps not."

"What do you mean?"

"Well you're making a lot of assumptions, and I don't know anything about you. In fact maybe you're looking to steal something from old Lerkein. Maybe you think I'm an easy target."

Lani shook her head. "Not at all."

"What you got in that satchel then?"

"Nothing for you, it's just where I keep all my clothes."

"Well what is it you're so keen to sell me? I don't buy clothes. If you're wasting my time then off with you, before I get one of my helpers to relieve you of your 'clothes'."

Lani tightened her grip on the strap of the satchel. "The type of things I sell are always very worthwhile and unique. If you'd rather I walk across the lane and try my luck there, that's okay by my thinking. This shop looks like it is down on its luck anyways."

"Let's not get too hasty there, lass, I didn't say I wasn't a buyer, but I don't just buy any old thing."

Lani slowly looked about the store, noting how much of it was quite ordinary jewelry and random items. She raised her eyebrows as if to say as much.

"What is it you've got then, let me see it before we waste the night completely throwing jabs at each other?"

Lani walked closer to her side of the counter, reaching into her tunic pocket and holding out the Enderk's ring.

"Oh sheez, look at that," Lerkein said. "That isn't something you see every day."

She held it closer to him then quickly pulled it back and put it on her middle finger.

"Like I said, I only sell quality and unique things, when I have them."

"And where does a girl like you come by such a pretty ring like this?"

"Does that matter to you?"

"It matters to me that I'm not about to have someone come wandering in here asking about their missing property."

Lani eyed him suspiciously. "No one will come asking about their missing property. I'm the owner of it and I am keen to trade its value for coin."

He held out his hand and she reluctantly handed it to him. Lerkein spent several minutes looking over the ring, holding up to the lantern nearest him, and several times looking back at her.

"This is amber and I think you know that. While it's rare, everyone knows where it comes from. There's few people that will pay to hold stolen stones."

"I told you the ring is not stolen."

"Stones, I said. There's no amber anywhere on Dharatan, lass. That means it's come from Enderk. One way or another." He put it down on the counter between them.

"So you don't want it then?" Lani grabbed it and started to put it back in her pocket.

"Hold on. I didn't say that." Lerkein rubbed at his eyebrow. "It's a question of price. As you can see, Lerkein, he's down on his luck. He doesn't have lots of coin to gamble on something few might want."

Lani chuckled. "I expected that. Of course you'd try to get it cheap. I'd always been told that rare things were worth more."

"There's rare, that you can show off. And then there's rare that you keep hidden. People pay differently for them. This, it's one of the latter."

Lani looked outside. What daylight there had been was disappearing quickly. She didn't want to be here much longer, she didn't know her way around and she was still carrying all of her things. She wished she'd left the bag back in the room now.

"Do you want it or not? Make me an offer, or I'll need to get to another shop before they close."

"Two silvers. That's all I can offer for it."

Lani put the ring back in her pocket and rearranged the satchel on her shoulder. "Sorry, I thought you'd make me a decent offer. I guess I wasted your time."

"Four. I can go to four, but that's all I have. Seriously, I mean it."

Lani looked him in the eyes. She wanted to be away and back at her room, but the way Yerat had gotten all excited when she'd shown him the rings told her he would have paid at least double what this man was offering.

"It's not enough."

"What do you want then? Save me some time and tell me a figure. I can either meet it or I can't." He was fidgeting on his side of the counter. Lani was sue he would have more to offer.

"Eight silvers. Give me eight silvers for it and I'll haggle with you no more."

He scrunched his eyebrows together, as if he was confused.

"Eight? No way."

She stood looking at him, preparing to leave.

He turned and pulled open a drawer. He shuffled around in it and picked up what looked like coins. He placed them down one at a time in front of her. "One, two, three… four, five, six."

She looked at them sitting there between them.

"That's all I can do, lady. It's time I headed home. If you want to sell it today, I'm the only one left open now. Take it or leave it, but make your mind up now."

Lani looked between him and the coins. He had successfully delayed her now long enough that she had only those choices. If she didn't take the coins she was no better off than before and six silvers would last her a good amount of time.

He had a sneaky look to him and she still wasn't sure if he had some trick up his sleeve. She reached into her pocket and pulled the ring back out. Reluctantly she put it down on the counter and swept the coins back her way.

"I guess we have a deal," he grinned at her.

"We do." Lani looked around quickly to make sure they were still alone. "Until next time."

Lani stepped out of the shop still unsure if she'd got a good deal or not. She knew he wouldn't have bought it if he didn't think he could get at least double that, but where he'd sell it she had no idea.

Lani hurried back down the lane until she reached the main road and merged into the back of a group of people. Turning her tunic inside out she appeared different from behind, enough for now she hoped in case Lerkein had silly ideas to reclaim his money.

She didn't trust him to not try and send someone after her to take the coin back. While a fence wouldn't do that to someone they regularly did business with, he knew he'd likely never see her again, so he might try to double his gain.

She slipped into the inn as they passed it and made her way back to their room. Thankfully Arbery was still nowhere to be seen so no explanations were needed. Lani pulled out her coin pouch and added the six coins to it, a smile forming on her mouth at all her good fortune in the last few days.

43

LANI

"What a trial that was," Arbery said as she put two mugs of ale down on the table.

"The ale?" Lani asked, looking around the main room of the inn.

Arbery chuckled, "No, Tiber, getting that wheel sorted. The wainwright didn't turn up first thing like he said he would. I had to hunt him down. In the end I used my charms and convinced him it would be worth his while."

Lani raised her eyebrows at that.

Arbery almost spat some of her mead out as she laughed. "No, not like that, lass. I said I was happy to pay for an emergency, but that I needed to have it fixed this morning so I can get it loaded."

"Is it fixed?"

"Yes, I stayed until he followed me back. I think he just wanted to see the end of me. I don't care either way. Now I can head over to the warehouse district to get some wheat to take back."

"You aren't heading back today then?"

"Not likely. I plan to get a full load and set it in the yard here ready to leave at first light. They have a guard overnight, so it should be safe and all. It will take me the best part of two days with a full load, the horse can't go the pace we made on the way here."

Lani nodded as a girl placed their meals in front of them, a healthy serving of vegetables and some chicken in sauce with several big chunks of bread on the side.

The inn was filling up with workers coming through to get their middle day meal. The noise grew and the two spent most of the meal without words.

Arbery pushed her tray aside and looked up at Lani. "So what's your plan then, Tiber?"

Lani chewed her bread slowly, wanting to be a little careful about what she said. "I am going to go look for a ride south once we've eaten and see what I can find."

"I expect you'll find that none will leave until tomorrow. The room's here for another night, so you best stay here with me. You don't talk so much but you're not bad company."

Lani saw a small smirk on Arbery's face and let a smile form on her own. "Thanks."

After their meal they both headed out on their separate ways. The innkeep had pointed Lani in the direction of where the town's agents were based. After finding nothing at the first of them she entered the next, feeling a little less hopeful than when she had set out.

Lani approached the counter.

The man behind the counter had a pair of round spectacles perched carefully on the bridge of his nose. When he looked up he reached up and took them off.

"How can I help you?"

"I am in need of a ride south."

He looked her over quickly. Lani had been able to clean up at the inn, and was dressed as best she could.

"South, you say. Anywhere more specific than that?" He tilted his head and looked more intensely at her.

Lani felt uncomfortable under his gaze. "Yes… Ultimately I need to make Nedor, but I am willing to take whatever I can to keep moving south."

"Nedor," he repeated. He put his glasses back on his nose and looked down at the papers in front of him. As he ran his finger down the list he mumbled what Lani could only guess were town names. He turned to the next page. "The next carriage isn't for several weeks. Will that do?"

Lani shook her head. "No, I have to make haste." She repeated the story she had used before. "My pa is unwell and I am rushing to be by his side. I do not need a carriage, I can ride a horse or in a wagon."

"Hmm." He went back to the first sheet and ran his finger back and forth over several items marked on the paper. "No caravans or the like. There's one merchant caravan, but..." He stopped thinking over what he was discussing to himself. He took the glasses off his nose again and looked at her. "There's one, but I am not sure he will take any passengers. I can ask, although I wouldn't get your hopes up. Can I assume you have adequate coin for such a trip?"

Lani took her time to reply, as she didn't want to get charged too much. She had no idea what the cost should be and was entirely at their mercy. "What would the fees be for such a trip?"

"I can only surmise, miss. A carriage to Nedor would be most likely a silver coin. This ride wouldn't be of that quality but I can't say what they'd charge for it."

"I have the coin, and am willing to consider anything at this point."

"If you will give me a few minutes, I will see what I can find out." The man put his glasses down on the papers, and walked out of the room into the large yard beside.

Lani watched him approach a man helping to load sacks into the back of several wagons. The man stopped and was in what appeared to be an animated conversation with the agent. At one point the agent turned and pointed back at the office she was in. The way the man shook his head wasn't encouraging to her. He ended up waving the agent away and returned to loading the wagons.

The agent came back into the office appearing flustered. "I'm sorry, miss. The caravaner has no interest in passengers."

"Doesn't he have room?"

"He's not interested in having to cater to someone not working the load. And, as he put it, especially not a woman, who he would have to look after."

"I don't need no looking after."

"I'm sorry, but he's not interested at all. I even tried offering double money."

Lani raised her eyes at that.

"Like I said earlier, there's a carriage in two weeks, if you can't find anything before then."

Lani thanked him and left the office. She walked across the yard towards the man she had seen the agent with. She could hear him talking to one of the men.

"Like we need some lady interfering with how we travel. There's no coin worth that. That's the bloody reason I love this job, I get to avoid my wife talking at me all the time."

The other men loading the wagons with him all laughed. "Ain't that the truth, boss."

She turned and walked away, knowing there was no way he would take her.

When she got back to their inn she could see Arbery handing the wagon over to the stable lad. The back was empty, which surprised Lani.

She walked over to Arbery, who didn't appear to be in a great mood, "You don't have a load?"

Arbery turned around, a little startled, "No, Tiber. Curse the pests."

"What do you mean?"

"It seems the problems we've been having in Big Rock aren't isolated. The shortage has meant the suppliers here are struggling to fulfil demand." Arbery walked with her back into the inn. "I've spoken to all the suppliers, not just our normal one and there's nothing here to buy."

"What will you do then?"

Arbery opened the door to their room and Lani went in first. "I'm just going to have to wait."

"For?"

"They're waiting on deliveries from Nedor. I've been promised most of what I hoped to get. If I can get a deal with one of the others as well I might end up with a full load."

"How long will that take?"

"I'm not sure, yet. Possibly a week."

"Won't Dedrick be worried?"

"It's okay, I know some people here that will help me get word to him. There's not much point in going back empty-handed. There won't be anything to come into Big Rock very soon, so we'll either run out or Dedrick will have to start using emmer or the like."

"What's emmer?"

"It's a poorer grain, grown further out and by many of the smaller farms for their own use. It's a tougher grain and it hasn't been affected, it seems, mainly because the stores of it are kept near the towns and far away from the cities."

"But it's not so good?"

"No. It doesn't make breads like we are used to, and it's harder to mill and work with. Dedrick will be a grump for months if he has to bake with that, and we won't make much from it. The price we can charge isn't much more than it costs."

They both sat in silence for a while.

"What about you then?"

Lani had been debating on her way back what she would do. She was clear she wanted to get free of Arbery. The woman had been very kind to her, but something bothered Lani about that. She still wasn't sure if it was because she just wasn't used to it, or if there was something more. It had only been little things but she felt the woman was a little too interested in her.

"I've found myself a ride."

"That's great news. To Nedor?"

"Yes. There's a seat I've bought, leaving tomorrow."

"Well, that's you sorted then."

Lani didn't know what else to say. At this point she had nowhere to go, but it gave her excuse to go her own way. "Yes, it was very lucky."

"I imagine you'll be up and gone early then?"

"Yes, I will be planning to get my head down soon. You've been very kind to me, and still you haven't let me pay for anything."

Arbery waved her hand in dismissal. "Nothing to pay for, Tiber. You've been company and that's worth something on its own. Let's hear nothing more of it. If you want to settle in for the night we best go and eat."

After their meal they both retired. It didn't take Arbery long to fall asleep and Lani could hear her heavy breathing from her bed across the room. As she lay awake worrying about what to do, an idea came to her. For several hours she played the idea around in her head as she talked herself out of it, then back into it.

Once all the noise from the inn had stopped and the town had reached the late hours, she made up her mind. She sat up slowly and edged her way along the bed. Gathering her clothing, she dressed as quietly as she could.

At one point Arbery snorted and appeared to begin sitting up. Lani froze, not wanting to say goodbye or explain why she was leaving at this time. It was a false alarm. She stood and lifted her satchel, hooking it over her shoulder.

The door proved the hardest thing to do without noise. Lani felt bad that she would be leaving it unbarred, but unless she woke Arbery there was no way to change that.

She slipped out of the inn and looked to see if anyone else was around. Everything appeared quiet and she made her way back to where the agent's yards were. She kept to the sides of the roads and used the deep shadows to hide her movement.

When she reached her destination she could see the yard was blocked by a large gate. A heavy chain and padlock hung around the gate. She waited for ten minutes tucked out of sight in a lane entrance to see if any guards were around.

The idea that had formed in her head had come from a mental snapshot of the yard and surrounding buildings. When she'd been tossing and turning in her bed she had noticed the small building alongside the yard. As she remembered in her vision there was a wall close by that Lani believed she could climb and get onto the roof of the building. From there she could get into the yard.

Once she'd made the climb, she lay flat on the roof looking down into the yard. It was not empty. There were no merchants or teamsters there but there was a guard. He hadn't moved much but he was definitely awake. She could make out in the moonlight the wagons of the caravaner were still there. There were at least four that were all filled the same. In the middle were bags and cloths, while the outsides were lined with sacks stacked on top of each other.

Lani lay still for at least an hour waiting for the guard to move or fall asleep. He stood up and stretched out his body. He picked up the mug from the table beside him and walked off across the yard.

She couldn't wait any more and turned around on the roof, edging backwards over it. Her legs hung down and she crept further until she was hanging just by her hands. She looked back over her shoulder but couldn't see the guard.

Letting go, she dropped to the ground. To her the sound seemed to boom across the yard. Lani turned and crouched where she was. She crept under the covered part of the yard where there was less light and waited for the guard to return.

As she heard him walking back she moved in the opposite direction around the barrels she had hidden behind. She could now see a line to the wagons she wanted to reach.

There was a loud banging on the gate, causing the guard to jump slightly and nearly spill his drink. He hurried over to the table and put it down.

"Who is it?" He reached for the sword hilt at his hip.

"It's Siden, I'm the caravaner with all those wagons. Your boss should have told you we'd be here early. We need to be out of town before sun-up."

"Bit earlier than I was told."

"We couldn't sleep, what's a few hours to you? Unless you've been sleeping."

The guard had walked over to the gate and was taking a chain off his neck. "Fat chance of that."

Lani had no time left. Using the distraction she sprinted across the yard and up to the back of the third wagon in the group. She clambered up onto the back and started trying to wedge her way down between the sacks on her left and the bags in the middle.

She could hear the guard. "Here, use this key and open the lock, then we can get this all open."

The sound of the gate sliding open caused Lani even more alarm. She didn't know if they would recheck each of the wagons but until she was underneath something she would easily be spotted by the wagon driver.

As best she could she worked halfway up the wagon and pulled some of the bags over her. They were heavy and there wasn't much movement in them. Right now the best she could hope for was they'd get a long way out of town before anyone might see her. She could hear people approaching the wagons and gave the big sack beside her another last pull.

It didn't want to budge as she gave it all her strength. Just as she was about to give up it moved a little. She gave it another effort and the heavy bag collapsed on her. It only partially covered her head but the rest of her was trapped there now.

She could feel someone climbing up into the front of the wagon and within minutes they started to lurch forward. The driver turned the wagon and she could tell they were out of the yard as he picked up speed.

There was nothing else she could do now but lie there. She closed her eyes and figured she might as well catch up on some sleep.

44

LANI

What had seemed like a good idea in the dark of night had become a prison with the light of the new day. At first Lani had been able to change the position she lay in with the cover of dark. That changed once daylight emerged.

She could make small adjustments to her position in the safety of the space she had created but anything more than that would have exposed her to the driver of the wagon directly behind hers.

For several hours she had lain on her back feeling every bump and hole in the road through the wooden floor. Her first relief came when the convoy stopped so the drivers could have some breakfast.

Once she was certain there was no one within sight of the back of her wagon she had adjusted the space she was in to give her a little more room and shifted how she lay. Her stomach grumbled a little and the skin she carried in her satchel was empty, presenting her with another problem.

While the way she had lived in Barnen as an urchin had prepared her to go without food for a day or more, not having anything to drink would test her. Now that the sun was up she had started to sweat. The tight space had kept her warm in the chill of the early morning but was now cooking her. She dragged her partially dry tongue across her lips and wished she had prepared better for the journey.

Lani repositioned herself onto her stomach with a cloth under her elbows. With her head propped in her hands she looked out over the open countryside. Her view was narrow through the small gap in the sacks.

The drivers must have been close by as she could hear parts of their chatter now. One voice she recognized from the caravaner who had done all the talking to the guard at the agent's yard.

"Don't forget what you're doing..." Lani guessed he must be moving around when he talked, as some words were much clearer than the others.

"...The only cargo that really matters ... sacks tied off with the red cloth. The salt bags ... items ... for show. We don't talk to anyone ... won't be stopping in any town."

"Where we going, Sider?" Lani heard a different voice.

"You don't need to know. This cargo stays safe no matter what ... Or you'll pay. Got it?"

Not long after, they got back on the road again. All Lani knew was they were heading south, but not the actual destination. She hoped they wouldn't veer away from the main road much.

The trip continued throughout the day, with only small stops for their meals. By the time they stopped to make camp for the night, Lani was desperate. She needed to relieve herself and she was feeling ill from having had nothing to drink. Her elbows felt battered from trying to prop herself for part of the trip and her legs had cramped more than once. She was feeling very dispirited and trapped.

Once the horses had been unhitched from the wagons and the sounds of the group were away to the side, she risked getting out of her hiding spot. She moved one of the sacks, being careful to do it slowly so there was no sudden movement in case anyone was nearby. Lani placed it in a way she hoped she could get back in quickly if she needed to.

After waiting for several minutes she climbed up towards the front of the wagon. On the driver's bench there were several skins. She tried both but to her despair both were empty. There wasn't a single drop in either.

She crawled over the sacks to the back of the wagon and lowered herself to the ground slowly. It took her a moment to stretch out her legs and back. Relieved by being out, she crept to the side of the wagon and could see a fire thirty or forty paces away. It looked like there were about ten men sitting in a circle around the fire. One of them appeared to be cooking on it.

Lani moved back to the other side of the wagon and looked around. They were parked on land between the river which turned sharply here and the road that shadowed it.

The wagons created cover for her and she moved towards a small clump of shrubs near the river's edge. She desperately drank from the cool water before washing her head in it. While the skin in her satchel wasn't big, she filled it so she would have enough to sip on the trip tomorrow.

The evening landscape was dappled with moonlight through the cloud above. Even if Lani could have seen more she wouldn't have been able to tell where they were, as this was all new countryside to her. She was further away from Barnen than she had ever been.

Leaving Little Big Rock was important. Lani had known that anyone looking for her from Barnen would soon check the neighboring towns. She had known when she left Barnen she couldn't stay in Little Big Rock. She hadn't thought about where she would stay after that.

Riverbend had seemed okay but she didn't want to wait around with Arbery. Lani still wasn't sure why, but something about that woman bothered her. Maybe she wasn't used to someone being so nice but there was something that nudged at her instincts and she had chosen to follow it, even if it meant she wasn't entirely sure where she was going to. The thought of seeing new places excited her.

Would Nedor be as exciting as the tales she had heard? In the end it would come down to being able to sell the amulet or the rings. She would need money to survive when she got there. She had to get there first anyway.

There was no way she could ride these wagons all the way there. Her body couldn't take too much more of it. Tomorrow she would need to be ready to get out at any town they passed through. If she was alert she could jump out and run off before anyone stopped to catch her.

If what she heard was true, they'd likely just ignore her and keep going. That might play to her advantage. She crept back to the wagon she had traveled in and cautiously climbed back into it. Once back in her hidey-hole she pulled the sack over her and settled in for a long night.

Lani awoke to the sound of the wagoners hitching the horses and preparing to leave. She had managed to sleep for large portions of the night. If nothing else, the cramped space was insulated and warm. Without delay they wagons set off again with only tiny threads of sunlight crawling across the dark sky.

Several hours into their journey the caravan stopped. If it was like the day before, Lani knew this would be their time to eat some breakfast. Using the noise of the carts to hide any noise she adjusted her position.

The wagons stopped and she could feel and hear her driver climbing down from his bench. A leg cramp caught her by surprise. Her right calf locked up and instinctively she pushed her leg out straight and reached out to grab it. She let out a sharp cry of pain before she could stop it and then bit her lip to hold in her discomfort.

"What was that?"

"What you going on about, Rowdry?"

"I heard something."

"You probably heard the sound of your first thought."

"Funny, Brek. In your wagon. I heard something, sounded like a person."

"For real? There better not be a stowaway on here. Siden will have my neck if we've brought an extra."

Lani lay locked in her spot. Her eyes filled with tears as she held her calf in pain. She just hoped they didn't look too hard. The sacks at her feet were dragged away and her feet poked out visible to the men. A strong hand grabbed her ankle and she was pulled across the wagon floor. She tried to wriggle free but as she neared the back of the wagon other hands grabbed her and pulled her off the wagon and upright.

As soon as she was on her feet another hand locked around her mouth. A surly voice called out from toward the front of the convoy. "What are you fools up to back there? Come and eat or you'll get nothing."

The man in front of her looked at her with angry eyes and held a finger up to his mouth. "Nothing, boss, just rearranging a few things. Don't wait on us," he yelled back at the man.

"Don't you damage the goods. I warned you what was at stake."

He leaned into Lani, his sour breath clogging her nose. "Try anything or say a word and Brek here will stick you with that knife of his. Got it?"

Lani could see the knife Brek held. She nodded as best she could against the strong grip over her mouth. They marched her over to the bushes protected from view of the rest of the group by the line of wagons.

"We don't have time for this shit, Rowdry," Brek muttered under his breath.

"I ain't going to have her, fool. But we can't leave her on the wagons, he'll have our hides. No one is meant to know what we're carrying or where."

"What's your great plan then?"

Rowdry didn't say anything straight away. He looked at Lani and back at Brek several times. She could see him trying to work it out.

"Go and grab some rope and a cloth."

"What for?"

"Just do it, Brek. If you don't hurry Siden will come looking for us. Then what?"

Brek nodded and left, but was back quickly.

"Right, gag her with that cloth. Once that's done we'll just tie her up and leave her here. We'll be long gone soon enough."

The two men roughly handled her and edged a cloth that smelled of bad wine into her mouth and tied it off behind her head. They laid her on her stomach and tied her feet. They then tied her hands behind her before pushing her deep into the bushes.

"Where are you two? We're leaving in ten." The boss's voice carried across the wagons to where they were.

The two men had started walking away, then she heard footsteps returning. It sounded like Rowdry's voice. "You should have stayed out of our wagons, girl."

The last thing she remembered before she went unconscious was the sound of something swinging through the air. Whatever it was hit her in the side of the head, and then everything went black.

TILLANDRA

*P*ravat had been and gone. Gimbden had been able to sneak him into the inn without anyone being the wiser. The Mayor was a frustrating individual to deal with and Tillandra had struggled to not lose her temper with him.

It was left in no uncertain terms what he was to do. He was to block the Envoy from any further progress on the matter, and insist that they were still discussing it. He could use Tillandra's injuries to apologize for her lack of presence at the meetings, but he was not to let the Envoy know, in any way, that she was out of town.

She hoped that would be enough for now. The best case scenario for her would be that Reyes took her absence as an affront to proper protocol and left Watersend. Until she got back from Midderbuilt that would have to do.

While she had been lecturing Pravat on his stand with the Envoy, Gimbden had been out trying to secure her a ride north with the camel owners. He returned with good news and had then taken Pravat back to his residence.

There had been little else to do but repack her small bag, then she retired early, having eaten alone. She had tried to contact Goran and frustratingly he hadn't been able to talk. She'd lost too many days and her only hope was that the girl was moving towards him. She had to fix this, but it would have to wait until she reached Midderbuilt now. As the sun began to sink in the sky, Tillandra dressed in her traveling clothes, then lay down in bed to catch as much sleep as she could.

As promised Gimbden was waiting outside the back door when she hobbled out. The sky was still dark but broken with the first shards of light from the distant horizon. He shook his head, as he watched her hobbling across the ground, and came over to take hold of her arm and give her some support. They made their way very slowly down the back alley behind the inn until they came to a small plot between two storage buildings.

Two men stood with six camels tied together in a train. Both men were covered from head to toe in wrappings, with only their eyes visible. Tillandra could see them run their eyes over her, observing her wounded gait. Neither said a word but dipped their heads towards her in respect when Gimden introduced her as the important delivery. In turn she nodded at them, and thanked them quietly for taking her.

Her height made horses impractical, but she could ride on a camel. Given her injuries they would be much faster than if she traveled by foot on this stretch of road to Midderbuilt.

The desert roadway, if that described it, was unstable and difficult underfoot. Camels seemed to make easy travel of it, which made them the fastest albeit least comfortable method to reach Midderbuilt. There weren't enough people on the road to pay for full oasis so a system of way stations had been created. Refill caravans went each way once a month and left supplies for travelers in small shelters that gave respite from the relentless sun and dangerous sand storms.

The remote city sat on a strange ledge at the foot of the mountain range dominated by Qum, The Spire of Sand. The strange peak surrounded by moving sands was a difficult landmark to look at. The rugged cliffs and mountain side around Midderbuilt made it a difficult place to gain access to. The town itself was built on a large flat platform cut into the side of the mountain high above the desert below.

Tillandra and Gimbden had been clear that no one should know she had left town, and had instructed the team that they wanted as little noise as possible so as to not attract any nosey watchers. The camels' padded feet were almost silent and they slipped out through the workers' gate in the north eastern corner of the city walls.

Before long the camels had settled into their rocking gait traveling across the packed roadway, throwing sand up as their feet moved over the ground. When the sun fully crossed the distant horizon the team was well north of Watersend. The three humans on the camels leaned into the motion, staring ahead, only their eyes exposed to the sun.

There were six camels so that they could swap beasts and ride harder and further than normal. The goal was to be at Midderbuilt within three days, a relentless and hard ride that would rattle their bones and leave them worn. It wasn't a journey for the faint-hearted but was a fast way to cover many miles.

They stopped for no more than two hours a night. Just enough time to take a break from the ride and to take care of their needs. The camels stood about gathering their energy while waiting for the riders. They used the way stations to rest and replenish their own water. With little other cargo to carry they had been able to bring their own food.

They passed well-guarded caravans of jewel merchants heading back to Watersend. Tillandra noted the caravan guards were all on edge as her small fast-paced team hurried by. On the third day Qum had become visible and Tillandra had marveled at it as she always did, the massive mountain climbing to the sky dwarfing its smaller siblings. The mountain was a spiral of ever moving sands spinning counter clockwise. A series of ridges ran from the bottom up, with no clear beginning or end, a myriad of yellows, reds and browns flecked with white and black.

The spinning of the spire of sand made it difficult to look at for long periods of time. It had an unusual beauty to it that Tillandra never tired of. She knew there was powerful magic causing it which they had little understanding of.

Tillandra still did not know if there was a rock mountain under the shifting sands. The spiral was so all encompassing that you couldn't see, and the residents of Midderbuilt spoke little of it. To them it was their protector, their supplier. The mountain seemed to spit out the many jewels that were to be found in the surrounding quarries and clefts although she suspected there was more to it than that.

Access to the town of Midderbuilt was by invitation only and the only pathway up to it was heavily fortified. All visitors had to enter via the quaintly known Travelers Rest, which was more of a heavily fortified outdoor camp. It extended out from under the large rocky overhang into an open holding area on the sands before it.

The team slowed as they approached Travelers Rest, dismounting and approaching the guardsmen. Tillandra hung back with the second of her guides while the other spoke with the guards.

"My companion is checking that we can pass quietly and without notice into the camp," her guide said almost inaudibly.

Tillandra nodded and waited until the other man returned with a frown on his face.

"Trouble?" Tillandra asked him.

He used his eyes to point out to Tillandra the holding area in the far corner of the camp. The massive boom and platform that was winched up and down to carry heavy items to Midderbuilt was crowded with workers and others as it was unloaded. Tillandra could make out two horses larger than most, being walked off the platform that appeared to have just finished descending. They were being led by two Skarian knights and she nodded to her guide that she understood.

"Master G told us there were others looking for you."

"That's unexpected. It seems they were not just in Watersend and Fort Layden."

The other guide beckoned to his partner and her to follow him through the gates. Once they were away from guards he turned to her. "We will take up lodgings in the back of the camp out of sight."

"I had wanted to be up in town today," Tillandra replied.

"If you don't want to be seen by people like them, then you will need to wait. You will stand out walking up the ledge or on the platform. It's not for me to tell you what to do but our spot to camp is okay for the night. Maybe they will be gone by the morning."

Exhaustion taking over, Tillandra could do little but nod in agreement. "Let's go then."

She hobbled along between the camels, out of sight. In a spot at the back of the space created by the overhang, many small tent like rooms were packed together. It was ideal, with little light and no room for strangers to wander around.

She was frustrated at the extra delay, every day she lost had the potential to cost her on the return journey. She had to be back in time for the Audition, the deadline of the second full moon was absolute. If they didn't induct a new member then they lost that ring forever. They didn't have enough as it was already, she wasn't going to be the Mother that lost a ring.

The knights being here in Midderbuilt concerned her. She had had plenty of time on the ride to think about what was really behind the Envoy's trip. She didn't like how aggressive a move it was sending these armed soldiers into this realm.

It highlighted how others saw them. Sahro had never held an army of its own. Each city and town had their own guards. There had been no reason for anything else. Clearly King Ahn felt there was an opportunity to expand his lands and influence. *But why?*

One thing was for sure, when she got back to Anderwell this would be high on the topics to be discussed. Either the Maltzer priests, King Ahn or both were up to no good and it was another thing she needed to deal with.

The routineness of her life over recent times was rapidly changing. The threads of their day-to-day life seemed to be unravelling. She had been reminded of the dream of the wall of knights. No good could come from a barrier of Skarian knights in Sahro, or anywhere else. A statement would need to be made.

She was concerned that Beantic hadn't raised the tariffs in Vodotok. That was a very hostile and deliberate move. Her colleagues, like her, had fallen into a repetitive pattern of handling day-to-day business without suspicion.

Things were changing, and they would need to be more responsive or they would lose the upper hand.

She hoped Tingfurlew would answer the question of the stranger with the ring; at least if she could solve that riddle she would have one less thing to manage.

With a small meal of dried fruits and nuts and some crude ale she fell into an exhausted slumber anticipating her meeting with Tingfurlew.

46

TILLANDRA

*E*arly that morning Tillandra had watched with relief as the knights left the Travelers Rest and headed back towards Watersend, on the Midderbuilt Road. It meant she didn't have to hide her entrance into the city.

The walk up the ledge road was hard, as she had no animal to help her and only a staff to lean on. Her feet were sore and her inability to walk at full stride meant her hips and back tightened the further she climbed, increasing her discomfort.

The road switched back and forth as it cut into the shale and rock creating a difficult and awkward path made worse by the constant heat from a desert sun. No one could easily attack this small town up this narrow path from below. As you approached you could see it had none of the typical walls or barricades, just the natural protection of its position. Tillandra had always mused that the residents all knew that the only likely attacker was the mountain so no defence they could build would protect them.

A massive pulley and boom system, over the ledge, allowed for the raising and lowering of bulk supplies and goods. Tillandra had left her guide team in their lodgings below, and the camels would rest in the animal compound, while they waited for her to be done. Whatever other things they were delivering she didn't know, nor did she want to know.

Near the top of the long path stood the gates, the only semblance of a normal town. She was able to gain entrance because she held a 'Friend of Midderbuilt' pass. The guards at the gate gave no quarter to those who weren't allowed in. If you weren't a resident, or didn't have a correct pass, you did not enter.

Many a merchant had lost their livelihood from offending the Master of Midderbuilt and having their trading pass revoked. In some cases they leapt off the ledge to their deaths far below, the loss of the pass meaning the end of their entire business.

In all of Dharatan no other place provided such quality of jewels or workmanship. To become a craftsman here was to reach the pinnacle of your craft. To have a pass to purchase and trade the same jewels was possibly the most prestigious, if not lucrative trading pass, anywhere on Dharatan.

Once inside, Tillandra took a break to regain her breath, and to take in the sights of the town. There was never a time when she wasn't awestruck here, looking at the rock buildings nested below the spinning sands. She tried to shake off the dust of the desert, the yellow sands that coated everything. Despite wearing a cloak and hood to protect her robes, she still couldn't truly keep the sand out. It worked its way into all the fabrics and worse.

Her destination was in the south western corner of the town, built into what was known as mini-mountain. It was a strange rock face that disappeared up into the sands. The building that she was visiting was attached to that wall.

The structure was like a protruding cave. Part of it was in the small mountain behind and part sat outside. The only openings for light were high and narrow. No person could fit through them and the long drooping eaves kept out any bad weather. The door was made of heavy timber braced with steel, and firmly shut.

Hanging high in the middle of the door was a large orb of stone set in a brass lever, which Tillandra lifted and dropped three times. The large cracking noise reverberated through the door and most certainly alerted the occupant.

She stood and waited patiently, facing the door.

A shrill voice came through the door after many minutes. "Go away, I don't do tourist shows. *Go away!*"

Tillandra stepped forward, and knocked three more times, a small smile settling over her tired face.

"Do you only listen to your own head?" shrieked the voice. "I said, no store. Go away!"

She could hear the latch sliding on the other side of the door.

The massive door opened, creaking deeply on its hinges as it did. There, standing in the opening, stood a man many times shorter than Tillandra, his bright yellow tunic a mismatch with a pair of rusty orange pants. Tillandra waited for him to look up at her. He lifted the strange goggles from his head, and squinting from the sun behind her, raised his head.

"You! Why didn't you say so? Come, come in. I've been expecting you." He turned, and disappeared inside, leaving Tillandra at the door. She followed him in, closing the door behind her. The dark, lamp-lit main room was filled to the brim with tables, shelves and cases of jewels sparkling in every color. Further into the room lay weapons, cases, boxes, plates and jugs.

Tingfurlew had gone back to his large work desk and climbed up onto a tall stool, filled with plush cushioning and closed sides. It was on rollers so he could move back and forward along the tables without getting down.

"Mother Folly, here so quick. Much of what was in my dreams, now true. Make us drinks, Mother, you look travel worn."

"Good to see you too, Ting. Yes, I'll fix us something to drink. There is much to discuss." Tillandra smiled at being ordered around by her strange companion.

"Yes, yes. But I must finish lovely brooch before the next merchant leaves." He put his head back down to the work in front of him.

Tillandra found some fresh wine jugs and relatively clean goblets made of silver in what pretended to be a kitchen space. His workshop was also his home, and she could find no order to any of it.

She poured them both a drink and then sat waiting for him. She was content to rest and watch him while he worked after so many days on the road. He swiftly dragged his stool from table to table, dipping the setting in steaming liquids before cooling it and working on it with his tools.

His pace of work was always so impressive to her, and the quality was unbelievable. His work was known throughout Dharatan. People paid a lot to get something made by him, yet Tillandra could see no evidence of any great wealth. It was one of the mysteries surrounding him; what he did with all the money he made, and his age. Rumors existed that he was very, very old, and yet he never seemed to look any older than he already did. Tillandra had never thought to ask him, she accepted that whatever magic helped him make the rings also gave him other benefits.

"There, there. I am happy now. That's done. Yes, it's done. Good, now wine."

He climbed down and went to the door. He dragged it open and called out, "Fepret, Fepret, where are you?"

Within a short time a man came running, and Tillandra saw Tingfurlew hand over the package to him.

After locking the door he walked to Mother Folly, his springy steps almost comical. Picking up one of the goblets, he affectionately tapped her hand several times with his other hand, before sitting on a bench beside her.

"So, Mother, tell me why you have rushed to see me. I can see you rushed, don't argue, it's written in your face. So much sand about your robes, and you hobble."

He spoke as fast as he worked, and Tillandra smiled warmly at him. "You know I have to come each year, Ting."

"The stone? Is it that time already? So soon, so soon. Has it been a year?"

"Almost, Ting."

He shook his head at her and fidgeted with his tunic. "So much time. It all goes, and I never see it. When I work it just goes. I never know if it is today or tomorrow."

"You need to get out more."

"Out? Out, where? Who will make the things?" He stared at her with wide open eyes. "Besides, it's all just sand. I hate the sand, never walk the sands again."

"You picked a funny place to live if you don't like sand, Ting." Tillandra chuckled.

"Yes, yes. Mother Folly so funny." He poked his tongue out at her, and jumped off the bench. "But why such a rush? Did you let it run empty?"

She shook her head. "No, Ting, but there are was another reason for me to hurry here than just the Mother Stone."

Tingfurlew was perched up on his seat, his legs tucked under him backwards like a youngster. He leaned toward Tillandra, his little eyes peering expectantly at her, his left hand twirling at his wiry long mustache. "What reason?"

"I need a new ring."

He looked up at her, startled. "A new ring, oh no. Who was lost?"

Tears formed in Tillandra's eyes. "Ashantha, Ting. Dear Ash has passed."

"Ashantha? So sad. Sad. His connection with you was very strong was it not?"

"Yes it was. And I have struggled with his loss since I found out and not just because of that."

"What happened?"

"Well there's a lot to the story, it's not straightforward. He had been away."

"Away?"

"Yes, Ting, I sent him on a mission to Enderk, I'd not heard from him in much more than a year."

"Enderk, of all the places, there is much strange over there. Did he die there?"

"No he did not, but that's part of why I am here."

He focused back on her, his hand dropping, leaving his mustache alone, and peered at her expectantly.

"His death is sad, yes, but there's more for me to be worried about. Several things are causing me concern, which seem connected. Let me give you the whole story and then I will explain what worries me."

Tingfurlew sat back on his heels and nodded at her. Tillandra drank a little more before continuing.

"You know that each of the Court have a skill?"

"A little I know, but not all."

"When we pass the Audition, one of our skills is boosted. We do not get to choose which one but the change is significant. For me that is my dreams, or premonitions."

"You see the future?"

"I wish. I see things but they are never clear, they do foretell events in the future, usually."

"Usually?" He had started twirling his mustache again.

"I don't always get it right, so I am unsure if it is me understanding the message wrong or it wasn't a message at all and just a dream. When they come, and I never can tell when they will come, I have to try and uncover their meaning so I can act on it."

She stopped talking and had another sip of the wine.

"For many months I had a persistent dream of a frail, ancient man standing with his hands pushing against a massive wall of orange. The best I could tell was that he was holding it back. Every time I tried to latch on to the meaning of it, or stay in the dream, it would slip from my grasp. Over those months I began to recognize that the man I saw was a Derk."

"Is that why Ashantha was in Enderk?"

"Yes. All I could make sense of was that either the Derks were under threat from something or that they were being held back from us." Tillandra shook her head. "It's the most frustrating part of it, Ting. I can't know for sure what anything means until after it has actually happened, so I can never be sure about my decisions until it's too late."

He said nothing but nodded at her, and grabbed a handful of nuts from the table, munching noisily on them.

"In the end, and after many debates at the Council table, I made a deciding vote to send him there to learn what he could of this 'Orange Wall'. Due to the nature of the trip there was no way we could communicate. I knew nothing about his wellbeing or if he had learned anything of importance."

"You cannot speak across the water?"

"No, and there was the danger that he could be found out."

"Wouldn't his ring stand out?" Tingfurlew asked.

"He wore a glove that hid it, it looked just like the skin of his hand but hid the ring and blocked its powers. As he was clearly a foreigner over there he assumed he would be a slave and anything like jewelry would be taken from him if it was discovered."

Tingfurlew nodded vigorously. "Yes, yes."

"To be honest I had almost forgotten he was there. The first I knew he was back on Dharatan was the whistle."

Her eyes filled with tears as she recalled the sound arriving. She breathed in deeply, sighing as she exhaled, and brushed her arm across them to wipe away the drops.

"It devastated me, Ting. That it came without warning and without hearing from him made it all the worse."

"Oh, Tillandra, I am so sorry for your loss."

"For our loss, Ting, we are all in this together!"

"Of course, Mother, of course. You know what I mean. So what happened? "

She held up her hand. "There's more. I followed the whistle back to its source and found him in the north of Malamig, dead in a cave. When I saw him he'd been stabbed through with a blade. That in itself was surprising, as you know he was a master with the sword, but what was more surprising was I could see there was someone else in there, a woman, and she wore his ring."

At this Tingfurlew leapt up to his feet and onto the floor. "That cannot be. The ring cannot be worn by another."

"I assure you it is true, Ting. The young woman somehow had removed his ring and was wearing it on her hand. I was able to watch her for a short while."

"Watch her? What do you mean?" Tingfurlew asked.

Tillandra didn't answer immediately. She grabbed a handful of the nuts and fruit on the table and chewed on some while she thought about how to explain to him what she meant.

"I am unsure how much of what we can do you know?"

"I have learned through the time some of it. I am not with you very often, or those before you, my role is the rings. That's all. I help you but I am not like you."

"I know, Ting. Let me tell you some of it. With our masks we can communicate to each other over distance."

"This I know."

"Let me finish. You also know that the person who starts the communication must bear the cost."

"The rat?"

"Yes, the rat. The rat becomes the sacrifice that powers the ability to speak to another. You may or may not know that one of my roles in the Council is to learn of our magic?"

"That I did know." He had climbed back up on the bench next to her.

"I found an old journal from a previous 'Mother', a man in fact."

"Percival?"

"Yes, how did you know?" Tillandra looked startled.

"You forget, Tillandra, I have been here for some time." He smirked at her.

"Yes, but… that was several hundred years ago."

He winked at her and waved his hand. "Carry on, what next in this story?"

Tillandra looked at him curiously but held back a question about what he had just said for another time. "Percival had made some notes about a way to see, not just talk to, each other. It's very much like what I can do when I hear the whistle. When they pass I latch on to the remnants of their life force to locate them. That's why I must do it straight away before that life force disappears into the void."

Tingfurlew shook his head at her and was shifting uncomfortably on the bench.

"When I read the journal I began to figure out what he was experimenting with. How we use the rats made sense, we grab their life force and use it to talk. Percival used the same method but sought out someone to watch, not talk. It takes a lot more energy to do it and is very tiring to learn, but each time I've got better at it."

"What you mean, more energy?" His brow was creased in concern.

"More than one rat."

"Oh. How many?"

"At first four, but since I have got better I can use just two."

He shook all over. "I do not know how you can do that?"

"It is very unpleasant, Ting. You've seen how sick it makes me."

He turned away from her and grabbed his wine goblet, emptying it in one go. When he went to fill it up again he nearly fell off the bench as he lifted the large jug.

Tillandra laughed at the sight and reached out to help.

"Very funny, am I? Leave me be, I don't need your help."

"Sorry, but it did look funny."

"Yes, yes. So what did you see?"

"This young woman has his ring and was wearing it on her hand."

"Perhaps you were mistaken?"

"I am sure, Tingfurlew! She also has his mask." Tillandra again shook her head; the more she thought of it, the worse it seemed. "How can she wear his ring? Has it not always been that the mask wearer is bonded to the ring?"

She could see his face was twisted with concerns, and he was busily contemplating what she'd just told him. She waited for him to speak for what seemed an age; it was most unlike him to not have an immediate response to anything.

"This is troubling, very troubling. We both need answers. I know you came looking for one from me, but I do not have one for you."

"What do I do then?"

He held up his hand. "Just wait. I will need to seek answers. You have to wait here until the stone is restored, do that and I will find out more on this."

He stood up and grabbed her hand and pulled at her to stand. "Go now," he said as he started to nudge her towards the front door. He pulled a key from a pocket in his tunic handing it to her and saying, "to your room."

Tillandra left through the big wooden door, turned right and headed over to a small hut that also sat against the back wall of the city, that was known as Ting's Guest House. It was nothing more than a single room with a bed and table but it was all she ever needed whenever she came to Midderbuilt.

47

UKSOD

Things had become precarious for Uksod. For years now he had kept everything under control. He served Yantarnaya's will but there was little he could do to resolve her predicament. She was trapped until the amulets returned, that was the deal she had made, and for his whole life there had been no sighting of them.

He had been left to run things, which had suited him nicely. Schevenal was crazy and they had managed to keep him confined to the palace. In truth he rarely left the Amber Room and he made little sense if anyone talked to him.

The boy was almost ready to replace Schevenal, but there was still time before that needed to happen. Enderk had been his to control. The role as Regent was a nice compromise, he had the power but could assign blame elsewhere if things didn't go to plan.

Not so with Yantarnaya. She was a different beast altogether, and she was growing increasingly unhappy with him.

That had all changed once she had felt the pulse of one of the stones. Each of the amulets had been carved from the Debrua stone, which lay deep underground below En Carta. Few knew why the capital of Enderk was located where it was, but the draw of the stone was strong. Those who ruled here felt its influence whether they knew it or not.

The amulet had been freed from whatever prison had hidden it from her, and now she could sense it. That only made matters worse. Beforehand she had been trapped, waiting, with no timeline on when she might get free. Since it had been found, that had changed. Every day she called to him and demanded to know more about what was happening.

He had been excited to tell her they were retrieving it and even that it was on its way home. That plan had been going well until the interference by the slave. Uksod couldn't understand how a slave could have uncovered what it was they were transporting over the Stepping Isles, and then steal it. What good were his Vrah if they could be outsmarted by a slave?

He believed what he heard, the guardsman who had been in charge of the retrieval had lain on the stone table in his work room, as Uksod interrogated him. By the time he had finished there was no doubt about the events, only wonder at how such a low one could have got close to the amulet.

His Vrah had failed him then. There should have been no way that such a possession should have been left alone, nor so easily replaced. All four of the guards had been put to death. Failure was not a result that the Vrah were allowed to accept.

Her fury directed toward him had been immense. The headpiece he wore, set with its own piece of amber, provided her direct access to him. She had poured her anger through it, causing him to black out. For nearly a week he had been unconscious.

Since he had awoken she regularly threatened him with what would happen to him should he fail again. Until it was retrieved she would not be happy, and so far anything that could go wrong was going wrong.

He had sent two teams of the Vrah, their elite special soldiers, to hunt the slave. They traveled in threes and one of the teams had informed him they were closing in on the man believed to have taken the amulet.

Then nothing, suddenly they had gone silent. He had tried twice to connect to them, and there was no response. He had been able to pick up faint signals showing them moving south. Someone had the rings. Someone who wasn't the Vrah, or else he would be able to communicate to them.

"Master?"

Uksod turned to see two of the Vrah, holding an unconscious slave. "Bring her in, up on the table, like normal."

The two men, both wearing tight dark clothing emphasising their muscular builds, dragged the slave to the table before lifting her and chaining her into position.

"That will be all." Uksod waved off the men and looked at the woman lying on the stone table. "Unconscious, well, you won't feel a thing. Which is a shame, but time is of the essence."

He stroked her hair off of her forehead before placing his left hand there, and his right on her heart. On each of his fingers he wore identical rings, an amber stone set into a black setting. On his bald head a gold headdress was wrapped round his skull, with a central band joining back to the front, where a large amber stone pressed into the skin above the bridge of his nose.

The stone on his forehead began to glow, and one by one each of his rings began to illuminate. The body beneath him bucked before falling flat again, and he lost himself in the light. He moved his vision into the place outside of his body, and sought out the rings.

To reach such a distance he had to use a person, there wasn't enough life force in an animal for what he needed to do. Across the darkness he began to see the orange lights. There were three different groupings. Three of the lights were together, their signal strong, another two were weak and moving away, and the last one was not moving and was pulsing then fading.

He focused in on the three lights until he could sense who wore them. He pushed his mind into that one, until the man's face appeared before him.

"Master?"

"93?"

"Yes, master."

"Where are you?"

"We are outside a town called Riverbend."

"Why are you there?"

"This is where the trail has been leading. It is hard to locate the person we seek."

"One of the rings is near to you. It is alone, someone is trying it on."

"Can you point me closer?"

Uksod focused on the other ring and was able to describe to 93 the building, and the man who had the ring. "There is just one man, he doesn't look a threat. It would seem whoever had the others, has sold this to him. He has the look of a trader."

"I will locate him."

"Retrieve it, 93, there is no option."

"Yes, master."

"No one that has seen the rings should live. And all of the rings must be retrieved. None left behind. *Is that clear?*"

"Yes. What of the others?"

"Something is masking them, I only get glimpses of their location, but they are still moving south."

"Then we will follow."

"There is no room for failure, 93."

The man didn't reply immediately.

"93?"

"I never fail, master."

Uksod broke off the connection and moved his mind back into his workroom. The jolt back from the darkness he always enjoyed. Almost as much as feeling the last of someone's life slipping away beneath his hands.

The body lay dead and he raised his hands above his head and gasped in deep breaths, acid burning in his stomach and throat, but he swallowed it back down and savored the flow that had passed through him.

The light in the rings faded out and he slumped to the floor, exhausted.

KYRO

yro looked up when he heard the knock on his door. "Come in."

The door opened and two boys were pushed through, followed by Markahm. Kyro recognized the bigger of the two boys, although he didn't know his name. His face looked twisted as if half of it was lame, making him easily recognizable.

"Sorry for the interruption, captain, but I thought you'd want to know what I found out."

Kyro put his quill down and sat back in his chair. "What's that then?"

Markahm closed the door and turned to the boys. "I think they might have something to tell us about Lani."

"Oh, and what's that?"

The smaller boy looked like he was bursting to say something but looked at the bigger boy, who stared him down. Kyro waited for them to speak but they held their tongues.

"Nothing to say. She's not in any trouble, you know. We just need to talk to her."

The bigger of the two boys kept his eyes firmly on the younger one.

Kyro stood up, startling both of the boys, "Why don't we take you two to get something to eat? We always have something left over, let's go and see what we can find."

The boys seemed to relax a little, Kyro looked up at Markahm and nodded. They took the two lads into the guards' quarters and sat them down. Markahm sent one of the junior guardsmen to get water and food for them.

His outward appearance was all surly and rule bound, but Kyro knew the life these boys led was likely a short and hungry one. He knew he would get more sensible information from them when they were fed.

When they saw the meals the lads' eyes lit up, as if it was the finest banquet they had ever seen. They launched into it without question as soon as it was placed in front of them. Kyro's heart fell a little at the sight, watching them look up from their bowls protectively, as if someone would take it from them.

"Don't you be rushing, lads, that food's all yours and no one here has any need to take it from you. You'll just make yourself sick if you rush that."

His words only paused them a little, so he gathered himself an ale from the table, and sat waiting until they were done with the meal.

The smaller of the boys burped out loud and absently covered his mouth with the sleeve of his tunic. He looked sheepishly about, unsure if he had just committed a crime inside such a place.

"Do you boys have a name?" Kyro asked

The smaller one look up from his plate, gravy dribbling down his chin, "Ilker, captain."

"You boys live at the old stable in the guild quarter, don't you, Ilker?"

He paused eating and looked at Dorted as if they had been caught. Dorted just shrugged.

"Ah...Yes. Mostly. Yes," Ilker replied.

"It's okay, son, we know about that place. It's fine for you to be there; we'd rather you all have somewhere safe to live than trying to find shelter on the street."

Ilker looked at him cautiously over his bowl, tearing strips of bread and wiping up what was left of the stew.

"Let's talk about Lani, shall we, you do know her, don't you?"

"Yes, captain. She's like our big sister, not real, like, but she treats us like that. You know what I mean?" Ilker asked.

"I think I do, Ilker. She looked after you as if you were her real kin?"

"Yes. Yes that. She used to call us all her kin. We not as good without her."

Kyro paused so as not to push the young boy.

"What do you mean, without her?"

"She's gone, captain. She hasn't come back. It's been like, forever."

Kyro was also keeping his eye on the bigger boy, who said nothing. Looking at the way his face was mashed on one side it was probably not easy for him to talk. He was like the muscle and Ilker the mouth.

"So has she gone before and not come back?"

"No. The most she's ever been gone before is just a day or two. Never for weeks. She makes our meals and tells us what to do. If she won't be there to make our dinner she always tells us. She didn't tell us. She doesn't go normally for this long."

Ilker's face was showing his concern, small tears were welling in the corner of his eyes which he rubbed at with his grimy sleeve and looked down at his bread.

"Easy there, lad, don't go worrying too hard just right now. Maybe she got sick and where ever she goes to stay, she's holed up there."

"She was fine when 'he' came to look for her," Ilker replied, looking up at Markahm standing off to the side. "She wouldn't go to Little Big Rock if she was sick."

Kyro looked sideways towards Markahm. "Little Big Rock? Why do you think she'd go there?"

Ilker stopped and looked at the bigger boy.

Dorted spoke, albeit slowly and with great effort, his face crushed so that only one half worked. "Sometime, she go."

Kyro waited to see if he had more to say.

"Not long. Just day...two." He sucked in a breath, "N'food Lani brings. None to eat."

"Markahm sounds to me like Lani's kin need some help with leftovers. Have a word with cook, will you, and see if we can help."

"Right-oh, captain." Markahm left the room and closed the door after him.

"So you saw Lani when my guards were out checking for her?"

"She wasn't there then, not then." Ilker said almost apologetically.

"Okay, but she was okay when you saw her?"

"Yes," the bigger boy said. "She said… be back soon… Not soon… Too long."

Kyro waited to check he didn't have any more to say. "We'll find her, don't worry. Let me worry about that. Right then, tonight you'll have a meal to take with you. Markahm will walk you back and check things out. If I find out more I'll tell you. For now you boys need to take up Lani's role. *Okay?*"

They both said nothing and looked downward. Dorted spoke up. "Thankful. Sir. For Food, thankful."

Kyro nodded and left them in the room and went looking for Markahm who was making his way back from the kitchen.

"All sorted, Kyro, I've organized a few sacks of stuff from the cook that they can have. Our lord will be none the wiser."

Nodding, he replied, "Good, that's one thing sorted. Sounds like we might have to check out Little Big Rock from the sounds of it. If she was scared off by Harsop then maybe she headed that way?"

Markahm scrunched his face briefly, "You don't think she killed Harsop, do you?"

"I don't know what to think," Kyro replied curtly. "I thought I knew what was going on around here. The murders out at the cave, Harsop's murder and her missing at the same time seems a bit coincidental, don't you think?"

"What we going to do then?"

"Right now? You're going to take those boys back with the food and put word to our men that we want them kept an eye on. Then we'll talk about heading south if we can't turn up a trace of where she might be."

Markahm nodded and Kyro watched him head back to the room with the boys in it. He stared down the dark hallway, the only light a single wall lantern further down, wondering about what he needed to do next.

He'd failed at this one simple task he'd been asked to do. So much time had passed and he had simply got stuck in routines and forgotten why he was even here in Barnen. He'd become so consumed with being the captain, that the commitment he had made all those years ago had slipped into the background.

If she had left town, or worse had been taken away, then he would have to leave Barnen and hunt for her. That wasn't going to be easy to explain to Lord Barnen. Kyro didn't know how much of the truth of it he could share with him, nor how he would react. It might be easier for him to resign his post and not have to tell the truth of it. He couldn't imagine that would go down much easier.

He headed to his private quarters and went to his long box, moving clothes and books off it. He pulled out a number of things that lay on top of the items he was looking for. The leather capsule he lifted out, and pulled out the small scroll contained within. Thankfully it was still readable.

Next he lifted the long curved knife that sat on the bottom of the box. The black handle and blade still made his skin crawl. He lifted it up and stared at the symbol etched into the handle. The same mark tattooed on the wrists of the Derks' bodies. He dropped the sword back, before putting everything else back on top. He sighed and closed the box.

Kyro stood up and left his room, walking out through the guards' building and across the large courtyard to Lord Barnen's residence. This wasn't going to be easy, but he had to do it.

49

KYRO

*L*ord Barnen was standing outside his reception room looking across the gardens that the house encircled, when Kyro approached him.

"Any more news to tell me, Kyro?" he asked turning to face him as he entered.

"Only some information about a missing girl from the old stables, that we've been wanting to question."

"It doesn't sound of much importance to me. Don't let me tell you what you should or shouldn't do, but I don't see how a missing urchin has much bearing on these filthy bandits terrorizing our lands," Lord Barnen said, turning back to the gardens.

"Well on the surface you'd be right, m'lord, but there's a little more to this story than most would know."

Lord Barnen turned back to face Kyro, his eyebrows raised as he faced him full on. "More?"

"Indeed. Perhaps you might recall the last time we had an event similar to this in Malamig?"

Kyro waited while Lord Barnen thought over the question.

"You mean the murders on the RaMar trail?" he asked incredulously.

"Yes, them," Kyro replied.

"But what's that got to do with all of this and a missing girl? That was more than ten years ago, how on earth does it relate?"

"Well I wouldn't have thought it did but for two things now. That was back when your father still was alive and was of course the lord here. You were away in Nedor, at the time, if I recall, studying with the King's stewards. What you probably didn't know was that I was based at RaMar around then and was the first patrol to arrive at the scene."

Lord Barnen shook his head. "That, I didn't know. How thoroughly dreadful that must have been. I still don't understand how that affects us today? Didn't the murderer get caught and executed?"

"I'm getting to it, m'lord, but there's a few things that fill in the gaps. We publicly told everyone that someone was caught and punished, but if you were to ask anyone here or in RaMar you'd not find anyone that saw the murderer caught or hung. We simply let it be known that was what happened."

Before Lord Barnen could interrupt again, he continued. "There was a culprit, or so we believed. We found a man, a Derk, who had been wounded in the attack. The attack was far more than one man could have done. Best we could tell was that the others he was with left him to die once he'd become injured. We interrogated him brutally but he never told us anything. He died from it."

Kyro shook his shoulders and head, loosening his neck. The memory was still unpleasant even after all this time.

"To all but a few of us, no one survived the massacre. Twenty-four men, women and children were killed in the senseless attack. Their wagons abandoned, but not rifled for goods, the attackers were there only to kill and they did it brutally."

"You said, 'to all but a few of us no one survived' so I am to presume that someone did in fact survive?" Lord Barnen asked.

"When we returned to the site after the outlander died, we undertook the gruesome task of burying the bodies. There were too many to transport to any city and some of them had been beheaded or gutted, so it was decided no one else needed to see what we saw. We sent most of the guards back and only myself and one other remained.

"For the entire day we toiled, not a word spoken. It was getting late when I heard sobbing, and underneath the last pile of bodies, we found a little girl, hugging to the body of what we assume was her mother.

"She was unhurt, but obviously terrified. She was distraught and very confused and we could get nothing from her. She would have been all of about four years old."

"This girl, is she the same girl?"

Kyro nodded. "Yes, Lani, as we named her, was that girl. Due to her age we had to assume both her parents were killed that day, and no one came forward once news of the deaths spread to convince me otherwise."

"But, but how is it she is here and not RaMar?" Lord Barnen blurted.

"There's a lot in the answer to that question. We did initially return to RaMar. The Prince and his counsellor decided that it would be best she didn't stay there. There was some reasoning, although I didn't understand why, that due to Derks regularly passing through RaMar it might be traumatic for her to see them. That's when the Prince decided she should be moved to Barnen."

"My father was aware of all this?"

"Yes, it was agreed between the Prince of RaMar and your father. And at the time a family offered to foster her, although there was some hiding of the fact of how she came to be brought here."

"How very odd indeed. One can't know the reasonings of others, although I doubt I'd make the same decision. Why then the concern now, and from you?"

"I was given the task to watch over her and see her through to adulthood. I was given my orders by the Prince and sent here to be captain the guard and to ensure no trouble found its way to Barnen. At the time none of it made much sense to me, I was still only a year or so out of Nedor and not from around here."

"I had never thought to ask what you brought you here."

Kyro continued, "At first it seemed a good result. Over time she left the family who had fostered her, she was apparently very willful. She ended up with Despring first at the church rooms before he moved her in with the other urchins. I kept my eye on her to start with, and tried to ensure she was okay as best I could. I wouldn't say I've done a particularly good job of being her carer."

Lord Barnen appeared slightly bemused by this story that had unfolded in his own town without even his knowledge. "So how are they connected?"

"The Derk we caught carried the same mark as these latest ones do. The tattoos on their wrists were the same as one he had. I don't know what it means, but I have a blade in my office that bears the same symbol. Whoever these Derks are, the mark connects them, then and now. To my mind if Lani has disappeared there's a connection between her and them and I don't know what it is."

"This is all very interesting but I am not sure what more we can do about it? It would reinforce to me that we need to keep our town closed and our forces alert, more than anything, if I'm not mistaken?"

"These Derks are killers, that I am sure of, and yes I agree, we need to stay very alert. I have been trying to convince myself otherwise but I think the two events are connected somehow. I don't think it was a random attack, although that's only my gut talking, I have no other evidence. I am not sure if she knows more either, she can't be found."

"Well she should have come forward when we warned everyone. If she knew more she should have come forward back when we gave everyone a chance. She might already be dead for all me know. *Another body!*" He sighed.

"I don't think I can just leave it at that," Kyro replied.

Lord Barnen turned back abruptly to face him. "What do you mean by that? I just explained what I think about it all."

Kyro took the capsule in his hand and opened it, pulling out the scroll. "Like this or not, my lord, my orders on this matter come from a little further afar. I was charged with her care, and as this scroll will attest, now that she is either in danger or lost I must report back to those whose orders I was to obey." He walked over and handed the scroll to Lord Barnen.

"What is this nonsense, you do what I pay you to do." He stopped as he read the scroll, Kyro assuming the Prince's seal on the bottom probably pausing his outburst. "This is all bloody outrageous. We've got murders and attacks happening just outside our walls and now my captain is going to abandon his post."

"I am not abandoning my post, my lord, but as you can see the Prince laid a charge with me which now I must report back to them on. We know the Prince was on his way to Nedor when he passed through here, so I should be heading there to tell them."

Lord Barnen stood, staring him down.

"The full guard will be here. I'll leave Markahm in charge, he's as good as I am and we are already on alert. It's easily a week's, or more, trip each way but those that need to know need to hear it from me. I was charged with that responsibility back when this all began. Little did I realize then that we'd ever see this again. "

Both looked at each other, the tension in the room very palpable.

"There's a possible chance it won't take the whole trip, though?"

"What do you mean?"

"I've just heard that she often goes to Little Big Rock for a day or two. It's possible she's hiding out down there, which would be much easier than traveling to Nedor. I will try to locate her there first, and if I do, we'll return and get to the bottom of anything she knows."

Lord Barne broke the silence, "It seems as though I have little choice, I don't like it at all, and you and I will need to have a longer conversations about this when you return. You've served me well, Kyro, but I don't like the control of my town being taken away from me. Now I have you to worry about as well. Is it prudent you travel alone?"

"I'll just be another lone traveler on the road and moving fast. I would think I am an unlikely target and no one is after me. My goal is to either find Lani first or make it to Nedor as fast as I can."

"I assume you'll be leaving soon?"

"As soon as I can make myself ready and let Markahm know."

"Send him to me when you're done with him, I need to make sure he understands what I expect from him in your absence."

"I will at that. I will see you when I return."

Lord Barnen turned and went back to looking outside. With nothing more to be said, Kyro left the room and made his way back to his quarters to gather his things.

50

LANI

It took her a moment to remember what had happened. Her head felt foggy and as she licked her dry lips all she got was dirt on her tongue. She went to bring her hands to her face as she tried to spit it out and they caught on the ropes holding them.

Lani opened her eyes, looking for the two men. The sunlight immediately caused her eyes pain and she squinted to protect them. She managed to wriggle upright and brought her tied hands beneath her and over her feet so they were at least in front of her.

She listened for any sound of the caravan but there was none of the sounds it would have made had it been close. Lani couldn't hear any voices either. After backing up to a small tree, she used the trunk to help herself stand.

No one was close by and she could see no one along the roadway in either direction. Tears formed in her eyes and one started to run down her cheek. She wiped it away with the rope around her wrists and shook her head.

The pain when she moved her head stopped her momentarily. The right side of her forehead was very sore and inside her head she could feel one of her headaches forming. Part of her wanted to slide down the tree trunk and curl into a ball until it passed. Lani knew she couldn't do that. If she didn't get free now she wouldn't be able to do anything once the real headache came.

She hopped out of the small clump of bushes and onto the road, every jolt causing pain to shoot through her head and eyes. The satchel flopped against her side as she jumped, and she was glad the men hadn't taken it from her. Thinking about the satchel reminded her of the small knife that she had also taken off Ashantha's body. It was inside the satchel if she could get her hands to it.

She hopped off the road over to a pile of rocks, and dropped down against them, the movement further aggravating her head. She looped the strap of the satchel over her head awkwardly, unable to get it out from between her hands. She pulled the bag open and dug around inside until she felt what she was looking for. Several times she tried to pull it out but was unable to get a good grip in it.

In the end she tipped the bag upside down and let everything fall out. The knife fell on top of Ashantha's journal and she picked it up. There was no easy way to cut her hands free but she was able to hold the knife and work it back and forth on the rope around her ankles. By the time she had cut through the first of the loops she was sweating heavily. The throbbing was growing in her head and she was thirsty.

Once she was free of the foot ropes Lani stood up and moved around to see if she could find something to help her with the hand ropes. In the distance she could hear the sound of a horse, running at pace. It was still a distance away but it made her anxious.

Lani went back to the satchel and started to push everything back in, starting with the journal and mask. She began to grab the smaller items and push them in as well. The horse sounds were close by now and she looked up, expecting to see it appear soon.

As she kept one eye out for it she finished packing the bag, and closed the flap, tucking it over her head. She picked the knife up again and held it out of view as the dust neared her. Within a minute a man riding the horse came from the north and pulled the horse to a stop when he saw her standing beside the road.

"Whoa," he called at the horse as he pulled back hard on the reins.

Once the horse had come to a stop he looked at her and then around the area.

"What have we got here?"

"I was on a caravan, and the crooked leader robbed me and left me here."

"Is that so? That's terrible, lass." The man climbed down out of his saddle, and brushed off his jacket. He was as tall as the horse and very thin. His brown tunic was dirty as if he had been on the road many days.

"Can you help me cut these ropes?" Lani held out her knife.

"Of course." He walked towards her and took the knife from her hands. He looked at it and laughed, "That's hardly a knife." He dropped it on the ground and reached around his side, sliding a large knife out from the sheath tied to his waist. "This is a knife."

He grinned at Lani as he held one of her forearms and sliced through the ropes. "There you go."

"Thank you so much." Lani went to remove her arm from his grip, but he held it tighter. He moved the knife closer to her, pointing it at her face.

"I think I deserve me a reward, I do." His eyes lit up as he evaluated her. "Yes, I think I've found me a very nice reward for my good deeds." He laughed at his own words.

Lani pulled against his grip but he just gripped harder.

"*Stop it!*" He held the knife right up to her eye. "Unless you want me to cut you?"

"No, please don't."

Without warning he pushed her hard so she fell back onto her butt. "*Ow!*"

"Don't move an inch, girl. Understand?"

Lani grimaced and gave him a little nod.

"Now hand me that bag."

Lani gripped on to the strap, not wanting to let him have it. "Just leave me."

"*The bag!*"

He stepped towards her, bringing the knife closer. She pulled the strap over her head and handed it up to him.

"Now, just sit there and let me see what goodies I've earned myself." He held the bag with his knife hand and opened it with his free one. "What on Thenis is this?" He held up the mask. "Creepy."

He tossed it on the ground and did the same with Ashantha's journal. "You've got a lot of rubbish, girl." He pulled out the coin pouch, "Now this is more like it." He shook the pouch near his ear, "If I'm not an ass's tail that's silver in there too." He had a big grin on his face now.

He pulled out the gray pouch which held the amulet, and saw the alarm on Lani's face.

"Ah hah, something interesting is it?" He dropped the satchel on the ground and sheathed his knife. "Let's see what it is you didn't want me to find."

He opened the pouch and pulled it back over the top of the amulet. "Ohhhhh! Now that is some fine piece of jewelry. Very fine. I think that will look very pretty on my lady's neck, that will. I will be very popular."

Lani could see him ogling the stone and she could feel it reaching out to her. Or that's what it seemed in her mind. Like something reaching for her.

The man plucked the amulet off the cloth and clenched his hand around it. He looked down at her and she could see his mouth starting to form words but nothing came out. Suddenly his eyes rolled back in his head and he dropped to the ground.

Lani jumped up and back from him, waiting for him to recover but he never moved. She moved around him and when she saw his face she recognized the same look that had been on Yerat's face. *Surely not?*

Lani grabbed the satchel and picked up the mask and journal, stuffing them back in. She went over and picked up her knife and slid it in the side of her boot. The man still hadn't moved so she felt she was okay to get closer to him.

Leaning in, she tentatively touched the skin of his neck. It felt eerily cold. They were out in the middle day sun and Lani was sweating, yet her fingers went very cold when she touched his skin. She pulled her hand back and rubbed it on her tights. Moving around his body she had to force herself to open his hand and pluck the amulet out using the felt pouch.

It can't be a coincidence that Yerat and this man dropped dead when holding this. But I took it from Ashantha and held it no problem at all. Nothing happened to me. I don't understand.

Lani put her finger on the stone and all she felt was warmth. She quickly pulled it back, noticing her forearm had tingled when she touched it. She shook her head and was reminded of the headache that had been growing.

I can't keep this thing, it's dangerous. Why did Ashantha want me to carry it?

Lani closed the pouch and put it in her bag. She retrieved her coins from the man's tunic and put them in there as well. It was far too open to leave the body lying out here in the sun but she didn't have the strength or any tools to dig a grave for him so she grabbed his ankles and pulled him towards the bushes she had been left in.

It used most of her remaining strength to get him into the hiding spot, and she knelt down to catch her breath when it was all done. Sweat dripped off her and her head was pounding. Dragging herself up she trudged back along the road to where his horse was grazing.

She calmed the horse and hauled herself up into the saddle, lying forward on its neck. Nudging it to move, she got it into an easy trot as she draped her arms around it. Her head was throbbing badly and Lani knew she needed a dark place and sleep to get rid of it, but for now this would have to do. She needed to get away from yet another dead body.

51

LANI

The horse dipped its head down, dragging Lani's arms with it. She slid forward and landed on the ground with a jolt on her side, causing another surge of pain in her head. The sound of the horse lapping up water from the creek beside her head sounded like a waterfall. She pulled her hands up across her ears, and crawled forward until she could dunk her head under the water.

The coolness of the water helped relieve the pain enough that she could drink a little and sit upright. She looked around and saw the horse had brought her away from the road beside a low lying creek.

She used the reins to help pull herself upright and walked with the horse towards a small copse of trees. She tied the reins to a sturdy branch and lay down on the ground, out of the sun, and closed her eyes.

The horse nudged her with its foreleg, startling her awake. As she sat up in alarm it licked her. She shrugged it off and wiped the slobber from her face. Her headache had almost gone, thankfully, and she cautiously stood, leaning against a tree trunk.

It looked to be early morning, which meant that she had slept through the night. She quickly pulled the satchel around her body and checked inside. Everything appeared to still be there.

Relieved, she untied the horse and walked it to the creek, so they could both drink. For the first time she inspected the horse. There was a bag strapped to the saddle. Inside she found a skin of wine and several dried meat strips.

Lani thought back over what had happened yesterday. She pulled the amulet out of the satchel and rolled it around in her hands. *Why can I touch it without it harming me?* None of it made sense to her, except she had seen both yesterday's assailant and Yerat die from touching the stone.

Her original plan had been to sell it for as much money as she could, and be done with it, but that couldn't happen if everyone who touched it died. At least the rings didn't harm anyone. She could still sell them.

Was this what Ashantha meant when he said it was evil? He wanted me to take it to his friends, but even they might not be safe. I don't know if I want to be carrying it anywhere.

After refilling her small skin with water she mounted the horse and set off south to whatever lay ahead. There had been no time to learn what towns were ahead of her when she'd stowed away on the caravan nor how far they were. She only hoped she could get to somewhere soon without anyone else attacking her.

The first town she came across was large enough for her to go unnoticed and she stocked up on food. Over the following days she traveled as fast as the horse allowed, only stopping at towns and villages for food as needed.

Each night she would sleep rough on the outskirts of nearby towns. That way she didn't need to spend her remaining money, but she still was close enough to people to feel safer. If the only way to dispose of the amulet was to make it to Callet she'd need to conserve the money she had. Lani didn't know how long it would take to get there. She would have to sell the other rings no matter what.

After learning she was only a day's ride from Nedor, at the last town, she joined on to the back of a slow moving caravan. No one seemed to mind her riding along and by the middle of the day she ended up riding alongside another woman who would occasionally chat to her.

Lani was looking at a massive forest, far across the river to her left. Even at this distance the deep green and browns were visible to her. A short distance above the treetops was a stretch of clouds that seemed to end on either side of the forest. The white clouds just hung in the same spot, seemingly unaffected by the wind or anything else.

"I'll be hoping we make Nedor shortly, before that ill looking weather comes this way," the woman beside her said.

Lani had been so lost in her own thoughts she hadn't seen how the surrounding sky was changing. It had become gray with patches of darkness spreading towards the forests she had been looking at.

"Those clouds are unlike anything I've seen before. That forest looks as if it is about to come alive and move this way," Lani replied.

"Well the white clouds of KapuaMa are a myth all of their own, girl. They linger there throughout the year, then disappear following the great summer storms, for a time of one moon and then come back anew. Some say it's a magic of some sort that makes it so, but few say it aloud in company."

Lani glanced at the woman and back at the distant sky. Over the woman's shoulder they had just left behind the last of the Sisi range, with only large hills that rolled from their base towards Nedor. Through the lowest hills the Axin river was flowing strongly, racing to where it joined the Emmer river. They'd followed the Emmer all the way from Little Big Rock. Despite there still being miles between them and the Axin, the sound of it rushing was very apparent. The noise was more similar to the ocean tide crashing against the shore than a typical river.

"You believe in magic?"

"Hah. Do I believe? Maybe, maybe not. What I reckon is, if it exists, then none of it's good. I'd stay away from it if I came across any. No, it's just what some folk say about those odd clouds over there on those treetops. I don't know if I believe it, but I don't know any other clouds that just hang around as if on a string from the Gods. No, I don't. If nothing else, it doesn't seem natural at all."

Lani didn't reply and they entered another long period of silence before she spoke again.

"Have you ever seen one of these storms before?"

Lani shook her head. "No, this is my first time here."

"Oh, well they're something else, let me tell you. I've only been down here once during one of these storms and they aren't for the faint-hearted. You'll not want to take long to find a boarding house to batten down in."

"A boarding house?"

"Right, you've not been here before. In Nedor they have lodgings just for women, called boarding houses. They are normally better than an inn, and safer, if you take my meaning."

Lani nodded. "Thanks for the information. Where's the best place to start?"

"Inside the gates we'll go through off to the right, there's a bunch of them. They're all different, some are cheaper than the others. I have family here so I don't need to stay there but you'll be right if you haggle a bit on price."

"Thanks."

The sky seemed to lower down on them the closer they got to Nedor. Before long it hung across the river and farms just outside the city walls like a damp blanket, leaving them feeling closed in and damp despite the lack of actual rain. Winds from the east had been building over the last hour and as they joined the line at the city gates everyone was starting to grow anxious to be inside before the storm hit proper.

The arrival of the weather hurried the guards at the gate, and they rushed through their checks. It appeared they had no desire to be caught outside in the storm any more than the people lined up.

Lani waved the lady goodbye as she turned right and headed in the direction they'd discussed. A sudden crack of thunder above made her horse rear up in fright. She managed to hold on and calm it, although it flicked and kicked under her. Lani slipped off it as best she could, and gripping the reins tried to calm the frightened animal.

She could see the fear in the horse's eyes and looked over her shoulder to see if there was someone to help her manage it. Everyone else was running for cover as she tried her hardest to drag it up the road. A flash of lightning lit the dull sky followed by another loud boom of thunder. The horse leapt free of her, the reins pulled from her grip, and bolted off up the road.

It raced away without stopping and Lani knew she wouldn't catch up to it. With the weather closing in, no one paid her any attention. Store owners were latching down shutters and boards as gusts of a foul wind rolled over the walls and down the roads. Anyone else was hurrying to their destinations.

Large drops of water were beginning to fall from the sky, kicking up puffs of dust as they landed; not enough had yet fallen to moisten the roadway, nor turn it to mud.

A large carriage swung through the gates as the guards finally finished checking the latecomers. When it was through they closed the large ironclad gates and dropped the bolts. The carriage turned and made its way slowly up the street three buildings from the gateway. It pulled to a halt outside what looked to Lani like an inn.

Several men rushed out from the inn, talking to the driver of the carriage. A flurry of activity ensued as they worked on gathering all the baggage and helping some women from the carriage.

As she approached the coachman was explaining to one of the ladies that this lodge was the best he could do at such short notice. With the weather the way it was, and if he didn't get to the stables shortly, the carriage was likely to be damaged.

Lani used the wind gusts and ever increasing rainfall to slip inside the foyer ahead of the ladies trying to gather their things.

As she made her way into the foyer she was greeted by a well-dressed woman with a stern look on her face. "Who are you?"

"I…I need a room."

"We have none, sorry, girl. This lot won't even fit in here properly. Best you hurry before everyone locks their doors."

"But… I have money."

"It's not about money, girl. I have no room." Lani watched her turn to the women from the carriage as they came through the door. There were all wearing dresses and capes, and one of them looked at Lani in her dirty clothing and sneered. "Never mind her, ladies, she's just leaving."

"I would hope so and all," the new arrival said as she turned her back on Lani.

The hostess nodded at one of the men, who put down the bags he was carrying and moved over to Lani, grasping her high on her arm.

"On your way, girl."

"Let go of me! It's about to storm out there." Lani tried to wrest herself free of his grip.

The man squeezed harder. "Then best you find yourself somewhere else, and fast." He shoved her out the door. "Don't find your way back here again. *Off with you!*"

Lani stumbled down the front step, clutching her satchel about her chest. The rain was increasing and the street was emptying fast. She turned to her right and headed up the street, trying to find another inn. All the doors were either closed or quickly being shut and barred. Most of the lower windows were already shuttered so she couldn't even see in to find what she was looking for.

The carriage driver came running out of a side lane and almost bowled her over. "Watch where you're going, girl," he yelled at her as he pushed away and raced back the way she'd just come.

She looked down the lane, but it was too dark to see what was down there. Lani looked around her, there was no one to be seen. There were few options left to her, as she cautiously entered the lane and listened for any signs of danger.

A loud crack of thunder above her was quickly followed by a flash of lightning, which gave her enough light to see what was ahead. The high gates of the stables where the driver had left his carriages blocked the end of the lane.

Lani hurried toward them and looked along the length of them to find a way in. She was already drenched by the rain, and the cold was settling in. The fence was solid and there was nothing to climb onto, not that she wanted to climb up anything in this weather.

There was another laneway to the side of the stable which she hadn't seen, which was blocked by a wagon. She pushed her way past it and headed along. A smaller set of gates had a gap between them. By pushing the gates apart Lani could squeeze through. The chain holding them together was enough to stop them opening but not enough to stop her.

The rain ran off the roofs, splashing everywhere in the small court-yard. Soaked to the skin, Lani sloshed over to a small hut with a flimsy door that was flapping in the wind. Inside was dark, too dark for Lani to see what it was used for. That didn't matter, she slid down the wall onto the wooden floor and used her legs to hold the door closed.

At least I am safe here for the night.

TILLANDRA

With her back against the closed door, Tillandra took in several deep breaths. She could sense the faint pulse of the mountain vibrating up through the floor. She closed her eyes and let the feeling move through her.

People spoke of Qum as if it was something bad or a form of evil magic, yet to Tillandra every visit felt a little like coming home. There was a strange comfort and peace whenever she was here, almost as if it was not just the Mother Stone that got recharged.

She pulled the stone out and held it between her hands, letting its warmth soak through her. Each year when she brought it back she could sense the change in its touch. It too liked being back where it had come from.

There was another reason for Ting's guest house, one which only the current Mother and Ting knew. Tillandra stood up and pulled the bed away from the wall. The room was so small that she had to climb over the bed and push it right up against the door before she could access what she needed.

She held the stone out, touching it against the rock wall.

A loud click sounded before a door popped out of the wall just a small amount. Tillandra pocketed the stone and pulled on the handhold exposed in the side of the door. What should have weighed too much for her to move, slid out with ease, filling what little space there was in the room.

Tillandra squeezed through the opening into the darkness beyond and brought the stone back out from her pocket. She held it in front of her and it glowed with a white light showing her the way.

The passage wound deep under the mountain, the air stale and heavy. There was no way she would easily be able to find her way back out, but she wouldn't leave until the stone was ready anyway.

When she got to the large chamber near the center of the mountain, her legs were heavy and she knew she had been walking for hours. The stone in her hand had brightened, the closer to the chamber they had walked, and now it was as bright as the Citadel Stone that stood before Tillandra.

A massive crystal stone stood shaped like a tear drop reaching far out of sight up into the cavern above. At the level she was standing it bulged out, taking up much of the space of the cavern. Directly in front of where she had walked in was a dark spot, marking the hole that the Mother Stone came from.

She walked up and placed her tiny stone into the hole, and the sound the Citadel Stone made brought tears to Tillandra's eyes. A soft sweet sound filled the chamber in what she could only explain was like an audible hug. The first time she had completed this task it had brought her to her knees. The feeling of love that emanated from the stone, and the sound, had caused her to sob for many hours.

Whatever power this mountain jewel had was so powerful that Tillandra felt insignificant next to it. She simply felt glad to be able to experience it, even though she couldn't mention it to anyone.

A small alcove lay in the opposite wall and Tillandra made her way there, wiping the tears from her face. A tiny stream of water ran from a hole in the wall, into a small pool in the floor. She drank from it and felt her energy restored. She then went and sat on the cushions that made up the rest of the space.

While the Mother Stone was charging Tillandra would meditate. This time she had much to contemplate and hoped for some insights that might answer the questions she had. Most of all she knew that her dreams wouldn't bother her here.

Time disappeared as she sat on the cushions, lost inside the space in her mind, absorbing the feeling of the stone and being again at peace. The constant worry she normally carried throughout the day was gone, and in its place she felt complete calm.

When she saw the woman coming toward her she felt confused. She knew she wasn't asleep and it didn't feel like a dream. The woman glowed like the Citadel Stone and Tillandra could almost see through her. Her eyes were still closed and yet it was if she was staring at her walking across the cavern to her.

"Tillandra," she said, her voice low and soft. "All is well."

Tillandra couldn't talk, she felt like she was underwater and that if she opened her mouth she would drown.

"Just listen, child. If you have questions just think them, you cannot talk here."

"Where are we?"

A warm smile formed on her narrow face, "We are here. Is that not enough?"

"Who are you?"

"Worry not for names, child. You have enough to worry about."

Tillandra could feel her calm begin to slip away.

"Not now, but in your future. Times have changed, and you have much to do."

"What?"

"Not all of it is clear but I will help where I can. The stone you see before you, is but half of a whole."

"There is another?"

"Yes, unlike this one, it is very different. And it doesn't want the same things we want."

"What does it want?"

"I wish I truly knew. The pair of stones have been here for longer than anyone can know."

"You are not the stone?"

The woman laughed at Tillandra. "No, child, I am not. I am using it to come to you because you cannot resist me this way."

"What do you mean?"

"Your dreams, Tillandra, they are messages from us. You fight us so much you are breaking the messages. That's why you have little faith in them."

"They are all from you?"

She paused for a while before responding, "No. There are dreams you may receive that come from other places. I cannot see them, nor guide you on them."

"What messages do you send?"

"Do you recall when you first met Ashantha?"

A tear formed in Tillandra's eye at the mention of her friend.

"Oh, child, do not be pained. Ashantha has passed now, he is in no pain. He served his role."

"But… I sent him away, and now…"

"You did as you were bid, Tillandra. He served what he was made for, as should you."

"What do you mean?"

"We brought you together to fulfil a role, what you are leading is very important for this world."

Tillandra didn't know what to say.

"Can you recall if meeting Ashantha felt different?"

"Yes, I dreamt of the circus, and when I went there, it felt unusual."

"How so?" the woman asked her.

"It's hard to remember but I knew I had to be there, and things, some of the things looked different."

"That was the path being lit for you."

Tillandra realized what the woman was saying.

"That sense, and dream, coupled with the light, that's how you know our messages. They all have that sense to them. The same when you made the decision to send him away. It was what was needed. Stop fighting them, Tillandra, we need you to understand. You will need all the help you can get."

The woman appeared to be fading. "Wait, don't go."

"I must. Ask Tingfurlew about the Occultation."

"The what?"

"He will tell you. It is time."

"What of this girl?"

"She is a danger to you."

"What do you mean?"

"You must get to her, Tillandra. If you need to speak to one of your own, you can use the stone, in here, it is possible…" Her voice was little but a whisper now and her form had receded into the stone.

"Stay," Tillandra pleaded.

There was nothing but silence. Tillandra opened her eyes and looked around the cavern but there was no one there. Had she dreamed that? Or had it actually happened? She couldn't tell the difference.

The experience had been very strange but the information about her dreams was helpful. Maybe now she could use them and not resist the messages. If nothing else, she could tell useful dreams from any others.

Tillandra suddenly realized that she had not contacted Goran to tell him of his task, she'd wasted valuable time, distracted by the journey here, and the complications along the way. Cursing herself she reflected on the message the woman had just told her, that she could use the Citadel Stone to communicate with others.

She needed to speak with Goran, she had left it far too long. If she could use the stone, that meant she didn't need to sacrifice an animal, and hopefully the reaction she felt afterwards.

The sound of the Citadel Stone began to hum around the cavern again telling her the Mother Stone was ready.

Focusing back on the space between her eyes, Tillandra dropped into the void and sought out Goran's likeness.

GORAN

$\mathcal{I}$t had been days since he'd had a clear head, the last couple of weeks had disappeared in a blur. Being back in Nedor hadn't been good for Goran, and he knew he would need to get out of there soon, or he'd end up in more trouble.

His head was groggy, from the weed and all the red wine he'd consumed last night. He knew it needed to stop but his motivation to change was low. He was tired of being a courier, and being on the outer.

He stretched out on the bed before swinging himself up to a sitting position. The windows were still shuttered from last night's storm.

He stood and opened the window, letting the morning sunlight stream in. The smell of fresh rain and wet mud rose up from below, and he looked at the mess in the courtyard below.

As he looked across the wall of the yard into the main street he could see a lone horseman heading their way. The rider pulled up at the gate and after dismounting led his horse across the muddy yard.

Goran recognized the courier and a smile crossed his face. *I wonder what news he brings. I could do with something new to deal with.* He left his room and headed downstairs.

"Shrever, good man, how are you?" Goran greeted the man as he came into the main room.

"Goran, just the man I was looking for."

"Oh? Why is that?"

"I have a message just for you."

Goran smiled. "Now that's good news, I've been looking forward to something to do for a while now. What is it?"

"I'm not sure what's in it, Goran, I was simply told to give it to you." The courier reached into his bag and handed over a letter; the wax seal of the Jester's face matched the stone token the man wore around his neck.

"Thanks. I will look this over. Anything else urgent to tell?"

"Nothing that can't wait. I got caught in that storm last night, and had to shelter on the road. I'm in desperate need of a bath and some food. Can I update you later?"

"Yes, off you go."

Goran climbed the stairs and went back into his room. He sat at the table and broke the seal on the letter and read the message.

The Keeper in Riverbend, Nahele, had written him a note about a woman from Little Big Rock that had come to see them. The woman, Arbery, claimed that a younger woman had come to their bakery wearing a Jester's ring.

Nahele went to great pains in his message to say he had questioned Arbery extensively about what she claimed to have seen. Nahele didn't understand it, and thought she had to be wrong. He did agree with her, that despite having difficulty believing it, it was best to pass it along.

Goran pulled at his dreadlocks, running his fingers over several beads.

How very strange. There's no one new in the Court, I would have been told. Wouldn't I? Surely if someone had died I would know. This can't be true, that baker woman must be desperate to get on our good side.

He put the letter back on the table and stood up. At the window he looked back out at the day, wondering what was the truth of it all. He knew that since the problem at King Nordahl's court he had been kept on the outer by his colleagues. But not that much on the outer. If someone had died and a new member added to their Court, surely he would have been told. He thought back over the past month, trying to recall if he'd missed any connections, and forgotten to get back to them, but it was all a blur.

Too much of his life of late had been lost in a blur. He wasn't happy with what he was doing, and he was enjoying the other side of life too much. It wasn't usual for one of them to be traveling around collecting and sharing information for so long, but he knew it was his punishment for being shut out of the palace here in Nedor.

The knocking came unexpectedly. In his head the sound was like someone knocking on a thin piece of wood, but it came from right between his eyes.

He moved over to the bed and slid over so his back was supported by the wall. After folding his legs in front he began to slow his breath and calm his heart rate. It took a little time to bring his focus to the place between his eyes where the knocking came from.

With his eyes closed he focused on that spot and slowly slipped into the void. It was neither dark nor light, there was a sense of calm there which Goran could never find in the real world. As he held his attention there one of the many faint shapes that floated across his vision slowed and started to become bigger. He could see it was Tillandra's face.

"Goran..." Her voice was faint. "Goran," she repeated, this time much clearer. "In All Jest."

"In All Jest, Mother, how are you?" He knew she hated the price of initiating the contact.

"In All Jest, Goran. I am good. Your signal is weak, are you okay?"

He paused. "I am well, all is good here," he lied. "It has been a long time since we last spoke, Mother. Last time was not so pleasant."

She took a while to reply.

"I wish today was more so, but I don't think it will be."

Goran's heart dropped, he nearly fell out of the connection, and had to calm himself and breathe deeply. "What is it?"

"We have lost one of our own, Goran. Ashantha has been taken from us."

He could hear the sadness in her voice and was stunned by the news. "Oh my Thenis. What on earth has happened?"

"He was killed somewhere to the north in Malamig."

"Killed? How, Mother?"

"It's not easy for me to share the news, Goran." She paused before continuing. "I do not know who he was killed by, but I am guessing someone must have followed him back from Enderk."

"Is that where he was? I knew he was away, but wasn't sure where."

"Yes, that was where. Unfortunately I did not hear from him when he returned."

Goran was struggling to understand everything she was saying. "Why would he be followed and killed? What was he doing over there?"

"That's the thing, Goran. Without his journal we won't ever know now. I am unsure why he never contacted me, but he never did. We have to get his things!"

Realization of what she meant hit Goran. "Oh, of course. The mask. He had a journal?"

"Yes I was able to see it when he passed, and he had been writing something there. We need it. You have to go get them, Goran."

"Me?"

"Yes, you. You're the only person close enough to try and find his things."

"Right." Goran wasn't sure if he was happy that they'd chosen him or sad that it was just because they were desperate.

"Do you understand how important this is? If someone uses his mask, the harm will be terrible. My hope is that his journal would be coded to others but it worries me what might be in there that shouldn't be read by others."

"Yes, Mother, I understand."

"This is your chance, Goran. There are those still unhappy about your last transgression, you can show them you take your role seriously by fixing this."

"Will that never be forgotten?"

"It will be much easier if you show your willingness to do something not just for your own interests. Speaking of which, why on Dharatan are you in Nedor?"

Goran had forgotten their locations were visible in the map room. "I have changed my appearance, Mother. No one but our kind would recognize me." He knew this wasn't completely true, but he was certain his current appearance wasn't recognizable to the King's men. "I needed a break from the road through the winter, but ended up stuck here a little longer than planned. I had an infection in my bad leg."

"Is it better?"

"Yes. I was planning to be gone very shortly."

"Some feel you're chancing your luck just being there, it reinforces their view of you."

"Some wouldn't change their view of me no matter what I do."

"You know I advocate for you, Goran. Please, we need to be united, especially now."

"Why now?"

"There's more to the story. There was a young woman in the cave when I scryed Ashantha. She took up his ring and put it on."

Goran couldn't help his outburst. "She what?"

"She put on his ring."

"I thought that wasn't possible?"

"And I. That's why I've traveled to Midderbuilt to speak with the Ring Master."

"That changes everything."

"What do you mean, Goran?"

"I just received a message from Nahele in Riverbend, several days north of here. It comes from a new contact I've been developing from a town called Little Big Rock. She told Nahele that she had come into contact with a young woman wearing a ring like mine, but who didn't identify herself to use their lodgings. I was just trying to understand how she could have been so confused, but from what you're saying it's most likely true."

"That's interesting. It might be the first bit of luck we've had around this. Did she tell you where she was?"

"The girl is on her way here, that's her best guess. She left Riverbend, and there's nothing of interest between there and here. I'll need to work out the timing but it's possible she's already here."

"Then maybe your decision to be in Nedor has worked in your favor. If she's there then you can put an end to this quickly. I think she has his ring, mask and journal."

"Then I need to get them back?"

"Yes, and quickly. Her as well."

"Her?"

"She cannot be left with any knowledge of what she has found, Goran."

"You want me to use the mask on her?"

Tillandra didn't reply for a minute, Goran was thinking through what he thought she had just suggested.

"No, Goran. She must be brought to Anderwell. How she could take the ring is important, and if it was her that killed Ashantha then the court can decide how to punish her. For now we need all her memories intact. Unless…"

"Unless what?"

"Unless you can't get her to Anderwell. If there's any chance of her getting away, she cannot be left knowing what she might have learned. Understood?"

Goran let sink in what was being asked of him.

"Understood, Goran?"

"Yes, Mother. Understood."

"Good. Beantic will contact you to tell you where the ring is. I need to go, be safe, my friend."

"And you, Mother."

Her face started to fade and receded into the blur of shapes floating across the void. Goran sat there for a moment or two, before pulling back out of the void to the spot on his forehead. Slowly his sense came back into the room, and he opened his eyes.

Sweat had formed on his brow and he stood up and wiped it away with his sleeve. His day had just taken a major turn and he wasn't sure if he was happy about it or not.

54

LANI

The storm raged through the night, killing any chance of Lani sleeping. At times she began to drift off to the sounds of the heavy rain, her head rested on the side wall in the corner of the small hut.

Then another thunderclap would scare her awake. She would sit upright looking for the threat, just as the flash of lightning would follow. The small bursts of light helped her see a little of the dark hut.

Her ability to guide herself in the darkness required her to have seen it before. The hut was unknown to her, but in the flashes of light she could see that it was some form of washing room, with a big tub at one end.

Progressively the weather moved away and all that was left of the booming was an occasional rumble in the distance. By the time the first trickles of morning light had shone through the gaps around the door, the rain had also ceased.

Lani was still soaked through and exhausted from shivering. It had been a long while since she had been forced to survive on the street, and she missed the safety and warmth of her warren. *Even the old stable in Barnen was better than this.*

Several times throughout the night she had broken down into tears.

Everything she had was now gone, and she was lost, in a big city far away from her home. Having the kin around her had always helped to keep the feeling of loneliness at bay.

It dawned on her that she had used them for that comfort, without even realizing it. The sense of emptiness, her lack of family or connection, had always haunted her. Those dark feelings had come back to her through the night, and she had been unable to fight them off.

It seemed no good would come to her, her lot was hopeless. Even her poor life in Barnen had been better than being stranded here, and that was gone now. If she deserved better then she wouldn't be stuck in such a mess. Lani knew she should get up and move but the gloom in her mind removed her will to move.

A door swung open close by, and Lani could hear someone walking heavily down some stairs. She heard three or four steps then the sloshing of someone in the yard outside. The fear of being discovered pulled her out of her self-pity and she lifted her knees to better prepare herself to stand. The door opened ever so slightly, allowing splinters of light into the space.

The footsteps approached the hut and then the door swung open, crashing into the side of Lani's legs before stopping and returning in the direction it came.

"What in the sewers of Nedor?" a woman said.

Lani started to stand but her feet slipped on the wet floor. The door opened again, more cautiously this time, and a thick wooden staff poked through. Before Lani could grab hold of it, it was pressed into her chest pinning her against the back wall.

A stout woman eased the door open with her shoulder, and stood over her with the staff firmly gripped between both hands.

"*Don't you move a muscle!*"

Lani wasn't sure she could if she wanted to, as between the cold in her bones and the staff that was causing her difficulty to breathe, she was trapped where she sat.

"Please...?" she forced out.

"Please, what? What are you doing in my laundry?" The woman's eyes bored in on Lani.

"The… the storm." Lani was struggling to talk. "My chest. I can't breathe." She felt the pressure ease a little.

"There, now speak up."

"I only just made it through the gate last night. The storm hit, and my horse threw me. I had nowhere to go, everywhere was closed." Lani tried to put on a pleading face and look as if she was about to cry. "I found your gate a little open. Please, it was horrible, the storm. It was all I could find."

"You're a girl? Oh, Thenis!" Her face seemed to soften and she started to pull the staff back, before pushing it forward again. "You being serious, girl, or you just trying one on with me? Where you from?"

"It's the truth, I swear. I come from a city far in the north."

"What's it called then?"

Lani looked at her. "Barnen, it's a long way from here."

The woman pulled the staff back and placed one end of it on the ground beside her, using her other hand to reach up and pull her hood off her head. She bore little resemblance to the Mals that Lani was used to.

"Go on, get up. I won't hurt you. If you're a traveler then you can afford somewhere to stay?"

"Yes, I can. But everywhere was boarded up last night, and the only place I tried threw me out in the street, because of my dirty clothes." Lani had to slowly push herself up the wall, her knees were locked from the cold and her muscles didn't want to respond.

"Look at the state of you, you must be freezing. Here, what's your name?"

"Lani."

"Well, Lani, I'm Merta. Let's get you inside and we'll see about a room for you."

Merta was wide and plump, not as tall as a typical Mal, but not short either. Her skin was a chocolate brown, and faded a little across her broad arms, one of which grabbed Lani to help her out through the door.

"Is that your only bag?" Merta raised her eyebrows over the wide squat nose that dominated her round face.

"Yes," Lani shrugged.

They walked back across the yard, and up the stairs into the back of the building.

"This is my lodge for ladies, although you don't have to be a lady to stay here, just a woman." Merta burst into a deep laugh and she patted Lani on the back. "Don't mind me," she said when Lani didn't laugh along with her. "You'll be safe here, but you'll need to clean up. A bath suit you?"

Lani nodded, a small smile forming on her face, the dark feelings from overnight beginning to lift. "Yes, please."

"I don't have many rooms left, it's a choice between a suite or I have a worker's room. It's only small and not so easy to get to, up on the top floor, but it's cheap, and it's got a decent enough bed."

"Cheap sounds good."

Merta laughed again. "Sorry for scaring you, girl, but I can't be too careful. There's those in this city would steal the cape off a woman's back, standing right next to her, they would. Thieving in this city just been getting worse. Grow, grow they say, makes for more trade. More trade for taxes and thieves is all it seems."

Lani found it strange to hear her talk about thieving as if it was normal. Captain Kyro had always made such a big deal out of stopping it, and punishing those that did. *Maybe I can find some extra coin while I am here.*

By the time she had cleaned up, Merta had taken away her dirty clothes and left her with a dress to wear. It took her a lot longer to put it on than her usual tunic and tights and the weird feeling of her clothing, moving separate to her as she turned, bothered her.

Normally she didn't consciously think about what she wore, it lay against her skin and she never had to think about it. Things felt very different when she was dressed like this and she wasn't sure she liked it. She had removed the blue brooch from inside her tunic, before Merta took them away, and it was pinned on the inside of the dress against the skin of her chest.

Even that felt unusual, it was usually pinned inside the inner pocket of her tunic, and never sat against her skin. She had carried it for so long it was just part of her, the only connection she had to her past, but one she knew nothing about. Captain Kyro had never explained to her what it meant, and now she would never get a chance to ask. If nothing else, she was certain that she wouldn't be going back to Barnen any time soon.

The room she had rented was on the top floor and wasn't much bigger than the hut she had spent the night in. Standing at the window Lani could see far across the city. The view amazed Lani. There were buildings and roads as far as she could see. Nedor was obviously much bigger than Barnen, or the other towns she had seen on her way here. It had to be at least double the size or more.

Far across the city a grand structure stood out. It was surrounded by its own wall and there were many towers on it. That would have to be the palace where the King lived, she guessed. She looked at in awe for some time, taking in its size and shape.

Lani swung herself up onto the window ledge and sat with her legs dangling above the alley below. She felt embarrassed as she swung her legs out and the dress billowed in the breeze, quickly pushing it down. She shook her head at herself, there wasn't even anyone around to notice.

The sky had mostly cleared of cloud with only small pockets still visible. As she looked across the many rooftops and streets Lani wondered what to do next. Things had been happening so quickly for her and the journey she'd set out on had taken on a life of its own. In some ways it felt like a lifetime ago since she had left Barnen but in reality it wasn't long at all.

Her original plan had been to sell the rings, and the amulet too, if she could, and find somewhere away from Barnen to live or wait it out until it was safe to go back.

Yerat's sudden death had caught her by surprise and she had hurried away from Little Big Rock quicker than she had planned. She knew she couldn't have stayed there if people from Barnen were looking for her, but her journey had now taken on a life of its own.

Things felt out of control like they were a runaway wagon with no driver. She needed to have a plan, or she wouldn't last here or anywhere else. The cost of this room would eat up her money before long, and that was without buying any food. If the city wasn't as heavily policed as Barnen then she knew she could steal food, to keep her costs down, but she needed somewhere to live. If she was going to stay in Nedor.

That was the choice she had to make and it all came down to the amulet. Selling it seemed out of the question now. Two people that had handled it had died, that was too much coincidence for her to ignore it.

But why can I handle it? That doesn't make any sense. And what did it do to my arm?

Her bare arm looked no different to the other one. There were no marks on it from when she had felt the amulet burning into it. She turned it over and back again several times, comparing the two arms and rubbing her skin to check.

Without the gloves on her hands Lani looked closer at the ring. It still wouldn't budge, she still couldn't get it to come off.

Did it protect me somehow? Are they connected?

None of it made any sense to her. Whatever magic it was that she was wrapped up in, she wanted to be rid of. So far it had brought her nothing but bad luck. Lani could remember the feeling she had first had when she had seen the amulet and thought how all her luck had changed; that was before Ashantha had broken whatever spell it had on her.

Nothing since then had been good for her, except maybe selling the ring with the amber stone. She needed to sell one or both of the rings here in Nedor, if she could. That would buy her enough time to work out what to do about the amulet.

Something had changed that day back in Little Big Rock when it had stung her arm. Lani was struggling to understand it, but it was like she could always tell where it was. The sense of it reaching out to her, that she'd had that very first night, was always there now. But it wasn't like it was reaching for her, it was like it was connected to her. There was something always in the back of her mind, almost like a picture of the amulet, reminding her of itself.

It wasn't a feeling she liked and now that she knew it had killed others she wanted to be rid of it. It didn't matter what Ashantha had said, she wasn't going to take it to Callet. She needed to be rid of it, and in a way that no one else would be harmed by it. She had no idea how to do that and once she had sold another ring she'd start figuring out how to get rid of the amulet.

Another gust of wind came and billowed up her dress, breaking her from her thoughts. She batted it down again, and climbed back into the room.

Whatever I do, I'm not doing it in this dress.

55

LANI

~

*L*ani almost didn't recognize her clothes when they came back from Merta's cleaners. It wasn't like she had never washed them before but they looked completely different now, and smelt like fresh cloth.

She was glad to be out of the dress, and back into her clothes. She wanted pockets and clothing she could feel against her skin. It was a small thing but with everything else in her life changed she clung to the few small things she still seemed able to control. The brooch went back inside her tunic, and she considered whether to carry the amulet there as well.

Lani weighed up the risks of taking the amulet with her, or leaving it behind. This inn seemed safe enough, so if she left it hidden in here, the chances of someone stumbling on it were slim. She was going to head into the slightly shadier parts of town to find a buyer for the ring, and if she took all her belongings she would be a bigger target for the types that she assumed she would meet.

A thought crossed her mind that the amulet could save her if she got into trouble, and she had to shake her mind free of that way of thinking. She didn't want to kill anyone, the amulet wasn't a weapon.

In the end she put the amulet in the hidden pouch alongside the brooch, and put an amber ring into each of the two pockets in her tunic. She also pocketed one silver piece before stowing the satchel behind the robe.

Merta had given her directions to where the large central markets were. Lani stepped out of the inn onto the street and headed that way.

The main road was heavy with mud from the overnight rain. A few horses and carriages were making heavy work of it traveling up the street. Thankfully there was a path of paved stones on this side, set higher than the road level.

The road initially followed the line of the outer wall, several streets across, but as she walked it straightened and headed directly north-west towards the heart of Nedor. The closer to the center she walked, the more stores she saw, until the palace walls became the focal point of all she could see. In front of them was a massive city square, the stalls and buildings dominated by the walls they backed onto.

Once she reached the cobbled square Lani found herself having to weave her way through people hurrying about their business, and the aggressive market sellers trying to drag people to sample their wares. Some were way too persistent for her liking and she found herself pushing one off before making her way to the outer edges.

Part of her was swept away with the excitement of traveling in a new place, and wanting to learn more about it, while the rest of her was cynical and wary of any potential threats. There seemed to be many travelers from lands further afield, many that she had never seen before.

Nedor market was a kaleidoscope of people, their dress and color as varied as the wares on sale. She sat off to the side and watched, trying to learn anything she could about the people in this city. After half an hour of watching it all unfold, Lani scanned the area seeking anyone that might have been paying her undue attention.

None of the pickpockets she had seen trying their hands amongst the travelers gave her any attention, but she spotted one that she felt she could follow. If anyone was likely to know where a fence was, then that was a pickpocket.

She waited patiently until she saw her get her mark, carefully lifting an item from a stall and slipping away. Lani was up and moving swiftly, keeping out of the line of sight between the thief and the stall. As expected the only place the thief looked was back over her shoulder to the stall.

The route the thief took followed several main roads, and then some side lanes. Lani was able to guess the general direction and not lose sight of her, without having to directly go down the same lanes. At one point she thought she'd lost her before catching sight of her between several older boys. Probably part of her crew, Lani thought.

As she had guessed, the section of the city they came to, while still full of stores and other businesses, was not the same as the main streets she had walked earlier. There was less light with the buildings crammed closer together. The people around here weren't dressed as fancily as in the main streets, and there no one was standing around idly.

Lani watched the girl and her companions go into a store but not come back out, while she hung around to watch. After a while Lani hunted the streets for a similar looking store displaying jewelry and other trinkets. She stopped in front of a small shop front; the glass window was coated in dust, but she could still see some chains and silver items on display.

It looked a likely candidate and she pushed the door open and stepped inside. She walked into a cloud of smoke filling the shop, the only person inside leaning up against the counter, puffing on a pipe.

"I help you, miss?"

Lani held back a cough. "Maybe."

"How so?" He put his pipe back in his mouth and puffed on it a few more times, more smoke rising into the room.

"I have a ring that I'd like to sell."

"A ring, hey?" He raised his eyebrows before sweeping his spare hand over the top of the glass counter top. "I've got loads of rings already, miss."

Lani walked up to the counter, and spent a moment looking left and right viewing the different jewelry he had on sale. She looked up at him. "Not like my ring if this is all you have."

The man chuckled at her. "Oh… You've got something special, do you?" He shook his head and stood upright, "That's what everyone tells me when they desperate to sell."

"I'm not desperate."

"Then why do you need to sell it? If it's so special why don't you keep it?"

Lani didn't say anything for a few moments. "I don't need it and it's worth good coin, I reckon."

"Go on then, miss, don't keep wasting my time." He looked around his shop and laughed. "Either you're going to show it to me or you're not."

Lani took out one of the rings, and placed the small cloth parcel on the counter before opening it.

The man jumped back from her. "What on earth? An amber ring, don't be bringing that in here."

"What are you worried about? This is a rare piece, you could do well with it."

The man, was mumbling to himself as if saying a prayer. "Amber is cursed, don't you know that? I don't want any amber in here, not a ring or anything else."

"There's nothing wrong with this ring." Lani held it up and turned it in the dim light.

The man regained some of his composure. "Like I told you, as far as I'm concerned that stone is cursed. We've not seen any of that for a long time and no good came from anyone that had it."

"It's just a ring with a stone set in it."

"I don't know where you got that ring from, but all the amber can only come from one place, Enderk. I won't touch the stuff, and you'll find few who will. Especially since word arrived yesterday."

"Word?"

"A trader, up north in Riverbend, had been touting he had amber to sell. They found him carved up in his shop. Them that told me, we all agreed, same as happened years ago. You get amber and you get trouble. Simple as that. Take that and go, I won't be buying that from you nor will anyone else around here."

Lani wrapped the ring and put it back in her tunic. "You said few who will. Does that mean you know someone who might be interested?"

The man looked at her for a minute, occasionally shaking his head. "You should just throw it away and move on."

"It's worth good money, it is. Do you know someone that might be interested?" she repeated.

He looked away from her again, before seeming to make his mind up. "You'll not find anyone in Nedor that I know will touch it. The only person I know, he has a place in Nkuku. You know where that is?"

Lani shook her head.

"South, to the south, in Morska. On the border with Lletem, or thereabouts. You want to sell that, then head to Nkuku. But mark my words, that ring will bring you trouble. I don't want any more of it."

"Nkuku, thank you. How would I find them?"

"Eastern part of the city, you'll find what's known as Jobber's Lane. If you can, find Robatch. Good luck to you! He's not my taste of ale, but he'll likely buy that from you. Now get that out of here and don't come back."

He had come around the counter as he was telling her the directions and shepherded her out the door. Lani could hear him bolting it on the inside. A shiver went up her spine thinking about what this fence had told her about the trader in Riverbend, and his concern about the ring she had shown him.

The reaction to the ring still surprised her; the trader in Riverbend had been excited by it, as had Yerat. Unsure if it was just this man's fear and nothing more to it, Lani moved further along the lane until she saw another target shop.

This time the reaction was even swifter. The shopkeeper pushed her out of the shop and she fell heavily onto the ground as she stumbled down the stairs.

"Don't waste your time down here with that, girl! No one with any brains will touch what you've got." He slammed his door shut and again she could hear the sound of it being locked.

She got to her feet feeling foolish, and saw people who had seen what had happened turn and hurry away. The lane she was on now was completely empty and Lani felt unsafe and exposed. Turning to the right she hurried away, heading back towards the main street.

LANI

When Lani returned to the market it was bustling with activity. As was typical even in Barnen, entertainers had taken up a spot at the edge of the city square and were drawing a sizeable crowd. The lure of the entertainment was strong and she made her way closer to where they were playing.

She needed time to think about what had just happened. The reactions to the ring weren't what she had expected. Not only did they not want them, but the talk about the amber being cursed had shaken her confidence. If no one would buy them her plans were useless.

Without the money from the rings she was going to run out of coin very quickly. When that happened she wouldn't have the safety of her warren and the job with Bragg. Nedor was big, too big for her. She had wanted to see the city but the thought of living here, stuck on the streets, was not what she had planned for. At some point she needed to find a base and find a way to survive.

She smelt fresh food from the stalls around her and her stomach grumbled. Her mind flicked back to a very similar scene in Barnen, and how that decision to take the pastries started her on the path she was now on. First Harsop catching her, then Ashantha and the amulet.

The sight of pastries on a stall counter caught her attention and a shiver ran up her spine.

Not again!

Laughter from the crowd snapped her back to where she was. Lani found a spot off to the side where she could stand on some steps against the wall of a shop. She tucked in behind a group of smaller children that climbed up there to see over the top of the adults. They were laughing and thrilled by the antics of the clowns that were performing.

Lani felt very lonely suddenly. She had never had family so there was always part of her that knew she was on her own but being in the company of the kin had always been a buffer from the outside world. The children that she was next to highlighted that loss to her. She really was on her own.

She looked back at the entertainers. One of the clowns was as tall as Lani had ever seen and, ridiculously, had stilts strapped to his leg that made him even taller. He towered above everything in the square, wobbling and careening around the space, rushing towards the crowd as if he would fall on top of them. At the last second he would right himself and turn to catch balls thrown by a squat companion lying on the ground. The contrast of the two, and the antics of the taller one, had the crowd laughing and gasping at the well-practiced chaos.

The skill of the stilted clown had Lani in awe. She had never seen someone who in one moment seemed so hopeless but in the blink of an eye could move and catch and juggle seemingly without any effort. His companion lay on his back in the middle of the ground, pretending to be half asleep. He had to have trusted his partner completely because with great regularity the stilts flashed over the top of him, the tall one missing his head and sides by small margins, as he dashed back and forth. He threw the balls with great precision and as they came back juggled them, sometimes on his feet, without what appeared to be a care in the world.

So enthralled was the crowd that they had started clapping along with the performance, speeding it up or slowing it down in sync with the routine.

As the show continued, Lani saw a number of soldiers arriving singly or in twos. They began positioning themselves around the square, in what appeared to be a deliberate pattern.

Not long after they had reached their positions another group of heavily armored soldiers marched out, protecting one whom Lani could only guess was the King. The crowd parted, albeit reluctantly, to allow them space, and attendants rushed forward with a small seating platform where he sat to watch the entertainers.

The crowd had lost some of their energy while this happened but the entertainers didn't miss a beat. They continued on in more earnest, if that was even possible, the stakes of their show even higher now. The clown on the ground was up and aimlessly wandering about, throwing balls over his shoulder into what seemed random places. The clown on stilts was catching them all, or batting them immediately back at him.

It didn't take long for the crowd to pick up the clapping again and Lani lost herself in the atmosphere. When the show ended she felt better for the distraction. The melancholy that had set in earlier had been replaced by a feeling that she would be okay. She didn't know why, but she knew she had survived this far, despite the events she had faced.

Nedor meant nothing to her, and getting upset because she couldn't sell the rings here was pointless. She needed to sell them and if she could believe the trader, Nkuku was as good a place as any. He had given her a name and somewhere to look, that was more than she had when she had arrived here.

Her choice would come down to cost. She either had to look for another buyer in the city, that didn't share the same fears as the two she'd already encountered, or get a ride to this other place. It was a risk, the trip could burn through what she had left, and if she couldn't sell them she would be in a new realm, and with even less money.

Her stomach reminded her she was hungry and Lani wandered back over to the stalls she had passed earlier. One of them was a possible target for her to take food from, especially when the show finished and the crowd would be pushing through.

The stall owner looked up and saw her. "Hungry, girl?"

She nodded and walked over. She decided to buy, now that he'd noticed her, and traded in the silver piece she had for a spiced pastry. It only cost a few coppers and having the change in smaller pieces would be easier for her.

"They smell so good."

He chuckled. "My partner, he does the cooking. Has a magic touch he does, everything he cooks, tastes like it came from Thenis's hand."

Lani smiled back at him. "Maybe you can help me?"

"How's that?" He looked a little guarded now.

"I want to find out about getting a ride to Nkuku, but I'm not from here. Where would I find the agents?"

His faced relaxed again. "Oh, that's an easy one to answer." He turned and pointed to the south. "Follow Southgate road until you see a mighty white temple on the left-hand side. Turn right at that junction and you'll find the bulk of them a short walk from there."

"Thank you."

The man nodded at her and turned to serve the next customer. Lani moved off and ate as she walked, heading in that direction.

It took her three agents to find one that wasn't just organizing shipping caravans. There was a line inside the store, with several people waiting to talk to the surly man behind the counter. They all were booking carriages and when she heard the prices her heart sank.

"You're next, young lady. What can I do to help?"

Lani approached the counter. "I need to get to Nkuku."

"Speak up, girl. No need to be secretive. Nkuku. Let me see." He flicked back a sheet on the book in front of him and ran his finger down the list. "No carriages going that way, I'm sorry."

"I don't need a carriage. I'm happy to ride, or on a wagon."

He looked up from his book, and peered at her. "A wagon? Dear lord, we don't do wagons, young lady. This is Thurodges, we move people, not things." His voice had taken on a condescending tone.

Lani blushed. "I was just saying I only need a simple passage. I need to get there sooner rather than later."

"Hmm... Hold on a moment, there is one option." He turned and walked over to a companion seated at a desk. The other man looked up at her as the first spoke quietly to him before responding to him.

"We do know someone that offers the sort of ride you are looking for. It's not usual for our customers to request such a thing," he said, the haughty tone returning to his voice, "but he runs a horse service between several locations."

"Oh, great. Does he have one going to Nkuku?"

The man laughed. "I wouldn't know, young lady. We don't book his services, but you can find him three doors that-a-way." He flicked his thumb to his left. "You'll know it when you see it. A little less refined than us."

"Well, thank you, anyway."

He lifted his eyebrows, and went back to his book. Lani left the store and made her way down the road until she found the place he had mentioned. It was a fenced courtyard with a covered area on the left-hand side. A woman was sitting there, watching the horses that were tied up at the back of the yard.

"What have we here then?"

"I was told that you do rides to Nkuku?"

The lady sat up from her slouch and looked Lani over. "Who told you that then?"

"A man back up the road. Thurodges, I think he called it."

"Ha. Probably Carl. No doubt he scoffed when he mentioned us, did he?"

Lani nodded.

"Thinks he's one of the King's men, he does. Doesn't realize he just books rides same as us. Nkuku?"

"Yes. I can't afford one of his carriages, and I need to get there as soon as I can."

"We do have a run going there, but it's not for a few days. Hordan, that's my man, he's the one that leads the rides, and he's off on one of his benders. It'll depend on when that finishes before we get this lot south." She nodded towards the horses.

"You deliver the horses?"

"Yeah. That's what we do, we saddle up any that we have rides for, otherwise we just take the horses. It's nothing flash, let me tell you. No fancy inns and boarding houses. You ride all day, camp out at night, and head off again at the break of day."

Lani shrugged. "That doesn't bother me. How much?"

"That's up to Hordan. I'd say it will be a silver though."

"A silver?" Lani made sure she sounded surprised.

"Yeah, but then he might go soft on you. Not for me to say."

"How will I find out for sure?"

"Like I said, only when he gets off this bender and comes back. Til then I can't tell you much more. Best you show up each morning, and check in. I'll let him know but he won't wait about. When he decides to go, he'll go."

"There's no one else?"

"Not that I know, but wouldn't be smart me selling you on someone else now, would it?"

"I guess."

"You want me to tell him you're interested, or not?"

"Yes. I'll come back in the morning, and see."

"What's your name, so I can write it down on our waiting list?" The lady laughed; she hadn't moved from her seat.

"Lani."

"Don't mind me, I get bored sat here all day looking after horses. Once he takes them, then I can go have my own bender, until he gets back."

"I'll come back tomorrow." Lani turned and headed back up the road.

57

GORAN

The main room was quiet and the mug of ale Goran was sipping on had helped clear the remnants of last night as well as the thirst he had developed talking to Tillandra.

He knew she watched over him and balanced the views of the others, especially Junther. They had never gotten along, they were night and day to each other. In Goran's view, Junther was too serious for his own good.

The Bard's Bell Inn was away from the main traffic of eastern Nedor and Goran was watching the empty road through the open window. He'd spent too long doing exactly this for the last month and even if the Tillandra hadn't given him instructions he would have needed to move on anyway.

As he daydreamed about where this young woman could be, another knock arrived. He was so surprised he nearly spilled his ale down his tunic. He stood up and left the mug on the table as he hurried up to his room.

Hopefully it was Beantic, otherwise two contacts in the one morning meant something was wrong.

It was a relief to see the diminutive figure of Beantic come into view once he had returned to the void.

"In All Jest, Goran."

"In All Jest to you, Beantic. At least I have had you to speak to from time to time."

She smiled at him. "You know there are a few of us that still can't put the past behind them."

Goran decided there was little to say in response so just smiled in return.

"Have you heard from Mother?"

"Yes. Only a few hours ago."

"Sorry to burden you with a second contact so soon, but it is important."

"It's fine with me, Bea. I'd rather more than the absence of them of recent times."

"While your choice of location might not have pleased everyone, it appears you might have been lucky."

"The girl is here then?"

"Oh, what do you know?"

"Sorry, of course, I only just told Tillandra. A courier arrived early this morning from Riverbend, with a message from Nahele. Do you recall the baker and his wife from Little Big Rock I've been developing?"

"Yes, but not their names."

"Arbery and Dedrick."

"That's them. You have told me before."

"Arbery turned up in Riverbend with a story about a young woman from Barnen and she was wearing one of our rings. Of course Nahele didn't believe it, but thankfully he sent a message anyway."

"That is good work, I will make a note to send recognition."

"The word from him was that it was likely this girl, called Lani. Darn, I forgot to tell Tillandra her name. Anyway, she was most likely heading here to Nedor."

"She is. I checked the map this morning, and she's definitely around there. As you know I can't say a specific location, only a general one."

"If only it could point her out to me."

Beantic laughed. "We're lucky to have this much visibility. If she didn't have the ring we'd be blind to her location."

"I will start the hunt. Not many know I am here, but I will need to reach out to some old contacts."

"Be careful, your old patron would be very happy to lay his hands on you."

"I know, I know."

"While you are there, tell your keeper and everyone there that we are going to yellow."

"Yellow?"

"Yes, these Derks are a worrying sign. Ashantha, bless his soul, was over in Enderk because we had some hints they were up to something and wanted to know more. Tillandra wants the circuit on alert and looking for anything unusual. Particularly all information about any Derks."

"Okay."

"I'll let you know if the girl moves. Do you have anything else for me?"

"No, Bea. I'll be in touch as soon as I have news."

"Til then."

Goran watched her fade from view and returned to the room. This time he felt the fatigue of holding the connection. His eyes took a while to focus properly and he wasn't able to stand up straight away.

It was all up to him right now, there was no escaping that. He was going to have to visit a few old friends and adversaries if he was going to find this girl. There were so many questions he had, and neither Tillandra nor Beantic had told him enough to answer any of them.

He thought about Ashantha, bringing a memory of his face to mind, and was engulfed in sadness. Goran wanted to know who it was that had killed him and why.

Find them and kill them. The voice in his head startled him. It laughed at its own words. *Kill them all!*

Goran leapt up, he didn't need to switch. Not now, and not around those that knew him. He opened a drawer and pulled out a pipe. He sat in a chair and packed the pipe with the zongle weed from a pouch he'd also taken from the drawer.

He lit it quickly and drew in the smoke, letting it roll down into his lungs, before he exhaled. He closed his eyes and drew more in, the laughing slowly dissipating. By the time it was shut out completely he had emptied the pipe and felt very relaxed.

I don't need that now, I need to stay focused on what I have to do.

That was the thing he couldn't tell his colleagues, they wouldn't understand what he meant. It wasn't him that had seduced the princess, it was the other him. The one that had come with the mask.

His skill had been to perform, and even he knew that when he was acting out few could resist the performance. When he had been in Nordahl's court people would travel from far around to see the King's Jester put on a show.

The mask had made it even better than when he had been a student, but it had brought with it a side he didn't understand. The other performer, Zoran he had named him, came out randomly without warning.

When he came he was stronger than Goran and he was always angry at someone or something. At first it was something Goran had learned to live with, especially away from Anderwell. No one he knew noticed it, and he adapted his behavior to hide it as best he could. Mostly Zoran came out if there was a threat.

Then, one day, he had come out when Goran was sitting with the King's daughter, and had begun to seduce her. Because Nordahl was overprotective of his beloved daughter, she rarely met with people on her own, despite being almost twenty years old.

Zoran gave her attention and played to her needs in a way she had never received before and she fell in love with him. Goran had been stuck between the two different parts of himself. He didn't mind being with the princess. He naturally loved being around ladies, but Zoran was deliberate.

After they had been caught together it was Zoran who had escaped the palace. Using all of his aggression and daring he had climbed out the window and leapt to safety. Deep inside, the Goran persona had his eyes closed.

When he was back in control he had found himself in a dingy bar on the outer northern edge of the city. That was when he had first tried the weed and felt the first relief from the constant other person in his head.

Over the following months, he had left Nedor and sought safety elsewhere and used the weed to shut Zoran out. When the Court had sought answers from him about what had happened and how he had let it happen, he had shrugged them off and given them unsatisfactory answers.

If they knew the truth of it they would have ordered him back to Anderwell, and who knows what would have happened.

He wouldn't let that happen. He was seeking someone that might be able to help him understand it. So far no one had been able to help him but he would keep looking.

Where would this girl be?

He thought about the current problem. He knew he needed to go look for her, but the grip of the weed was on him. He finished off another pipe and then went and lay on his bed to rest.

I'll get to finding the girl later. I'm tired after all those connections, I deserve a rest.

58

TILLANDRA

Speaking to Goran had given her a small piece of good news. She still couldn't believe she had let so much time pass before contacting him, but if the girl was where he was, then little harm would come of it.

Using the Citadel Stone to communicate was much easier than the usual method, and much more pleasant. She could hear it humming, meaning the Mother Stone was ready. She stood and went to check. The small stone was protruding from the Citadel Stone and Tillandra pulled it out, feeling heat surging through her.

She turned and held it out in front as she returned down the long tunnel back to Ting's guest house. When she arrived back she closed the door, letting it click back into the wall, invisible to the eye. Tillandra restored the room to how it had been before. Every time she came the walk back seemed to take only minutes, although she knew it was the same distance each way.

She packed the stone away in her bag and checked her feet, which felt surprisingly good. They had completely healed, something she had not experienced before when she had visited. After replacing her boots she walked down the small road to Tingfurlew's main building and let herself in.

His high pitched voice squeaked out from his main work table. "I thought you had gone home already."

As she approached his table the Ring Master stood expectantly on his stool, his mustache gleaming as if waxed. He was wearing a bright green robe that hung to his ankles.

"Funny, Ting. You know that it takes time to do what I have to do. How long was I there?"

"Two nights."

"Two? It always feels so much less."

"Well two it was and it was good for me, I had much to study."

"About the ring?"

"Yes. No. Not the ring. The other stuff."

"What other stuff?"

"Did she not tell you?"

"Who?" Tillandra was getting very confused. "I thought you were going to find out about the ring this woman is wearing."

"Yes, I did."

"But you just said you didn't."

"No, I did not. You asked me if I studied about the ring, which I did not. There's little to study. I studied about that other thing."

Tillandra shook her head. *"What other thing?"*

"Did you or did you not meet someone new?" He waved his hands behind his head as if indicating up the hill. "Up there."

"Oh. Yes. How do you know?"

"She told me."

"You saw her?"

"Yes."

Tillandra paced around the table, feeling confused about everything. She hadn't been entirely sure she hadn't just dreamt about the woman, until now.

"When do you see her?"

"Very rarely, but she came to me while you were there."

"What did she tell you?"

"She told me if you asked me about anything I knew then I should tell you what I know."

"Stop talking in riddles, Ting."

"It's not a riddle. I am not allowed to discuss it unless under these conditions. I couldn't say it even if I tried." He shrugged. "Believe me, I've tried."

Tillandra had to think back about what it had been called. "The Occultation. That's what she called it."

"Wasn't so hard, was it?"

"I'm not sure what you mean. What about the ring and this Occultation?"

"I think we should sit. I have a story to tell you."

As they turned to go to the soft seats, Tillandra noticed a new set of shelves built into one of the walls. It wasn't even as if they were new, it was like she was seeing them for the first time.

"When did you get them?"

"What?"

"Those books, that bookshelf."

"Oh, that. I've always had that. Now you can see it?"

"Yes." She walked over to it and ran her hand over the spines. The shelf was covered in dust and the names of the books were faded and hard to read.

"Now that it's been named to you, many things will become visible, which before you could not see."

Tillandra turned back to see him propped up on his cushions, a goblet in his hand. He patted the seat. "Here, come and sit."

She walked over and grabbed the other goblet as she sat.

"It is all part of the story and those books hold as much of it as I know."

Tingfurlew leapt down from the seat, hurried over to his table and pulled a book down from it before coming back to his seat. Once he was settled back up there he opened it.

"I need to go back over it all, it has been a long time. A long time since I last thought about it all. It has been going on for so long, I don't have much need to remember."

Tillandra just shook her head; after the appearance of the goddess, or whoever the woman was, and the confusing story Ting was trying to tell her, she was feeling as if she knew nothing.

"The Occultation happened straight after the Seven Realms battle."

"You're going to have to help me, Ting, I don't know what you're talking about. What seven realms?"

"Let me tell it, just sit. Drink."

"I forget, you are so young, none of this would you know. There was a time when only seven realms existed on Dharatan. The ten you know now, formed after the battle."

He flicked through the book until he found a drawing and turned it to her. It showed a massive field full of tents and people.

"That was the last Great Fair."

"Great Fair?"

"Yes. Every four years the leaders of the seven realms would meet to hold a Great Council. During that time they would discuss and resolve all of the issues that they had with each other. From what I have read it was put in place as a way to settle all disputes and avoid the many wars that had come before."

He had some more to drink before continuing.

"Over time, and as each ruler brought more and more entourage, they became not only a council meeting but the Great Fair. Trade, entertainment, and sport amongst the many things that happened between all who attended. It became an event for the ages."

"What happened?"

Tillandra noticed he wasn't reading from the book, he spoke as if it was something he knew.

"In that year, an invitation had been extended to the High Prince of Enderk. His name was Schevenal. In an effort to increase the relationship between Dharatan and Enderk the council had decided to see if he should become a member."

He twirled his mustache and was lost in his thoughts for a minute.

"Sorry. Schevenal accepted the offer and he came to the Council bringing with him seven gifts. In fact they were all the same, seven beautiful amulets, set with a large amber stone." Tingfurlew flicked back and forth through pages in the book until he found another drawing.

"Here, this." He stabbed the page with his thick little finger as he turned the book so she could see. "This is one that the High Prince wore. Word was they were one of the most beautiful pieces of jewelry anyone had seen."

"I am surprised that they invited a Derk."

He shrugged. "I don't think the people back then felt the same way about Derks. That came after."

"After the Fair?"

"After the battle. The books have only sketchy details of what happened next. Many people were killed. So many of the people that were there died and all of the leaders except for Schevenal."

"How? Did he bring an army?"

"No, he didn't kill them. I still cannot work out from the different books, what made everyone seem to go a little mad, but that's what it reads like. Each of the rulers turned on each other, their soldiers and aides, all of them, became enemies of each other, like a disease had spread through all of their minds."

He closed the book on his lap. "They all turned to fighting, and a battle, unlike any seen on Dharatan, before took place. The Derks fled when it first started and by all accounts made it back to Enderk, just before the land bridge was destroyed."

"Slow down. The land bridge?"

He raised his hand. "I'll get to that. The battle raged and everyone there was being slaughtered. Out of nowhere a massive storm blew from these very mountains, tearing over the land lifting everything in its path. When it reached the site of the Fair, somewhere between where Afon and Gogledd are today it engulfed everyone still alive."

Tingfurlew took a big breath, and put the book down on the small table and took up his goblet. He drank from it and chewed on a date.

He waved his hands in a big circle. "This mighty desert is what was left behind."

"Really?"

"Yes, there was already some desert here, but not like this. The storm destroyed the land, and Qum as you see it now was formed. Back then people said that the storm came back here and was left as a reminder of what the land will do if provoked again."

Tillandra found his story a little hard to comprehend. "This sounds like a bard's tale."

"Not all bards' tales are fiction, Mother. You, of all people, should know that."

"What happened to the rulers?"

"Disappeared. All seven gone, not a trace of them to be found. The survivors cleaned the site, it took weeks and then they all returned to where they had come from. Only a few scholars had survived and this book is one of but a few that survived, before the Occultation."

"That word again."

"The dream lady, the same one you saw, she told me they did it for everyone's safety."

"What?"

"They hid the memory. Of everything before that moment, it slowly disappeared from people's minds. These few books have been blocked so no normal folk can ever see them. You couldn't even see them when you came."

"How were they blocked?"

"If she's a goddess, like I think, then how would I know? She told me it's called the Occultation and it shielded the past from everyone. Think about what you know, about the past. How far back does the history of Dharatan go?"

Tillandra stood up and stretched herself out before walking around the room. "That's something I have been bothered about this last year. It's almost as if I have only just realized it for the first time. I have been trying to find what came before."

"Until now you would find very little. The Occultation blocked everyone, even you, from remembering and as the people who were alive back then died, their memories died with them. Now she has taken the block away from your mind, you will be able to find more about the history."

"I have found little pieces of information before, I even discovered a book, but it's badly damaged. It has taken a lot of work to even read a small part of it. None of it ever made sense to me but I was drawn to it."

"I think the veil, or whatever it is that blocks people from seeing, has broken. Or it weakens. Maybe this is why she has given you this understanding. Things are different, and I am not sure they are for the good. I can feel parts of that past reaching out to me."

"That past?"

"That was the time when I came here, Tillandra. Back then."

"What? How long ago was this?

He held his hands up, palms towards her. Then he beckoned her over. "Come sit back down. It's much to learn all at once, I know."

She did as he bid her.

"I forget it's been so long." He seemed to be trying to calculate it in his mind, his eyes flicking up and down, left and right. "Maybe eight hundred, eight hundred and five years."

"You jest."

"I do not."

"How can that be? Aren't you a Beng? I haven't ever known a Beng to live more than seventy or eighty years."

"This is true. Don't ask me how, Tillandra, I cannot answer. Ask the Dream Lady, maybe she knows."

"Who?"

"The Dream Lady. Who you just met. She's never told me her name, and I've never asked. She usually comes to me like a dream so that's what I call her. I think it relates to the deal I made."

"The deal? What deal?"

He chuckled. "Well that's another story."

TILLANDRA

"Maybe we should eat as we talk." Tingfurlew stood and went to the space that most resembled a kitchen.

While he was busy Tillandra thought about what he had just told her. She had always instinctively known that something wasn't right about the world's history, but whenever she'd tried to think about it, it slipped away. Knowing that magic was being applied to make that happen made sense to her.

Tingfurlew came back with a large platter which he placed on the table beside her. He climbed back up into his seat and smiled at her.

"Eat, Mother. You must be hungry."

"Not so much, Ting. When I am in here I only get thirsty, but thank you."

She watched him tear his bread apart and dip it in the different plates of spreads, chewing noisily. He ate with his mouth open as he continued to add and chew food in a nonstop motion.

When he had had enough he gulped down more wine and wiped his face on the back of his sleeve before he started his story.

"Where to start. You know now about the Great Fair, and the battle. I was but a boy when that happened. I think, maybe…" He twisted at his mustache as he thought about it. "Ten, ten and a half. I was this size already but young to look at. Us Bengs, we don't grow so big."

Tillandra smiled along with him.

"I hail from Wishter, on the far coast in Thabeng."

Tillandra knew where it was but had never been there.

"My father, he was a jeweler, and his before that a jeweler too. I was not his best pupil, I took much time, *always slow, Ting* he says, *always slow*. But every piece I made sparkled in some way special."

Tingfurlew's pace of speech was so fast he needed to pause and breathe.

"I never knew why, I just played my heart song, let my way flow. Everything I made I needed to see it first, in my mind. A picture, then I made it. Sometimes the picture took the longest. When I could see it then I could make it.

"My father was the jeweler to the King Chief, even though he lived in Wishter and not Motse. Every year he would be gone a long while back to Motse to deliver his goods for the King Chief. Each year he would come back with many monies and we lived well."

He had stopped for a moment, staring at the far wall.

"Wishter, on the sea it is, and I miss the breeze of the sea so. Not like this wind of grit."

"Have you not been back?"

"No. I cannot." Tillandra had started to ask another question but he held up his hand. "Let me tell."

"That year of the Great Fair he never came back from Motse. He sent word that the King Chief wanted him to travel to the Great Fair and show off his works. The King Chief wished to trade our Beng style of jewelry and boast of his master jeweler."

Tingfurlew paused again.

"My mother, she glowed, so proud of him. But he never returned."

"I'm so sorry, Ting."

He shrugged. "It is what it is. So long ago now, he would be dead many times over by now, fair or no fair. The King Chief and many of the Bengs who went with him never returned. Those that made it back were injured and scared. Little was ever said of it.

"Not long after this was when Thabeng split in two and Rohumaa was born."

"Thabeng split in two?"

"Yes there were but seven realms, like I said. After the battles many kin fought with their own or they no longer trusted each other. What was seven became ten. Now you only know of the ten realms, but Daskare and Kysten, they also split to make the ten."

"When they split into two, fear was everywhere and there was little need for a jeweler. Trade had stopped and soldiers were only to defend towns not protect merchants.

"I began to live like a beggar when the Dream Lady came the first time." He shook his head, looking back in his mind to his own memories.

"What of your mother?"

"She died from grief and starvation. There was nothing for us for such a long time." He covered his head with his hands for a few moments.

Tillandra topped up their goblets from the jug still on the table.

"That was the first time she came to me. It was such a dream. I told others but no one believed Ting, they thought my mind had gone with my loss. Her words so simple.

'You, Tingfurlew, have a lone and hard path to follow. Take your tools and cross the mighty desert that now lies between you and its mountains. You must go soon and follow the stars of the night sky. Only you will be able to see it, and each night stop when it goes out. Your new home is in a remote town called Midderbuilt on the mountains.'

"It was such a strange message, but her image was so clear and real, so un-dreamlike and her voice demanded I listen, as if I had no choice.

"I blindly ignored those around me and packed a small bag and left. I had no one left to live for. I started to walk and the lights in the sky were there. Every night I walked and every day I rested, I can only say that my trip was guided. I saw almost no one for months on end. The journey I made on foot was very slow. Every night when the stars went out I would find myself with food, drink and shade in the strangest of places."

"I thought little of what I was doing, the journey became my trance. I just followed the path every night, my mind ignoring almost everything else. I lost track of time and where I was, but I crossed the desert like I should never have been able to. Each day there was a cave or hollow to rest in, cool from the sun. This mighty desert," he spread his hands out towards the east, "was new and there was still a path through it. This was why she rushed me, I know. While there was still a way.

"I came here, back when it was young and smaller. More a town than the city it now is. There were only a few of the jewelers and less of the stones. Everyone was frightened of the mountain that had begun to spin from the great storm. They all talked of the great storm that built the desert and changed the mountains.

"This house was empty and I took it as my own. I was so young back then, so very young. It has been such a long time, I have lost count of the years. I have seen many Mothers and heard of rulers that have come and gone."

"I still don't understand this deal?"

"Oh, the message to come here wasn't the deal. She came back again to me, once I was here. Not at first, but once I had begun to settle."

He got up and walked over to the far wall. On a bookshelf he shuffled a few things around before grabbing a long wooden box and carried it with him back over to where she sat.

"I began to make jewelry when I settled here but I had only several tools with me. The walk was too long to carry much more. My work was good; good but slow. And there were other jewelers. I survived with what I made but that was about all. I wondered why I had come all this way."

He cradled the box in his lap, and took a moment to catch his breath.

"She came again in another dream. I hadn't expected her, and maybe it was because I had considered leaving.

'I have a new task for you, Tingfurlew. You followed my word last time and I will give you the reward for this but there is a contract to go with it. When you wake you will find new tools, these tools will make you even better

than you are today. Your work will be known everywhere and you will want for nothing. The price of these will be that you will be the one to crafts the fool's rings.'

"You must remember this was all in a dream, I never knew I could talk to her back then, I had to make sense of it.

'You must take my word on this, if you open the box, you will forever be the Ring Master. Until they exist no more – only you can make the rings. This will be a long burden to carry, Tingfurlew, think on it hard. We need you, they need you, but you must do it of your own will.'

"She told me about how I would make the rings using the sands from the mountain and a silver that only I can access. It was the strangest dream of them all and I woke immediately after it to find a box sat on my table. I spent a whole day staring at this."

He held up the box he had been cradling. When he opened the lid Tillandra could only see one item in it. The reverse stamp of the Jesters' mark, the outline that Ting used to create their rings.

"Is that all?"

He laughed. "No, Tillandra. The others I use every day. Amazing tools they are. Never do they wear. This is just the one part that is used only for your rings. She told me that there would be twelve once they were all made, and one spare."

"Spare?"

"You think I'm a magician?" He laughed. "If someone dies, their ring takes time to return. I cannot use it when it comes back, usually it is a silver coin. I must return it to the source. While I wait the spare is given and I fashion the new ring for the replacement."

"I thought you just made them as we needed them."

"No. There are rules I follow, I do not control them. I have been thinking on these rules trying to understand how this new girl can wear Ashantha's ring. It was so long ago when she told me, all the time you were in the mountain I went back over everything she told me.

'One ring for the line of one. Only their head can collect the ring, and it must be placed on the new fool within two moons, or it will pass. Once passed no ring can be replaced. Once all the rings have passed, Tingfurlew, your service will be done.'

"That last part I did not know.

"I have wondered when that might be, but after so many years I have had to accept that my service will be a long time. That's the deal I took, and whatever magic Dream Lady puts in the tools she puts in me as well. The only other part to the story was that I could never leave here. Midderbuilt is bound to me and me to it."

"Did she say what would happen if you left?"

"No, but I can't. I tried once, I cannot get past the gate." He laughed and stretched his hands above his head.

"What of this ring then? You agreed that she said a ring can only be worn by the one person. How can his ring have not returned and be worn by this other woman?"

"I didn't see it at first, but the more I repeated her words, the more it stood out."

"What?"

"One ring for the line of one, that's what she said. *The line of one!*"

"I don't understand."

"What if that means a family line?"

The sudden realization of the meaning startled Tillandra. "Surely not?" She stood up and walked back and forth, trying to understand what this meant.

"He didn't have any family."

"Can you be sure?" Tingfurlew asked.

Tillandra shook her head. "No, I can't."

Tingfurlew just shrugged his shoulders at her.

"It would make sense as why he might have given her his things, if she was someone close to him. I am sure he would have told me."

"When I saw Dream Lady before I tried to ask her more. She was not sure. She said to me, *'She is quite unusual. She was unexpected'.*"

"She said something similar to me!"

"When I tried to ask her what that meant, she didn't answer and left. I can't tell you the answer you want to hear. At best guess, this woman is related to Ashantha."

Tillandra stopped her pacing and looked at Tingfurlew for a long time, occasionally shaking her head.

"Ashantha had a daughter? I can't believe it."

TILLANDRA

"I have questions, Ting." Tillandra was standing at his table.

"Me too."

"I am not sure there are answers for them all."

"Answers not my specialty, rings I can do," he replied with a cheeky smile on his face.

"So there is a new ring for me to take back?"

Tingfurlew started shaking his head. "No! I went to check while you were in the mountain, but the spare has not been provided."

"What do you mean?"

"Like I told you earlier, when a ring returns I give it back and it's given back to me when the time is right."

"How do you know?"

"I don't. But when you turn up, and tell me someone has died, then I know."

"Oh." Tillandra rubbed the temples on her head. "And there's nothing there?"

"No, and I can only guess as to why."

Tillandra came back over to sit beside him.

"If this young woman is wearing Ashantha's ring, then to the rules, the ring is still alive. So there would be no new one to be made, twelve are still in play."

"But she's not one of us. I don't understand how a novice could take up a ring, without the Audition, or mask?"

"These things are more than I can know, Tillandra. All I can do is make the rings."

"I wish she had told me about this girl. If I get this wrong the Balance will be thrown out. I can ill afford to lose one of my team and not be able to replace them."

"I know the rules, but not how they apply. Maybe you will hear from her again?"

"I wish I knew. I came here to replace a ring and start the process for an Audition. Instead of answers and solutions, I've picked up multiple new problems, not the least, that we've been living a lie."

"Not a lie, Tillandra, just not seeing all the past. Life has been peaceful, has it not?"

She nodded. "It has, that I will agree, although I feel those days might be behind us. Several rulers have been getting restless and extending their reach, one I discovered while coming here. King Ahn is trying to grab parts of Sahro. If my hands weren't already full, they're about to get even fuller."

Tingfurlew looked intensely at her for a few minutes. "Take advice from an old jeweler?"

She laughed. "Of course."

"I can only make as much as my tools and resources allow. Tis the same for you. You are twelve, not just one. These tools of yours are to be used, each must be here to help, or they would not be provided. That is how I look at what I was given. Don't forget, your resources are limited, but all of you together have much more." He brought his hands up beneath his chin and pressed them together, touching the tips to his chin, and nodded to her.

"Wise words, Ting. Thank you."

The loud banging of the knocker on his door boomed through the room.

Almost as if on cue Tingfurlew leapt to his feet, and his high-pitched voice yelled out, "Go away, I don't do tourist shows. *Go away!*"

He headed to the door nonetheless, and opened it.

"Fepret, I have a guest. What do you want?"

"A message, Tingfurlew, for your guest. Her guides down below have sent word, they must leave by middle day. She has two hours to join them or they will have to leave her to her own ways."

Tillandra made her way to the door.

Tingfurlew turned to her. "It seems your time is done with me, Tillandra?"

"I think so, much as my feet are healed, I would preserve my strength for the long leg home from Watersend." She looked at Fepret. "Tell them I will be there, and thank you for bringing me the news."

He bowed and left. Tingfurlew closed the door.

"Come, let's fill you with food, and finish what we were discussing."

"I am not sure there's much more to say, Ting, without the ring, I will need to find this girl. If she passes, or the ring leaves her, I am not sure if I would be able to get back again in time."

"Let's hope if that happens, the clock starts again. This I don't know, never before have we had such a thing."

"Let's hope. Thank you for what you have told me, and your hospitality. I wasn't aware of the burden you've carried for so long. It is obviously important, or we wouldn't be doing this. I only wish I could make more sense of it all."

She readied her bag and was preparing to leave when he brought her a box.

"This was the other thing she told me, I almost forgot. Silly Ting. She told me you would need this, soon. That you would know why, when the time came."

Tillandra took it from him, and opened it after struggling with the silver clasp. "It's just a box?"

"This is what I was told to give you, it has been here for so long I forgot I had it."

"Where did it come from? Did you make it?"

"I do not know, and no. I just know it's been there on my shelf since the first day. It was already here. I've never had a reason to use it, and

I've never been able to open it. So now I know it was meant for you, you can open it."

"More mysteries. Thank you, I think." She forced it into her bag and kneeled down to hug him. As he always did he leapt onto her and hugged her as if he would never see her again.

"Be well, Mother. I hope to not see you for another year."

She chuckled. "And you, Ring Master. I hope so as well."

With nothing more to say he turned and went to his table and began to work on a new piece. Tillandra looked at him fondly, soaking up the feeling his house had, grateful for the things she had discovered here, despite them not answering all the questions she had.

The walk down to Travelers Rest was much easier than her walk up, and she met her guides with plenty of time to spare. They were glad to see her earlier than their deadline and with little discussion they all left on their way back to Watersend.

Once she had settled back into the rolling gait of the camels, Tillandra started to let what had happened float across her mind. There were many things to sort through. The idea Ashantha had a daughter was the one she had the most trouble with. She had always believed they were close friends, having shared much of their lives working together. For him to have kept such a secret was hard for her to accept.

If it was true then she would have to accept that things weren't completely as they seemed. If she didn't truly know him, then what else might he have hidden from her? Was that why he never contacted them?

Could she really believe he would come across his one child by chance on his return, just before he was killed? Her biggest worry was why he'd kept his return a secret. There were too many threads to this that she struggled to understand.

Oh, Thenis, if she is his, then I have to tell Goran. He must protect her and be sure to bring her to us. She would know much more than I realized.

There was no place to reach out to him, the earliest she could do that would be in Watersend. On the trip up to Midderbuilt the team had only stopped for an hour or so, never long enough to sneak off and enter the void to talk to someone. It wasn't something she could risk others knowing about anyway, she'd have to hope no harm came to the girl before she reached Watersend.

GORAN

He lay on his bed for several hours, lost in the comfort of the zongle weed. The voice was blocked and the concerns everyone had laid on him sat in the background. His conscience fought against the drug-induced complacency until it had enough leverage on him to get him to move.

Finding this girl mattered, he knew that, it was just it mattered a little less than keeping the voice at bay. He didn't want to hear it or live with it, and the weed was the only way he knew how to hold it back.

He would get a day or two's respite now, which would help. Slowly he pushed himself upright and started to think more clearly about his options.

Since his demise as the King's fool, Goran had left them at a disadvantage as to insider information about the King's court. Whenever there was a lack of insight to what Nordahl was up to, Mother Folly would give him a piercing stare or sarcastic remark to remind him of the cost to their network his mischief had caused.

While much of the work when he was here full-time was to monitor what happened with the King, Goran had developed a useful network of contacts throughout the city. The few times he had come back through Nedor he had avoided those contacts. While he trusted most of them he couldn't be sure who might fancy a reward for turning him in.

That would have to change now, he was going to need help if he was to find this woman and get Ash's things back. There were insiders he could ask first and he sought out the market square where one of their own network would be performing. When he arrived, a crowd was beginning to disperse and he could make out the performers on the far side of the square. He followed them discreetly to an alehouse close by, where they would spend a few hours mingling with locals, before slipping away and back to the Bard's Bell where they were staying.

The use of the traveling entertainers as communicators was very important to the circuit. Only the Jesters, the upper court, could communicate over distance, and not all liked the method that was needed. Taking the life of the rats shouldn't bother anyone, Goran mused.

They're filthy disease-ridden pests. We do everyone a service when we do it.

None of them knew why you got sick from it, whether it was the reaction to taking on their life force, or if you absorbed something bad from them, but whoever made the connection was almost always ill straight after.

It wasn't something any of them used every day, and much of the information that needed to reach the working circuit was delivered by traveling entertainers. It was a clever system in of itself and allowed the court to monitor events around Dharatan without anyone the wiser.

These two were regulars in the northern quadrant and would work their way up the Nedor road all the way to Saudur in the north, then back down the great eastern coast road through Ngahere. If they were back in Nedor then they would have come from Callet and would have swapped news with those from the south.

Not everything needed to get back to Anderwell in a hurry, but anything important was shared by couriers on more direct routes.

Having eyes across the different realms allowed the court to manipulate things and to help keep the peace. Timely influence at the right time had avoided numerous wars between rulers.

The alehouse wasn't big and was crowded, packed mostly with men who had been working in the square and were now refreshing themselves. The tables were full as was most of the standing room as well. A couple of stern looking women were working the floor, running fresh ale to the tables and trying to deliver food as well. Those standing were expected to get their own drinks from across the bar where the Keeper was serving and keeping an eye on things.

Goran could easily see Portna the tall clown, who stood an easy head or so above anyone else in the room. He was in the far corner of the room standing over a small table which had only two occupants. Goran made eye contact, a slight nod toward Portna and worked his way toward the table. He didn't want to wait until late evening to make contact with them and this was as good a place as any.

Sitting at the spare seat at the table without asking, he smiled a greeting at Labut the dwarven partner to Portna. Labut, slightly surprised, grinned back.

"Be forken right, Lordy turns up for his cut," Labut said.

"Fine to see you too, young Labut, I see your humor is as perky as usual," Goran smirked.

"'No doubt some ale you want too?" Turning to one of the serving women who was clearing the table behind them, he said, "three more ales please, lass."

Portna pulled the chair back a bit from the table so he could sit, his knees still above the edge of the table even when he sat.

Goran chuckled. "You Humaas always make me laugh sitting at human tables."

"My job is but to make you laugh, a clown, am I not?" he replied.

"Indeed you are. In All Jest!"

The two men leaned in and quietly responded, "In All Jest."

Goran looked cautiously about the room, especially at those closest to them. No one stood out as paying any more attention to them than normal. No more than anyone who found the Humaas different and stole themselves a longer look. Portna was tall even for a typical

Humaas, and his face was as horse-like as any Humaas Goran had ever seen. No doubt this alehouse was as safe as it had always been to talk business.

"What news are you bringing north?" Goran asked.

"Things have been quiet up until now, Goran. We came here by way of Callet about two days ago."

The ales arrived much to Goran's relief, he could at least sip his ale while listening to Portna finish his news.

"Not much to tell. There's good rumors, not verified, that the Queen might be carrying a baby." Portna took his own drink and sipped some to quench his thirst.

"That should be easy to verify. Did you come through Manawa on your way around?"

"Filthy place that," Labut spoke, "Pests and sweat is all that muddy city has to offer."

Portna continued, "Yes we have been on the long journey. We wintered some in Laumua until it was time to move on. Queen Vika is much stronger than even time last we were there."

Goran shrugged at the news, it being of no consequence on its own. The Queen was a powerful woman who had impressed most who met her, few would question her within Ngahere. "What of your next step?"

"We are back here at the start of the route. Waiting on word to confirm we are to go back to Anderwell for a break from the traveling. Being on the road through winter is hard."

"Nice change, say I," Labut threw in.

"I might have bad news then."

The two entertainers put their ales back on the table and looked at him their faces frowning at his comment.

"What news is that then?"

"We're on yellow alert level."

Goran leaned in to them. "There are Derks that have attacked some people in Malamig. It seems to be something coordinated, but we're blind to why. We need ears and eyes alert and everywhere. Any Derks are to be reported in."

"What is it you want from us then?"

"While I wasn't told specifically to keep you out on the road, someone needs to share what we know around the circuit. I need an experienced team to do that."

"You want us to do the route again?"

"I am not sure I have many other options."

Goran watched the two of them exchange looks, words probably not necessary between them, having been on the road together for the better part of eight years.

Labut spoke up. "If it's to be done then best we do it. Not sure you've told us all we need but I can see the worry you carry about it. We'll do it."

"We need word of anything untoward, even small things that are unusual."

"Such as?"

"That is hard to know. Look for things out of place, scratch any itches your instincts give you looking for oddities. Especially as you come back through Ngahere and RaMar. Any of the ports or landing spots that might suit the Derks. You'll need to get that word on a messenger."

The two acknowledged his requests.

"I have one more request of you."

Labut rolled his eyes. "More ale, no doubt. We'll have nothing to give back to the Keeper at this rate."

Goran chuckled. "No. I need to find a woman in Nedor."

Portna spoke up, "I thought you would have learned your lesson?"

Goran frowned at him. "Nothing like that, Portna. She's a traveler who would have just arrived in Nedor, from up north. I have no idea how to locate her, any suggestions?"

"Pincer?" Labut asked. "Wouldn't he be the best to find someone?"

Goran nodded. "That was one of the people I thought of. I'm trying to not alert too many people to me being here, the new look has mostly kept me unrecognized."

"Fair. I'd say he's your best bet. If it's urgent, that is. If not, well maybe you could buy some knowledge on the street, but that is less reliable. Should we be looking for her?"

"You'll need to be on the road tomorrow, but thanks. I'll solve it."

He stood up to go.

"Stay safe."

"And you," the two replied.

Goran slid his way through the crowd, around the side of the bar down a small corridor to the back of the kitchen area, and out through the open door into a dark courtyard. No one was about but he still sidled along the outside of the building until he could squeeze through the back fence into a laneway that ran behind the alehouse.

GORAN

*M*aking his way down a dark lane, he was glad to leave the noise of the inn behind. His next stop would hopefully be more fruitful; while their network knew many things, much of it was at the surface level. When you wanted to dig deep there were those who could find what you needed.

Goran had sent word that he would be visiting through one of the pickpockets lurking in the square, when he passed through earlier.

There was minimal moonlight to help him see him in the dark narrow lanes he traveled, switching behind workhouses and other industrial buildings. The cloudy sky didn't help and many would feel unsafe in such places; not so Goran.

If you knew your way through the maze you were fine to use them as long as you could tolerate the stench of refuse and waste piled up on the side. Workers left it there by day, and at some time in the night, shifters came with their carts to take it away. The lanes were wide enough for the rubbish and a cart and not much else.

He noted his destination a short distance ahead, the gateway easily noticeable by the two large men standing guard in front of it. Those without invitation or right of passage would be foolish to head any closer. Given he looked different to the last time he had been here, he used a little more caution as he approached.

Neither guard moved as he approached, their large frames blocking the entry. The one on the left called out, "Easy, stranger, you've no place being here, head away now."

"I have a meeting with your boss, Hussad. You might not recognize me as I am."

The guard peered at him through the dim light. "It can't be. I see the limp and I hear your voice, but you do not look like the unpopular fool I knew."

They made Goran approach so they could see him better. He could see the scar running from Hussad's left eye across his nose and down his right cheek. If his size wasn't enough, the scar made him look even more menacing.

"It is I. My falling from popularity was long enough ago, everyone should have forgotten it by now," Goran replied.

"I'm pretty sure the King hasn't forgotten. I'm not sure this look would attract all the ladies, but perhaps that's a good thing for you," Hussad joked back as he stepped aside. "You're expected, second level down. You'll be met."

"Many thanks. May your night be quiet and profitable." He nodded his head as he went through.

Goran walked across the courtyard leading to the warehouse sided to the city wall. Despite being high above the river the sound of it rushing over the rocks below could be heard even with the solid wall. He knew the warehouse led down several levels to where the men inside had their own access out to the waterway.

He went through a plain wooden door where several men were waiting sitting at a table playing dice. Behind them a partial wall blocked most of the view of the warehouse. With the nod of a head they pointed to the stairway on his right. The stairs went down several floors. At each landing he passed more guards.

If you didn't know better you would think they were very casual and relaxed but he knew it was only because he was expected. He reached the second level and was led into a large room, where many men were working rolling barrels and carrying other cargo.

At a table to the side sat the man he had come to see, surrounded by several pretty young women.

The head of the thieves' guild in Nedor walked his way. Pincer was of average height, and lean. His arms were disproportionate to the rest of his body, large muscles rippled from his shoulders down to his hands. They were the source of his name, it was said his grip was impossible to break.

Local legend said he had snapped swords in his bare hands in an attempted arrest many years back, laughing at the King's guards and beating them unconscious. He had avoided capture numerous times since, and there were multiple compounds around the city that he moved to. The underclass in the city spread word to his men if anything was brewing, Pincer had always shared the spoils of his work with those who had no income, or struggled to survive.

He sponsored a number of places where the poor could eat and get shelter when in trouble. Whether it was the loot from the nobles that his men robbed or the goods he shipped into the city out of sight, there was plenty to go around. Pincer had learned what King Nordahl had not, that looking after the weak brought more loyalty than force.

His deep voice echoed through the room. "Goran, our lost fool, how good to see you, although you look a lot different than I remember."

Walking to him, Goran held out his hand, but Pincer grabbed him and wrapped his arms around him in an affectionate hug.

Crushed for breath he forced out, "It's good to see you, Pincer, too."

"Come sit with us and enjoy some wine. I have some of the finest wines from Daskare here."

Goran pulled up a seat close to Pincer and took a brass goblet of wine a young woman offered him. Pincer flicked his head at the women and they all got up and moved away, taking their drinks.

"This is a soft drop indeed," Goran offered, raising his glass.

Pincer leaned over and touched goblets, "Soft it is. Soft as the touch of a woman's naked breast caressing your tongue. Hmmmm."

He laughed a deep hearty laugh.

"Now I know you didn't come down into the bowels of our great city to talk breasts, you want a favor of me, Mr Goran, I assume?"

"I did and I would be extremely thankful for any help you can give."

"Well you know how I like to help, it can be a very profitable business."

Goran couldn't helped but smirk; he had known there would be a price. Now he would find out what the cost was. "As always, and how profitable would this bit of help be for you?"

"Now that depends on what it is you need to know."

"I seek someone from out of town, that is in Nedor. I don't have much time to find her."

Pincher's deep laugh rolled around Goran. "Always a woman with you, good friend. That's the thing we have in common."

Goran shook his head. "Not for me. She has information I need."

"You know I always like to help another friend. An urgent request like this will cost a lot." His face beamed with a wide grin.

This was the part Goran was dreading, what it would cost him. If it was money that would be easy, but Pincer had enough money. It meant he would want something he couldn't do himself.

"You need someone found and I need to get back something lost."

There it was, Goran immediately knew what Pincer was going to ask him.

"The dagger, Goran. My lovely dagger, that the King's men recovered the last time they tried to capture me. I do believe it's in the palace, the one place I have never been able to get into."

The attempt to capture him had been costly to Pincer, he had been cornered with a small group of his men, and the King's soldiers had lain in wait for them. They had surrounded him with crossbowmen up on roofs and started firing without warning. He lost all but one of his men, and had taken a bolt through his left arm, causing him to drop the dagger. It was only his strength that allowed him and the other survivor to break through a barred door, and find an escape. Goran knew deep down he seethed about it, although on the surface he never showed any anger.

"You know as well as I do that it is there, Pincer. I told you it was."

"That's the price of this favor, Goran."

"It seems a little steep compared to finding out where a young woman is hid up in the city."

"Value is all relative, my friend, and I wouldn't want to undersell the value I have. If of course you don't wish to find your woman so quickly then that's okay. Although I think this price is likely to be the one for any favors I need for the foreseeable future."

Goran knew this would come when he first revealed to Pincer the location of the dagger. He didn't know what it meant to Pincer, but it was a source of anger in him that the king had it. Worse that he displayed it as a showpiece.

"That task is not something I can accomplish in a short space of time, as you know. You'd have to trust my word that I'll take care of it when the time is opportune."

Pincer's face lit up with a wide smile. "I knew you could see reason. Yes, I know you are good to your word but we need to not let this go on forever. One year, you need to do this for me within the year, then we can call this deal resolved."

He held out his hand to shake on the deal. Goran hated shaking hands with the man at the best of times, and this was not a fair deal. He looked Pincer in the eyes, and disliked the grin on his face, but shook it anyway. He had little choice if he was to find this girl quickly.

"I love a good deal. Let's drink a toast. *To a dagger of a deal!*" This time the laugh grated on Goran. He raised his goblet and drank.

Sensing his concerns, Pincer leaned closer. "Worry not, good friend! I know you will find a way to deliver what I want. You of all people know that place better than anyone. And I will find who you are looking for. Now tell me who she is."

They spoke for a little longer until there was nothing left to tell him.

"Where will I get a message to you?"

"The Bard's Bell."

"Ah, yes, that inn. Something about that place intrigues me, I never can seem to learn much about it."

"Nothing much to learn," Goran carefully replied. "It's quiet, that's why I like it."

Pincer looked at him for a moment longer than Goran thought he needed to. "We're done then?"

Goran nodded and excused himself. One of Pincer's crew guided him out through another exit. No one came and went into the guild headquarters the same way, and the back ways were always hidden. Goran was blindfolded once he left the room and led to another location in the city. When he took off his blindfold the two young lads with him wandered off up the street, not giving an inkling of where they had come from.

63

GORAN

It had been very late by the time Goran had got back to his room in the inn. He slept until morning and waited impatiently in the main room, hoping word might come from Pincer soon. Sitting around inside wasn't going to help him find the girl but if he missed a message it could delay him even longer.

Before he had to make the choice, a messenger delivered news that a young woman fitting the description he had given might be staying at Merta's lodging house. He'd sent his thanks back to Pincer that the deal was good if it was the right target, or else they'd need to keep looking.

He had met and crossed paths with Merta a few times, when he had been in the King's retinue, as she often hosted foreign guests who arrived unannounced looking to gain access to the King. The safety and discretion of her accommodation was well known, which would make it harder to confirm whether the girl he sought was there. How to pry that information from Merta was the question he had no answer for right now. His days of royal leverage were long since departed.

There was no subtle way to make his approach, but the yard at the back of her building was a better approach than the front door. Men were generally not welcome in the lodge and there was a guard always out front.

As luck would have it there was no guard out the back and he found Merta coming out of her laundry hut carrying a basket, as he squeezed through the opening in the gates.

"Hey, get out of here, those gates are locked for a reason."

"I'm sorry for the intrusion, Lady Merta,"

"Don't be calling me Lady anything, I'll call the guard if you don't go." She placed the basket on one hip, keeping it between her and him.

Goran bowed in mock humility, sweeping his hand before her. "But, Merta, you are a lady and one of great renown in our fair city"

He could see a flicker of recognition in her eyes.

"Surely not? How well you hide who you are, except to those who know better. If I not be fooled it is you, is it not, Goran?"

"One can only fool those who allow themselves to be fooled," he replied.

"What are you doing in Nedor? Word is your head has been fitted for a lovely wall mount in the King's Palace."

Goran self-consciously rolled his shoulders, as if he was checking there was nothing separating his head from them. "Well the King doesn't seem to smile so much at my jokes, that's true. I don't think I'll be paying him a surprise visit. As to why I am back, I miss my old city. Here, let me help you hang that and allow me a question of you, if I may?"

Merta looked at him furtively from the corner of her eyes, but handed him the basket none-the-less. "Over there," she said, pointing to the back of the lot," That line there is where they go. I doubt I know anything likely to be of interest to you, but there is no crime in asking. Unless you're asking the King's daughter to a quiet room that is!" At her joke she burst out in hearty laughter.

"Will no one let me forget?"

"Why should we forget, it is still the best story going around the ale houses. I hear several bards have a fantastic ditty about the fallen Jester."

Goran rolled his eyes at hearing that. Following Merta's example, he shook out the laundry before pegging it to the line with the wooden pegs hanging in a bag. He waited until he had hung several items up before he spoke again.

"What I need to know is very important so I won't try to dance around the topic."

Merta flapped a larger sheet of cloth in the air and continued to peg it up amongst the other laundry.

"A young woman arrived in Nedor just a few days ago, a lone traveler who has come into possession of some things she would be best not keeping. Word about town is that she has been staying here."

Merta stopped what she was doing and turned to look hard at him. "And these things would be better off in your hands then, I assume."

"Not exactly." He thought carefully about how to word his reply. "The family to whom they belong, would like these things returned. They hold strong sentimental value."

Merta hadn't moved, her hands firmly on her hips, her gaze directly on him. "Is that what you are now, a messenger for people who've lost things?"

"One has to make a living, Merta. These people reached out to me to help them, that's all that I am trying to do."

"And be rewarded, no doubt?"

"Well, of course I would like a reward from the family, if it's earned."

"It doesn't sound worthy of your talents, Goran. Such a shame to be reduced to this, the man who could hold an entire court in the palm of his hand."

He shrugged.

"So, if I believed you, and if, I say if, such a woman was staying in my lodge, what exactly is it you are asking me to do?" she asked him.

"I just want to meet her and find a solution to the problem. I've been given ample compensation for the items, so she wouldn't be out of pocket."

Merta had returned to finishing off the last items on the line. She said nothing else and finished loading it all, looking up at the morning sky, a mostly blue backdrop with small patches of fluffy white clouds gathered in small groups. As if satisfied no foul weather would come and ruin her laundry, she gathered the basket and turned back to him.

She stopped in front of him, the woven flax basket between them, and with her dark brooding eyes looked right at him.

"I'm not sure whether you're telling me the truth or not, Goran. The one who could act himself out of the executioner's axe could simply be spinning me a great tale. What I do know is that I keep my guests' privacy. Who is here and who is not here is not something I will share with you, nor anyone else."

Goran feared this would be her response. "But all I am asking for is a chance to meet such a woman. What harm can come of me being introduced to her?"

"It's not my job to match people up with my guests unless they ask for it, and I haven't said such a person is staying here. I think you've been given some bad information."

"Oh I trust the source, they specialize in knowing these things. If I can't convince you otherwise, I understand. Don't blame me for trying."

"Well you've asked more than one question and now you're delaying me. My patience has worn thin, Goran. It's time for you to move on, I have work to do."

Goran couldn't hide his disappointment, but knew better than to push her too far. "It's been my pleasure to be in your company, Merta. I shall leave you be." He did his dramatic bend and sweep of his arms, before turning and leaving via the back gate.

He always felt he could read people well and unless his senses had failed him, Merta knew who he was talking about. Pincer's information was correct, now he had to determine how to get to her before she slipped out of his grasp.

He loitered in the back lane and looked up at the back of the building. There were only two ways in and out of the building and if Merta warned the girl then she might make a move. He could only watch here or the front, not both. If he left to go and get help he could miss her completely.

Hedging his bets he went back towards the next crossroad, where he could see the back of Merta's building and also people walking along the main road. He had to hope if she left via the front she would pass that way, and perhaps he might notice her. He had little to go on, and doubted he would be able to see the ring at a distance.

He could do with some luck right now, or another set of hands. He slunk back into the spot he had found out of sight, and settled in for a long day.

64

LANI

Despite the guards outside the lodge, and her room being on the top floor, Lani had still moved the table to block her door before she went to sleep. The last few days had unsettled her and she was feeling exhausted from the stress.

She slept the best night in a long while and her mood was better when she woke. Her focus for the new day had to be arranging a ride, and the only hope she had so far was Hordan and his strange wife. If he was leaving soon that was a good option but she wasn't sure she'd trust a sole man on a trip all by herself.

For now, she didn't have to make that decision, until she knew whether he could offer her a ride. There were a few other agents to try and the hope that one of them might be able to get her to Nkuku was enough to get her moving early.

When she arrived back near Hordan's yard, she stopped at the sight of a number of soldiers. Lani could hear a lot of shouting coming from inside the yard, most of it sounding like the woman she had spoken to yesterday.

She moved to the side of the road, beside some people who were also trying to see what was happening.

"Leave him alone, he's done nothing wrong. *Leave him!*" the voice screamed.

A deep voice cut through her shrieking, *"Enough!* Stop your shouting or you'll be coming with him. We're taking him to the cells and he'll face a judge on the morrow."

The woman burst into sobs, and Lani watched two soldiers march a scruffy looking man out of the yard, holding an arm each. The man had dried blood down the front of his tunic, and his face showed the wounds of a fight. The rest of the soldiers formed up around him and the group marched back up the road.

Hordan's wife, whom Lani had met yesterday, followed them out of the yard, quickly pulling the gate closed and chaining it up, tears still running down her face. Then she took off after her husband. "Hordan, my Hordan, what have you done?" She wailed as she followed the soldiers.

The onlookers broke up and went back about their business. Lani walked up to the yard and looked through the gap between the wall and the gate. The horses were still in there, but they were no use to her without Hordan.

Frustrated, she turned and walked back up the road, checking all of the other agents for a possible ride. The last one she came to was a large warehouse with a yard twice as big as the building. As she approached she was nearly run over by a wagon hurrying out the gate. Two others followed it, and by the time they had gone she was covered in dust.

She brushed off what she could and spat dust out of her mouth, before walking into the office at the front of the warehouse.

"You picked a bad moment to walk by, miss." A man only half as old as her again was standing in the foyer."

Lani brushed her mouth but there was still dust in it. "Yes."

"How can I help you?"

"You work here?"

"I do. My father owns the business, I manage the bookings. You're looking for someone or something?"

"Well, yes... I am trying to get a ride to Nkuku."

"Ah. We're shippers, not carriers, sorry. We move goods by wagon, you need to try some of the carriers for a carriage."

"They're all a bit more than I can afford. I'd take a horse but the man that had some was just arrested."

"Hordan, yes? I saw them walking him away earlier. Not the first time he's been in trouble, no doubt it won't be the last. "

"Do any of your wagons take a passenger? I'm no trouble, and I can pay, just not what the carriages want."

"Very few will take a passenger, most don't want to have to care for anyone. The others will make you work for it, that way you take care of yourself."

Lani's eyes lit up. "That would be fine by me. I'm not afraid to pitch in. I just need to go south to Nkuku, and I'm stuck on what to do."

The man smiled at her. "Okay, let me have a look, I'll see what's on the list." He walked to a high bench against the wall, and looked over the papers there.

"There is a wagon master heading off in three days, he's a safe one to go with, he's my uncle and I could have a word with him to see if he'd mind."

"Would you?"

"I can't guarantee it, but it's the only option I can see for now. He doesn't mess around though, he pushes the horses hard, sleeps rough and gets where he needs to fast."

"Like I said, I just need to get there."

"I will see him later today, come back just before sundown and I'll have an answer for you. What's your name?"

"Lani."

"Pleased to meet you, Lani. I'm Barrick, I'll try my best but don't count your coppers yet. It'll depend on what mood he's in whether he agrees or not."

"Thank you. I'll come back later."

She left and walked back towards Merta's. It wasn't what she had wanted, to have to pay for another two nights or more. She needed to check her coins and count out what she had left.

When Lani walked back in through the front door she saw Merta standing behind the counter.

"There you are, Lani."

"You wanted me?"

"I do, but let's go upstairs, where it's more private."

That comment concerned Lani and she became very alert as they climbed the stairs. Merta let her lead the way into her room, and shut the door behind them when they went in.

"What's the problem?"

"I'm not one to judge, be noted, but someone I know was around earlier looking for someone a lot like you."

"Who?"

"A man who carries a little mystery with him. He used to be the King's Jester until a year or so ago. He had an unhealthy relationship with the King's daughter and had to escape before the King locked him up."

"How do you know he was looking for me?"

"I don't for sure, but the description he had, albeit a little vague, best suited you. Now don't worry, I didn't tell him anything. I denied anyone like that was here."

"Thank you."

"It wasn't personal, dear. I don't share anything about my guests. People come here for their privacy, if they heard I couldn't be trusted, these rooms would all be empty."

Merta moved over to the window and looked out across the back lane before turning back to Lani.

"Like I said, not for me to judge, but he said this person was holding some things that didn't belong to them, and the family that they belonged to wanted them back."

Lani hoped she hadn't changed her facial expressions when Merta said that, and continued to play ignorant to what she was saying. "I don't understand?"

"I don't care so much for the man, but I do care that he doesn't cause any trouble here for my guests. I hope you won't be the cause of bringing undue attention here, especially that from the city guard?"

Lani shook her head. "I've done nothing wrong."

Merta looked at her, and Lani could see her trying to establish if she was telling the truth.

"Not for me to say, girl. You did show up here in a strange way, that's for sure. What I will tell you is he won't have taken my word for it. He'll be out there somewhere keeping an eye on who comes and goes. If you are of interest to him, you best be very wary about how you come and go."

"Thank you for the warning."

"One other warning. If trouble does arrive here looking for you, then you'll be out before you know it. Understood?"

"Understood."

"And if there's a chance it might come then you'd be best moving on before it comes. Right?"

Lani nodded and looked away from Merta, who turned and left the room.

The room seemed very small all of a sudden, and Lani went and barred the door before sitting on the edge of the bed.

She had no idea what was happening. A Jester looking for her rang warning bells in her head. She pulled off her gloves and looked at the face on the ring she had taken from Ashantha. What had he said? Trust no one but Bossu.

Was this man one of his kind? The chance was high, but Ashantha told her not to trust anyone. To that point she wasn't sure she should be trusting Merta either. What reason did she have to protect her? For all Lani knew the man night be waiting for her next time she left.

Merta was concerned about keeping her other guests safe, just not Lani. One thing she had to remind herself was she was alone, and trusting strangers like her could only lead to trouble. She needed to smarten up and look after herself. If it profited Merta to turn her over to someone, she would.

Lani retrieved the satchel from under the bed, and took out the coin pouch. There were still four silvers which was a little more than she thought were in there. Her cautiousness was paying off. She could afford a couple more days here if she needed, but now she wasn't so sure about Merta.

Three days was a long time to wait, and more than enough time for Merta to change her mind. It would probably be best if she moved to another inn, and kept her head down until then. If she timed it right she could do that today when she went back to check on the wagon ride.

65

KYRO

*S*everal days into searching Little Big Rock and Kyro was no closer to finding any scent of Lani. He had sources here but they offered no news at all. It was possible she had not come through here or if she had, only fleetingly and not enough to be seen.

Caught between the decade-old commands he was compelled to follow and his wish to make her safe, he was running out of time. His anger at himself had spilled over several times, taking it out on the people he sought help from. That no one had seen her wasn't their fault, but not looking after her and ensuring her safety was his.

Despite trying to focus on what he could do, a constant thought kept burning in his head. *What good as a leader am I if I can't follow my own code yet expect others to follow it?*

He had run out of time now, and needed to be on the road to Nedor. He needed to at least fulfil this part of the task he had been set, and deliver news to the Prince. While it was more than ten years ago that he had been given the instruction, he doubted the importance would have diminished. There was something he didn't know about what had happened back then, and where Lani fit into it.

He and his horse had been housed at the barracks in town and last night he had spent the evening with the head of the guards there, Qwipen. They had always enjoyed each other's company and unfortunately the wine he had shared was some of the best he had tried. Kyro's only regret now was that he had stayed as late as he had drinking it.

Today's ride would be much less enjoyable for his dry mouth and stinging eyes.

His rested horse made good time throughout the morning, as getting away from town early meant a mainly empty roadway ahead.

As it neared middle day he came over a small knoll and then down to some flatter road where he saw a cart off to the side. As he closed on it he could see there only appeared to be a single lady standing beside it.

Naturally cautious, he slowed as he approached but went on alert for any threats that might exist. The lady stood beside her cart, holding one of its wheels upright.

"You trying to do that all on your own?" he called out.

She leaned the wheel back against the side of the cart, her brow sweaty with effort and her face flushed. "Aye, there's not a lot of folks on the road."

"You traveling alone?"

She looked at him warily. "I am. Why?"

Kyro recognized the change in her posture and tone. "Just concerned for your welfare, ma'am. I'm the Captain out of Barnen, and there's strange things afoot, not the best of times for a woman to be traveling on her own."

She appeared to relax a little. "That might be so but there's things you can control and things you can't. I needed to get this load home to Little Big Rock and Thenis himself didn't turn up to carry it back for me."

Kyro chuckled, "He never does seem to do the heavy lifting when you need it, does he?"

She smiled back at him. "This wheel came off, I think my load is too heavy. I wedged that log there under the cart but I fear it's not quite high enough for the wheel and it's taken much of my strength to get it to here. I'd rest here tonight but I've been away from Little Big Rock long enough and its close enough I can almost smell it."

"Let me find something else to help us, take yourself a rest there while I see what I can find."

Kyro wandered back towards the knoll, and down towards the river, finding a few study logs around the banks which he brought back. With a combined effort, the extra wood helped raise the cart back up, and Kyro hoisted the wheel back onto the axle before setting the spigot to keep it there. Once done he knocked out the logs and dragged them out of the way.

The cart appeared it would travel the rest of the distance now, once it was loaded again. He started lifting the sacks back into the cart that the woman had emptied so she could raise it.

"You should be all set to keep moving once I get this lot back in."

The woman helped him lift the sacks up, which didn't take them long. Kyro grabbed one of his water skins and offered it to the woman. He waited until she had taken a drink then quenched his very dry mouth.

"You should be all set to get back now but I'd not push too hard. That's a bit of weight in there but you don't have too long to go. I'd be wary with your load of flour too, there's those that'd take that with the shortage."

"Thanks for the water and your help. Can I say your reputation doesn't do you justice?"

He looked sideways at her. "Why's that?"

She appeared reluctant to say any more.

"I'll not bite."

"Well, you're known as a heavy hand. Word in Little Big Rock is clear that you run Barnen with an iron fist."

He grinned. "Fair. Not that I run anything, I do Lord Barnen's wishes. But I don't tolerate law breakers, that is true."

"Not that there's wrong in that. I'd have you guard this load for me if I could, this wheat shortage is making everyone edgy. The whole trip has been a bit strange, I'm probably anxious for no reason. It was easier going to Riverbend, at least I had some company."

"The wrong way, sorry, but if you head off soon you'll be in before nightfall I think you'll be okay, I saw no one loitering on my way here. Where's your companion then?"

"It was a young lass, as it turns out, she was from Barnen too."

Kyro perked up at the conversation. "A young lass, you say? That is odd, I'm looking for a lass from Barnen. I thought she might be laid up in Little Big Rock but I had no luck spotting her there. I have a message, from Lord Barnen to deliver to Nedor, so I had to move on."

The lady looked at him carefully.

"Is the girl you been looking for in some trouble then?"

"No not really."

"What does that mean?" Kyro noticed she had become a little more cautious than before.

"We think she might have been caught up in something she doesn't realize and some unseemly types might be looking for her," Kyro responded.

The women said little, brushing down her dress and hat from all the dust she had ended up covered in. After seeming to contemplate him for a while she spoke again.

"You sure you aren't going to harm her?"

He shook his head. "I only punish those that deserve it. I just want to make sure she's safe. Can you tell me more about where you took her?"

After another minute she finally spoke up. "I'm Arbery. I live in Little Big Rock, my husband and I run the bakehouse that serves the Meet Markets." She nodded to the cargo in the cart. "Hence the need to get this wheat."

"I'll trust your word you won't harm her. Not that I know her well but I got the feeling she wasn't wanting to harm anyone, just get away from something. I'll share this with you for what it's worth. The lass I delivered turned up from north and she definitely said she was from Barnen. She was slight taller than me indeed and pleasant enough to look at if you could wipe the dirt and chip from her shoulder."

"She called herself Tiber, she did, though I told our Dedrick that I'd gamble all our ovens it wasn't her real name. She said that her da had needed her down south, not that she told me where, and she was in need of rushing there. We originally traveled to Riverbend together, but there was no wheat there so I ended up waiting for it to arrive there from Nedor. She bought herself a ride to the capital and left the day after we arrived. I've not seen her since."

"Tiber, you say. She sounds about the right height, she'd be a lean thing then but wily and street smart, with green eyes you'd not forget?" Kyro said.

Nodding her head back to him she replied, "Indeed she would. She appeared as if she was on the street, to be honest, but her way was pleasant enough and she'd chance enough to take from us but never did. She claimed to have plenty to pay her way too but I didn't see her with much coin."

"You've just made my day, Arbery, let me tell you. I was torn between seeking her in Little Big Rock and having to deliver my message. I am very worried for her safety. Meeting you though was fine chance indeed. Very fortuitous that I rode out today, and that you had this mishap. When did you last see her?"

"It be six days gone by already, I would say. Your help was more welcome to me than me sharing a little information, I am glad to be able to pay you back. She did me no harm, that girl. Her up and disappearing at the end was strange but I figured she was hiding from something or someone. I hope that someone isn't you."

"I hope to find her and protect her, that's all. Thanks again and let's hope you have no more trouble with that wheel. Safe travels to you, best you set off now if you want to be there before dark."

Kyro mounted and rode on, pushing his stead hard. As good as the news was, he now knew how much gap there was between them. Finding her in a place like Nedor might be impossible, and there were too many different places to head to from the capital, so he might never find her.

At least he knew more than when he set out this morning, more he could share. He thought it interesting she had taken on another name. What did that mean, or was she just being cautious? Was she aware of the danger she was in? There was nothing he could do now but ride hard for Nedor.

There was much he didn't know about her now she had grown up.

He had left her with Despring as a youngster but he had said she wouldn't fit in, much of her time she slept rough and kept to herself.

What was it about Lani that mattered so much to the Prince and his advisor? He might never know.

Nedor was a hard ride over three days if he could keep up a good pace, so Kyro settled in and focused on the meeting he would need to have once he got there.

66

LANI

*L*ani had spent the late afternoon in her room sitting at the window watching the back lane and yard. The view wasn't of anything much but it was better than staring at the walls.

She was feeling troubled and was trying to resolve what was bothering her. While she was frustrated about the lack of a ride, it was Merta and the man she had told her of that seemed to be unsettling her the most.

It had spun around in her head a hundred times, and she had decided that if Merta was going to hand her over, she wouldn't have bothered to tell her about it. And yet her gut simply wouldn't buy into what her mind was rationalizing, and it made her fidgety.

The day was fast slipping away and she had almost forgotten about going back to see Barrick to find out if his uncle would take her. She decided she'd use the window to leave this time, using the ledge that gave her access to the roof.

Earlier Lani had tried using it and found she could move over a number of roofs to a place that allowed her access down and back up again. Still undecided if she'd come back or not, she unbarred the door from the inside but left it closed, slung her satchel over her head and climbed out.

The route took her a little longer than she planned and by the time she'd reached the agent's yard the sun had almost set. The office she had been in earlier was closed, as was the yard, and no one could be heard inside.

With tears welling in her eyes, Lani paced back and forth trying to work out what to do next. All she had wanted was knowledge of the ride south, but the frustration at the complications was building up in her.

She would need to find a new place to stay or go back to the inn before it got too dark, and she was less confident about using the roof in the dark. It felt like there were too many decisions to make, life had really been much simpler before. Wiping her eyes with her sleeve, Lani decided to walk back down the road and see if she could spot an inn on one of the side roads.

Something around here would likely be more functional than fancy, which would mean cheaper, and being close by would be better for her to come back in the morning. Now that everyone had gone for the day this section of the road was eerily quiet.

As she approached the last junction, she looked down at Hordan's yard. The gate was closed and there was no one around, so Lani chanced taking a closer look. She peered through the gap to the fence and couldn't see anyone inside. The sounds of the horses shuffling inside was all she could hear.

Looking back up the street she could see it was still empty, so she made a snap decision, and reached through to lift the gate latch open. Slipping through the gate she quickly closed it behind her and turned, expecting someone to call out.

There was no one there but still she stood there frozen still. Once she was convinced it was just her and the horses she headed to where they were tied up. The covered area that housed them was pretty basic, with random piles of hay and horse droppings everywhere.

In the back corner lay a workman's bench and equipment for tending to the horses. There were half a dozen saddles hung on the wall. One of the horses snorted at her as she passed, making her jump. Lani laughed at herself.

Scared out of my wits by a horse.

The impulse to take a horse and go came over Lani. She knew stealing someone's horse wasn't a great way to go unnoticed, but the chance of Hordan or his wife knowing who took it was next to nothing. She thought back on her last impulse, which was stowing away on the wagon, and how that had turned out.

She knew this was different, she would be in complete control now, and on her own. Before she rushed on with the idea she went and hid near the saddles and thought her way through what to do. The biggest obstacle was finding her way, all she knew was it was south. She thought that would be easy enough to manage if she followed the main road south. There would be villages and towns she could get help at.

Water and food she could manage, the only other obstacle was getting out of town without being caught for stealing. Going back to Merta's made no sense now, and she knew this was likely her best chance for days.

It had been a while since she had saddled a horse but she knew enough, and picked what appeared to be the calmest of the horses. He was tied up separately and Lani hoped that was because he was Hordan's riding horse.

She tied on a couple of small saddle bags and stuffed one with some hay and the other with some skins she found. One was empty and the other had something that tasted like a weak mead. The horse followed her willingly and she headed to the gate. This was the riskiest part of her plan, she needed to open the gate to walk the horse out. If anyone came by and challenged her she'd be in trouble.

Taking a deep breath she opened the gate and walked the horse out. No one called out, and Lani saw no one up the road, the dusk light providing her some cover. She struggled to latch the gate with one hand while she held on to the horse with the other.

When that was done she breathed a sigh of relief and quickly mounted the horse. She didn't linger and started towards where she thought the south gate was. She needed to get through it before the sun fully set and the guards closed the gates.

Pushing the horse as fast as she could through the city, she found the gate she was looking for. There was only two guards watching over the stragglers coming into the city. Lani knew it wouldn't be long until they pulled the gates and kicked the horse forward, making a dash for it.

The guards looked up as they heard the horse hooves rushing down the roadway. Lani heard them call out, "Easy there, rider, no need to rush."

She didn't ease up and pushed harder towards them, as one of the guards stepped over to block the exit, waving her to slow down. She leaned forward and steered directly at him, while all the time his colleague was yelling at her to stop.

At the last minute he leapt clear of her, and she rode through the gates brushing past some people lined up outside. Lani could hear the curses behind her as she kept pressing the horse down the hill and away from the city walls. Once she was out of sight she eased up and let the horse settle into a more comfortable trot, keen to make as much distance as possible from the city while there was still a little light.

Lani rested in the cover of some trees a good distance back from the road, until dawn arrived. She knew it was dangerous to ride in the dark but was unable to sleep out amongst the myriad of sounds around her.

She started riding as soon as there was enough light, her plan being to reach the next town and learn more about where she was heading. The road south was wide at this point and gently wound its way amongst fields of vegetables and rows upon rows of greens.

She came to a water crossing where the road to Nkuku crossed the Axin river. It was unlike any Lani had seen before, made from heavy cuts of wood and as wide as seven or eight carts side by side. Large numbers of people were able to easily move across it at any one time, without the typical bottlenecking that happened at the bridges she had crossed so far.

The horse was able to maintain a solid pace throughout the morning. At regular intervals she passed through outpost stations full of soldiers. Lani didn't know why there were more soldiers down here than in northern Malamig, but their presence was noticeable.

The sun rose to their left as they rode along the river. It had been joined by the Emmer river and flowed swifter than they could ride.

Not long before dusk she reached a fortified border town surrounded on three sides by wooden walls. The fourth wall was the garrison itself, but while it was fortified, even Lani could tell it wouldn't hold out a serious attack. It seemed more decorative than effective.

She hadn't eaten today and wanted to find somewhere in the town to spend the night rather than sleeping rough again. At worst she'd buy food and head out again. Just inside the entrance to the town she saw a large camp area, where other travelers were setting up for the night.

A woman stood by the entrance to the roped off area, and called out to her. "Single copper gets you a cot and somewhere to tie your horse, two and you get food as well."

Lani stopped and looked at the camp site. It was as good as she needed, so she dug into her pocket trying to pull out her coins. She had to pull her glove off to do so and was able to separate two coppers from the coins she had.

"Here you go." She handed them to the woman.

"Go to the left side, there by that wagon. Women stay on the left, men on the right. Food in the center, an hour after sundown." The woman handed her a square wooden token. "Hand this in for your meal. Lose it and you'll have to buy another. Got it?"

Lani nodded and walked into the compound. She tied her horse up within sight of where she'd be sleeping and found some water and feed from the supplies available.

The meal was a stew, thick and brown. Hot was probably the best thing about it, Lani thought, and she was used to taking what she got. The women all sat at tables together while they ate, and an older woman sitting next to Lani had started chatting to her.

"I wish I was brave like you, lass."

"What do you mean?"

"Traveling on your own, I'm too afraid for that."

Lani didn't know what to say.

"We're heading to Nkuku, what about you?"

"Me too," Lani replied. "Are you from there?"

The woman laughed, "No, dear, I'm Mal like you. You've not been there before then?"

"Ah. No." Lani felt like she'd said something wrong. "Why?"

"Oh, you'll see when we get there. They are a different type, quite a different look to us Mals."

Lani ate some more of her stew. "Is it a straight route there?"

"Yes, dear. The road we came in on crosses the border, then you'd have to fall asleep to lose your way." She patted Lani on the back. "You'll be fine, won't be getting lost if you stick to the main road."

When she finished Lani excused herself and retired to her cot. A scratchy blanket was provided and the cot looked like it had never been washed. Without any sleep the night before, it didn't take long before she drifted off. She woke several times through the night due to all the noise and people moving about.

She rose early and grabbed some of the hard cheese and bread put out on the table. When the first of the travelers left the camp, Lani followed after them and was on the road as the first rays of the sun crossed the road. She trailed several other riders for much of the day. By late afternoon they crossed through a border station and the road turned sharply to the west and away from the Axin.

As the day began to wane the sight of massive white walls came into view, the afternoon light gleaming off their surface. They were taller than anything manmade that Lani had ever seen. She pulled her horse back to a walk and marveled at them. It was still a long ride from her and yet their presence reached out across the wide open land.

She picked up the pace again, hoping to reach the city before nightfall. As the sun fell behind the city she neared the river crossing still a mile or two from the city. She eased her horse to a walk and approached the guards at the bridge; a long tree trunk spread on legs blocked her passage.

"We're closed for the night, miss."

"Really? I wanted to reach the city tonight."

"No chance of that, we close this when the sun dips below the wall." He pointed to the camp she'd ridden past. "That's the place for tonight, there's plenty of places to stay."

"What time will you open?"

"Once the sun comes over those trees." He was still pointing in the same direction. "On your way."

With little choice Lani climbed off her horse and walked back to the camp, and this time she got a small tent all to herself.

The camp was more like a small town, Lani realized. It centered around a market and trading zone, with semi-permanent accommodation surrounding it. It lay on the banks of the Three-way Lake which was surrounded on two sides by heavy forests.

It made sense that border trade would be done here outside the city walls, without all the prying eyes and city levies. What caught her by surprise was the mix of races of people, freely moving throughout the market place.

She had seen a number of different races in Barnen, but only in single or small numbers. It was too far north to attract all but the ardent traders. Here the camp was alive with people from all over, some she'd never seen the like of before.

The meal was better here than the night before and the cost the same. She ate by herself and avoided meeting anyone's gaze. Lani didn't want to answer anyone's questions, and as soon as she had finished she got up and walked so she could see the city walls in the distance.

They were still easily visible even in the limited moonlight. She tried to imagine what it took to build them, and how long. Tomorrow at least she'd get to go inside and see for herself.

67

TILLANDRA

*J*f she never rode another camel for the rest of her life Tillandra would be happy. Riding wasn't something she took to naturally, and while she understood why others rode horses, she preferred to be on her feet.

She could have made the journey on foot herself, but knew she would be pushing herself hard back to Anderwell, along Death Road, and her newly healed feet could do with the rest. Tillandra also liked being accompanied on this leg, just in case the knights were still on the road.

The whole journey back to Watersend she'd focused on the problem the Envoy from Daskare presented. She'd think more on the things she'd learned from Ting on her journey along Death Road. Pravat had to go, there was no question about that now. He'd always been weak, but there'd been nothing to concern anyone about this lack of strength before.

Watersend was an important link from East to West Sahro, and perhaps the Court had not spent enough time thinking about who should be controlling the city. That would change now, and she'd make that top of her agenda for the next Court meeting.

As for the Envoy, he needed to be gone, there was nothing clever she could think up to delay it further. The answer needed to be a clear no, and she wanted him gone from Watersend before she left.

Sahro had always operated under a veil of individual independence, each of the cities and towns administering their own jurisdictions without an all-powerful ruler. That was the external view, but it wasn't true. The Court controlled everything, and the Mayors or town leaders reported to Beantic.

Tillandra reflected on the fact that Bea rarely traveled anymore, and maybe that was part of the problem. Someone needed to be visiting each Mayor at least once a year, or else the Mayors would fall into the mistaken belief that they were totally in charge.

It was the very dark hours of the night when her camel team had arrived back in Watersend, and they dropped her where they had started. As promised she had paid the team well, and when they saw the bonus coin she added they were most grateful.

She arrived at the back door of The Clown Prince and knocked quietly, patiently waiting to attract someone's attention. As it turned out she didn't have to wait long, and Wessen was the one to unlock and open the door.

"Mother!"

"Wessen, sorry for the unannounced arrival."

"No, no problem. It's late, I assume you want your bed?"

"I do, but I need something else first."

"Oh?"

"I know I'm being difficult, but I need a rat."

His face dropped. "Now?"

"As soon as you can, yes. Sorry."

"Can't be helped. I'll get it to you in your room?"

Tillandra nodded.

"Come on in, let's get you up to your room."

She stepped through the open doorway and let Wessen close it up behind her. She turned to him in the dim hallway, speaking softly. "Everything been normal while I've been away?"

"Well, normal." He grinned at her. "Not sure what normal is, but you stirred up the bats cave with those knights."

"What do you mean?"

"There's been one around this inn most days. Not inside, but loitering in the vicinity, according to Gimbden, they would be looking out to spot you."

"Interesting. I told that Envoy, Reyes, to keep them close by, but it seems they aren't to be easily contained. I'll head up."

"I'll be back as quick as I can, I'll need to go wake a ratter."

"I'll need a bucket, too, Wessen."

He shook his head. "I know. I'll bring one."

Tillandra knew he didn't truly know what happened with the rats, nor did he ever ask, but he expressed his displeasure each time nonetheless.

The conversation with Beantic was short, Tillandra didn't want to bring up all the matters that needed addressing this way. She only had the one rat to use, and there was a limit to how long you could talk. She told Bea to get word to Goran that the young woman, Lani, had to be brought back to them, in one piece. She repeated that to Bea, and told her that Goran had to understand that he was to do nothing to her that would cause her any harm.

Tillandra told Bea why, but asked her not to tell Goran. She didn't want him distracted from the main goal she had set him.

She dropped the dead rat and sack out the window, as arranged with Wessen. The thud in the dark of night sounded louder than she had wanted. Thankfully, no one seemed to react to it, and she closed the windows and retired to her bed.

The few hours of sleep she got was enough, and she woke ready to deal with Pravat and the Envoy. Surprise was going to be her main tactic, and she slipped out the back door and made it to Watersend council buildings unimpeded. As she approached the buildings she was pretty certain that she'd noticed someone dart away. Most likely a spy watching out for her arrival.

She found Pravat in his private chambers, enjoying some breakfast. His face dropped when she burst through the door, and he spilled some of his drink down his front at the surprise.

He stood as quickly as he could. "Councilor!"

"Pravat, sit down." She waved her hand at him and quickly sat herself across from him.

"You're feeling better?"

"Yes, Pravat, much better. We don't have long because your friend the Envoy will no doubt be here within a short while, his spies rushed off at my arrival." Tillandra leaned forward and helped herself to some grapes from his platter. "I've made my decision about recent events."

"You have?"

The more Tillandra looked at him and his weak manner, she wondered how they'd ever chosen him to be the leader in Watersend.

"Yes. As soon as Reyes arrives, we'll meet him in the chambers and inform him there will be no deal. He'll also be escorted immediately from Watersend, his knights included, and followed until they've left Sahro."

She didn't realize Pravat's face could get any paler, but it did. He looked like he might pass out in front of her.

"That's very confrontational, Tillandra, is that wise?"

"What's not wise is leaving you here running things," she snapped back at him. His eyes nearly popped out of his head at her tone.

"W...what do you mean?"

"We know all about your vices, Nion, the young woman. You've spent the best part of your time running Watersend from your bed."

He went to object, but Tillandra waved him silent. "You will ensure that my command is followed, and nothing goes wrong. Then we'll discuss what happens next. Should another young woman be seen in your company, you will find yourself spending time in the cells at Fort Layden. Am I clear?"

He nodded feebly at her.

"I didn't hear you?"

"Yes, Councilor."

Tillandra didn't need him to know this was his last task, she wanted him focused on achieving it, so she could move Gimbden sooner rather than later.

A knock sounded at the door.

Tillandra spoke quietly to him. "No doubt the Envoy is here already."

"Come," Pravat called a little weakly.

One of his aides, entered the room. "Mayor Pravat, Envoy Reyes has arrived and wishes to meet with you as quickly as possible."

Tillandra spoke for him. "Take him to the chambers, tell him we'll be there shortly."

When they arrived in the chambers, the Envoy and his attendants were preparing to seat themselves.

"There won't be need for you to sit, Envoy, this won't take long." Tillandra's voice filled the room.

Envoy Reyes looked at her, his face showing his dislike of her involvement. "You do not even know why we are here."

"Let's not waste time, Mister Reyes—" her choice to not use 'envoy' was deliberate "—there's only one matter at hand. Your request about the access to Sahro."

The Envoy looked at the Mayor, who was partly hiding behind her, but Pravat had his eyes to the ground.

"And you've made a decision?"

"I have. Any roads in Sahro will be determined by the Council. At this stage we see no immediate need for such a road to be developed hastily, but will take it on notice and seek ways to improve travel conditions along this route. *Ourselves!*" She heavily emphasized the last word.

"I see. You know that the King is very willing to fund this."

"And his offer is appreciated, but as I'm sure he'll understand, I doubt he would allow such an intrusion into his own realm by us or others. Nor shall we."

"Intrusion?" The Envoy tried his best to appear offended.

"You can use whatever word you choose when you advise him."

"Perhaps we can meet again and I can find some new options we could present you?"

"No, there's no need. My decision is final. And besides, you're leaving today."

"Excuse me?"

"Mayor Pravat will be ensuring that you, and your unwelcome guards, will leave Watersend before sundown today."

"That's totally unreasonable. I am not ready to leave at this point."

"I think you misunderstand me, Envoy!" Tillandra walked over to him, looking down on him. "You haven't been asked, you've been told. You're no longer welcome in Watersend at this time, and your knights are considered a form of aggression on the part of Daskare. I will be making a formal complaint to the King about you, their presence and this whole process."

"He will not be happy at my treatment."

"Should you remain, he'll be much less happy. Especially when he discovers you locked up in the cells at Fort Layden."

For the first time Tillandra saw the man's face drop.

"And for clarity of my intent, you will be escorted to the border."

"This is outrageous!"

"Call it what you will, but if I was you, I'd be more worried about packing and preparing than arguing with me. The clock is ticking."

The man didn't even pretend to be happy, he bowed and excused himself, before hurrying from the room.

Tillandra turned on Pravat next. "Do you understand my instructions?"

"Yes, Councilor."

"You're to send at least twenty armed men to escort them," she said as she turned to catch the eye of Gimbden, who had quietly slipped into the room. "And I want a fully armed camp within range of the border by the next full moon. You're to set up courier way stations and horses, so messages can be relayed quickly from the camp to here. Now go."

When the mayor had scurried from the room, Tillandra spoke quietly to Gimbden. "Until we have someone here that can communicate to the court, you're stuck, but like I said, it shouldn't be long."

"I understand. You're leaving?"

"As soon as I know they've left the city."

"Travel safe."

Tillandra nodded and left the room. She had packing of her own to do.

GORAN

Goran had spent the rest of the day watching the back of Merta's place. He had been uncomfortable and bored as he sat waiting for something to happen, and was close to giving up for the day when he caught sight of someone climbing onto Merta's roof from a back window.

To his mind it was highly probable this was the woman he was after, and as he'd guessed, Merta had warned her. He couldn't make out anything defining about her over such a distance, but he could see which direction she headed on the roof top.

He still was concerned about not attracting any attention of his own so while he hurried he was careful not to run. When he reached the end of that line of buildings he found a place to watch for someone making their way down, but failed to spot her.

There were few places she could have come down from and he checked all of them but couldn't see anyone of interest. Goran spent a good while pacing the area until he knew he had missed her. Cursing his luck, he gave up and headed back to the Bard's Bell where he was staying.

It wasn't going as easily as he had hoped, not that much had since his stint here in Nedor with the King. While he was still one of the Court, there was no way to remove the mask while you lived and he had been ostracized from the inner circle. Tillandra and Bea were the only ones he had spoken to in over a year, and they had kept him working out on the road, part courier, part supervisor, which was beginning to take its toll on him.

He could sense the voice in his head, clawing its way trying to get free. The depressed feelings always seemed to feed it and bring it forward, so he tried to focus on something positive.

At least he had this task, all he needed to do was find her and bring her in, or as Tillandra had said, find a solution. Then he would be back on side with everyone, there was no way they could ignore him solving this problem for them all.

In his room, he prepared another pipe. It had been a couple of days now and he knew the voice would keep picking away at his thoughts until it could get free, unless he dampened it down again. It only took two inhales and he felt the peace flowing through his body, first his mind then into the muscles of his shoulders and arms.

Another benefit of the zongle weed had been how it relieved him of the constant pain and aching in his bad leg. That's what everyone else called it, 'his bad leg'. To him it was just his other leg, shorter and poorly formed, but it was still his leg. He'd lived with the pains in it since he could remember and the smoke eased that, even if only for a few hours at a time, but it helped him sleep.

His mind was drifting on a sea of smiles when he heard the knock. At first it seemed as if someone was at the door, and he muttered, "Go away." It kept coming and grew louder in his head, until he realized it was someone calling him, and he sat up with a start. He took in a few deep breaths and tried to clear his head before he entered the space between his eyes.

The usual calmness as he entered the void was replaced by a woozy feeling and Goran struggled to maintain his focus. Beantic's face was a little more blurred than usual.

"In All Jest, Goran. Are you okay?"

"In All Jest, Bea. Yes, why?"

"Your form is distorted, as if your connection is weak. I've not seen you like this before."

"Perhaps it is because I am very tired, Bea. I've been up through the last night looking for our target," he lied, trying to settle into the space better.

"Make sure you maintain your health, we need us all at our best. I have news."

"Oh?"

"Where are you now?"

"Still in Nedor."

"Oh, well your target is on the move."

"Darn. What have you seen?"

"She's moving south, or the ring is."

"What do you mean?"

"It's the ring that shows on the map, Goran, not the person."

"But I thought it showed as blue when it was worn, and a different color if it was returning to the Ring Master."

"That's true, and it's still blue, so this means she has it and is heading south. Unless…"

"Unless?"

"Well, she shouldn't be able to wear it so if she can, then whatever allowed her to do that could possibly be passed to someone else."

"That's a lot of ifs."

"My belief is that it's her and she's heading south."

"Nkuku?"

"It's hard to tell, Goran. That's the most likely place, and I'll watch it every day in case there's a change, but for now that's all I can say."

"Best I make travel plans then."

"Don't linger, Goran, she's already got a head start on you."

"I know, Bea."

"I think it's best you get out of Nedor anyway, you might like the risk, but we don't need any more complications right now. I have news from Mother as well."

"Oh?"

"She has been to Midderbuilt and sends this message. The woman,

Lani, is to be brought to Anderwell, *in one piece.* She wanted me to emphasize that last point, that no matter what had been discussed before, they need you to make sure she is found and protected. Understood?"

"Yes, I understand."

He signed off and brought his focus back into the room. Being in the void had strangely cleared a lot of the effects of the weed he had smoked. By the end of the connection his head had cleared and he could see Bea clearly.

You messed up again, Goran. Let this girl get away. The laugh that followed in his head was sinister and he was surprised it had come back so quickly.

Goran knew he needed to make plans and get on the road, but it was almost nightfall, and traveling in the dark was never a great idea, unless absolutely necessary.

He fought off the voice and thought through his options. Beantic would have expected him to set off immediately, he was sure, but he needed peace in his mind if he was to do this properly. He filled his pipe and lit it, before breathing in deeply on the smoke.

The anxiety he had felt just before eased and he was able to shutter the voice.

Tomorrow will do just fine, I'll set off tomorrow, the woman will be stopping now for the night herself.

He slumped in his chair, happy with his decision, listening to the muffled sounds of the inn filter through the walls and door. Once the pipe was emptied he stumbled his way over to his bed and lay down, ready to drift off to sleep. He knew he'd forgotten to eat, but that was okay, he'd get something in the morning before he left. *Leosa really should be told,* he thought, *so she can prepare the horse.* He shrugged.

Tomorrow, that's all for tomorrow.

He closed his eyes and started to drift to sleep.

The thump on his door forced him to open them again. He rubbed his forehead as if he could feel a connection coming. The thump came again, twice in quick succession, Goran realized it was the door.

"What?"

"Quick, there's trouble." It sounded like Leosa's voice.

He rolled upright and wobbled over to the door, unbarring it.

Leosa stepped in and closed it quickly behind her. "There's King's Guards out the front, and they're looking for you."

"Me?"

"Yes, they say they have word you're in the city and are doing inspections. Paunly is holding them off briefly at the door but they'll be in soon. You need to go, now."

He rubbed his eyes. "Okay."

"Are you alright? You look groggy." She sniffed the air. "You've been smoking again, haven't you?"

"It helps my leg. Leave me be."

"You've got a few minutes at best. I sent one of the lads out to the stable to get a horse ready, he'll put it out the back lane, through the back door of the stable, but they'll get out there soon enough too." She shook him by the shoulders. "Do you hear me?"

Goran nodded. "Yes. I'm going."

He kneeled down and grabbed his bag, and stuffed his few belongings into it, he could pack it better later.

She pointed to the window. "You'll have to go out that way, are you steady enough?"

"I'm fine," he snapped back. "Leave me to it and go back to what you need to do. Thanks for the warning."

"I'll do what I can to keep them busy downstairs for as long as possible. Stay safe, Goran."

"And you."

He climbed out the window and held on to the ledge above him while he worked across slowly towards the back wall. The fresh early evening air helped him wake up, but even so he was glad to get to solid ground once he had climbed down the wall.

As promised one of the lads held a horse for him in the lane behind the Bard's Bell, and he thanked the boy before mounting and setting the horse to a walk.

The guards turning up to where he was staying was no coincidence, he knew that, and there were only two possibilities for who had informed on him. It was unlikely Pincer himself would have done it, especially if he wanted him to fulfil his end of the bargain. That didn't mean there wasn't a plant inside his organization feeding information to the King. The only other person was Merta, and he wondered what favor she had hoped to gain from snitching on him.

He brought his concentration back to the task at hand, getting out of the city without being caught. Merta would be something he'd need to address another time.

LANI

*L*ani peered out the tent flap as the first vestiges of light broke the night. She felt on edge from the hot weather. It had been hot and sticky throughout the night and the morning air was just as heavy and damp. She had never been in air that hung across your skin like a drape while the temperature didn't seem to change at all.

It wasn't long before everyone else was leaving their tents and readying for the short trip into Nkuku.

As they crossed the toll bridge Lani's focus was the walls of the city and massive gate they were approaching. She couldn't take her eyes off the massive white marble walls. They were something to note from a distance but were incredible up close.

The early morning light hit the upper walls and ripples of color rolled across their surface, bringing a smile to her face. The high panels of marble were all carved, some with ornate designs and others with images. It was hard for Lani to pick them all out but she could see there were many gems laid into the carvings and they were gleaming in the light.

To enter Nkuku they passed under a massive arch, made even more impressive by the size of the opening doors. They were made from large panels that looked like single trees, bound together with steel bands and bolts, faded from years facing the sun.

The size of the archway and doors dwarfed the people walking through. The groaning of chains and hinges finally stopped as the doors finished opening. On each side Lani saw bullocks connected to chains, around a set of wheels, that were linked by more chains to the doors.

As she rode in the city unfolded before her eyes, with roads leading off in many directions amidst a multitude of buildings. The one directly ahead seemed to run straight with no visible ending. Even at this early hour, this section of the city was swamped in a mass of people, a mix of arrivals and those looking to sell their wares to them.

It was even more amazing to Lani than Nedor. She had grown up hearing about Nedor her whole life, and while it was different to what she had imagined, in her mind there was still a familiarity to it. This was something different entirely. Until just a few days ago she didn't even know Nkuku existed, but even if someone had told of her it, she wouldn't have believed the scale of it.

Not long ago her whole world was made up of Barnen and everything around it. She'd never heard stories about other cities, or none that she could remember. She wasn't sure she could explain it to her kin, or anyone else, and do it justice.

A small touch of sadness hit her as she realized she didn't know if she'd ever see the kin again.

Following the line of people that had come over from the camp, Lani stopped sightseeing and turned her mind to what she needed to do. Her only goal for now was to find somewhere to stay.

She took a top floor room, out of anyone's way, in a small inn, the woman in charge paying her little notice, which suited Lani. She was glad to house the horse in their stable, the upkeep was part of the cost of the room.

Her room was clean but smelled a little musty, as though hardly used. There was a small window on the far wall and she opened it. Puffs of dust blew in off the sill as a breeze rushed in. Lani could see out across the back of the property, the small outbuilding and stables backed up against the side of a large building.

She could see they were only a few streets back from the wall's edge, and even though she was several floors up the height of the wall pressed down on her, it was massive. There was a ledge to the side of the window, and Lani put her bag on the bed and scrambled out onto it.

Standing out on the ledge, she could see a way that she could get up onto the roof. It would be a perfect way to come and go if she wanted to get out without being seen. That would need to be at night though, she would attract too much attention clambering across roofs in the daytime.

Lani emptied the satchel onto the bed and sorted her things. She took the two rings and placed them to the side; this morning she was going to try and sell them. The sooner she traded them for coins the better she would feel.

As she ran her hand over the mask, a chill ran up her spine causing her to pull back from it. It was a strange object and Lani wasn't really sure why she had kept it, except that leaving Ashantha's face behind seemed the wrong thing to do. She quickly returned it to the bag along with the cape she had worn. After flicking through the journal and laughing to herself that she still couldn't read, Lani picked up the pouch holding the amulet.

Even in the gray felt pouch she could sense the stone inside. When it was out of sight she didn't think about it, but seeing it she felt compelled to pick it up. There wasn't a noise or a voice but Lani could have sworn that the amulet called to her. It was so subtle she hadn't noticed it until the last few days when she had been on her own.

Without thinking she opened the pouch and the amulet seemed to gleam in the light. She could feel her forearm heating up from it, and pressure in the spots where she had felt it in Little Big Rock, when Yerat had died. It was enough to break her fixation and she quickly wrapped the pouch back over it. She shook her head and went to put it in the satchel, but at the last minute decided it was safer to carry it with her, and tucked it into the hidden pouch in her tunic.

She put the remaining things including the coin pouch back into the satchel and hid it in a small nook in the wall behind the robe.

Out on the street she moved into the flow of people. She had kept her traveling clothes on, and her hair was tucked up into a cap. She looked as much a boy as a girl. The sun was high above the walls now and Lani noticed how bright it was inside the city, with many of the buildings made of a light colored stone and not wood.

The gate she had come through was on the eastern wall of the city and she hadn't ventured far from it to find her inn, which meant she was close to where the trader had told her Robatch was likely to be found.

Unsure who to ask for directions, she decided to use an old trick she had learned in Barnen. She pretended to be busy looking left and right and deliberately stepped into the way of someone walking the other way.

"Oof!" The man stopped in a hurry. "Watch where you're going, girl."

"Sorry, mister. I'm just trying to find somewhere, maybe you could help?" She tried her best to look confused.

The man straightened his jacket. "Where's that then?"

"Ah... I think it's known as Jobbers Lane."

His eyes widened with alert and he frantically checked his pockets, patting them down, checking he had all his things. "All there," he said to himself. "You don't want to be going there, off with you." He hurried away from her, looking back several times as he went, still patting his jacket pockets.

A little surprised at his reaction, Lani chose the next person a little more carefully, making sure they were wearing the clothes of someone who looked to be working close by. As she made contact with them, she fell backwards, deliberately mimicking the action of being knocked over.

The man stopped and bent down towards her, offering his hand. "You all right? Sorry about that. I wasn't watching where I was going."

"That's okay, nor was I," Lani said as she stood up. "I'm trying to find somewhere but everyone gives me strange looks when I ask."

A small friendly smile formed on his face, "Oh really? Where's that then?"

"I think it's called Jobbers Lane."

The man laughed, "Yeah, well I can understand why people look strange at you. That's not the place many would want to go to, it has a reputation."

"Oh? What kind?"

"Let's just say it's the sort of place where the stores trade in things that maybe they shouldn't." He winked at her. "I'd suggest you stay away, if I was you. There'd be those down there that might take advantage of a stranger."

Lani slumped and frowned at his words.

"I'll tell you where it is though. Two blocks that way, make a right, head along three or four crossroads, and you should see a clock tower. Go right there, and you'll find what you're looking for. But like I said, I'd give it a wide berth if I was you."

"Thank you."

"Nothing to thank me for. Watch where you're going as well." The man hurried away, leaving Lani smiling at how well it had worked.

The tower the man had mentioned was easy to see and she heard it ringing before she saw it. She had never learned to read a clock, for what she needed she had always just used the sun's location in the sky to know what time of day it was.

Jobbers Lane was narrow and darker than the roads she had been on. The tall buildings on each side blocked much of the light. It was busy with people and she started walking along, taking in the different stores she passed.

She knew the only way to find Robatch was to ask, so she walked into the next store she came to displaying jewelry. As she entered, an older man standing behind the counter looked up from his work, tools in hand.

"What you need?"

"I'm looking for someone."

"Who's that?" He looked back at the necklace in his hand, through the large eyepiece attached to his head.

"I have a ring to sell and someone told me to find a man called Robatch?"

The man put his work down on the counter and looked up, pulling the glass up from his face. "Robatch, you'd want to watch yourself around him. He's a crafty snake, that one."

"Do you buy rings?"

The man shook his head. "No I don't. I make everything you see here, and things have been slow of late, so I'm not needing anything else."

"Do you know where I can find him?"

"Down the lane a ways, you'll know it by the snake sign above the door. Is that all?" He looked back towards his counter and pulled the glass back over his eye.

"Thanks." Lani left the shop and headed further down the lane. She found the store easily enough, the carved wooden sign above the door was of a snake leaping out towards you. It was the least welcoming sign she'd ever seen over a shop.

The door was closed and she held her hand up to the front window, trying to see if anyone was in. She knocked several times on the door but no one came to answer it.

"Not seen him for days."

Lani turned to the voice and saw a man standing across the street, outside another store.

"Oh, I heard he might be interested in what I have to sell."

"He's always interested, whether he'd pay is another matter altogether. What is it you want to sell Robatch?"

Lani stepped over to the man; he was a little shorter than her, and very thin. He was wearing a dark brown tunic marked with stains.

"I have a ring I've brought with me from up north. It's quite unique and I was told he was the man to see."

"He's not the only person that buys jewelry and things, girl. I'm always looking for new pieces, if they're as unique as you say." He stepped into his store and beckoned her in. "Come in and we can talk off the street."

Lani followed him in and he went and stood behind the counter. There were several display cases on top about half full of rings and necklaces. She made a show of looking them all over; none were amber.

"So, can I see this ring?"

Lani dug into her pocket and pulled out one ring and held it up for the man to see. He blinked several times and looked carefully at it.

"You're right, this is unique. You know what that is?" He pointed at the stone.

"Amber?"

"Yes, amber. You know how rare that is?"

"A little, just what someone told me."

"It's rare alright, this is a fine piece."

"Are you interested?"

"I'd love to take it off your hands, but no, it's not for me. Whoever sent you here was correct, Robatch is the man you need to see."

"How come?"

"I couldn't offer you what this is worth, and I think you know it's not just a simple ring. So you won't take any cheap offer from me. Besides, Robatch is the one who'll know who to sell this to. He deals in the unusual."

Lani couldn't believe it. She was in the right part of the city and had found the place she needed to be but couldn't sell the ring.

"How do I find him? I want to sell the ring before I leave."

"Like I said earlier, he's been gone a few days. You'll just need to come back again tomorrow, and the day after, until he shows up."

Lani shook her head; this wasn't the result she had hoped for.

"Sorry, girl, nothing I can do for you." He handed her back the ring, and she put it away in her pocket.

"Thanks for your help. If you see him tell him I'll be back."

"I'll be sure to do that, don't you worry."

Lani left his store and turned left back towards the clock tower. She kicked at some rubbish on the lane out of frustration.

Does no one want these rings?

70

LANI

It wasn't the start to her stay that Lani had been hoping for. Rushing to Nkuku had been in the hope of making a quick sale and getting more money. She was feeling frustrated, not just with her situation but with herself.

She felt a little like she'd been gullible and followed the word of a strange shopkeeper rather than thinking for herself. Maybe she shouldn't have come here, was it all just a lie? Robatch did have a shop here, and the man she had spoken too told her he'd be back.

If nothing else she was going to have to learn to be patient. She wasn't going to just take one person's word, that was a silly mistake. She had to remember anyone trying to help her wasn't really looking out for her, they were just looking after their own interest. That's what she needed to do too, look after her interests.

There would be other jewelers and traders in this city, not just the ones she been to just now. Lani stopped and looked around.

She'd been so busy thinking she hadn't paid much attention to where she was heading. She'd wandered into some narrower lanes and roadways that looked a lot more like the darker parts of Barnen than the main roads she'd meant to go back to. A few querying eyes looked out of doorways or windows as she passed, but no one spoke to her.

Something had triggered her to stop and she tried to look for any danger. Nothing obvious stood out to her, but she was now on full alert. She paid more attention as she started walking again, a little more purposefully now, towards what she hoped would be a way out of the area she was in.

Several times she felt like someone was watching her. Not just those that peered out of their windows but something more deliberate. She looked over her shoulder multiple times but couldn't see anyone following her and in the end put it down to her anxiousness.

With no idea what to do next, Lani's stomach made the decision for her. She was hungry and the best place to resolve that would be some sort of market square. Thinking that every other city she'd been in so far had a square in their center, she aimed to where she thought that might be.

As it was she chanced on several stores off one of the side streets that stocked jewelry. Every time she showed the ring she got almost the same reaction, an excitement in the eyes of the store owner that they tried to disguise, and then they'd say they weren't interested. She could tell they all knew it was a valuable piece but none were interested in buying it. When she asked if they knew anyone, most said no, while one told her to go to Robatch.

Something else was at play, it had begun to feel as if they knew she was coming before she got here. That meant she was in danger of being targeted and having it stolen from her.

Lani left the last store and moved as quickly as she could without running until she merged onto one of the busier roads. There were plenty of people moving along the road and once she had settled in alongside a loose group of them she started monitoring for followers.

Several of the jewelers had appeared a little frightened, which meant someone had made it clear to them to move her along. No one stood out to her but then locals would blend in if they had any skill to them.

All she could do was stay vigilant. Her next task was to get something to eat and find information. This city was new to her and she couldn't afford to take another misstep, having already stumbled onto potential trouble.

As she moved along with the throng of people she was able to take in more of the city sights. Her home of Barnen was almost entirely wooden, in contrast to Nkuku, which was predominantly stone.

Most buildings were at least two stories high with many being three or more. There was no reason for the differences, except none of the tallest buildings sat on the outer ring near the walls.

There were a lot more people on the road now as they neared what must be close to the middle of the city. Lani could hear a lot of noise ahead, where the road disappeared around a building to the left.

As she rounded the corner she viewed a large open area filled with people and noise. The main square was a hive of activity. A paved outer ring circled the inner main square, and it appeared to her that this path was how people quickly moved around the outside.

Dominating the center of the square was a large statue, gleaming orange in the sunlight. It was of a fierce looking warrior, very broad of build, hunched into a fighting stance, with a long sword raised in his right hand. It had a rounded face with a flat nose and prominent brow, and long hair flowed down its back.

It was the biggest statue Lani had ever seen and it made her feel a little intimidated. She'd never seen a battle or heard of any. Maybe down this way there were more armies and battles, which explained all the soldiers she'd seen.

Her attention was drawn to her right, where a solo musician was camped against the side of a building on the square's edge. His lute played upbeat tunes that lifted her spirits a little, despite not knowing the words he sang.

Lani worked her way slowly through groups of people, avoiding those hurrying in other directions until she found some food stalls. There were those selling baked goods, and she was able to get a roll of bread and cheese from several stalls close together.

Taking her food she moved towards a spot against a building beside the stalls, where she could keep her back protected, and watch while she ate. People watching, those moving about the square, was entertainment enough for her. Some just wandered with what seemed no purpose, others picking up items and leaving immediately and some like her getting food to eat.

Scanning the way she had entered the square, she noticed the face of a young man about her age who seemed to be loitering about the square without much purpose. His face triggered a reaction in her mind, which meant something. She knew no one from here.

Taking a moment, she closed her eyes, and brought up the snapshots her brain constantly took of her surroundings. Lani found the same face in several other streets she had walked along, when she'd quickly turned her head to look behind. It had been too fast in real time to notice but her mind had spotted it. She had no idea why her mind worked this way, but when she discovered that no one else's did, she paid more attention to what it told her.

Lani had thought that someone would be sent after her from the jewelers she had visited and she was right. The young man was waiting to see if she went back the way she came.

Reaching under her tunic she checked the knife was still tucked in her belt, hidden from sight. As best she could tell at this distance, he was shorter than her and probably a few years younger.

Despite wanting to leave immediately, Lani took her time to finish what she was eating. Every so often she would casually scout the other sections of the square to see if he had any helpers. One person was enough of a problem, multiple would be extremely dangerous for her.

She couldn't spot anyone else which meant either they were very skilled at hiding or he was alone. She hoped it was the latter.

While she had been monitoring what was happening Lani had decided that the best way to get out of the square was the access road to her left. It was a wider street heading towards the city wall on this side. There were plenty of buildings between the square and the wall, so she figured that there would be a number of roads or lanes she could choose from to use.

She had purposely kept a handful of scraps from her food, and as she stood she tossed them into the grassy area to her right. A small flock of pigeons roosted nearby raced to get there, their wings flapping and the rush of noise making enough of a disturbance to give her a head start.

Lani slipped out of the square and down the road. As she turned the corner she started running to put some distance between her and the guy, if he was going to follow. At each lane she came to, she slowed and quickly looked at her options. They were neater and safer looking than the earlier ones she had come down, but mostly no wider. She took enough time, without looking back, so that if anyone had followed her they would see her duck down the lane on her right that she finally chose.

Once she had turned that corner she sprinted until she got to a tight alley behind a set of houses, far enough back from the road to be unseen. She stepped into it and backed tight against the wall on the street side and caught her breath as best she could. Slowly she calmed herself enough and pulled the knife from under her tunic, clasping it firmly in her right hand, and waited.

LOSPA

*L*ospa was angry, and he was upset. Sitting up high on the rooftop, filled with hate for Chacka, he played through scenarios in his mind where he got to belittle him instead of the other way round. Mostly it involved smashing him in the face and knocking him down in front of everyone.

Up high he was safe, no one followed him up here. He pretended he was ducking and weaving, throwing out ghost punches and seeing a different result than what had happened earlier.

It was always the same. Chacka would come in angry about something and look to take it out on whoever happened to be in his way. Lospa seemed to be that person more times than not. Being the bottom of the ladder was the worst, and he wondered when he would get a chance to move up the pecking order.

The pretend fighting on the rooftops always helped him calm down, and slowly the anger receded and his humiliation eased.

After a little while he propped himself on the edge of the roof, his legs dangling over, his head in his hands and elbows on his knees. He could sit for hours like this, peering across the streets below, creating stories in his mind. They were meant to be Watchers and that's what he did up here, he watched.

He'd wondered many times if this prophecy was true, they had been keeping their eye out for something for as long as he knew. To him their group, or gang, was all he had. They'd taken him in when his mother had died, and now he was one of them.

At first he didn't pick out the person below, he'd been too busy in his imagination and had lost focus. They were moving though the back lanes and didn't look like they belonged down there. They were not Morskan, that was for sure, taller than normal and lean. Nkuku had plenty of foreigners that came through, but they never ventured down these lanes. This was the Watchers' and allies' highway, not some common roadway.

Lospa tried to think through who it might be. Who would be brave enough to enter their zone? This might be his chance to show his worth, gather some important information and bring it back to base.

That would get him credits with the Watcher, for sure. That was his best way to get back at Chacka. He smirked to himself; smarter, that's what he was. Much smarter than dumb Chacka.

He quietly moved along the rooftops, following the person below, keeping them totally unaware of his presence. This was his domain, he knew these roofs better than anyone. He knew where they led and all the up and down routes. It was like his own "high" way, he always enjoyed saying that to people. Some people didn't get the joke, but then he was smarter than most of his lot.

The person went into several stores that Lospa knew. They were all safe shops and fences. Whenever their crew came across something of value that's where they took it. The person didn't stay long in any of them and hurried away from each one. He'd have liked to have dropped down and asked the storekeeper what they had wanted, but he'd lose the trail if he did. His best bet, he knew, was to follow and watch, he could always come back and ask later.

The line of roofs was coming to an end there was no crossway ahead. They were nearing the center of the city so most buildings on this side ended on Teepol road. The second last house had a lattice that ran up the entire side of the building, and while it had a thorny vine on it, Lospa had made a pathway through it. He quickly scaled down avoiding any of the thorns, as big as a nail, having learned that lesson well before.

Once he was in the lane he slowed down and tried to blend in, as just another person going about their day-to-day activities. He tried to follow a path that used the shadows and buildings, to obscure himself from view, and settled in behind the person as they made their way towards the city square.

He couldn't tell much but it looked like someone about his age, a lad taller than him wearing a cap that hid much of his hair.

His target approached the Square of Kimsto, the famous Morskan warrior of eons ago. So long ago, in fact, that few knew what battle he had fought in, or why he was a symbol of their mightiness.

Lospa's crew were the Watchers, and as their name implied, his lot did lots of watching. He thought he had been getting pretty good at it, and lately he'd passed all their tests. All he needed to do was keep following this lad and see what he could learn. Who knew what type of reward that would bring?

The lad he was following bought some food from the market traders and was perched against a wall on the other side of the square, limiting Lospa's options to get a good view. He had no money to buy food of his own and thought about stealing something, but didn't want to risk getting caught, not when he had something this important going on.

Lospa pretended to be looking at the wares of some of the other stalls and moved slowly, keeping an eye on the target from the corner of his eye. All of a sudden a commotion erupted in the open garden, with birds flapping and attacking each other. Distracted by the noise he nearly missed seeing the foreigner scurry out of the square and down the western gate road.

Without thought for why he had run, Lospa followed quickly, and got to the street corner, pausing to look around it, not wanting to be made so easily. He saw the figure hurrying down the street not looking back and then disappearing down a laneway. Thanking his luck to have not missed them, he hurried down to where they had turned.

He slowed as he approached what he thought was the right laneway. He was anxious now; what had seemed a good idea at the time now was becoming more dangerous. Maybe he should just let it be and go back to his high spot. His face flushed at his cowardice, the words of Chacka earlier mocking him for being too scared to do anything useful.

He forced himself around the corner and finally took a breath when he saw the lane empty ahead.

There's nothing here, you chicken. See? What were you getting all worked up about? It's empty and you can fight them anyway. What were they doing coming down here? They are probably just some delivery person, and heading back to their boss. But why did they run off? Doesn't make any sense. Unless. Unless they saw me following them.

He punched his other hand, berating himself for his carelessness. He was so focused on his thoughts and berating himself, he walked right by a small lane without noticing the person standing there. He only knew what happened when they wrapped their arm around his throat and pulled him into the small laneway.

He tried to struggle but as they pulled him back in they dragged him over their leg and he fell backwards hard onto the cobbled lane. The solid impact forced his breath from his lungs, made only worse by the assailant kneeling on his chest, and placing a sharp knife blade against to his throat.

"Why you watching me, boy?" the person hissed at him.

Lospa struggled to gather his wits, his head a little startled from knocking it on the lane as he fell, the knife at his throat definitely taking up a lot of his attention. The boy looked very un-boyish, and he suddenly realized that he had just been bested by a girl.

Stuttering from lack of breath and his surprise, he said, "I... wasn't following... I wasn't ..."

The blade pressed a little deeper at his throat; he wondered whether it was going to cut through, the steel felt like it was already cutting in, but he couldn't feel any blood running down his neck.

"Don't lie, boy, you've been watching me for a while. You're trapped so cut the bull unless you fancy not getting up from here again," she hissed at him, glancing about quickly to see if anyone was watching.

"But I was just curious, curious was all. You're not from around here," he blurted out. He need time to work out how to get free with his arms and body pinned by her weight. She wasn't as heavy as Chacka, but more than strong enough in this small lane to keep him subdued.

"Who's your master, boy? Don't mess around. I know you're not smart enough to live on your own, you're a lookout if nothing else."

Lospa didn't know what to say. Her threat to kill him seemed real enough, but he didn't tell strangers about the Watchers. He knew that much. He wished he'd just stayed put on the roof, he'd be still there right now watching the sky, and safe from this crazy girl.

"I can't, no. I can't, you'll have to kill me. I don't have no one. I won't talk about my friends neither. I'm just a boy from the streets is all." Lospa hoped this might buy him some more time. He still wasn't sure if she'd actually cut him.

She seemed to look at him hesitatingly as if unsure what to do with him. He knew that if they stayed like this much longer someone would notice them. That was his only hope of getting free right now. Maybe she was thinking the same thing, which was why she was looking about.

"In a moment I am going to let you up. Maybe you're telling the truth, maybe you aren't, but I don't believe you're on your own. Not in a place this big. You might actually be useful. I need information, so maybe you can actually help. But try anything when I let you up, and your only use will be for feeding the rats. Got it?"

Lospa nodded, feeling relieved, as the blade was slowly removed from his neck. She pushed into his chest to help get herself up, then stepped back and pointed at him with the knife to get up.

As he stood she moved in toward him to corral him down the lane. In a split second he made his decision. It wasn't courage, and it wasn't even from thinking clearly, he just wanted to be free. He turned and started to run.

He felt her hand grab at his tunic and spun his left arm around to wrestle free, forgetting about the knife. As his elbow whipped around he felt it connect on something hard.

Her grip fell free, so he started to bolt away, before he heard a body slump to the ground. He stopped and looked back. She lay on the ground, unconscious. His elbow must have caught her in the head and knocked it against the wall or something. She was out cold.

Now he really didn't know what to do. Most of him still wanted to just turn and run and forget this ever happened. No one need ever know. That small part of him craving attention, though, hoped she was someone that Watcher might want to know about.

He cautiously crept back to where she lay. Her knife was off to the side so he picked that up and slipped it through his belt. She was pretty lean, despite being taller than him, and he knew he was strong, all the years living with older boys had made him work hard on being stronger.

He stood over her and awkwardly lifted her heavy body upwards. She might be lean but an unconscious body was heavier than an awake one.

Crushing her against the wall, he squatted down so he could sling her over his shoulder. Not thinking much else, he stumbled down the alley heading back towards home base. He knew he couldn't keep this up for long and she'd wake soon enough so the closer he was to help the better.

Two turns later, his luck changed for the good. Two of his own cohort were heading straight towards him.

Between them they bound her hands and legs and gagged her mouth before sharing the load back.

LANI

*L*ani came around poorly. Her head hurt and her jaw ached. With both her hands and feet bound there was little she could do and her brain was foggy. She was being carried by two men and their rough handling was only making her head worse. When she tried wriggling into a more comfortable position, a jab to her stomach ended that quickly.

"Lay still or you'll get more of that," a gruff voice said from alongside her.

That meant there was more than two people. Lani wanted to cry, her eyes began welling up at her foolishness. Why had she bothered taking on that lad? She was doing well enough and she could have just lost him and gone back to her room. Now she was strung up like an animal, caught by who knows what group, her luck deserting her. Everything had been going bad for her, she should have known she couldn't sell the rings and have money. Stuff like that never happened to her.

The lanes they carried her through were narrow and dark, the walls of the buildings tall and close together. Occasionally they would bump her feet into a wall, as they turned or clambered over crates and rubbish left in their way. Her head had begun to throb, never a good sign, which meant one of her bad headaches was coming. As if she needed things to get worse.

Not only was she caught, and being taken somewhere she didn't know, but her ability to escape was going to be zero within a few hours. Painfully she kept her eyes open, letting the tears slowly clear, so she could see something of where she was being taken.

Trying to rest herself as much as she could, she let her body relax, knowing it would be better for her and worse for the carriers. Every lane seemed the same as the last and being face down, she had little chance to capture landmarks in her mind.

It had to have been one of the stores she went into, or all of them, the boy she had grabbed was no doubt a scout for them and although she had caught him first the others must have been close by. She had taken her luck too much for granted, selling the other ring had gone so easily she had assumed doing it again would be just as easy.

Her only thanks were that she had chosen to leave her satchel in her room so that it wasn't with her for these thugs to take away. Then she remembered she had the most valuable items on her, the amber rings and the amulet.

Lani wanted to slap her own head for her stupidity. She had only just rebuked herself, to pay more attention and be smarter now that she was so far from Barnen, but the first thing she did, she had messed it up and got herself caught.

Abruptly the carriers stopped, and seemed to be waiting for something. Lani could hear more noise and tried to wriggle her way free of their grip with the hope of attracting someone's attention.

She copped another jab in her side for it. "I told you, lay still or there'll be worse than a jab."

Now her side ached, he had hit something tender and with her head throbbing, more tears formed in her eyes, dripping down her cheek. Thankfully the carriers were ahead of her face and couldn't see her.

All of a sudden they started to run, sprinting across a wide open street, with her bouncing on their shoulders. Lani struggled to see more of the street, her head aching more for it, before they entered another lane. If anyone noticed her being carried, none called out or followed them into the side lane.

While her captors might not have wanted to be seen, most of the normal folk on the street probably knew better than to get involved with the street gangs.

The only thing Lani could tell from her brief view was that daylight was starting to fade now, as dusk was falling in Nkuku, and the lanes they were in were more ominous looking for it.

They came to a stop near a building and one of the men knocked on something wooden. Lani could hear wood sliding, then there was some mumbling, between the person in front holding her feet and someone on the other side of what had to be a door. They carried her through the door once it opened before it quickly closed on them.

The smell of oil lamps burning was strong inside, and she was carried a little way further before they stood her on her feet.

"I'm going to remove the cords from your feet, lass, but be careful about thinking of kicking out or trying to run. You're not going anywhere in here, and we'll skin you first and ask questions later, if you get what I mean. Do as you're told and no harm will come to you, for now." Lani didn't like the way the man said the last part.

The one who Lani had cornered said nothing and stood to one side, and she could see his right hand resting on what looked like her knife, tucked in his belt. He carried a silly smirk, as if he was pleased with himself for capturing her, even if it was a chance blow she had not prepared for.

The third of the captors prodded her in the back and pushed her forward, once the cords had been removed. They passed through a sliding stable door into a much bigger room that seemed to be a mass living area for a large number of men, from teenagers to middle-aged.

Makeshift tables and benches were spread about the warehouse - some appeared to be for eating, while others were occupied by groups playing games, with much shouting and raucousness. On one side was sleeping quarters, separated from each other by thin half-height walls. As they passed by she could see several beds or mattresses laid in each pod, a couple with people resting in them, but most were empty.

Lani scanned the room trying to make out what she could in the gloomy light. It was difficult to see too far, through the haze of smoke. Lamps burned on every wall, and pipes and hookahs being used around the room added to it. There was a sweet and bitter smell that she found hard to inhale.

The majority of the inhabitants in this room were Morskans, Lani could tell that. They were shorter in general and had a distinctive head structure, their brows more prominent. A token couple of Mals, as well as several other types of peoples Lani had never seen before, made up the rest of the gang.

Her captors led her across to the right-hand side of the big room, towards a more secluded section with three half walls and a big table. Sitting around the table were several men, mostly older than the rest. As they approached, a broad-armed man stopped them, barring their way towards the table.

"He busy. Bugger off," the guard said to them.

"Not for this, Brainless," the taller front man of their group spat back at the guard, their eyes squaring off at each other. "The Lopsided one seems to have done something useful for a change, and found us an interesting little prisoner."

The guard looked over his shoulder and noticed Lani for the first time, his eyes running up and down her as if evaluating something. "Wait here."

Lani's headache was getting worse, she could feel it coming quickly. The room was beginning to rotate and her head felt like the big warrior from the statue was crushing it with his massive hand.

Her eyes came next, they always felt like someone was trying to push a needle into them. The sharp pain was made worse by light and even the dim lantern light was triggering them. She closed her eyelids for some relief, and struggled to stay standing, only the firm hand on her arm keeping her up.

"She doesn't look so well, what did you do to her, Lospa?" the lad holding her right arm whispered to the one on her left.

"Nothing but a knock to the head, shush or you'll get us clipped," he replied.

The guard made his way to the table and leaned in to talk to the three seated men, who were deep in conversation. Lani couldn't hear any of what was said, but it didn't take long before the guard returned.

"Take her to him. Be quick! Waste his time and I'll discipline you," he sneered.

When they reached the table Lani could see who they were all deferring to. Sitting behind the table was the broadest man she had ever seen. His shoulders made him look as wide as two men, his arms were thick with muscles and large strong hands. His forehead dominated his face, and if his hair was longer, Lani could have believed he was a replica of the statue in the square.

His voice was as deep as his eyes, but gentler than she expected, "I don't like what is brewing amongst the wheat traders. I need it stopped, Timron, understood?"

"Yes, boss." The man pushed his chair back and stood. "Nothing else?"

"No," the man he called boss replied. He turned to face the other man. "When whatever this is, is over, go and sort the crews out. There's too many people down here messing about, surely there's jobs to be done?"

"I'll sort it."

"Chacka, I'm busy! Who's this, and why did you bring them down here?"

The front one bowed slightly and answered, "Sorry, Watcher, but Lospa found this one up to something on Prendle Way. When he caught up to her, she tried to knife him. I thought you'd want to know."

Lani was pushed forward closer to the lights hanging around the table, which caused her more pain behind her eyes, so she forced them closed again.

"Who is she?"

Lospa answered, "All I know, Watcher, is she was in and out of some of the shops down on Prendle Way, seemed suspicious is all. I just kept following her until I caught up to her and she jumped me."

The man laughed, "You got sprung by a girl, Lospa? Lad, what will we do with you?"

Everyone but the lad beside her burst into laughter. Lani cautiously forced her eyes open to see what was happening. She found the large one they had called Watcher was looking straight at her. Forcing her eyes to stay open was all she could do, and at that point she was glad for the two hands holding her arms, or she would likely have collapsed to the floor.

"What did you hit her with, Lospa, she looks ill?"

His response to Watcher was less confident than to his peers and he almost stammered, "Just my elbow, boss, she seemed fine before."

"What's your name, girl?"

Lani wasn't sure she wanted to reply, but she could hardly stay conscious now the headache had fully come. She needed to find a flat dark place to lie down.

"Well?" He stared at her some more. Watcher waited in silence, then looked at the three lads that had brought Lani forward, and back at her. "Have you searched her?" he asked.

Chacka seemed to shrink a little; he turned and looked at the others before turning back. "Only the knife she had attacked Lospa with, we not touched her since."

Watcher nodded to the man beside him, who got up from the table and came over to Lani. He stared at her with his cold marble gray eyes.

"Stand still, girl," he hissed at her. He roughly ran his hands down both her legs and moved upwards, caring nothing about her gender. He reached her pockets and pulled out the contents, dropping them on the table. He removed her cap, looking it over before roughly placing it back on.

He then ran his hands over her back and then ran up her front, catching on the lump hidden in the inside pocket of her tunic. "What's this then?" He poked it again.

"What are you doing, Rifkin? She's not sport."

"No, boss. There's something hidden there." The man seemed uncomfortable after the Watcher's comment.

Watcher spoke to Lani again. "Take it out, or I'll order him to. And he won't be minding your modesty when he does."

Lani dragged her hands free from the men holding her, and reached up under the tunic and turned the amulet out, her hand hidden by the cloth. No one could see the brooch still pinned in there, and when she pulled her hands free, dropping her tunic back down, she kept it out of sight.

Rifkin grabbed the gray pouch from her hand, and dropped the item heavily on the table.

"You don't want to touch that," Lani said weakly.

"She speaks," Watcher replied. "Why's that now? You going to do something if we do?"

"Not me, it."

"Well now you've got me intrigued. Rifkin, let's see what you've found."

Rifkin sorted the few coins that had been in her pocket, and slid them with his fingers to one side before unwrapping the rings. "Oh!"

Watcher stood suddenly, and leaned over the table, picking up one of the rings. "It's her! She's the one been trying to sell these amber rings." He looked at Lospa. "Looks like you did good, son. We got word just before, from Jobbers Lane, that someone was about with an amber ring."

He rolled it around in his hand and then grabbed the second, whistling through his teeth as he did.

"Who are you, girl? To have two of these rings, that's a worrying thing."

Lani said nothing. She knew she was now screwed. Without the rings and amulet she was broke and far from home. All she could do right now was fight the pain in her head, she just needed somewhere dark to lie. She almost toppled forward, the two men on either side reacting quick enough to save her face planting into the table.

"Get her a chair. She doesn't look so well," Watcher barked at them.

Being thrust into a hard chair had never felt so good, and the relief of not having to support her weight let her catch her breath slightly. Lani cradled her head in her hands, with her elbows on the table's edge. Her head felt as heavy as bricks but she knew it was just the pain.

"I've not seen a ring like that before, boss."

"Me either, Rifkin, but amber is amber. What can you tell me about this, lass?"

Lani didn't look up, she knew there was little she could say. She didn't have a convincing story ready to tell and she doubted they would believe the truth. Staying quiet seemed her best option.

"You're not going anywhere, so staying quiet won't help your cause. I need to know where these amber rings came from, or should I say, who?" He sat back in his chair and pointed to the gray pouch. "What's in there, Rifkin?"

Lani raised her head to look at him. "You don't want to do that!" her voice crackled from her dry throat.

His face turned serious. "I don't think you are in any position to tell me what to do."

Rifkin opened the pouch and let the amulet slide from it onto the table.

A collective gasp went up from everyone gathered around. Rifkin reached forward to pick up the amulet.

"*Don't!*" Lani struggled to get the word out, the throbbing in her head grew and she dropped her head into her hands again.

Rifkin stopped and looked back at her, before turning back to the amulet. "Silly girl…"

His words drifted away from her, and she struggled to hear what was being said; her last thought was to put out her hands as she toppled from the chair before slipping into the blackness.

73

LANI

She was lying down, that much she knew, but where she had no idea. As Lani came to she kept her eyes closed. She had learned that lesson before, avoiding the reflex to open your eyes immediately on waking. The headaches were too severe for that, and rushing the waking cycle normally brought the headache back worse than letting her body adjust more slowly.

Whatever she was lying on smelt old and dank, and using her hand she could feel it was like dry straw. The smell was a bit like urine but not quite, most likely from it getting wet then drying over time. There was some form of blanket draped on her; she tugged at it and pulled it up to shield her eyes, allowing her to open them.

She was still in the same room with the large table but in a corner, out of the light. As she became more conscious the mumbling voices became clearer.

"We've put his body downstairs, boss, for now. What do you want us to do with it long term?"

Watcher's voice stood out, and Lani could hear a mix of anger and sadness in it. "I don't know. I'll decide later, alright?"

"Yes. Sorry."

A voice closer to her said, "She's awake, Watcher."

"Get her up then."

She had closed her eyes again to ward off the light, and she felt hands grab her around her armpits, dragging her off the mat she was on and up into a chair. She was at one end of the table, to Watcher's left.

"I don't know who you are, girl, but whatever was going on before, it is very different now."

Lani felt like retching, the pounding in her head was still there, albeit diminished from earlier when she had blacked out.

By choice she would have kept herself in the dark, but whatever had happened here, they weren't going to let that happen.

"What … happened?" she struggled to get out, her voice scratchy.

"Get here something to drink!" Watcher's voice was agitated as he barked instructions at someone.

"You know what happened. You warned Rifkin about it, so you knew what would happen when he touched that amulet."

She had opened one of her eyes and as she squinted at him, noticed her right forearm was warmer than the rest of her, and tingled. He was pointing at the amulet sitting in the middle of the table, out of the gray pouch.

With her eye partly closed she thought she could see several wispy orange tendrils originating from the amulet. One reached out to her arm, the other had weaved its way out of the room.

"You should cover that up," she said. One of the younger men placed a wooden cup in front of her and stood back quickly. Lani picked it up and gulped down what was a weak ale, happy for the liquid.

"We're not touching that. Not after what it did to Rifkin," Watcher replied.

"What did it do?"

"You want to play stupid? Fine. He just dropped dead as soon as he touched it. It was like a shock went through him and he dropped it where it is and fell to the floor. Now you can put it back in the pouch."

From behind her, hands lifted her out of the chair and she shuffled over to the pouch, grabbing it and sliding the amulet into it before drawing the cloth closed.

"How can she touch it, boss? Is she a magician?"

"All good questions, Chacka. We'll find those out soon enough."

Lani was shoved down in the seat where she was, the jolt triggering more pain.

"Bring that drink down here for her, and get us some food, Lospa. The rest of you, be ready for anything, if she can use that thing, whatever it is, who knows what else she might try."

"It's not me."

"What's that?"

"It's not mine. The amulet, it's not mine."

"You expect me to believe that? How is it you can handle it but Rifkin died from it?"

"I wish I knew."

Lani slowly opened her second eye and shifted in her chair, sitting a little more upright. She took another drink from the cup, emptying what was in it. Watcher sat across the table, his dark eyes unflinching, staring at her. She gently turned her head from side to side, looking at who else was in the room. There were at least four she could see, and two of those had short swords in their hands. All were watching her carefully.

She didn't know how to feel about the man who had died. When he had grabbed at it, she had warned him. Several times. It wasn't her fault the amulet killed him, she had no control over it. She did blame herself for carrying it with her, though. That was dumb. She knew it was dangerous, she was definitely going to have to get rid of it, if she could ever get out of this situation.

"You're not making much sense, girl. Do you have a name?" Watcher broke the silence.

Lani realized that even the warehouse behind her was quiet now. Whereas before it was filled with laughter, shouting and the sound of chairs and people moving, now there was a deathly silence.

"Lani." She saw little point in using a false name. Her chances of getting out of here weren't great, unless she could come up with a plan or something they might believe. She didn't think Watcher would fall for a tale easily.

"So, Lani, perhaps you can explain for me what exactly that amulet is?"

"I don't rightly know."

"You'll need to do better than that."

"It was given to me, and I was warned it was evil."

"Who by?"

Lani pointed at her cup. "Can I get some more… please?"

Watcher looked to her right and nodded. One of the men brought a jug and filled it up.

"Eat if you want as well. You're not going anywhere right now, so you might as well recover from whatever ails you."

"It's my head. The knock, it causes bad headaches. It will pass." Lani reached forward and took a handful of the nuts and fruit on the platter in the middle of the table. No one spoke while she ate; Watcher simply stared at her, his eyes never moving from her.

"How long was I out?"

"Several hours. Now the amulet, I need to know more. If you don't tell willingly we'll try another method."

Behind Watcher a large tapestry hung on the wall. Woven into it was a massive battle scene, warriors alive and dead lay everywhere, rivers of red spread throughout the wool. In the scene Lani could tell it was set in front of the massive walls of Nkuku.

Watcher turned his head to see what she was looking at.

"That's outside the city?" she asked.

He nodded. "Yes, it's part of a story we've been told. A prophecy of sorts."

Lani looked more at it. "A prophecy?"

"Don't worry about that. Nice attempt to change the topic. The amulet?" He looked hard at her eyes.

"I found a man, up in the north of Malamig, where I am from. He had been stabbed in a fight, and was dying. He gave it to me and told me I had to deliver it to a place far to the south."

"Where?"

"Barnen."

"Where's that?

"North in Malamig." She screwed up her face, she'd told him that.

"No! Where to the south?"

"Oh. A place called… Callet."

"Callet?"

"Yes, that's what he said. I don't know where that is."

"It's the next major city south of here, across the Simpans river." He stopped what he was saying. "Why there?"

"I don't know. Just someone he knew there."

"Who?"

"Some man, but I don't really know. He died while he was trying to tell me. He told me it was evil, and the man would know what to do with it."

Watcher said nothing for a while, looking between the gray pouch and her. He reached into his pocket and pulled out the two rings and placed them in front of him. "And of course these. He gave you these as well?"

Lani looked at the rings; she knew that there wasn't an easy way to hide where they came from. Maybe if her head wasn't pounding she could come up with something he might believe, but she had no ideas right now.

"Not exactly."

He raised his eyebrows at her.

"They were on the men he killed."

"I thought you said he was killed?"

"He was. He killed the men first but took a fatal wound."

"Who were these men?"

"I don't know."

"You're not being very helpful, Lani."

"I don't know much. They were Derks, that's all I know, and they were dead."

"Why did you take the rings?"

"They looked valuable to me and I got good money from…" She stopped, realizing what she was saying.

"Go on."

"The other one, I sold it."

"Where?"

"A town called Riverbend. In Malamig."

"It was these that alerted us to you."

"What do you mean?" she asked.

"The amber, it's very rare. All the traders, well at least at this end of the city, know to tell me if they see any."

It dawned on Lani now why they had all been reluctant to buy from her.

Watcher raised his arm and swooped it in the air above him. "This part of the city, is where I have many friends." He smiled. "We look after our own, and they keep an eye out for what I am looking for as well."

"Why are you looking for amber?"

He picked up one of the rings and poked the tip of one of his fingers through it. The ring didn't go far up his wide finger, and Lani saw the flickering lamp light reflecting on the dark black surface.

"I'm not sure you need to know what we are doing, Lani. Right now, I need to know who you really are and what to do with you."

"Let me go, you can have them. I don't want any of them anyway. They were just a way for me to get money."

"But the amulet?"

"I didn't want that either. It was only when I tried to fence it I discovered it killed. I don't want it, it's dangerous. Bury it, I don't care. I just want to go home." Lani hoped he'd believe her, she forced her eyes to water, trying to play on his emotions. She had no idea where home was now, and without the money she was stuck in Nkuku for now.

"So you say. I'm not so sure. But we'll find out more soon enough."

"What do you mean?"

"Someone's coming who should be able to help fill me in more about all of this."

"Who?"

"He's one of the people we call the Eyes. He has an ability to see things that aren't easy to see."

"A Teller?"

Watcher chuckled. "A Teller, yes, that's a northern term. Same thing."

"Why a Teller?"

"I don't trust you, girl. That's why. And you killed one of my men."

"It wasn't me. You heard me warn him, I told you both."

Watcher looked back at her, and shrugged his shoulders. "If you've got nothing to hide, then there's no reason for you to worry."

74

LANI

$\mathcal{W}$atcher had left her sat at the table under guard. Lani could hear him in the background instructing people to get out of their base, but she couldn't properly hear him from where she was sitting.

She didn't like her chances of getting free from her guards, and she always felt weak from the headaches. Normally it took her a full day to recover. After staring at the tapestry for what seem an age, she turned around causing her guards to flinch. She turned her chair so she could look out into the open warehouse. None of them stopped her.

Lani didn't know if she would get a chance to try an escape but knowing where she was mattered to her. Her ability to map spaces out in her mind required her to have seen the space clearly before. When she'd been led into the building earlier the knock to her head had stopped her from paying attention to her surroundings properly.

She looked over everything that she could see from her seat. With so many people in the building the only chance she'd get would be if they turned the lights out, to sleep. She didn't like her chances but it was the only plan she could come up with right now.

Whoever this group was, Lani wasn't sure they'd let her go easily. Any chance she might have had ended earlier when their man died touching the amulet. Even if it wasn't her, she sensed they wanted to make someone pay, and she was the only candidate for that.

Her mind started thinking about the Teller. She had never seen one for real, she'd only heard stories about them. People spoke of them in muffled tones, and behind hands across their mouths, as if the mentioning of one would bring them to focus on you.

There were those on the street in Barnen who proclaimed to have seen one and that they were harmless except for what they could see. Lani knew little else about them as there wasn't one that lived anywhere near where she had grown up. She was in no rush to meet one now either, even if she had told Watcher mostly the truth.

All she'd wanted was to sell the rings and the amulet. Even though she knew no one would be able to take the amulet, part of her kept trying to convince herself she could get money for it. It was almost as if it she was being driven towards Callet, always heading south.

Could the amulet really control you like Ashantha had said? That made no sense to her, it hadn't come from Callet so why would it drive her there? She couldn't sell it anyway, no one lasted long enough for her to pull that off. She'd have more luck stealing money than getting money for it.

She didn't understand any of it. Ashantha had warned her about it getting into the hands of anyone she didn't know. He had said it was evil, but he could have warned her it was more than just evil.

Without thinking, she rubbed her forearm.

What did it do to me? Why can I touch it?

Why would this Bossu be able to handle it? She would have to force him to leave it in the pouch before she handed it over.

Lani laughed at herself, making the guards look at her. If she was going to get out of here, she needed to stop having fanciful dreams and focus on how to get free.

The atmosphere out in the warehouse suddenly changed, and it went quiet again. Watcher walked alongside someone dressed in a long green robe. As they got closer Lani could see it was a teenage boy, much taller and skinnier than Watcher, but his face looked only thirteen or fourteen.

They came into the room and Watcher led the boy to the end of the table on Lani's left, where he sat himself down.

"This is Cideep," Watcher told her.

The boy lifted his head and pulled the hood off, the light in the room fell on his face and Lani let out a gasp before she could even attempt to control it.

His eyes were gone and there was nothing to replace them, the empty sockets seeming to look at her. His hair was shaven down both sides, and the short spiky strip down the middle was a dark black. The skin on his head was a pale white and he reminded her of the Derks.

Watcher chuckled. "You truly have not seen one of the Eyes before, then. Cideep is going to help look into the story you've told me, and maybe more. Perhaps he might start with the ring you brought to us..."

"You stole," Lani interjected.

"That you brought to us," he continued. "And he will tell us whatever he sees. Isn't that right, Cideep?"

The boy spoke quietly but in a voice that was deeper than the age he appeared. "What sits in the middle of the table?"

"There's some sort of amulet," Watcher told him.

"Why can't I see it properly?"

"It's in a pouch. Somehow it shelters it. The amulet is dangerous, one of my men handled it and dropped dead in an instant."

Lani saw the face of the boy frown in concern.

"Do not hand it to me, but take it from the pouch."

Watcher looked at Lani. "Do as he says."

Lani reached over and emptied the amulet from the pouch onto the table. She could feel it grabbing at her as soon as it came free.

"*Get her away from it!*"

Watcher sat up in alarm. "What?"

"Put it on the table but get her hand away from it."

Lani pulled her hand back and left the amulet face up on the table.

"What is it, Cideep?"

The boy sat as if looking toward the amulet for several minutes. "The rings?"

Watcher pulled them from his pocket and placed them in Cideep's open right hand.

Cideep muttered and mumbled for many minutes.

"You don't want these rings." He spoke firmly to Watcher. "They are beacons, those who they belong to can sense them. They will come for them."

"Who?" Watcher asked.

"Derks, the dark ones."

"Not the orange ones, then?"

Cideep turned to face him.

"The orange ones. The prophecy we follow, about the wave of orange coming. That which we watch for, to protect our people from."

"Watcher, this is the orange." He held up the rings so the amber showed in the light, and pointed at the amulet. "The orange comes. It leads the dark ones. They are who you must stop."

Lani was confused by what they were saying. She assumed the dark ones were the Derks in black, but she didn't want to ask anything. She preferred not being the focus of Cideep's attention.

"But, all we knew was…." Watcher was less confident than any time Lani had seen him. He was taking in this new information.

"They come. It has begun and now they come. They want what is theirs and they will take it all. They don't care who is in their way. You should not have these things. Especially that." His voice almost hissed as he spoke of the amulet he pointed towards. "That is evil and they will know where it is."

"We are no easy fodder, Cideep, we've been training for this fight for a long time."

"You do not know who you face. They will come soon, and they will kill many. They are shadows, black like the ring. They are not to be seen. They come like a cloud. You can see it from afar but not once inside it. Be warned, they come to take back what is theirs. They do not buy. All should be worried about these people."

There was silence, no one else in the room would speak, although Lani could feel the tension in the air.

"What of her?"

Cideep turned to face her. "Bring her to me."

Someone came behind her and dragged her chair closer to him, the scraping sound seeming to set everyone on edge.

"Your hand?"

Lani reluctantly placed her right hand in his; she wasn't sure she could have resisted his command even if she had tried. The whole time he held it he shook his head from side to side slowly. She wondered if he could see the smoke-like tendrils reaching out from the amulet.

He let go of her hand. "Wrap it up, quickly."

Lani moved back towards the amulet and did as he said, feeling better for the amulet being back in the pouch. While her arm seemed to like it being out of the pouch, she could feel the amulet influencing her thoughts. It was subtle but she could sense it, and while it was out she felt a clear direction to kill everyone there.

"So?" Watcher sat expectantly looking at Cideep.

The boy shook his head again. "This is strange, very strange. I would speak to my mistress about this."

"You must tell me, Cideep, even if you aren't sure what it means."

"She has a lock."

"A lock?" Watcher asked.

"A lock. Her mind has been locked to one such as me. I cannot see into what has been, only remnants of recent events. Things that aren't behind the lock."

"Is that normal?"

"No. I have heard of such a thing but have never before seen one."

"What does it mean, how do we know who she is?"

"Ask her," the boy remarked in a flat and dry tone.

"What remnants can you see then?"

"I can see her finding these things. I see she wears the mark of another. This has broken the Balance."

"What mark?"

"The ring on her hand."

Watcher turned to look at her. "Her gloves, take them off!"

One of the guards stepped forward and wrestled with Lani to pull her fingerless gloves off. And held up her left hand showing Ashantha's ring.

Watcher struggled to focus on what she was wearing as if it was hard to see. "What is that? Whose mark?"

"Those who do not wish to be known but they are all around. They too seek her."

"Who seeks her? Cideep, I do not understand you."

"Those of the clown face, this ring she wears, is their mark. She is not one of them…yet." He paused. "She should not have that but it too bonds to her."

"What else does she bond to?"

"That," he spat as he faced the pouch again. "It too has connected with her, she cannot leave that if she tries."

"What do you mean?" Lani had to ask.

"You must take it with you wherever you go now, it will not let you leave."

Lani shook her head, not understanding what he meant.

"Can you not feel it, how it touches your arm?"

She didn't want to admit it, but she slowly nodded.

"Can you take the ring off?"

"No."

"Nor can you rid yourself of this amulet."

"This makes no sense." Watcher had stood up and had his hands firmly pressed down on the backrest of his chair.

Cideep opened his hands and held them palms up. "I just tell you what is. Test it."

"How?"

"Take her from this room."

Watcher gave a small chuckle, and nodded to one of his men. Two came forward and lifted her from the chair and marched her towards the main warehouse. They got twenty steps from the table before they walked into an invisible wall. The group stopped abruptly and could not proceed.

"What the—" one of the guards said. They stepped back and moved forward again with the same result.

Watcher left the table and went towards them. He walked straight past them without issue. "Let go of her."

The guards did, and he beckoned one of them forward. The man walked toward him without issue.

"Now you," he said to the other. He too was able to walk to him. "Lani, now you."

She tried to move but was frozen in place. She stepped back and to the side, before walking forward again and stopping abruptly in line with the same spot as before. It felt like a soft blanket she couldn't push through.

Watcher moved to her and reached for her hand. He could grab it but not move her, despite his strength. She could feel his grip on her wrist and see the strain on his face, as his arms began to bulge with the effort and a bead of sweat formed on his forehead.

He finally gave up and pushed her back towards the table. "What in Maymun's name is happening here, Cideep?"

"Your god might be the only one who can tell you, Watcher, but I cannot. I just see what is."

Lani sat in the chair, as confused as everyone else. She had been worried about what the amulet had done to her when she had first felt it burn her, but this was more than she could have known. This changed everything.

LANI

*L*ani had no idea what time of the day, or night, it was. Since Cideep had left them she had sat in the room, alone but guarded.

She was still thinking through what she had heard the Teller say. She wasn't comfortable calling him the Eyes, the memory of the empty sockets made her feel queasy.

Watcher walked back in, his manner less confident than earlier and he seemed agitated.

"You're a problem, Lani. A problem I'm not sure how to solve."

"What do you mean?"

"Who are you? I know your name. That tells me nothing about you, if it's even true."

"It's my name. I'm from the city called Barnen, in Malamig. That's it. I lived with other urchins there, and that's all. Or it was."

"Meaning?"

"Until I found the man and he gave me that amulet."

Watcher sat back and looked hard at her. "Was it him that shielded your mind?"

"I don't even know what that means. What Cideep said was news to me. If it keeps him out of my head though, then I'm happy to have it."

"That I can understand, but it still means you know more about us than we you."

A young lad came into the space carrying fresh jugs and placed them on the table, picking up the empty ones.

"We'll take some food too, I think we're going to be talking for a little while."

The boy nodded at Watcher and left without speaking.

"Can I ask you something?"

He looked at her. "You can, although it doesn't mean I'll answer."

"Who are *you*? I get they call you Watcher but what are you watching? You seem like thieves hiding out here, but that's a strange name. And what about the prophecy?"

He laughed. "Well we probably do look like thieves. But we don't, in fact we do the very opposite."

"What does that mean?"

"We watch out for those of our own. Have you ever been to Morska before?"

"Never," Lani replied shaking her head.

"Morskan society is made up of many strata. We have positions that you are born into. A class, if you like. There are five levels. The very bottom of which are the Parya, the outsiders. They survive on the streets, their lives are meaningless to the Nukhba, those at the top. The watchers protect and provide for the Parya, we don't follow the rules of our rulers."

"Okay, so that's what being Watcher is, watching out for these people?"

He smiled. "No, but that's what we've become. The term Watcher relates to the prophecy you heard about before. Let me finish explaining more of what we do now, then I will explain the rest. I need to think more about what to do with you anyway, maybe an answer will present itself."

He took a drink and gathered some food in front of him.

"The higher levels believe they have the right to take from those below them. They believe it's their divine right, laid upon them by

Maymun, our god. I don't agree with that. My followers also believe as I do, that everyone should be treated equally. So we offer protection from those who would take from them. In return they give us small rewards. Many small fish make for a big meal."

He laughed as he said it, then ate some food.

When he had emptied his mouth he continued, "All of this is paid for by that work we do. We give to the Parya as much as we can, we run food carts and offer sleeping areas and housing. It's little but more than they would have without us. We've been doing this for a long time, while we wait for the orange wave."

"The prophecy?"

"Yes, although Cideep has changed my understanding of what it was."

He stood up and walked to the tapestry. "This is a prediction of a great battle to be fought defending our city from those of the orange wave. Now if I understand it better, the orange referred to was the amber that controls them, and the people are Derks."

He scratched his head and looked at the tapestry for some minutes, before returning to his seat.

"The Watchers were formed when a small group of men came across an old ascetic, in the northern Sisi mountains. The biggest mountain is called Mt. Beruk, and in the shadows of this mountain the ascetic lived in a small cave. The men had been out, scouting and exploring the mountains, based on a dream one of them had been having every night. It was so vivid that it drove him to go and look."

"They were camping at the base of the mountain when, as the story goes, the ascetic floated down from his ledge above, startling them all. The story says that he was many hundreds of years old and as pale as the moon, almost transparent."

Watcher took a drink from his wine before continuing.

"This strange creature was not a Morskan, and the men knew not what race he was. He spoke in riddles, repetitively. He would only say more when they repeated and recognized the meaning of what he had said prior. He instructed them that they were to become *watchers*. That they should keep their eyes to the east, from where a great evil come. He said if no one prepared for it, they would sweep across the land

and all would fall to them. He had chosen them to watch and prepare for this."

Lani was fascinated by the story, although it sounded more like the tales told for coin in inns. She'd never heard anything like this one before.

"They were told that someone must be watching or the false peace would be shattered beyond repair. That was all that he said before returning to his ledge. As our history of the event goes, he floated back up to his ledge, where none could reach. Over time, others have sought out the ascetic, but none can find such a place."

Lani spoke up. "Are any of these men still alive?"

Watcher shook his head. "No, this was many years ago. I am the third Watcher, and their story only lives on my word."

"Watcher, Watchers?"

"The one chosen to lead is known as the Watcher. All of us are known as Watchers."

"Ah." Lani nodded now that she understood better. "If this role is so important to Morskan defence why is it you seem to be hiding out here?" she asked.

"The Nukhba do not believe this story. They believe it offends our god, Maymun, and is the work of another god trying to steal his people away. They have banned all talk of Watchers and we live in a constant struggle against each other. They have tried to eliminate us, but for now we hold much of this end of the city and they wait planning some way to roust us. My men are trained well, and we are always prepared for a fight, from them or the prophecy."

He shook his head.

"If they believed us, good men would not die needlessly, and we'd have more to fight the enemy when it comes."

"Sounds like it's already begun?"

"If Cideep's words are to be believed, then you've brought the enemy to us."

Lani sat up straight. "I did not know."

"So you say."

Watcher sat quiet for a bit, taking food from the platters and chewing on it mixed together, sipping wine in between mouthfuls. Lani followed suit, her hunger catching up with her now.

"Why did you bring this thing to us? Where are you really heading with these rings and amulet?"

"I've already answered this for you."

"You say something that sounds believable but then magic surrounds you. That ring and that amulet you are connected to, this cannot be by chance."

"Believe me, after what's happened since I found them both, I'd hand them to you if I could. Up until Lospa caught me, I was planning to throw the amulet away. All I wanted was to sell the rings for money. I have almost nothing left, and have no home to go to."

"What of Barnen?"

"They believe it was me who killed this man, and a guard. I had to flee there. It was one of these Derks. He saw me, and the guard. I ran away but the guard must have been killed. I ran away from Barnen and have been running from trouble ever since."

Watcher shook his head and placed his hands flat down on the table. "I feel like I should believe you but still I cannot. If this is connected to my destiny then you could be the very start of what I am meant to protect us from. Until I am convinced otherwise you will be held here."

"But…" she started to say.

He stood up quickly. *"Enough!* Men, take her to the lock room downstairs. Do not mistreat her but keep her there until I say otherwise."

76

LANI

They had moved Lani into a small room down a set of stairs. There were two similar rooms that she could see when they brought her down. The room held only a cot bed for her; the door had been left open, which pleased her, but a guard sat at the bottom of the stairs, holding a large knife and watching the doorway.

Lani sat on the bed trying to understand what was happening. Despite the open door she was their prisoner, and she had little choice right now on what she could do. Watcher had said he needed time to think things over, and that she could rest down here, where he'd feel more comfortable about her.

There were too many things that didn't make sense to her. Ashantha could use magic, she had seen that, even though she'd never seen it before, he could do things others couldn't. But the ring was stuck to her. She tried again to pull it off but still it wouldn't budge. And the amulet had some connections to her. But she wasn't like Ashantha. Or was she?

How did he know my name?

She hadn't given that any more thought until now, she'd taken his word for what he said. Maybe there was a connection?

Cideep had said the Derks would know where the rings were and would come. Lani had to assume they also knew about the amulet. Was that what she saw creeping out of it? Did those tendrils reach out to the men in black and attract them to it?

A shiver crept up her spine as if something had clicked into place in her mind. Did that mean they could track her too? She rubbed her forearm, and then pulled her sleeve up. There were no markings on it, nothing that showed what it had done.

Lani pulled the sleeve back down and stared back at the wall. The sound of running footsteps and raised voices came from the floor above.

The sound of Watcher's raised voice made its way through the growing cacophony of sounds. Lani's concern grew as she heard barking calls to arms. The movement above accelerated and she heard many people rushing over her head.

Watcher's voice boomed down the stairs. *"Bring her to me, Jiren!"*

She didn't know what it meant but the urgency in his voice was clear. Jiren came towards her brandishing his blade. "Out!"

Once she left the room she could feel the point of the knife in her back, terrifying her. If she slipped going up the stairs it would go straight through her. As she stepped off the top stair onto the floor above she breathed a sigh of relief, the blade no longer so close to her.

The sound of fighting was coming from above and there were several large crashes. Watcher and Lospa stood before her.

"It looks like they have come already, Lani. Who would have known it would arrive on the tail of just one person."

"I didn't know."

"I'm not sure what you do and don't know, Lani, and am less than certain you'd tell us anymore now besides." He turned to the man that had been guarding her. "Jerkin, go arm up and head up above. We need more men up there."

"Yes, boss." The man took off running.

"Dark clouds are following you, woman, are you positive there's no more you can tell me of this?"

Lani looked at him, thinking on his question; she did know more and helping him was probably helping her. If the Derks got in here she was more at risk than ever.

"I will tell what I can."

Watcher finished what he was doing, carrying a knife in his hands as he came back to the table standing beside it. "Now would be a good time!"

"The dead men I took the rings from looked like trained fighters. They wear black clothing that makes them hard to see in daylight, impossible in the dark. They killed other men before the one who gave me the amulet killed them. He said it was a lucky strike that killed the last of them."

"Is that all?"

"They carry a mark, it was tattooed on their inside wrist, all had it on the left arm. I don't know what that it means."

Watcher looked at her carefully as she said it. "Come here, quick!"

Lospa followed them at a distance back to the room with the tapestry.

Watcher went over to a cupboard and pulled out an old parchment, rolled up, and held with a silver ring. He opened it, and marked in ink on the paper, was the very symbol she had seen.

"This?"

Lani shivered. "Yes. Where did you get that?"

"It was left behind when the ascetic left the group I told you about. In his place after he floated up was this parchment. No explanation, just this."

"I have no idea what it means but they all had it."

"It seems maybe what we have been watching for has arrived and we didn't even see it coming." His face was creased with concern now, and Lani stood waiting for what to do next.

He looked back at the table where the gray pouch was still sitting alongside the rings. "If Cideep is right, they want those. And if you can't leave the amulet they will try to take you or kill you. I wish I knew what you are up to, or what this means but there's little time to find out."

He paused at the sound of a series of large crashes from the levels above.

"They won't defeat us, this is not the battle foretold, but I won't chance them getting what they seek. Your luck has turned your way, Lani." He looked behind her. "Lospa, come forward."

"Lad, I'm trusting her to you. You know the rooftops, they will be the safest way out. Take her where she is staying and help her stay safe until this is over."

The lad seemed shaken but the request. "Yes…Watcher," he almost stammered.

Watcher nodded at Lani. "And take that amulet. I'll not touch it, but I'll keep the rings."

Lani screwed up her face without thinking; they had been her only source of money.

"What?"

"I was going to sell them, I have no money."

He rolled his eyes at her, and reached into his pocket, pulling out a small pouch. "There's only a few coins in there, but that will have to do. If you don't hear from me, money won't save you, this city will be in trouble. Otherwise we can discuss more when we this is over."

A massive crash above and the screams of men interrupted him.

"Go, I must get to the fight." Watcher rushed out of the room, grabbing a sword as he went. His massive frame ran awkwardly, having to twist at his hips to propel himself forward. Lani wouldn't want to be fighting against him.

Lospa looked at her but appeared too scared to talk.

"How do we get out?" she said.

"Oh… We'll have to go down to get out now."

"Down?"

"We can't get to the roof from up there." He pointed up the main stairs where all the noise was coming from. "If we go out the drains, we can access some buildings a street over and go from there."

Lani suddenly felt her hopes rise. Drains she knew, if they were anything like Barnen, there would be plenty of places to get away. She also knew Lospa wasn't very likely to stop her getting away. She grabbed the pouch Watcher had dropped on the table and picked up the amulet. She put the amulet back in the inside pouch beside her brooch and the coins in her pocket.

As she turned to Lospa, a blast of air blew through the warehouse.

It was like a gale, throwing small things in its path. All of the lanterns went out and the warehouse became pitch black, making the battle sounds above sound even more ominous.

"Shit," she heard Lospa say.

"It's okay," Lani said to him. "I can see."

"What?"

"I can't explain. Here, where are you?" She held out her hand. "I can't see you, but I can see the room."

"Really?"

"Yes." She felt his hand and grabbed hold of it. He was shaking and the anger she held towards him for trapping her eased a little. Her mind flashed back to Barnen, and she realized she could be holding Ilker's hand. This lad was probably alone on the streets when Watcher took him in, catching her was paying him back. "Walk with me, I'll find the way if you tell me where we need to go."

"The downstairs you were in before. We need to go there."

Lani started walking, the fine grid lines in her mind mapping out the dark in front of her. She had never understood how this worked but knew no one else who could do it. You just had to watch out for fixed objects like pillars, that only showed up when you almost walked into them.

More screams came from up above and the clash of steel was ringing throughout the building. They reached the small stairwell down to the rooms below. "I'm going to let go now, we are there, the rail is to the left."

"Okay."

When she got down below, she realized the only space she'd been into was the one cell and she hadn't seen any exit there."

"Where to now, Lospa?"

"The right-hand room."

They walked over to the closed door of the other room, almost walking into it.

When they got inside Lospa spoke again. "It's under the cot. There's a grate, we need to drag the cot off."

Lani looked around, and realized even though the grid lines

weren't showing she could still tell the light differences in the room. She could make out roughly where things were.

The cot was easy to move and they lifted the heavy grate together, dropping it to the side.

"Is that smoke?" Lospa asked.

She smelled the air. "It is, we better hurry. What's below?"

"It's a straight drop to a wide drain. Only as long as this cot. It'll be wet."

Lani dropped first and braced her legs for the landing. It was a horrible feeling which thankfully didn't last long, waiting to hit the bottom without being able to see it.

She moved aside and called Lospa down.

He landed heavily beside her.

"Where now?"

She could just make out his head turning left and right, before replying, "This way."

He didn't seem very keen to lead, so Lani again grabbed his hand and encouraged him on. "Let's go, before anyone else comes down."

GORAN

The Good Companion Inn sat in the south western section of Nkuku and was like many lesser prominent inns, indistinguishable from others. Above the main door a well-worn sign swung in the gentle breeze.

Goran briefly looked at the faded, and peeling, masks on the sign. To some they looked creepy, to him they were five different expressions of the same face.

He slowed his horse and dismounted, heading to the right of the building where a gate was closed. It had taken him longer to get here from Nedor than he would have liked. His horse had done well, but there was a limit to how much they could ride at pace.

The gate led to the stable yard, and he used his left hand to ring a small bell hung there. A young face peered through a gap in the gate several moments later, looking him over. Goran held up his hand showing the ring he wore, the lad nodded without saying anything, and the gate begun to swing open.

"I thought it was you, Mr Goran. Welcome back," the lad greeted him.

"Hello there, Itto. Look how you've grown, son. Good to see you again. Is your master in the house today?"

The boy smiled at Goran's words and stood a little taller. "Yes. Leave the horse with me, I will see to it, you know your way."

He made his way around the back of the inn and into the rear of the kitchen, then out into the hall that led to the main room. It was empty, which he was happy about. He was exhausted after his ride here and having to deal with strangers wasn't something he relished.

There were several stools beside the bar; he draped his coat over one, and pulled out a small bag of normal tobacco and his pipe from an inner pocket. He went behind the bar and filled himself a mug of ale before sitting on the other stool, packing his pipe and lighting it.

He sighed out loud, after a big gulp of ale. He'd run out of water last night and had ridden today on a dry mouth. Several more sips later, and he started drawing on his pipe with more vigor, the smoke starting to drift about the room.

He hoped Itto would be able to tend to his horse, as she was starting to limp the last part of the ride, and he'd have preferred to have not pushed her like he did. While he'd feel bad if she went lame, he had to catch this woman, and she had a healthy start on him.

A change in the smell of the room, a sweet subtle perfume, alerted him that he was no longer alone, and turned to see Voince behind him.

"I'd know that smell from one hundred paces it's a dead giveaway, Voince."

"Look what we have here. Mr Goran himself, looking happy with all the free ale he's helping himself to," she replied.

Goran stood up and they came together in a warm hug.

"If I wanted you to not know my presence, Goran, be sure you'd only know when it was too late," she smiled as she stepped behind the bar.

"I am sure that's true, Voince, no need to scare me," he said.

"Let me fill up this jug for you, seems you dried the thing all out," her rolling speech continued. "What pleasures does Nkuku have to see you again?"

"Not so much pleasures, Voince, and much as I like to sit and joke, I need your favor as quick as we can."

Voince placed the now full jug back on its platter on the bar, and leaned on her elbows, cupping her face in her hands as she leaned in towards him.

"What do you need?" She spoke quietly, despite the empty room.

"How quickly can you get Hallendell to visit with me? I have something to discuss with her of much importance," he asked.

"Tricky indeed, Hallendell only arrived back this very day from Asema. The Master General had her with him on his visit to the White City. They've been gone many a week now, and only back but a few hours ago."

Goran sighed, realizing that it was unlikely Hallendell would have any news to help him, but he would need to update her none-the-less.

"She probably can't help me then." He puffed on his pipe some more. "Who's the guy that runs the dissidents here?"

"You mean Watcher?"

"Yes. That's the one. He might know what I need answers to, can you get me to him?"

"We'll be unlikely to see him."

"Why's that?"

"There's been trouble in the city overnight. Watcher's headquarters was attacked by some foreigners. He lost many men and he's not been seen since."

"Foreigners?"

"That's all I know right now, I'm just been out scouting the city, to learn what I can. The soldiers of the Master General are blocking a good portion of that area off, they don't seem much wiser either."

"I need to get more information, this could be related to why I'm here."

"Related?"

"I can't say. I might have to go visit Hallendell myself. I need to speak to her."

"Aye, me lord. It is rare for strangers to be in there it would be not good for Hallendell to have you meet her there. We can get word to her, but you mustn't go to her. Don't spoil what is working well."

Goran nodded his understanding. "Then what do you suggest?"

Voince was quiet for a moment. "It's that urgent?"

He nodded. "It is."

"Then let's put your stuff in a room, and let me change, before we go and send a message to her. If it gets through she'll come meet us, if not we'll need to wait until tomorrow."

They set out through the roads casually winding towards the citadel in the middle of the old city. Nkuku had expanded around itself over many years, and what had once been a fortified citadel inside a small city perimeter, now had several extra layers of walls added.

Like all the open cities in Morska, being led by military commanders, they were fortified despite the lack of any wars or battles in living memory. As the city expanded around the outer walls, the Master General of Nkuku had seen it necessary to protect the whole city by wrapping extended walls further out.

The belief that any exposed living areas were a potential easy target, and threat to exploit, was the primary reasoning. It did mean, though, that every twenty years or so debate raged within the council about the extensions and if more were needed, particularly as Nuku had swelled.

Many of the outermost quarters held non-Morskans, an enforced but not spoken about rule of the city. Only true Morskans were allowed to live within the inner walls. It made Nkuku a unique city, with pockets like mini foreign villages, all living within one bigger city.

One could find one's way in the middle of the Ngaherian quarter or Bengs' just by walking down a different street. For some traditionalists, it was a threat to their way of life, and they feared and avoided these sections. For others it was a sign of a modern city and they loved enjoying the food and culture brought in by their foreign residents.

Passing through a small section of the city backed up to the first inner wall were mostly Morskans. Voince slowed occasionally and appeared to inspect the food stalls and have casual conversations with some street vendors. Goran played along with her as she did. She kept checking to make sure no one was following or paying them too much attention.

When she felt they'd wasted enough time she briskly hurried him across several streets and into a narrow laneway, between a smithy and a wagon warehouse. Avoiding some cases and barrels, she guided him down the entire length of the building before squeezing into a deep recessed doorway.

They waited several minutes, Voince counting under her breath, listening for any trace of a follower. When she was certain no one was around she stepped out from the recess. Looking left and right, she nodded to Goran and they headed further down to the back of the building and around a corner into what appeared a blocked door. Taking a key from a pocket inside her dress she lifted what appeared to Goran to be a fixed bar on the door and unlocked it.

As the door swung inwards they both stepped through quickly before she locked the door and, using a lever, dropped the outside bar back into place. They were standing in a dank smelling dark passage with only a sliver of light making its way under the door. Goran watched her feel her way to the wall and grab a flint and stock before lighting a small lantern she clearly kept there for such visits.

Tamping the lantern as low as practical, she led him down the passage as it headed directly across the back of the building. There was a wooden trapdoor in the floor, and using a timber slat propped it open so they could get back out.

Voince climbed down a ladder into the narrow tunnel below, and signaled Goran down. The smell was unpleasant but he trusted she knew what she was doing. Along the near side ran a ledge for most of the length of the tunnels, allowing the adept passer to avoid stepping down into the sludge that slowly passed along the tunnel floor. No one chose to stand in the mix of water, sewerage and muck.

The tunnels that Voince followed led toward the center of the city and under the original walls to a spot directly below the citadel. Taking a small side tunnel Voince climbed up to a grate that sat in an outside passage at the back of the workers' buildings of the citadel. She told Goran to wait below.

She was gone only momentarily before she climbed back down again.

"What did you do?" he asked.

"There's a loose brick in a wall up there. We're in the back of the citadel. Hallendell knows to check it every evening she's in town, I just hope she remembers today."

"It's a message?"

"Yes, if I leave it a certain way it means I need to see her."

Voince checked the position of the grate looked correct before taking the lantern back off Goran.

"Now all we can do is wait and hope."

She turned and started back the way they had come, as Goran took off after her.

78

HALENDELL

*S*itting in her room in the citadel Hallendell felt exhausted, despite it only being early evening. The trip afield to the White City with the Master General had been tiresome and hard on her.

While she had survived many trips on the road in the past, keeping up appearances around the clock in a military procession was demanding, and the soldiers' ideas of travel comfort were non-existent.

She had planned to retire early from the citadel central hall, and by chance had returned via the workers' quarters, checking the signal post that was there. The brick had been turned which meant Voince had been here. More importantly though, the direction it had been placed signaled an urgent need.

This raised a challenge; she couldn't leave the citadel via normal means if she was retiring due to tiredness. That would raise suspicion with the Master General. While she'd been his companion for some time now she never felt like he trusted her. He was suspicious of everyone around him and her being an outsider even more so.

In the end she had little choice but to make her way out into the city, but tonight she determined that stealth would be the best option, over her usual extravagance and showiness.

She carefully arranged her bed that it would appear she was asleep should a casual observer intrude into her room. She did not totally trust that her door bar was entirely safe from external manipulation.

Wearing dark pants and tunic with a thin cloak over the top, Hallendell climbed out her window and stepped onto the roof, before quietly making her way to the side wall of the citadel. Suddenly with a sharp burst of speed she ran on an angle to the wall along the roof, hitting a stone parapet with precision, and sprang outward in a full somersault landing precariously on the wall's edge, before using the momentum to complete a forward somersault, coming to an abrupt halt.

Catching her breath, her legs locked in balance, she stepped off the side of the wall and dropped a few feet onto a small ledge that was just wide enough for her feet, one in front of the other. Only an acrobat of extreme skill could have pulled off these maneuvers. She took out a slender sturdy coil of a rope made from a Kabel vine.

The vine could only be found in the shared forest between Daskare and Vodotok and few knew the correct way to cut and gather it. Even fewer knew how to weave it into the lightweight, strong rope that Hallendell carried. For most people that had to live with the Kabel encroaching on their farm lands, it was just a cursed weed that nearly choked life from any decent plant.

Attached to one end was a three-pronged hook. She had to contort herself and maintain her balance to secure the hook to a loop, attached to the ledge, her tired muscles aching as she did. Once the hook was set, she slipped off the ledge, her gloved hands sliding down the rope to control her pace, while her booted feet ran soundlessly down the wall backwards.

As she neared the bottom she slowed her descent, and swung out a little before landing with a muted thud on the paved laneway below. Her hidden exit was a necessity she used when she didn't want anyone to know she was away from the citadel.

The rope, hooked onto a latch on the lower wall, was almost invisible in the evening light. Should anyone come across it, it would appear like it belonged there. Hallendell brushed her clothes straight, pulled on a black cap and tucked her hair into it, before crossing the laneway and heading down an alleyway.

Despite her weariness she set off at a jog down the alleyway, skipping over rubbish littering the path, and avoiding the puddles and muck that would mark her clothing. There were several designated meeting places that she had arranged with Voince, but there was only one for an urgent summoning.

Leaving the old city and entering the second city she passed through a section where the poorest in Nkuku lived. Here the least maintenance and repairs had been done. The ramshackle wooden buildings had rotted and fallen into poor use, but were still inhabited by many workers who struggled to eke out a living in the strict military city.

On the eastern fringes of this slum a few ale houses catered for those with little to spend, most of them funded by Watcher or other unknown patrons that ensured the poorest had something to look forward to. Behind one of these was a small stable that housed a few horses and a delivery wagon. In the very back of the stable was what appeared to be a tool and storage shed.

Hallendell pried the door open and closed it behind her as she made her way in. A dull lantern burned in the center of the shed, emitting just enough light for someone inside the room but none that was seen outside. At the back of the room a stack of crates appeared to prop up the side wall. Slipping behind them, she knocked on an obscure door.

A panel slid open at eye height but only enough that a set of eyes could inspect her. The panel closed, a lock or bar was lifted and the door opened inwards. As she stepped in, the door was quickly closed and barred by Voince, the keeper of the Good Companion Inn.

"Good to see you could make it, Hallendell, we were only going to wait until the half-moon sat high," Voince said warmly as she made her way back to a table in the center of the room.

As Hallendell followed her, stepping into the well-lit center of the room, she realized they were not alone and seeing Goran across the table her face lit up.

Goran got up and came around the table to embrace her warmly, she returning the favor. "Oh, Goran, if I had known you would have been here I would have brought my knives."

Stepping back and looking her up and down, he replied with a smirk, "Don't worry, I have enough for the both of us."

She held out her right hand that held her ring, and he lifted his as well, touching them together. "In All Jest," she said.

"In All Jest, Hall," he replied.

"Apologies, Hall, I know you've been on the road but Goran had need of an urgent meeting."

"None needed, Voince, a signal was sent, and received, so I came. All the better for the additional company, not that I don't enjoy our rendezvous, but had it not been urgent my weariness from my recent travels would have left it ignored." Hallendell could see the silver token hanging around Voince's neck, that marked her as a keeper in their network. The symbol engraved in it matched the one on the face of Hallendell and Goran's rings.

"Fate has played its hand well then. My apologies for bringing you out after your journeys but I need your help, and I have to update you on some unusual matters." Goran spoke less cheerily as he sat himself back at his seat.

The room was only big enough to hold six people around the table and little else. They all sat and Goran began to discuss what he needed Hallendell for.

"I'll be direct to keep this as short as possible. There's been trouble in the lands to our north and we think they are spreading. Forces about whom we know little have been active and there's been deaths. We've lost one of our own as well."

The two women stared at him, waiting for him to continue. He needed a moment to gather his breath, his throat tight; the news still brought a sadness to his heart.

"Ashantha appears to have been killed in a fight in Malamig."

Hallendell and Voince both gasped at the news.

"How has this come to be?" Hallendell softly asked.

"I don't know every detail of it. He was wounded in the fight and died some time after. More than that though…"

Goran took another moment to calm himself down. "… he had

been away, in Enderk. I don't know all of the details, but he had not spoken with anyone since his return. Mother believes Derks might be responsible, based on other reports we're getting. A young woman, going by the name Lani, was there at his death."

His voice still cracked a little at the talk of his friend's death.

"Even more concerning, this woman appears to be wearing Ashantha's ring."

"What?" Hallendell burst out. "How can that be? We all know the rings only belong to the one they are fashioned for."

"I have no idea. Mother has seen it to be true. No one knows why and she is on her way to the Ring Master to seek answers." Goran subtly moved his eyes at Voince and back to her before continuing, "And this girl has his other things."

"Other things?" Voice spoke up.

"His belongings," Hallendell jumped in. She knew exactly what Goran meant, Ash's mask. "How can I help?"

"I don't know her location, Beantic can see the movement, but I only find out once she's moved on. She was heading here, to Nkuku, so she's either here or moved on. I need help to find her or information about her."

"I've been gone for weeks as you know, I'm not sure what help I can be?"

Goran got up and stretched his back before standing behind his chair, his hands upon the back of it. "The man, Watcher, he would be our best chance of getting information, would he not?"

Hallendell nodded in reply. "Yes, good idea. Sorry, my brain is weary."

"It's okay, however there's a complication. Voince told me that there was an attack on his headquarters by foreigners."

"An attack, here in the city?" Hallendell was worried about what that meant for her; once word of it reached the Master General he might call for her, back in the palace.

"Yes. I can't get any more word from that section of the city, it's blocked by soldiers," Voince added.

"Watcher's crews would have eyes on any outsiders passing through the city, so he may have information that can help. This news bothers me, I may have to hurry back to my room, they might come calling for me."

Hallendell rubbed her temples and tried to steer the impending headache away. "I will need to try and find Watcher quickly. Is he still alive, Voince?"

"Sorry, Hall, I couldn't get anything from my usual sources, everyone's gone quiet."

"I need to know if the girl is still here or left already, Hall. I'm sorry to impose, but it's very urgent. Mother *needs* me to find her and get Ash's things back."

She nodded at him. "I know, I know. Goran, you go back to the inn and wait. You'll stand out too easily, especially if there's soldiers patrolling, the area. Voince, I know a way in, but I want you to stay here until I come back. I'll pass on what I know to you, and you can tell Goran. If I can't find the Watcher quickly, though, I'll have to leave. I can't chance being found absent, it will break what little trust I have."

"Thanks, Hallendell. I wish we could spend more time together enjoying a fine wine or two but for now an answer on where this little bird has flown to or where she rests would be of great benefit to us all."

They hugged again and Goran was let out a door opposite the one that Hallendell had come in through. It led into the back of an alehouse that was full and rowdy, allowing Goran to disappear amongst a group of people.

Hallendell bid Voince farewell and left through the other door. She pulled her cape up over her head, wishing she was back in her bed resting, before setting off towards a place she thought she'd find Watcher.

I go away for a few weeks and the world falls to pieces.

79

GORAN

Goran was edgy as he waited in the main room of the Good Companion. He had remained in the alehouse, for an hour or more, enjoying an ale and chatting to some of the locals who were well on their way to a bad headache. Not wanting to be seen leaving the area at the same time as Voince and Hallendell, he'd found some interesting locals to sit with and see what news they would share the looser their tongues became.

While he wasn't going to be remaining in Nkuku, you never knew what tidbits of information you could pick up from a random conversation, especially when alcohol was involved.

He was able to play the part well; he never actually drank that much, but could mimic those around him, and fit in to any group. His mind was still flitting through the few things he knew about Lani, knowing his responsibility to collect the things she had that were not hers. What happened after that wasn't his concern.

By the time he got back to the Good Companion it was closed, apart from those up in their rooms. He waited in the main room alone until the silence was broken by the back door opening and Voince walked in.

"I guessed you'd be lubricating yourself."

"A man has to keep himself hydrated, Voince, we couldn't have me collapsing from lack of fluids."

"It wouldn't be the lack that made you collapse," she said, her grin lighting up the dull room.

"What news?"

Voince looked around the room and came closer to him on the other side of the bar. She grabbed a goblet from under the bar and poured some wine into it, taking a long sip before answering him. Her face was grim. "All bad."

"Did Hallendell not find Watcher?"

Voince said nothing but took another drink.

"Well?"

"She couldn't talk to him."

"Oh, no." Goran imagined the worst.

"He's alive but unable to talk. She spoke to one of his lieutenants."

"And?"

"They were attacked by an enemy they could hardly see, in the dark their attackers were almost invisible and seemed to flow around them like they could ride the wind. It took Watcher to wade in to the battle, taking wounds constantly, to break the back of them. His strength allowed him to hold his ground and save the rest of his men, but at a price."

"Did he say who it was?"

"Hall got shown the dead. The attackers were Derks, dressed all in black."

"How many were there?"

"Four dead bodies was all she saw."

"Just four? How many men did Watcher lose?"

"More than twenty, less than thirty. They are still looking. Others were injured either from the attackers or in the damage to their building and some were arrested out on the streets."

"Soldiers?"

"Yes."

"How bad is Watcher?"

"Bad, he may not survive."

"So nothing of the girl, then?"

"There is news of her. She was there when the battle started."

"With them? How come?

"From what he told her, this young woman, Lani, I think Hall said her name was…" Goran nodded. "She had some rings she was trying to sell."

"Rings?"

"Sorry, I don't know more about them."

"Okay."

Voince continued, "She ended up getting caught by one of Watcher's men. They wanted to know what she was up to. She killed one of his senior men."

"Killed?" This piqued Goran's curiosity. This was the first news of this woman being violent, apart from her possibly killing Ash.

"I didn't understand all that Hallendell told me, I'm just trying to relay the words. I think she said, 'She had an amulet with her, made with a large amber stone, and when he picked it up he fell dead on the spot, but the woman she can hold it'."

Goran shook his head, trying to understand what this meant. An amber amulet. It made no sense to him.

"Is she still there?"

"No, apparently Watcher sent one of his men to take her back to her inn, so the amulet wouldn't get found by the attackers. It seems they had a warning, about them wanting it."

"A warning?"

"The Eyes."

"Is there one of them here?"

Voince nodded. "Yes, but I do not know where."

"Very interesting." Goran knew of the group of seers known as the Eyes, but he had never met any of them. This was even more intriguing. "Finding them could be helpful, if they know about what is happening."

"I do not know where they are but I could try and find out."

"So, back to the young woman, Lani. She's safe then?"

"Potentially yes. She and one of the Watchers escaped before the worst of the fighting but they haven't been seen since. No one has left the headquarters, they're still tending to the injured and handling the dead."

Goran took a deep breath, followed by a mouthful of ale. This was all turning messy and the girl was being exposed to people that did not need to know anything more about what she carried. The amulet was a dangerous twist to the situation, and he'd need to get news of that back to Anderwell.

"What chance of finding where she's staying?"

Voince looked at him, her face looking tired, "I was thinking you'd ask me that. Once I've had something to eat I will handle that myself. I think I'll need to call in some favors to get information on guests, but I'll find her, it will just take time."

"How can I help speed it up?"

"You can't. No one knows you so they'll turn you away or worse bring you to the attention of the soldiers. You're going to have to leave this to me."

"I don't believe she's ever been this way before, so she would have come through the main gates on the north wall. If we start up there, that's probably your best bet."

"We?"

"I'll keep you company, so I'm not going stir crazy sitting here."

"Okay."

Goran needed to find Lani quickly. If Derks were following her she was putting his colleagues and him in even more danger. They couldn't allow Ashantha's mask and journal to fall into others' hands, and he needed to get his hands on the amulet. Not literally, but he needed to get it, and her, to Anderwell; how, he'd have to figure out once he found her.

GORAN

Goran and Voince had covered as much ground as they could but to no avail. He'd known it would be a long shot that anyone would be able to recognize a lone woman amongst the myriad of people that moved through the gates.

The city guards were more concerned with the events of the previous day's attack on Watcher. Goran didn't know enough of the politics here, but it was clear the guards were happy someone had done their work for them. Voince tried to sort the rumor from facts of all the information they gathered but there was little useful information to be heard.

He tried to think through what he would do if he was in this woman's position, but he couldn't get a read on her. It was likely she was hiding out after what she'd just been through, but finding her might be an impossible goal.

If she had left town then there was only one way to find out and that was to reach out to Beantic. Either way, she'd be able to tell him where Lani was, and that was what he needed to know.

Making the connection to Beantic was not the most enjoyable way to start the day but he had little choice. He definitely needed to do it before he ate or he'd lose it all, as the side effect of the process was unpleasant, to say the least.

Goran found Voince out the back of the inn.

"Morning, Goran."

"Voince, you're up early."

"Always something to do, Goran. Just because we were up half the night, doesn't stop the work. You need something?"

"I do."

"And?"

"I need a live rat."

Voince turned to him with a quizzical look.

"You know not to ask, Voince. It's urgent."

She finished emptying the bucket she been holding. "How urgent?"

"Now, urgent."

"Where do you want it?"

"My room," he said almost apologetically.

She shook her head. "Leave it to me, go back there and I'll get it sorted."

"Thanks, Voince."

"Whatever," she replied, and headed back into the inn.

Goran followed her, and saw her head through the back of the kitchen. He continued straight and upstairs, back into his room. Voince returned with a small sack containing a rat, and left him without further discussion.

He settled on a cushion in the corner of the room by his bed, and slowly calmed his breathing. Over years of practice he was able to ignore the distraction the frantic animal made, they always were desperate when captured. As he centered his focus on the spot between his eyes he laid the hand with his ring firmly onto the squirming body of the rat. The ring had to be in contact with the crea-ture to access its life force.

He moved into the void, the experience when you made the call, different to receiving it. You could sense what was flowing into you from the animal, and the feeling was uncomfortable. The sensation of energy it gave you powered the connection, but it came with a companion. In his mind he saw it like black ink that intertwined around the green of the energy, thinner and lesser but still there. Tillandra had explained that she believed this was what made you feel sick afterwards. It was like a poison, the cost of taking something's life in this manner.

Goran brought Beantic's face into the void, bringing it from his memories, and pushing towards it. Now he had to wait, hoping she could take the connection. Sometimes you did all this in vain, with the receiver not able to stop and talk, but right now he needed her, he hoped she'd be able to answer.

He didn't have to wait long, as the image of her changed from a flat memory into a live view of her face.

"In All Jest, Goran."

"In All Jest, Bea. I wish it was."

"What?"

"All jest."

"What is happening?" she queried, concern forming on her brow.

"This chase is becoming increasingly difficult."

"How so?"

"Wherever this woman goes, trouble seems to follow. I'm in Nkuku and there's been an attack."

"What sort of attack?"

"Details are sketchy about the who, but I believe it's Derks."

"Derks attacking Nkuku?"

"Not exactly, do you know of the Watchers?"

"A little, we're aware of them, and parts of their story."

"The Derks attacked their base, there were a lot of deaths, and damage. It appears they were seeking this woman there."

"Really? Did they catch her?"

He could see the concern all over her face now. "No, it seems she's escaped, which is why I'm reaching out. I need to know where she is."

"You called at the right time."

"How so?"

"I'm in the map room. She's not there, sorry. I wasn't sure who had moved, but now that I know it's you in Nkuku, then the other person is moving south."

"South? Towards Callet then?"

"I can't say, but where else?"

"True." He tried to understand why she would be heading there, but had no idea. Beneath his hand he felt the rat had gone limp, which meant there wasn't long left in their conversation. "I don't have long, I have more to tell you."

Beantic said nothing.

"Hallendell was able to learn from the Watchers that Lani, this woman, has an amulet."

"An amulet? What does that mean?"

"I don't know. Apparently it kills those who touch it."

"But not her?"

"I got this second-hand, Bea, so I can't tell you more, but that it was an amulet with a large amber stone set in it."

"Okay, I'll let the others know. Anything else?"

"No, I'll need to leave straight away. If she veers off from Callet, let me know. That's where I'll head."

"I will. Be safe, Goran, it sounds like she's more dangerous than we imagined."

"Yes. I know."

Beantic floated out of his vision and he slowly brought himself back into the room. Even knowing what would come, he still wasn't ready for the physical reaction. The nausea overwhelmed him and he flung the sack to the side as he reached for the pail he had left beside where he sat.

Once he had finished vomiting, he washed his mouth out and took the sack and pail outside and disposed of their contents. He had no time to waste, he needed to get back on the road.

LANI

With the light filtered down from the street through what few grates there were, Lani's eyes could see enough to guide them. Lospa had let go of her hand once he too could see a little better, and followed quietly behind.

When they had reached the way out that Lospa had told about, they found it was blocked. They didn't know why, so they kept going further away from the Watchers' hideout.

The grate above her now seemed as good a place as any to get out of the drains. Her boots and the bottom of her tights were wet, and she didn't want to think about what they had been walking in. The smell down here was not pleasant, and nothing like the drains she had used in Barnen.

She climbed up and listened until she was sure there was no one close by. When they were up on the street, they moved into a dark lane and stopped.

"Where are we?"

Lospa looked around and pointed. "Prendle Way is just over through there. Where are we going?"

"I'm not sure about you, but I want to get back to my room."

"That's what I meant. Watcher told me to take you back there and watch over you, but where is that?"

Lani explained where she was staying and this time he led the way, and they started back towards the inn.

"I'm sorry," he said out of nowhere.

"Sorry for what?"

"For knocking you out."

Lani laughed. "Your lucky elbow."

"It wasn't lucky, I meant it."

"Sure. It's okay, I should have been smarter."

"Where you from then? I didn't hear all that was being said with Watcher."

"Malamig. A city called Barnen."

"Oh, never heard of it."

"It's a long way away. Are you from here?"

"Yeah."

"Your family?"

He was silent for a while, and Lani didn't push it any further. She used the quiet to think about how to get rid of him. She had already bested him once, and she thought she could do it again, if she had to, but she needed to figure out what her plan was.

Since the revelation from the Teller that the amulet was bound to her, everything had been out of control. She needed time to think about what she should do. She still had the horse she'd arrived with, and Watcher had given her a little extra coin. There was nothing in Nkuku for her now, Watcher's men knew who she was and she no longer had the rings to sell.

He had said Callet was the next major city to the south. If it was anything like the distances between the last cities that was another two or three days' ride. That; she could do. Maybe Bossu could help her get rid of the amulet. Would he know what to do?

"They all died. Watcher took me in." Lospa's voice startled her.

"Oh, I'm sorry."

He shrugged his shoulders' "It is what it is."

"Here it is." Lani saw her inn ahead of them. "Now what?"

"He wanted me to wait with you until everything was safe, so I'm coming in."

No one bothered them as they went up to her room, and Lospa pulled the chair over to the door and sat down, blocking her exit.

Lani took off her wet boots and turned them over to dry. She wanted to change out of her tights but there was no way she was doing that with him in the room. She climbed onto the bed and sat against the wall. He had his eyes on her, and while she wasn't threatened by him, she wished she was alone.

Neither of them slept through the rest of the night, nor did they talk. Lani had tried to think of ways to get rid of him, even briefly, but by the time the first rays of sunlight crept through her window there was only one way she could think of.

Lospa stood and stretched, as he had done several times throughout the night. While he faced to the wall, leaning into it to stretch his calves, Lani reached into her tunic and took out the pouch holding the amulet.

She put it in her hand, hating the way it made her arm feel, and stood up.

"You know what this does, right?"

Lospa stood up and moved back from her. "What … are you doing with that?"

Lani could see the fear in his face. She hated herself for using it like this but it was all she could come up with. "You know what happens if it touches you?"

His small stammer had come back, "Y- yes."

She waved it out in front of her towards the center of the room. "Down on the floor."

"W-what are you going to do?"

"Down on the floor!"

He moved cautiously away from her and lay face down on the wooden floor. Lani stepped around him and pulled out the saddle bag and rope she'd fortunately brought up when she arrived.

"Give me your hands."

She tied his hands together behind his back and then looped the rope around his ankles and tied them too.

"Watcher will kill us both."

"Watcher can do what he likes with you, Lospa. I won't be anywhere near here when he finds you."

He grunted and dropped his head back on the ground.

When Lani was finished she retrieved her satchel and put everything on the bed.

"Please, don't do this."

Lani didn't want to hear anymore from him. She went to get her knife and realized he'd taken it from her. She turned him part ways over and grabbed it from his belt, glad he'd been happy to wear it like a trophy.

She cut a strip of his tunic off the back and forced it into his mouth, tying it behind his head. He tried to buck under her, but she grabbed the amulet again and waved it near his eyes. He stopped resisting then.

"You'll be fine, someone will find you before long. Sorry, but I can't be waiting around for your crew to come find me."

Glad that was over, she quickly put the amulet back in the pouch. It felt wrong to have used it for her own benefit, and her arm had tingled the whole time she held it. If the Derks were behind the attack on Watcher's place that meant they were here in Nkuku. If any had survived last night's attack then they could probably track the amulet. She needed to go, and now.

Lani knew if she left with all her baggage then the landlady would likely come and clean the room, she needed time between when she left and them finding Lospa. She hung both bags over her shoulder and climbed out the window onto the ledge. Once on the roof she found a safe enough place to climb down into the yard.

She found her horse, and gave the stable lad a small coin to thank him. "I'll be back later today, once I've had a look around," she lied, hoping if he spoke to the landlady it would suffice for them to not check her room.

Riding out of the yard, Lani looked back at the window of her room, "Sorry, Lospa, but that's payback."

With a firm grip on the reins she trotted the horse out of the city through the gates she already knew, unsure about any others. Once outside she turned the horse southward and set off at a gallop, keen to get out of sight of the walls.

When she stopped to rest later that day she felt minor relief at not being able to see Nkuku behind her. Each mile she had ridden brought Lani closer to Callet. With that realization she felt a growing sense of anxiety about what lay ahead. It had never been part of her goals to come this far south. Now what had seemed some fanciful place off in the distance was fast becoming a reality.

Callet wasn't just a destination, it was the center of the quest Ashantha had wanted her to take. He'd charged her with delivering the amulet to someone she had no idea how to find.

The amulet sat in the inner pocket in her tunic. She didn't know why but that was the only place she couldn't sense it. With it so close to her skin, she'd thought she'd sense it more, but she didn't. Whenever it was out of there, she could almost sense it, despite the pouch. It was as if it was itching her skin, and several times she found herself scratching her forearm.

Ashantha had warned her that it was more than just a jewel and at the time she'd thought him crazy. After all the things that happened and what the Teller had said, she knew it to be true. She had no idea what it really was, he had called it evil, but she didn't like it and didn't like that it had bound to her.

Taking it out in the room wasn't a great idea, she knew that. The sense of people seeking it was always there when it was free, and the tendrils that reached out worried her. She had to keep it in the pouch, so no one knew where she was.

Since leaving Barnen everything about her life was a series of strange events and new experiences. Her life had been flipped on its head since she'd stumbled across Ashantha in the cave.

Her life had taken on a frightening, and somewhat exciting taint, but there were definitely forces surrounding her that she didn't understand. There was a world out here far bigger and complex that she could ever have imagined, back in her life in Barnen.

Every day had been the same back there, mostly just about surviving. The rest of her kin thought of nothing but food, shelter and avoiding those who would do them harm. Lani had always wanted more, she set herself a goal to learn everything Bragg knew and be able to run her own shop in the future.

That was all changed now, she doubted she could ever go back to Barnen after what had happened. In the blink of an eye everything had changed. Yet she didn't even know why she was doing what she was doing, or for whom.

She'd felt like she'd been pushed down this path she was on, without having made the choice herself. Part of her wanted to believe that Ashantha's story was just a lie, and she was carting some rich person's stolen jewel across Dharatan. Whoever seemed to be looking for it was just working for its owner. It would be worth a lot of coin so it would be only reasonable to expect people to hunt it down, and for there to be retribution.

But she'd seen what it had done, the people it had killed. And the experiment with her being unable to leave it behind showed that it wasn't just a jewel. There was magic involved, magic she didn't understand.

She looked at the ring on her hand. Who were the people behind this ring? The Teller had called them, *'those of the clown face'*, whatever that meant. She didn't know anything about them, or the Derks that followed her.

Was she walking into a trap? Ashantha had said not to trust his own kind and to deliver it only to one person. Thankfully being caught by Watcher's men had turned out alright, but only by chance. It had shown her how out of her depth she was.

In Barnen she would never have been caught out like that, but then she knew everything about Barnen and its people. She knew how to survive there. Out here in the wider world there were many dangers, as she was learning, and not even from those who might be seeking her.

She had to find this Bossu, he would want Ashantha's things. Maybe he could solve the two biggest problems she had; getting the ring off and how to get rid of the amulet.

She continued her journey, learning about her destination from other travelers the closer she got to it.

Callet was on the southern side of a great river, in the northern part of Lletem, on a vast open plain. Across the river, to the east, sat the town of Waena, a Ngaherian outpost. Callet was also a border city watching those who would come into Lletem.

Unlike Nkuku though, it was too far back from the river to be able to halt the progress of anyone wanting to cross.

Where Waena marked the end of the great forests of Ngahere, Callet was the centerpiece of the great wide plains that stretched south from the river.

Lani had progressively felt the weather change as she rode south, more and more stickiness clawing at her skin. The River Bwyd provided no relief, her skin constantly sweating and the air heavy with moisture.

She'd never felt anything like it in her life and had begun to think she was unwell until she had heard others complaining about it also, in the last town she passed through.

Lani reached the gates mid-morning on her fourth day from Nkuku. A small column of people, horses and carts were making their way in through the city gates under the very casual watch of the guards.

Once inside she set off in search of a place to stay. Her body was glad to be off the horse, but the hard trip had made her weary. She needed rest so she could work out a strategy to find what she was looking for.

Taking lodging at the first inn she came to, she landed a spacious room at the back of the first floor, overlooking a small stable area and work yard. Locking herself in, she made for the bed and was asleep within minutes of lying down.

KYRO

Kyro eased his horse through the gates of Nedor, taking in the sights of his home city for the first time in many years. He had grown up here and his family was still here, all except his pa, who had passed away, their relationship never having been repaired from his decision to become a soldier.

He was happy to be back in some ways, although the reason for his return wasn't one that brought him joy. While he was anxious to see his ma, he knew he didn't have the time to spend there, it would need to wait until this work was done.

Right now his only priority was getting a meeting with the King, not such an easy task for a remote city guard, as tradition decreed a visitor like him needed to present himself to his superiors, the captain of the King's guard.

This should be interesting, he thought, as he slid off his horse and, grabbing the reins, started walking towards the palace.

Knowing protocol he had deliberately stayed out of the city last night, sleeping hard outside the walls. He planned that his best chance of arranging a meeting at such short notice was to present himself early before anything else got in the way.

What was equally as important was that Dante, the Prince of

Malamig, was still here in Nedor. Kyro knew Dante had passed through Barnen several weeks prior on his way here, and he had traveled with him for a day to rekindle their acquaintance. Dante hadn't mentioned any other plans than visiting Nedor to see his parents, but that didn't mean he had told Kyro everything about his trip.

RaMar was the closest big city to Barnen, their key ally, and over the years Kyro had ensured the friendship the two men had formed in Nedor in their early years was kept alive as best it could be, with Dante second in line to the throne. Kyro knew it might come in handy some time in his future, if for nothing more than calling for help in Barnen.

As he walked along the main road to the city square, he recognized how much growth had happened within the city, buildings now several stories high, some reaching up towards the tops of the outer walls. Nedor was always going to be pressed for space, with rivers on both sides locking it to limited land. That meant it had to grow upwards to contain all the new people.

Before the city square Kyro turned right and headed down the palace road to its main public entrance gates. The guards outside were wearily waiting for their replacements and the main wooden doors were still closed when he walked up. They didn't give his dirty appearance any importance and paid him little attention.

"Greetings, good men," Kyro broke the morning silence.

"The palace is closed and strangers don't get past here without royal invitation," one of the guards snapped back at him.

"I see the King no longer welcomes guard captains from his kingdom then, soldier?" Kyro tersely replied.

The guards changed their posture at his reply, their attention now focused on the trouble they'd be in if they'd not paid a superior office due respect.

"Well look at that, it appears the real guards turned up," he mocked as they stood tall. "Go tell your captain that Kyro Beguillan, Captain of Barnen's Guards, presents himself to the capital."

The previously silent soldier spoke this time. "Yes, Captain Beguillan, please wait here while we rouse the Captain, and have the gates opened."

"I shall indeed, soldier," and raising his eyes at the second man, he said, "if you could find me something to drink while I wait I am sure I will kindly forget our introduction."

"Yes, sir, as soon as a replacement shows for me, I'll see to it myself." Still smarting from being caught out in their post, he looked everywhere but at Kyro.

Kyro watched the people in the streets bustling to get to their tasks as the morning moved into full swing, and waited for the gates to open. He doubted King's Captain Feros would come to the gates in person, no doubt the soldier would be told to bring him to the guards' rooms.

The guardsman had made good on his promise to bring him drink as soon as the morning shift had arrived. As he quenched his thirst with a skin of honeyed mead, the sound of the winches moving announced the opening of the gates.

Within minutes they had pulled back and the palace forecourt was before him. The guard who had been dispatched to announce his presence returned, and as expected, took his horse from him and led him inwards to the guards' quarters.

The last time Kyro had been in these palace grounds had been more than a dozen years before and he had been a young soldier who had struggled to keep his head calm in the confines of a palace guard. It had been determined that his strong nature would be best suited aiding a northern town and while it had been a mark down back then, Kyro knew it had been a smart decision by Feros. He wondered what the reception would be like as this was his first trip back.

They walked through a winding, arbored pathway to the back of the main pavilion, to the right of the forecourt. Next they came to the stables where the soldier handed the horse to one of the stable boys, with instructions to freshen it and put it with the other officers' steeds. Attached to the stables was a large heavily fortified building where the guards' quarters were housed. They entered this and made their way down a long hallway towards the rear.

The door to the captain's room was open and the man sat behind the desk inside was the same imposing figure Feros had always been. As he got closer Feros rose to his feet and stepped around the table.

"Well, isn't this quite the surprise! Captain Beguillan indeed, look at how well the north has treated you."

He grasped Kyro's hand and then, pulling him closer, embraced him in a strong hug. As they separated Kyro noticed the flecks of gray throughout Feros's heavy head of hair and the age that was setting in his face.

"It has been quite a while, Captain Feros, I appreciate the warm welcome. Truth be told I had wondered how it would be to come home after so long."

"Don't be so daft, you're always welcome here, Kyro. You are one of our own. From my reports the best thing I ever did for you, son, was to set you loose in the north. Elsewise, you would most likely have ended up in the stockade, having torn some guileless lad apart from frustration at being caged here in the palace."

Feros turned and walked back behind his desk sitting in the hard chair behind it, pointing to a similar chair on Kyro's side.

Kyro sat in it and let his breath out, gathering his composure before he responded. "I wish it was all in good times that I came back, but Barnen keeps me busy, and events have taken a turn for the worse. You know of the incident several weeks ago?"

Nodding, Feros answered, "The dead bodies up your way?"

"I wasn't sure if word would be here already or not."

Feros rubbed both sides of his chin and cheeks with his hands, looking hard at Kyro. "What don't I know?"

"I believe my message told you that they were Derks?"

"Yes it did."

"All of the Derks that we found outside town bore a similar mark." Kyro turned his left arm palm up and tapped his inner wrist. "A tattoo right here."

"Do you know what it is?"

"Unfortunately I do, but I need to speak with the Prince first. He knows this mark from a long time ago, and I am not sure I can say any more without his agreement."

"Is that why you are here then?"

Kyro nodded. "He came through our way several weeks ago on his way here, I've not seen him return and am hoping he's still here?"

"He's still here, he's been stirring up the King good and well. Those two always clash when they are together too long. I can see why you and the Prince always got along, hotheads the pair of you."

Kyro avoided the look and comment directed at himself.

"You look as if you could do with a wash and some food, you going to stay in the guard house or finally visit your ma?"

"This is too important for either, much as I'd usually want to present properly to the King, I need to see the Prince before anything else. It's that urgent!"

Feros appeared a little taken aback by Kyro's last words and he rocked a little in his seat, looking at the man before him.

"Calm down, son. You might think it's important, but you'll need to give me more than your word before I can just rush in on the King for no good reason."

Kyro stood up and pulled the scroll from his bag, handing it to Feros.

The King's Captain opened it and read it. "Right. We better catch up to them before they head out, they had plans to go hunting this morning, and once they are outside the city they won't be back until sun fall."

Kyro rose and they headed out of the room. Feros shepherded him through a door outside to the grounds and across a paved courtyard that led to the side of the grand palace.

83

KYRO

The palace itself was a grand sandstone structure with multiple turrets on the main structure. Smaller sections of the building clung to it like needy toddlers, each with smaller and lesser turrets and parapets.

The guard at the back door nodded as they passed. They headed along narrow workers halls before coming out at the main hall. A small gathering of nobles and servants was forming in the foyer beside the front palace entrance and the two guard captains swept around them, before heading up the central stairs towards the King's sitting rooms.

The two guards outside the sitting rooms stood a little straighter as they saw Feros approaching.

"Tisot, is His Majesty in his rooms?"

"Yes, sir, he is. He has the Prince as company at this time."

"Very good. Stay your post, I will announce myself." He rapped his knuckles on the large doors and opened them without hesitating for a response from inside.

He stepped cautiously into the room, ducking his head as he greeted the King. "Your Majesty, please forgive my urgent intrusion, but I have a messenger with urgent news to deliver."

King Nordahl was standing, his hands on a chair in front of him.

He stopped his conversation with Prince Dante, who was seated to his left. "Accepted, Feros. Come in and bring the messenger with you."

Kyro followed Feros into the room, much less comfortable in the setting than Feros appeared to be, although seeing Prince Dante's familiar face calmed him a little.

"Kyro, while it's good to see you again so soon, if you're the messenger I am suddenly very nervous about the reason," Prince Dante said, as he stood and walked over to shake Kyro's hand.

"Father, meet Captain Beguillan of the Barden guard. He is the reason the north has been so quiet up until recent weeks, his firm hand of justice has prevailed where others have failed."

"Your Majesty." Kyro dipped his head as he faced King Nordahl.

"Captain, it is my pleasure to finally meet you, your reputation precedes you. Both your earlier one as my son's playmate, and more importantly the one keeping our northern regions safe from rabble. Like the Prince I am also concerned as to what brings you to our city."

The King took a step towards him and shook his hand. Kyro sensed immense strength in his grasp, despite an outwardly lean appearance to his frame.

"Your Majesties, I do have news and I shan't beat about the bush, if you will bear with me, as I may not have the graces and formality for the situation I find myself in."

Nordahl waved the statement away. "As you need, Captain Kyro, I would prefer you told us what brings you here with such haste rather than trip over your words."

A steward had rushed in with another chair and placed more cups on the table. He hovered near Kyro who was still standing awkwardly his hands on the back of it to keep himself steady.

"So what exactly do you need to tell me?"

"In fact it is for the Prince as much as for yourself, Your Majesty. It concerns a matter that I am not sure many know about." Kyro paused, looking at the Prince, then back at the steward who was busying himself around the room.

The Prince nodded in return and quietly used his hands to signal to his father.

Nordahl dismissed the steward. "Leave us, until summoned,

please, and close the doors as you go. Now sit, Kyro. You look like you could use something to eat and drink. You'll have to serve yourself though."

Kyro took his seat and poured a goblet from the jug in front of him, taking a healthy drink from it before he started.

"Dante, I haven't told Captain Feros here why I have come. None know the full reason behind it. Lord Barnen had to be told enough to allow me leave to travel. This relates to a matter from over a decade ago and the attack that we have not spoken about since. I assume I can speak freely of this matter now?"

Dante leaned forward in his seat, his arms now resting fully on the table, "Indeed you can, although you might have to remind me as well."

Turning towards the King, Kyro continued, "Your Majesty, this involves an event near RaMar some twelve years ago, a brutal murder of a caravan on the road between Barnen and RaMar."

Nordahl interrupted, "I recall this. It was quite a butchery and all the caravan were murdered quite brutally. I had forgotten that had even happened, we've had nothing like that until these recent events, am I right?"

Dante jumped in, "Your memory is correct, Father. In the story that's told the whole caravan was murdered, and we killed one of the attackers in the fight. The others escaped while he appeared to sacrifice himself to hold us off."

"You say 'In the story that's told', why do I get the feeling that there is something more that hasn't been told?"

"There is some more. There was a survivor from the caravan."

"A survivor?" Nordahl exclaimed, "How did I not know about that, Dante?"

"Father, at the time I determined it was not something that needed to be shared, and she was only a small lass. She was found, hidden under the bodies of what was believed to be her parents. She was obviously distressed and it was the best the soldiers could do to hold her still, she couldn't distinguish between friend and foe. Rightly so, one would expect, in the circumstances."

A tense silence now held around the table. King Nordahl looked as if he was about to burst; he wasn't known for his patience, and he glared at his son the Prince.

Kyro spoke up. "I found her amongst the perished. I had set my soldiers to digging a place for the dead, we had no way to transport them to either city, and we weren't going to leave them to be found by unwitting travelers or hacked apart by the wildlife."

"I came across them with my guard on our way through there, and we helped clean up. The lass was in a dreadful state as I recall," the Prince added.

"It was your counselor, Dante, if I remember rightly, he was the only one who could settle the girl. He sat with her and spoke to her in private, she calmed as soon as he was done and not once again did she speak of it. I know he spent more time with her that night and the following couple of days but it was him that handled her."

"Your counselor, Dante?" Nordahl asked.

"At times he was, other times he played a fool."

Nordahl grimaced at the mention of the fool, it was well known he had a very negative view since the incident with his daughter.

Dante paused, looking upwards before continuing, "Hembleth, that was his name. We called him Hem for short."

Kyro continued, "Whatever his role, he did an excellent job calming her down. We were just guards, not parents. If my memory serves me correctly, and I've been running through it the whole trip down here, we then met to discuss what to do with her. We had no knowledge of who she was and it was very likely her only family were all killed in the attack. No one knew why this caravan was heading for RaMa nor why it was attacked and everyone slaughtered."

Looking back at Dante, Kyro added, "It was determined that no one else needed to know about the extent of the slaughter, nor the involvement of the Derks."

Nordahl almost burst cutting in, "So who made these decisions?"

"I did, Father. I listened to the guidance of those present. On reflection it reminds me how I felt at the time that Hembleth had more than his share of influence in that meeting. At the time I didn't notice it nor how he did it."

"I don't trust these fools. We should never have let them in our court. Where is this Hembleth now?" Nordahl asked.

"He stayed in my court for a good number of years. Perhaps three years back he left RaMar and took off to be a Tellerman, as much as I know. He was quite the odd fellow, but in his time in RaMar I appreciated much of his counsel, despite your feelings, Father. He seemed to have a worldly knowledge that is hard to replace."

'You say that, but maybe he was as bad as the one I had here. What was the decision about this girl and if I am not confused I still don't understand your message, Captain Kyro?" Nordahl asked, getting visibly more agitated.

Dante answered, "RaMar is a well-traveled city, Father, as you might recall. There are small numbers of Derks that come through there from time to time. I decided that potentially the sight of them might cause this girl harm. Frankly, if I'm honest, if she remained in RaMar I felt she'd end up on the streets. There's only so much I can do for those without family or money."

Kyro cringed at the comment, he knew he hadn't done any better.

"Lord Barnen's father was still alive back then, and he'd requested help in quelling crime around the growing town. I was already planning to send Kyro there, but was not sure when. This event triggered me to act, I sent him there to run the guard, and to take the girl with him and see to her wellbeing."

Nordahl turned to Kyro. "I hope we are getting to the point of this soon; much as I like a good story, I don't like a long one."

"I did take charge of looking after her. We named her Lani, because she gave us no other. She's used it ever since. Before I left with her, Hembleth came to me. He spoke to me about her in a tone that was extremely serious, and charged me with her protection, not just to get her back to Barnen, but long term. I have never told you this before, Prince Dante, forgive me, but you left before I had time to see you again, and since then life's just carried on normally."

All eyes were back on him, with Captain Feros the only one speechless in the entire group. "Hembleth told me back then that there was something about the murders that rang alarm bells but he wasn't sure what that was. He said once you and he had figured it out he'd let me know. He said it was the tattoo on the man's arm, the symbol that was also on his blade, that he didn't like the look of. I never did hear from him again. Did you work it out?"

"No, this is the first I've heard of that. I would recall if he had discussed the symbol with me." Dante, too, was beginning to sound frustrated.

"He told me things back then that only on this ride south have I actually recalled. To be honest it felt almost like I was dazed when he told me, my memory was very hazy. He told me that this girl's family had been the target of the attack, and if they learned of the girl she would be in danger. I was to make her part of Barnen, fit her into someone's life, so she hid in plain sight. No one should know of her family. At the time I just went along with what he said. I can only assume he was manipulating me although I have no idea how."

He took a drink, gulping down a few mouthfuls to quench his parched throat. "I fostered her with a noble family, labelling her a rural orphan. She was a quiet one and said little, which unsettled many including the family that had her.

"As time went on she ran away from anywhere I could house her and ended up living with the street kids in Barnen. I tried to watch over her from afar, without bringing any unnecessary attention to her from me being focused on her. We tried to ensure these kids were fed as best we could. As time passed I had pretty much forgotten all of this. I certainly came to believe your fool was just that, an old fool. Up until now."

Kyro needed another drink from his goblet; the other men about the table all had their eyes on him.

"How so?" Dante asked, as curious as the others.

"It seems Lani might have been present at the recent deaths, or soon after. The bodies of the Derks we found all carry a tattoo on their wrists. It's the exact same mark."

Kyro took a big breath and let it out.

"It seems too coincidental to me that we now have multiple events concerning Derks bearing this mark, which I know nothing of, and they both seem related to Lani. I am worried for her safety, if she even still lives. More than that, if there's something more to it then I don't understand it at all. I had hoped you might know be able to answer more, Prince Dante?"

"Why is that?" Dante queried.

"Because of the scroll you gave me." Kyro felt confused by the lack of understanding from Dante.

"The scroll? Remind me."

Kyro pulled out the scroll he had carried with him and passed it to Dante.

Dante read it, his face confused. "I don't ever recall writing this. Where did you get it?"

"Hembleth gave it to me, it's signed by you, so I assumed it came from your hand. It told whoever was in my way that I was to see you, or in your absence, the King, immediately without delay in such an event."

"Show me that," Nordahl demanded, reaching across the table for it. He read it quickly. "This is most concerning. Our very men are being subverted beneath me to keep secrets from us and given false documents bearing royal seals. That is not good, Dante! Why didn't we know about this threat back then?" Nordahl was done with his patience now and had become very agitated. "Who or where is this Hembleth?"

84

KYRO

 sudden loud knock at the door stopped Nordahl in his tracks. "I said to not interrupt me until I was done," he shouted at the door.

"So why did you call me then, oaf?" an impertinent and older voice returned fire.

Nordahl's face was flushed red now and he stormed over to the door swinging it open. As it did a short man with long red hair and a wide girth confidently pushed his way into the room, avoiding Nordahl completely.

"Of all the leaders I've ever known, Nordahl, you were always the quickest to smart but the slowest to be smart."

Nordahl reached out for the man but he was past him before he could grab him. If Nordahl's face was red before, it was now crimson, and his eyes looked ready to burst from his head. He slammed the door shut and turned towards the stranger in the room.

"Who the hell are you, old man? I didn't say you could come in here!"

Feros had risen from his seat, readying to take action, his hand had gone for his sword, but he had no weapon on him.

"As I said, not very bright. Did you or did you not just call out

'Who or where is Hembleth?' Here I am, and yet you stand around yelling, like a town fool."

While this exchange had been continuing, Kyro and Dante had also risen to their feet, but were now looking back and forth at each other and the dwarven man in front of them.

"Hembleth, is it you? In Thenis's name what are you doing here?" Dante asked.

The short man grabbed a cup on the table and poured himself ale, before sitting in Nordahl's own chair. "Of course it's me, don't you be daft as well. I've been here for quite some time, keeping an eye out for this very thing you all are now awake to."

Nordahl stood, still in some shock, staring at the man now sitting in his seat. "I recognize you, you're the kitchen steward."

"You're half correct, Nordahl. I work in the kitchens, as a steward, but I am not a steward."

"I haven't heard anyone call you Hembleth down there?"

"Well what sort of hidden person would I be if everyone knew who I was now?"

Kyro sat silent, not quite sure what was going on. Hembleth was again seemingly able to influence everyone in the room, or his aura was such that he commanded everyone's attention, King and servant alike.

"Besides, that lovely cook of yours, Greta, is well worth being around. I should say, she can cook a mighty feast, but her cheeks are a better sight for me than the food she prepares. I shall be sad to not look upon those rosy cheeks every day when I leave."

"LEAVE!" Nordahl steamed, "What makes you think you are going anywhere?"

Hembleth sat back in the chair and swallowed his wine in one large swig, before belching in mock laughter at the King.

"Son, rest assured, you could bring the Captain's entire brigade in here and I would still walk out that door without a soul stopping me. So find yourself a stool, and either shut your trap while the adults talk, or behave like the leader you are going to need to be!"

"Hembleth, restrain yourself," Dante said. "Have some respect for the King or we will get nowhere with this matter."

Turning slowly to face Dante, Hembleth lowered his voice, "My dear Dante, I have no time to respect people that treat everyone like their personal slaves and that have done nothing of value to earn it. It's time to let you all know, this 'matter' you speak of will happen with or without you, so it's best you all take my words seriously. You need to focus on this, and not whether or not your good father's pride is smarting from a fat old man calling him for what he is."

Kyro was aghast at the frankness of Hembleth. Despite having met him before, he hadn't seen him like this. He also had his eye on Feros, who remarkably had remained quite calm. He knew there was a lot of truth in what Hembleth was saying about Nordahl, but even so, no one ever said it to the King's face.

"Alright, let's get to it, I no doubt expect there are a lot of questions to be answered, but to keep it short, whatever name you'd like to call me is fine, I have gone by a few, but Hembleth seems to be the favorite around here."

"Why are you based in the kitchens, Hem, I thought you had taken back to the roads?" Dante asked.

"I had, I was, and I was particularly enjoying it. Until I started to detect that all was not well and the trouble ahead was going to need my influence. This palace seemed as good as any to set up base. You can learn anything you want here, and come and go as you please. Sorry, Feros, but you've got more holes in your security than there are drunks in East Nedor."

"Trouble? What do you mean trouble, old man, whatever you call yourself?" Nordahl responded.

"Exactly the trouble that young Kyro has just been telling you about."

All eyes turned to Kyro. "I'm sorry, Hembleth, I know you charged me to take care of Lani. It was a double-edged sword, she was like a caged wolf always looking for a way to escape. I should have had my eye on her better but there has been nothing to be concerned about until these events."

"I'll deal with your lack of diligence another time. While I know many things, I don't always know the specifics, so update me on what has happened to her, and others, and where she is now."

Kyro repeated his story of the recent murders near Barnen, the extra body found and the location, and his belief that Lani was being chased by Derks bearing the tattoo.

When he finished there was complete silence in the room. Hembleth sat back against the chair and seemed to stare off into the wall.

"This is strange. Where to start?" He went quiet for a minute, before suddenly releasing another loud belch. "Much better. There's a complicated history to this land, one which my brothers and sisters might have had a hand in."

He held up his hand as if to stop them talking.

"No questions about that. There's things you will come to learn soon enough that will undermine what you think you know about Dharatan, and those people to the east."

"The Derks?" Nordahl asked, more calmly than earlier.

"Yes, the Derks. I won't rush that process, it's happening anyway and it has been suggested to me—" he rolled his eyes as if pained "—that I might not be the best person to be educating people on it. So for once I'll heed that and tell you what you need to know."

Everyone looked at him without saying a word.

"Lani, as you call her, seems to be more than we thought."

"We?" Dante asked, knowing his father would likely start trying to grill Hembleth again.

"As I said earlier, my brothers and sisters."

Dante shook his head; Kyro understood why, he was just as confused as them all.

"Well what did you think she was?"

"A girl, Dante, the daughter of a woman that the Derk assassins hunted. They're called the Vrah, so you know."

"Who is?" Kyro asked this time.

"The Derks you refer to. That mark on their arm is not worn by just anyone, they are a nasty, bad lot of Derks."

"There are good Derks?"

"Yes, Kyro, just like there are bad Mals, you also have your share of rotten eggs too. Why else do you need a stockade or hangman's noose?"

Kyro understood what he meant.

"You only see the ones they send over here, life over there is not like it is here. They are controlled and influenced by a woman related to my people." Kyro watched him shift in his seat uncomfortably, and look to the ground

"Who is she?"

He coughed, and looked around the room as if he hadn't heard Nordahl's question.

"Tell us, old man!"

"Alright. She is my sister. One of them. I didn't like her much anyway. She's been gone a long time, I thought she was busy just being the selfish woman she always was. We think maybe she's been busier than we thought."

"What do you mean?" Nordahl's temper seemed to be heating up again.

"These Vrah are her doing. They've been training and building their numbers for decades, or longer."

"Longer, how old is she?"

"You should know it's not polite to ask a woman's age." Hembleth gave off a weak smile as if to break the mood. "That's not important. What's important is Lani. Can we focus back on her?"

"Alright, what about her then?"

"They don't know she exists."

"Who, the Vrah?"

"Yes, and my sister. The mother was the reason they attacked the caravan all those years ago. I was up your way, Dante, because we had a sense something was going to happen, but I was too slow in working it out. I couldn't stop the killings."

He stopped talking and stood up so he could reach the goblet. He filled it and had another healthy drink from it. Hembleth swept a bunch of hair back across his head that had fallen forward and looked the group over.

"Why did they want the mother?"

"I'm not sure why, Dante. Like I said I was too late…" He repeated what he said earlier.

"So why is this girl so important?"

"Well, that's what we need to find out."

"It seems like you know more than us, can't your family tell us what's going on?"

"It's not that clear cut, Nordahl. We see things up very high—" he motioned off up to the sky "—and only get the detail when we're up close. But I can't stay here long, and half the time the good bits happen while I'm away. It's bloody inconvenient, let me tell you."

"So what's the point of all this?"

Hembleth folded his legs up on the chair and took a moment before continuing.

"I need to know why the Vrah are roaming all over Dharatan. I haven't been able to make it out, and the *why* is important. We're missing something."

"We?" Nordahl asked.

"My brothers and sisters, mostly. There's a piece missing and I don't know what it is. That's why I am here."

"But *WE* don't know what you're even talking about." Nordahl was standing and he was very agitated now.

"Hembleth, when I found the dead up in Barnen, there were a few things that struck me as strange."

The old man turned on his chair and stared at Kyro, "Such as?"

"The faceless man, for one."

"The what?" Hembleth asked, opening his eyes very wide.

"One of the dead men, he was alone in the wood cave, had been stabbed multiple times and bled out. But he had no face. He had a head, but his face was missing, it was just a lump of skin."

"What on Dharatan? You didn't think to tell us this in your message, Kyro?" Nordahl had turned his anger on him.

"Enough," Hembleth interjected. "Now that is interesting. I know what that is, but I can't tell you right now. What else, Kyro?"

"All of the bodies had been looted, there were things missing, such as the Derks, I mean the Vrah, had rings missing from their fingers. I don't know what else was missing but it wasn't something I could answer. My gut tells me Lani was involved somehow, I'm not sure why, but if she looted them, and has these things of theirs, she'd be in danger."

Hembleth said nothing for a minute. His eyes never moved from Kyro, making him feel extremely uncomfortable.

"That would explain why they are still here. Those rings would matter to them, and yes, she's in danger. She's walked herself into the middle of a right old mess. As we all are. You did good coming here, Kyro, you've helped give me enough information to make some decisions."

"What decisions?" Dante asked.

"There's only two that affect you right now." He turned to Nordahl "You need to hunt for these Derks and rid your land of them. I doubt they can get through Ngahere at the moment, so you're their gateway to Dharatan, and they need to be stopped."

Feros, who'd said nothing up until this point, cleared his throat. "Finally something I can do. We'll route them out soon enough."

Turning to face Feros, Hembleth continued, "We'll see. Your toy soldiers have been on show for so long, will they know what to actually do against those trained to kill?"

Feros stood, his discomfort at sitting through all of this evident. "These aren't some pretty lads in steel, my men are well trained, and ready to do their job."

"Trained they may be, but when was the last time you had to battle anyone, Feros? Never, in your lifetime!"

Hembleth let that sink in, before continuing. "In all your lifetimes there has been no threat, no war, no battles for the very lives you protect. You sit here in battlements and castles handed down through generations, enjoying the surety they will stand forever but without the history of why they were even needed. You do not know what a true battle is, and certainly not against a foe that wants to see you wiped from the face of the land."

He cleared his throat and stood.

"You can take my advice or leave it, that choice is yours to make. The consequences of letting these Derks get a hold on Dharatan will be deadly to your realm if you ignore me. They do not care about their lives like you do about yours. They will kill without care, and whatever it is they want they are likely to keep sending more until they get it."

The room was silent.

"The second thing is, I would like your help in finding the young woman, Lani."

Nordahl spoke up. "If nothing else I am in complete agreement that these Derks need to be flushed from our shores. As for our help finding this woman, what exactly are you asking?"

Hembleth turned and pointed at Kyro. "Him. Let Kyro continue to look for her, he's the only one that knows what she looks like, and who she would recognize. There will come a time when she will welcome a familiar face. If you can spare him to carry on the search I will guide him as I can."

Nordahl looked first to Feros, who shrugged, then to Kyro who was still staring at Hembleth. "I doubt Lord Barnen will be happy about this, taking away his Captain for the sake of a hunt."

"An important hunt. If she is caught by the Vrah then I fear much more is at risk than we yet know."

"Hunches and guesses, old man? How do you expect me to convince people on guesswork?"

"Not hunches. Don't be pig-headed, Nordahl. I've told you all I can for now, I need to find this girl and get her to a safe place. You need to get rid of these assassins from Malamig. Is that not enough for now?"

The king looked at Kyro. "And your wishes on this, captain?"

"I serve you, Your Majesty, and will follow your command on this matter. I do feel she is in danger and partly I'm to blame for that. I would like a chance to protect her if I can."

Nordahl rubbed his head, then turned to Feros. "You need to find these Derks and flush them from our lands Feros. All Derks, not just these we've been discussing, we can't trust any of them. Lock the ports, and any we can capture, I want them interrogated. Understood?"

"Yes, Your Majesty." Feros dipped his head to Nordahl.

He looked at Kyro. "I'm unsure about this, Kyro, but your leave to pursue this woman is granted. Go where you need, and I'll offer whatever help we can provide. Get coin and equipment from Feros as you both agree."

Kyro nodded back at him.

"Kyro, go to Nkuku, that's your next best bet to find her. I do not know why she is heading south, but that's all I know. When you get there look for someone they call the Eyes."

"The Eyes?"

"Yes, he's a seer. His name is Cideep, when you get to him, tell him I sent you. Be honest with him, or he will tell you nothing."

"Thank you."

Nordahl turned to Hembleth. "Do you have any more demands, old man?"

Hembleth laughed, "As much as I'd like to stay and put special herbs in your meals to irritate you, I must be away. I've been treading time waiting here in your kitchens, and now I know why. I had to wait for this information. I have other places that need me now and I have little time left in this visit."

"I think now I've met you, the last place I want you is on the inside of my kitchens. I believe our meeting is done then. Feros, Dante, we need to meet as soon as you've seen Kyro on his way. Today's bird hunt is off, it seems we have bigger prey to catch."

85

LANI

*L*ani sat upright with a start. She looked around anxiously for any danger. Her brain struggled to place where she was, as she sat up in the bed that was in the corner of a large room.

Daylight was pushing past the shutters on the window, and she could see the room clearly. She was in Callet, finally, and this was the inn she had taken a room at.

There was no one else here, that she could tell, only the bright morning light beating through the window.

Standing and stretching out all the kinks in her body from the horse ride, she rummaged through her kit to find a skin with some water still in it. It was wet enough to clear out the furry feeling in her mouth but she'd need more than this soon and something to eat.

She went to the window and looked out over the street nearby. Lani marveled at how busy the city was already and how much noise there was in general.

While they were riding towards the city Lani had noted how different it was. She'd only ever seen large cities bound by water or rock, not sitting in the middle of open land. Where Nedor had been built at the wedge of two rivers, and Nkuku facing the lake, Callet lay alone, surrounded by plains on all sides.

Sitting some ten miles from the Bwyd river, and the accompanying border with Ngahere, it appeared close enough to both for practicality but far enough to see all who came near.

The walls held none of the majesty of Nkuku, but wrapped around the city entirely, giving a sense of its size. She was no wall expert but they didn't look particularly well made, more a barrier than anything for defense. The closer she got to them, the worse they looked, their state of repair was low and Callet as a whole appeared more shabby than Nedor.

As Lani looked across the city that she could see her opinion remained the same as it had the day before. It looked like little was spent on the upkeep of buildings here. The city itself appeared to be very long and wide, and she wondered at what point the walls had been built. It would have been quite empty in the early years, where now buildings ran up to the walls on both sides she could see. One building stood out, right in the center of the sprawling metropolis, and it gleamed where everything around it was dull. It must be the central palace, Lani assumed.

She grabbed one of two chairs in the room, and placed it by the window. Sitting, she continued looking out across the part of the city she could see, contemplating what she was to do next.

Several weeks before she had set forth, more from desperation than any desire to do this task. She'd not really thought about coming to Callet. That was Ashantha's wish, not something she even really considered. Yet here she was.

Despite her original intentions, she'd ended up here. Thinking back over the series of events, each on its own seemed significant, but altogether it was if she was propelled against her will. Now she was where he'd asked her to go, not really knowing what she was here for.

The amulet was the reason now, whether or not it was for the same reasons as he had wanted. Lani wondered if Ashantha had known what it would do to her. Had it done it to him? Once he had died did it latch on to the next person? He had called it evil, but she wasn't sure he'd experienced it like she had. She'd never know now.

A thought came to her, and she looked in her bag, pulling out his journal. She flicked through it but was still unable to read it. He had been writing in it when she had found him, maybe he'd explained more about it in there. Perhaps Bossu might be able to read it.

There were so many questions she now had, and part of her was hopeful about finding Bossu. Could he explain to her about the ring, and the mask? What else did the journal contain? How did Ashantha know her name?

What did he know? How even did he know her? He had known her name the moment they had met, as if she had it written on her head. Yet she had no knowledge of him. Was he related to her?

He had looked like a Mal, albeit gaunt and weary. Had he come looking for her? What a cruel twist of fate would it be that he was her family but died as they met. No he didn't have the blue eyes she had. That and her reddish hair, the very things that marked her as an outsider in Barnen, he didn't have.

Now, such a long way from the only home she had known, a gloom fell over her. Could she ever go back there? She'd be a wanted criminal now, over Harsop's death. She'd run after being accused, and the only person who could prove it wasn't her was a Derk criminal, who wouldn't tell anything to help, not that she would know where he was.

The guards in Barnen hanged all murderers, that she knew. Captain Kyro set that as the law of the city. He'd warned her that the next time she got into trouble she'd be treated like anyone else. That would mean hanging her, if they judged her the killer.

Her journey was over, if she could find the person Bossu and get rid of the amulet safely then she was done. What then? Where would she live? If Barnen was off limits to her now, then where would be a good place to go?

Lani stood up and shook off the black feeling that was wrapping itself around her. There was no point in dreaming up fancy lives when she had no idea what lay ahead. She was alone, as she had always been, and feeling sorry for herself wasn't going to resolve anything.

I need to get rid of this ring and amulet. That's all, then what comes next, will come next.

Opening up her satchel and laying the contents on her bed, Lani made herself laugh at the strange collection of things.

The mask that still looked like Ashantha, she turned face down. She couldn't look at it without chills running up her spine. The coin pouch looked small, and she put the other one from Watcher alongside it. She took the amulet out of her tunic and placed it alongside the journal and the other items.

Lani could feel the pull of the amulet, she still found it strange that when she took it out of her tunic it always felt stronger to her. There was nothing special about her tunic and only the small blue brooch was in there, pinned to the inside.

She reached in and turned the pocket out, looking at the brooch, running her finger over it, a sense of warmth radiating into her hand. She let it go and studied what was on the bed again. She combined the contents of the two pouches, not feeling very good about how little was left. Maybe Bossu might reward her for delivering the things from Ashantha.

Again the amulet seemed to call to her. Lani could almost hear her name being called softly, as if it was speaking to her. She shook her head again, she had to be imagining it.

Hesitantly she opened the pouch and tipped its contents onto the bed. The jewel fell out onto the bed. The orange hue of the amulet brightened in the light of the room, drawing light into itself.

Again she could see the tiny strands of light creeping out of the stone, one to her arm and the other heading out the window as a wispy swirl. The amulet fascinated her to look at it, it drew her eyes and mind into it and it took some concentration to look away from it.

She reached over and grabbed the pouch and, fighting with herself, managed to force the pouch over the stone and pushed it into the opening and closed the ties tightly.

The air in the room seemed to withdraw into the pouch and a fresh light filled the room, as chills ran over Lani's skin. The effect the amulet had was very real and clear to her. It had been easy to forget the influence it had on her the few times it had been out, but this time it was very apparent.

Whatever it was, it felt wrong to her. Ashantha was right, whatever he was part of, the amulet was wrong.

Ashantha's dying words ran through her mind, their meaning unclear; was it a place she would have to find out?

'*Song ... Weaver*'

What did that mean? This was her only clue. It had to be a place, something to do with music. Hopefully it would be well known, but she'd need to be cautious about how she asked. She'd run into enough trouble looking for help on this trip. She needed to smarten up her thinking and be clever.

Lani knew the street, yes this was a different city, but she needed to go back to what she knew best. There would be those she could relate to here, they existed everywhere.

With at least some hope in her mind she stashed everything but a few coins and the amulet into her satchel and then hid it as best she could in her room. She put the amulet back in the inside of her tunic and the coins in a pocket.

Taking a big breath as if to brace herself, she then exhaled and opened the door.

Time to end this.

GORAN

"One would hope you've found better ale than the swill you usually serve," Goran called out as he strode into the main room of Follies.

The man behind the bar, his back to the room, turned at the sound of the voice. His scowl quickly softened when he saw the scruffy man, his dreadlocks flapping as he walked. "We do for all our good customers, but for you we save up the cheap swill."

Goran chuckled, plonking himself onto the nearest stool, dropping the bag from his shoulder, "Well that will have to do then, Brando, I guess."

"And it's mighty fine to see you again, Goran. I'm surprised to see you round here this time of year!"

"As am I to be here. Enough chit chat, I've been riding non-stop for a week. I'm dying of thirst here."

Brando filled a jug with ale before using it to fill a mug in front of Goran, placing the jug beside it when he was done.

After a few mouthfuls Goran sighed happily, "Definitely better than your usual!"

"Now I might be able to get something useful out of you," Brando replied.

"There's a lot afoot, Brando, a lot! I've come almost straight from Nedor. You know how much I despise riding, hopefully I might get to use my feet for a while now."

"Well I doubt you'll be filling me in on all the details. Sounds like you'll be here for a few days then at least. I don't have many people here so your favorite room is empty and clean, make yourself at home."

Pretending to fall off the stool, Goran spat out a little of his ale, "Clean rooms now too, what devil are you and where is the real Brando?"

"Ha ha ha. For a clown you're about as funny as three cats in a sack."

"In all seriousness, I won't loiter around here much today except to change my clothes. There's people to see, and I'm trying to locate someone that should have arrived here a few days ago."

"What can I do to help?" Brando asked.

"Can you find Zeresse for me? I know that can be a challenge at the best of times."

"Yeah, a challenge indeed. I'll set to the task as soon as I have finished up here. What's the message?"

"Meet me here for an evening meal if she can, it will take me a while to hunt down some others," Goran answered.

"Right you are, Goran. Don't finish that jug then, you'll be no good to anyone."

Goran eyed the already half empty jug, glanced back at Brando and nodded. He put down his mug, grabbed his bag off the floor as he stood, and headed out through the rear door towards the upper floor.

Goran stepped out the front door of Follies feeling better for the drink and being able to change his clothing. The inn would be his base while he stayed in Callet. Their circuit inns made life a lot easier, knowing you had safe lodgings.

Callet wasn't one of the places he ever stayed in for long, but being central to Dharatan most of the circuit passed through here if they were coming from or heading back to Anderwell. That meant Follies had to accommodate a lot more people than most of their inns around the realms, and stood out more.

It also meant that Follies wasn't an ideal place to conduct meetings, or handle their business. Brando had advised that there weren't many in the inn that weren't one of their own, but nonetheless this was too sensitive to be discussed there.

In cities like Callet, the circuit held other safe houses that enabled their business to be protected. The safe house in Callet was where Goran was heading now, he needed to know who from their family was in town and where he might find them. The roster of entertainers changed regularly so Henri would be the best source of information.

The streets were typically busy and despite all the people out, a dullness hung over the city, mostly due to the heavy cloud hanging around.

It had been a while since he'd been in Callet; it seemed like he was always between places at the moment, not staying anywhere for very long. He hoped that capturing Lani and getting Ashantha's things back would clear the record for him, and he could settle into a new role. Being on the road like this was tiring, he was getting very sick of it.

Not that he wanted to spend any length of time here; the last time he had, his habits had taken on a life of their own and his health had suffered for it. Lletem as a whole, and Callet more specifically, weren't places high on his list.

He had always wanted to see the White City, the capital back in Morska. But then all of the court did, it was rare that any outsiders could make it in, as Morskans there didn't like foreigners. You only ever went to Kamasa if you had an invitation from one of the Masters or, if lucky, in a trade expo. He was jealous of Hallendell's recent visit and made a mental note that he should discuss it at more length with her when he got back to Nkuku.

Focusing back on the task in hand, he headed through the eastern section of the city towards the link road. He always thought how the city must look to the birds above, like a wheel with a hub in the middle and all the spokes fanning out from it.

Goran entered the sector of the city called Harkaitz. It was like a district all of its own, with its own 'rules' and accepted behaviors. While Callet was extremely liberal and open, Harkaitz was the place where everything was taken to the extreme. If it stayed within this district most turned a blind eye to it.

Harkaitz was always busy, at all hours of the day and night, and today was no exception. The boundaries of the district were clearly outlined, with colored paving across the streets and similar markings up the corners of buildings, to at least head height.

Every laneway and alley was alive and fed off the main streets. Unlike many cities these weren't back alleys full of rubbish and despair, but access points to smaller venues, or rooms that held all sorts of activities.

It was often said of Harkaitz that no matter what you wanted to do you could always find it there.

His destination was one of the large attractions in Harkaitz and a place he had spent many hours drinking and enjoying the entertainment that attracted many.

The circuit had placed its safe house here long before the district had become what it was and by then it was too late to move it. As it turned out it appeared easier to hide in plain sight than in some far-flung location.

The main part of the standalone building was a large bar and entertainment venue, behind which stood a section which held guest rooms used for the entertainers and staff. Behind this, the rest of the building appeared to be a storage facility or little used space.

The truth was different. Goran left the main road and used an indirect route that led to the back of the building. A large heavy door was set in from the lane. Apart from the robust look of it, it could have been any other door in the city. To its right hung a black chain, unnoticeable from the street, unless you knew it was there. A small knob was attached to the end of it, the chain disappearing into the wall above. Goran pulled down firmly once, and could only just hear the ring of a bell from inside.

He waited. You didn't pull the chain more than once. A small hatch opened behind a rusty grate just above his eye height. A pair of dark eyes peered out at him.

The voice behind the eyes was gruff. "Not expecting you."

The hatch closed and he could hear a key turning. The door opened enough for him to step through before it was quickly closed, locked and barred.

"Master Goran, Henri didn't expect to see you this time of year."

"Henri, me either, but it's good to see you, man."

"No doubt you need something from Henri, it doesn't look like you have anything for me."

Goran reached into a deep pocket in his coat. "That's where you're wrong, Henri."

He pulled out a small package wrapped in paper. He handed it to Henri, using his left hand. It was a curious thing that none of them understood but Henri could not touch anything of theirs that was of magic, like their rings.

"What Henri think it is?"

"I think you'll like this. I came across it in a strange town. It's called toffee, it's too sticky for my liking but each piece will have you sucking for hours."

Henri opened it and his eyes lit up. It took him a few moments, as if he was deciding what to do, before he closed the paper and went to a sideboard and hid it away in a drawer.

He nodded multiple times. "Henri thanks Goran."

"See, I didn't just come for my own benefit," he smirked.

Henri moved to the big table in the middle of the room and sat, waiting while Goran followed suit.

"So what are you here for?"

"Like always, straight down to business. Good, as I have little time. I need two things, the first is to know who is working in Callet, which relates to the second. I am seeking someone who has come to town and will be as hard to find, I think, as water in the desert."

Henri reached over to a large leather-bound book on the table, dragging it over in front of himself. He opened it at the place his marker was set. He turned the book around and pushed it to Goran, pointing to a place on the page.

"Here, those are everyone Henri know of."

"Doesn't everyone have to report in when they are in Callet?"

Henri flicked his eyes side to side, his head rocking a little. "This they say, but there are those who sometimes try to be smart. Mostly

Henri find them. Not good for them when Henri do, but who is to know, maybe Henri not so good at his job now he gets old."

"Ha! You're not old, Henri, you'll be still here long after I have gone to dust. I will seek them out and see if they can help. Thank you."

"So who are you looking for?"

Goran paused; he wasn't sure if Henri knew about Ashantha or not. Ashantha lived in the spare room upstairs whenever he was around. They had been close.

"Have you heard from Anderwell in the last few weeks, Henri?"

He shook his head.

"Then I have bad news, my friend. Ashantha has died."

"Not true, *not true!*" Henri shook his head and stood up angrily. "Henri don't believe you. Ash not dead."

Goran stood and reached out to him, placing his hand on his shoulder. "It is, Henri, I'm sorry. We're all upset, just like you. Sit back down, I need your help, Henri."

It took a few minutes for him to settle again.

"Henri not happy."

"I understand, Henri."

"Change topic. What did you need from Henri?"

"A young woman, from Malamig. She was the last to see Ashantha before he died. She has come here, and I need to find her."

"What do you need her for?"

Goran couldn't tell him the specifics of the things Lani had, no one else needed to know that much detail. Only those who had passed the Audition knew about the mask. "She has something that doesn't belong to her, we'd like it back."

"I just need you to tell everyone who comes here we're looking for a young girl from the north and if they notice someone send the word. I doubt there'll be too many down here."

"Henri can do this. Shall Henri look too?"

"No, Henri, your job is here. I have to go now."

"Of course." Goran could see Henri looking hard at him. "Leave by the secret door, not this one."

"I will, Henri. It was good to see you, enjoy that toffee."

Goran climbed the stairs to the first floor and walked along the hallway. There was a lot of storage up here, including clothing, weapons and a couple of rooms, one of which was where Henri lived. The other had been Ash's. Goran was tempted to look in there, but knew he'd only get sadder. He could feel the voice speaking in the back of his head, of course it wanted to brood about his death. Goran kept moving, he would need to smoke some more weed if he was going to keep that at bay.

The actual safe was in the basement and only Henri had the key to that. At the end of the hall Goran turned and went down a narrow set of stairs, sideways. At the bottom he was facing a door that led out into the accommodation entry of the building. He pulled the hidden handle, and could hear a gentle click before the door opened a fraction. He listened for the sound of anyone, before stepping through and closing it quickly.

He came out from under some stairs in the entertainers' reception area before leaving via the building side door. He walked around into the main entrance of the Song Weaver. It was time for another drink. The first person he wanted to see was here and it would serve as a great starting place for his search.

KYRO

$\mathcal{I}$t had been years since Kyro had been traveling for such a length of time. His butt and legs ached from all the riding, and his horse was struggling with how hard he pushed it. He doubted it could carry on further without a decent rest, and as he rode under the massive walls of Nkuku he hoped he could take a break from riding.

He had never been this far south of Nedor, and he was amazed at the size of Nkuku, knowing that it wasn't even the Morskan capital. The white marble walls towered above him, and he'd stared at them for hours as he approached from the distance.

One of the city guards had pointed him in the direction of suitable accommodation and he took refreshments before he ventured out into the city. He still had half a day of light left, and didn't want to waste any of it.

Kyro was amazed that Lani had made it this far on her own. He'd not spent much time with her, the few times he had was usually when she'd been caught up to no good, and he'd been berating her. He knew she was resourceful, or crafty, but she would never have been this far before either.

She probably had no idea the danger she was in, if he was to believe Hembleth and his own memory of the Vrah. He needed to find her, and hoped he could protect her.

When he asked about where to find Cideep, he was met with strange looks. It was clear people knew who he meant but it seemed the normal person in Nkuku didn't go seeking him out. Cideep lived in a small wooden hut at the back of a small garden space on the west side of the city. The garden belonged to a temple to the god Maymun, that the Morskans worshipped.

When he approached the entrance, which appeared to have no door, a gentle deep voice spoke to him.

"Welcome to Nkuku, Kyro."

He was taken aback by the knowledge of his name. "Hello, are you Cideep?" He still couldn't see into the darkness in the hut.

"I am. Why are you here?"

"Can I come in?"

"First tell me why you are here, then I will decide."

"A man called Hembleth, he told me to seek you out."

The man inside the hut did not reply for several minutes. Kyro stood out in the sun, waiting.

"You may enter, but leave your weapons outside."

Kyro took off his sword and knife, and laid them on the ground outside the hut. He walked inside. A young looking man waved his hand to a cushion opposite where he was sitting.

"You seek the woman?"

Kyro struggled to speak at first; the empty eye sockets facing him made him uncomfortable. "I do."

"Why?"

"She is in danger, that's what I believe, and Hembleth told me to find her."

"You do everything he commands of you?"

"He's … very convincing."

"So you have no free will?"

"No, I do. It's just…" Kyro felt like he couldn't get the right words out.

"Why do you truly seek this woman, Kyro?"

"I feel like I failed at protecting her. I was told she was to be protected, and I forgot my responsibilities and lost myself in my work."

"Now you are at least being honest."

"Be careful from whom you take direction, many have interests that are their own. You must remember to do what is your truth, not just others' wishes."

Kyro wasn't entirely sure what he meant, and remained silent.

"No more lectures. She is not here, she has gone on the journey she must take."

"What journey?"

"To the clown people."

"Who?"

"Those who wear the mark of the clown. You will know when you meet them."

"Where will I meet them?"

"Many questions, but I am not to tell all, some of it is not yet clear to see. You will follow her south. You have little time to waste. She is many days ahead, and her future catches up to her. The dark ones get close. Hurry."

"Hurry to where?"

"South, Kyro. To Callet. That is all I can tell you."

Kyro was pretty sure the dark ones were the Vrah. He didn't know how long it would take to reach Callet, but he was behind everyone, and was useless to Lani right now. "Thank you, Cideep."

The young man just nodded at him but said nothing more. Kyro rose and quietly walked out of the hut, collecting his things as he left. At the outer edge of the garden he turned and looked back at the small wooden structure. Hembleth's contact had helped, fortunately, but now he needed to swap out his horse, if he was to make Callet quickly.

LANI

*L*ani had never thought about how different cities could be from one another. Each time she had explored a new place it seemed to be a new revelation. Her experience in the world was limited, and it showed.

The road in front of her seemed to head directly to the city palace, which was outlined in the sky ahead of her, sitting higher than any of the buildings surrounding it.

Either side of her the buildings were a mixture of shop fronts and accommodation. Occasionally there were small warehouses wedged between shops on either side. As an occasional thief, they were the places you tended to be more aware of. That's where the more practical goodies could be found. Many thieves focused on the high priced items, but they were generally better protected, inside living quarters and much harder to offload.

The warehouses held everyday items and often, if you were as smart enough, you could remove items without the owners even knowing. Lani had only ever taken what improved her life, she'd never been greedy to make a big profit. Well not until she'd found this amulet, that is.

With the shops preparing to open, the warehouses were open as the storekeepers restocked their shelves. Guards stood at the open entrances. It appeared to Lani that many of the warehouses were shared between the local shops, which seemed to make sense. It would keep the costs down and one guard could look after many.

There were more people on the early morning street than Lani was used to. Not all were workers busy with their early morning tasks. There seemed to be many revelers still active from the night before.

They flowed in and out of the numerous ale houses and vintner bars that seemed to be everywhere. Coupled with the general activity, their lively presence added to the overall noise on the street.

The landscape changed around here despite her still being on the same road. The shops diminished and it became what she could only understand as an entertainment district.

Now there were more and more ale houses, brothels, massage parlors, specialized eating houses and inns. At different intervals there were small wooden floating platforms set and she could see a musician setting up at one.

In one section of the road a small group of street entertainers were running through a routine with a couple of extremely short men being thrown through a flaming circle to bounce on a skin stretched tight across a frame, and bouncing up into the arms of a very tall woman. Lani thought she was strangely tall, her legs looked as if they weren't real.

The sound in this section of the city was even louder than elsewhere. Lani couldn't believe this was morning. In Barnen those up at this hour of the day were workers only, but here it seemed like a perpetual party.

She struggled to focus on mapping out the city in her head, with all the noise and distractions. While the ability was useful, it still required her to intentionally snapshot the images of where she passed, which required some concentration.

Mindful of what had happened in Nkuku she stuck to the main road, intending to inspect other lanes and roads later, once she had a bigger overview of the city.

The closer to the center of the city she got, the less entertainment there was. It was now mostly houses, which made it a lot quieter. The road she had followed joined a circular road that followed the walls of the palace. As she walked around it she could see in all directions there were other major roads that all led onto this circle road.

Lani walked entirely around the circle road watching carefully everything she saw. The palace walls were in much better repair than the city walls and there appeared only two gates into the whole complex. The main gates faced south while a side gate to the north west was smaller but seemed more regularly used by workers and merchants bringing deliveries.

A gathering appeared to be going on inside the walls, and from the main gates she could see a large garden where a group of people were gathered under marquees and covers. Lani reflected how everyone in Callet seemed to be at a party or coming from one. Even the palace guards seemed more interested in watching the happenings of the garden party than watching outside the palace complex.

She returned her focus to the outer streets and headed down one on the western side, which branched away from the circle road in as near to a straight line as it could.

This close to the palace the road was predominantly filled with houses and boarding properties followed by some services, a baker and a cobbler amongst others. To her left was a large open square where semi-permanent carts and stalls were set up. As Lani slowly walked between the stalls her mind wandered to thinking about Arbery and how they'd met in the Little Big Rock market.

She hoped Dedrick and Arbery wouldn't think too poorly of her for disappearing after all the help they had provided. Maybe she'd get to explain another time if she headed back that way.

In Little Big Rock the market had cleared out each day whereas this market seemed to be permanent. A fixed set of stalls and wagons, each appearing to be lockable, didn't appear to be movable at all. The area was clean and still fairly quiet, an array of aromas greeting Lani. Her stomach let her know that she hadn't eaten in some time.

Lani spent the rest of the day searching Callet on the off chance she'd walk across it herself, but to no avail.

Her feet ached and her calves were tight, having walked all over a large portion of the city. She'd observed the changes to the ebb and flow of the city, which while never truly quiet had its moments.

Right now just past dusk there was a calmness about the area she was in. It was clearly defined from the rest of the city marked out by color, and within it was the busiest areas of all. In passing she had heard this section of Callet referred to as Harkitz. She felt strangely safe within its confines, despite most of the people being a little influenced by one thing or another.

Once she left Harkitz the roads quietened a lot, much as if everyone was indoors taking a deep breath before the full night activities began in earnest. She felt more exposed now and learning from her foolishness in Nkuku was being a lot more cautious.

She was unknown here but a single young woman out on her own was a target in any city. She found a recessed entry and paused in the dark, waiting to see if anyone else was interested in her.

Almost ready to move on, she felt compelled to stop. She didn't know why but chose to stand still nonetheless. Fully on alert she watched the road and spotted a lone man, making his way furtively on the far side of the road. He appeared to be dressed entirely in black and had a hood covering his face.

She could see little else in the poor light but he moved efficiently and looked dangerous, enough that she stood frozen in her spot trying to keep her breath calm.

He never looked her way or seemed to realize where she stood, but Lani was very aware of him. The light was poor but that wasn't what stopped her being able to focus on him very well. She knew it was his clothing, it was the same as the man in Barnen, the Derk who stared at her through the window. There was something about the clothing that stopped you seeing it easily. He also was clearly sober and walked with intent.

What was a Derk doing all the way down here? Was it simply a coincidence he was here? She recalled the dead bodies outside of Barnen, and the symbols on their wrists. As she thought about that mark she felt pressure in her head, similar to when she'd seen them on the dead men.

It was if her mind was fighting with her, or her memories. There was something she couldn't recall, something related to that symbol she could see. The pressure was as if something was fighting to break free.

The Derk had disappeared from sight now, but this time she wasn't rushing out of her cover. The chance of them just being here at the same time was too slim, she needed to be extra cautious.

She centered herself, using her breath to calm her nerves and heighten her awareness. The spot she was standing in was dark and she could hide there safely, she was sure. Glad she had stayed put, she saw another hooded man coming along the same path as the earlier one. He was using all the cover he could, carefully trying to be seen by as few people as possible, not that there were many around right now.

This one was shorter but dressed exactly the same. He was more observant than the other, constantly looking around as he went, like a hound trying to pick up a scent.

As he came nearer to her position she was able to see his face as he turned looking in all directions. Her heart stopped in her chest, and she only just halted a gasp about to escape her lips. The short black goatee was clear to see, and she could have sworn it was the same man who had looked at her through the window in Barnen.

His eyes passed over her hiding spot without stopping, and he kept moving along the street before turning at the same place as his colleague.

That was two now. Two too many, for Lani's liking. She had to make a decision and fast, in case a third was coming. Staying here wasn't possible, she needed to get back to her room, but they were clearly seeking something around the same area. If it was her they were looking for, she didn't want to make it easy for them.

She left her hiding spot very slowly and without any sound. Sticking hard against the walls she headed opposite to where they had gone, but towards where they had come from. She only went in short bursts stopping in dark lanes, alleys or recesses, to wait and watch.

As she made her way into a narrow lane between two shops, little more than a gutter for water, she heard faint footsteps and stopped abruptly. Only a minute later the first of the two hooded men came back into view, still looking for something, as he made his way along the street before heading down the same path he had followed before.

All Lani could think was that they were seeking her inn, and had somehow found her, despite the care she had taken all day, in watching out for any traps. How did they even know she was in Callet?

She decided to wait and see if they came back around again. As she waited she replayed her memory over the day's events, carefully looking over each picture in her mind seeking out who might have been a scout or identifier for them. Her skill at replaying the pictures had helped her in the past, maybe it could give her a clue now.

She scrolled through the day looking for anything, slowing to inspect scenes that might provide more information but nothing stood out. After a little while the second of the two men, 'Goatee', appeared again on the roadway, continuing along the road as he had before.

Lani didn't understand what they were doing, they were obviously hunting her or someone else, but typically you would lie in an observation spot and wait until you saw your prey before showing yourself. She could only think they didn't quite know who or where their prey was.

The road was again empty and quiet except for a distant clicking of horse hooves, echoing down the streets on such a still evening. Lani probed her memory again, starting at the moment she had first woken.

Forcing herself to do it slowly, she watched as she had inspected her things on her bed. She replayed taking the amulet out of the pouch and shivered involuntarily as she recalled how it had made her feel.

Then she saw it. In the image there was a wispy orange haze like a smoky tendril creeping out of the amulet. The other tendril had gone off on its own and out the window. She couldn't see anything more of it, but both tendrils snapped off when she put it back in the pouch.

It triggered her to remember she had seen this multiple times. Each time one of the tendrils reached out for her, the other off into the distance.

Now she thought back about each of those moments, within a short space of time the Derks had shown up near where she was. Now it made sense, somehow they could sense where the tendrils had reached out from, but because it was hidden in the pouch they couldn't find its exact location.

Ashantha had warned her they would find her if she didn't use the pouch. She wished he had told her more before he died.

If it was inside the pouch then they couldn't find it. Armed with this knowledge she felt a little safer. Only a little though.

That had to be how they found Ashantha in the end, she guessed. Why he had it out of the pouch she would never know, maybe he was studying it to learn more about what it was doing. Maybe he didn't know much more than her anyway, just that it was evil. He was dead now, only his journal would likely hold any other clues. Maybe Bossu would know.

One thing she knew for sure now was that they were hunting for her, whether they knew it or not. They were after the amulet and had followed her here. Leaning against the wall she sighed; she wanted to get back to her accommodation, but if Goatee saw her face she doubted he would not make the connection.

She squeezed her way further down the narrow gap between the buildings hoping she'd be able to find an exit.

LANI

The lane was pitch black with such a little gap between the tall buildings letting no moon light in. Each step was tedious and slow. She didn't want to make an unexpected sound to alert her hunters that someone else was about.

Lani came to the end of the gap between the buildings, which led to a small courtyard at the back of the building on her left. There was a part wall to the right separating the two areas. The wall between the two neighboring courtyards stepped up every couple of feet until it matched the height of the back wall. In the courtyard where Lani was standing there was a large gate in the wall, closed and barred. The heavy door didn't look like it would open without making noise, so she walked up the middle wall between until she stood on the high wall at the back.

Unsure what to do, Lani sat on the high wall, her legs draped over the outer side, and allowed herself time to think through her next options. The knowledge about the amulet was useful in its own way, but also scary. Not only did it confirm what Ashantha had told her, these hunters were real, the Derks were everywhere, it seemed, and they wanted this amulet.

She was right to have felt she was being watched, and to have been cautious, although she wasn't sure these hunters were going to use traditional ways to find her. How much they knew she had no idea. While she had more information than earlier today, it raised as many questions as it answered.

If her instinct was correct the hunters were searching the areas behind her, so she needed to hang out in Harkaitz and find somewhere to hole up there until tomorrow.

She dropped down from the wall into the laneway at the back of the courtyards. Landing in a crouch she looked left and right, waiting for any sounds, before she slowly stood.

Which direction to go was like rolling a dice, there was nothing either way that made more sense to her. She chose left. Lani was feeling tired, her emotions were strung out and she'd been trying to focus on multiple things for hours now. It was important that she kept her guard up and didn't make a mistake, and as soon as that thought crossed her mind she tripped over a cobble in the lane. Shaking her head, she did her best to focus on where she was.

You're so stupid, Lani, pay attention.

She wasn't quite sure where she was, most of her exploring had been during the day, and everything looked different now. It took a lot more time to compare daytime memories with how they looked now. There were more people out now which made her feel a little more comfortable. It would be easier to hide out amongst a crowd. She could pick up the sound of music that had drifted down the small road she was on.

Approaching a larger intersection she decided to go right, deeper into Harkaitz, as left would have headed back towards where the hunters were last. She still hung closely to the right side of the road, watching the groups of people out starting their nights. Staying as inconspicuous as she could she stopped every so often, stepping back into a doorway and taking stock of everyone around her.

Every group of buildings she passed, the crowd seemed to grow and with it the noise. People wandered up and down on their own, in pairs or groups.

This wider road was well lit with street lamps which created a different atmosphere. Ahead a small corner stage was wedged between two buildings and some musicians were playing to a small crowd. Those watching were cheering them along while a couple of them danced in the street.

Each of the buildings in this part of town were marked distinctly, some clearly ale houses, others hookers' dens, smoke pits and food halls. There were also inns and boarding houses mixed amongst them, though Lani was glad her lodging wasn't in the middle of all this noise.

Diagonally across from her stood a large standalone building, making it unique to the others around it. It had a distinctive flair to the way it had been adorned, the wooden face decoratively created across the front.

Outside many people were lingering, mostly men carrying cups of ale and bumping into each other as they swaggered about, cheering at the nearby music and goading each other in humorous banter.

There was a sign out the front declaring its name, an image of a single woman surrounded by some words. As if on cue the sounds of a woman singing started to come from within, accompanied by string instruments. The sound of her voice was captivating to Lani, she wasn't sure why but it was one of the sweetest voices she could recall hearing.

The drunkards outside recognized the music and hurriedly turned and headed back inside. Lani used all the sound and movement to cross the street. She stepped up onto the front deck and looked through a window. At the far end the woman singing stood on a stage that took up the whole back wall. Down most of the right-hand wall was a bar, and the rest of the space was a mix of tables and people standing. The whole bar was packed with people watching the woman in awe. Lani stepped back from the window and looked around, spotting a man staggering her way.

"Can you help me?"

"Yesh indeed, lassy," the older man said, making his way towards the doors.

"What's this place called?"

"Everybun knowsh this be Sung Weeper." He stopped and looked at her, his head bobbing back and forth as he tried to stay still.

"The Song Weaver?"

"Yesh, what I said."

"Okay, thanks," Lani said, a grin on her face.

"It's from down south, shesh southerly, but my lass, shesh sings the best." He had taken to leaning with his right arm against the front of the building.

"Is this just an ale house for the songster?" Lani queried him.

"No, lassish, bout the back there, workers rooms and stuff. Not for us though, just workers. Best me catch her, she not much more songing."

He bumped his way along the front and in through the main doors, the music from within streaming through as they opened.

She partially opened the door and looked in; a crowded room lay ahead packed with men and women now cheering on a large woman in a flowing green dress, up on the stage. She had the most captivating voice Lani had ever heard and she was tempted to step in and enjoy the show.

She broke free of the trance of the song and stepped back outside again. She wasn't here to watch music, she needed to find Bossu. Lani backed away from the door, letting it close and hurried around the side of the building.

This was the place she was meant to find, but where was Bossu?

GORAN

The Song Weaver was one of Goran's favorite venues in the whole of Dharatan. As a building and bar it was only unique in that it stood alone, unconnected to anywhere else. It had been built for this purpose, or so it seemed.

What made it special was the music, or more specifically the singing. The Song Weaver attracted the best of the best, and many of those who thought they had it in them to be the best. On any given day, or night, you could hear the sweetest and widest range of singing talent anywhere.

Some people came to Callet purely to listen to certain artists, and its reputation was known in many quarters throughout the realms. Some Kings and Queens tried to solicit the key performers to attend their courts but the smarter singers knew that they were better served performing here.

A number of the singers had performed here almost every week for decades. They lived and breathed the ethos of the Song Weaver, created by the very first song weaver, Nina. Her haunting songs were still sung by many of the performers, years after her passing.

It was said that several rulers over the years had arrived dressed in disguise and enjoyed the music hidden to all but their protection. In the times he had been here, there had never been such a visit, he was sure he would notice. Myths helped the mystique of such a place and who was he to prove or disprove anything that made it the special place it was.

He stood at the doorway for a moment surveying the room, and the musicians on the stage at the far end of the room. On the right wall coming back from the stage a long bar ran almost the length of the wall, behind which two women were pouring ale and wine. Goran made his way there and, taking a small jug of wine and a wooden goblet, walked across the room settling into a table on the opposite wall.

He watched as a lady who had been propped on a stool near the stage stood and made her way over to his table. He took his first sip of the wine, and looked at her crossing the room. Her torso had a permanent twist to it, so her left shoulder sat back behind her neck, and the arm on that side was mostly missing, with no hand on the end.

She wore a jade green dress which reflected the color of her eyes. They were a deep green that seemed to sparkle as if sprinkled with glitter. In her right hand she carried her own goblet and placed it down towards the jug as she sat.

"Be a good boy and fill that then, Gor," she smiled flirtatiously at him.

"You only ever want me for my wine, Leola."

"If that were true, I'd die thirsty," she chuckled. "It's good to see you, Goran, but why so soon after the last time?"

"It's always more pleasure for me," he grinned, letting his right eye wink a little. "There are things afoot that demanded it."

"Oh mystery and intrigue, how super, tell me more."

"Let's just leave the details out, but I need your people to be on full alert."

"Oh?"

"There is a woman in Callet, or who may have been here and left already, that I need to find. I need your help to get the word out," Goran continued.

Leola put her goblet down and savored the wine before responding.

"I will need to know more than this. There are a lot of women in this town and many don't want to be found."

Goran chuckled, "Yes, I know, Leola. You're jumping ahead as usual."

She crossed her arms and, turning her head slightly, peered at him with a scowl on her face.

"She is taller than my height, more like you, slightly tall for a Mal but is typical in much of her look. Her hair has the strangest red tint to it and she's less polished than a city woman, she appears to be from the street."

"So far you've explained a red-skinned girl, with reddish hair, that is a normal height, not exactly anything specific that will help us find her," Leola repeated back at him.

"She will be wearing one of these." He held up his ring to her. "And we have no idea why she can."

Leola look at him, a little dumbfounded. "If we get close enough to see that, we're likely to be in more danger than it's worth."

"I don't think she is likely to harm anyone herself, it's her that's in the most danger. She's managed to find herself in possession of some things that aren't very good for her long-term health."

"Nothing else to go on?" Leola asked before taking another drink of her wine.

Goran shook his head. "We don't really know why she is in Callet. I don't think she's ever been here before, so she might stand out for that reason alone. I don't want her leaving town though, I've been chasing her from place to place already."

"You like to give a girl a challenge, I'll say that." Leola looked about the room and Goran watched her taking everything in that he had told her, despite it being of little help.

"There's others that seem to be hunting her, and they will stand out."

Leola raised her eyebrows at him.

"They're Derks."

"Derks are a rarity here, Goran. They would stand out."

"In Nkuku they attacked someone most would have avoided, and they left a lot of dead bodies behind. You do not want anyone approaching them."

He watched Leona as her face tightened at the last comment, her deep green eyes staring at him unflinchingly.

"This isn't your usual task, Goran. I'll send the word out but I'll be warning my lot to keep themselves at a distance, I've no need to lose anyone. Where will I find you?"

"Here, or at Follies. Either will work. Pass the message, I'll find you," Goran replied.

Leola nodded and stood up, quickly swallowing the last of her wine. She walked away from the table, gathering a couple of people as she went and disappearing out through a service workers' door.

Goran sat and enjoyed the music. The current performer was a broad Beng woman of average height. Her ebony skin shone in the lamp light around the stage, her voice a deep rich tone that sounded as if it was coming from an injured soul sharing its pain. It almost made Goran want to fall into his own melancholy, but he had heard these types of tunes before and they were a release, not a call to despair.

Her voice sucked in everyone's attention, the whole room drawn to the performer. That was the thing with this bar, it was if its very being enhanced the music and the shape of the room made the performances even better.

He wasn't sure if it was the melancholy of the song, or simply the number of days since his last smoke but the other voice had been triggered.

Look at that fine beauty over there, in the yellow top. I want to get to know her, she'll be a lovely way to spend the evening.

Goran looked at the empty goblet in front of him, and the jug beside it. The other voice loved alcohol and things that gave it energy. His arm wanted to fill the jug and lift the goblet.

We deserve some fun, Goran, you're taking yourself far too seriously.

"Shush," he said out loud.

A man at the table next to him, turned and looked quizzically at him.

Goran held up his hand apologetically, then stood up and forced himself to leave the room. He didn't have time for this, and worse, the solution meant a foggy head. He needed to finish this thing. If he caught the woman and collected the things, everyone would be happy with him.

Not me. I'm not happy with you at all. You've become so tedious… Girl this, girl that, but no actual girls.

The laugh the voice made caused chills to run down Goran's spine. He squeezed the flats of his hands against his temples as he walked, muttering to himself as if to distract this brain. If anyone he knew saw him they'd think he was crazy.

Back in his room, he opened the window so the smoke could get out. Being Callet, he doubted anyone would comment at the smell of the weed, but he didn't need the room full of it.

The voice hadn't let up the whole way back, pointing out the brothels and bars he passed, several times almost convincing him to go it. He made it to his room but felt exhausted, the battle in his mind taking its own physical toll.

He hurried to pack the first pipe and began to relax after he was able to draw in several quick puffs of the smoke. He'd rushed it too much and coughed after the second puff, his eyes watering a little.

Slowly everything became muted around him. Anything he looked at lost its hard edges, as did his mind. He wanted to stop and just let these couple of inhales calm his head, but deep down his body called for more.

Closing his eyes he drew in a large breath from the pipe, holding it in for a good while before slowly exhaling it out the window. When he had finished the whole pipe he went to his bed and lay down, tucking his knees up and cradling them.

She can wait, let the others find her for me. I've been traveling, I need a rest. A nice long rest.

Part of him wanted to stand up, and go back to the job he had to do, but he had little willpower to follow through. The zongle weed was much stronger and had already engulfed his mind. A smile was fixed on his face, his eyes staring out into the dark of the night.

Inside he knew this was better than the voice. He couldn't let the voice out, he didn't think he could put it back again if he did.

LANI

*L*ani stood pressed back into a deep doorway several lanes away from the Song Weaver. She had found the place she was looking for and was excited by it.

She was so close to getting answers, hopefully, and she'd nearly forgotten about the Derks who were still looking for her.

When she'd walked past the building she wanted to just go in and ask for Bossu, until fear of getting caught drove her away.

As it stood she only had Ashantha's word about Bossu, she didn't know if he was a friendly, or if this was a trap. Lani rubbed the ring on her hand, through the gloves she still wore.

His people, he had said, a private group of people. She wasn't sure if they would welcome her or see her as a threat. Either way she needed them to help her get rid of the amulet.

They would want their ring back, that was for sure, if they knew how to take it off. She flinched as a vision flicked through her mind of someone cutting her finger off to get the ring.

After what she had been through they should reward her, this journey had been dangerous.

The Teller had called them the people of the clown face, and she'd briefly looked to see if she could find a symbol like that on the side of the building. It had to be the place, Lani felt sure that it was.

She should have asked the drunk if he knew a Bossu, she kicked herself for not doing so. It had been such a surprise to have found the building, she didn't think to ask that.

The sound of footsteps and a muffled voice brought her attention back to the laneway she was in. It sounded to Lani that they were coming directly toward her. She pressed into the recess as hard as she could and held her breath.

A man slowly walked by. He was talking to himself and had his hands squeezed against his head as he shook it. Lani felt sorry for him, he seemed crazed.

She caught the sight of a ring on his hand only briefly, but as she did it was as if time slowed down. Slow enough so she saw it. He was gone as quickly as he had arrived, and Lani leaned her head out of the recess to watch him as he limped away. One of his legs was clearly shorter than the other, and was twisted.

Had she seen correctly? Pushing back into the dark she flicked back through her mind looking at the images of what had just happened. There it was, a copy of the ring on her hand. She could make out the symbol on the face of it, he too was wearing a ring like Ashantha's.

What was wrong with him? He seemed crazy, had Ashantha also been an idiot? Maybe the ring marked fools so others knew who they were? *Why is it on me then?*

She had to decide whether to follow this man or keep looking for Bossu. Would the man she'd just seen lead her to Bossu? But he was walking away and Ashantha had been clear, she was to trust no one but Bossu.

Standing here wasn't going to solve anything, Lani knew she needed to find out how to locate Bossu. It would be too easy simply to ask someone, but it would alert them to her coming. Before she just turned herself over to them, she wanted to know more about who they were. Or what they were.

She had escaped from Watcher, but whether he would have let her go on his own without the Derks attacking, she didn't know. If she had learned anything on this trip it was do *not* believe or trust anyone. She had to look after herself, no one else would.

Lani made her way back the way she had come, walking behind some others heading in that direction. Approaching from the back of the building she was able to see there were no easy ways in, it had few windows and only one heavy door, recessed in from the street. As she slowed walking by it, Lani could just see a small chain hanging beside it.

She kept walking. Along the southern side there was a single door, about one third of the way back towards the front.

Lani stepped inside, knowing she was risking getting caught, and readied herself to turn and run if needed. She entered a small hallway. On the left side a stairway led up to the floor above; the right half was narrow and didn't seem to go anywhere.

Step by step she crept up the stairs to get a view of what was above. There was a landing at the top of the stairs with a closed door to the right. A small sign was fixed to the wall beside it, but she couldn't read what it said.

Lani didn't hear anyone, so tried the door handle. It turned and the door opened inwards. As she started in, a short woman standing behind a small desk turned to look at her.

"Who are you? You can't be here!" she said abruptly.

"Who lives here?" Lani stuttered in response, unsure what to do.

"Not you, these are only for the singers. Go get away or I'll call the men!" She had turned completely around now and had a serious look on her face.

"What about Bossu?"

The woman looked at her as if she didn't understand what she'd said.

"*Go!*" The woman started to come around from the desk.

"Sorry. I'm sorry." Lani quickly stepped back through and pulled the door with a bang. She hurried back down the stairs and out onto the lane. She didn't think the woman recognized the name. All she could tell with the quick look was that there were a series of rooms up there. Was that where Ashantha lived? He didn't seem to be a singer, so it was hard to think he would have had a room in there.

Another group of people were swaying their way up the lane, and she followed them back to the front of the building. She crossed over to the other side of the street where she'd perched earlier and stood in the dark watching the bar.

Thinking back over what she had seen, she could tell there was another part to the building, but it was only accessed through the solid door at the back. There was no way into it from the room's hallway. She could see no windows and no way up onto the roof.

Who in this building knew about Bossu? Was he in the Song Weaver or the place at the back? Lani had to assume it would be that section at the back of the building.

Whatever this building was it was the key to finding the answers she needed. While she wanted to rid herself of the things she had, she didn't have to solve it all in one night. Maybe she should take a lesson from the Watchers.

Lani chuckled to herself; maybe now she had found the location, she could sit back and watch, and let them reveal themselves to her, not the other way around. That meant she needed to find somewhere to watch the building and see what she could learn.

With that decided she walked several more laps around the Song Weaver, through the different access lanes and smaller roads. Then she chose a spot that looked like it would be the best place to keep watch from. She would be able to see the back of the building and down the entire side lane.

Choosing it was easy, getting up there was going to be harder. Unlike Nkuku, these buildings didn't naturally create a walkway between buildings that would make it easy to move from one to the other.

Once up on the first roof she climbed or leapt from one to another until she was only one roof away from the building she wanted to be on. The roof she was on was almost flat, which would allow her a small run up. The gap between them wasn't large thanks to the wide eaves but she still needed to psych herself up for it. It was the pitch of the other roof that gave her the most cause for concern.

The slope looked steep enough for someone to slide on and the tiles didn't look very well maintained. She took a couple of big breaths and then rushed forward, leaping across the gap. Her back foot landed heavily and she felt the tile give way beneath her. The tile had split in half and the lower half was slipping back towards the edge, causing her to slide with it.

She was half crouched, her arms waving madly in different directions trying to stabilize herself enough, to lean forward against the slide. As her slide stopped she froze, afraid to move in case she slid further. There was only a single tile between her and the edge.

The broken tile had gone over the edge and she heard it smash on the ground below. Lani waited for the sounds of doors opening and people looking for the cause of it. Her landing had made enough noise if anyone was directly below her they would know someone was up here.

No voices called out towards her, and no one appeared to look towards where she was. She held her position for another minute before daring to crouch and then creep up the roof.

The small moon lit enough of the roof that Lani was able to move over the ridge safely, and choose her spot. It was quite exposed, the chimney stack wasn't on this side, so she was going to have to lie out flat, and hope no one would look her way.

She lay down on the roof and edged forward, until she was at the right angle to see over the edge and down the lane beside the Song Weaver. From this spot she could also see the small doorway at the back of the long building. She couldn't see everything due to the edge of the roof but she hoped what she could see would be enough.

LANI

The first light of day burned Lani's eyes. She'd remained awake the entire night, except for the occasional mini nap she hadn't been able to control. Now her eyes felt like they were full of grit and her mouth was parched.

She knew she should have planned better before attempting something like this. It wasn't the first rash decision she'd made since leaving Barnen, and she needed to be more careful if she wanted to stay safe.

From her position up on the roof Lani could see carts and people moving along the main road as they crossed over the entrance to the lane beside the Song Weaver. The only people with any chance of noticing her were those first turning into the lane, and even then she doubted anyone would have a reason to look up this high.

This lane and the other one that bordered the back of the building were her main focus, and her position directly above them meant anyone heading along them would be easily visible to her.

Lani was none the wiser as to who Bossu was, not that she expected to be from what she'd been doing, but she did have more information about the building than she had yesterday.

Whatever was hidden behind the back door appeared to be some sort of base for a number of entertainers. Different groups or pairs came and went through the night, either collecting instruments and props, or returning them. They came and went at all sorts of times, and she was thankful they had, otherwise she would have found it hard to stay awake.

Once or twice in the earliest part of the morning she had dozed off, only to be jolted awake by the sound of a drunken singer crashing their way down the lane, or loud voices as a group left the area. Thankfully she hadn't rolled sideways while she nodded off, or she would have fallen.

Lani stretched her legs out and tried to ease the kink out of her back. It would get too warm up here soon and without anything to drink she wasn't going to be able to last for too long.

She was certain that someone was always in the back of the building. Whenever anyone turned up they knocked and waited to be let in. She had no direct line of sight on the recessed door from her position, although once she had seen something curious.

A group of three were outside waiting to be let in. The one in the doorway had turned back to talk to his friends, and as he stood there he reached under his tunic and pulled out some form of necklace. Lani couldn't see what was attached to it from this distance, but when he turned back to the door he held it out towards whoever was there.

She didn't know what to do with that information, but there was nothing Ashantha had been wearing like that. Lani wasn't sure if it was some form of pass key or not, but she knew any extra information she had was better than none.

Two more of them had arrived at the door and waited to go in. Ten minutes later, they came back out, dressed differently with one carrying a lute. They turned right and walked away from the Song Weaver.

That was another curious thing, when the entertainers arrived, they came from the same direction as everyone else. They all came from the westbound lane that she didn't have full sight of. Once they left the building they went off in numerous directions, to do their day's works. When they returned, all finished for the day, they went back in the same direction they'd arrived from.

Lani thought that was unusual, almost as if they were all staying at the same place. She didn't understand what it meant, but she always noticed patterns, and she knew sometimes that observation came in handy later.

There hadn't been any music drifting up from the Song Weaver for three or four hours now, but it didn't look like they were closed. Patrons seemed to come and go all night and the staff were still there.

A barmaid carrying a pail came into the top end of the lane and roughly threw its contents into a gutter against the wall in what was probably a daily routine. Lani had seen a number of men throughout the night use it as a place to empty their bladders, before heading back into the bar, and no doubt in the heat of the day it would add to the horrid smells surrounding Callet.

At the sound of a door opening she changed her focus to the side entrance. Two women stepped out into the lane before heading up to the main street. As they were in street clothes she couldn't tell if they were staff or singers. Throughout the night people had come and gone through the door as their shifts changed.

Those that worked at the Song Weaver never went to the back of the building, it was always other street entertainers or musicians that came to the back. The side entrance always seemed to be for the women who sang in the bar. Some would stay inside after they finished their shift, while others appeared to have changed and went out into the city.

The back lanes were quiet again now and the grumbles in Lani's stomach were growing. Only three weeks ago, she was lucky to get a meal every couple of days, and now she had become accustomed to eating much more regularly, and real food, not just scraps.

Not only was it changing her expectations but the regular food was having other side effects as well. Her figure was filling out in ways it had never before, and her clothing was beginning to pinch. It would become a little harder to masquerade as a male if she kept eating like this.

She was beginning to get pretty bored of her watch now, and had started to think about the best way to get back down. She'd be much easier to notice now, in the daylight, as she leapt across the rooftops, but at least the sound wouldn't stand out.

While she wanted to get rid of the amulet and get answers, she didn't want to rush into anything again. The truth was she didn't really know anything about Ashantha, and originally she didn't have any intentions of ever coming here. Lani didn't believe he had any special concern for her either, she was simply the only person around that could help him do what he needed doing.

Rushing in on this group of people could end just as badly as getting caught by Watcher's men. She needed to be prepared as best she could, and to have some idea of what she was getting into. Another afternoon and evening up here might help her gain some more insights and come up with a plan.

She was about to get ready to leave when she spotted a man limping down the laneway. He had been here several times through the night, and had stayed inside much longer than the others. He had long matted hair that flapped about his chest and back as he moved. Lani had nicknamed him Locks because of it, her mind trying to amuse itself through the long watch.

He stopped at the side door, looking up and down the alley, and Lani thought he was going to go in, but then it opened and a group of women stood talking in the open doorway. He started walking down the lane immediately and Lani lost sight of him when he went under the eaves. Locks showed up at the door at the back of the building and was let in soon after.

That was interesting, she wondered why he was going to go in there? Or perhaps he had heard the voices of the women and was simply listening in. He was always on his own, which differed from the other people that visited the building, and he remained in there longer too.

Could he be Bossu?

Ashantha had been very clear that she should trust no one but Bossu. If the amulet wasn't as dangerous as it had turned out to be, she might not have worried so much about what he had told her, but now she felt differently.

When she found Bossu, she needed to be able to speak to him alone, and show him it. There didn't need to be others around for that.

She was still no clearer about how to identify Bossu. She couldn't just loiter near the door, it would be way too obvious.

If she couldn't get inside, her best bet was to find a quiet part of the day to approach the door.

Locks still hadn't left and Lani became more curious as to whether he was her target. With the morning getting into full swing she watched a steady stream of the entertainers come through the building. Each time she watched carefully to see if he left with any of them, but so far he hadn't left.

Her hunger and thirst had been forgotten and she sat watching, running ideas around in her head on her best way to approach him.

The back of her neck started to burn with the sun behind her, and sweat ran down her back. She knew she couldn't stay up here much longer without cooking. Lani was preparing to give up and go back to her room when the side door up the lane opened, and Locks stepped out.

Now that's interesting. How did he get out there?

He briefly looked up and down the lane before he headed up towards the front of the Song Weaver. Lani was certain she hadn't missed him leaving through the back and going in the side, which meant somehow he'd passed through from the back.

When she'd been in that side entrance yesterday she had seen no doorway between the two parts of the building. The way he had carefully stepped out and taken in his surroundings, hinted to Lani that maybe he was using an alternative exit. Maybe the long night on the roof wasn't such a waste after all.

That might be the most useful knowledge she acquired all day. Perhaps she could get in without having to go through the main door after all.

LANI

Getting back to her room in the inn had taken Lani time, she hadn't forgotten about the Derks and was extra deliberate about how she approached it.

She never saw them once, and she felt like they were more likely to use the night to do their hunting. While Callet was a jumble of people from many different races, the way the Derks dressed, in that strange black clothing, would have made them stand out in the daytime.

She'd taken a meal and slept, a broken sleep, and the dream of Ashantha had come again. It was an unpleasant dream and thankfully she always woke quickly when it started, his face staring at her, eyeless.

What she had seen yesterday was hopefully going to help her today. She needed to get inside the Song Weaver and try to find what or who Bossu meant. No matter what happened she wanted to get rid of the amulet, then the bandits could chase Bossu or whoever he gave it to. She'd be happier to give Ash's mask back to them as well, she still wasn't sure why she'd carried it with her, and she rarely thought about it, except after the dreams.

It hadn't occurred to her now, but maybe that's why she was

having the dreams. If she didn't have the mask she might not get the nightmare?

There were too many things to worry about, but none mattered until she got inside the building. It was time to go, or she'd be stuck in here brooding over everything for another day.

The noise of the busy street, the different setting and walking helped change her state of mind. Lani chose an eatery just up the road from the Song Weaver and ordered some food. She picked at her meal for a long while, watching the people coming and going along the road. Music drifted up from the bar, adding atmosphere to the surrounding businesses. She knew this was the big moment in the whole trip and she could feel herself avoiding doing what needed to be done.

Waiting didn't help, the longer she'd sat there the harder it became to get up and get started. She hadn't seen anyone familiar, Locks hadn't shown, nor the Derks, it was only her own mind holding her back.

Finally, after building herself up to it, she left the eatery and crossed the street before turning right at the side of the Song Weaver. The lane was empty, which made her more nervous than if it had been busy. When she neared the side door, she paused and looked back over her shoulder to the main road. Right at that moment the side door opened, and she turned in surprise, stopping in her tracks. Looking up she came face to face with Locks stepping out of the hallway.

"Oh sorry, lad, didn't mean to frighten you."

Lani's voice caught in her throat she coughed to cover her surprise. "It's okay," she said, as she continued on down the lane. She wanted to run but forced herself to maintain her calm and hoped he wasn't following her.

The sound of the door closing caused Lani to hold her breath again until she was almost certain the footsteps she could hear were going the other way. When she reached the back of the building she chose to step right, behind it, and leaned her back to the wall, gathering herself.

Her heart was racing and she couldn't believe she'd nearly walked right into him.

"You alright?"

Lani turned to see three men walking towards her along the back of the building. "Ah, yes. Just catching my breath." Two of the men were about half her height, their thickset smaller bodies reminding her of the juggler she'd seen in Nedor. The third carried what looked like a lute, but he was walking with a severe limp.

"Don't stare, lad, it's just a stick."

Her face flushed as she noticed his left leg was missing and he had a special foot attached to a stick where his leg should have been.

"Sorry, I just…"

"Don't be, but you should move along now."

They stopped at the back door of the building, the lute player stepping into the recess. Lani turned her back to them and began to slowly move away. She could hear what was being said.

"Who is it then?" A surly deep voice.

"Us three again, Henri, just like yesterday," said lute man.

"All three of you then?" Deep voice again.

"Yes we've had a good haul today."

Lani had reached the edge of the building and turned; if any more was said she missed it, but she heard the door shut firmly. The lane she'd come down was currently empty and Locks was nowhere to be seen. She had to make a quick decision. If he'd just left then he wasn't going to be inside and he hadn't used this side door to come in previously.

She stopped at the door and turned before grabbing the handle, pressing down on the latch with her thumb and opening the door inwards. Stepping inside, she closed it quietly and waited.

The hall in front of her was lit with a single lamp which cast enough light to see where you needed to go but threw plenty of shadows as well. There was no outside light in here. There was little sound of any sort, it seemed to be isolated from the bar and nothing came from upstairs.

The light was going to be Lani's biggest issue, to find any special way in she'd need to be able to check out the walls carefully. She needed to get the lantern down from the wall and use that, but if anyone came in she'd be caught red-handed.

To reach it she needed to go halfway up the stairs, which she did one tread at a time, trying to be as soundless as she could. Her first instinct was that there was no door down here, so it must be upstairs where the accommodation was. That meant getting past the woman she'd seen before.

Stepping only on the outside edges of each tread she reached the top without any of the boards creaking. The landing wasn't the same and when she put her weight onto it a board squeaked.

Lani froze, listening for any response, ready to sprint down and out of the building. There was no noise. She waited for several minutes and heard nothing at all. Taking an even bigger risk she slowly turned the door handle and opened the door into the upper level, poking her head around the corner to where she'd seen the lady earlier.

She relaxed a little when she saw no one there. Thankfully there was no sound at all up here, although she could hear music filtering through the wooden floor from below.

Lani quickly looked to her left where the wall connected with the back part of the building. It was filled with shelves and stores. It was not well lit but she couldn't see anything that would easily move to allow someone through.

She stepped back onto the landing, closing the door very quietly behind her. The landing wall was also solid, and running her hand over it she couldn't feel anything that might give away a secret entrance.

There was a ridge, like a bannister running down the wall, which Lani had never seen before, but enabled her to pretty quickly tell there was no seam giving away a hidden door. Halfway down, she reached out on her tiptoes, and grabbed the lantern off its hook.

At the bottom Lani used the light to check the entire length of the wall. There was nothing she could find that even hinted it was used for access. There were no marks on the floor, and no obvious seams that gave away something not quite in alignment.

The color of the paneling all matched, each aged and marked as you'd expect they would over time. It even had the strange bannister ridge running along it like the stairs. Standing back to look at the wall again, she saw the only place left was under the stairs. She walked over there and saw that the stairs were closed in underneath by a solid wall.

The floor down here was as clean as the main foyer, which meant it was also swept regularly as well. She was surprised there was no storage under here although she guessed that with the door unlocked it would be a likely easy place to steal from.

Again the wall seemed intact, the single lantern helped her to see but was still imperfect. If she hadn't known Locks had come out of here she might have given up, but got closer to the wall and inspected it more. The bannister ridge ran along this wall too. Running her hand along it, her woolen gloves got caught on something. A small bit of wood snagged on them. She freed her hand and held the lantern where it had happened. She could see the tiniest of lines, a seam in the wood. She almost called out in joy.

The cut in the ridge aligned perfectly with the wood panel up the wall. She tried to push against it to no avail.

Lani knelt down and used the lantern to look at the lower wall. Under the bannister ledge there was a small hole cut into the panel. Without decent light and being overly curious, no one would never see it.

She carefully poked her finger into it, checking that there wasn't anything sharp in there to trap her. There was a story she had heard in Barnen about a lord who had poisoned sprung needles in his locks. If someone unwittingly put their finger in, they were pricked and left unconscious, so he could catch them.

There was a strange shape inside the hole, which she couldn't describe despite running her finger over it many times. With some dexterity, she held the light above her head, while she twisted on an angle so as to not create a shadow.

What she saw brought a smile to her face. She quickly pulled off her glove and looked at the ring on her finger. It still wouldn't come off, but she was able to twist her hand into place and push it into the small hole, the face of the clown matching the shape inside, and clicking into place.

The wall panel popped out towards her, just a small amount.

She admired how cleverly it was built, the bottom of the panel was cut at the top of the wooden strip running horizontally along the wall. That's why no scraping mark showed on the floor.

She pulled the panel further back towards her, and it slid out on a series of connected beams down the middle. There was just enough room for someone to get in beside them. She looked inside using the lantern and could see a standing space and what looked like a more obvious door on the inside.

Lani went back up the stairs and put the lantern back where it was. As it slipped onto the hook, she recognized the voice of the lute man and another voice outside the door to the street.

Without hesitation she ran back to the secret door and stepped inside, pulling on the panel behind her.

With it almost closed she heard the voices carry on past the outside door. She breathed a sigh of relief, then the panel seemed to close itself. She was standing there in total darkness.

LANI

There was no light at all in the space under the stairs and there wasn't much room for her to move around. The dark didn't bother her at all, and she slowly edged herself around to face the back wall. Lani was excited with her find and held her hands out in front as she took a step forward, stopping as she felt the wall.

She started at roughly the same height the lock had been on the outside panel, feeling the wood for anything similar. Without the benefit of light she had to carefully work her way along sections of the wall and then up and back again. Her hand hit something and she ran her fingers over it. The dowel she had felt came out of the back wall and had a short wooden handle on it.

Lani tried to pull it but nothing happened, though she noticed there was play in it. Slowly she twisted it to her left. There was almost no resistance at all and the handle turned fully to the left, quickly, opening the back wall. It swiveled around a pole attached to its middle, creating enough room for one person to step through.

Had it made any noise? Lani wasn't sure, she'd been so surprised by the movement she hadn't noticed any loud sounds.

Enough light filtered in that Lani could see it led to the bottom of a narrow set of stairs that climbed to her right. She poked her head through enough to see the steps were narrow and they led to the end of some sort of hallway. She'd have to get to the top to see what else there was.

Lani stepped through, and reluctantly had to close the door so she could get past. It closed with a small sucking sound. It was such a tiny noise, Lani doubted it was loud enough to carry anywhere. Before she headed up the stairs, she decided to find out how to reopen the door from this side, in case she needed to get out in a hurry.

Locks had come out this way so she knew it was openable. It took her a few minutes to work it out. Above the door, a ridge ran along the wall, and part of that was a handle which probably was very obvious in full light but would have been hidden to anyone not in the know.

She opened and closed the door several times, to make sure she had could do it easily in a hurry, before turning and heading her way up the staircase.

The space was very narrow, forcing her to turn sideways as she walked up the stairs to avoid her shoulders brushing along the walls.

Two steps before the top Lani stopped and listened. She was inside the back portion of the building now but still had no knowledge of what or who was in here. She knew one name, Henri, and sought another, Bossu. It was clear that many people entered the lower room but she had no idea what this place was.

Almost on cue she heard the sounds of someone moving around. The sound was a little distant, like a chair being slid over a solid floor. Lani had to guess it was downstairs at street level, it didn't sound close enough to have come from the wooden floor she could see.

Very cautiously she stepped up another level and then put her head around the corner, ready to turn and rush down the stairs if spotted.

Seeing no one in the open area she exhaled, and took another step until she was completely on the upper floor. The space in front of her was a hallway. To her left were two doors, both closed.

On her right there was a solid wall, with a hanging barn door. It was a wide door and looked heavy. The far end of the hall was the landing for the stairs down to the floor below.

A bell sounded from downstairs. Again she heard the sound of a chair grating across a floor, followed by heavy steps and then the noise of something being slid across.

"Who do you serve?" a deep voice came from inside.

"We serve the Court, Henri, and we come for our tools of trade."

"Are there the four of you?"

"Yes, all of us."

"Hold back then."

Lani could hear the sound of something small being slid again, then a latch, before she heard the sound of a bolt being moved and then a key in a door.

"Inside, and be quick with you."

"Always rushing, Henri, always," the same voice spoke back to him.

"You know the rules here, it's Henri's place, and Henri's rules. Henri can't afford to be letting just anyone in. So what instruments do you want then?"

"Same as usual, although we might try a new spot in town today." A different voice answered the man called Henri.

"Henri hopes you make more than you did yesterday. Wait here, while Henri goes and gets them. And don't touch anything."

Lani quickly stepped back, into the dark of the narrow stairs, and listened to the heavy footsteps coming up the other stairs. They headed her way before stopping, then she could hear him roll the heavy barn door, followed by more muted footsteps.

She knelt forward and chanced a look around the corner. Through the barn door opening she could see into what was a large storeroom, filled with shelving. The shelves were crammed with all sorts of items, and she could make out racks of clothing as well. All she could see of the person she assumed was Henri, was his shadow as he moved around the back of the room. When she saw it turn back towards the doorway Lani slipped out of sight.

The barn door closed slowly, to the sound of Henri grunting with the effort, then Lani could hear his footsteps as he made his way back downstairs. Lani crept back up to the upper level and moved along a bit closer to the void, so she could hear what was being said.

"There it all is," from the deep voice.

"Thanks, Henri, it's much safer leaving it here than having to worry about it at the inn."

"Henri will see you when you come back with your take later then. How much longer do you think you'll be in Callet?"

"The crowds are good this year, so we'll try and take as much as we can before we tire on them. It's always a lean time when we go west but we need to be heading that way within another week, I guess."

"Have you seen Master Goran? He tells Henri to make sure everyone gets the message?"

"No, we haven't. What's the message?"

"He looks for someone here in Callet, a woman from…" there was a pause. "…Malamig. She is from the north. He wants anyone that sees a Mal young woman to tell him."

"There was a bit of talk about something in Follies, it would be good to know fact from fiction."

"Master Goran will be helping to sort that out. Right, out with you, Henri has things to do," he ended their conversation.

Lani could hear people moving around downstairs, and edged back towards the end of the hall. It sounded like the main door opening and then closing after the group left. She heard the sound of a key and bolts and then only the heavy footsteps downstairs.

The barn door on her right wasn't fully closed. The man called Henri had been grunting when he was closing it. Maybe with his arms full it had been too difficult.

She moved across the back of the hall, trying to avoid the middle floorboards. There was just enough space between the barn door and the frame to squeeze her head through. With her head through it then just took some twisting to fit everything else through. She didn't want to budge the door, given how much noise it made when it moved.

As she worked through the gap her tunic got snagged on the door, her left shoulder pinned in place. She was already precariously squatting on her inside leg, to stay under the door latch, and her right arm was useless with nothing it could grab on to. She pushed back slowly on the frame, trying to brace herself, while she moved back out the door a little.

The tunic moved along the snag but hadn't come free. With herself balanced on the frame she was able to bring her right hand back through and free the cloth. As she did she heard footsteps down below and then on the stairs.

In a panic she worked herself through the gap more, avoiding the snag. She had to get down on her right knee and quickly drag her left foot through the gap, hoping she'd got it out of sight quick enough before Henri, or whoever it was, had got to the top of the stairs.

No one called out, she had to hope she was still unseen, and scrambled over the floor before standing. Lani made her way behind some of the shelves and dropped down out of any sight lines.

The footsteps appeared to stop outside the barn door. She could hear someone breathing outside, then they moved, Lani wasn't sure in what direction, but they were still upstairs. It went quiet again. She didn't dare to try and see what was happening, hoping that whatever they were doing they'd soon go back downstairs.

More footsteps and then she could hear the barn door creaking and sliding until it was closed. It clunked as it stopped, leaving Lani alone in the storeroom.

She crept over to the door and listened. Through the heavy wood she was sure she could hear the sound of someone breathing, and she froze. She waited, holding her breath, until the person walked away. Lani could hear the footsteps appear to head towards the stairs and descend, getting quieter as they went.

There was no easy way out of here now; if she opened the door anyone in this part of the building would know she was there.

LANI

*L*ani took a minute to catch her breath and take in her surroundings. The storeroom was filled wall to wall with shelves, hanging racks and chests. It looked like Henri ran the storage for entertainers and musicians. There were instruments, apparatus and clothing that best suited those who played to the public.

One lantern hung on the back wall and provided just enough light for her to see around the room. Parts of it were dark with shadows and Lani struggled to see what was in the boxes.

She was cautious with every step she took, trying to not cause the floor to squeak, but Lani had no way of telling which boards were solid or not.

Some of the racks were covered in dust while others were more recently used their items clean and polished. The chests were stacked against the back wall alongside a tall cupboard. They all looked heavy and had padlocks looped through them.

The tall cupboard was also locked and Lani couldn't find any keys in the room to help unlock it. A rack of masks caught her attention and she went through each of the masks. Some were only partial faces, others were closer to full face masks. None of them were anything like Ashantha's mask that was back in her room.

There was nothing of use to her in this storeroom, she was just wasting time trapped in here, and needed to get out.

Lani heard movement again outside the room, and crept back to the door to listen. She brushed her face to wipe off a little of the sweat that had formed and realized her hand was bare. She was only wearing one glove and checked her pocket for the other. When she had used the ring to open the secret door she had stuffed it in her tunic pocket.

Frantically she retraced her steps in the storeroom to check if it had fallen out anywhere, but couldn't locate it. Had she dropped it outside the door when she'd gotten stuck? Or was it down in the space under the stairs?

She went back to the door and listened. There was definitely more movement but Lani couldn't hear any voices. It must be Henri moving around. She held her ear to the small gap between the door and the wall trying to identify what was happening. The sound of a key being used and the bolts that she recognized from earlier, told her the door was being opened.

Lani waited to hear voices but there were none, and then she heard the door close but no bolts. There seemed to be one other faint noise but she couldn't make it out.

Has he gone out? Please let it be true.

She waited, listening for any other sounds, but nothing came. It sounded like a floorboard creaked, but nothing else, and there were other groans from the old building that it seemed to fit. How long could she wait to try the door? He might only be gone a short time, this was her chance to free herself from the room.

There was no ideal amount of time for her to wait. She needed to get free and the risk of opening the door wouldn't change. When she opened it she needed to be ready to run out and down through the secret door before anyone could catch her. Timing would be critical, she'd need to get through that and out onto the street before they had time to react.

Bracing herself and taking a couple of big breaths, Lani pushed hard against the barn door. At first it hardly seemed to budge before it began to slide on the old wheels it hung on. The loud scraping sound broke the silence and she doubled her efforts to force it wide enough open.

She didn't hear any noise coming from below and stepped through the gap she had created, trying to work out if she needed to close it again or if she was best to just escape.

Lani didn't see the hand that grabbed her throat. It grabbed her neck with immense strength, lifting her onto her toe tips.

She was turned to face an older man, with a pockmarked face that had a scar running down from his left eyebrow to his chin. The scar had a hard pink ridge that did not match the brown color of his face.

His blue eyes bore directly into hers, his face angry and threatening.

"Thief, how did you get in here?"

Lani tried to answer but she couldn't speak, his grasp cutting off her voice and airways. He lifted her further and thrust her towards the stairs, ignoring the room she had been in.

The man marched her down the hall and then half pushed and half lifted her, down the stairs to the main room. In the middle of the room he slung her into a chair and brought his other hand up holding a long knife which he placed against her throat.

Lani sucked in air now that her neck had been released and her eyes cleared; they had misted over as she felt herself nearly passing out. Her other glove sat on the table in front of her.

"You nearly choked me," her voice cracked as she protested.

"Lucky Henri didn't use this first on you, girl," he growled, pushing the blade a little harder against her throat.

Lani flinched and stared up at him. With his stoop the front of his tunic fell open, and hanging around his neck was a silver token, hanging on a silver chain. Engraved into the token was the same symbol as on the face of her ring. 'Those of the clown face', Cideep had called them.

"Not such a good thief, are you? Leaving your glove where I can see. No one is allowed in here unless Henri let them pass. Henri didn't let you in, where did you get in?"

"The back door."

"That door is sealed and locked, how did you unlock it?"

"The ring. On my hand."

She was unable to look down at her hand because of the knife. Every movement she made she could feel the blade against the skin on her neck. He never once eased the pressure.

"Hold it up, turn to Henri," he demanded.

Lani slowly lifted her hand and turned the palm towards herself. Henri pulled the token around his neck out into the open and up to the ring. The symbol engraved in the token began to glow a strange blue, and he let go the token and grabbed her wrist. He looked closely at the ring, before dropping it back to the table. Lani could see the symbol on the face of the ring glowing in the same blue, but fading quickly.

"Who are you and where did you get this ring?"

Lani wasn't sure what had just happened, but the symbol on her ring glowing must have convinced him it was a real ring. She had to do something, there was no way she could overpower this man, and he'd cut her before she could move. She had to pretend she belonged, whether he knew her or not.

"Do you always treat us like this?" she sneered at him with as much arrogance as she could.

Her tone worked on him, she could see him thinking about the situation. Henri took a step back, removing the knife from her throat, but still holding it menacingly in front of him. Lani grabbed at her throat with her right hand and rubbed where the blade had been.

"A fine welcome it is here, threatened and manhandled."

"Henri doesn't know you. You've come into Henri's place. It's Henri's place and Henri's rules. Henri only let in those he knows. Henri doesn't know you! That ring gives you one yard, that's all."

Lani didn't know what the symbol meant but she had remembered what Cideep had said, and the warning he had given Watcher. He was one of Ashantha's people, but he wasn't Bossu, and there was no one else here. She took in more air, trying to calm herself. His piercing blue eyes made her spine shiver. He was standing over her and she knew she was on thin ice.

"You used the other door, why?"

"Do I not wear the ring that gives me access to this place? And yet you still threaten me?"

He didn't answer, she could see him trying to work out what to do with her.

"People come to see Henri, they use the front door."

"Well I'm not here to see you, Henri."

"Who then? Why are you here?" he asked her, less aggressively but still in a growl.

"I am here to find someone." Lani still knew nothing about these clown people, and Ashantha had been very clear, to trust no one but Bossu.

"Who?"

"Not you."

He still hadn't moved. Lani tried to take in everything she could about him. He would stand tall if not for the permanent stoop that his upper body forced on him. She didn't need to see the size of his arms and shoulders to know how strong he was, she'd felt that already. Without thinking she rubbed at her throat again where his fingers had been.

"You're a Mal!"

"Yes, what of it?" She knew what he was probably thinking.

"Goran tells Henri to watch for a Mal woman, you're her." He waved the blade in his hand accusingly.

Lani was glad she'd heard the conversation earlier. "No, he's looking for someone else."

"How does Henri know?"

"Did he say she was one of us?" Lani held the ring up again.

Henri shook his head but said nothing. He sat in a chair at the table, still close enough to reach her.

"Why did Goran not tell Henri? Henri should have been told."

Lani shook her head, wondering who Goran was. That had to be the one she called Locks. "Told what?"

"New ring bearer." He pointed at her hand. "Henri should be told, surprises aren't good."

"I can't tell you why. I have a message for only one person. And you aren't that person."

He looked up at her, a frown across his brow. Lani's stomach flipped on her. She was trapped here at a major disadvantage and he wasn't the man she was meant to find. She looked at the long knife he had placed in front of him on the table and then back at him. She doubted she could get to her feet and away from the table without him reaching her first.

The stairs behind him were her only hope, he wouldn't be able to match her pace up there, and she knew the door in this room would be locked to the street. That would be her only advantage if she could get out through the panel at the other end of the building. If the other one he had called Goran came back then she would have no chance of escape.

"Henri can't tell you where to find this person because you won't tell him. So we have ourselves something of an impasse. Henri cannot let you leave here until he can be sure who you are. We will wait, see who comes to visit Henri."

He sat staring at her, as she tried to hold his gaze as long as she could, and every time she looked away then back again his blue eyes were still locked on her. He said nothing.

LANI

enri stood abruptly, surprising Lani as he broke the stalemate. He had been silent watching her for minutes and all it had done was raise her concerns. One thing she had learned on her trip was that things could change quickly, in your favor, or against you.

"Henri think we need to go visit a friend so we can determine what is to happen here."

"A friend?" Lani asked.

"Yes a friend. If you are truly of the ring then Henri's friend will be your friend as well. Of course if you aren't..." He shook his head, making a twisted expression with his mouth.

"Who is this friend?"

"You won't tell me who you are, Henri not tell you about his thoughts either."

"My name is Lani, and I will tell who it is I am meant to tell and no one else."

"Why is that?"

"I was given very clear instructions. I was only to trust one person with my message, you aren't who I was told to tell."

"Why here? Why Henri's place?"

Lani looked at him he stood at the end of the table. He picked up his knife again and held it out in front, pointing at her.

"Ashantha told me to come here."

Henri's face went ashen. He stepped back towards her.

"Ashantha, what do you mean? He is dead."

Lani was surprised he knew, "Yes… I know. Before he died, he gave me a message and told me to come here."

"It's you. Why Goran not explain to Henri about the ring." He had become more aggressive in his stance again. "Stand up!"

Lani wanted to defy him just because she could but she also knew sitting here wasn't going to help her escape. If they were going to leave the building it would be her best chance out of here.

"He should have told Henri more, we'll go see him. Solve it all, and save him the hunt."

Lani flinched at the word hunt, it sounded as if the man Goran was already looking for her. Why? What did he know?

"Let's be clear, you make any silly moves and it won't end well for you. Henri doesn't trust you yet and ring or no ring you are in here unwelcome, so let's just go see our friend and learn what we can."

She had no real choice so she stood up from the chair, straightening out her clothing. Henri stepped back to the wall, and put the knife down on a ledge for a few moments while he pulled a coat on. He sheathed his knife into a leather scabbard sewn on the inside of it and then beckoned her over to him.

Henri moved behind her, working her towards the door. He gripped her right arm with his left hand, the pressure he used sending her a clear message. With his other hand he reached into a pocket on his coat and took out a large key which he placed into the door lock.

He turned the key and opened the door. He pushed her out and stepped through himself.

Henri had to let go of her as he twisted around to lock the door. "Don't move!"

Lani did as he said, waiting until he was pulling the key back out and his focus momentarily diverted to stowing the key in his pocket.

She pushed off him quickly using the momentum to get her into the laneway. Her agility was always going to be her best advantage and outside she had room to use it. She started to run.

"Fool," she heard him call, unsure if he meant her or himself.

She knew it was only a short distance to the intersection of the lanes. The lane to the left led to the front of the Song Weaver, this time she needed to get away, and charged straight ahead. By the time she saw something to her right it had already collided with her.

She was propelled across into the corner of the opposite building, her head banging on the wall. Dazed and winded, she slid to the ground.

"Whoa, girl, whach-you-do," a male voice seemed to be talking to her.

Lani opened her eyes to see a startled boy about her age sitting on the ground beside her.

"Where you going in such a hurry?"

He stood up and brushed himself off, before reaching out a hand to help her.

As she stood, Henri reached them. "She's with me."

The young man turned at the growling voice and saw Henri. "Oh." He raised his hands to Henri. "All yours then, Bossu, although I didn't think she'd be your type." Laughing at his own joke, he carried on up the lane towards the main road.

"You're Bossu?" Lani asked, brushing the dust off her coat and reaching up to her head.

"No, Henri, but they—" he waved his left arm in a big circle "— they call me Bossu, for this." He pointed over his shoulder to his back.

Lani wasn't sure she understood but part of her was relieved, the other worried now about her head and the headache that would come.

"But, you're who I was told to find."

"You're not making sense, girl." His tone was angry and he stood blocking her ability to run again.

"Ashantha, he told me to find Bossu. Not Henri, Bossu!" Her hand rubbed at the back of her head now, and she winced a little as she felt a raw bump through her hair.

"He never used that term with Henri, he always called me Henri."

"He was quite clear I was only to trust Bossu, no one else. Those were his last words."

Henri was silent for a moment studying her. "You don't look so good. Can you trust Henri now and not make to take off again?"

"If you are Bossu then I have to trust you, but no one else. I had to run, you were trying to take me to see someone else. Ash was very clear, that not all is what it seems. I am only to trust you, who you trust is up to you but I can't be seen by anyone else."

He stood back and quickly looked down the lanes. "Then we should go back inside and maybe you can tell me what it is you know. It will be some time before anyone else comes."

Lani's head was throbbing, making it harder to think. She didn't need the headaches now. After everything she'd done to get here, to find him, she wanted it to be over, but within the hour she would be in a bad way.

"Not here, I can't chance anyone else seeing me." She had to take a breath and rub her head.

"You don't look so well, girl. That knock to your head has shaken you."

"I get bad headaches when I knock my head. Soon it will make me very sick. Help me get to my room, and I can give you it."

"Give Henri what?"

"What Ashantha gave me to give to you."

Lani could see him trying to decide what to do next. "Please."

He grabbed her arm, this time more gently as a guide not a grasp. "Where to?"

"This way." Lani started walking back up the side of the Song Weaver. Henri walked beside her, his gait steady but labored. His body was strong in some ways and twisted in others. His heavy footfalls were not as much from his size but the way he had to move.

"Henri doesn't understand why so much secrecy?"

"Nor do I, but I had little choice, and what I have seen since he died hasn't made me any more trusting."

"What do you mean?"

"I am being chased by bad people. Ashantha said they want what I have. They don't take prisoners." Lani stumbled a little; her headache was coming now, she could feel it.

"Is it far?" he asked.

"Close, it's close."

LANI

*L*ani was thankful for the strength that Henri had this time, as her headache closed in on her and the stress of the day unwound. She felt weak and unstable on her feet. Crashing into the outer wall of the building had caused a small split in her head; the blood hadn't run for long but her hair was matted where it had bled, and there was a lump there that ached, the pain throbbing through to the back of her eye.

"There are Derks that have been hunting for what I have. I saw them scouting near here yesterday." It was the first either had said since he had agreed to come to her inn.

"Derks?"

"Yes. Pale men, from across the northern ocean."

"Why would they be hunting you?"

"I don't know as much as I would like to and only what Ashantha told me. They seem to know where I am or where I am going."

"Maybe it's just a coincidence."

Lani stopped causing Henri to nearly lose his grip on her. "It's not a coincidence. Ashantha died at the hands of Derks just like them."

Henri twisted towards her, his face dark with anger. "What do they look like then?"

"They all wear dark hooded tunics and tights. Not usual cloth like yours or mine, it has a …" she paused as she thought of the word "… shimmer or something to it. They can be hard to see. They all carry a mark on their wrist."

"A mark?"

"A tattoo, a symbol of intersecting lines."

Lani indicated the inn she was staying at, they entered and made their way upstairs to Lani's room. She quickly closed the shutters in the room, to block out as much light as she could, before taking refuge in a chair. She leant against the wall and pressed against the other side of her head to try and lessen the growing pain.

"You don't look well, girl."

"I will pass out before long. I get headaches that make my stomach turn and everything seems to close in on me. Any noise seems ten times as loud. I just have to sleep it off."

"You better tell Henri what he needs to know then, before that happens. Henri isn't happy that no one told him of Ashantha's death and none of what you've told him makes any sense."

"I was with him when he died, I am not sure anyone else would know. He was a long way north, alone."

"There's ways to spread the message, you should know that. Master Goran he was here but he didn't tell Henri you were there."

Henri seemed to pause for a moment.

"He did tell Henri about you though."

"What do you mean?"

"He told me there was a woman he needed to find. She had something that wasn't yours." He looked at her hand again. "The ring!"

"It's Ashantha's."

He stared at her suspiciously now. "What do you mean? You wear the ring, only the Court can wear those rings, that's what Henri's been told."

"I don't know about that. All I know is this is Ashantha's ring, which I got when he died. It went onto my hand and now I can't take it off."

Henri came closer to her, and held her hand up by the wrist. "How does Henri know you didn't kill Ashantha? That's why Goran is looking for you!"

Lani could see his face had become more concerned.

"Why would I kill him then come here to you to tell you about it? Think it through. You can take it off if you know how, it won't move for me." Lani pulled at the ring with her other hand, desperately trying to loosen it, but it wouldn't budge. She held her hand out to him but he just shook his head at her.

"No. Won't touch the ring." He said nothing else and Lani decided not to push it any further.

"I didn't kill Ashantha. He was killed by the Derks. Why is Goran looking for me?"

"He only told Henri you had something you shouldn't have. He wanted to find you."

"How would he know? Ashantha died a long way north in Malamig. I've been traveling for weeks, he wouldn't know about it."

"They can talk over distance, they have a way."

"Oh?"

"I don't know all of it, I just do my role. You shouldn't be able to wear that ring, and you know more than you should." He paused and walked the room. "Mother will have told him."

"Mother? Whose mother?"

"Ha, you truly don't know anything, do you. She's like our Queen, but that's not the best way to describe her. She leads the court and runs the college. Mother Folly."

"The college?"

"In Anderwell, where we are based. Her role is oversee the Court and the travelers, we serve her and the cause."

Lani's head was hurting too much for all this new information, so she cradled her head and rubbed her temples. "This headache will stop me soon so I will tell what I can for now." She told him only of Ashantha and how she found him, and what he told her she should do, not of her journey here. She still wasn't sure what he would want to do about it, and at this very moment she was not going to be able to escape anyway, soon she would have to sleep.

Henri had sat down opposite her as she had told her story. Lani had her eyes closed tight to keep the light out, but she could hear him quietly breathing as he took it all in.

"This amulet, why did he want it brought to Henri?"

"All he said was to find you and give it to you. He said you were safe. I don't know what that means. All I know is ever since I met him I've had bodies following me alive and dead."

"Henri is the gatekeeper of the safe. He doesn't have the ability to speak to Mother. Henri would have to tell another."

"You have to take this to her then. You can't tell another."

"Henri cannot. Must not ever leave his post here in Callet. Henri not a traveler."

"Ashantha's words were clear, to not trust anyone but you with this." Lani paused for a brief moment. "But that's not my problem once I hand it over. His parting words were to bring it here, I just want to be rid of it. That and his other things. All I have had is hunters and dead bodies following me where ever I've been."

"His other things?"

Lani got to her feet unsteadily and went to the spot where she hid her satchel. She dragged the chest of drawers out from the wall and pulling the bag out from behind it.

"Henri can help."

"It's done." She went back to the bed and opened the satchel, tipping out what was in it. She turned away from him and reached into her tunic and retrieved the pouch from the pocket within. She brought it over to the table.

"The amulet?" Henri asked her as she sat back down at the table.

"Inside here, yes. This pouch Ashantha gave to me to protect me from it. It has magic, and it's dangerous. It has killed two people just by touching it. But it also does more, the pouch, it seems to block that from happening."

Lani could see Henri looking at the pouch with cautious eyes as if she held a snake in her hand.

"The pouch, how does it protect?"

"I am not so sure how much it protects, but if the amulet is out, it reaches out. You can feel it in your mind. I can see things coming off it, one of them always seems to go off into the distance, I think it tries to call to the Derks."

"Calls to them?"

"I don't know. There's another thing."

Henri looked at her curiously.

"I can't leave it."

"What do you mean?"

"Something happened to it, to me." She shook her head as she recalled the way it felt, and instinctively rubbed her forearm. "It seems to have connected to me, I can touch it and carry it, but I cannot leave it behind."

"Henri doesn't understand."

Lani put the pouch on the table, and got to her feet slowly. "Help me walk."

Henri stood as well, "Okay, where?"

She leaned against his arm, grateful for his strength, again. "Just outside."

They stepped out into the hall and walked along a bit further, until she walked into the invisible wall. Henri walked past her not realizing what was happening and stopped as her arm wouldn't move.

"What is happening?"

"I don't know, Henri. Try pulling me."

Henri couldn't budge her, and once she could see he understood they went back into the room.

"Henri doesn't understand."

"Don't ask me, I have no idea. You need to stop that."

"How?"

"I hoped you would know."

Henri shook his head. They sat in silence, as he looked at the pouch without moving.

"Henri doesn't know what to do. Henri can't fix magic."

Lani shook her head. "But how can you be the one Ashantha said to deliver it to? I want rid of it."

"Henri doesn't know. He's also not sure why he would want it brought to me, not to Mother."

"This is too much to take in." Her head was pounding now, and she laid it down on the table, hardly able to talk.

She felt his strong hands around her shoulders, lifting her up and half carrying her, half walking her to the bed. There was nothing she could do to stop him, the pain in her head was too much now, and she collapsed onto the bed as he lowered her.

"You take rest now, Henri needs to think on this thing."

She heard nothing more, as the blackness came and consumed her.

LANI

*L*ani became aware of her surroundings slowly. Her headache was mostly gone although the residual pain behind her left eye was still there. Her tongue was stuck to the roof of her mouth which was dry. She never knew why her mouth tasted foul after one of the attacks but it always did, she needed some water.

The room was much darker than she remembered which meant it was probably night now, but on which day she wasn't sure. She struggled to recall what set off the headache. It came back suddenly; Henri, or Bossu, and the accident.

She forced her right eye open and could see he was still in the room. He was sitting at the table. She slowly rolled over and sat up on the edge of the bed.

Henri turned to look at her. "Do you feel any better?"

"Yes. Sleep fixes most of it." She stood slowly and shuffled over to get a drink. Her mouth felt better for it, and she put her empty cup down and turned to talk to him.

She shrieked at the sight of the amulet sitting on the table in front of him. "What? Why is that out of the pouch?"

"Studying."

"Studying what?"

"Henri wanted to learn what he could. You say things about it, but he needed to see for himself."

"It's dangerous. How did you get it out? You didn't touch it, did you?" She was agitated at the sight of it, and recognized the warm feeling in her forearm. Lani rushed to the table and jammed it into the pouch.

"No, Henri didn't touch it. Why are you so concerned, it's just a stone?"

Lani had seen the tendrils emanating from the amulet, one to her arm and the other out the window to who knows where.

"I told you before, it reaches out to them."

"How?"

"When it was out there's lines…wisps… like smoke." She was frustrated trying to find the right word for it. "They're orange, like the amber, and they reach off to the distance. One comes to me, to here." Lani pointed at her arm.

"Henri doesn't see them."

"I can't explain that. Like I told you, Ashantha didn't tell me anything much about it. He sure didn't tell me it would link to me."

"Was it linked to him?"

"I don't know. Maybe. Maybe when he died the link broke which is why I could take it. I don't know. I don't know."

"Lani, it's okay. We'll get help, sort this out."

She was pacing the room, she knew that they could somehow locate it. "How long was it out of the pouch, Henri?"

"Several hours, Henri couldn't sleep, he watched over you. He got bored, wanted to know more about this."

"They will come. They will know where we are."

Henri stood and made his way to the window, slowly opening one of the panels looking out onto the yard and street. "We will need help."

"Who?"

He touched his hand to the token around his neck. "There are many of us, hidden, but around. They will help us."

"I just want to be rid of it."

"Henri doesn't know how, it's magic, they will know. Henri needs help, you need help, and…" He stopped.

"And?"

"Never mind."

"What, Henri?"

"You have the ring, this you shouldn't have. Henri thinks the Court will want to meet you."

"The Court? What's the Court?"

"It's the people that run who we are. Mother will want to meet you. Now you know more than you should."

"You're keeping me prisoner?"

He shook his head. "Not a prisoner, it's for your protection. You wear that ring, and have this amulet. If the Derks want you, then you're too valuable to let go or let be harmed."

Lani laughed.

"What's so funny?"

"You called me valuable, that's the last thing I am. I don't need any protection, I've survived so far, haven't I?"

"So far, yes. But what now, you said they will know it's here. What if there are many of them and they do know who you are? Can you defend yourself against them? You told Henri they were killers."

Lani knew he was right. Her whole journey here had been fraught with danger. On one hand it had seemed lucky, finding help or escaping capture, but on the other hand it had seemed doomed. She'd been responsible for people dying, and was being held captive by a jewel. The one person she'd been told she could get rid of it to, didn't know how to help her.

The thought she'd raised just before about Ashantha knowing about the bond, bothered her. Had he known all along what it would do? How could he have known she could touch it, without it harming her? Maybe he didn't know, and it was just more bad luck.

Staying with Henri was about all she could do right now, maybe someone in his group could solve it, remove her from it. If not she'd need to escape and find somewhere to hide until she could find a way herself.

"We should go." His voice brought her back into the room. "The safe house is strong and there's no easy way in. I can send for help once we are back there, but we should go now."

Lani nodded. "I don't want to go anywhere. I want to just have it gone, Ashantha said to just give it to you."

"You know Henri can't take it. You have to come. We'll be safer there, until others come."

She couldn't stop it, the feeling crept up on her, and she slumped and her eyes filled with tears.

"Why me?" she muttered, tears rolling down her cheeks. "I just want it gone. I've had enough."

Henri stepped over to her, and his arms wrapped around her. "You'll be fine, Lani. You did good, look what you've done. How many other people could have made it here, like you did? That stone is dangerous, you know that, but you made it here. We need to get it safe."

She stood back up and out of his hug. Wiping her eyes with her sleeve, she looked up at him.

His blue eyes now offered only a plea, not the hardness of yesterday. He seemed smaller than before, his stoop more pronounced, and she realized he had been awake all night, looking over her and the amulet.

"Let me gather my things and I'll meet you downstairs, then we can go. Okay?"

"Henri wait outside the door, he doesn't want you making off out the window nor anyone else getting in. Alright?"

She shrugged at him and took another drink from her cup. Henri stood up and eased out the aches and stiffness from his joints, then unlatched the door and closed it behind him.

Lani tried to think of her options but there wasn't anything else to do, she didn't want this amulet anymore and she needed to be somewhere safe. The Derks would be close now, it had been out too long.

The back of the Song Weaver was as good as any place to hide. What had he called it? The safe house? Lani had no idea what that meant but it was a well-hidden place and could be protected easier than here. She stuffed her satchel with her things and put the amulet back into her tunic, before bracing herself and opening the door.

Henri stood there, his arms folded, leaning against the hallway wall, a small smile crossed his face as she stepped out. "Let's go then.

It's still dark, which should help us for now, but we'll want to go out the back way and then hurry away."

Downstairs the inn was almost quiet, and there were still, surprisingly to Lani, people drinking at this early hour. Lani and Henri quickly moved past the entrance to the main room, and headed down the hall, past the kitchen, before finding themselves at the back door.

Henri opened it cautiously. They made their way into the yard, and headed to the gate in the back wall. Up until this point they'd been almost soundless, but the gate had a heavy wooden bar locking it. Henri easily lifted it but there was no way to do it without making noise. The scraping made Lani more anxious than she already was.

He opened one of the gates and looked out. "It looks clear, we'll go to the right," he whispered to her.

Lani nodded at him; he knew best, whatever he said, she'd follow.

He reached into his coat and pulled out a knife, smaller than his blade, but it still looked sharp. "Here, you might need this."

Lani raised her eyebrows at him.

"Henri's being safe, we don't know who is looking for us. Make sure you don't stab Henri."

She took it and slipped it into her belt. She was still feeling weak from the headache, and the pain behind her eye was still there, so if it came to a fight she wasn't sure how much help she would be.

Henri took the lead and they moved into the laneway. It wasn't very wide, at best a cart would have just squeezed down it.

They turned and crossed into another small lane, Lani was lost but Henri seemed confident in where he was going. These lanes were all narrow and littered with rubbish, leaving them only wide enough to go single file.

Lani couldn't see what stopped Henri but she collided with his back. "Back," he hissed sharply at her. As she took steps backwards Lani saw Henri draw his blade. Over his stoop she could see the hooded man beyond.

Lani took out her own knife in one hand and slipped the satchel strap over her head. She was of no use in this fight unless the attacker got past Henri and then it might be too late.

"Back up slowly, careful you don't trip, and watch Henri's back, there might be more of them," he said quietly.

Lani did what he said, not liking her back to his, unable to tell what was happening. He bumped into her again and she moved away a little more.

"On your way, friend, nothing to see here."

Lani turned and could see past Henri, there were more than just one of the Derks in the lane. "There's too many, Henri."

"Henri can't outrun them, girl, you might be able to if you go now. This is a fight Henri has to have."

She shook where she stood. She knew the Derks were lethal, she didn't like Henri's odds.

"I'm… I'm staying, I'll watch back here."

From down the alley one of them spoke. "You have something of ours, you shouldn't have it. Just put it down and walk away, and no one needs to fight for anything."

Henri had stopped beside a small brick protrusion from the side wall. It made the lane narrower and gave the attackers less room to work with.

"Don't know you, friend. Turn and leave, what we have or don't have is none of your business and you don't look like you belong around here. Leave while you still can."

The first man laughed. "You think we're worried about one old man and a little girl? Fight if you want, it won't take long. We'll have what's ours either way."

Henri turned his head to Lani. "Go now, girl, and get it to the safe house." He pushed a key into her hand. "This will get you in. Just wait until someone comes that can help, you'll need to trust Goran, or you'll never survive."

Lani took the key and pocketed it but didn't move. "There might be more out there, I feel better here with you."

"Don't be daft, there's two of them and only one of me. Henri can hold them but he's not sure if he wins. You'll be long gone before they get by. We'll walk back to the corner there and you slip away while Henri keep them busy."

Lani shook her head. "I need you, there's too much I don't know about the amulet."

"Keep moving back, girl," he snapped.

She nearly fell over some rubbish as he bumped into her, quickly propping herself against the side wall.

"I'll go if I can get help, but who is close by?"

"The inn is too far, Follies, that's where Goran would be, but this will be over before you ever get there."

"Who else?"

They had reached the intersection; the lane they were on continued a distance before ending against a wall. The lane to their right was no wider than the one they were on. Lani and Henri both looked down it.

"Frak!" Lani said.

Henri didn't reply. Another of the Derks was standing at the end of that lane blocking the exit to the street. Lani either had to get past him or they were now blocked in.

"We can't retreat down this lane any further, or we'll be pinned in. Henri needs you now, there's nowhere to go and you'll need to watch his back. We have to chance it against that one, better than these two."

They moved into the shorter lane, heading back towards the main road. Before they turned the corner Lani could see the reflection of light coming off the blades of the two coming towards them. She knew the only way out of this was to fight but she wasn't sure she could help Henri much.

Her hand was white from gripping the handle of her knife. Inside all she felt was dread. She'd seen what they'd done before and didn't like her and Henri's chances.

As she looked back toward the single bandit she could see his teeth, as his nasty looking smile took over his face.

99

LANI

The sound of running feet caused Lani to turn and look. Henri hadn't followed her as far along the lane and was standing waiting for the attacker near the entrance.

As the Derk appeared at the corner Henri was able to grab the man's wrist, stopping him from using the knife he carried in that hand. Lani knew all too well how strong Henri's grip was and heard the man grunt in surprise.

Henri pulled the man around using his momentum and slammed him into the wall of the lane. The Derk recovered quickly and burst forward, up the side wall, letting his pinned arm help him spin. As he came down off the wall he punched Henri in the side of the head.

Lani watched, helplessly as Henri wobbled slightly before he slammed the Derk back into the wall. She could hear the air forced out of him as he crashed into the wall, but again he seemed to recover quickly.

The attacker had broken free of Henri's grip, but his knife was out of reach and he swung a kick at Henri's head. It made contact with Henri's shoulder. While it didn't move him at all, it did present Henri with an opening. He slashed in with his knife, forcing the Derk to use his arm to block it. Henri's blade sliced deeply into the arm.

The Derk didn't appear to flinch at all, but Lani could see a lot of blood running from it, and the arm hung limp beside him.

At that moment the other attacker turned the corner.

"Henri! Watch out!"

Lani felt like everything was slowing down, she could see everything frame by frame as if she was replaying it all in her mind.

Henri moved closer to the bleeding man, grabbed his other arm and swung him around using him as a shield. Before the injured man could react, Henri pushed him into the second man, and drove his blade through his stomach. He twisted it several times, and as he pulled it out, pushed the man away with his other arm, and stepped back towards Lani.

"Eat that!" he snarled.

The body slumped into the other Derk, who just pushed it out of the way before coming at Henri.

Lani recognized this man from Barnen, his cold stare and goatee beard instantly recognizable. He didn't even look at her, his attention solely on Henri. She turned to check on the other man behind her. He hadn't moved and blocked the far end of the lane, leaving the fighting to his comrades.

Hearing a rapid exchange of blades clashing, she turned back. Henri was facing a withering attack from the Derk, it was all he could do to block each strike with his blade. Lani struggled to even see the strikes, the speed at which he thrust and moved so quick.

"How much room, girl?" Henri called at her.

"Twenty paces, a little more, that's all."

"Just keep your eye on him, Henri doesn't need more surprises."

Lani didn't like having the fight happening behind her, but turned to watch the man further up the lane. As she did so someone walked around the corner and bumped into the back of the Derk.

"What's going on here?"

The attacker turned immediately and thrust his knife straight upwards into the stranger's throat. It happened so quickly Lani doubted the man would even have known what happened before he died, dropping to the ground as the Derk pulled his knife out, before turning back to face her.

Blood pooled around the body, and Lani had to choke back a gasp. The hand holding her knife shook, and she knew if she had to fight, she was done for.

"He... he just killed a stranger," she called over her shoulder to Henri. "If he comes I can't stop him."

Henri didn't answer so she turned fully around to look at him. He was pressing towards his opponent, which created more room behind him but it looked like he was tiring. His face was sweating and his breathing was labored.

The Derk feinted to his left, before lunging forward on his right and punching his knife in and out of Henri's upper arm.

The grunt Henri made was loud. He pulled back, trying to avoid the next attack.

"You okay?"

"Let Henri focus, girl," he snapped back at her.

Whatever ground he had made for them was lost again as she moved to give him more room. If they killed Henri, she had no chance, they would kill her easily. These men knew how to fight.

She felt Henri's back just behind her and took more steps forward, a small lane entrance she hadn't noticed before appearing on her left. Her momentary excitement was destroyed when she looked down it and saw it was blocked by a wall that had been added to stop people using the lane as a thoroughfare.

If they went down there, they were trapped.

"There's a lane here but it's a blocked part way down."

He didn't answer. She turned back to see him; there was blood dripping off his left hand, and that arm was hanging limply by his side.

"Take it."

"But it's..."

"TAKE IT!" he cut her off.

She went down it and Henri quickly followed her. If nothing else Lani was glad that she could walk backwards and keep her eyes forward on what was happening.

Lani tripped over something and fell down, letting out a cry of alarm.

She saw Henri turn to look but yelled back at him, "I'm okay!"

As he turned back Goatee had seen his opportunity and stabbed at him again, catching him in his side, his tunic opening above his hip.

Henri brought his arm down just as fast and his knife sliced across the forearm of Goatee. The attacker pulled back a pace, a sneer on his face the only sign he felt anything.

Lani looked at what she had tripped over, and saw some broken bricks left in the lane. She stood up, and grabbed one, before yelling, *"DUCK!"* at Henri. He dipped enough, and she launched the brick over his head. Her throw wasn't great but it still clipped Goatee on the cut arm as he sidestepped, causing him to flinch a little.

She bent down and grabbed another brick, hoping for another chance to do something. Blood was starting to pool under Henri and she couldn't see how they'd get out of this.

The other Derk had joined the fight now and stepped in front of Henri. He was fresher than Goatee and taller than Henri. His longer reach showed, his first move landing a glancing cut across Henri's barely usable left arm.

HENRI LEANED TO THE LEFT TO PROTECT THE INJURED ARM, ALLOWING Lani space to throw her brick. This time she hit the attacker on his thigh, causing him to stop his next movement.

She fumbled down at her feet for another brick, almost banging her head on the wall. The next one she grabbed was a little smaller, there were only another few left that would be big enough to bother the Derks.

Henri turned to face her and spoke as quietly as he could. "Aim for his head, stand right behind Henri, and be ready to throw it."

Lani did as he said, moving in close behind him and readying her arm. She could only partly see past him and waited for whatever Henri was planning.

Henri thrust out at him several times, blocking the return thrusts. The narrow lane stopped his attacker from being able to do much more than a frontal attack. Goatee stood behind him waiting for his turn. The lane had become much darker now, the walls of the buildings on each side restricted what light reached the lane and the two attackers were blocking any that had been seeping in from the outside.

Without warning Henri ducked, and Lani threw the brick, which sailed past the shoulder of the bandit and hit Goatee in the chest.

"Crap."

"Again," Henri grunted.

Lani stumbled back and picked up another brick, there was only one more left she could use. As she stood up, she put her left hand on Henri's back, so he knew where she was, and readied again. It wasn't long and she hurled the brick, watching it fly straight into the face of the bandit. He stumbled backwards, raising his hands to his face, his nose flowing with blood.

Henri didn't wait, racing forward and plunging his knife into the man's stomach then pushing him off and stepping back, bumping into Lani who'd overbalanced behind him.

They almost went down together, before Henri fell sideways onto the wall keeping himself upright. Ahead of him, Lani could see the bandit now bent over, a hand on his middle, blood seeping through his fingers. He looked up with a dark stare at them.

He charged forward, his blade moving fast. Henri blocked and blocked again, but Lani could sense Henri was struggling. He'd been losing a lot of blood and was already tired from fighting them all himself.

The Derk struck him again, and Henri groaned, he wobbled in front of her. He waved his blade out in front keeping the attacker back as best he could, but there was only so much he could do. "You …have… to go, Lani. Henri cannot… last long." He struggled to get his words out.

Behind the man facing Henri, she could see the one with the goatee beard, waiting for his turn again. He turned to his right suddenly, and Lani could hear voices shouting from the lane. She could only hope enough help had arrived to save them, she didn't think Henri could last much longer.

She brought her eyes back on the Derk facing Henri; he hadn't rushed back in, and she could see he had lost plenty of blood as well. He was struggled to stand upright.

Henri forced himself upright again and squared off with his opponent. Lani's attention was distracted by a rainbow that appeared over the top of the buildings behind him. While the fight had been going on the sky had darkened, as if a storm was forming, and she could make out the colors faintly.

It triggered a memory of the strange trader named Rainbow. What had he said to her? Something about when it's dark and you need a little color. Lani remembered now, he had given her the little pouch of chalk or something. She had never actually opened it so wasn't sure.

Whatever it was, the sight of the memory, and the rainbow in the sky, she took as a sign. She pulled her satchel around and fumbled around in the front pocket looking for the pouch.

The sound of blades distracted her as Henri and the Derk started back on each other. Frantically she tried to find it but dropped the satchel instead. She bent over and tried to calm herself, finally pulling the pouch out. And looked up.

Henri had taken another glancing slice to his other arm, and was propping with his left against the wall. Lani closed in behind him and grabbed a pinch of the chalky substance in the pouch. As the Derk moved in again she reached across Henri's shoulder and flung the chalk in his face.

Nothing happened. Some yellowish chalk flew from her fingers causing him a little surprise and landing on his face and tunic.

"Bricks... not bloody dust!" Henri gasped at her.

Lani knew there were no more bricks and stepped back, disappointed the chalk had done nothing. It was a stupid idea, she knew, but she was desperate. Suddenly a bright yellow light appeared. It was strange, like a small globe of yellow had circled his head emitting a bright light which caused Henri to flinch and look away.

The Derk was trying to get the light off, both his hands up by his face, shaking his head frantically. Lani pushed Henri and without thinking drove her knife into the attacker. She pulled it out and stabbed him again. She started to madly stab him over and over, all her anger boiling over.

His knife tumbled out of his hands to the ground, and he fell to his knees, stopping Lani in her tracks. She felt hands on her shoulder pulling her away. "Stop, Lani. He's… dead."

Shock took over and Lani started trembling, her hand and knife covered in blood. She dropped it to the ground and couldn't stop shaking.

Henri dropped to a knee behind her. She turned to him.

"Henri!" His face was pale and he was slumped against the wall of the lane.

Lani turned to shouting behind her from the lane where the other Derk with the beard had gone.

Henri grabbed her tunic, pulling her towards him.

"Run now, girl, and get away, while you have time. You have to get that stone away from them… now!"

His breath was ragged and his eyes a little glazed.

"I can't leave you, we're winning."

"If this is winning, thank Thenis we didn't lose." He snorted, some blood spurting out of his mouth. "Henri can't help you, take the key and get to the safe house."

"But I don't know what to do with the amulet. Ashantha wrote something in his journal but I can't read it. I can't do it."

"Girl, you must. It's too late now, Henri can't help you anymore."

"You'll be hidden back there. If you have to run there's money in the safe."

"Safe? What safe?"

"Basement… we keep the money and things there."

Lani put her hand on his side, trying to block the blood seeping out. There was nothing she could do for him.

His eyes closed a little. Lani shook him. "Don't close your eyes. Stay here. Don't go."

"Help Henri up… then go."

He started to shove himself backwards up the wall. Lani looked and could see Goatee was now at the junction of the two lanes. He was definitely injured but was in much better shape than Henri. He took a look at his comrade and saw he was gone, before looking back at her.

Henri stood for his last fight and shook her off. "Can you climb it?"

The brickwork of the wall wasn't smooth like other walls. Some bricks jutted out and there were edges she could probably use if she had to. She'd need some luck but if she could jump up to the first holds she could probably climb over them.

She looked at Henri. He was hardly able to stand. Goatee had turned back to them now; either he'd finished off the unknown strangers down the other lane, or they'd backed off.

Suddenly more shouts came from the side lane. Goatee turned and looked at her, like he was weighing up his options. He glanced back from where the voices were coming from. Then he looked back at her, moved forward and pulled something off the hand of his dead comrade, before turning and sprinting away.

"*Go!* You can't get … caught… by anyone. No… guards. No… one."

"But I can't leave you now."

"Henri is done. Go!"

Lani looked at him; his eyes stared back at her with little light left in them. "No."

"*Now!*"

Lani could hear other voices coming along the lane. She looked at him, and nodded, before turning and running at the back wall, and leapt. Her fingers grabbed onto a hold up the wall, but only just. She used her momentum to pull upwards and was able to get her left hand higher, gripping onto something wider.

A voice yelled out behind her, "Hey, you. *Stop!*"

Lani didn't know who it was and she didn't care, she pulled herself up. Scrambling across the top of the wall, she rolled over and fell down the other side, landing on her feet with a jolt.

Feeling bad for Henri, Lani knew she had to get out of sight, she was covered in blood and now multiple people were dead. If she'd been a likely suspect in Barnen, now she was a prime one here.

She started to run down the narrow lane, listening for anyone who was going to follow her.

100

GORAN

Everywhere he turned he ended up empty-handed. The stress of what he had been asked to do was pressing Goran in ways he wasn't used to. He wasn't just trying to redeem himself with his colleagues, he knew that things were escalating. The woman, Lani, was both in danger and dangerous to the Court, as well as others.

On top of it all the more stress he felt, the more the other voice seemed to appear. It appeared to thrive on the tension within him.

He had lost precious time battling the voice, since the first night in Callet. It had been okay up until yesterday, but then he needed to shut it down again. It meant he wasn't out on the street hunting her, he'd had to leave it to others.

None of them had found this woman anywhere. His last communication with Beantic, was clear, he thought. She would only let him know if he was off track, or going in the wrong direction. He assumed that meant Lani was still in Callet. But where? And why?

Goran had no idea why she was on the road, but if she hadn't moved from here, then there was some reason she had stopped here. Who was she meeting? He wished he knew what the amulet was, he didn't like the report from Hallendell about it killing. The limited magic they had was restricted to their few, and none of them had something that was this powerful.

He looked out the window of the inn, letting the noise of the people in the main room wash over him.

Where are you, Lani?

The keeper, Brando, hurried over to him. "Goran, come quickly."

He leapt up and followed Brando out into foyer. "What's up?"

"I'm not sure, but there's talk of a major fight happening over near Merryway."

"A fight? Why am I interested?"

"Apparently there's Derks involved. And it's pretty ugly."

"Derks?"

"Yes. But I've only heard a quick report from one of my runners. What do you think?"

"I'm stuck doing nothing right now, we might as well go. Let's take arms, though."

"Agreed."

The two men hurried away from Follies, and towards the rumored fighting. As they got closer to Merryway, Goran could see a crowd had formed. They nudged their way through, Goran letting Brando use his size to clear them a path.

Down a long lane he could see a group of men, one of them fighting a man wearing black clothing. Goran could only really see the hood, he was taller than the men he fought, but something about the clothing made it difficult to see. It didn't make sense to Goran, but it was like the clothing shimmered and was always blurred.

He recalled what Hallendell had told him about how the men who had attacked in Nkuku had almost been invisible in the dark light. It had to be the same clothing, that's what made them seem invisible. The men fighting would be in trouble if the Derks were all as dangerous as those that attacked Watcher.

He pulled on Brando's tunic, saying, "let's not go down there, come on over to your right, we'll come around the side." They moved away from the crowd and made their way quickly along some side lanes. As they circled around towards where the fighting had been, a woman dashed across the road they were on, shoving through a small group of people who called out in alarm.

As Goran reached them he could hear their complaining.

"She looked frightened to me, as if she'd been attacked," a man said.

"Looked to me like she was the attacker. Did you see all the blood on her hand and arm?" another replied.

"Not my issue," the first answered. "I'm not going looking for trouble, bravery's a young man's game. At my age I'm happy enough just to find a good ale. Let the watch find her."

"True enough. With everyone out gawking at what's happening we should be able to get ourselves a good table somewhere. Let's go."

Goran signaled Brando on, and they headed towards the scene of the fighting. He wondered who the woman was. They came upon a group of men, swords out, standing over a dead body, while they bent over a man on the ground. Goran recognized him and rushed over.

"Henri, no!"

Henri barely opened his eyes to look at him. He didn't seem to recognize him. Goran looked at the state of him, and all the blood, not liking what he saw.

"It's me, Goran. What happened?"

A flicker of recognition crossed Henri's eyes.

"The girl."

"What girl?"

"The one…you wanted."

"She did this?"

Henri weakly shook his head.

"Derks…did…this." He coughed, blood dribbling down his chin. "She got…away. She…needs you."

Brando leaned in and handed a small vial to Goran, "It's one of Zeresse's, he needs it."

Goran plucked the stopper and held Henri's head, while he tipped the liquid down his throat. Henri coughed again after he'd finished.

"Brando, we've got to get him back to Follies. Help me."

It took all of their strength to get Henri upright, and he winced at the pain. By the time they had him up, a little light had returned to his eyes. He'd turned to Goran. "Henri saved her. But there's more...of them. They want..." he leaned close to Goran's ear "...the amulet."

Goran nodded, "Okay. Don't speak, let us get you somewhere safe."

"Where are you taking him?" one of the men in the lane asked.

"To a healer, now get out of the way," Brando snapped at the man.

The man went to block their path but must have seen something in Brando's eyes, and backed off.

Goran knew the watch would come, they'd deal with them later, right now they needed to get Henri back to Follies. He doubted he'd survive his wounds, but then had to do something. This was not going to be the sort of news he wanted to tell Tillandra. He shook off the worry and focused on trying to support Henri's weight.

By the time they arrived back at Follies, even Brando was struggling. Goran was exhausted. Henri was not a small man, and he'd not been able to support himself, despite the tonic they'd given him. No one got in their way, most saw the blood and hurried away, quickly. Callet was a fun town, not a place you went to get into fights.

They laid Henri down on a bed in a spare room near the back of the ground floor. Brando went to get help, while Goran sat with him. He knew the woman he'd seen rushing away had to have been Lani, but he was glad he'd not chased her. If they'd gone Henri would never have made it. Hopefully Henri could tell them more, right now he'd drifted out of consciousness and there was nothing Goran could do but hope he survived.

Goran wasn't religious, he didn't believe any god was watching out for anyone. If they were, Henri would have been the person to protect. All he could do now was wait and hope Brando could get a healer.

101

LANI

Lani turned at the first corner and ran away from the trouble behind her. If Goatee changed his mind and came for her, she knew there was nothing she could do. He must know now she had the amulet. Did he recognize her from Barnen?

He looked almost the same as the man she had seen through the window. His stare was chilling. There was nothing kind in him, she knew he would kill her without a second thought.

She was so caught up in her thoughts she nearly plowed into a group of people. They all jumped back as she lurched towards them, screaming out. Lani realized she must look like the attacker with blood all over her. She shuddered, thinking about what she had just done.

There was no shout for her to stop, the city guards thankfully hadn't caught up to the action yet.

Where to go? She had already checked out of her room, and Henri had given her the key to his place. She slowed her pace, taking more care and trying to stand out less.

Thinking about Henri brought tears to her eyes. Lani had to shake her head, she had no time right now to lose it. The safe house as he called it, the back of the Song Weaver was where she needed to go. She had the key and no one else could get in there, she could block the secret door and be safe for a while, until she figured out what to do next.

Lani stopped and tried to figure out where she was; she'd been so busy getting away she hadn't thought about where she was going. She looked around and could recognize some familiar buildings, thankfully her instincts had carried her in the right direction.

She started walking again but more cautiously now. While she needed to get out of sight, she didn't want to walk into a trap either. She felt her chest, and the amulet was still there, out of sight, and wrapped in the makeshift pouch.

Instead of heading directly to the Song Weaver, Lani circled around the area, using a few different lanes on her approach. She saw no one familiar, and the Derk she'd named Goatee hadn't appeared either. Now she walked up to Henri's door.

As she pulled the key out of her pocket, her trembling hands dropped it at her feet. Cursing herself, she picked it up and put it in the lock. It was stiff but turned, and the door opened. As Lani pushed against the heavy door, she realized how tired she was.

Thankfully there was no one inside, so she closed the door and used the bolts to ensure no one could get in from the outside. The room was still lit from a lantern Henri must have left burning, everything felt ghostly, and as she looked at the place Henri had called home, tears formed in her eyes.

Lani dropped to the floor and burst into tears; she had watched Henri die, and killed a man with a knife. So many people had died because of her. After a while her eyes ran dry and she leaned back against a cupboard in the kitchen area. She pushed herself up and found a drink.

A small side room held a wash basin and water in a barrel, which she used to clean herself up as best she could, wiping the blood off her hands and face. She ate and drank sitting at the table staring at the door, knowing full well Henri wouldn't be walking back through it.

She remembered the secret door then and jumped to her feet. Looking around the room, she saw the only thing useful was a chair. She carried it up the stairs. It was then a tight squeeze to get it down the other steps to the hidden door.

When she got down Lani realized that it was the wrong way round to block the door properly, so she had to work her way back up dragging it with her. She turned it around and this time had to scrape the walls to force it down to the bottom.

She looked at the chair, and felt safer knowing that no one was getting through there.

Once back up on the upper level Lani went into the storage room and hunted through the clothes racks until she found something suitable to change into. She left her stained tunic and leggings on the floor and dressed in the new outfit.

Back downstairs she took up the key Henri had given her and went looking for the safe he had mentioned. He had said the basement but she couldn't see any other stairs. There were no other doors either.

Knowing what she knew about the secret door Lani went and checked under the stairs by the main door. There was no cupboard there, but on the back wall she could see some marks. She went back and grabbed the lantern off the wall and carried it into the darker space.

With the light she could see a patch of the wood that was worn, or marked, as though it was regularly pushed. She pushed it with her opened hand and the panel clicked and popped back slightly towards her.

The open door revealed stairs leading down into the darkness below. Carrying the lantern in front, Lani carefully headed down. At the bottom she made a sharp right turn and before her was a solid wall with a metal door. She had never seen a door made from metal like this before. Thankfully it had a key hole set in it.

Lani rushed back upstairs and grabbed the key off the table and headed back down. The key fit and with a twist it unlocked. She sighed with relief, and swung the door open. Stale air blew back from the room beyond.

As she stepped in she could see the room was broken up into two sections. On the left, was a set of bags, tied closed. She opened one and inside stared at the large pile of coins. This bag was all silver, and she opened several more and found different types of coins in each.

She could tell that the color of the bag identified the different coins, the silver ones were made with a dark green cloth. The entire side of the room held racks of these bags. No wonder the place was called the safe, there was enough money here for a city.

On the other half of the room were shelves and racks. She rummaged through the boxes, finding an array of trinkets and valuable items. Silver goblets, gold candlesticks as well as countless jewelry. There were a few weapons, and knowing she had lost her knife, she chose another small one from a shelf, tucking it into her belt.

A box partially hidden on a shelf caught Lani's eye. Engraved on the outside was the same symbol of the face of her ring. She pulled the box down and opened it. Inside were a number of the tokens Lani had seen before. Henri had worn a silver one around his neck, but there were also others. She picked up a stone token polished almost smooth, with the same symbol carved into it. She held it to her ring, and it too glowed blue, like Henri's had done. She held her ring into the box and as she brushed over the tokens they all emitted the same blue light, even the round wooden ones.

Lani took a stone one out of the box, and pocketed it. She didn't know if it would come in handy, but she might find a use for it. She closed the box and put it back on the shelf.

Henri had told her to take some money, so she did. She filled her pouch and took several more from a shelf. She made sure she had plenty of silver coins, knowing she was all alone now. There were no rings to sell, and she'd have to go somewhere safe to work out how to live with the amulet.

She picked up the lantern and headed back up the stairs, locking the safe behind her. There was little else for her here, and she decided that Henri's people would need to be able to access the safe. Lani knew she needed to get away from here, they would come to protect this place once they found him, and she didn't want to have to explain her role.

He might have said to trust Goran, but she was told by Ashantha only to trust Henri. She'd survived so far, now she needed to get away somewhere until all of this settled down. She left the key on the table, and after moving the chair blocking the back door, exited that way.

The only people that could access Henri's place would be ring wearers, so she felt it would be safe enough.

She pulled the hood of the jacket she'd taken from the dressing room up over her head, and left through the building's side door. No one was paying her any attention and she turned left at the main road, away from where all the trouble had been. She needed a place to stay, away from everyone, while she worked out what to do next.

102

KYRO

Dressed in a nondescript tunic and cloak, Kyro was just another traveler arriving in Callet. While his guard's uniform from Barnen would have meant nothing to anyone down here, he didn't need to be singled out as a lawman on his hunt for Lani.

The journey here had been rushed, and he hoped he'd be able to stay put for several days. He was no longer used to spending days in the saddle and he now hurt all over.

There'd been no sighting of any of the Derks, and none of Lani, though everything pointed to her being here, or worse further south. Finding her wouldn't be easy especially if what he'd heard about Callet was true.

Arriving across the plains it presented as an impressive city, but once inside, the surface level impression was deceptive. He could see there were multiple walls within; as the city had outgrown itself, the original outer walls became part of the city as new ones were constructed.

The latest walls didn't look like they were there for much more than presenting an impression. It appeared they didn't even encircle the whole city yet, and much of what he saw looked poorly constructed.

The guards on the gates were definitely not there for anything other than show. As he rode through it appeared they were likely under the influence of drink, and more interested in being left to rest than doing anything practical.

It was all he could do to not get down off his horse and berate them.

No one needed to know who he was or why he was here. And all he would do would be embarrass himself. Some foreign captain trying to be a big shot.

He hoped that there were other guards inside the city who took their role more seriously, especially if it came to a confrontation with the Vrah. They were brutal and seemed to have no problem with killing. Kyro had never understood how there were those who took a life without any care.

The few times he had been responsible for taking another life, justified by their laws or not, it had caused him much grief. He still carried the upset deep within himself, occasionally having to face it when it surfaced. On those days only a large jar of wine seemed to help him resolve the internal pain it caused.

Droplets of sweat ran down his face, the hotter southern temperatures distinctly different to the cooler weather in Barnen. It was only mid-morning, but he could tell it would be another scorching day, the back of his neck felt burnt from his travels.

There seemed to be two types of people on the streets; those who clearly were going about their work, mostly trying to avoid the main roads, who ducked in and out of the many laneways that ran off the major thoroughfares, and then there were those who were in party mode, whether still going from the night before, or starting fresh for the day. Kyro couldn't believe how many people were in the mood for entertainment at this time of the day.

There were those quite clearly worse for their efforts, some asleep propped against a wall, while others had literally slept where they fell. He had to remind himself it wasn't his city and this was normal for here.

Callet's reputation as the City of Excess appeared well earned. His horse walked slowly through the heavy mass of people, and other riders. They passed inn after inn, ale houses, wine bars, brothels and even dens of game. Those were definitely not allowed in Malamig, King Nordahl forbade any such gambling.

Kyro knew that gambling went on around Malamig, but all behind closed doors. Here it was everywhere. It surprised him there wasn't a more visible city guard, given how much money must be changing hands, someone had to be protecting it.

Being a little more observant than the regular citizens, he did start to notice some discreet private guards as he moved through the city. That made sense given the state of the public guards he had seen so far.

The only buildings that seemed to be well maintained were what appeared to be the more popular venues. The rest of the city look poorly maintained and dirty.

There was a surface level presentation to keep people happy, but underneath that façade, Callet seemed to be unloved.

He dismounted to make it easier to move through the thickening crowd. After adjusting to being off the horse, he was glad to be walking on his own again. He was now near the center of Callet and had no idea how he would find Lani or even if she was still here.

He was a fish out of water in this place, a city he didn't know and with no contacts or method to locate anyone.

Throughout the ride here, he had been plagued by guilt on how he'd not looked after young Lani. He'd been too caught up in his role, and how that stroked his ego, and had handed over a frightened young girl to others to care for. Having to admit it to Cideep had brought it right to the surface.

He lectured others about having values and being honorable but in the wash-up he'd put his job over the safety of someone that he'd been charged with the care of.

Hembleth had said little, but the look he had left him with was very clear. This mess was of his making, and he'd failed in his duty.

Kyro still didn't know how Hembleth had influenced him, but despite his strange appearance, he commanded respect. Even Nordahl had bowed to it, albeit reluctantly.

Lani was old enough now to take care of herself, but that wasn't always the case. If she didn't have to eke out an existence on the street would she be in this situation? It didn't matter how much he spun it around in his head, he always came out feeling worse for the thoughts.

What he needed to do now was find her, somehow. First job was to get rid of the horse, and his bag, and that meant finding an inn that didn't look like a complete dump.

He chose one that appeared, on the outside at least, to have been cared for, and used his room to get changed before heading out to get a better sense of the city.

Without any particular goal he continued heading towards the city center, and chose another road to follow. There seemed to be a small tide of people actively heading towards something, and up ahead he could see a group of people, standing focused on something he couldn't see.

The movement of people slowed the closer he got and he couldn't get through it easily. He took a side lane and aimed to see if he could sweep around the side of the crowd and continue forward.

He saw a figure rushing away up in the distance. He couldn't tell for sure, but the black clothing with hood up reminded him of the Derks' outfits. The person was in a hurry to be away from whatever was happening, which drove Kyro to approach with more caution. He felt for his sword and rested his hand on the hilt, comforted by it.

Several members of the guard were talking to a small group of men, all focused on several bodies lying on the ground.

"You said there was another one dressed like this?" one of the guards asked.

"Yes. These two didn't make it, but the third took off that way." He turned and pointed past Kyro.

"Oi, you there. Come here," the guard beckoned Kyro over. "Did you see someone in black?"

"I did, sir. Just before as I came along here, he was sprinting through that lane."

"He was alone?"

Kyro nodded.

The guard looked back at the first man. "What about these others?"

"Like I told you, two men turned up, and helped the wounded guy away."

"This was the man who been fighting the men in black?"

"That's how it looked, we didn't get here until it was over."

"What about these other bodies?" The guard turned and pointed up the other alley.

"They were ahead of us, fighting to stop the one that got away."

"He must have been someone, there's three there."

The man who'd been answering all the questions just nodded.

"So who was it that took the injured one?"

"I don't know. One of them was big, really big. The other limped and his hair was all knotted and beaded. Long, it hung down past his shoulders. Don't forget the girl."

"What girl?"

"The one that got away. She climbed up that wall. Well at least I think it was a girl, it happened so quickly. Her face looked girlish but she was dressed just in a tunic and tights."

"And you don't know anything about where they took this guy then? The injured one."

"Not really, but one of them said something like… Folly."

The guard seemed to know what he was talking about, nodding his head. "That'd be Follies, it's an inn on the other side of town. I'll need to check it out. You've been helpful, but you lot can clear out now. I've got more men coming to clean this mess up."

Kyro turned and walked away. Partly he was relieved; if the girl was Lani, then she was still here, and she was okay. He had no idea if it was her, but he didn't believe in coincidences and Derks and a girl all in the same place, meant it was most likely her.

At least he had a clue, Follies. He didn't know what the men would know about her, but he needed to find out.

TILLANDRA

Tillandra burst through her kitchen door and nearly frightened Milfred to an early death.

"M-m-mother, you scared m-m-me."

"Oh, Milfred, I'm sorry. I'm just desperate to be off my feet."

"You have just got back?"

"Yes. Right this very minute."

"Here, sit. Let m-m-me get you something to drink."

"And food, please?"

He nodded and started shuffling around the kitchen. Tillandra was exhausted from the trip back across Death Road, but she was strangely energized as well. There was so much to do, she had a checklist in her head, and the most urgent of them all was to place the Mother Stone back where it belonged in the tower.

She needed to get up to speed on developments over the last week, even though she knew if Lani had been caught, she would have been contacted. That meant they were still chasing her, whatever she was up to. She'd have to gather everyone together to catch up on all the news, she required information now more than ever.

The glass of wine Milfred placed in front of her, she drained in one gulp and placed it back on the table.

"That bad, is it?"

"Just very dry, Milfred. It's been a long couple of weeks."

He replenished her glass and laid a plate of breads and cheeses before her, which she picked at as well. Whatever magic had replenished her at Qum was now exhausted, and she needed food.

"What do you need, M-m-other?"

She looked up at him.

"A bath? Clothes?"

"A bath would be good, first I am going to visit my study, I need to record some notes. When I am done I will wash and change, then I'd like a meeting with everyone. Can you arrange it for two hours' time?"

"Yes, M-m-other."

Taking the cup of wine and her pack to her study at the back of the house, she sought out a book from the many lining the shelves here in this secluded room.

The book she sought was *The Times of the Council War*, a very old manuscript that had not survived well over time. Every time she had tried to read it had been a struggle. Now she knew why.

Her understanding of everything about the past had changed since Tingfurlew had told her his history. It was now apparent that most of their oral history had been scrubbed from everyone's memory.

For some reason this book had become visible to her, but not all of its contents. She had read nothing about wars before and had become fascinated by it, so much so that she stole it from the City Library of Okeans. It had been with her for just about a year, and she still couldn't make sense of most of it.

Much of the book was either missing or badly damaged. It was clearly very old, and according to the inside cover it was a written account from the year 4101, and the Great War of that year.

The book had always been difficult to read, and she assumed, with her new knowledge, that this was probably due to the magic blocking her mind. On top of that it was written in a broken Humaas dialect that few had any experience in.

It was as much a poem as it was a true recording of the time. It was only in fairly recent times that historians had begun to appear in many realms, producing books that were more fact than fiction. Prior to that much of the written word was just a person with the capability to write recording the stories heard by bards and tellers.

Placing the delicate book on her desk, she put her cup on another side table; Folly forbid that she spilt wine over the contents and lost even more of it.

It was painstaking work and normally she would have given the task to her historians in the college who were more patient than most and had tools to handle and restore damaged works. For reasons she didn't understand, she'd never done that, and kept it all to herself. Tillandra hadn't even informed her colleagues or Milfred when she had recovered it.

She kept it in a spot behind a row of other books, hidden away from anyone looking. She doubted anyone would ever be in the room to look, but her instinct told her the content was best kept to herself. Reflecting on what she'd learned in recent weeks, it might have been more than that. As if some magic was trying to keep it hidden from everyone.

They needed to know what it contained now. She and the rest of the Court needed as much information as they could. Things had shifted, and change always challenged you to think differently and modify your actions. The best way to be ready for change was to have more information.

Today she opened the book towards the back and sought out the pages she had seen once before about a Great Fair.

There has been several mentions of Great Fairs in it, but there was no other mention of these in anything else she had read.

～

AND EACH DAY MORE PEOPLE ARRIVED TO HELP SETTING THE LIVING TENTS and stadia in place for the mighty fair. From all the eight realms came the stewards and senior aides of each kingdom.

～

IN THE SECOND WEEK MUCH WAS READY FOR THE GREAT FAIR OF 4100, AND the weather gods have been most kind, the Sun shines but does not fire those on the ground. No rain has fallen since the weeks before the start of this campaign and much excitement has been building amongst those here.

~

TODAY THE FIRST OF THE ARMED GUARDS FROM THE EAST AND SOUTH started arriving, taking over the finishing of their camps and setting up the great marquees brought with their builders. Within days these will stand and the colors will start to show about the great plains.

~

TILLANDRA MARVELED AT THE SOUNDS OF SUCH AN EVENT AND TRIED TO imagine where something of such magnitude might have been held. Ting had told her it was where desert now lay, to the northeast. She couldn't imagine what that land would have looked like before it was all sand.

Even more interesting to her was mention of the eight realms. Tingfurlew had mentioned seven realms. This book talked of eight. Did they include Enderk as one of the realms? She wanted to know what the realms were and where their boundaries were.

A number of following pages were almost empty; there were some small drawings on them, but any words that once lived there had been lost over time. Some of the next pages were broken, dry and crumbling, and several looked to have been ripped or torn from the binding.

~

WORD HAS ARRIVED TO THE COUNCIL THAT THOSE FROM ENDERK HAVE BEEN held up but will be here within days most likely just behind those from Malamig who also were delayed by weather.

~

So, as Ting had told her, Derks were at the Great Fair. That accounted for the eight then. Derks were now excluded from Dharatan, apart from small groups of travelers, and the seas between were very difficult to navigate.

How did the Derks make their way in such numbers to the Fair or was it a small delegation that attended? Ting had never finished that story about a land bridge. She should have pressed him more on that. It made more sense as to why the Derks were considered enemies. Even though people might not mentally remember, the feelings about them had clearly been passed on from generation to generation. She had not seen any of this content before, and reading it now fascinated her.

~

The arrival of all the remaining rulers and attendees from the North complete the arrival of the 4100 Fair and the host Truegen of the Kystenites declared the Fair open.

~

Much talk and joy has been had by the gifts that Schevenal had bestowed on the seven other rulers, these amulets of much beauty have been worn by all with great pride.

~

The next pages said little else apart from talk of feasts and games, that were part of any fair. A lot of it was broken with whole sections missing.

Tillandra noted the mention of the amulets; it seemed every one of the rulers received an amulet from Schevenal. This name had been here before, she was sure, but it had been like smudged text, and now it was clear to read.

It dawned on her that maybe much of the ruined text she'd tried to read before was just obfuscated. If nothing else the name on the page had stopped hiding itself. She'd broken through that part of the block.

Carefully closing the book again, she wrapped it in the silken cloths that had helped preserve it, and hid it again on the shelves.

Tillandra left her study, and washed. Milfred had left her a perfectly heated bath, and by the time she was done and changed she was ready to work. Sleep would have to wait.

The amulets were a significant part of the old story and it was bumping against the edge of her mind. They had amber stones, and she knew that what amber there was came from Enderk. It made sense that the amulets were made from it, but there was something more. She couldn't figure it out right now, but she knew it was important. She'd ask others once she dealt with more important things first.

Where was this Lani? And of course they would need to discuss the implications of there not being an Audition. She breathed deeply, that was what worried her the most. Then she and Junther needed to discuss the whole situation with King Anh. That was just the beginning.

She could feel the past was rushing to catch up to them, she now wanted to know more about other history that had been hidden from her. The library in Okeans was another place she should go, hopefully they hadn't noticed the book she took. Of more concern would be getting into Daskare before King Ahn took her handling of the Envoy situation personally.

He would still be on the road, so perhaps if she went soon, she could be done before they realized. That and a visit to the carver to see if they had any more to explain than Ting had.

She needed to know more, and she wasn't going to get it from the Circuit. Their network could only tell them of what was understood and being seen right now, not the past.

So many things she needed to do, and with so little time. First, her colleagues, it was time to let them know what she had learned.

LANI

By nightfall Lani was, safely she hoped, locked in a room in a small inn on the south side of the city. She'd not attracted any unusual attention and sat in the room trying to push the memories of the fight away.

The way she'd stabbed that Derk frightened her, she'd never actively killed anyone before, and she'd vomited again thinking about it.

Even taking a meal and something to drink down stairs hadn't been enough to lift the heavy feeling she carried.

Lani washed her face using water from the pail in her room, ducking her hair into it before drying it the best she could with a rough towel hung over one of the chairs.

Rubbing her temples she tried to understand what everything meant. She was stuck with the amulet, and had no idea how to get rid of it. She'd seen yet another person die, and poor Henri had given up his life for her, and he hardly knew her. Why?

Why had Ashantha sent her to him if he couldn't solve the problem? And who on Dharatan were these people with the clown face symbol? There were more than just a few of them, and they had considerable wealth, and yet they didn't live extravagantly.

It was all too much for her to understand right now. She touched the amulet through her tunic; it was wrapped up which meant the Derks couldn't track her. As far as she could tell anyway.

She didn't know if Goatee had any more helpers close by, but he'd been hurt, she knew that much. Hopefully it would buy her some time before he looked for her again.

What came next? How could she get away from these people? Where would she go next?

Maybe everyone would just stop chasing her, and she would live happily ever after. Lani scoffed. There was no happy ever after for a girl like her. She was a long way from the only home she'd known, and they wouldn't have her back now. She was a wanted murderer back there, at best a thief.

She was still on her own, same as always. Nothing would fix that. Whatever magic Ashantha had used to know her name, he'd probably been able to force her to take on the amulet. He didn't care about her, he'd just wanted someone to deliver his things.

Lani punched the bed in frustration. She'd been on her own and would still be on her own.

Slumped against the wall on her bed, the tiredness became too much and she huddled down on the bed and let her exhaustion overtake her.

The dream returned, it had become a common event now. Lani wasn't sure she'd ever get used to it.

She had been running and running at the beginning, not sure why but always having to run. Her arms and legs were a heavy weight, and the movement seemed to take every ounce of energy she had, but she made little progress.

Then out of nowhere she ran straight into Ashantha, or more correctly his skeleton. He stood in front of her, mist swirling around his bones, straight upright not moving, but his face was intact.

His head wasn't bone, it was his real face. She would always remember his face. She tried to talk to him but no words came out, and he said nothing. He beckoned her to him.

Lani knew it was wrong, but even with her mind screaming at her to stay away, she took a step towards him. Then another. His bony fingers were calling her to him.

The face, Ashantha's face, smiled at her, almost friendly, but something wasn't real about it. Then the face changed and went completely black and it became the mask that she carried in her satchel. Now it was the mask on the skeleton, not smiling, just staring at her. The finger curling, still, inviting her forward.

She froze as the hand reached up and lay upon her shoulder. She could feel strength through the hand, and had she tried she wasn't sure she could have pulled away. Her mouth had gone dry and her heart raced in her chest. Her brain told her to escape but her body was locked in place, going nowhere.

Then, without warning, the other hand reached up and pulled the mask off his face, exposing the skeleton beneath.

Lani cringed, the whole thing reminding her of Ashantha's real face, missing back in the cavern. The dream had started the same as always but she'd never gotten to this point. This was the furthest she'd ever been in it. Normally she had woken before he touched her.

Sweat dripped down her back, even though everything around her seemed cold, dark and covered in mist.

The mask in his hand looked exactly the same as the one in her satchel. She looked directly at the skeleton; there was nothing there just empty eye sockets. Before she knew what was happening, the skeleton moved its hand up and placed the mask over her face, with such speed it caught her unawares.

She woke in a fright, gasping for breath. Reaching up, Lani grabbed at her face, almost poking herself in the eye. There was no mask on her face. She gulped in air, she'd been holding her breath in her sleep, just like in the dream.

Standing up and shaking off the chills she felt, Lani paced the room. The dream was haunting her, making it hard to get any rest. She had no idea what it meant. Maybe she should never have taken the mask, it was cursed. Was the mask haunting her? Maybe she should just leave it behind. It wasn't like the amulet, she could leave it here and then it wouldn't invade her dreams.

Lani couldn't remember a time, before finding Ashantha, where dreams had plagued her sleep. Maybe it was because her sleep was always broken or fearful, she didn't know, but now she dreamed almost every night.

Her life had changed so much, in such a short space of time, everything was so different to how it had always been. Damn Ashantha, damn Harsop, damn them all. Why couldn't they have just left her alone? How on earth was she meant to do all of this on her own?

Despite being awake and her eyes open, she could still see the skeleton, its image imprinted in her mind. The bony hand reaching up as it put the mask on her face. She shook as she remembered it.

Wanting to be sure she still had it, Lani grabbed her satchel and tipped the contents onto the bed. Reluctant to touch the mask as it came out, she used her knife to flip it over on the bed. The shape was a replica of what she had dreamt. It lay there, doing nothing, just a static wooden object.

How it came to be was as confusing as the dream. Could a wooden mask be part of a face? Was this normal in any way? She had never been around dead bodies much before so she didn't know, but she had never heard anyone speak of masks.

Lani moved a chair over near the bed, and sitting backwards on it watched the mask, half expecting it to leap up and fly at her. She wasn't sure how long she sat staring, but nothing changed. The mask was just a mask lying on her bed. Hard, lifeless, doing nothing.

It was the first time she'd spent any time looking at it. It had spooked her when she first saw it, and she'd stowed it her bag ever since. There was a weird softness to it, mimicking those elements of Ashantha when he had been alive. It wasn't smiling but it also wasn't frowning.

The thought crossed her mind to put it on, like in the dream. She sat back a bit and a shiver ran up her spine. What a crazy thought. She wasn't going to put it on. How creepy. That would be just weird. It was his face, it had come off him. Well it wasn't his face in truth, just a replica of his face.

The longer she sat staring at it, the more the compulsion grew. She almost felt like it was more of the magic at work, drawing her in. Was that what the dream was about? Telling her to put the mask on? But why?

No, that couldn't be good. It felt like it was hypnotizing her. She stood up and went over, grabbing her satchel. It would be best to just put it back out of sight, like the amulet when it was tucked away, it couldn't cause any harm.

As she put her hand on the mask to push it into the satchel, everything changed around her. The room seemed to slide backwards away from her, and her hand with a mind of its own picked up the mask, turned it around and began moving it toward her face.

Lani tried to duck from her own hand but it was if she was back in the dream and couldn't truly control what was happening.

She held her breath as her hand came towards her face, blocking her view of anything else.

When the mask touched her face she half expected her skin to burn, but all she felt was a coolness, a soothing coolness like when you stick your head in a stream on a hot day, and all the heat just slips away.

There was a faint sound of a click, as it settled onto her face. The room seemed to come back into focus now, but she felt different. Everything had a different look and feel to it.

She looked down at her hands and saw her normal hands, but she saw them differently, as if it wasn't her looking. She struggled to understand the difference.

She put her hands on her face, expecting to feel the mask. All she could feel was a normal face, except it wasn't her face. She knew what her face felt like. This face felt different, her nose was bigger and her skin felt coarse along her jaw.

Frantically she ran her hands over her head, even her hair was different, longer and thinner. She went to the corner of the room where a small mirror hung on the wall. What she saw caused a scream from her mouth.

Looking back at her was Ashantha, very much alive and very much male. She turned, and shook herself and the image in the mirror mimicked her every move. Her face was Ashantha's. There was no mask on her. She wasn't her. She was him.

Turning away from the mirror horrified, Lani madly grabbed at her face and head, searching for the mask. Everything felt just like a head, smooth and skin-like. Then she detected a slight ridge across her hair line, at the top of her forehead. Using one of her fingernails to lever under it, she again heard a small click and suddenly the mask was in her left hand.

Racing back to the mirror Lani could see herself again. She turned and flung the mask over onto the bed and slumped down on the floor, her back against the wall. Wrapping her arms around her knees, she tried to breathe, tears rolling down her face. What on Dharatan had just happened?

For much of the morning, Lani sat where she was on the floor, staring at the mask on the bed. Everything about what had just happened scared her. She had no prior experience of anything like this, she doubted anyone did.

Before this had all started she had never experienced magic at all. All she'd ever heard had been fanciful tales that bards told, in alehouses. Mostly, common folk talked of magic only to blame it for the bad things that happened in their lives.

Lani hadn't really ever considered magic anything real. Until now. Now she was caught inside a world of magic, that was weirder than any tale she'd ever heard.

Part of her wondered if she was losing her mind. Or was she really just having vivid daydreams, that weren't actually real? Wasn't that how people described the cracked and crazy ones? That they lived out the strange dreams during the day and not just in their heads when they slept.

Except she knew what was happening was real.

It was the lack of a logical explanation that bothered her the most. How could her face have changed into his? How did his face turn into a mask, and how could she put it on and turn into him? It felt wrong. She could actually sense his thoughts. It was too hard to understand.

She wondered if her actual voice sounded different with it on. Would she sound like Ashantha or like herself?

Standing up, Lani went over to the window and looked out across the city. Low gray cloud cover blanketed the city. The gloomy view didn't help her feel any better. Looking back at the mask and her small collection on the bed, she felt lost.

A dark mood was plucking at the edges of her mind, trying to draw her in. She was feeling helpless and very much alone. The magic was frightening to her, even when she benefited from it. Not knowing what was going on was the worst part of it all.

What next, was the big question? Her dreams had been leading her to putting on the mask which now she'd done. To what purpose? It was clear that the dream wanted her to put on the mask, but all it had done was frighten her.

Maybe she needed to try it again, to get calm with it, and see if there was something to learn from it? The thought made her shiver and she grabbed the satchel and smothered the face, as if she could kill it. She let go of the satchel, leaving the mask covered and sat at the table, placing her head in her hands, wanting to scream, but instead she began to cry.

LANI

The room seemed too small, and she felt an urge to leave and run away. If only she could. As it was, running away had started this whole fool's errand. That moment, when she had run from Harsop, triggered the events that led her here.

Now she couldn't get away from the amulet if she tried. She needed help, but didn't know who to trust. Nothing about her journey here and the events surrounding it had been easy. Her life had been endangered and she'd seen so many people die.

Lani had left to get away from the trouble she was in, but it had followed her. She'd never intended to come to Callet, and yet here she was. All she'd been trying to do was get away from Barnen. All she wished for now was to be back there, tucked up in her warren.

Now she was stuck with the amulet, in a foreign city, surrounded by people who wanted to harm her and with nothing to show for it, except some coins and a creepy mask.

She looked over at the bed again and remembered there was also Ashantha's journal. She moved the satchel to the side, trying to avoid the mask, and grabbed the journal taking it back to the table.

The letters on the cover meant nothing to her, nor the pages of writing inside. Lani flicked through the pages, looking for anything that might help her, but there was nothing. She had never been taught to read. Maybe if Henri were here he could read it and tell her what it said.

She had hardly known him and still the thought of what he had done for her, and his death, upset her. Tears spilled down her cheek, and she had to remember to breathe.

In frustration she slammed the journal back on the table, making everything on it jump. Ashantha had done nothing to help her so far, why would this journal be of any more use? If it wasn't for him, she wouldn't be here.

He had sent her into danger and given her nothing. Even what he had told her was wrong. Henri couldn't help her. "Hear that!" she sneered at his mask. "I can't trust you or what you said, there's nothing here for me. Why did you lie to me?

"How did you even know who I was, and choose me to do this dirty work? It was all dumb and stupid. See what happened. If you cared about Henri you wouldn't have got him killed. Asshole!

"Why did you lie to me?"

It still creeped her out having an exact replica of his face in the mask. Even his death had been strange. She half expected it to answer her, like some other form of magic Ashantha had been hiding from her. Nothing happened.

"Nothing to say, dead man? Of course not."

Lani got up and paced the room. Despite her anger at him, Ashantha's journal was still her best bet to learn something more. Who could she get to read the book? Was there anyone safe she could trust to read it and not tell of her to others? What if Ashantha had written it in code? Maybe a code only their people knew. Then showing it to anyone else would be pointless, and just endanger her.

The fewer people that knew where she was the better. She wasn't even sure if she was safe in this inn, let alone going outside and meeting people.

If only Ashantha had told her what he wrote, then she might know who else she could trust.

She stopped dead still.

The mask.

The idea hit her like a physical jolt.

She knew it was a dumb idea and she had hated the feeling when she put it on before, but it made sense. It made a lot of sense. If it was his book then maybe only he could read it. If her face turned into Ashantha, when she put the mask on, could she read like him too?

She rolled her shoulders and paced back and forth in one spot, trying to decide if she could do it. Nothing bad had happened last time she wore the mask, and wasn't that what the dream was telling her?

In the end it might all come down to this. Without Henri, the journal and mask might be her only answers. Lani walked cautiously to the bed, and picked up the mask, holding it away from herself.

Back at the table she sat with the journal in front of her, and took several big breaths, steeling herself.

Her hand was shaking and she felt a little queasy to the stomach but she also knew she had to try it. The mask was face down in her hand, she closed her eyes, then opened them and quickly swung the mask up onto her head.

Just like the time before she felt the coolness spread all over her head and the clicking sound as it snapped into place.

Her skin felt strange, everything felt strange and her brain fought against what she was doing. She felt for the ridge line again to pull it off and noticed the journal on the table.

She could read the letters on the cover.

Embossed into the leather ever so lightly were the words 'The Jest Book' and underneath two initials. 'A.P.' He had told her his last name but she couldn't remember it, Lani guessed these were his initials. Ashantha P.

She turned the cover, and inside all of the words lay before her, and she could read them. She could hear his voice in her head, reading each word.

Her crazy idea had worked, and as Ashantha she could read his book.

Ashantha had been writing when she found him, and he made her wait while he finished, in his dying moments. Lani flipped to the back of the book to see what it was he had written.

~

MY LIFE IS SLIPPING AWAY, I THOUGHT I WOULD HAVE MORE TIME BEFORE *they found me, but it seems they can trace the stone. I wrapped it in the glove I was given to hide my ring. I had hoped it blocked it from them, but I do not know.*

Once or twice I have opened the pouch to look at it, I can almost hear it, calling to be free, but I have been able to resist it.

No matter what, they found me, and the wounds I have suffered will not heal. My time is short. I write these words in the hope that somehow they will find their way to those who can understand them.

~

THE AMULET MATTERS. I AM NOT SURE IF THIS WAS WHAT I WAS SENT TO *find, but it's connected to the ill that rules Enderk. The amber they adore, seems to be more than just something to wear and use. I always felt like it affected me, there was a dulling of my senses when I was around it.*

If I was out of the cities, away from any concentration of amber, I felt my senses return. I am unsure what that means, I did not have the means to learn more. En Carta is intolerable. When I was there I could think of nothing but their goddess, and I felt I could see why they all moved in unison. Their minds are not their own.

I am only thankful my time there was very limited.

The amulet is something else, it feels very wrong. I do not know why.

~

I FOUND THIS THING PURELY BY CHANCE, I WAS WORKING ON ONE OF THE *islands that link our lands. They are building bridges that will allow them to cross in numbers. One night a small team of the assassins landed on our island with an elderly woman who seemed lost to her mind. These men are known as the Vrah. One avoids them when living in Enderk.*

They stayed away from us and when most were asleep I was able to get close enough to hear talk of what they had. This woman had found a box carrying a relic of great importance, they had been directed to fetch it by their high priest. One of them murdered the old woman when she slept, apparently as part of their orders. The others slept while a lone guard watched over the box that they had brought with them.

≈

I HAD NO TIME TO PLAN ANY BETTER. SOMETHING DEEP DOWN DROVE ME. I knew this object was something that shouldn't be taken back to Enderk, I can't say why but deep inside I could feel a sense of foreboding. I was able to steal what was inside the box from under their noses and left them the box without them detecting it.

When the Vrah returned to their bosses, the theft would have been discovered, I pity what will happen to them. Punishment in Enderk is brutal.

≈

WHATEVER GUIDED ME KEPT ME FROM TOUCHING THE AMULET. I USED THE special glove I had been given, to mask my ring, as a pouch to take the amulet. Since I could no longer cover my ring, it would have not taken long for me to be exposed, despite the theft of the amulet.

I had no choice then but to flee. One way or another I knew they would come after me. A missing slave might not be noticed, but the stolen amulet would be something else altogether.

≈

I TOOK TO THE SEAS AND BATTLED THE HARSH WINTER CONDITIONS TO GET back to Dharatan, I was weak and that is why I have not made contact. I doubted I could sustain the method to talk to someone, and I couldn't afford the chance I might be found.

≈

IT WAS THE VRAH THAT EVENTUALLY CAUGHT UP TO ME.

≈

THE WORD VRAH TRIGGERED PAIN IN LANI'S HEAD, SHE HAD NO IDEA WHY, but each time she read the word it caused her agony. She had to close her eyes as the pain passed, and in the darkness the symbol of the tattoo floated across her vision.

Were they the Vrah?

Again she felt the pain in her head before she turned back to the pages.

~

I HAVE FAILED. THEY FOUND ME, AND WE FOUGHT. ALL MY YEARS OF training and it wasn't enough. There were three of them, they were so quick. I thought I was good enough but I wasn't. I put two of them down, but by then I was tired. If it hadn't been for the help of the men from around here that were also in the fight, I would never have lasted as long as I did. The third had been waiting, saving his energy.

When it was just the two of us he didn't let me rest, he came at me. When his sword cut into me I managed to also strike a telling blow. He didn't survive. Neither will I.

~

I'M IN THE CAVE, WHERE I LEFT MY THINGS, BEFORE GOING TO ENDERK. THIS journal, my satchel, I left them here for when I returned. I had hoped it would be after a successful mission. I must try and bury it all back in the hole where I left it before. If anyone else finds this amulet we are doomed. I hope you will see where my ring is and find my remains, before anyone else does.

Whoever reads this first, be wary of the amulet, do not expose it or they will hunt you too. More than that, there is evil in that stone, I am sure of that. You can feel it, it is not right. Do not touch it.

~

OF MY MISSION TO SEE WHAT WAS STIRRING IN ENDERK, I BELIEVE THEY SEEK to come for Dharatan. They have been training many soldiers, and building the bridges to connect the Stepping Isles. It is slow, and they lose slaves all the time in the building of them, but they care not of that cost.

If no one finds this journal then not only have I failed but you will not know what comes until it is too late. I am sorry that I have failed you. I just wish someone would come that I could give this to.

~

Lani paused. These words must have been before she found him. Why had he not told her all of this? Maybe she might have thought differently about what she was doing. It didn't matter now. Reading it was hard for her, reading these words brought the memory of his dying moments fresh back into mind.

There he had been, knowing he was to die, all alone until she had found him. Sadness swept over her.

~

The girl has found me. I know not how this has come to pass. She is the one. I was told I would know her when she came. I wish I had more life left in me. She looks familiar, but I do not know how.

Before I pass I must tell you what I was told. Before I left for Enderk, I met a strange man, he was known as Rainbow. His face was filled with color, from all the chalk he handled.

It was the strangest meeting, and I had forgotten until just now, but he told me, at the time I ask for help, at the time I most need it, a girl will appear. Her name is Lani. You will give her what it is you need delivered. I thought he was a crazy old fool, but I heard what he had to say anyway.

All of my recollection of that meeting I had forgotten until now, but a girl has appeared here. Her name is Lani.

I write this hoping now she can get this to Henri. I am unsure how much to tell her. I cannot tell of her character, but such coincidences I must trust. I have told her to get the amulet to Henri. Henri, if you read this, then she has done well, old friend.

We will never meet again, and I will miss our companionship. Be well and see this amulet to Anderwell. Mother will have to solve the riddle, for I cannot. I know you will be unable to either, but you can see it on its way.

❧

LANI PUT THE BOOK DOWN, AND STOOD UP. REACHING UP TO HER FACE SHE found the spot on her hairline where she could slip her nail under and pulled the mask off.

She put it on top of the book and wiped the tears from her eyes. She was reading it as Ashantha, she could feel his last thoughts and feelings, she was him, reading those words. More than that, memories of his time with Henri had flashed across her mind, and she was able to see his past. It was heartbreaking.

She cried for a while, then tried to understand the part about Rainbow and herself. How had Rainbow known about her? This made no sense at all to her. How did he know about her, she had only met him for the first time in Barnen, at the markets, when he'd given her the chalk?

His pouch of chalk was still in the pocket of the satchel and she pulled it out. She looked inside and all she saw was chalk, but that chalk had saved her life. It too had been magical. What did it all mean?

Her skin was all clammy, and she felt exhausted from the experience. It felt like she had walked all day up a mountain carrying a heavy bag.

There were still more pages of the journal that Ashantha had written on, and Lani knew reading his final moments would be hard. She'd been there and it was hard enough, but to feel them as him, she didn't know how to handle it. She had little choice, she knew. She had to know what he said.

❧

HENRI, IF LANI CANNOT READ THIS, PLEASE READ IT FOR HER. I DON'T KNOW how, but I have a feeling that if you can survive the task I set you, Lani, then you will find a way to read this. I was told you hold the key to much of our future. Don't ask me how. My friends and I, the Jesters, we think we know a lot but we also know so little.

For a long time we have been good at keeping the peace, manipulating those who are easy to fool. I am not sure if that will be enough in the future.

The amulet I will give you, you must keep it safe. If you are here, you will know Bossu is Henri, I had to misdirect you, I don't know who to trust anymore. I thought our family was safe, but now I think there are those inside who are not on the same path. I will not write why it is I think that, in case this falls into the wrong hands. I hope it will come out on its own.

Henri won't be able to touch the stone, he can only put you on the path. Your quest isn't to take it to him, but it's as much as I could ask at the time. You must get it to Mother Folly, she is the only one who will know what to do with it.

With it, you must deliver this warning. The Vrah and their masters are coming. Enderk seeks to conquer us. They won't be stopped. They have a vast army and powers that they seek to unleash on Dharatan and control us all.

I don't know why, but I know that much. In time they will have a bridge. We are not ready.

I am not sure how I will get you to deliver this to Henri, but if you read this then I will have not failed at everything.

You are not who you think you are. You are not alone, Lani.

I can only tell you what I know. This strange fellow Rainbow was not of this land, that much I do know. He slipped me a note, I only found it once he was gone, and I destroyed it after I read it. It was in riddles, which seemed to be his way.

He knew your mother, and what she gave up for you. She risked much so that you could live, and be free. Even in her last moments she protected you.

He wrote that he knows your father as well. That you have family, but that your new mother will have to help you solve that puzzle. They did not expect you to be who you are. You live in two places, and your choice will always be between the two.

It is hard to recall the exact words that he wrote, now I wish I had kept the note. Keep her away from the Derks. The past will come back to the future. I think that is what he wrote. It is so hard, to remember. There is so little time left.

I FEAR I HAVE PUT YOU IN MUCH PERIL, BUT I MUST TRUST WHAT IT IS THAT has occurred. Coincidences do not happen by chance, learn this lesson well. You will need friends, good friends. Find Mother, she will protect you, as much as your own did, even if she too does not know why.

Thenis be with you, Lani. I wish I could help you more.

LANI TOOK OFF THE MASK AND PLACED IT ON THE TABLE. SHE WAS LOST, floating in a lake of emotions, unsure which direction was the closest to a safe shoreline.

Rainbow, of all the people, knew her parents. Why had he never told her?

Ashantha's words seem accurate but he was relaying a message he tried to recall, Lani could feel the angst in his thoughts, as he tried to write an accurate recollection of what Rainbow had said. Had he remembered it correctly?

Her father was still alive? That was how it sounded. He wrote, 'you have a family'. What did that mean? Grandparents? Uncles and aunties? Was it true?

She was angry. Angry at Ashantha for dying without telling her the truth. Despite knowing the pain of his final moments, she struggled to forgive him for keeping things from her. The whole trip here was never about delivering it to Henri, it was about getting it away from the north, and ultimately to this woman called Mother.

If Rainbow knew so much, would he know how to break the bond of the amulet? Where would she find him? He had been north in Little Big Rock the last time she'd seen him, and said he would be heading towards Nedor. Lani didn't know if he was there, or where else he might go. She had no idea how she might find him.

All her life Lani had believed she was alone, that's what she had been told. Or if not specifically told, it had been implied. She knew for sure her mother had died, and it had been suggested her father too, but if he hadn't, then why had he not come for her? Who and where was he? What family did she have?

The book said her new mother could help her solve the puzzle. Why had Rainbow not said where her father was? It said he knew him, but not where he was. Maybe he didn't know.

Lani assumed that 'her new mother' referred to the woman Henri had called Mother Folly. The person that led these people, Henri, Ashantha and the man called Goran. Henri had made it sound like there were many of them, but she still didn't know who to trust.

Henri had mentioned this Mother Folly, too. Lani trusted Henri, he had done nothing to deceive her. In the end he had given up his life for hers. Lani still didn't understand why. He didn't have this information, why did he care to save her?

She was no one special, despite what was in this journal. Why Rainbow had known she would meet Ashantha and be able to help him concerned her. There were these people who could use magic, that had involved her in their world. Now everything was spinning out of control.

Just as she thought she could be done with it all, she found she was still trapped. After all she had been through, she'd made it to Callet but for nothing. Even that goal had been fake.

Was the woman Mother Folly going to be able to help, or was that another fool's errand? Someone had to know how to break the bond of the amulet, so she could be safe. If Mother Folly could help solve the puzzle, as Ashantha had written, she had to take that chance. Didn't she?

There had been too many lies.

Holding her head in her hands, she gave in and let the tears fall. Everything had built up, ever since she'd met Ashantha, his death, the others, and now Henri's and the thought of her mother. Once they started she couldn't stop them, it was years of grief just flowing out of her. Her body felt tiny, and tired. She sobbed and hugged herself.

I have a family?

It was like a thin ray of sunlight breaking through the stormy sky. It was enough. She could see the shoreline, it was still a distance away, but she knew what direction to head now. There was someone waiting there for her.

THE END

ACKNOWLEDGMENTS

Many thanks to my editors Fleetwood Robbins for helping make my debut novel the best it could be. Also to Rachel Amphlett for continually providing support and encouragement through the challenges of such an ambitious debut novel. To Jane Dixon-Smith for the cover design, Tiffany Munro for the initial map design work and Lauren Atkinson for creating what it is today.

To all my family and friends who have endured me talking about this novel for so many years, continually willed me on and provided constant encouragement, thank you all. It helped, more than you might realise.

To Fletcher, Samuel and Piper thank you for all your support in all the little ways you might not even remember.

I can't ever thank my wife Gill enough, she's pushed me when I needed it, helped me step back when it became too much, encouraged me for all this time, and provided invaluable feedback along the journey.

FROM THE AUTHOR

In All Jest,

First of all, I wanted to say a huge thank you for choosing to read *A Fool's Errand*.

When I sat down to write my first fantasy novel, I pulled out a set of notes that I have nurtured for a decade or more. Every time I tried to start writing that story, another one kept popping into my head.

That was a story which revolved around not just one Jester, but a society of them. In the end, I put the other story away and let the *In All Jest* idea take over. Since that time it has grown into the world, it now is, and this novel is book one of six. I've fallen in love with a number of the characters as it has the story has taken on its own life.

I hope you've been taken in by some of them as you read the book.

If you enjoyed *A Fool's Errand*, I'd be grateful if you could write a review. It doesn't have to be long, just a few words, but it's the best way for me to help new readers discover the book, and my series, for the first time.

If you'd like to stay up to date with my new releases, as well as exclusive competitions and giveaways, you're welcome to join my Reader Group at my website, www.kingdarryl.com.

Best wishes,
Darryl King

ALSO BY D.E. KING

The In All Jest series

Fool Me Twice (Book 2)

Spire Of Fools (Book 3)

The In All Jest World

Cut In Half (Book A)